G000115897

CRYSTAL FROST

ALICIA RADES

Copyright © 2017 Alicia Rades

All rights reserved. No part of this book may be used or reproduced in any matter whatsoever without written permission from the author except in brief quotations used in articles and reviews.

This is a work of fiction. Names, characters, places, and incidents are either the product of the author's imagination or are used fictitiously, and any resemblance to actual persons, living or dead, business establishments, events or locales is entirely coincidental.

Published by Crystallite Publishing.
Produced in the United States of America.
Edited by Emerald Barnes.
Cover by Clarissa Yeo of Yocla Designs.

FIRE IN FROST

ALICIA RADES

CHAPTER 1

*M*y knees buckled and my hands trembled as I reached for the door to the school. An invisible weight came crushing down on my lungs as I gasped for air.

"What's wrong?" Emma asked with urgency. "Crystal, you look sick. Are you okay?"

I paused, unable to move or speak because I was afraid I would collapse if I did. The truth was, I didn't know *what* was wrong with me.

"Crystal," Emma prodded, resting a hand on my shoulder.

I blinked a few times and finally caught my breath. My voice was hoarse and barely there. "Yeah, I think I'll be alright. I just have a weird feeling."

Once I found my legs, we entered the building. The commons took on a different role today. Instead of everyone seated at tables waiting for the bell to ring, most were crowded toward the far end of the room. It was quieter than normal, too, as if a tragedy had just taken place.

"What's everyone doing?" I asked in a near whisper as I stood on my toes to get a better look.

"I don't know," Emma started, but she cut off. "Oh, yeah. Remember the fundraiser they're doing today for Olivia Owen? They must have started already."

Now that Emma pointed it out, I remembered yesterday's announcements reminding students about a fundraiser in memory of Olivia. I knew Olivia's story. In a small town of 3,500, *everyone* knew about Olivia's tragic death that happened last year.

I approached the table where the crowd stood and moved to the side so I could see. When I got a clear view, I saw two girls sitting behind the table, Kelli Taylor and Justine Hanson, the co-queen bees of the school. Athletic, beautiful, straight A students, these girls were pretty much the poster children for perfection. In front of them sat boxes of candy bars they were selling for the fundraiser.

Informational flyers and pictures of Olivia scattered the table. There was even a large framed photo of her junior volleyball picture taken just weeks before her death. She stood with a confident stance in her number 17 volleyball jersey with the ball resting on her hip. Her blonde hair was straightened, and her dark brown irises made her eyes appear larger than they should. She looked more like an angel than a student. *It's sad, I thought, that she didn't live long enough to finish the season—or even to graduate for that matter.*

I grabbed one of the flyers from the stack and began reading.

Fundraising for Burn Victims: In Memory of Olivia Owen

By Justine Hanson

Olivia Owen was once a loving daughter, student, and athlete. She was a straight-A student who set an example for her fellow classmates by becoming an active member of the student council and the community service club. Her athletic abilities surpassed those of her fellow junior-year volleyball players despite her asthma, and if she would have made it to the end of the season, she would have undoubtedly claimed the title of MVP. Olivia was a spectacular human being, volunteering when she could, helping the community with things like the Peyton Springs Halloween Festival and the Fourth of July Parade.

But more than anything, Olivia was my best friend. I knew her and loved her like a sister, and it pains my heart each day to know that her life was cut short at only age 17. When Olivia forgot to blow out a candle before she fell asleep, her curtains caught fire, and she suffered an asthma attack before she could escape the smoke or find her inhaler. I can't imagine the physical pain she must have endured that night.

Because of this tragic tale, Olivia's family and friends decided to honor her life by helping raise money for other burn victims and their families who have survived house fires. Today, on the anniversary of Olivia's death, we ask you to contribute by purchasing one of our fundraising products (candy bars, baked goods, and other donated items) or by simply dropping $1 into one of our donation jars located throughout the school.

Olivia's mother and her friends thank you for any and all contributions, and we hope to continue raising money for families like Olivia's. Thank you, and God bless!

"What's it say?"

I jumped. I didn't realize Emma had followed me to the table.

"It's just a flyer explaining the fundraiser," I told her.

Olivia's story was sad. I felt like I couldn't just leave the flyer there, one that told her story to the world. I wanted to contribute in some way, but I didn't have any money on me, so I simply folded the paper up and slid it in my pocket, hoping that would show I cared.

The thought of death crushed my heart, so I kept my eyes down, avoiding gazes so I wouldn't tear up. I didn't know Olivia that well, but since we were both on the volleyball team—although she was Varsity when I was on the freshman team—I'd spoken to her a few times.

I blinked back tears as I thought of Olivia's tragedy. The whole idea of death brought a lump to my throat and resurfaced memories that I thought I'd gotten over. Emma rubbed my back to comfort me because she knew the subject of death was a touchy one.

As I stared at the floor, afraid to look up for fear that tears might start falling, an invisible force—something unknown willing me to look—pulled my chin up. My gaze fell upon the empty hallway to the right of the commons area where students hadn't yet been released to roam for the day.

In the middle of the hallway stood a tall, beautiful girl with blonde hair and dark brown eyes. She looked at me across the distance, her eyes full of emotion. I couldn't pinpoint exactly what she was trying to say with her expression, except that I knew it was urgent.

As soon as I spotted her, the bell rang, announcing that students could now go to their lockers and prepare for class. The crowd dispersed from the commons into the hallway and blocked my view of the girl. The students hurried down the hall as if they didn't see her. I kept my eye on where she was standing, but I didn't see her again.

"Crystal." Emma's voice seemed far off, a distant hum in my confusion.

The faintness I felt just moments ago returned. My heart pounded in my ears, and for a second, my knees felt unstable. I gripped the edge of the fundraising table for support.

Emma snapped her fingers in front of my face. "Crystal," she said again as her voice came back into focus.

I was suddenly whipped back into reality, dazed. "Wh—what?"

"Are you okay?" Emma asked with a tone of serious concern. "You look like you've seen a ghost."

I let the statement sink in for a moment. "Yeah," I said. But I wasn't answering her initial question. I was agreeing with her latter statement.

But I didn't see a ghost. I couldn't have. An odd sensation stirred as a chill spread from my spine to the end of my fingertips. This was the same type of chill I used to get when I had my imaginary friend Eva over for tea before I started kindergarten. *I'm imagining things,* I told myself, mostly as reassurance.

But I had seen her clear as day. Olivia Owen had stood in the hallway and begged for my help with nothing but an expression. Yet how could that be when she died a year ago?

Emma took my arm and led me to our lockers as I silently assured myself I wasn't crazy.

CHAPTER 2

A s we neared our lockers, I rationalized what I had seen.
Whatever bug I'm catching sure is making my imagination run wild.

I took a deep breath, willing my bad mood to go away, but a tension headache was already forming. I tried putting Olivia out of my head. Easier said than done.

We arrived at our first class, which was my favorite class of the day because it was the only one where Emma, Derek, and I had class together. Plus, Mr. Bailey always left us to our textbooks and let us talk with our group. Needless to say, there was more goofing around than working on geometry homework.

I walked in with a frown on my face. Derek noticed immediately. I moved my desk so it was facing my two best friends, forming a triangle so that we could get to work.

Derek shifted in his chair and looked up at me. "What's wrong?" he asked gently, obviously concerned.

"It's just not a good day," I murmured. With that, I actually opened up my textbook and began reading.

I could see Derek's expression out of the corner of my eye as he looked to Emma for an explanation. She simply lifted her shoulders and opened her own textbook, but I could still see her stealing glances at him.

I apologized for my behavior when the bell rang, but I still couldn't shake off my mood. I seemed to walk through the hall in a daze, blinking back tears and cursing the knot that was forming in my chest. Was I getting sick, or was it something else altogether?

When lunch rolled around, I quietly found my spot next to Derek and Emma at our usual table. We normally sat with the other JV volleyball players but mostly kept our conversations to ourselves. Derek was freely welcome at our table. Last year when he tore his ACL in basketball, Emma and I begged him to join the team as our manager.

Besides, he didn't really have the typical basketball player physique. He was shorter than most of the other players, although his attractive bright blue eyes and curly brown hair made him blend in with the other good-looking guys at school. He hung out with Emma and me more than any other guy, though.

Emma and Derek were arguing next to me about some issue I didn't care to weigh in on, so I blocked them out as I picked through my food. When I lost interest in it and glanced up, I noticed the long table set up against the far wall of the commons.

Kelli and Justine sat behind it, still selling candy bars and taking dona-tions. I watched in awe as they ran their campaign and encouraged passing students to purchase a candy bar or to spare a few pennies. The way they held themselves bit at my own self-esteem.

Our school wasn't very big. In a small town like Peyton Springs, you couldn't expect a large high school. Everyone knew everyone else here. It was so small that some of our team members—like Emma—had to double up on JV and Varsity.

I had talked to Justine and Kelli in volleyball once or twice, but they still intimidated me. Not only were they seniors and at the top of the social hierarchy, but they were gorgeous. Kelli was petite like me, but she'd had more time to fill out, and her gorgeous smile reflected her confidence in her beauty. Justine had a similar smile painted on her face, but her body was one to *really* be jealous of. She had long, slim model legs that she kept in shape with volleyball and weight training, and her tan skin and shiny dark hair had me cursing my pale skin and plain dirty blonde locks.

I had zero curves to speak of and a pencil-shaped body that puberty had not yet had a chance to fill out. I was willing to bet I was the only girl in my grade who hadn't started her period yet. Granted, I was one of the younger students in the sophomore class with a summer birthday. I was nearly a year younger than Emma, who already had her driver's license, but that wasn't any excuse for the universe to slow down the onset of my menstrual cycle.

I wanted to hate these girls. I really did. As much as their mature bodies and full confidence bit at my self-esteem, I couldn't hate them. They'd always been friendly to me. I didn't have any legitimate reason *to* hate them.

I was still watching them when Kelli's boyfriend, Nate, came up to her from behind and embraced her. She flinched at first in surprise. Then she tilted her head back to nuzzle against his shoulder. From this distance, they seemed to make a great pair. They were the designated "It" couple of the school, the two everyone thought would last long after high school. They looked good together, too, with her small but athletic frame and his tall, muscular body. Their blonde hair and blue eyes complemented each other. I couldn't help but take note of how I'd like a boyfriend like that.

While admiring the girls, my mind thought back to Olivia. What would it be like if she were still here? Would she be sitting at that table with them fundraising for some other good cause?

My thoughts drifted back to those I was trying desperately to suppress. *Did I really see Olivia this morning?*

No, I thought, poking at my spaghetti. *I was just stressed and had an image of her face fresh in my mind. I have a wild imagination,* I rationalized. *I don't really know what happened this morning. I'm just remembering it wrong,* I told myself.

With all these thoughts racing around in my head, I hadn't noticed how much time had passed. The buzz of the bell pulled me from my reverie, and I sprang up in surprise. I pushed through the crowd and dumped my tray of uneaten food. Before I let it all fall into the garbage, I grabbed the piece of garlic bread and shoved it in my mouth. I knew if I didn't eat something, I'd be curled up with hunger pains before our volleyball game that night.

The rest of the day continued in a haze, my mood lifting only so slightly in band class, where I fully enjoyed playing first-chair clarinet. When the final bell rang, my stomach called out to me, clearly upset that I didn't eat my lunch. "Oh, shush," I scolded my belly, which earned me a few odd stares.

I shoved my notebook in my locker and took several deep breaths. I needed to calm down if I was going to do well at the game tonight. Our JV team hadn't lost all season, and there was only a week of games left. I wasn't about to lose one because of a bad day, which wasn't honestly all that bad anyway. Gosh, what was up with me?

"Ready?" Emma said cheerfully as we walked toward the locker room to gather our equipment.

"Ready as I'll ever be, I guess." I gave her a smile in hopes that it would cheer me up.

CHAPTER 3

*W*hen we got on the bus, I quickly claimed one of the empty seats near the back and placed my book bag on my lap. Emma sat next to me the same time Derek popped his head up over the seats at the front of the bus as he climbed the stairs.

"There are my two favorite girls." He smiled, taking the seat in front of us. "Chin up, Crystal."

I knew he was trying to get me to smile, but the way he touched my chin as he said this simply annoyed me further.

"Knees and nose," I said, pointing to the front of the bus while repeating the phrase the teachers used to tell us in elementary school. "Knees and nose to the front," they'd tell us for safety reasons.

Derek backed away from me with his eyebrows raised. "Someone woke up on the wrong side of the bed."

I glared at him in warning. I loved Derek like a brother, but I wasn't in the mood for his bubbly attitude. "Yeah," I snapped.

He held his hands up in surrender. He turned away from me and pointed his knees and nose to the front. "Well, it's obviously *someone's* time of the month," he muttered, intentionally saying it loud enough for me to hear.

I rolled my eyes while silently thinking to myself that I *wish* it'd be my time so that I could finally grow into my body.

"Are you okay?" Emma said when we were on the road traveling over the flat terrain of southern Minnesota.

I tore my gaze from the window to look at her. "Yeah. I just... I don't know. I feel weird. I just woke up in a bad mood, and it's been following me around all day."

"I know what you mean." She rolled her eyes. "Talk about being a teenage girl."

Derek popped his head back up over the seat. "And what exactly is that like?"

"Knees and nose," Emma scolded. I laughed as they teased each other, and they joined along in my giggles.

"Maybe I just need a girl's night," I said once our conversation was private again.

"Sure. Tomorrow night?"

"Yeah. It's your turn to host, Emma."

Emma crinkled her nose, which made her look more like a chipmunk than normal. She ran a hand through her dark curls. "My house? Are you sure? I mean, Andrea is way cooler than my parents."

"My mom's great, but I really like your house. You have way more fun things to do. Can we please stay at your house?"

She seemed reluctant, but she finally agreed.

It didn't take long to reach our opposing team's school. Coach Amy must have not noticed my bad mood because she put me in during the first set.

This was certainly not a good day. I bent my knees, ready as the serves came over the net, but I felt so disoriented that I couldn't seem to hit the ball just right. I knew where the ball was going to go before it got there, but my motor skills took a nose dive.

My first serve slammed into the net, and when I tried bumping the ball over on the third hit, the net caught it again. To avoid this the next time, I sent the ball to the other side of the court with a set, but one of the girls on the opposing team spiked it. The ball soared past me before I could process what was going on. A whistle blew, and I knew Coach was rotating me out before she stood from the bench. I slumped over to the boundary line and gave Jenna a high-five as she took my spot.

"What's up, Crystal?" Coach Amy asked as I returned to the bench. "You're not at the top of your game like normal."

"Yeah, maybe I should just sit this one out."

And I did. Coach didn't put me back in for the second or third set, either. I was so out of it that I hadn't noticed when the game was over. When I looked up, all I saw were the disappointed looks on my teammates' faces. I didn't have to look at the scoreboard to know we lost our first match of the season. My shoulders slumped in disappointment to meet the expressions of my teammates.

Coach called us together before we left the court. "I don't want you girls to get too disappointed over this. You've done great this season. You played well tonight, but we can do better next week. Let's keep this as our only loss this year, okay? Team Hornets on one, two, three."

I kept to myself on the bleachers as the Varsity team warmed up. Emma was throwing serves over the net with them, and Derek was catching balls, so I didn't have my best friends to talk to. My eyes fixed on the girls warming up, but I didn't fully process the picture until I saw a blonde ponytail swishing around on our side of the net.

I know that ponytail. It shouldn't be there.

As the girl with the ponytail turned, her brown eyes locked on mine. The other players were moving so fast that in an instant, the girl with the blonde ponytail disappeared.

I felt woozy as a shiver ran down my spine. My heart was beating so hard as if it might escape from my chest, and for a few moments, the sounds in the room ceased to exist. I bent my head down and rested my elbows on my knees, taking in slow, controlled breaths.

Finally, I regained my composure. The sounds of the gymnasium began to come back to life. I looked around uselessly, thinking for a moment that I would find an explanation somewhere in the gym.

But there was nothing. In that moment, I knew I had seen Olivia Owen for the second time that day.

No, I rationalized. *I didn't see her. I imagined her.* I watched the girls more closely and wondered if I mistook one of the other team members for Olivia, but no one looked remotely like her. Once my heart beat settled, I shook off the bogus idea. *Maybe I am going crazy*, I thought to myself.

Time flew by, and before I knew it, our side of the gym erupted into cheers for the Varsity's win.

The bus ride home wasn't exciting since most of the people fell asleep. After working on a few homework problems under the light of my cell phone, I nodded off with them. When we arrived at the school, I deposited my equipment in my gym locker and changed back into my normal clothes.

"See you girls tomorrow," Derek promised when we came out of the locker room.

"Bye, Derek," Emma and I said together. Emma smiled back at him, and I couldn't help but notice that she batted her eyes a bit when she did it. We walked most of the way home together but took our separate ways at our normal corner. I wondered briefly if I should tell Emma I was getting sick, but I didn't want to worry her.

"See you tomorrow morning," Emma waved. "And don't be late."

"I won't. I promise." I actually cracked a smile at that.

When I walked through the door, the smell of brownies hit my nose. I dropped my backpack instantly and raced into the kitchen. There on the counter sat a scrumptious-looking pan of freshly baked brownies. Well, they looked good if you could get past the crusty edges, which I was okay with at the moment. Without bothering to say hello to my mother, I dug in. Sweet, delicious chocolate after a day so sour felt great.

"Hungry?" my mom teased.

She was more like a friend to me than a mother.

"I had an awful day. Back off." I narrowed my eyes at her, a warning that I might bite her hand off if she touched my brownies. It was a light-hearted glare, and she knew it. Even I couldn't hide the smile twitching at the sides of my mouth.

"How did the game go?"

"We lost."

I felt bad that my mom couldn't be there for my games, but she had a business to run, and with Halloween just around the corner, it was the busiest time of the year for her. Mom owned a small shop on Main Street called Divination that specialized in everything Halloween, from costumes and decorations to candy and crystal balls. She and her two friends, Sophie and Diane, kept the business going by selling homemade candy and supernatural products like tarot cards throughout the year.

My mother let out a long yawn. "Well, I'm going to bed. I just wanted to make sure you made it home safe. And, you know, I had to make you brownies. I had a feeling you'd need them tonight."

My mom was always so considerate and somehow knew exactly what I needed when I needed it. Right now, double chocolate brownies were my solace.

"Mom," I said. "Can I stay over at Emma's tomorrow night after practice?" I knew I didn't have to ask, but I did anyway to be courteous.

"Sure."

Once my mom left the kitchen and I felt like I'd eaten enough brownies, I covered the pan and went to get ready for bed. I flipped on the light in the bathroom and brushed my teeth. When I sat on the toilet, I thought I was imagining things.

Nope. My underwear was clearly stained. I had finally started my period!

So that's what my bad mood was all about, I thought. *If that's what PMS is, I'm not sure I want to be a woman anymore*, I joked with myself.

I searched under the sink for something to help me with my issue and found a half-empty package of pads. Soon afterwards, I crawled into bed and fell asleep.

CHAPTER 4

I woke with a start. My legs were tangled around my sheets, my whole body was wet with sweat, and my heart was pounding hard against my chest. I knew I had woken from a nightmare, but the details of the dream now eluded me as I struggled to remember what had terrified me.

I lay in bed for several long minutes until an image of my nightmare resurfaced in my mind. I remembered the sound of a car door shutting. I recalled the way the interior light lit up my face in the side mirror. No, not my face. It was the face of a young girl—maybe six—with brown hair and big chocolate eyes full of terror. As quick as I saw the image in my mind, it was gone.

When I finally calmed down, I made sure to fully dress before leaving my room because I could smell eggs and bacon. That only meant one thing: Teddy was here. The first time my mom's boyfriend came over in the morning to make breakfast for us, I made the mistake of coming out of my bedroom in just a t-shirt and undies. I really should have made the connection that there wasn't the smell of charred breakfast in the air, which meant someone other than my mother was cooking. Needless to say, it was a bit embarrassing.

When I entered the kitchen, I gave Teddy a hug. I was glad he was cooking since my mother was known to burn food and I had the tendency to over salt everything. I was fine with just a bagel, but I could take bacon and eggs any day.

Teddy and I got along well. Mom had been dating him for a few years, but he hadn't filled that hole in my chest where my father belonged. I was sure he never would, but I still liked him.

An image of the crash replayed in my head as I thought about my father. It wasn't a memory of the real car crash since I wasn't there, but rather a memory of a dream I had before it happened. It was strange that I dreamt that my father died in a car accident and then he did. Young children do have wild imaginations.

"Yum," I smacked my lips. "Bacon and eggs."

I reached into the cupboard and pulled out three plates and set them on the table.

"Almost ready, Kiddo."

Normally I would hate if people called me kiddo, but I really didn't mind when Teddy did as long as he let me to call him Teddy Bear whenever I wanted as a way to embarrass him. He didn't mind, even when he brought me to the police station once to show me around and I'd called him Teddy Bear in front of his coworkers. They just laughed, but he managed to laugh along, too.

"Mom!" I shouted down the hall. "Breakfast."

Teddy and I took our spots around the table. He didn't live with us, but he might as well have since he spent most of his time here when he wasn't at work.My mother entered the room. The way Teddy gazed at her in awe told me he really did love her. In a flash, an image of a diamond ring popped into my mind, but it was gone before I could process it. *I hear wedding bells,* I thought silently.

"So how's everything going with planning for the festival?" Teddy asked my mother.

I was intrigued to know this, too, so I listened carefully.

"Most of our responsibilities are set up, but there's another meeting before the festival, and we still have to get a few things together for our booths."

My mom was talking about the booth she and her business partners set up at the Peyton Springs Halloween Festival every year. Since they're the experts in town on Halloween, they graciously volunteered. Plus, it was really good for business promotion.

Mom ran a fortune telling booth and dressed up as a gypsy every year. She knew all about the superstitions with tarot card readings and crystal balls, but it was, of course, all just for fun. A lot of people raved about how accurate she was, but that was just because she was so involved in the community that she knew everything about everyone. It was actually kind of funny to see people talk about how great she was when she was really just faking it, but I guess people wanted to believe in that kind of stuff around Halloween.

Sophie and Diane helped out with other things at the community festival like the haunted trail, carnival games, and other fun things.

"We have some really awesome ideas this year, and the haunted trail is going to be better than ever before," my mother continued. "There are lots of people willing to help out, and Sheryl and Tammy are really doing a lot to make this year a blast."

Sheryl Stratton and Tammy Owen were the co-heads of the festival, but they were always begging my mom and her friends for help, which I found odd. My mom should have just taken over the festival. *But then again,* I thought, *maybe Tammy needs it this year to help her get past this difficult time.* After all, we had just passed the anniversary of her daughter's death, which left me feeling kind of bad for her. I applauded her for how she was holding together and getting so much done with the festival.

"I'll try to be there," Teddy said, "but I can't make any promises. We've had a lot of work at the station lately."

I crunched into my bacon. It was like heaven in my mouth. I moaned, causing my mom and Teddy to stare at me. "What?" I said innocently. "It's good."

The kitchen went silent again when we dug into our food. Teddy was the one to break the silence. "I was wondering if you girls are busy tomorrow night."

My mom and I exchanged a glance. "No," she answered. "What did you have in mind?"

Teddy shrugged, but it didn't feel like honest nonchalance to me. He seemed nervous about something. "I just wanted to take you girls out. We haven't gone out in a while."

"Is it a special occasion?" I asked.

"No. I just thought it would be fun."

My mom looked at me again and nodded lightly. "Sounds great."

I left the house in a much better mood than the day before and made it to the corner the same time Emma approached. "Looking better," she complimented.

"Feeling better," I agreed.

As we strolled to school, I was reminded of the scene we walked into yesterday with the fundraiser. I thought about Olivia briefly and wondered again if I should tell Emma that I thought I saw her in the hallway. I decided not to. It would just come across sounding as if I was crazy. When I told people in my kindergarten class that I had a friend named Eva, who apparently no one else could see or talk to, my classmates called me crazy. All it took was me telling Eva to go away before I made friends with Emma and passed the phase of imaginary friends. Maybe I could tell Olivia to go away and her face wouldn't appear in my mind. *That is, if I ever see her again, and since I'm not crazy,* I told myself, *I don't believe that I will.* I didn't say anything to Emma.

I had a much more successful day at practice, killing my serves and reacting quickly.

When practice ended, I was about ready to eat a horse. I mentioned this to Emma. "Ugh, I want food *now,* but I still have to go home and get my stuff for overnight."

"Why don't you go get your stuff, and I'll go home and start the pizza," she offered. "It should be ready when you get there."

"Deal," I agreed.

Emma and I walked to our corner. In our privacy, I again considered telling her about what happened to me. I still wasn't sure about talking about Olivia. *But I should at least tell Emma about getting my period, right?* I thought. *Perhaps that's something best saved for girl talk tonight, or maybe that's too private to mention.* I tried thinking back to when Emma started her period. I couldn't remember if she'd told me right away or not. The thought of what I should and shouldn't say still nagged at me as we went our separate ways toward our homes.

When I entered the door to our one-story house, Diane and Sophie sat in our living room.

"Girls night for you, too?" I asked before they had a chance to greet me.

"Yep," Sophie answered as she bounced up from the couch. She held me at arm's length. "Is something bothering you, sweetie?"

"Does being a teenage girl count as an excuse?"

Diane laughed from her spot on the couch. "Sure it does."

Sophie embraced me, which helped soothe me. I wrapped my arms around her small frame. Sophie was about my height with curly brown hair and bright eyes. She always seemed upbeat and happy.

Diane, on the other hand, was completely her opposite, which helped balance them out as best friends. Diane was a bigger woman with long, thick auburn hair that she always piled on top her head. She was less laid back and more serious.

"It's great to see you guys, but I have to pack up my stuff and head over to Emma's."

I went to my room and filled a bag with overnight supplies.

"Do you want a ride, Crystal?" my mom shouted from the kitchen when I reentered the main room.

"No, Mom. I'll walk."

She poked her head around the wall separating the two rooms. "Are you sure? It's getting dark."

"Mom, it's only a few blocks. I'll be fine."

"Okay, sweetheart. I'll see you tomorrow."

"Bye, Mom. Catch you later, girls."

It really wasn't a long walk to Emma's house, but I found myself second-guessing if I had packed everything I needed. I mentally ticked off all the necessities in my head. As if the cramps in my abdomen were trying to tell me something, I knew immediately what I had forgotten. Even though I was nearly to Emma's, I turned back toward my house.

CHAPTER 5

hen I arrived back home, Sophie's car was gone. *They must have gone to the shop to play cards*, I thought. I never understood why they went there instead of playing at our kitchen table. There was plenty of room. I didn't fret on it too much.

I knew it wouldn't take me long to get what I came for, but when I looked under the sink in the bathroom, I found nothing but an empty package. I must have taken the last pad this morning without realizing it, and I had used the last one in my backpack for volleyball practice.

I stood from the sink wondering what I was going to do. I could ask Emma, but that seemed almost embarrassing, and I didn't want to just take her pads without asking. Plus, I knew Emma used tampons, and I was *not* ready for that. Weren't they uncomfortable?

I headed to the hall closet where we kept linens and extra bath supplies, but no matter how far back I dug, there weren't any feminine products around.

The gas station wasn't far. Maybe I could go pick some up. That plan seemed like a good idea until I remembered that I didn't have any cash. Maybe Mom had some stashed away, but I was not the kind of girl who would steal money from her mother's purse. Besides, my mom probably had her purse with her.

That left only one option. I would have to go to the shop and ask my mom for a few dollars. She'd have to find out eventually that I'd started my period. I might as well tell her sooner than later.

The shop wasn't far from our house. It was only three blocks down to Main Street and then a few more in the direction toward Emma's house.

The gas station was on the corner. It would hardly take me out of the way.

When I arrived at Divination, I wasn't entirely sure my mother was there. The lights were turned off, and it seemed quiet. When I cupped my hands around my eyes and pressed my face to the front window's glass, though, I could see a faint light creeping out from one of the doors in the back.

I headed around to the back of the building and tried the door. Sure enough, it let me in freely as if it was willing me to join their girl's night. When I stepped into the hallway, I didn't hear the giggles and commotion that I expected from my mother and her two best friends. Normally they'd be loudly bickering and accusing each other of bluffing while laughing hysterically, yet those weren't the sounds I heard coming at me down the hall.

Instead, I heard a quiet humming noise that I couldn't place and smelled the faint scent of a familiar aroma. I guessed it was incense or a candle of some kind, but I didn't know exactly what scent they'd lit. A sense of eeriness overcame me, and I was suddenly afraid of what I might find. I neared the door with the light shining around the corners. It caught me off guard for a moment.

They wouldn't be in there, would they? I thought. *That's the storage room, not the break room. Or am I wrong? What if they left the door unlocked by mistake and someone is robbing their storage room?*

My heart raced as I considered this possibility. A shiver ran down my spine, and I felt a shift in the air. Still, my body sweated nervously. I considered turning around and fleeing for a moment, but I was too curious to turn away.

What would I do if there was someone else here, though? I would scream, I decided. *I would scream and run as fast as I can.*

My heart pounded on the walls of my chest, reverberating through my ears as I neared the door. I began to feel faint. I grabbed the handle with my damp palms and twisted slowly, and then in one quick motion, I whipped the door open.

My heart beat slowed when I found nothing in the storage room but a bunch of boxes. I switched off the light and let the door fall shut with a click.

Once I was back in the dark hallway by myself and ready to leave, the humming noise caught my attention once again. What was that? I followed the sound and pressed my ear against the door that led to the break room.

I could hear muffled voices, but I didn't see a light under the door.

Who was in there? The sound, I realized, was a woman humming a stagnant note.

"We're here to help you," Sophie's voice rang over the humming.

I didn't take a moment to consider what they were doing behind the door. Once I was sure it was my mother and her friends, I wasn't scared anymore.

I had only a split second to take in the scene. The three girls sat in a circle around the break table, their hands connected as if in prayer. Candles lit up their faces. Just beyond the table stood another girl with blonde hair and brown eyes. Olivia Owen's ghost stared back at me with that same look of urgency.

"Help," she mouthed, but I didn't hear any sound come out.

The sight of Olivia lasted only a moment before the women jerked their eyes up at me in surprise and pulled their hands back, breaking their circle. Olivia disappeared.

My jaw dropped. *What is this? What are they doing?*

"Olivia," I murmured before I could stop myself, although I wasn't sure they could hear me. My racing heart returned, and my fingers quivered against the door knob. I felt hot and sweaty all over at the same time a chill overcame me. I was frozen in place and holding my breath.

I am *crazy*, I thought.

My mother smiled at me innocently like I hadn't just walked in on some satanic ritual. "Can I help you with something, sweetie?"

I couldn't find my mouth to formulate my words. I stayed where I was, unmoving for several long seconds as my eyes fixed on the empty space where Olivia stood only moments ago. When I regained my composure, I simply spat out, "I need some cash."

My mother rose from the table, grabbed her purse off the hook near the door, and led me out into the hallway. "It'll just be a minute," she assured her friends as she guided me out of the room.

My whole body trembled and felt weak as I tried to make sense of what I had just seen. I knew what I had seen, and I couldn't deny the fact any longer. I *was* crazy. Olivia's ghost? What was Olivia doing in my mother's shop? Could my mother see her? Did I imagine her?

"Wh—What? Did I—? Were you—?" I spattered, unable to put my thoughts into words. Did they know Olivia was there? I couldn't quite understand what had frightened me so much. Was it the fact that I saw Olivia? Was it the fact that I knew for sure that I had seen Olivia at school the previous day? Or was it because I started believing that I was going crazy?

"We were just meditating," my mother said.

"Meditating," I said without inflection, still trying to catch my breath.

"It helps relieve stress."

Really, meditating? Because to me it looked like you were conducting a séance. But this kind of stuff is just for kicks! It isn't real, right? I tried to rationalize.

"I just need some money for pads," I managed to say almost normally.

My mother smiled at me as if relieved. She reached into her purse and pulled out her wallet. "Here you go. This should be enough."

I grabbed the bill and thanked her before I turned my back and headed toward the door.

"Have a good night, sweetie." She disappeared back into the break room.

When I reached the back door, I paused for a moment and crept back to the break room. I pressed my ear against the door to listen.

"I don't know what she thought," my mother said. "I mean, she can't know what's going on, right? Then again, she just started her period. Maybe there is still hope for her."

Hope? Hope that I'd finally grow into my breasts and my hips. If only.

~

The gas station sat another block down, and when I went in, I used the extra money I had left over to buy a bag of chips. I knew I'd be late to Emma's. I was hoping this would be enough of an apology. I picked out her favorite, Old Dutch dill pickle chips, even though I didn't really like the flavor.

When I got to her house, I knew she was about to scold me for being late. I lifted up the bag of chips, and that was enough to make her squeal in excitement.

"I totally forgive you for letting the pizza go cold."

I smiled back at her, and within minutes, my bad mood from the previous day and fright of what I'd seen earlier melted away. I felt completely comfortable at Emma's. Once we started gorging on pizza, soda, and chips, I was back to my normal self.

"Where's your dad?" I asked, half expecting Emma's father to come around the corner and make a silly joke like normal. Her mother was sitting at the kitchen table going over some paperwork and ignoring us. Her younger sister Kate was in the living room, but their family didn't feel complete without John there.

"He's not here," Emma answered as if I was supposed to know where he was.

Oh, well, I thought.

We spent the rest of the night tackling homework and goofing off in Emma's room while ignoring Kate's pleas to play with us.

"We don't *play*," Emma insisted.

When we sent Kate to watch a movie in the living room, she fell asleep almost instantly, leaving us alone upstairs to read magazines, listen to music, and try out different makeup techniques. Emma was great with makeup whereas I had a difficult time putting on eyeliner.

I was trying, and failing miserably, to put on a dark line across my eye when Emma turned off the radio.

"What was wrong with that song? I liked it."

Emma wrinkled her nose. "I hate that song. Let's listen to some real music." She sifted through her stacks of CDs to find one she liked. "Crap. I can't find the one I want. That was my favorite CD! Oh, well. We'll listen to this one instead. You can pick something if you want."

I sighed, finally giving up on my eyeliner. Emma returned to the mirror and began powdering her dark complexion. I switched spots with her and shuffled through her CDs. Where I collected owl décor, Emma collected CDs. I recognized several that I'd given her from birthdays and Christmases in the past as I ran my hands across the cases and read the artists' names. Suddenly, an idea struck.

I stood up almost too quickly and fell back down at her open closet.

She turned to look at me in confusion. "What are you doing?"

I didn't know how I knew, but I knew where she had lost her favorite CD. I threw clothes out of the way that she had let lay on her closet floor —the only part of her room that wasn't pristine—and flung myself deeper into her closet. I couldn't see what I was doing, but sure enough, my hand finally fell around the corners of a CD case. I pulled it out and looked at it in triumph.

"Is this the CD you're looking for?" I asked, holding it out to her.

"Oh, my gosh!" she squealed. "Yes! I don't know how it got in there. Thank you."

We ended the night by watching scary movies and falling asleep in her queen-sized bed around four in the morning. I woke up around 10:00 a.m. and checked my phone for messages. There was a text from my mom telling me to be home by noon because I had chores to do. After chocolate chip pancakes, I said goodbye to Emma and headed home.

"Thanks for staying the night," she said. "I don't know what I'd do Friday nights without you."

As I neared my house, the memory of the previous night at the shop came flooding back to the forefront of my mind. Did I really see Olivia in my mom's shop? How was that possible?

I contemplated telling my mother about what I had seen in case I needed help or something. What if I started seeing other people, like my dad? I was sure that would make me go crazy for real, and I needed someone there to support me when they put on the straight jacket.

When I entered the house, my mom was already preparing lunch.

"I'm not hungry," I told her.

"That's fine because I didn't make you any food. I figured you would have eaten already."

I watched my mother set her grilled cheese sandwich on the table. It was charred in the middle. How had she not learned how to cook yet? She paced back around the counter and pulled one of the glasses from the drying rack.

Should I tell her? I wondered. My hands shook and my stomach knotted as I tried to work up the courage to say anything.

"Mom," I managed.

"Yeah?" she said as she turned from the sink and took a sip of water from her glass.

I paused for a moment, unsure if I should admit I was going crazy, but in the next second, I knew I had to say it. I spat it out before I could stop myself.

"I saw Olivia Owen last night."

My mother's eyes widened, her jaw dropped, and the glass in her hand fell to the floor and shattered.

CHAPTER 6

"*How* ow could you hide something like this from me?" I stared at my mother in disbelief, trying to process what she'd just said. I wanted to be mad at her for keeping this a secret, but I just couldn't.

An expression of guilt fell over my mother's face. She sat across from me at the dining room table after we'd cleaned up the glass shards. She had just told me the truth about my heritage.

As much as some people would run from the house screaming that my mother was a crazy person, I believed every word she said. Perhaps it was exposure to the paranormal through her business, even if I always believed her crystal balls and tarot cards were fake. Whatever the reason, I wasn't terrified. It was comforting to know that I wasn't actually going crazy.

"I'm sorry. I didn't think you had the gift. I wanted you to live a normal life."

"What do you mean?"

"Crystal, you have to understand," my mother pleaded, trying to justify her actions. She really didn't need to. I wasn't mad at her. I was just confused. "Being psychic is hard. People will hurt you. It's not all rainbows and butterflies."

"Hurt me? How?"

She took a deep breath. "They'll either think you can give them something you can't, or they'll shun you because you can do something they can't. Sweetie," my mother said urgently, grabbing my hands from across the table. "You can't tell anyone. You know that, right?"

"Why not?"

"Some of them will call you a witch. Others will take advantage of you," she continued.

"But Mom, you use your gift every year at the Halloween festival," I pointed out. It was odd to think that all the fun she was having didn't originate from the town gossip but rather from her honest-to-god gifts.

Mom averted her gaze from my eyes and curled her mouth up guiltily. "Everyone thinks that's just for kicks. Even you didn't believe I could do it for real."

She was right. No one really believed she was a fortune teller. She played her role well, a woman who wasn't psychic but pretended to be. Except that she really was.

"What I'm saying," she continued, "is that you have to be careful. I'm carefully hiding out in the open where no one will notice."

I found that a bit ironic, but she was right. "Okay," I agreed. "I'll be careful, but can I at least tell Emma?"

My mother sighed. "I would advise against it. It's your own choice, but you have to be prepared for the consequences. You have to make sure she doesn't spread it around. I don't want people to hurt you." My mother's eyes brimmed with tears.

It took me a few seconds to realize the meaning behind her words. If I told anyone, it would put her secret at risk, too. Still, she was giving me that choice, which is something I really respected and appreciated.

"Mom, Emma's not like that."

"I know. I'm so sorry I didn't tell you, but you understand, right?"

I smiled. "Yeah, I understand, but how come you didn't think I had the gift? Did I not show any psychic tendencies?"

I could see it in my mother's eyes that she was looking into the past. "Do you remember your imaginary friend, Eva?"

"Of course I remember her."

"When you first mentioned her, I was happy and devastated at the same time. At one level, I wanted to share so much with you about the gift, but on another, I wanted you to live a normal life away from the supernatural. When I asked you if Eva was real, you said she wasn't and that you made her up. I assumed that she really was a figment of your imagination. It's not uncommon for children, especially those without siblings, to create imaginary friends at that age."

My mouth fell open in disbelief. I remembered the moment she was talking about. I had been in my room having a tea party with Eva when my mother knocked on my door.

"Who are you talking to, sweetheart?" she'd asked.

"Eva," I said in my high four-year-old voice.

My mother bent down beside my chair. "Sweetheart, who's Eva?"

"Eva's my friend."

"Where is Eva?"

"Right there." I pointed to the chair across from me. I knew by my mother's expression that she didn't see Eva, my first friend my own age. In fact, I knew that no one else could see Eva because none of the other kids at daycare could. When I had asked my babysitter if she could save a seat for Eva at lunch, she had a long talk with me about how Eva wasn't real and that I was imagining her. She told me that it wasn't healthy to have imaginary friends and that I should play with other kids at daycare. So when my mother looked me straight in the eyes and asked me if I believed Eva was real, I put on my best lying face and told her no, I had made Eva up. It was the only time I can remember blatantly lying to her.

"I told you she wasn't real because I thought I would get in trouble if I believed it," I told my mother.

She smiled at me across the dinner table. Then my mother erupted into laughter. I simply stared at her for a moment, unsure of what was so funny. When she didn't stop, I joined in the laughter.

"After that," my mother admitted, "you never really gave me a reason to believe you had a gift. I almost thought you were psychic when you guessed your birthday presents before you opened them. Remember that on your eighth birthday? You were so accurate, but then I figured you peeked before I had a chance to wrap them. I didn't want to ruin your fun, so I didn't say anything."

I hadn't ever peeked.

"There were other times when I thought... maybe... but I convinced myself that I was *looking* for reasons to tell you about my—our—gift."

Memories flooded back into my mind, and suddenly, so much more about my life made sense. "I guess I must have hid a lot from you."

"Like what?"

I picked at my fingernails and kept my head low.

"Like what?" she prodded.

"You know when Dad died?"

"You saw his ghost?" she squealed in shock.

I was taken aback by this statement because it never occurred to me that my father roamed the world as a ghost. "A ghost? No. Is that what Eva was? A ghost?"

My mother stared into the distance for a moment. "Most likely. She could have been your spirit guide, but I'm guessing she was just a lonely girl who needed someone to play with."

"My spirit guide?"

"Everyone has one. They're like angels who guide you in the choices you make in life. I speak to my spirit guide all the time."

My spirit guide? I may have had psychic visions in the past, but I'd never spoken with a spirit guide.

"What happened with Dad?" my mother asked.

"Well, before he died," I started reluctantly, "I dreamt of the accident before you ever told me about it."

My mother gasped. "You—you saw your father die before it happened?"

"Yeah. I think so. I mean, I always thought it was just a coincidence. Do you think it was a vision?"

My mother's lips pressed together deep in thought. I gave her a moment to digest this.

Her next words came out as a whisper. "Do you know what this means?"

"No," I whispered back. Where was she going with this?

"Crystal, there are different types of psychics. Some can predict the future. Others can see the past. Some psychics see ghosts while others hear voices. Do you see where I'm going with this?"

"No," I admitted.

"Crystal, most people don't see spirits *and* predict the future. I mean, we can communicate with them—it's easier in numbers, and that's why séances work—but rarely do people like me *see* them. You clearly have an amazing ability. More amazing than any of us could have predicted. What else should I know?"

I thought for a moment. "That's pretty much it. I can usually tell who's calling before I check caller I.D., but I always wrote that off as luck. Besides, you don't need to be psychic to know who's calling these days."

My mother smiled at this.

I continued. "I always know when it's going to rain, but I took that as a sign that I would make a great meteorologist."

My mom laughed. "Anything else?"

I froze. I knew she would believe me, but saying it out loud made me feel like I'd have to admit it was real. But it was, wasn't it? I took a deep breath. "I've seen Olivia Owen's ghost three times now."

My mother didn't call me crazy, and she wasn't about to contact the mental institution, either. "Three times?"

"Yeah. I saw her at school Thursday morning, at the volleyball game, and in the break room last night."

"You saw her last night." It wasn't a question, only a statement to mull the idea over.

"Yeah, when I went to go get money from you," I clarified even though I didn't need to.

"Are you sure?"

"Yes." Why was she grilling me? "Why?"

She closed her eyes to soothe herself. "We've been trying to contact Olivia for weeks, but we couldn't get through to her."

Why was my mother trying to contact Olivia? "Is Olivia in trouble?"

"Maybe," my mom started, but she was cut off by the sound of the front door opening. Teddy was here already. "We'll talk later." Before Teddy came too far into the house, Mom added with a whisper, "Teddy doesn't know."

Teddy entered the kitchen and looked from me to my mother and back again, and we shot him stares of our own. He held his hands up in defense. "Whatever girl talk stuff is going on here, I don't care to know."

*N*ow that Teddy was here, Mom and I couldn't continue our conversation in case he overheard. It was only about one o'clock, so we had plenty of time to kill before he took us out to dinner. When I walked into my bedroom, I understood completely why my mother wanted me home early. I really did need to do some chores and clean my room.

My bedroom was my place of solace. The walls were white since I'd painted over the pale yellow a few years ago. I'd added a wall decal beside my bed of two colorful owls sitting on a branch together. There was other owl décor spread throughout the room. And it was utterly a mess. Clothes, both clean and dirty, were strewn around along with pieces of homework, books, and other crap I hadn't realized I'd even used recently.

I started with my stuffed animal owl collection in the corner, straightening their wings and setting them upright on their shelves. I took special care of the gray one I called Luna, the one my father had given me that had started the collection. I set her next to the larger black one I'd named David after my father.

My collection brought me back to the memory of my father's death. He used to be a math teacher at the middle school. That night was parent teacher conferences, which meant he was working late. Perhaps if he wasn't out so late, he wouldn't have been hit by a drunk driver. I doubted my father even saw him coming before the full-sized pick-up truck hit him head-on.

Maybe if I'd said something about my dream, we could have warned him.

The thought only wounded my heart further. I knew there was nothing I could do to change what had happened nearly a decade ago.

I forced down the lump in my throat. When all of my owls were in order, I turned back to the rest of my room and prepared myself to tackle it.

I slowly organized piles of clothes and other random belongings and then walked down to the basement to do my laundry, all the while trying to sort through the overwhelming information I'd just stumbled upon.

I was psychic? I was really psychic? How powerful were my abilities? What could I do? What would Emma say when she found out? How would I tell her? Would I tell her? Why was it so easy for me to believe in this nonsense? Was it nonsense?

So many questions raced through my head. I let my clothes sit next to me in the basket as I took a seat on top of the dryer. I folded my legs and rested my hands on my knees. I closed my eyes and took in a deep breath.

How do I use my abilities? I tried focusing on my breathing to relax myself, but it didn't work. I thought maybe if I focused, I would be able to see something, maybe even see Olivia again to find out what she needed, but nothing came. There was still too much confusion clouding my mind.

What good is being psychic if I can't see things at will? I thought as I hopped down, annoyed, and threw my clothes in the washer, not bothering to separate the whites from the colors.

When I went back up to my room, I suddenly lost all forms of motivation I'd had from earlier. Although my room was only half clean, I fell down on my bed, intending to sort out the thoughts in my mind.

Moments later, my mother was knocking at my door. She peeked her head into my room and frowned at the mess, but she didn't say anything about it.

"Crystal, it's time to get ready to go."

Go? Go where?

I glanced at the clock on my nightstand. Holy crap, I'd fallen asleep for nearly three hours. Where had the time gone?

"Teddy wants you to dress nice."

My mother closed my door quietly, and I got ready to go out. I put on a sun dress with blue flowers, which seemed to be the nicest thing in my closet. I let my hair fall down around my body and slipped on a pair of fancy sandals. I applied mascara as a final touch.

"Don't you have anything nicer to wear?" Teddy asked when he saw me.

I looked down at my dress. I thought it looked fine. "Nicer?"

He laughed. "I'm just kidding, Kiddo. I think you look great."

My mother came out a few minutes later looking as gorgeous as ever in a blue halter dress that showed off her slim figure. She had twisted her hair up and applied some makeup. I could tell she hated it. "Why so fancy?"

Teddy rose from his chair and held out his elbow for her. He was wearing sleek black pants, a button down shirt, and a tie.

Why is he doing this? I wondered. *He said this wasn't a special occasion.* Before I could finish the thought, I knew exactly what the special occasion was.

~

Teddy didn't bother telling us where we were going, but it didn't surprise me when we reached the city and stopped outside of Amant. My mother clearly had no idea what was going on as Teddy led her through the front doors.

"Why so fancy?" she asked again.

Please, Mom, I thought. *If you're psychic, how can you not see what's happening?*

Teddy shrugged. "I just thought we could use a nice meal." He gave my mother a peck on the lips before turning to talk with the host about our reservations. I got the impression that Teddy had this planned for quite some time but was still trying desperately to keep things casual. It wasn't working so well for him.

The host led us through the restaurant to an elegant table set with a romantic blossom centerpiece. We took our seats and ordered drinks before searching over the menu. How could my mother not see what was going on, especially with these prices? Steak and fries for $30? *It better be a pretty good steak*, I thought.

I decided to order salmon the same time our drinks arrived, and I silently sipped on my lemon water while Mom and Teddy chatted about the menu.

"I was thinking about getting the lobster," my mother announced.

"I was thinking the same thing. Maybe I should order something else, and we could share," Teddy offered.

My mother gazed up at him and smiled. They ogled at each other from across the table for what seemed like forever before finally deciding on what to order. I tried not to blush at their obvious flirting.

We ordered our dinner and talked about trivial matters while we waited. Teddy was a great guy, but he could get a bit dull at times, so I tuned him out. I let my mind wander, again exploring the implications of my abilities while trying to sort through all the questions I still had. I thought of Olivia again. What did she need help with?

When our food came, Teddy finally quieted. I sat in peace listening to the tranquil music in the background and savoring my delicious fish. I watched as Teddy and my mom shared food, actually feeding each other. My first instinct was to gag, but then I reminded myself why I was here. I smiled, wondering when the excitement of the night would climax. This was a memory I was sure I wanted to hold onto, so instead of letting my mind wander, I focused on the couple before me, so happy and in love.

As the food on our plates began to disappear, our mouths started moving more. When my mother asked about Teddy's parents in Florida, she set up his speech far too well, and he took advantage of this.

"I'm glad you asked because the last time I talked to them, they suggested that we all go down there for Thanksgiving, their treat."

Mom's face twisted as if she didn't know how to answer the question.

I thought it was a great idea. We didn't have family in the area. The only reason we lived in Peyton Springs was because my parents moved here to partner with Sophie and Diane on their business. Sophie was the only one with family in the area out of the three of them. Teddy had family nearby, too, and I'd met most of them, but his parents retired to Florida and traveled the tropics most holidays. We still hadn't had a chance to meet them, so it only made sense to leave Minnesota on Thanksgiving weekend. Getting away from the chilly November weather and lying on the beach sounded fantastic to me.

"I—I guess we'd have to think about it." My mother shot me a nervous glance. "I'd love to meet your parents."

Teddy scratched his head. "The thing is, I don't want you to meet my parents for the first time and have to introduce you as my girlfriend and her daughter."

"What do you mean?" she asked.

Teddy shifted in his chair and reached inside his pocket.

"Your other one," I whispered, unsure of where that came from.

He shoved his hand in his other pocket and pulled out a small black box. He nodded toward me as a thank you gesture while he pulled his brows together in an expression that begged the question, *How did you know?*

"What I mean is that I'd rather introduce you as my future wife and future step-daughter." He hesitated for a moment before rising from his chair and bending down onto one knee beside my mother.

My mom's hands flew to her mouth, and her eyes widened in surprise. How did she *not* see this coming?

Teddy opened the box, and even under the soft glow of the restaurant lights, the familiar diamond I'd seen in my mind shined with every facet. Their eyes locked in a lover's stare.

"Andrea Mae Frost, will you do the great pleasure of being my wife?"

A small sound escaped my mother's lips, although I wasn't sure it was meant to be an answer.

Teddy raised a pointer finger to stop her and placed the box beside her on the table. He reached into his pants pocket again and pulled out another small box and turned to me. When Teddy opened the box, tears welled up in my eyes. Inside the box sat a gorgeous pendant of an owl, its body outlined in blue and black gems.

This was the most touching gesture. Now I understood how my mother didn't see the proposal coming. I had no idea Teddy was planning this for me, either.

"And Crystal Rhea Frost, I would be honored if you would give your mother and me your blessing and that you wouldn't mind if I became your step-father." He glanced toward my mom. "That is, if your mother says yes."

Was he trying to bribe me? Or was he saying that I was just as important to him as my mom was? I wasn't sure. All I knew is that my heart swooned at the gesture and that I loved Teddy enough to want him to marry my mother and hope she said yes.

My mother's eyes were still wide, but she let her hands fall to her lap. "Teddy, I—I." She glanced at me nervously. "I think we need to talk about this." She looked around at the crowd, who was beginning to stare, and then back at the ring. "I'm not saying no. I'm just saying it's a big step, and I think we should all talk about it privately."

Teddy rose from his place on the floor, his shoulders slumped as he sat back in his seat. "I completely understand," he said, although his fallen face told me this made him nervous.

"Let's just get the check," my mom insisted.

I reached toward the middle of the table where my beautiful necklace sat, box open, and snatched it up, closing it and placing it in my purse. I wanted to put it on immediately, but I couldn't predict how my mother would feel about that. If I could see the future, shouldn't I be able to tell?

"You have *my* blessing," I whispered, unsure if I had a place in the conversation.

I gave Teddy a sympathetic look when my mom wasn't watching, and he raised the corners of his mouth in reply. Neither of us had to be psychic to share a telepathic conversation.

Sorry about the way my mom answered, my expression said.

I was expecting a yes, but there's still a glimmer of hope, Teddy's eyes replied.

The car ride home was silent except for when Teddy asked if we could talk now.

"I'd like to speak to both of you separately," my mom answered.

When Teddy pulled into the driveway, he hesitated when getting out of the car. "Should I come in, too?"

My mom climbed out of the passenger seat and looked back at him. "Yes, please."

Teddy hung his head as if Mom was mad at him even though she clearly wasn't. I assured him of this when she was out of earshot, and he gave me another smile of thanks.

My mother left Teddy in the living room and led me into her bedroom to talk. When the door clicked behind her, she let her emotions run.

"I want to marry him so badly!" She danced about the room and plopped down on her bed. "Ugh, I don't know what to do."

I stared at her. My mom and I got along great, like best friends, but I'd never seen her act so much like a teenage girl.

"Why didn't you say yes, then?"

She stared back as if I just didn't get it. I really didn't understand. If she wanted to marry him, why did she crush his spirits in the restaurant?

"It's not that simple, Crystal. In marriage, you shouldn't hide anything."

"Hide anything? What are you hiding?" I knew the answer before I finished the sentence. Teddy didn't know she was psychic.

"I love him so much, but before I can say yes, I need to make sure that he can live with my secret. I hate to put this responsibility on you, but I need you to help me figure out how to tell him."

CHAPTER 8

"*D*idn't you see this coming?" I asked. I wasn't referring to the fact that my mother was psychic. I was referring to the simple fact that she and Teddy were meant to be together. My dad died nearly 10 years ago. My mother and I were both ready to move on, and Teddy would make a great addition to our family.

"I may be psychic, Crystal, but I can't see everything."

"Why don't you just come out and say it?" I offered. "Just tell him about your ability, and if he can't deal, then tough luck. But Teddy loves you. He won't just *leave*."

My mother twisted her hands in her lap and fiddled with her purse strap. "I'm not sure he'll believe me. What if he thinks I'm playing some sick joke? What if he's scared of me?"

I didn't know how to answer my mother's questions. It was a lot to take in, and I wasn't used to my mother leaning on me like this. I wouldn't have believed her ability myself if I hadn't experienced it. Plus, I wasn't entirely sure what Teddy's take on religion was. I knew he didn't go to church, but if he wasn't open-minded about an afterlife, would he believe in the paranormal?

"Well, can't you just look into your crystal ball and figure out what to say?" I asked, half joking.

She twisted her face at me. "It doesn't work that way. I may be able to see the future, but I never get visions about my own future."

I moved across the room and sat next to her on the bed. "What if you could prove it by telling him something he doesn't know?"

"No," my mother whined. I gently rubbed her back to calm her. "I'm only partially clairvoyant. I only get feelings about the future. It's Diane who can see past events."

"What?" I practically squeaked. "Diane is psychic, too?"

"And Sophie," she said.

"But... how?"

My mom gave me a look that begged the question, *Really, you haven't figured it out yet?* She turned toward me and stared into my eyes intently. "How can I tell Teddy?"

"Well, I don't know the future, either!"

She looked at me seriously. "Crystal, I'm not asking your advice as a psychic. I'm asking your advice as a person, as my daughter. Normally I'd ask Sophie or Diane how to handle this, but I've learned that teenagers can have some pretty great insight, too."

She reached up and tucked a strand of hair behind my ear, and I suddenly understood. She was asking me because she wanted me to be part of the decision, of all of this. If she said yes, if she told him her secret, it wouldn't be just her secret she was telling him or her life she'd be affecting. Every move from here on out was sure to affect both of us.

I swallowed, stalling to come up with a good solution. "Mom, what does Teddy believe in?"

"What do you mean?"

"Like, does he believe in God?"

She cocked her head. "You know, of all the things I know about Teddy, this is one subject that we've never really talked about." She dropped her head guiltily. "I guess I always avoided it because I didn't want to reveal my secret."

"Mom, if you love him so much, why did you even hide it from him?"

Why did you hide it from me? I added in my head, but I didn't say it out loud.

"Crystal, you know your dad wasn't the only guy I dated, right?"

"Yeah," I said slowly, unsure where she was going with this.

"Well, I've told other boyfriends my secrets before, and you know what they did?" She didn't wait for an answer. "They left me, called me a witch. My high school boyfriend told everyone, and the bullying got so bad that I had to transfer schools."

My heart dropped. I didn't know my mother had ever been bullied. I was briefly reminded of kindergarten when my classmates called me crazy for having an imaginary friend, except I hadn't imagined her.

"I've always been careful about telling people since then, but your father still loved me after I told him, and he believed me." She blinked at me, holding back tears. "And now I hide behind the business and 'make believe' fortune telling just so that I can use my talents without telling anyone. It's so pathetic." She dropped her head, pulling her self-esteem along with it.

"No, Mom," I assured her as I reached out to rub her shoulder. "It's not pathetic."

"What if he doesn't believe me?" Her voice cracked.

"This is Teddy we're talking about. I think he'll love you no matter what you are. He loves you so much, he'd probably still marry you if he found out you were a dude."

My mom giggled and lifted her head to look at me. Her eyes sparked with tears that threatened to spill over her lids. "Maybe I just shouldn't say anything."

"Come on," I said, patting her shoulder. "I'll be there to help you, but you have to tell him. No more secrets, okay?" I hoped she knew I meant no more secrets from me, either.

"Okay."

"Now let's take a few deep breaths. Then we'll tell Teddy that we'd love him to be part of our family."

She smiled and wiped her nose as she let out a nervous giggle. "I'm sorry I dragged you into this. It's not a burden a mother should put on her child."

I continued rubbing her shoulder. "It's okay, Mom. It really is. I'll help you, okay? Let's go tell Teddy your secret." I paused. "Our secret," I corrected, which made my mom smile.

When we came back into the living room, Teddy was waiting patiently on the couch. He perked up as we entered. My mother hesitated, but I nudged her forward.

"T—Teddy," she started as she approached him hesitantly, and then she knelt down beside him and took his hands. "The reason I didn't say yes right away is because I can't go into a marriage having secrets."

They both glanced at me for a brief moment, my mother looking for encouragement and Teddy searching for some indication of what she was talking about.

"There's just something about me that you don't know, and if you can't accept it, I can't marry you."

Teddy squeezed her hand tighter. I watched from the corner, playing my role as observer. He stared into her eyes dreamily, speaking words of honesty. "Andrea, there's nothing you can say that would stop me from wanting to marry you."

That made my mother's lips twitch into a small smile. "It has to do with what I believe in. Teddy, what do you believe?"

He furrowed his brow. "You mean, do I believe in God?"

"Yes. What do you believe?"

He shifted. Perhaps the subject never came up because it was uncomfortable for him, too. "Well, I believe anything is possible."

I released the breath I didn't know I was holding. My mother did the same.

"Teddy," my mother addressed her soon-to-be fiancé but paused for a brief moment before continuing. "I believe there's another side out there. I believe there are spirits, family members waiting for us on the other side."

He gave her hand another tight squeeze. "Of course there are."

"I also believe that we can communicate with these spirits. Sometimes they tell us about the future. Sometimes they show us things we don't want to see. Sometimes they come to us for help."

Teddy nodded. "A lot of people believe in prophecies."

"Teddy," she said slowly. She paused for a moment, taking in a deep breath. "I believe I am one of those people."

She finally said it. The tension in my body waiting for this moment let go in quick release. I was proud of her. I only wished that when the time came, I would be able to muster up the same level of courage.

"One of what people?"

My mom shifted. "Someone who can communicate with spirits." She hesitated again. "Teddy, I'm... I'm a psychic."

Teddy looked from my mother, to me, then back to my mom. "You girls aren't joking with me, are you? I mean, I know you're into that supernatural stuff with the shop and the Halloween festival and everything, but you're serious?"

The tension in my body returned. He didn't believe her?

My mother dropped her head. I knew she was scared of what would happen next, but when she lifted her head to meet his gaze, she simply said, "Yes."

The next few moments stretched into an eternity, leaving me far too much time to think about the next possible outcomes. Would he storm off and call us crazy? Would he think we were still playing a joke on him? Would he hate us? The clock above the couch ticked, but it seemed too slow, each second pulsing in my ears, a thumping in my body. What would happen next?

Teddy stood and pulled my mother up from the floor. He placed a hand on each of her shoulders and looked her directly in the eye. "I can live with that," he said with a grin. He embraced my mother so hard, I could practically feel the hug in the air. My mother's face lit up, and she beamed at me. In a quick twitch of her head, she motioned for me to join them. I wrapped my arms around their bodies in a group hug.

When they finally pulled away from each other, my mother shouted,

"Yes, yes, yes!" Teddy pulled the box from his pocket once again, knelt to the ground, and slipped the ring over her finger. "Yes!" she cried again as they embraced once more.

Once they settled their excitement, we all sat down, the happy couple cuddled on the couch while I sat on the matching chair. We talked about future plans, like when they would get married and where they would have the wedding. I pulled the box Teddy had given me out of my purse and put on the necklace. It was the perfect length.

I still wasn't sure if Teddy believed us or not, but he at least seemed to accept that we believed it.

My mom suddenly pulled away from Teddy and looked him in the eyes. "Move in with us," she begged.

He smiled back at her. Without hesitation, he agreed.

It was nearly 11:30 when I started nodding off. They wanted me to be part of the planning stage, but I couldn't keep my eyes open anymore to process the plans they were making. My mother was going on about her dream cake when I excused myself. When I closed my door and finally had privacy in my room, I pulled out my phone and immediately texted Emma and Derek.

Mom and Teddy are getting married!!!

It wasn't even a minute later when I heard the familiar chimes notifying me of a text.

OMG!!! You woke me up, but that is AWESOME! Tell them congrats for me!

I was pleased by Emma's excitement and a little disappointed that Derek wasn't awake to send back a text. I felt like I'd been rude to him the other day, and I liked our texting conversations. Even so, I was really tired.

I wanted to tell Emma more about the big night and how it all went down, but I didn't know how to tell her without revealing my mother's, and now my, secret. I figured I'd tell her eventually, but I couldn't discuss something like this over text message. Plus, I was far too tired to stay awake texting, so I changed into my pajamas and fell asleep instead.

CHAPTER 9

$\mathcal{I}$ woke up to find Mom and Teddy at the breakfast table. I poured myself a bowl of cereal and joined them.

"Well, I have to take off," Teddy announced. He rose from the table and carried his dishes to the sink. "I have some paperwork at the station I need to get ready before the week starts. You girls have a good day."

My mother smiled up at him. She'd once told me that having a policeman as a boyfriend made her feel like she was dating a super hero.

Teddy's eyes fell on the owl necklace around my neck as he exited the room.

"You have a good day, too, Teddy Bear," I called after him.

When we were alone with our last few bites of breakfast, my mother spoke. "So, how are you holding up?"

"Holding up? I think your engagement is awesome. I love Teddy."

She set down her fork and looked at me across the table with a serious expression on her face. "That's not what I meant. I want to know how you're handling your abilities. Sometimes growing up can bring them out a bit."

What? Is she saying that I saw Olivia because I started my period? I had to admit, the events did seem to coincide.

"I think I'm fine," I answered. "It's just all so confusing."

"I know," she agreed, adding a sense of *I've been there before* to her tone. "It's just that we didn't get to finish our conversation, and I wanted you to be able to ask questions."

I thought about this for a moment. What *did* I want to know? Did I even want to be psychic, to have this burden over my head, this secret

41

that I would have to hide from everyone, even from the people I loved the most? Did I want to go through what my mother went through? Maybe I could suppress my abilities. I had lived in Peyton Springs my whole life, but what if people found out? What would happen to Divination if the community discovered that the owners were really psychic? Would they drive us away or welcome us with open arms?

At the same time, I knew there had to be some good to come from it. If I could prevent a tragedy like my father's death by learning how to recognize my dreams as visions, then that was something I was willing to do.

As much as it confused me, I wanted to be psychic, to embrace the world beyond this one and to not run and hide from who I was. I met my mother's gaze again, knowing exactly what I wanted to ask.

"Will you teach me?"

Her face lit up.

～

Mom was talking too fast to process anything she was saying.

"Slow down," I begged as we neared Divination. Sophie was the one running the shop this weekend, but mom wanted to bring me in and teach me about the art of being psychic.

It was early on a Sunday morning, so there weren't a lot of people out shopping yet. When we entered Divination, there were two girls who I recognized from the middle school trying on costumes in the dressing room. Other than that, the shop was void of customers.

When the bell above the door rang, Sophie looked up from the costumes she was organizing. "What a surprise! Have you come to take over my shift?" she joked.

"No," my mom laughed as she gestured to Sophie to follow her toward the back. "Crystal, can you stay here just in case anyone comes in and needs help?"

I had worked at the shop in the past, but since I started high school, I rarely came in here.

My mom walked toward the break room while I took a seat on the stool behind the front counter. The shop looked a lot different than I remembered since it was Halloween. Any typically empty spaces on the walls were covered in fake cob webs, and the normal contents of the store were gone, replaced with rows of costumes.

I glanced around and focused on the girls trying on costumes.

"Oh, my gosh. Look at this amazing Roman costume," one of them raved from the dressing rooms toward my right.

"I hate this fairy costume. It's so itchy," the other one said. "I'm going to find a different one." She exited the dressing room and roamed the shop on her own. Clearly she didn't need my help.

Seeing as I wasn't needed, I rose from my chair and slipped around the counter. I ran my fingers across some of the costumes, but none of them stood out to me. I wanted to dress up for Halloween, but I was too old for trick-or-treating. A lot of people dressed up for the community festival. Maybe I could find a costume for that.

I flipped through the costumes on their hangers but found nothing interesting in that row, so I turned to the row behind me. From out of the corner of my eye, I noticed something sparkling from the next room. The building used to have several shops in it, so there was a wall separating the two main rooms with an open entryway between them. The other room was usually full of things like tarot cards, crystal balls, and magic kits.

As I peeked over the clothes rack, the sparkling caught my eye again as bright waves of light danced around the other room. *What is that?* I wondered. I was too intrigued to let it sparkle without investigating.

The young girls' laughter near the dressing room faded into nonexistence as I carried myself into the other room. The light glowed in my eyes, pulling me in. It played tunes of blissfulness and tranquility in my head. Without realizing it, I reached out and wrapped my hands around the source of the light. In my hands sat a glowing crystal ball. Its energy reached out to me and sent waves of happiness from my head to my toes. For a moment, it seemed as if the crystal ball and I were the only things in the world.

"Crystal," my mother called, pulling me from my trance. The other objects in the room returned to my vision, and the light emanating from the ball faded. All that was left in my hands was a regular crystal ball.

I turned around to see her standing in the doorway.

"Mom," I answered, dazed. "Can I get this?" I held out the crystal ball, showing her my new-found treasure.

"It's just a regular crystal ball." She inched into the room and headed over to the fancier balls they had on display, the ones with elegant bases or unique colors. "You don't want one of these more decorative ones?"

"I want this one," I told her, showing it to her once again as if it were a five-pound diamond. My next words came out as a whisper. "Mom, it speaks to me." I didn't think she heard me.

She waved her hand like she didn't care. "Sure, get whatever crystal ball you want."

I jumped in excitement and snatched up the base from the display. It was a simple stainless steel base with four legs. I exited the room and placed the ball on the front counter so I would remember it when we left. My mother followed behind me with a few products in her hands.

Sophie had returned and was again organizing costumes on their racks. I eyed her. Sophie was psychic, too? What kind of abilities did she have?

"What did you talk to Sophie about?" I followed my mother into the break room, which was a small room about the size of my bedroom with hooks and lockers against one wall and a counter against the other. In the middle of the room stood a square table with chairs placed around it.

"Well, I told her I was getting married. I also told her why we were here."

My mother set down the products in her arms on the break table and gestured for me to sit down. The first thing she grabbed was a deck of tarot cards.

I pushed myself away from the table. "Mom, I don't want to do this whole tarot card thing."

She already had the deck out of the box, and as soon as I said it, her face fell. Tarot card readings were her thing. I knew I'd hurt her the second I said it.

"It's just, you've tried showing me this stuff before," I explained, remembering years ago when she tried to get me to help with the Halloween festival, "and I just don't like doing it. I want to learn more about *my* abilities. I don't think I'll ever be a tarot card reader."

She put down the deck as if she understood. "Okay, maybe we shouldn't start with this, then. How about we start with questions?"

I had a lot of questions, but I wasn't entirely sure how to ask them. I decided to just start firing away.

"What type of abilities does Sophie have?"

"She's an empath."

"An empath?"

"She can perceive the emotions of others better than most people and oftentimes can even influence them."

"What about Diane?"

"Diane can see past events."

"Can she see it on demand?"

"No. We only see what we need to. Sometimes you can ask to see certain things. Other times unimportant visions work their way into your mind, but none of us are strong enough to completely control when we see visions or get feelings."

"What about you? Can you only see the future?"

"I can see small pieces of the future, but I rarely see things about myself or my family. I sometimes get vague feelings about things but nothing significant. I can also find things if I have something to touch. It's called psychometry."

I paused, digesting this. "And what about me?"

She shifted. "Well, from what you've said, it sounds like you're a medium, someone who can see spirits."

A medium? But I'd only seen two ghosts before. "I must not be a very good one," I said, wondering if that was true. A small part of me knew that it probably wasn't.

My mother raised her eyebrows. "Crystal, you have a natural ability, but using your abilities takes a lot of practice. Everyone is born with the ability to be psychic, but even if you're like us, born with a more natural connection to the other side, it takes practice to learn how to control and use your abilities."

"So let's practice."

"What?"

"Let's practice. I want to get better. I don't want this to scare me, because when I saw Olivia, I almost pissed my pants, Mom. I want to help Olivia."

The words shocked even me. Is that why I was so eager to learn about this? My heart felt for Olivia; it really did. I knew by the look in her eyes that she needed help and that only I could help her.

"You didn't see her in here the other night, did you?" I asked my mother.

"No," she admitted. "With all of us put together, I was sure we could at least talk with her. But we just didn't have it in us."

With this, realization struck me like a ton of bricks. "Why were you even trying to contact her?"

My mother dropped her head with shame and avoided my gaze. "I feel really bad about it."

"What, Mom? Why does she need help?"

"It's just, I wasn't supposed to hear. I was eavesdropping."

"On who? What did you hear?" My voice was full of urgency even though the situation wasn't that dramatic. But I just had to *know*.

"I overheard Tammy talking to Sheryl about Olivia at one of our festival meetings. When I heard Olivia's name, I stopped and eavesdropped on them even though it was supposed to be a private conversation."

"What did she say?"

"She said that she was scared for her daughter. She admitted that she was having a hard time moving on. She said she could feel her daughter, like she was still here and hadn't made it to heaven yet." My mom pressed her lips together. "I know I have no place in this, but I just knew when she said this that Olivia needed help moving on..."

"And you thought you could help her," I finished. "Mom, don't feel bad. I think it *is* your place because of what you can do. You have a responsibility to help people in these kinds of situations."

"I don't know, though," my mom said. "I can't even see ghosts."

"Well, if you don't have a responsibility to Olivia, then I do. She asked me for help, and I *can* see ghosts."

CHAPTER 10

"This isn't working," I complained.

Mom and I had cleared a space in the break room and were sitting cross legged on the floor. It had been nearly 20 minutes of dead silence and darkness, all while focusing on my fingers to clear my mind. I didn't feel anything. My mom was trying to get me to open my mind so that I could better use my abilities, but I didn't feel any shift in energy or divine enlightenment.

"How's this supposed to help me become a better psychic?"

My mother didn't move from her meditative position and spoke in a calm voice. "The best way to contact the other side is to clear your mind."

This was a horrible first lesson. I had done all I could to relax my body, but I didn't feel any more psychic than when I entered the room.

"It takes time," she informed me.

Meditation gave my mind too much time to wander. "Mom, how can all of you—Sophie, Diane, and you—be psychic? Isn't it super rare?"

She finally shifted and pulled herself up from the floor, flipping the light on. She took a seat next to me. "Yes, it is very rare, but we found each other."

"How?" I asked.

"At college. Somehow we just ended up together and eventually shared our secrets." She smiled at the memories. "It was like fate. We even called our little group 'The Sensitive Society' because we all had abilities. Together we learned how to use them."

"So that's why you moved here and started this shop? Because you were all psychic?"

"Pretty much."

"But why Peyton Springs?"

"Well, Sophie grew up here. We thought it'd be a great place to raise kids. Plus, it's a good place for business."

"Why?"

"Sophie's family moved here a long time ago, so there's a lot of psychic blood in the area. Lots of people come in for our more 'special products.'"

"Special products?" I asked warily.

"Yeah, like the real deal. Things that real psychics would use."

Suddenly their extra back room full of herbs made sense.

"Mom, if you're psychic and I'm psychic, was Grandma psychic?"

She scoffed. "No, your grandma wasn't psychic. *My* grandma was psychic, but it skipped a generation with my mom."

"And you thought it skipped a generation with me? Does it always do that?"

"Not always," she answered. "Sometimes it skips a generation. With some generations, abilities can manifest more powerfully than normal." She pressed her lips together in thought.

I didn't care to ask more questions because I already had enough to think about. I had sat in this room on the hard floor long enough. I shifted and stood. "Can we have a break, Mom? Maybe we can do this some other time this week."

~

We returned home, my crystal ball in my hands, and decided to have macaroni and cheese for lunch. "I'll stand here and make sure you don't burn the water, and you can make sure I don't add any salt to the noodles," I teased as we prepared our lunch.

We both moved around the kitchen in sync. For some reason, I felt a deeper connection to my mother. Perhaps it was the bond that we now shared with our abilities, even if I wasn't sure what I was capable of yet. Our macaroni wasn't terrible.

Mom and I spent some time surfing the Internet for wedding ideas, and then I took the rest of the day to finish cleaning my room. When I felt confident in my new pristine space, I crossed my legs and tried meditating again, plopping myself down at the foot of my bed. I attempted to open my mind, but I didn't know what I was searching for. *Should I try contacting Olivia? Is that a good idea to do on my own? Maybe I could look into my future. Yep. Fortune and fame for sure.* I laughed at myself. *I don't even want fame. A good fortune would be nice, though.*

Once my mind started to wander too far, I gave up on my attempts to meditate. When I looked up, I noticed the crystal ball sitting on my desk. I pulled it down and placed it next to me on the floor and pretended to look into it, but since I didn't know what to look for, I didn't see anything, and it didn't glow. *How will I ever learn to use my abilities?*

I gave up, exhausted, and crawled under the covers. I twirled my owl pendant around in my fingers until I fell asleep.

∼

On Monday morning I met up with Emma straight on time. I expected her to ask about the engagement, but she didn't say anything.

"Emma, are you okay?"

She didn't answer but rather kept her head low as she watched her feet pound against the pavement.

"Emma," I prodded, concern thick in my voice.

"What?" She looked up at me, dazed. "Yeah."

"You okay?"

"Yeah, I'm fine. Why?"

"Don't you want to know about Mom and Teddy?"

"Oh, is there something more to tell?"

"No, I guess not," I admitted, "but Teddy gave me this." I held out my owl pendant to her.

She glanced at it and then looked back at her feet. "Pretty."

What was going on with Emma? Something was clearly bothering her.

I went through my day in a typical state of complete boredom. Having to do worksheets and read textbooks on my own did not interest me, so I took this opportunity to work on my abilities. I started out small, calming my body through meditation while focusing on different people in the classroom. Now that I knew what I was looking for, knowledge came easy to me.

By the end of the day, I knew that Mr. Hall would win $500 at the casino this weekend but spend $1,000. I knew where Mrs. Graham had lost her good pair of reading glasses, which were behind the Lucky Charms in the cupboard. And I knew that Lori the Librarian lied to students about her age. She was actually 52, not 45.

I thought a lot about Olivia, too. Would she try to contact me again? Would I be able to help her? What could she possibly want?

When I found my seat next to Emma and Derek at lunch, Emma was the one sifting through her potatoes today.

"You okay?" Derek asked Emma.

I shook my head at him in warning when she didn't hear him. I knew I shouldn't have done it, but when Derek left to dump his tray, I opened my mind and relaxed my body, focusing on Emma. The noise in the cafeteria made it difficult to figure out what was bothering her. Even so, I knew exactly what had happened before Derek returned to his seat.

I stared wide-eyed at Emma, unable to believe what I'd just seen. She didn't notice me staring. When Derek started talking, I returned to the present and continued our conversation.

"Uh," Derek started nervously, changing the subject. "What are you dressing up as for the Halloween festival?"

I almost didn't want to deal with this because I was too focused on Emma, but I didn't want to get too far into her business. I needed to give her time until she was ready to tell me herself. I tore my mind off her and looked into Derek's bright blue eyes as an anchor.

I shrugged. "I don't have any ideas yet. My mom has a box of costumes, so I guess I'll find something in there. What are you going as?"

"Well, I was kind of thinking..." he glanced down at his tray, avoiding my gaze. "Maybe if you didn't have a costume idea, we could do a type of duo thing or something." He paused. "I don't know, I thought it'd be creative."

"What about Emma?" I asked, glancing at her, yet she was still in a daze.

"Uh, yeah, sure. We could do some sort of trio thing."

"We could go to my mom's shop before the game tomorrow and pick something out," I suggested.

Derek dropped his shoulders. "I have to babysit my twin sisters before the game tomorrow because my mom has an appointment and my dad will be working. How about we check out the costumes before the game on Thursday?"

"Sounds great."

"Emma," Derek tried, attempting to get her attention.

"Huh, what?" she replied, looking up.

"Want to go pick out costumes for the festival on Thursday night?"

"Uh, yeah, sure. Sounds like fun."

Emma was not at the top of her game at volleyball practice. I knew exactly why, but I didn't want to say anything. Emma needed her space, and how would she react if I told her I was psychic? I thought she'd believe me, but I didn't think she needed that right now. Maybe I'd tell her tomorrow when the weight of the world wasn't hanging on her shoulders.

"Call the ball, girls," Coach Amy yelled when Emma made another mistake. It was certainly not her day.

When I arrived home, I immediately went to my mother.

"Do you think I should say something?"

"Crystal, I think if Emma wanted you to know, she would have told you."

"But she's so down about it, Mom. I want to help."

"Just give her some time." I knew my mom was right. "You shouldn't have been snooping around anyway."

"I just wanted to know what was bothering her!" I defended.

"If you do stuff like that, she's going to have a hard time trusting you."

"Do you know that for a fact?" I challenged.

"I know that if Emma wanted you to know, she would have told you. That's all I'm saying."

I crawled into bed cursing my mother for being right. I curled up into a small ball, feeling guilty for using my talents to figure out why Emma was upset. My mom was right. That was private. I had abused my abilities.

CHAPTER 11

W hen I met up with Emma on Tuesday, she seemed to be feeling better. I knew she wasn't over the issue—she wouldn't be for a long time—but I knew she was going to have a better day than she had yesterday.

"Won't it be weird that Teddy will be your dad?" Emma asked on our walk to school.

"I guess I hadn't really thought of it like that. I mean, he'll still be Teddy. I won't call him Dad."

She wrinkled her nose. "It's still going to be weird with him living there and everything."

"I don't know. I think it will be cool having Teddy live with us. I like him. Plus, he makes really good food."

Emma nodded her head in agreement.

We met up with Derek before the final bell rang and all walked to class together. Emma was still on the topic of my mother's marriage when we entered the classroom and took our seats.

"Yeah, that's got to be a big change," Derek agreed.

I shrugged. "I don't know. Teddy spends a lot of time with us anyway. He just doesn't sleep at our house."

"When are they getting married?" Derek asked. "And am I invited?"

I rolled my eyes at him. "They haven't set a date, and I'm sure you'll be invited, Derek. If you're not, you can be my date, but I'll be sure you're on the guest list."

He smiled at that.

"And me," Emma chimed in. "Make sure I'm on the guest list, too.

Then we can *triple date.*" She shot Derek a glance that I couldn't quite read.

"Yes, you'll both be invited. I'm sure your parents will be, too." When I said this, I immediately regretted it, but when I looked at Emma, she didn't seem fazed by it. She just smiled and opened her textbook.

∽

When I got to our table at lunch, Derek and Emma were arguing again.

"Wait, Dustin is dating Haley… or Rachel?" Derek asked.

"Actually," I intervened, ready to set the record straight, "Dustin broke up with Haley to date Rachel, and Rachel broke up with Brandon to date Dustin, but now Rachel is cheating on Dustin with Brandon, and Haley hates Rachel for taking her boyfriend."

They both stared at me with wide eyes. Crap. How did I even know all that? It just came out.

Emma grabbed for me, her nails digging into my arm. "We need to talk." Emma forced me to abandon my food as she dragged me to the bathroom and quickly checked the stalls to make sure they were empty.

"How did you know all that?" she hissed.

I honestly wasn't entirely sure. *Should I just tell her I heard it through the grape vine, or is this my chance to tell her about my abilities?* I thought.

"I—I just said it so you guys would stop arguing," I lied.

She shook her head. "No, you didn't. *I* know, but how did you know?"

Honestly, I didn't care who was dating who, but Emma was more into the social politics of high school.

"Wait, how did you know?" I accused.

"Becca told me at practice. Oh, the perks of being on Varsity," she mused.

"Look, Emma, it doesn't matter how I know about Dustin and Rachel." I stalled, unsure if this was the right time to admit about my abilities.

"Yes, it does," she said, digging her fingernails deeper into my arm. "Becca told me that in the strictest confidence. If people know you know, they're going to think I told you because we're best friends."

"Don't worry. I won't tell anyone that I know about it," I promised, and I really meant it, mostly because I didn't care who was dating who.

"Are you not telling me because you're mad that I didn't spill the beans to you? I didn't think you cared. But seriously, who told you?"

I sighed. "I don't care, and no, I'm not mad at you for not telling me. You can keep your gossip to yourself."

"Tell me," she begged.

I wanted to tell her I was psychic so badly, but I didn't think it was the time or the place. I took the next few moments to weigh the costs and benefits of telling her. I thought about my mother's bravery when she had told Teddy, and I tried to muster up the same level of courage.

"Fine." I caved. Even if this wasn't the time, my need to confide in her overruled that logic. I lowered my voice even though no one was around. "I'm psychic."

She rolled her eyes. "Seriously. Just tell me."

"I am serious."

Emma narrowed her eyes at me.

"I don't know how I know. I just do. Now will you please let go of my arm?" I pulled away from her, happy to have my arm back.

She pursed her lips and crossed her arms. "Come on. I know you probably promised someone not to tell, but I'm your best friend. You can tell me anything."

"Emma," I looked her dead in the eyes. "I'm being serious. I just know things, okay?"

"Prove it," she challenged. "Either prove you're psychic or tell me how you knew about Dustin and Rachel." She stuck her hand behind her back. "How many fingers am I holding up?"

"Two," I answered automatically.

"Lucky guess."

"No. I can see your fingers in the mirror."

She glanced over at the mirror, embarrassed. I let out a giggle. Emma joined in until we were engaged in a full on laughing fit.

I finally composed myself. "Look, Emma. I couldn't care less about who's dating who at this school, but I care about you. If you don't believe I'm psychic, then how do I know that your parents are getting divorced when you refused to open up to me yesterday?"

Emma's face fell and she gawked at me. Tears threatened her eyes. Should I have said that, or did I make a mistake?

"I—I'm sorry," she said quietly, her eyes still fixed on mine. "I just found out."

I pulled Emma into a hug. She didn't struggle away from me. "It's okay. I'm sorry I used my abilities to figure out what was bothering you. I won't do it again, okay?"

I felt Emma tremble in an attempt to hold back her sobs. A tear fell gently from her eye, and she wiped it away quickly.

"How did you know that? My parents wouldn't have said anything."

"I told you. I'm psychic."

Emma gave a half-hearted smile. "You sound crazy, you know that?"

I shrugged like it didn't bother me. "As long as you believe me."

She glared at me again in skepticism. "I'm not sure."

"Remember your copy of *Charlotte's Web* you lent to Derek a while back?"

Her eyes lit up. "Only my favorite book of all time!"

"It's in his pencil case in his locker, shoved in the back behind his books." Derek's locker was such a mess, I didn't know how he found anything in there. "Even Derek doesn't know he has it, so how would I know that if I wasn't psychic?"

"That little—I knew he didn't give it back to me. I have to get him to open his locker. If it's not there..." She didn't finish. I suspected it was because she couldn't think of a good enough threat.

"It'll be there, Emma, but I have to go to the bathroom." I turned to the stall and then back to her. "And Emma, please don't tell anyone. Not even Derek."

Emma rushed off as I entered one of the stalls.

When I was done and at the sink washing my hands, I noticed motion in the mirror. I looked up to see one of the stall doors opening. I swung around to find Justine Hanson standing in front of me, her dark hair perfect and jeans skin-tight. I hadn't heard her come in. Did she come in the same time Emma left, or had she been there all along? How much had she heard?

She stared at me and crossed her arms across her body as she leaned against the stall.

"Um... hi," I said, hoping to relieve the tension in the air. Her intense glare made me very uncomfortable.

"In case you're wondering, I heard everything you said to Emma." Her tone was difficult to read. It came off as a confusing cross between condescending and kind.

"I was just joking around," I tried, but my hands were trembling under the stream of water as I said it. I hoped this would convince her. I did not want this spreading around school and having to relocate because of being a "witch."

She moved over to the sink and twisted the faucet to wash her hands at the same time I turned to dry mine. "No, you weren't."

"Come on," I argued. "You don't really believe I'm psychic."

She shrugged. "I don't know. Maybe I don't have to believe it."

"Then why do you care?" I asked, crossing my arms over my own body to appear more confident.

She shut off the faucet and turned to me.

"Because whether you're psychic or not, Emma was genuinely surprised at what you knew. You must be a pretty good detective."

Crap. What did she want? Didn't my mother warn me this would happen if I told people?

"Not really," I tried, but she was so intimidating with her superior attitude and four-inch heels.

Justine grabbed a paper towel to dry her hands. "I need your help." She wasn't asking, she was demanding. "Meet me at my locker after school, okay?" She tossed her paper towel in the garbage and turned to leave.

"And what if I won't help you?" I challenged. It's not that I didn't want to help Justine. After all, she had always been friendly, even if she was currently frightening me on some level. The thing was that I didn't want this getting out the way it had on my mother. I didn't want a repeat of kindergarten. But what if she was in trouble and *did* need my help? Could I refuse that?

She turned back to me, her hand on the door. "If you don't at least *try* to help me, I'll tell the entire school that you're psychic. I know you don't want that, do you?"

No, I didn't.

"Oh, and one more thing," she said with a smile I couldn't quite read. "Don't tell anyone you're helping me."

There was nothing I could do but meet her at her locker after school and find out what she had in store.

CHAPTER 12

*W*hen I walked back to our lunch table, my mind was still on Justine. I always thought Justine was a nice person, but she seemed so menacing in the bathroom. My hands were trembling at the threat. Would she really tell the whole school if I didn't help her?

Honestly, I tried to rationalize with myself, *how bad could it be? Maybe she just wants me to help her find something she lost. But then again, she told me not to tell anyone. Does that mean whatever she wants me to do is really bad?* I couldn't seem to set my thoughts straight and ease my anxiety.

"Oh, my gosh!" Emma squealed when I reached the table, pulling herself from an embrace with Derek. She was bouncing up in her seat, holding out the light blue book toward me. I sat next to her. She leaned over to me and whispered so only the two of us could hear. "It was right where you said it was."

Derek rolled his eyes from the opposite side of the table. "I don't know how Emma knew where to look, but she made me open my locker so she could find the darn thing. I was sure I gave it back to her."

I picked up my fork and poked at my food, my thoughts still on Justine. What was going to happen after school?

"Crystal." Derek snapped his fingers in front of my face. "Don't you agree?"

"Uh, yeah, whatever." I didn't know what I was agreeing to, but it kept the conversation going between Derek and Emma. I was grateful when I didn't have to weigh in.

~

The final bell for the school day set off an alarm in my body, causing my heart to pound. Why couldn't I just look into the future and see what Justine was going to ask so I could either relieve this anxiety or avoid her altogether?

"Hey," Emma started nervously when we met after school. I was crouched down at my locker. Emma stood above me and twisted a dark curl around her finger. "Do you mind if I hang out at your house before the game?"

We had a home game tonight, which meant we had a few hours of free time.

"Sure," I shrugged, hoping it would hide my anxiety. I needed to meet with Justine. "Can I just go grab something from my gym locker?" I lied. "I'll meet you in the commons."

"Are you lying to me?" She narrowed her eyes accusingly.

"No. Why would you say that?"

"Because your eyebrow is twitching."

My hand flew up to my eyebrow. Oh, no. It really was twitching. "I'm not lying," I lied again.

"Why don't I just come with you?"

"No!" I practically shouted. "I—I mean, it's kind of personal."

"Oh," Emma said, elongating the word to show she understood. She winked. "Gotcha. So you're finally a woman?"

I let out a gasp and glanced around. "Emma!" I scolded.

She laughed. "Okay. I'll see you in the commons."

Students had fled the halls quickly to escape school, so they were empty when I made it to Justine's locker. I wasn't entirely sure which one was hers, but I had a general idea.

When I arrived, Justine wasn't there. I glanced around frantically, hoping to spot her. Had I taken too much time? Was she already on her way to telling the entire school my secret? It would only take a quick text to say, "Crystal Frost is a freak," to spread like a wildfire. At least Emma and Derek would stand by my side.

Just as I was about to turn and flee in hopes of finding her before she could tell anyone, I saw her coming down the hall. She had a notebook in her hand, and her heels clicked against the floor as she rushed up to me.

"I'm so sorry. I had to talk to Mrs. Flick about an assignment." Her voice emulated a tone of friendship. It was like she was a completely different person from the girl I spoke with in the bathroom earlier. She was beaming with excitement and energy.

Justine twisted her locker combination as she spoke. "I'm so glad you're helping me with this. I've been thinking about you all day and how we're finally going to resolve this issue." She sounded like I had agreed to help her decorate for prom or something. She was far more excited than I'd expected.

She continued jabbering at a million miles per hour as she dug around in her locker. "You see, I've been trying to investigate this for like a year, but I just can't find any proof, and Kelli won't tell me anything."

"Hold up," I said, stopping her. "I may be..." I glanced around, and even though I didn't see anyone, I lowered my voice. "Psychic. But that doesn't mean I have any idea what you're talking about."

Justine spoke softly and cocked a finger for me to come in close. Then she told me everything she knew.

∽

I didn't believe it. I just couldn't. Justine thought Nate was abusing Kelli, but they looked so happy together. They had the kind of relationship every girl in the school longed for. Was it possible that the school's hottest couple wasn't so hot at all?

"I've seen the bruises," Justine had told me matter-of-factly. "But Kelli always makes excuses and says she tripped or it was from sports or whatever. That's why she always changes in the stalls before practice. She doesn't want anyone to see. It's not just that, though. Everything about her is different. She's more reserved than ever before."

"Why are you even telling me this?" I asked.

"Because I need you to help me get proof. If we don't do something, he's probably going to kill her. I've done everything I can. I talked to Kelli, but she denies it. I told her parents, but they think Nate's an angel. I even tried to turn him in, but since Kelli denied it, the police said there wasn't anything they could do. I've never seen him hit her, but I've seen how nasty he can be. Once I was riding in the car with them and Nate called her a 'fucking bitch' just because we took a wrong turn and she was supposed to be navigating. It wasn't even a big deal. He's really smart about it, too, putting on a façade in front of everyone and hitting her only where her clothes can hide it."

She glanced around and lowered her voice even further until she was whispering. "Last summer, he must have done something really bad to her arms because she wore long sleeves for like two weeks and wouldn't come out boating with me. I haven't seen her put on a swimming suit since she met him. Sometimes she doesn't even wear her spandex shorts at games but puts on long athletic shorts instead."

Strangely enough, I had noticed that, but wearing spandex shorts wasn't a requirement for our uniform as long as the shorts were black. Could it be that she was hiding something under her shorts?

"It's only getting worse," she told me. "I love her like a sister, but we've hardly spoken since the fundraiser. In fact, we've hardly spoken all school year outside of volleyball practice. It's like something happened between them last summer. There were a few weeks there when I didn't even *see* her, let alone talk to her. Nate has more control over her than ever. She does whatever he says, and he doesn't want her hanging out with me. If you knew her like I do, you'd see that she's scared of him."

Justine sighed. "I think he used to be a nice guy, but after his parents divorced, he just became dark. And now, it's like he's got this god complex and thinks he can do whatever he wants without consequences. Like he thrives on power over women or something." She paused. "It's disgusting."

I couldn't figure out why Justine was confiding in me. Did she really think I could help her? I hardly knew how to use my abilities, and I was still trying to figure them out so that the next time Olivia showed up I could figure out what *she* needed from me, too. And then there was Emma, who I was really hoping to speak with about her parents' divorce. With school, volleyball, and everything else piled on top of that, it seemed like so much responsibility falling on me at once. Suddenly, the idea of being psychic made me want to run away from who I really was, but hadn't I said I was supposed to help people?

With this, I caved. "What do you want me to do?" I was concerned. I really was. At the same time, I honestly wasn't sure if I could help. I'd found out a few minor things about people by concentrating on them, but was I able to really know something this serious? Besides, where would I get the "proof" Justine needed? We couldn't go to the police with a psychic vision as our only proof.

"I want you to look into it, okay? Try to figure something out so we can save Kelli."

"Look, Justine. I don't even really know how to use my abilities. I'm sorry, but I don't know if I can help you."

She stared at me with a pout that even I couldn't refuse. I wasn't sure if it was an act or not, but I had to remind myself that if I didn't at least try, she was going to tell the whole school and I might be bullied out of town. I couldn't risk that with my mom's business.

"Fine," I gave in. "I'll try, but I can't make any promises."

She smiled, and then in a shocking moment, she pulled me into an embrace. "Thank you so much, Crystal."

CHAPTER 13

"*What* took you so long?" Emma complained when I finally reached the commons.

I didn't want my eyebrow to start twitching again. Emma was too good at telling when I was lying. We'd known each other far too long.

"I was talking to Justine," I answered truthfully.

"Justine Hanson? About what?" Emma seemed suspicious and rightfully so. I could probably count on one hand the amount of times I'd talked to Justine in the past.

I bit my lip nervously but quickly stopped so that she wouldn't notice. "She wanted help... with homework."

"Why would she ask you? You're not even in any of her classes."

I shrugged. "She just needed a second opinion." That wasn't a complete lie.

I was still nervous and overwhelmed with all the responsibility my new powers put on me, but I wasn't going to let that ruin a great time with Emma, so I put on a smile. "Come on," I said. "We need some girl talk."

On the way back to my house, I got Emma to open up about her parents' divorce. She told me about how she was sad to see her family break up but that it wasn't as bad as it sounded. She said her parents had tried marriage counseling, but they just couldn't stand each other anymore and had separated.

"But I don't want to talk about my parents. I want to know more about you and this whole psychic thing."

I smiled out of nervousness. What could I say to her about it? "Emma, I don't even know that much about it myself. I'm just learning."

"So, can you tell my future? Like if anyone is going to ask me to prom this year?"

I rolled my eyes at her. "Yeah, it doesn't work that way."

She kicked at a rock. "Aw, shucks."

When we reached my house, Emma went straight to the kitchen. "What should we have before the game?" she called, and I could already hear her opening and closing cabinets. I heard the buzz of the freezer as she opened it, and I knew she had found the frozen pizza.

We put the pizza in the oven and went to my room.

"Oh, no," Emma stopped in my doorway, alarmed.

"What?" I cried, afraid of what had scared her.

She turned to me, an expression of terror fixed on her face as she grabbed my shoulders and shook me. "Who are you, and what have you done with Crystal?" She swung around and pointed to my room. "I can see your floor!"

I laughed. "Don't scare me like that!"

"Seriously, though," she said as she plopped down on my bed. "Your room looks nice."

"I usually keep it clean," I defended, "but I've been busy for like two months with school and volleyball."

"And I haven't? I manage to keep my room clean." She was right, and that was part of the reason I liked staying at her place better.

"Oh. My. Gosh." Emma's eyes widened as she caught a glimpse of something across the room. "What is that?" She pointed to the crystal ball on my dresser.

"Oh, that," I said nonchalantly. "Nothing." But I knew it wasn't nothing. I took the few steps over to my dresser and picked up the ball.

"Are you, like, into dark magic?"

"Dark magic? No!" I pulled the ball close to me in a protective embrace. "I just saw it at Divination and thought it looked neat." I returned the ball back to its stand and stepped back to admire it.

"But can you, like, look into it and see the future?"

I laughed. "No. Not yet at least. I don't know how to use it."

"This is so cool."

"What is?"

"That you might be psychic. You're like a superhero."

"It's not a question of 'might,' Emma. I *am* psychic." I almost wanted to argue the fact along with her and refuse my abilities and the responsibility of it, but I just couldn't do that.

"Come on," Emma said, sitting up in my bed. "We'll play a game."

Really? Was she serious? I knew Emma wouldn't give up until I played. "Okay, but I won't promise that it will work."

Emma shifted excitedly. "I'm going to take an object and hide it somewhere, and you're going to find it."

"Emma, I don't even know how to do that."

She held out a finger to me and made noises until I stopped speaking. "It's just a game, okay? You stay here." She leapt from my bed and left the room, closing my door behind her.

Ugh. I plopped down on my bed and placed my arm over my eyes. She was going to find the smallest thing to hide and put it in an impossible place to find. I wasn't going to win this game.

I wanted to cry. So much was happening lately with Olivia, Justine, and everything else related to my abilities. But I held myself together.

Emma came back a few minutes later and announced that I could start looking. I didn't move from my spot.

"Well, aren't you going to look for it?"

"I am," I teased. I'd never found things before except her copy of *Charlotte's Web* in Derek's locker. Then I remembered how I had found her CD. Maybe I *did* have a gift for finding.

"Even with psychic powers, you'll never find it," she said smugly.

Suddenly, I was up to the challenge.

My mom had told me she could find things. *I can also find things if I have something to touch. It's called psychometry.*

I sat up in my bed and held my hand out.

"What?" Emma asked.

"Come here. I need to see your hand."

"My hand?"

"Yeah, the one that held whatever you hid."

I gripped her hand and closed my eyes, concentrating hard on the object. Within seconds, I knew exactly what and where it was. I hopped up from the bed.

"Not-uh. You do not know where it is." Emma raced after me.

I headed down the hallway and pounded down the stairs to the laundry room. There were two laundry baskets full of clothes, one with towels and one with whites. I picked up the one full of whites and dumped its contents onto the floor. Emma stood next to me as I did this, her eyes wide and her mouth open.

I only had to toss aside two pieces of clothing before I found Emma's sock with its signature pink stripe in the mess. I reached for her ankle and pulled up on her pant leg. She was missing one of her socks. I held it up triumphantly, and a victorious grin spread across my face that made me—if only for a moment—slightly prouder of my abilities.

She frowned and snatched the sock out of my hand before storming back up the stairs. Was she mad at me?

"Emma," I called after her, but she didn't say anything back. *What did I do wrong?*

I slowly walked out of the laundry room and found Emma at the top of the stairs putting her sock back on her foot.

"Emma," I said softly. "Are you mad at me?"

"Yes," she answered crossly. When she was done tying her shoe, she planted her foot on the stair and crossed her arms, giving me the evil eye. "I'm mad because hide and seek is never going to be any fun again." She couldn't help it when her lips curled into a smile.

When I realized she wasn't actually angry with me, I approached her and gave her a hug. "You always liked to be the finder anyway. I can hide from now on."

We laughed together.

"I'm not mad at you, Crystal. I think it's awesome that you're a superhero."

"I'm not a superhero. I'm just psychic. It's even weird to say that. I'm still getting used to it."

"Well, it's pretty cool." Emma stopped and sniffed the air. "Do you smell something burning?"

We exchanged an alarmed glance and bolted for the kitchen together. Smoke was coming from the oven. Our pizza was burnt to a crisp because we'd forgotten to set the timer.

"Maybe we should just stick with microwaveable food," I suggested.

We ate hot pockets before heading to our volleyball game. Justine kept throwing me nervous glances as if to ask if I'd found anything out yet. I sent her back a look that said, *Sorry, nothing yet.*

Both the JV and the Varsity won.

CHAPTER 14

*T*hat night, Olivia came to me in my dreams. I only saw her face for a moment, but she whispered something to me. "Help her," she said, but I woke up not knowing who "her" was. I felt a wave of guilt rush over me. I knew I should have been focusing more attention on Olivia than on other things. She needed me.

When I woke up that Wednesday, I made a list of all the people Olivia could possibly mean by "her," but I only came up with one name: Tammy Owen. Did Tammy need help moving on? I had heard she was holding together pretty well, but some people are better at hiding it than others.

I told my mother about my dream and my concerns about Tammy.

"I don't really know how to help her, sweetie. I mean, Tammy and I get along, but I'm not exactly her best friend."

"Oh." I slumped my shoulders in disappointment. I didn't know how *I* was supposed to help Tammy.

"I'll look into it," my mother promised, which made me feel a little better. "But you know what? The girls and I can get together Friday night again. Maybe we can talk with Olivia this time and see what she really needs. With you there, I'm sure it will be easier."

My mom was inviting me to a séance? *That should be interesting*, I thought.

"But don't you have to get ready for the Halloween festival for Saturday?" I asked.

"It'll be fine. We don't have to do anything for it Friday night."

"Okay, I look forward to it." Did I really mean that? The whole idea of a séance scared me yet seemed exhilarating at the same time.

That day at school, I spent most of my time focusing my energy on Kelli. I ignored my teachers as I concentrated on my breathing and tried to relax my body and connect with her, but I came up blank every time. Either there wasn't anything to find or I wasn't as powerful as I thought. Either way, I couldn't seem to get through to her.

At lunch, I spotted Kelli and Nate across the lunch room, which sparked an idea. Maybe if I focused on *him* I could find something. Since Emma and Derek kept asking my opinion about music and distracting me, I didn't have the chance to concentrate on him. To top it off, all my teachers decided to actually do something in class the rest of the day, so I didn't have the opportunity to find anything on Nate.

When it came time for volleyball practice, our last practice of the season before our final game, Justine pulled me aside in the locker room. Unfortunately, I had nothing to tell her.

"I'm trying. I really am. But I can't see anything. Maybe if I could actually talk with Kelli, but I can't just bring it up."

"Well try harder," Justine hissed. "I'm getting really worried, and you're my only hope to save my best friend."

"I'm sorry."

Just then, Kelli pushed through the door into the locker room. We both stood upright in surprise, immediately ceasing our conversation. Kelli eyed us suspiciously, but I didn't think she knew we were talking about her. How could she?

After practice, I came up with the perfect opportunity to speak to Kelli. I watched as she left the locker room. I reached into my locker and grabbed the first thing my hands found.

"I'll be right back," I told Emma.

When I caught up to Kelli, I grabbed her wrist. She swung around at the same time she took a step back to distance herself from me. I was expecting to see something, an indication of her relationship, but there was nothing. My plan failed miserably. Interestingly, though, my touch allowed me to feel her emotions. She was confused why I was there and upset about something.

"What?" she demanded when I didn't say anything.

For a moment, I couldn't remember what my plan was, and then I looked down to find a bottle of lotion in my hands. "I thought I saw you drop this." I held the bottle out to her.

"Well, it's not mine." Not only did she sound irritated, but I could feel the annoyance as energy sizzled between us.

"I'm sorry. My mistake."

Just as I was about to turn and leave, a car pulled up next to us. Kelli's emotions shifted from exasperation to something entirely confusing, a mixture of emotions that made it hard to pinpoint. A sense of love, it seemed, washed over her when she saw the car. I also took note of the fear she conveyed by the sight of it. As her pulse quickened, so did mine. I wondered for a moment if it was a family member driving the car.

"Are you okay?" I asked without thinking. It only made her widen her eyes at me in suspicion.

"I have to go," she said as she turned on her heel and flipped her hair over her shoulder.

I glanced at the driver, and even though it was getting dark, it was still light enough to see his face. Nate Williams sat in the front seat. After Kelli closed the door, he jerked his head toward me and glared, his eyes dark below his eyebrows and the muscles in his jaw tense. It sent chills up and down my spine.

He tore his gaze from me and drove off. *Holy crap. He is a bad guy, isn't he? And Kelli is afraid of him.* I turned back toward the school, discouraged that my plan didn't work. Or had it?

I didn't realize that I was frowning when I got back to the locker room.

"Are you okay?" Emma asked.

Suddenly aware of my posture, I straightened up and put a smile on my face. "I'm fine," I lied and turned away so that she couldn't see my eyebrow twitch.

"So whose house are we staying at this weekend?"

"Uh," I stalled. "This weekend? I can't this weekend." I didn't care how much Emma begged, I would not miss out on the séance this Friday. I needed to focus on Olivia, especially since I'd been neglecting her and she needed my help.

"Why not?"

I couldn't tell her, could I? I didn't know if it was right to tell Emma that Mom, Sophie, and Diane were all psychic, too. I decided to keep this one to myself.

I ducked down behind my locker door so she wouldn't see my face. "Uh, my mom kind of has a mother-daughter thing planned on Friday." That wasn't a lie. "Don't worry. I'll still be here when we turn in our uniforms and have our pizza party on Friday."

"Oh, yeah," she said, trying to hide her disappointment. "Yeah, that will be fun."

I suspected that Emma wanted to be at home as little as possible, but I had other people to help at the moment. Besides, she said that home life wasn't that bad.

∾

When I got home, I slumped onto my bed. I wanted to cry, to relieve the overwhelming knot in my chest, but no tears came out. When I finally gave up and lifted my head, my gaze fell upon the crystal ball on my dresser. Maybe that would have some answers, but I didn't know how to use it. I thought about waiting for my mom to get home from the shop, which was staying open later and later as Halloween approached, but the longer I waited, the more I felt I needed to take my abilities into my own hands. I decided it was time to turn to the Internet for help.

I pulled Luna down from the shelf next to my bed, holding her close for comfort, and snuggled under my blanket. I flipped open my laptop and typed "How to Use a Crystal Ball" into the Google search bar. The first few sites I visited didn't help me at all, but I continued my search anyway, clicking through links and trying to find some helpful information. I got excited when I found an article that seemed to make sense. It told me to set the mood with candles or incense, let go of expectation, and to practice discipline over the conscious mind. It also noted that I should listen to the more subtle voices of the universe, whatever that meant.

I wasn't sure how this was going to go, but I decided to take a shot at it. I mean, what could it hurt? Rising from my bed, I walked into the kitchen and shuffled through a few drawers before finding a stash of candles. I gathered the tea candles and a box of matches and headed back to my room. One by one, I lit three candles. I shut off the light and placed myself in my desk chair in front of the crystal ball.

I paused for a moment, mostly out of uncertainty. I wasn't sure I would really be able to do this, but if my crystal ball could help me help others, then it was something I was willing to try.

I held the ball in my hands and stared into it for what seemed like an eternity. I didn't see anything. *Let go of expectation*, I told myself as I tried to put both Olivia and Kelli out of my mind. For a brief moment, I almost believed that the ball had no power, but when I regained control of my mind, I allowed myself to do as the website instructed and opened my mind to all possibilities.

Discipline over the conscious mind. Control yourself. Let go of expectations.

I let my mind relax as I stared deep into the crystal ball. When it started glowing, I squealed with excitement. The light dimmed in reply to my squeal, so I tried again, doing as I had done before. This time when it glowed and the glass clouded over, I didn't let my excitement get the better of me.

I stared further into it, making the connection with my ball. When I was confident in our connection, I set it back on its stand. I allowed myself to fall deeper into my trance.

The fog within the ball began to dissipate, and motion passed across it as if I were watching a scene unfold on a television screen. But when the image became clear, I didn't see Kelli or Olivia.

No expectations, I thought in the conscious part of my mind, but I let even that thought fall as I pushed my mind to connect with the ball and find discipline over my consciousness.

The first image I saw was of a small bedroom. The walls were pink, and there was a collection of teddy bears stacked against the wall. Frilly lace curtains outlined the windows.

As the angle zoomed out, I saw her, the girl whom the room clearly belonged to. She was curled in a lump on her bed and looked cozy beneath the sheets. I couldn't see her face, but she didn't look very big.

Movement in another corner of the room caught my attention. A tall figure moved in the shadows. He was dressed in all black, so it was hard to notice him at first. He moved closer to the girl, and when he was close enough, he pounced, clasping his hand hard over her mouth so that she wouldn't scream.

The girl's eyes flew open, and the image focused on her face.

I pushed back in my chair too quickly, flinging the crystal ball to the floor. It landed on the carpet with a thud.

My heart pounded, and my hands trembled. What did that little girl have to do with me? Why did I need to see that scene? I'd seen her brown hair and big chocolate eyes in a nightmare before, but what did that mean? I knew deep down that it meant something. It wasn't about Kelli or Olivia, my intuition told me, but I couldn't help but ask myself the question: Why have I seen her twice now?

I didn't want to look into my crystal ball again, so I didn't. Instead, I wanted to toss it across the room. I held back that urge, afraid that it would break. I already felt bad about letting it fall to the floor. Questions continued to race in my mind. How could I help a little girl I didn't even know? Was the man going to hurt her? As much as I longed to do something, I didn't know enough to help. All I knew about the girl was what she looked like and her approximate age.

That's not much to go on, I thought. Besides, I had too much to deal with already and too many people to help. Why hadn't my crystal ball shown me something about Kelli or Olivia? That was what I really wanted to see —no, needed to see.

Discouraged for not finding anything to actually help anyone I knew, and not giving me enough information to help Chocolate Eyes, I blew out the candles and crawled into bed far too early, but I fell asleep instantly.

CHAPTER 15

*A*fter a sound sleep, I woke up Thursday well-rested. I still had problems to solve and a mystery from my crystal ball, yet I was relaxed and ready to take on the day.

I could hear Teddy talking to my mom from the kitchen. I quickly realized that he had spent the night. Did this mean he was already working on moving in? I didn't have a chance to check it out before I heard the front door close, indicating that he was already on his way to work.

I started the day by taking a warm shower and drying my long dirty blonde hair. The hair dryer left my hair straight, so I kept it that way, brushing it to near perfection.

"Crystal," my mother called from the other side of the house. "I have to go to work, but Teddy and I will be at your game tonight, okay?"

My heart flipped at the thought. Just one more game and the season was over, and I'd have more free time on my hands. I was excited and disappointed at the same time, but at least I would have more time to figure out my abilities and actually put them to use helping people.

"Okay, Mom. I love you."

"Love you, too. Bye!"

"Bye!" I shouted back. I gave myself a confident smile in the mirror.

Gathering my backpack and supplies for the day, I left my room and headed for the kitchen, popping a bagel in the toaster and pulling out some cream cheese from the fridge to top it with. Yum. My favorite.

I turned on the TV for a few moments to get the scoop on the weather, but when the news switched to a story about a local abduction, I turned it off. I wasn't in a mood to focus on more unfortunate mysteries than the ones I already had on my plate.

The house was quiet, and I was ready for school early, so I wiggled my way onto the counter and closed my eyes. It was bright behind my lids. I could hear the soft hum of the appliances and smell the delicious scent of a toasting bagel. It seemed so serene.

What will I learn about my abilities today? I wondered. I let my body relax as I focused on my fingertips like my mother taught me. My mind spun in an elegant dance through clouds as I concentrated on the other side to guide me in my day's decisions. I felt at peace.

In an instant, it all changed, sending me reeling toward something dangerous. A frightening roar reverberated in my ears as a shock of terror spread through my body. My bagel popped, snapping me out of it.

What was that all about? I thought as I hopped down from the counter-top. My hands were still shaking and my pulse threatening as I spread cream cheese over my bagel.

It was nothing, I assured myself, but I still couldn't shake the feeling that it was a sign of something to come, that someone was coming to get me and would take me by surprise. My sense of peace shattered.

I met Emma at our corner, my anxiety and paranoia just above its normal level, but I didn't let it show.

The moment Emma was close enough to me, she started speaking. "I was reading last night, you know, about your kind, and I was thinking—"

"My kind?" I eyed her speculatively.

"Yeah, about psychics and stuff," she said, waving a hand nonchalantly. "I was reading that to make your powers stronger, you have to practice them, and—"

"Why?" I interrupted again. I never expected Emma to ditch me as a friend when I told her about my abilities, but I didn't expect her to be so accepting of it, either.

She shrugged. "I don't know. I guess it's just intriguing. I mean, it'd be awesome if I were psychic, but if I can't be, then it's cool that you are."

"Actually you can be. My mom said everyone's born with psychic abilities but that I just have a stronger connection to the other side or something. Like how everyone has intuition. It just takes practice, I guess."

"Ohmigosh," Emma squealed, stopping in her tracks. "We should, like, learn together, and we could *both* be psychic."

Something about the idea intrigued me. It was cool enough that I had my mom to help me, but I would be much more comfortable with Emma by my side.

"That would be really cool," I said, smiling. "But I really don't know that much about how to do it. Maybe you could talk to my mom."

I threw my hand over my mouth. Was I allowed to tell Emma my mom is psychic? I didn't think it would hurt anything, but I should have asked my mom first.

Emma's eyes widened. "Andrea's psychic, too? I mean, a real psychic? I know she does all that fake voodoo stuff for Halloween, but she's real?"

I dropped my hand. "Well, let's just say it's not as fake as she leads people to believe."

Emma smiled. "This is going to be so awesome. When can we start?"

I bit my lip nervously. I wasn't sure if I wanted to include Emma in the séance right away. It almost seemed too much for *me*. I didn't want to overwhelm her and scare her away.

"Maybe it's best if we wait until after this weekend once we all have more free time. Then my mom will be done with the Halloween festival."

"Deal," Emma agreed.

We got to school too soon.

Emma grinned. "I'll tell you about what I read later. Maybe I could come to your house before the game again."

"Yeah, sure. That sounds great." Even as I said this, I wasn't entirely positive. I was eager for some more alone time to practice with my crystal ball again. I was hoping to see something I could use to help Olivia or Kelli.

At the same time, I wanted so badly to share my abilities with Emma, and maybe even Derek, but I didn't know what I should tell her. A wave of guilt rushed over me. I'd never hidden anything from Emma in the decade that I'd known her, so why did it seem like I was hiding so much lately?

⤳

My mind raced with thoughts of Emma and me during my morning classes, which left me little time to remember to worry about Olivia or Kelli. I was too busy day dreaming about what it would be like to share abilities with my best friend. I knew it was selfish of me, but it was hard to think of anything else when Emma kept throwing excited glances my way.

I wanted to talk about it with Emma in first period, but we were both smarter than to talk about it in front of people. I had told her to keep this to herself, and she had. On some level, I think she understood the importance.

When lunch rolled around, I met Emma and Derek at our usual spot. When my hair wouldn't stay behind my shoulders and kept falling into my food, I had to excuse myself so I could get a hair tie from my locker and put it back.

The hallway was vacant when I got to my locker. I put in my combination and reached into my backpack for a hair tie and the travel brush I kept there. I looked into my small magnetic mirror as I pulled up my hair. When satisfied, I returned my brush to its proper position.

My heart nearly jumped out of my chest when I closed my locker and found Nate Williams staring down at me, which was weird because he'd never talked to me before.

"Um... can I help you with something?" I asked. No matter how much I tried, I couldn't keep the nerves from my voice. What was he doing at my locker?

"I saw you talking to Kelli last night," he said casually as if we had been friends forever. It was hard to not look into his handsome face, a masterpiece really, but something told me that his bright eyes and grin was just a façade.

"Yeah... I just thought she dropped some lotion." My throat tightened, and my mouth dried as my pulse quickened at the encounter. I was not comfortable being in a hallway alone with him right now, no matter how friendly he was acting. A dark haze that I'd never noticed before surrounded his body as if warning me of danger. I considered running, but I decided to play it cool. *Maybe I can talk my way out of this,* I thought. *Maybe he really is being friendly.*

"She said you asked if she was okay."

"Yeah, I did. I was just concerned—"

"Concerned about what?" His tone shifted accusingly.

I took a step back, distancing myself from him.

"She said she's seen you talking to Justine. What did Justine tell you about me?"

"Nothing." I could already feel my eyebrow twitching. At least he didn't know that happened when I lied. "I was just trying to be a good friend."

"Well, don't be," he snapped.

I took another step back, larger this time, until I could feel the cool touch of my locker on my back.

Nate only came in closer, jabbing a finger in my direction. "You know, I'm so sick of people like you and Justine and Olivia getting their nose where it doesn't belong, okay?" His voice was quiet, but it was full of enough fury to make me tremble.

"I—I'm sorry. I didn't mean anything by it."

"Whatever you think you know," he snarled, still pointing a finger at my chest, "you're wrong. Kelli and I are fine."

I didn't need my psychic abilities to tell me that I wasn't wrong. The way he advanced toward me with a threatening tone told me he was used to dominating. The way he spoke his words said he had something to hide. I glanced around the hallway, but no one was going to come to my rescue. Being all alone, I decided it was best to defend myself.

"You know what," I said sternly, taking a stance. "I didn't quite believe Justine at first, but maybe she was right about you."

Crap. What did I just say? Why didn't I just play it cool?

I didn't see it coming. Suddenly, he lunged at me, pinning me against a locker. Its combination lock dug into my back. He wrapped a hand around my neck and held me in place, bending down so that his face was just inches from mine. The strange feeling I got this morning returned, and the roar rang loud in my ears, a sound that only I, a psychic, could hear.

He leaned in close so that I could feel his hot breath on the side of my face. He came in to whisper in my ear. "You mind your own fucking business, okay? Whatever happens between me and my girl doesn't concern you, so I'd advise that you stay away. If you don't," he paused for dramatic effect, which successfully quickened my pulse, "there *will* be consequences."

And then he dropped me, letting me fall into a ball at his feet. He glared down at me for a moment before walking away, a strut that showed his confidence from every angle.

I wrapped my own fingers around my neck and coughed, terrified by his threat. What was wrong with him? I pressed my head against the locker, calming my breath and slowing my heart rate. I knew I didn't need proof anymore to believe Justine's allegations toward him. But as much as I wanted it now than ever, I still didn't have anything that could save Kelli. What if I continued searching for proof, spying on him with my abilities? Would he honestly seek revenge?

With little hesitation, I decided that I would do whatever I could to prove he was a dangerous guy. I rose from the floor, clenching my fists. My eyes narrowed down the hall at his retreating figure. *Nate Williams, you just made this battle personal, and you're not going to hurt* this *girl and get away with it!*

J stayed silent when I got back to the lunch table, knowing full well that I couldn't tell my friends what had just happened to me. I was lucky that Derek and Emma were so great at getting in heated conversation that they didn't ask me to join in.

I only heard pieces of their discussion, but I didn't fully process it. "A girl from the elementary school... they don't know... just shouldn't happen in a town like this."

Instead, I tuned them out and stared at Kelli and Nate, intent on finding something that would prove he was a bad person.

But what *could* I do? Justine knew what was going on, yet she couldn't successfully help Kelli. No one would believe any proof I could give them, except for maybe Teddy, but there'd be no case. What if there was proof somewhere? Maybe there was a photo of Kelli's bruises. Wherever there was proof, I'd find it.

By the end of lunch, I still had nothing. I needed to find a quiet place to relax and open up my mind if I was going to find anything. I didn't honestly know when I would have that opportunity.

"Hey," Derek said as we rose from the lunch table when the bell rang. "Are we all still on for after school?"

"After school?" I asked.

"Yeah. Aren't we going to go pick out costumes?"

I glanced at Emma. I totally forgot about that, and I was really hoping to talk to Emma about what she had read up on, especially now that I was more interested in getting dirt on Nate. I really had to learn how to channel my powers.

Emma and I exchanged a glance, both disappointed that we wouldn't have the opportunity to talk about this issue for a while. I could tell she was excited to learn more about it, too.

"Yeah, I guess we all need costumes, don't we?" Emma said. "We'll head over after school, Derek."

~

"Ooh, I really like this one." Emma held up a sexy kitten costume.

"Emma," I complained from behind my rack. "We're supposed to be looking for something we can wear as a trio. I don't think Derek would go for wearing a skirt."

Derek turned from the rack he was looking at and eyed the costume. "Mm... I don't know, Crystal. I think it would show off my legs well."

I laughed at him. "If you say so."

"Derek, if you want to go to the festival in that costume, I won't be the one selling it to you," Diane joked from behind the counter.

I knew my mother was somewhere in the back, but I wished she was out here to help us find a great costume. We had already asked Diane for ideas, but she said Mom knew more about the costumes they had in stock.

"Maybe we could go as the three musketeers," I suggested, which made Emma crinkle her nose at the idea.

Derek turned back to his rack of costumes and headed down the aisle.

Emma watched him go. Once he was out of ear shot, she started whispering to me. "I really think you should tell him."

"Tell him what?" I asked, looking back over toward Derek.

"Tell him that you're..." she glanced around at the other customers in the store, but none of them were paying attention to us. She lowered her voice further just in case. "Psychic."

"I don't know. What if he doesn't believe me?" I glanced back at Derek. He was completely ignoring us. *But he wouldn't believe me, would he?*

"Well, I believed you."

"Yeah," I argued, "but isn't Derek's family Christian? Don't they, like, shun psychics or something?"

Emma giggled. "I don't think Derek would shun you. Especially because he likes you."

"What?" I squeaked, stealing another glance at him before lowering my voice again. "He does not."

"He *so* does."

"Oh, please," I said. "Like I haven't seen you batting *your* eyes at him. You can't get enough of arguing with that boy. Besides, I couldn't do that to either of you. I couldn't risk our friendship." I didn't have to add that I meant mine and hers as well.

She turned to another costume, shaking off my statement. "I still think you should tell him." I couldn't help but notice that she didn't argue with my accusations.

I took a deep breath. I really did want to tell Derek, but I was too nervous that he wouldn't believe me.

"I'll back you up," Emma encouraged. "I just think it would be cool if he knew, too. We wouldn't have to have secret conversations like this."

I caved, unable to refuse her logic. "Okay, we'll tell him."

"Hey, Derek," she called.

"What?" I hissed at her. "Right now?"

She shrugged. "Not necessarily. I'm just going to warm him up to the idea."

Oh, no. What did she have in mind?

"Yeah?" he asked when he made his way over to us.

Emma put on an innocent face. "You know all that stuff they have in the other room?"

They both glanced at the opposite end of the store.

"Yeah. They have crystal balls and tarot cards and stuff in there. What about it?"

Emma squinted an eye like she was thinking. "Do you believe in that kind of stuff? I mean, like for real. Do you think people can know things?"

"What? You mean, like, psychics?"

Emma nodded. "Yeah, like psychics, fortune tellers, astrologers, and whatnot."

Derek shrugged then began flipping through the costumes where I left off. "I don't know. I guess I'd have to meet one to believe it."

I was getting nervous.

Emma glanced at me, and with reluctance, I gave her a look of approval back, allowing her to divulge my secret to Derek. "But you have met one."

"Huh? I think I would remember that."

Emma looked around at the other customers again and decided we were safe from ear shot. "Crystal's a psychic, and I'm going to be one, too," she said proudly.

Derek rolled his eyes. "Yeah, and I'm Clark Kent."

That stung at my heart a little.

"I'm serious," Emma insisted, and we both stared at him.

His eyes shifted back and forth between us, gauging our expressions. "You're serious."

I nodded.

Derek crossed his arms over his body and narrowed his eyes the same way Emma had when I told her. "Prove it."

I smirked. "Challenge accepted."

Emma and I walked to the back of the store and entered the break room so Derek could hide an object in private. He insisted that Emma come with me so that we couldn't cheat.

"Make sure to hide it really hard," Emma told him. "Crystal is really good at this game."

Emma and I sat across each other on the table in the break room.

"I did not expect him to believe us," I said.

"I don't think he does," Emma admitted. "Not quite yet. But when you find whatever he hid, he'll have to. Derek was always good at hide and seek, but you were better. You know, now I understand how you always found us so fast."

Looking back on it, I always was great at finding them.

Emma and I both jumped when the door to the break room swung open. My mother jumped back, too, and placed her hand across her heart.

"I'm sorry, girls," she said as she entered the room. "I didn't realize anyone was in here. I just need to grab a snack from my purse."

"Hey, Andrea," Emma greeted, but I knew there was more she wanted to say. "Crystal and I were thinking that sometime next week you could teach us more about being psychic."

My mother didn't miss a beat in her step. She wasn't surprised that I'd told Emma.

"I want to learn, too," Emma continued. "I did a bunch of research on different exercises you can do to enhance your abilities. That's what I wanted to talk to you about this morning, Crystal. I wanted to tell you about all these different types of exercises I found and maybe do some together." She turned her gaze toward my mother. "Crystal said that anyone can be psychic with practice. Is that true?"

"If you really want to, then yes," my mom answered. "I mean, your abilities won't be as strong as Crystal's, but we can try."

Emma fist pumped the air. Why was Emma more excited about this than I was? Was it because I'd already had a small taste of what it was like and I wasn't too excited about all the responsibility? To Emma, it was just a game, but I knew it meant more than that.

"Why don't you join us tomorrow night, Emma?" my mom offered.

"Mom!" I hadn't told Emma anything about Olivia, and my mom had to go break it to her that I'd lied.

Emma glanced from me to my mom then back at me. "What's happening tomorrow night? I thought you were having a girl's night."

My mom bit off a piece of her granola bar. "Yeah, just not the typical girl's night."

Emma looked at me for explanation.

"You didn't tell her?" my mother asked in surprise.

"Mom!" I scolded again. I didn't want her scaring off Emma, but now I was kind of stuck. I turned to Emma. "We're holding a séance."

Emma's eyes widened. "Oh, my gosh. That would be so cool! Why didn't you tell me, Crystal?" She swatted a hand at me like I was a puppy that had been bad. She looked at me expectantly.

A wave of guilt flooded over me. "I—I thought it would scare you away."

"No, it sounds totally awesome. I might even see a ghost! A real ghost!"She looked back toward my mom. "You don't have to be psychic to join the séance?"

"Nope. The more believers, the merrier."

"So who are you holding the séance for, and why?"

Before we had a chance to explain, Derek opened the door. "I hid it," he announced.

~

If people kept playing this game with me, it wasn't going to be fun for me for very long. Just one quick touch of Derek's hand and I knew exactly where he'd hid it.

"You hid your pencil," I announced to add to the show before I reached into his sweatshirt hood and pulled it out. "Sneaky little…" I muttered.

Derek's eyes widened. "I thought that hiding place was genius. Now this explains why you were always so good at hide and seek."

Emma and I exchanged a glance and giggled.

"I'm still not convinced, but I will say that I'm amazed. Were you guys spying on me?" Derek glanced at his watch. "We'll have to try this again somewhere where you *can't* spy on me."

Figures, I thought. *I knew he wouldn't believe me.*

"Andrea," Derek said, "we don't have much time until we have to get ready for the game. Do you have any suggestions on a trio costume we could wear to the festival?"

She thought about this for a moment, and then without saying anything, she led us to a rack of costumes we hadn't made it to yet.

She handed us each a hanger. Derek held up a Cat in the Hat costume, Emma a Thing 1 costume, and me a Thing 2 costume. They were perfect.

"I'll see you at your game," my mom said after we purchased our costumes.

"Okay. Love you, Mom," I said, kissing her on the cheek.

"I love you, too, Crystal." She glanced at my friends then back at me. "Can I talk to you for a minute?"

My mom led me back to the break room.

"What is it?" I asked.

She sighed. "Look, Crystal. I really respect your decision about telling Emma. I trust Emma, too, which is why I don't have a problem with it. I can sense something in her." She paused for a moment as if thinking. "But Derek?" Her eyes looked at me for an explanation.

"Mom, he's just as much my friend as Emma is."

She stared at me seriously. "Men can be…" She paused to find the right word. "Different. I just don't want to see you hurt. That's all. I'm not saying that I think Derek is a bad guy. It's just—"

I pulled her into an embrace and cut her off. "It's okay, Mom."

She hugged me back. "Okay. As long as you know what you're doing."

I smiled. "I hope so."

CHAPTER 17

*W*e dropped off our costumes back at my house before heading out the door for our last game of the season.

After we made it to the school and Emma and I were finally alone before we had to warm up, we went back to the conversation I knew we were both dying to have.

"So who is the séance for?" Emma asked.

I took a deep breath, relieved that I could share this with her without her freaking out. "Olivia."

"What's up with Olivia?"

"I honestly don't really know. Mom said that Tammy said something about Olivia needing help, so we decided to do this to help her cross over, you know?" I wanted to tell her about Kelli and Nate, too, but Justine told me not to.

"Wow," Emma said in admiration. "You guys are so cool."

"And she kind of asked for my help," I admitted.

"Who? Your mom?"

"Well, yeah. And Olivia." I bit my lip, wondering how Emma would take this.

"You *saw* her?"

I shrugged like it was nothing. "Yeah, I saw her three times and once in a dream. She wants me to help someone, but I don't know who. I think it's her mom. Like she wants her mom to get over her death or something."

"Well, I guess we'll find out tomorrow night. Oh, and my best friend is so *cool*."

I smiled at this. "No, Emma, you're cool." I really meant this. Who could have any better friends?

Emma and I returned to the gym for warm ups. I caught a glimpse of my mom and Teddy in the stands and waved at them, glad that they were able to make my game. I didn't just have cool friends; I had an awesome family, too.

The game was intense. The score stayed close the entire way. We won the first set and lost the second. Coach put me in for the last set, and I was all over the court at the top of my game. The last point of the game, when we led the score, played through my senses in slow motion. Betsy served the ball, then a girl on the other team hit it back over on the first hit. Emma dove for the ball in the back, allowing Jenna to set it up perfectly so that I could jump and, with all my arm strength, spike the ball to the other side. The ball hit the gym floor, and the home team burst into applause. We won our last game of the season, and it felt fantastic.

As our team exited the court to allow the Varsity to warm up, Justine caught ahold of me and pulled me aside.

"Anything?" she asked.

Even with Nate threatening me earlier, the fun I'd had with Derek and Emma after school took my mind off of it. Boy, did I feel like a bad person at that moment. I should have been paying more attention to this issue rather than picking out Halloween costumes.

I shook my head. "Nothing of proof yet, but something did happen." Then I told her about how Nate threatened me.

"That guy really has issues. I'm really sorry that happened to you, Crystal, but we have to do something soon. Kelli's getting more distant, and I'm afraid it's getting worse. I can't even text her without him telling her what to say back to me. He's so controlling."

"I'll do my best," I promised, and I really meant it.

I found a seat next to my mom and Teddy on the bleachers. We all stayed and watched the Varsity play and were excited when the coach played Emma and she killed two serves in a row, but I was paying more attention to Kelli as she moved around the court. I caught a glimpse of Nate in the stands, but I was too afraid to watch him, scared that he'd notice I was staring.

Oh, Kelli, I thought, *how am I supposed to help you if you won't even let your best friend help?*

The game continued, and the Hornets stayed in the lead. The whole crowd drew a breath in sync when a girl from the other team spiked the ball. It soared through the air quick as lighting and smacked Kelli in the face, knocking her to the ground. She sat in the middle of the court and covered her face with her right hand while her left supported her weight.

Suddenly, I wasn't sitting on the bleachers in a crowded gym anymore. The scene shifted around me. The gym dissolved, and a bedroom with white walls and sports posters replaced it. I spun around, confused. Where was I?

When my eyes adjusted, I saw two figures sitting on the bed in the middle of the room. Both were facing away from me but seemed strangely familiar. The guy had blonde hair that was long enough to show a gentle wave to it. He seemed tall and athletic. The girl appeared young with long, dark blonde hair. She had her arm around him like she was comforting him. His head fell as if he was crying.

"I just don't know what's going to happen," the guy said. I knew that voice. He seemed younger than just moments before, but I knew it was Nate Williams.

I walked around the bed to the other corner of the room so I could see their faces. For a moment, I was afraid the couple would react to my presence, but I reminded myself that this wasn't really happening.

Sure enough, I was watching Nate and Kelli talk, only they were younger, and Kelli's hair was a darker shade of blonde. I was looking into the past. It must have been when they first started dating. Each of them had a younger look in their eyes.

Nate's jaw was tight, and he had a scowl plastered on his face. What was he so angry about?

"People get divorced all the time, Nate," Kelli said to comfort him. "I mean, my parents are divorced. Olivia's parents are divorced. It's really not that bad."

"Not that bad?" he practically yelled, his nostrils flaring. "My dad cheated on my mom, and now his whore mistress has split up my family. We had it so great until *she* came along. Now nothing will ever be the same." He rose from the bed in rage, pacing back and forth as he ranted. "My mom's too depressed to even take care of me and my brothers anymore. I mean, how can I trust her after what she did last week? You think that's not bad? Downing pills because this family is so fucked up. That's not *that* bad?" He came so close to her face that I was sure she might burst into flames from his rage.

Despite this, Kelli kept her voice calm. "All I'm saying is things might look up in the future. You have to look at the positive side of things. It might not be as bad as you think."

"How can you say that?" Nate spat back in rage.

Kelli stood to face him as her voice rose in annoyance. "God, Nate, would you just calm down for one moment?"

And that's when it happened. Even I didn't see it coming. How could either of them? One moment Nate was pacing back and forth, and the next thing I knew, he was yelling, "Shut up," and there was the sound of a slap ringing in my ears. Kelli had fallen to the bed. Her right hand held her face while her left was supporting her weight. The next moment, Nate was by her side apologizing.

"I'm so sorry, baby. I didn't mean it. I'm so sorry. Please forgive me. I need you right now." He put on a sad face and cuddled into her as if he was genuinely sorry.

Don't fall for it, Kelli, I thought, but the damage was already done. I was watching a scene that took place over a year ago.

Tears sprang to Kelli's eyes.

"Please don't cry, baby. I need you to be strong for me," Nate said.

"It's okay," Kelli said, stroking his hair. When she pulled her hand away from the point of impact, I could see a red hand-shaped imprint forming across her face.

What? How could she not see he was evil? Tears welled up in my own eyes, partially out of frustration and partially out of fear.

"I understand. You're going through a lot," Kelli told him.

The scene shifted again, pulling me back to the present. I didn't know how much time had passed, but Kelli was already off the floor, and the game was back in session. I stared at Kelli on the bench, a beautiful young blonde with a black eye that meant more to me than a volleyball injury. Someone had given her an ice pack, and she now pressed it to her eye. How could I help this poor girl? She'd comforted Nate in his time of need, but he never let her go.

I continued to stare at Kelli across the gym until a light figure formed in front of her. Olivia stood on the side of the court, her apparition barely visible under the gym lights. Her eyes found me in the crowd, and she mouthed those words again. "Help her!" And then she pointed a ghostly finger at Kelli.

CHAPTER 18

*S*o it was all about Kelli, but what did Olivia know that Justine didn't?

I hadn't even noticed my mother staring at me, her eyes wide. "I know that look," she whispered under her breath, horrified. Mom wrapped an arm around me. I wasn't sure if it was because she was comforting me or because she wanted to get closer to whisper in my ear. "What's going on? You look like you've seen a ghost."

I couldn't answer. My body froze, paralyzed by what I'd just seen. My gaze locked on Kelli across the gym. I couldn't take my eyes off her. Nate had slapped her hard that first time, but what had he done since? How bad had it gotten?

I just nodded at my mother.

My mom shook her head. "No," she insisted. "It's more than that." She gently took a finger and turned my head toward her, forcing my eyes off Kelli to meet her gaze. "You will tell me about this later," she said sternly with the authoritative tone a mother is supposed to have yet one I hadn't heard in so long.

I nodded my head. I *had* to tell her. Now that I knew Olivia wanted me to help Kelli, I had to tell my mother.

Tears pricked at my eyes. I was both overwhelmed by my responsibilities as a psychic and fearful for Kelli. Would Nate hurt her when he drove her home from the game? How much longer could this go on? How bad did it really get?

Maybe I could tell Teddy about it and he could save Kelli. Why hadn't I paid more attention to Kelli before instead of being so selfish? If both

Justine and Olivia came to me about their best friend, it had to mean this was serious.

The crowd burst into applause for the Varsity Hornet's final victory of the season. As people slowly began to descend the bleachers, I stayed put, still paralyzed in my spot. I could still see Kelli as Coach Kathy led her into her office. I guessed it was to check out her injury in privacy.

"Crystal, are you okay?" my mom said as she shook me a bit.

I nodded, but I couldn't speak.

She glanced back at Teddy, who was also looking at me. "We'll wait for you in the commons, okay?" she said. "Whenever you're ready."

I nodded again as a thank you for giving me my space. I stared at Coach Kathy's office and waited for Kelli to emerge. My mother and Teddy left me alone on the bleachers, but there were still fans chatting on the court, so I wasn't completely alone. I noticed volleyball players leaving the locker room from across the gym.

I wasn't sure what I was doing when I stood up and followed Kelli once she left the coaches' office. When I entered the locker room, it was silent. All the other players were gone, so it was just me and Kelli.

I heard a sob coming from behind the center row of lockers. I peeked my head around the corner to watch Kelli. She sat with her head down and gently touched the ice pack to her eye, which was swollen but not too bad. She sniffled. I wasn't sure if it was from the pain or because she had other issues going on.

"Hey," I said softly, coming around the lockers.

She jerked her head up at me in surprise but relaxed when she realized I was just another player.

"Hey," she greeted with a sniffle. "Am I in front of your locker?"

"No," I told her, sliding down onto the bench beside her. "I actually wanted to talk to you."

"Oh." She seemed disappointed. She clearly didn't want to talk to anyone.

"That girl on the other team really has a mean spike, doesn't she?" I said, trying to find some way to spark a conversation. Mostly, though, I didn't know what I was going to say to her.

Kelli let out a forced giggle. "Yeah, she does."

"Um... are you okay?"

"Yeah, I'll be fine. It's just a black eye. It's not like I've never been hit before." She hesitated. "You know, by a volleyball."

I gave her a sympathetic expression, yet my pulse quickened as I prepared for what I was going to say next. I wasn't entirely sure if it was smart to confront her with this, but I knew I had to try. "That's not really what I meant."

She glanced at me sideways and looked me up and down suspiciously. I continued. "I mean, are you okay in general? Do you need help?"

Her expression shifted to suspicion, and her voice rose. "What are you getting at?"

I recoiled, pushing my way down the locker room bench a bit farther for her benefit. I didn't want to appear overbearing, although I knew I'd already crossed the line. "It's just... some people aren't convinced that Nate is good for you." Before I could offer my help, she stood and cut me off.

"Some people? You mean Justine. I thought you two were talking about me that day in the locker room. Nate loves me. I don't know how Justine can't see that. Besides, what do *you* have to do with this anyway?"

I wanted to explain it to her, but I didn't think she'd believe me. Before I had the chance to say anything else, we heard the squeak of the locker room door and voices outside. We both looked toward the door, waiting for whoever just entered the room.

Justine emerged from around the lockers. Her gaze shifted from me to Kelli then back to me. I knew she was suspicious about what we'd been talking about, but she put on her best bubbly face to mask the awkwardness of the situation. "There you are Kelli," she said happily. "I've been looking for you. How's your eye?"

Justine walked past me to Kelli. I knew it was my cue to leave, but I stayed put.

"Some of the Varsity players are going out to celebrate. Are you coming?" Justine's question was directed toward Kelli, not to me even though my team had won our game as well.

Kelli took a few moments to answer. "I—I don't know. I guess I'll have to talk to Nate. He's my ride home."

"I can give you a ride home, Kelli," Justine offered.

Kelli shook her head. "Yeah, but Nate might get mad if I wander off without him."

Justine's tone grew angrier as they spoke about Nate. "God, Kelli, he doesn't have to be with you wherever you go, nor does he have to dictate when you are and aren't allowed to hang out with your friends."

Kelli hung her head, clearly aware of this fact yet too weak to fight it. "Let me just go to the bathroom, and then I'll ask him."

"You mean tell him," Justine corrected.

Once Kelli was in the bathroom, a separate room off the locker room, Justine spoke to me.

"Did you find something out?"

I shifted nervously. "Um... I know why he started hitting her."

"She *told* you?" Justine's voice was full of surprise. It was clear that Kelli never mentioned anything of the sort to her.

"No." I assured her. I lowered my voice. "I saw it. In a vision."

Justine cocked her head and studied my face to see if I was lying. She narrowed her eyes in thought. "You really are psychic, aren't you?"

I nodded because that was the only way I knew how to answer. The way she was quick to believe me rendered me speechless.

"What did you see?"

I lowered my voice to a whisper and told her quickly about how Nate became violent after his parents separated and how Kelli stayed to comfort him, but he never let her leave, and now he's obsessed.

"I knew most of that. There are even rumors that his mom tried to kill herself when it happened."

If she already knew all this, what was I doing here? What good were my visions if they didn't give us anything to work from?

"We need more than that," she insisted.

"Well, what do you want from me? No one is going to believe a psychic vision."

"I need you to find proof."

"But how?"

Before she could tell me, Kelli emerged from the bathroom.

Justine raised her voice so that Kelli could hear. She spoke casually as if we were speaking like this the whole time. "Yeah, the JV's invited too, so you should come celebrate with us."

"Yeah, maybe," I said, mirroring her casual tone. "But I'm really tired. I'll see you around."

I turned to leave. I wasn't out the door yet when I heard Kelli speak to Justine. "What is up with you hanging out with *her*?"

The door closed behind me before I heard Justine's response.

I was caught slightly off guard when I saw Nate standing against the wall near the locker room. He was watching for Kelli. His ominous eyes locked onto me for a moment, sending a wave of terror through my body.

"Crystal!" Emma squealed as she approached me with her arms wide open. I was thankful for this distraction. She pulled me into a tight embrace. "I've been looking for you. Did you see my awesome serves? Some of us are going out to celebrate. Do you want to come?"

"Isn't that what our pizza party tomorrow is for?"

Emma shrugged and grinned at me. "We can have pizza two times to celebrate for such a great season."

"I'm actually really exhausted. I'm going to go home and sleep."

"I wish you'd come, but I understand. See you tomorrow."

I found my mom and Teddy talking to other parents in the commons and told my mom I was tired. I exchanged a glance of urgency with her, and she quickly rose from her seat and said goodbye to the other parents. Teddy followed.

Mom gave Teddy a kiss goodbye, and I waved as we split up in the parking lot when he left to go to his own apartment. Mom and I walked side by side back home but didn't speak.

When we finally got home, she spoke first. "Tell me what's up. I know that face. You saw a vision of something, and it scared you, didn't it?"

I didn't say anything for a long time. How could I not tell her? She had to know who Olivia wanted me to help. After contemplating how to tell her, I finally broke down and told her everything I knew.

My mom stroked my hair as I wrapped my arms around her waist. We were sitting in her bed after I had divulged all my secrets—and my anxiety about the responsibility—while she held me and I sobbed into her arms.

"Well, sweetie, we have these abilities so we can help people."

I sobbed. "I don't know if I want that type of responsibility. How am I supposed to help Kelli and get her away from Nate? Justine said she already talked to her and that Kelli won't say anything about him. Justine keeps insisting that I get some proof to save her, but how can I do that?"

"Well, if Olivia knows something, we'll figure it out tomorrow night. Now go get some sleep. You really need it."

I returned to my room without telling my mom that I didn't want to wait until tomorrow night to contact Olivia.

Maybe I could summon her myself, I thought, but that idea scared me. Truth be told, I didn't know *how.* She'd always come to me herself.

And then the realization of the obvious hit me like a ton of bricks. Aside from the séance, Olivia only appeared to me when Kelli was around.

Only then did I realized something else. Olivia had come to me in a dream before. Maybe she would contact me tonight.

I fell asleep thinking about Olivia and hoping that would help me get in touch with her.

CHAPTER 19

They were fighting again. I can't stand the sound of them fighting. Fighting. Fighting. Always fighting.

I pressed my hands over my ears to block out the sound. "Stop," I begged, but my parents didn't hear me.

I looked toward my two brothers who were mimicking my actions. Tears were streaming down both of their faces.

"Look what you've done!" my mother yelled. "Now you've made them all cry."

"Me?" my father spat back. "You're the one always picking fights, Sarah."

"Please stop," I begged again, but my 8-year-old lungs didn't have the strength to make an impact over their screaming.

My mother's voice rang out over my own. "Well, if I could actually put an ounce of trust in you, maybe this family would start feeling like a family."

"Oh, please," my father spat back. "Like you do anything around here to make this place feel like a home."

My mother threw her hands up in the air and turned away from him. "I'm done. I can't handle this anymore."

"Don't you walk away from me!"

My father grabbed for my mother and pulled her back with all his force as his other hand smacked against her face. She sunk to the ground in defeat while he loomed over her in dominance.

My brothers' cries grew louder to mirror my own.

My father spun toward us with rage plastered on his face. "Nate, would you and your brothers just shut the fuck up?"

～

I was crying when I woke up and had to remind myself that it was just a dream. Those weren't *my* parents. I was okay. I was a bit disappointed that Olivia hadn't appeared to me that night. My mood lifted slightly when I replayed the dream in my mind and realized what it meant, that my abilities were giving me a glimpse into Nate's past. That meant another piece to the puzzle, albeit small.

I texted Emma that I wasn't going to meet her at our corner. Instead, I headed off to school early. Most people were already at school before I usually got there, so I had faith that Justine would be there early, too.

I arrived in the commons and scanned the tables. When my eyes found Justine, they locked onto her, willing her to look up and meet my gaze. Kelli and Nate were both sitting by her, and I wasn't about to ask her to talk with me privately in front of them. When she did look up, she noticed my stare almost instantly.

"Bathroom," I mouthed, and then I turned to go meet with her. When I opened the bathroom door, I was glad it was empty. I double checked the stalls this time just to make sure we were really alone.

Justine entered behind me. "Thank God. I've been dying to talk to you."

I told her about the dream I had about Nate.

"That explains a lot," she said, "but it's definitely no excuse."

"Justine," I said, really needing to get some questions off my chest. "What kind of proof do you expect me to find?"

She shrugged slowly while an apologetic expression fell across her face.

"Then what do you want from me?"

"Look," she said. "I don't know what proof there is, but I know there's something. Maybe a picture somewhere, but I've checked Kelli's phone and her computer, and I didn't find anything."

"How do you know there's something out there?"

"When I first caught on to what was happening and asked her about it, she got really defensive, almost angry, and then she said that I would have to go find the proof, like there was something out there."

"That's it?" I asked in disbelief. It didn't sound like much to go on. "And what if there isn't? Justine, why are we even playing this game? Why don't we just turn Nate in?"

She sighed. "You don't think I haven't thought of that? Crystal, Nate's mom works for the county courthouse. She knows how to pull strings, and if there isn't any proof, then there isn't a case. Not to mention that I've tried everything to convince Kelli to leave him. What am I supposed to do if she doesn't want help?" Justine began pacing back and forth and ran her fingers through her long dark hair. I could see the tears welling up in her eyes. "God, I just want to help my friend, and she won't even let me. Crystal, you're my last hope to save her."

But where was I supposed to find proof? I couldn't just go snooping through Kelli's house. Besides, Justine already did that and didn't find anything. I wasn't entirely convinced there *was* any proof.

"Well, maybe she doesn't need saving if she doesn't want out," I suggested, but even as I said it, I didn't believe it.

"Believe me, Crystal, she wants out. She's just too scared."

I understood all too well. I was reminded of the way I felt her fear when Nate drove up in the car after practice. She couldn't admit what their relationship was like or he would hurt her even more.

I sighed. "I'll try my best to find proof. I'll focus harder, okay?"

"Thank you, Crystal," Justine said genuinely. She turned toward the door.

"Justine." I stopped her, wanting to ask the question that had been bugging me.

"Yeah?"

"How come you're so quick to believe in my abilities?"

She shrugged. "My grandma was psychic, and so is my aunt," she said casually as if being psychic was an everyday occurrence. And then she left.

I stared after her in disbelief. What? Justine came from a line of psychics? Could that mean that she was psychic, too? She couldn't be or she wouldn't be asking me for help, would she?

I exited the bathroom and found Emma and Derek in the commons just as the bell rang. We walked to our lockers together, but I stayed silent as I mulled everything over. There was possibly proof somewhere that could save Kelli. Justine might have some psychic abilities. And I still had to talk to Olivia tonight.

"I was reading up on the stuff we're doing tonight," Emma said at our lockers with a low voice. "And what I read said it works better if you have something from the person. Like something that belonged to them."

I eyed Emma suspiciously. What did she have in mind? "But we don't have anything," I pointed out.

"But we could get something," Emma suggested.

If we could get Kelli, I thought, *Olivia might actually make an appearance.* But I knew Kelli wouldn't go for it in a million years.

I still wasn't sure what Emma was getting at.

"Don't worry," she said. "I'll take care of it. I just have to get Derek to help me."

"You don't think what we're doing tonight is going to scare him off?"

She shook her head. "No. Besides, he'll help me either way."

How many more people would I let in on this secret? I wasn't just concerned about telling people about my abilities, but I was nervous about mentioning Kelli. Justine told me not to tell anyone about what was going on, but since Olivia was somehow involved, I had to tell the people at the séance about who we were supposed to help.

When I entered my first class, a blissful sensation washed over me. I knew that we would soon have our answers to everything.

CHAPTER 20

I set my volleyball jersey next to everyone else's on a table in the commons. After a victorious season, our coaches were rewarding us with a pizza party after school, which also doubled as turn-in-your-equipment-and-do-inventory day. Luckily, I got to enjoy pizza while our manager took care of inventory.

I gave Derek an apologetic look as he entered the gym with a stack of jerseys. *Sorry you have to do that, and sorry I've been such a crappy friend toward you lately,* I tried to say with my gaze. I really had been ignoring him, and even though I had a lot on my mind, I was excited to dress up with him tomorrow assuming tonight went well and Olivia helped us fill in the missing pieces to the puzzle that was Kelli and Nate's relationship.

Seventeen hungry girls gathered around the lunch tables as the coaches brought the pizza to us. I grabbed a piece of double cheese pizza and bit into it. It tasted like heaven. I moaned in pleasure and exchanged a glance with Emma to say I approved of the delicious meal. She widened her eyes back at me in agreement.

After just one slice, Emma bounced up from the table. "I'm going to go check on Derek, okay?"

"I'm sure he's fine," I assured her, and with the glance she threw back at me, I suddenly understood what was happening. This is what Emma was talking about earlier about having Derek help her. She was going to get Olivia's volleyball jersey from the storage room where Derek was returning the other jerseys.

I wondered if her jersey would even be in there. Surely her mom would have returned it to the school even after Olivia's death. It could have been anywhere when her room caught on fire, therefore not burning with her. I had heard that the house suffered little damage and that Olivia would have been fine if she didn't have asthma. Even if it was in the same room with her, would it have burned? Then again, most girls left their uniforms in their gym lockers. The school would have taken it back before they even gave the rest of her belongings to her family.

I didn't have to wonder about the jersey anymore because when I was enjoying my second slice of pizza, I watched Emma walk out of the gym and sneak down the hall toward her own locker. No one would have noticed the balled up jersey in her hand if they weren't looking for it, and no one did but me.

Emma sat back down as if nothing had happened and casually picked up another piece of pizza. People talked and laughed about the season. I joined in where appropriate, but my mind was once again stuck on more important subjects. I couldn't stop stealing glances at Kelli and wondering how I was going to help her. What was going to happen at the séance tonight, and how was I going to tell everyone about Kelli?

As I tried to sort out my thoughts, a wave of terror overcame me again. The blissful sensation I felt earlier disappeared. My vision clouded, and I felt woozy.

"Crystal, are you okay?" Emma asked. "You look terrible again."

My vision returned without any indication of why I was feeling the way I was. "Yeah, I'll be fine." I didn't believe my own words. All I knew was that I wanted to get away from the crowd so that I didn't embarrass myself if a vision was coming on. "I just need some fresh air."

"Want me to come with you?" she offered.

I glanced at her half-eaten piece of pizza and then at the other girls. Emma was having fun. I didn't want to worry her. "No, I'll be fine on my own."

I found my way outside and steadied myself against the side of the building. The air was thick, but a strong wind helped cool me down. I slid to the ground and closed my eyes as I focused on my breath to ease my anxiety. I knew something was coming, but I didn't know what to expect. Was Olivia somewhere nearby?

"I've been looking for you," a menacing voice said.

I opened my eyes to find a tall, muscular figure standing above me. "Nate?" I asked in shock. "What are you doing here?"

"I'm here to pick up my girl."

I closed my eyes again. I didn't have the strength to deal with his crap.

"Did you hear me?" he snarled, crouching down to my level. He was dangerously close.

"No," I answered honestly.

"I said I've seen you talking to my girl again. I thought I told you to stay away."

"And what are you going to do if I don't?" I challenged, but I immediately regretted it. Even though I didn't think he'd actually carry out his threat, I was still undoubtedly scared of him.

"I'll make you pay."

I couldn't help but notice that he never made it clear *how* he would make me pay.

I was bold. I was *too* bold. Before I knew what I was saying, words escaped my mouth. "Well, if you don't leave Kelli alone, *I'll* make *you* pay."

He laughed. "A little girl like you? I'm so scared." Sarcasm dripped off his tongue.

I shook my head in disbelief and met his terrifying gaze. I didn't know where the courage came from, but I found myself saying, "You'd never go through with it. I'm not your girl, and I wouldn't put up with an asshole like you."

My own eyes widened in disbelief. I'd never swore at someone like that before. The words didn't feel like they were my own.

He recoiled, surprised that someone like me would stand up to him.

I took this opportunity to stand up. I turned away, prepared to get back to the commons where there would be witnesses. The clouds seemed darker than when I came outside, and the wind seemed to pick up.

Nate grabbed for me. He wanted the fight to continue, but as soon as his hand clamped around my wrist, a powerful gust of wind came crashing down on him. I caught a glimpse of a white figure. I watched Olivia's face twist in anger as her apparition lunged toward Nate, and he fell to the ground.

I took my chance and sprinted back toward the main doors while silently thanking Olivia for getting me out of there. I knew Nate wouldn't pursue a fight with witnesses around.

I steadied my breath as I returned to the table and replayed my own words back in my mind. I wondered if maybe the words I'd spoken *hadn't* been my own after all. I took one final calming breath. I was safe for now, but I still couldn't shake the feeling that this wasn't my last encounter with Nate.

CHAPTER 21

"What am I supposed to write?" I asked.

Even though I didn't invite Emma to stay the night, I was glad that she'd come over; otherwise I'd be all alone after our pizza party worrying about the rest of the night. On some level, I wanted to talk with Olivia *now*, but I was still nervous about doing it on my own.

Emma shrugged from where she sat on my bed. "Whatever comes to your mind. These exercises will help get us ready for the séance tonight."

Of course, we couldn't start until later, once Mom, Sophie, and Diane closed down shop, and since it was the night before the Halloween festival, I suspected they wouldn't be home until late, at which time we could finally bring our abilities together to contact Olivia. Since my mother had nothing to hide from me, we figured we could hold the séance at home. Despite my anxiety for tonight, I waited patiently and played along with Emma's games.

"How is this going to help me?" I cocked my head to the side and stared at her skeptically from my chair. I wasn't sure if she was serious about this exercise or if she was just avoiding our geometry homework.

"If we both write down three predictions, it will help us get in touch with our inner psychic."

"Okay, but what kind of predictions should I make?"

"Anything you want. The website said you should try making predictions for tomorrow, but I think you'll be fine with anything."

"Okay," I agreed reluctantly. "I'll try."

We both fell silent and bent over our pieces of paper. I closed my eyes and tried to get in touch with my "inner psychic." When nothing happened, I opened my eyes and stretched my fingers, then my neck, and then let my shoulders fall in relaxation. I closed my eyes again and reached toward a prediction.

I drifted as if I was no longer in my body. My mind wandered in a different realm. There was no sense of time there, just a peaceful ambiance that made me feel like I was floating. All of my thoughts left me as I found dominance over my consciousness. I didn't know how long I sat there.

"Those sound good." Emma's voice snapped me back into my body.

"What?" I asked, blinking up at her in confusion. She had moved from my bed and was now standing behind my chair at my desk.

"Your predictions," she said, pointing to my piece of paper.

I looked down to find words scrawled across the paper in my handwriting. I hadn't remembered writing anything.

"My predictions are probably just nonsense," Emma said, pushing her paper toward me.

I took it and read her predictions, admiring the perfect curves of her letters as I did so.

1. *I will fall in love within the year.*
2. *I will soon discover a food allergy I never knew about.*
3. *I will love pizza forever.*

"I just wrote that last one because I couldn't think of anything else more creative," she giggled as she took her paper back and bounced back to my bed to rewrite her predictions, which I knew weren't predictions at all. "This is really difficult and frustrating, though," she complained before she continued scribbling.

With Emma quiet, I took the opportunity to look at my own predictions. I stared down at my sloppy handwriting, took a deep breath, and read through them.

1. *The more answers you find, the more questions you'll ask.*
2. *Be patient with your heroic duties.*
3. *Put more faith in your friends. They might surprise you.*

"This is dumb," I complained to Emma. "These aren't even predictions. They're like cheesy things you would find in a fortune cookie."

Emma wrinkled her nose and stared at me seriously, blinking a few times. "You're kidding, right? Those are really good." She rose from the bed again and came to stand beside me to look over my shoulder at the choppy writing. "What do you mean by 'put more faith in your friends?' Are you lacking faith in me?"

I stared up at her nervously. Was I? I didn't really believe that she would magically turn psychic. Is that the kind of faith I was lacking?

To my surprise, she burst out laughing. It took me a few moments to realize she was playing around with me. I laughed with her to ease my anxiety.

"I'm going to keep practicing," she said. "Your mom said that anyone can be psychic, so I'll probably take up meditation or something. Maybe we could start doing yoga together."

The doorbell rang and interrupted her. Emma and I exchanged a confused expression.

"Who could that be?" I asked. We were only expecting my mom and her friends, but they wouldn't have to ring the doorbell, and they wouldn't be home for another few hours.

I rose from my seat to get the door, but Emma grabbed my hand to stop me. "This is a perfect opportunity to practice," she said.

"Practice what?"

"Your psychic abilities. I read about this exercise where you try to guess who's calling or who's at the door. It can help you improve your abilities."

The doorbell rang again, but Emma wasn't going to let me go until I at least tried. I sighed and closed my eyes as I focused on the guest at my front door. It only took a few seconds before I saw an image of the mystery man, a guy my age with bright blue eyes and curly light brown hair.

I took off down the hall so that Derek wouldn't think I was trying to avoid him. Emma raced after me. I came to an abrupt halt at the front door and took a deep breath.

"Sorry, Emma, but your game is far too easy," I teased, opening the door.

Derek stood on the porch with his Cat in the Hat hat on. When he saw us, his face fell. "Aw, man, you guys are having a party without me?"

I giggled at him as he entered the house. I was excited that he was here. I wasn't sure if it was because we hadn't spent a lot of quality time together lately or if I was simply glad to escape Emma's games.

"Why are you wearing that?" Emma asked, pointing to his hat.

Derek shrugged. "I'm a sucker for Halloween. And I thought Crystal would find it funny, but I didn't expect to see you here, Emma."

"What brings you over?" I asked.

"I don't have to babysit my sisters tonight since Mom is home, so I thought I'd escape for a while. You don't mind, do you?"

Emma and I exchanged a glance. He couldn't stay, could he?

"Um... give us one minute," I said, pulling Emma back down the hall toward my bedroom. "He can't stay," I whispered once I closed my door. "I mean, something like a séance will scare him off, don't you think?"

"I don't know," Emma said, a hint of wonder in her voice. "He seems like he's taking the whole psychic thing pretty well."

"That's because he doesn't actually believe us. Look, I want to share this with him as much as you do, but we can't have a skeptic here when trying to contact Olivia. There's too much information we need, so I need as much time with her as I can get."

"Maybe we could—wait, what information?"

I sighed. I knew I had to tell Emma about Kelli sooner or later, but I figured it would be easier when everyone was together. "I'll tell you about it later. Are we going to get rid of him or not?"

"I think you should let him in on it. Your prediction said to put more trust in your friends."

She had me there, but was my prediction true? Did I need to put more faith in them?

"Look, Derek might be a skeptic, but he won't be if we can prove your talents to him. Come on," she said, grabbing my arm to lead me back into the living room. Ugh. More of her games? She had me feeling like a lab rat.

"Okay, Derek, you can stay," Emma told him when we came back into the room. "But on one condition."

Derek sat on the couch silently, but I could tell he was wondering what we were up to.

"We can't have any skeptics here tonight, so you either fully believe Crystal is psychic or you leave." Her tone was so demanding that I almost felt sorry for Derek.

Derek raised an eyebrow. "You guys are serious?"

We both nodded our heads.

"Look," Derek started, "the finding the pencil thing was pretty cool, but I don't know if I can really believe you're psychic, Crystal. I don't know what you guys are smoking."

That stung, but I didn't let it show. "If I'm not psychic," I retorted, "how did I know where to find Emma's copy of *Charlotte's Web*?"

Derek raised both eyebrows. "*You're* the one who told Emma where to find it?"

I nodded, but by his tone, I knew he still didn't believe me.

"I want to prove it to you, Derek," I said as I came closer and knelt beside him. "What can I do to prove to you what I am?"

He thought about this for a moment while Emma moved and sat on the couch next to Derek.

"What kind of pet did I have when I was four?"

I rolled my eyes at him. "First of all, it doesn't work on demand like that. Second, I already knew you used to have a pet gold fish."

Derek snapped his fingers in disappointment and then stared me in the eyes. "I want to believe you, Crystal. I really do, but I don't know if I really believe in psychics."

I didn't know where it came from, but suddenly I was blurting out Derek's deepest, darkest secret that he hadn't told anyone about. "You're adopted."

My hand flew up to my mouth. Where had that come from? Was it even true?

Derek's eyes widened. "How did you—oh, my god. You are—you have to be. I mean, I just recently found out. My parents never told anyone. You—how long have you known?"

I looked at Emma for help, but her eyes were just as wide. Her jaw had practically fallen to the floor.

"I—I'm sorry," I said, shifting my weight and pulling my knees to my chest as my hands came up to cover my eyes. "I don't know how I knew. I didn't even know I knew. I just... I'm sorry. I didn't mean—mean to intrude."

Derek placed a hand on my shoulder to stop my babbling. He didn't say anything for a long time. None of us did. Then he bent down to my level and wrapped his arms around me. I felt warm in his embrace. He pulled my head to his chest and rocked me back and forth as Emma shifted her weight on the couch and came closer to stroke my hair. I was sobbing now.

"Crystal," Derek said, "don't cry. You don't have to cry."

"Please don't cry, Crystal," Emma sniffled. "Now I'm going to start crying."

When my sobs stopped, I released my hands and looked up at both of them. I wiped my eyes. "I'm sorry. I don't know why I'm so emotional. It's just, how can you trust me when I intrude on your personal lives like this? It's not fair to you."

Emma continued running her fingers through my hair. "It's okay, Crystal. We don't mind. Do we, Derek?"

Derek shook his head. "No, it's okay. I was going to tell you guys eventually. It's just that I only found out a few weeks ago. It was a bit of a shock."

As I looked back and forth between my two best friends, I realized how much we'd been hiding from each other. "No more hiding things," I told them, and they nodded back.

"Um... guys," Emma said after a few quiet moments. She looked down at her hands. "Derek, I'm sorry I didn't tell you, but my parents are getting divorced."

"Oh, Emma. I'm sorry. I'm sorry I didn't tell you guys I was adopted. I only found out when we went in to get my driver's permit, and they needed my birth certificate. My mom didn't want me to see it at first, but I looked at it anyway. I was just too surprised to say anything to you two, and it doesn't really change who I am."

"And I'm sorry I didn't tell you guys I was psychic sooner," I admitted. We all looked at each other and started laughing as if our problems were so trivial.

"Are you going to search for your birth parents?" Emma asked Derek after our laughter died down.

"No."

"Why not?" I asked.

"I guess the only reason I was put up for adoption was because my birth parents died. There's no one to go searching for."

"How did you end up with your parents?" Emma asked curiously, which put us on the subject of sharing our secrets for a long time.

I'd learned that Derek's parents thought they couldn't have kids, so they were quite surprised when they found out they were pregnant with twin girls. I also found out he wasn't upset about being adopted or that his parents hadn't told him.

The conversation soon switched to Emma's parents' divorce. We were on the subject of my abilities, which Emma was raving about how cool they were, when the front door opened.

"What are you guys up to?" my mom asked as she entered, followed in toe by Sophie and Diane.

My best friends and I exchanged glances and burst out laughing again, reveling in our own little secrets.

Mom rolled her eyes at us. Then her expression shifted to nervousness. "Is Derek staying?"

I looked between my best friends as they did the same. "Well, Derek, are you staying?" I asked. What I was really asking was whether he believed me or not.

He shrugged. "I guess so. What are we doing?"

"We're holding a séance," Emma said casually.

Derek's jaw dropped to the floor.

CHAPTER 22

I was honestly surprised Derek was taking this so well. After he picked his jaw up off the floor, he seemed pretty cool with it.

We all sat around the kitchen table, the blinds successfully leaving us in privacy, the candles set around the table, and the number 17 volleyball jersey spread out in the middle. Everyone applauded Emma's efforts for getting the jersey, saying it was a good idea. I scolded her for stealing, but she promised she was going to return it.

My mother sat me at the head of the table. She said since I'd seen Olivia before, this was my thing, but I honestly didn't know how to run the show. I took a good look around the table to make sure everything was in place. Looking at the candles in front of me, I was reminded of the way Olivia died.

"Look, guys," I said, interrupting the chatter. "I have to tell you all something." Everyone stared at me expectantly, but I didn't know how to start speaking. I took a few breaths to gather my thoughts. "I know we're here for Olivia, but it's more than that." I kept my gaze low, not wanting to look anyone in the eyes. I had promised to keep this secret, hadn't I? But I knew they needed to know.

Sighing, I continued. "Olivia asked me to help someone, and I think that's why she's still stuck here. Her friend Kelli is in trouble, and I believe that if we contact Olivia, she'll help us help Kelli."

I looked up to meet their gazes. They were all still staring at me and listening intently.

"Kelli has been in an abusive relationship since before Olivia's death, and I think Olivia knew about it. That's the real reason we're here."

There. That wasn't too hard.

But I couldn't stop talking. I had more to explain. "Justine Hanson came to me to help Kelli, but I didn't know until yesterday that Olivia wanted me to help her, too. Justine is convinced that there's some proof out there. I don't know how. Maybe she's psychic, too."

Sophie scoffed.

"What?" I asked, looking up to meet her gaze.

She shook her head but spoke in a friendly tone. "Justine isn't psychic."

"How do you know? She said it runs in her family."

"And I'm part of her family." She pointed to herself proudly. Realization suddenly dawned on me. Sophie was the aunt Justine was talking about. How was it that I never knew they were related?

I didn't have time to wonder. I shook off this newfound information and focused on the real issue. "Regardless of how Justine knew, she claims that there's something out there that can help us save Kelli, and I think Olivia knows where it is."

I looked around again. They all seemed to understand. I nodded, ready to get on with it and finally save the people I'd been sent to help. I looked back at the candles on the table, the ones that reminded me of how Olivia died. "Um, maybe we should get rid of the candles," I suggested. Everyone looked at me, but after a moment, they all completely understood. It just didn't seem right to have them lit when Olivia died because of a candle.

We blew out the candles and sat in total darkness—apart from the gentle illumination coming from the digital clock on the stove and the light from the street lamps seeping in past the curtains.

My mother sat opposite our oval table from me and explained how the séance would work. Even though you didn't need to link hands, we would hold hands to raise the energy in the room. She explained that we needed to set our minds free and to focus on Olivia. When she was done, it was my turn again.

"Um..." What exactly was I supposed to do? "Everyone link hands please."

I found Derek's and Emma's hands in the darkness. Once the circle was complete, I could feel the energy pulsing in the room.

I spoke gently. "I'd like for us to take a few moments to clear our minds. Forget about your troubles, be conscious of a wandering mind, and focus on Olivia."

It was completely silent for quite some time as I allowed everyone around the table to relax. I needed the time, too, so I cleared my mind and reached out toward Olivia. When I was ready, I finally spoke. "Olivia

Owen, we know you want us to help Kelli, but we also want to help you. If you're here, we ask that you make your presence known."

We all waited, but nothing happened.

"Olivia, you came to me for help, and I'm ready to help you. I want to help Kelli, too. What can you tell me about her? Olivia, please help us help you."

Still nothing. I continued by repeating several versions of my call out to Olivia, but I still couldn't get through to her. This routine seemed to last forever. I dropped my hands, which prompted everyone to open their eyes and look at me.

I stared back at each of them. "This isn't working."

Everyone exchanged glances, looking for someone to explain. Thoughts of self-doubt spun in my head. *Am I doing this right? Maybe I need more practice. What if I'm not strong enough?*

"What should we do?" Emma's voice cut through my thoughts.

No, I told myself. *I can do this. I believe in myself.*

That's when I realized that not everyone here did believe in me. I looked around the table nervously until my eyes fell upon Derek. All other eyes in the room followed.

Derek's face fell, and he nodded. "I get it."

"I am *so* sorry, Derek," I said. "It's just that we can't have a skeptic in the room."

He nodded again. His expression was one of apology. "I want to believe you, Crystal, but I guess I'm just not ready." He stood up. "I want to be here for you, though, no matter what I believe or what you're going through."

"I'm so sorry," I told him again.

"It's okay. Really. I'm the one who should be sorry. I'm screwing this whole thing up. You guys have fun, okay?" With that, he turned and left.

I wanted to follow him and make him understand, but I was more than ready to get in contact with Olivia. Olivia's need for me won out.

When I heard the front door close, I guided everyone back to our séance. I linked hands with Diane and took a deep breath.

We sat in silence for several minutes. It was so quiet in the room that I swore I could hear each of our heart beats.

"Olivia," I called out again.

After a few minutes of focus, I felt a shift of energy in the room. A chill spread out from my spine to my fingertips. "Olivia! She's here!" I shouted the words. I wasn't sure if it was because of my own excitement or to inform the others. Even though I could feel her presence, I couldn't find a clear image of her. She was weak, it seemed, so I pushed further, reaching out to her and pulling her back into our realm.

"Olivia, we need your help to help Kelli. What can you tell us?"

Still nothing. After seeing her so easily and clearly the first few times, this almost seemed like too much of a struggle.

"Please, everyone," I begged, "clear your minds and focus on Olivia. She needs us to be strong for her."

With this reminder, suddenly the energy in the room shifted. I opened my eyes to search for her. Everyone else in the room still had their eyes closed. Had they not felt the energy shift?

"Olivia, come to us. We're here to help."

I could feel her reaching out to me, so I reached back.

"Crystal," I heard Olivia's voice in my head. "Help. Please help."

Shivers ran up and down my body.

"I'm—I'm not very strong," Olivia whispered in my head again. "I've become so weak after protecting you from Nate."

My hands gripped tighter around Diane's and Emma's. I wasn't sure if that had caused them to send the squeeze around the table and intensify our energy or if it broke something inside of me, but suddenly, the energy in the room burst like an ignited fire. I watched as a glowing Olivia appeared at the opposite end of the table next to my mother. Her blonde hair and brown eyes were bright in the dark room and clear as day.

Olivia rambled with urgency. "Crystal, I don't know how, but you can see me when no one else can. I need your help. I was going to help Kelli. I was, but I died before I got the chance."

"Slow down," I pleaded.

"I can't. I may not have much time. I never do. Please, just listen. You're the only one who can see me."

I nodded.

"The video. I left it in my locker. My mom. She has it. She kept it when they gave her back my stuff."

"Video, what video? And who gave her back your stuff?" I asked in as much urgency as she conveyed.

"I know I'm not making any sense." She stopped and thought for a brief moment. "Maybe this will help."

Suddenly, I was whipped from my seat at the table, spinning out of control, everything a muddle of confusion. I was falling fast until I came to an abrupt halt. My mind was still in panic mode, but my body seemed fine, comfortable in the situation even. However, I couldn't control my body, and when I finally focused on what I was seeing, I realized why. I was in one of Olivia's memories, seeing it through her eyes.

CHAPTER 23

I recognized the room I was in. It was vast, with a high ceiling and bleachers lining the walls. It smelled like sweat, dirt, and the familiar extras that came along with volleyball season. A volleyball net was set up in the center of the room. I was watching over it from the top of the bleachers. I could hear the hum of the ceiling fans and the thump of music coming from the coaches' office.

A lone girl stood at the back of the court. I watched as she tossed a ball in the air, jumped, and sent it flying across the net.

"Awesome!" I shouted, only it was Olivia's voice I heard. "I got that on camera, so we can study it later to see what you did right."

I looked over at the camera sitting on a tripod next to me. *Yep, the frame is perfect so that we see what's going on with her body. It won't take long until she has her jump serve down,* Olivia's thoughts said in her memory.

I looked back to the girl. The part of me that wasn't replaying the memory—the Crystal part—studied her face. I didn't recognize her at first, but then I realized it was Kelli, only she had darker hair and a rounder, younger face.

Kelli threw another ball in the air and jumped. It flew straight into the net. She turned in frustration to grab another one.

"That's okay," Olivia's voice assured her encouragingly. "That's why we stayed after practice to video tape it. We'll figure out what you're doing right and wrong."

Kelli jumped again, this time sending the ball flying crazy fast into the opposite side of the court. Kelli squealed in excitement and gave a hop for her success.

She grabbed another ball from the cart and stepped up to the serving line, but something caught her eye by the door. She did a double take.

"What are you doing here?" Kelli asked kindly before I even saw Nate storm into the gym.

"You better have a damned good excuse," he snarled, pointing at her. When he reached her, he seized the ball from her hands.

She recoiled, stunned by his anger.

I felt Olivia's body shift as she sprung up from her seat in alarm, but she didn't move down the bleachers.

"What are you talking about?" Kelli asked calmly. "I didn't know I needed to tell you I was staying after practice to work on my serves."

"Well, you should have. I've been waiting for you." Nate's voice was full of rage. He kept pointing his finger in her face. I didn't think he saw Olivia at the top of the bleachers looking down on them.

"I didn't know you'd come to pick me up. I usually walk home from practice."

"We talked about this. From now on, you ride with me."

"I don't think that's necessary." Kelli's voice was still calm.

I couldn't quite understand why, but Olivia stayed put. Her thoughts told me she was afraid this was something she shouldn't get into.

"Well, it is," Nate spat. "You don't get to hang out after practice when I'm expecting to spend time with you. You do as I say, okay?"

"No, I don't," Kelli said, crossing her arms over her chest and raising her voice to challenge him.

I didn't know how to react in my own mind or in Olivia's body.

"I want to work on my serves," Kelli said through clenched teeth as she snatched the ball back from his hands.

That's when it happened. A strong hand came up. Olivia bolted down the bleachers, but before she could get anywhere, I heard the loud smack against Kelli's face. She fell to the ground. Olivia continued racing toward her.

Nate looked up and saw me—well, Olivia—for the first time.

"You asshole!" Olivia shouted, but it felt like the words came from my own mouth even though I knew I would never be so bold as to stand up to him like that.

"You stay out of this," he barked back while pointing that ugly finger toward Olivia. She was still coming at him. She was so close now.

"You asshole," Olivia repeated, pushing him as hard as she could. I felt the impact in Olivia's memory.

He stumbled back a few steps. I knew she hadn't hurt him, only stunned him. Olivia bent to console her friend, but she didn't make it all the way down before Nate was pulling her back up.

"You think that's funny?" he spat. He shoved Olivia's body, sending her stumbling over her own feet, but she quickly regained her balance. He was advancing. "Kelli is *my* girl. You don't get to judge me."

"Oh, I think I can," Olivia's voice rang boldly. I applauded her bravery and then felt her body shift as she spoke again. "I thought you were a good guy, but Kelli deserves a lot better than this." Olivia stopped and folded her arms over her chest to show she wasn't afraid of him.

You go, Olivia, I thought as I experienced her past.

He paused inches away from her. "Better than me? She's never going to find anyone better than me. I'm all she's got."

"She's got me," Olivia challenged. "You lousy piece of shit."

He raised his hands, but before Olivia could duck out of the way, they came down on her, pushing her hard into the gymnasium wall. Pain shot through her back as her shoulder blade collided with the concrete. My own conscious mind felt a stab of pain, too. Olivia's hands came up to comfort her aching shoulder.

"*Nobody* says things like that to me," Nate snarled. "You best remember that, bitch."

He turned away like nothing had happened. "Get off the floor," he mumbled to Kelli, and to my amazement, she rose and followed him. Before she left, she sent Olivia a look of apology.

I have to go after him, Olivia thought in my mind. She started toward them. Kelli shook her head like it was just better if Olivia stayed. *That's fine*, her thoughts said in my mind. *I have a video of his violence, and Coach Kathy is in her office. We'll be okay.*

I expected the memory to end there, but it didn't. Still watching from inside Olivia's memories, she returned to her camera at the top of the bleachers and stopped the video before packing up her equipment. She took special care of her camera as she placed it in her bag, and then she walked slowly back down the bleachers while both of our minds tried processing what had just happened. Olivia glanced up only to see the opposite end of the gym covered in stray volleyballs.

She set down her camera and grabbed the cart, pulling it to the opposite end of the court to collect the balls. I could feel that she needed something to calm herself down before she told Coach about Nate. When she had all the balls picked up, she returned the cart to the storage room and went to retrieve her camera equipment.

Loud music was still coming from the coach's office, so Olivia pounded hard on the door. Coach Kathy still didn't hear, so Olivia turned the knob and entered. Coach looked up from her paperwork, smiled, and spun her chair toward her radio and turned it off.

"You girls all done? You don't have to put the net away because the gym teacher asked us to keep it up for badminton."

"Actually, Coach, I was really hoping to talk to you about something," Olivia said.

Coach sat back in her chair to listen.

"About what? How are Kelli's serves coming along?"

"Pretty good, but I really need to talk to you about something else," Olivia said again. "About Nate and Kelli."

"And?" she prompted.

Olivia didn't know how to say it. "It's just... Nate's done something really bad, and I'm scared for Kelli."

"Nate Williams? No. He's a good kid."

I should have known, Olivia's thoughts said in my mind. *Coach is friends with his mom. She wouldn't hear any of this.* But Olivia tried anyway. "No, I'm serious. You have to watch this video."

"Look," Coach said, "I've known Nate and his family for a long time. Whatever happened, I'm sure there's been some misunderstanding. Nate's a good kid."

"But he's *not,*" Olivia insisted.

She wouldn't have any of that. "The janitors will lock everything up. I trust you can find your own way out."

Olivia stared at her, stunned. *I don't get it. Does she just not want to believe he's bad? Does she think I'm too young to understand?*

Olivia carried herself back to her gym locker in disappointment and slowly changed out of her practice clothes and into her street clothes. She glanced into the mirror to assess her injuries. Nothing. She shoved the camera into her locker, intent on showing another authority figure— maybe the principal?—the next day at school.

As soon as she slammed the locker, my mind was falling again out of Olivia's memory. I fell hard back into my own kitchen.

CHAPTER 24

Olivia was still standing in front of me. My jaw dropped. Holy crap. There really was proof that would help save Kelli.

"Where is it?" I insisted in urgency, staring into Olivia's brown eyes. Then she showed me something again, but this time it wasn't as fierce of a transformation.

Instead, she sent me floating through town until I came above her house. I could tell which room was hers because that was the part of the house with new shingles. I floated down through her ceiling until I felt like I was standing on solid ground. It didn't look like a girl's room anymore. There wasn't a bed. Instead, it was full of boxes. Her mother had turned her daughter's old room into a storage room.

Olivia continued leading me until I moved to the boxes. I could see into them, and I knew exactly which box the video camera was in. When I had this information, Olivia pulled me back.

"I lit a candle that night to pray for her," Olivia admitted in a quiet voice. "I didn't know it would be the last prayer I ever made."

My heart ached thinking about what she'd been through.

"My mom saved all my stuff, but she packed them away. The school gave her back the stuff in my locker, and she just tucked that away with everything else. She never saw the video, but now you can. You can save Kelli."

"I will," I promised.

Olivia looked at me with grateful eyes. "Thank you so much, Crystal," she said, and then she faded, the energy in the room washing away with her. Everything went dark again.

I released my hands from Emma's and Diane's, which caused everyone to open their eyes and look at me. "She's gone," I announced. "I —I don't know if she crossed over, but I can help Kelli now."

My mom rose and flipped on the light. "What happened?"

"You mean, none of you saw her?"

They all stared at me and shook their heads in unison.

"But she was standing right there." I pointed to the spot across the table where she had stood.

"Crystal," my mom explained. "You're the only medium here. We can hear spirits, but none of us can see them."

"All I heard was Crystal," Emma interjected but spoke softly in wonder. "It was like a one-way conversation."

My mother nodded in thought. "That makes sense since this is your first time and you don't have much of a connection to the other side." My mom turned back toward me. "I didn't hear Olivia say much, though. She must have shown you something."

I sat there completely stunned for what seemed like forever. From the seat next to me, a giant smile formed across Emma's face.

"This. Is. So. Cool!" Emma exclaimed.

I offered a shy smile because I wasn't entirely certain. Seeing dead people? Did I really want that? Emma seemed to want it more than I did, but it didn't matter what I wanted right now. I had the information I needed. After I took a few breaths to calm myself, I told them everything I knew.

"Do you guys think this is the right thing to do?" I asked warily. "I mean, I saw Nate hit Kelli. It was in a vision, but still. Couldn't we just turn him in?" I was instantly reminded of what Justine had said. She'd told me that she tried to turn him in, but without any proof, there was nothing they could do. But what was I even doing? What if Kelli didn't want help? Somewhere deep inside of me, I knew that she did by the way she was overcome with fear when he picked her up that day after volley-ball practice. I wasn't even sure there would be a case against him if Kelli didn't want that, but maybe Justine could convince her otherwise.

All this went through my head in a few moments. My mother's words snapped me out of my thoughts. "This is what Justine asked you to do, isn't it?"

"Yeah."

"Then I think you need to stick with it," she said, and I knew she was right.

Now that I had answers, I only had more questions. How was I going to get it? What would I do with the video when I found it?

Emma spoke next. "Well, let's go get it."

"What? Now?"

"Yeah," Emma said. "It's only, like, nine. It's not that late."

I figured it wouldn't hurt, and we were only a few blocks away. "Okay," I agreed.

Emma and I found Derek sitting on my front steps.

"How'd it go?" he asked.

I thought about this for a moment. "Really well, actually."

"I'd still like to help if I can," he offered.

Several minutes later, Emma, Derek, and I were walking through the streets in the dark, led only by street lamps. My mom, Sophie, and Diane stayed back. They said this was my problem to deal with. I'd have been more comfortable with an adult coming along, but I had a feeling they were trying to teach me something.

I explained things to Derek as we walked.

I knew the house when I reached it, not just from the dream, but because in a town like this, you know who lives where. I walked up the porch steps and rang the doorbell. My best friends remained safely behind me. It took a few moments, but then I heard motion behind the door, and the porch light turned on.

Tammy Owen opened the door. She was wrapped in a robe and slippers. Her blonde hair was wet, and she was makeup free like she'd just taken a shower.

"Um. Hi, Mrs. Owen," I greeted nervously. She stared expectantly behind the screen door, so I continued, not quite sure what to say. Crap. Why didn't we come up with something good to say?

"Hi," she greeted with a smile. "You're Andrea Frost's daughter, aren't you?"

"Yeah, I'm Crystal, and these are my friends." I gestured to Emma and Derek. "I'm sorry it's so late, but we're looking for something really important."

"I'm not sure if I can help you."

"It's about Kelli Taylor."

"She was Olivia's friend. What about her?"

"Well, I think you have something that could really help her."

"Why?" Mrs. Owen asked seriously. "Is Kelli in trouble?"

I glanced back at Emma and Derek for help then turned back to Mrs. Owen. "Sort of. We were really hoping we could go through Olivia's boxes to find it."

She didn't wait for a further explanation but rather crossed her arms over her chest and glared at us. "No. I hardly know you. If Kelli needs something, she can come and get it herself." She reached for the door.

"Wait," I called, but the door slammed, and the porch light went out. I whirled around to glare at my friends. "Why didn't you guys back me up?"

They both gave surprised expressions.

"I'm sorry," Derek said.

"We didn't know what else to say," Emma apologized at the same time.

I pushed past them down the stairs and started walking back toward my house. What was I thinking? How could I think she would just let me dig through her boxes?

The only other possible way I could think to get the video was to get Justine to ask Tammy for it. Surely Tammy was still on good enough terms with Justine, one of Olivia's best friends.

"I feel like I should call Justine and tell her about everything we found out," I confided in my friends as we walked. "I think she might be able to help us get the video, but I don't even have her number."

Emma's face lit up as pulled her phone out of her pocket. "I do."

"What? How did you get her number?"

She shrugged. "When I got my new phone, it put in all my Facebook friends' contact numbers."

"Oh, you're friends with Justine?"

"I'm friends with practically everyone on the volleyball team. Here you go," Emma said, holding her phone out to me.

I took it and hit the call button. I knew it was getting late, but it was also a Friday night, so I suspected Justine wasn't asleep yet. She seemed wide awake when she answered.

"Hello?"

"Justine? This is Crystal Frost."

"Oh, uh. Hi, Crystal. Do you have anything new?"

"Yeah, I have lots. I know where your proof is, but my friends and I still need your help."

"Your friends?" she squeaked into the receiver. "I told you not to tell anyone!"

"It's okay, Justine. They helped me find the proof."

That seemed to make it okay with her, and she calmed down. "That's great news, Crystal. Do you have it?"

I bit my lip nervously. "Not yet. I was hoping you could help us get it. We need someone like you who Tammy can trust."

"Tammy Owen?" Justine's voice wavered a bit. "You mean, the proof is at her house?"

"Yeah. It's in Olivia's bedroom."

Justine hesitated. "You have no idea how much I want to help you, Crystal, but I don't think I can go there. Not after what happened to Olivia in that room. I haven't even been able to pass her house since it happened. Look, I trust you. Do you think you can get it without my help?"

My heart froze in my chest. In my mind, I was thinking, *No, no I don't think I can.*

"I want to help Kelli more than anyone," Justine said. "If you don't think you can do it without my help, maybe I can—"

"No," I cut her off. I couldn't force that upon her. I knew exactly how she felt. I still avoided the intersection where my dad died. If someone had tried to make me go back there... I couldn't finish that thought.

"Um, just one sec." I placed my hand over the receiver and spoke quietly to my friends as we walked. "She says she can't face the place of Olivia's death. What are we going to do now?"

They were both silent for a few seconds as if thinking, and then Emma spoke. "There's only one more thing we can do."

"Yeah. Turn him in," I suggested.

"No," Emma continued. "We could steal it."

"What?" I squeaked and looked at her in disbelief.

Derek was giving her the same expression.

"Stealing? No. I don't steal," I said.

"But it's so perfect," Emma insisted. "Tammy will be at the Halloween festival tomorrow night, so her house will be empty. You said you know where it is. We can get in and out of there in a matter of minutes."

"She does have a point," Derek agreed, and I gawked at him, unable to believe that he was considering this.

"You guys have got to be kidding me. I don't steal things, and I certainly don't break in."

"Since no one locks their houses around here, it's technically not breaking in," Derek pointed out.

I stared back at them in skepticism. What else could I do, though? This was my responsibility, wasn't it?

I sighed. "Fine. But someone needs to be at the festival to keep an eye on her, okay? I don't want anyone catching us." I looked between them both and wondered who would volunteer.

Derek raised his hand. "Okay, I'll keep watch. You two can do the sneaking. If I notice anything, I'll text Emma."

My mind continued to contemplate the ethics of this decision. How did I get dragged into this, and why was getting ahold of a video the best solution? It didn't make any sense to me.

I sighed and brought the phone back up to my face. "Justine, I'll get it for you."

She squealed excitedly into the receiver. "Thank you! When can you get it to me?"

"You'll be at the festival, right? I can give it to you then."

"Yeah, I'll be there. I'm helping out with some of the booths, so if you walk around, you'll probably see me. I'll be in a butterfly costume. I can't wait! We're finally going to get him, and I'll have my best friend back!"

Her excitement was palpable. It made me feel great that I was able to help, which for the first time since she'd asked me for help made me feel welcoming about my abilities.

"I'll see you tomorrow," Justine said, signaling the end of our conversation.

"Wait," I said, stopping her.

"Yeah?"

"What are you going to do with the video?" I asked.

"It's a video!" She seemed even more amazed. "Wow. You really are a good detective, Crystal. You know what I'm going to do with it? I'm going to use it to send the piece of crap to jail."

I wasn't sure if that was even possible, but even so, I figured it would help to at least get Kelli out of the relationship. Maybe Justine and Kelli could use it as blackmail against Nate.

"Thank you so much, Crystal. Seriously."

"I'm glad I could help."

I hit the end call button and handed Emma back her phone.

Emma and I said goodbye to Derek when we got back home. We found the fold-up cot and set it up in my room next to my twin bed. Emma and I lay side by side facing each other and talking about the situation we were in.

I was feeling better that this was almost all over, but when my head hit the pillow, I reminded myself that I still had to break into someone else's home. That sent a sickening sensation throughout my body.

CHAPTER 25

*E*mma and I couldn't sit around with nothing to do all day, so we tagged along with my mom to help with the festival. My mom didn't mention anything about our adventure. I didn't think it was because she didn't care but rather because she was so busy.

I wondered why Emma and I couldn't just go to Tammy Owen's house now. She had to be here somewhere, right? When I spotted her, I understood why it was a good idea to wait. I watched as she hopped into her car and announced to a few other helpers that she had to pick up more supplies from her house. I didn't know how many trips she was going to take, but I didn't want to risk the chance of her catching us.

Emma and I spent most of the morning helping set up tents at the park, moving around supplies, and decorating. Some people from the community brought all the workers sandwiches for lunch, and Emma and I sat by the creek as we ate. We didn't talk about our plans for that night or being psychic because we didn't want anyone to overhear, so we kept our conversation casual.

As we put up more decorations and more people showed up to set up their booths, the Halloween festival really started looking amazing. There was my mother's tent for fortune telling, some carnival games, food vendors, apple bobbing, a kissing booth, and even a huge stage for a band.

Around three o'clock, Sheryl tested the microphone on stage and began barking last-minute orders since we only had an hour until the festival officially started.

"Why aren't you girls dressed yet?" I heard a familiar voice behind me and turned to see my mother with caked-on makeup, curly hair, gaudy jewelry, and flowing clothes. She really had the gypsy look down.

"We don't have our costumes with us," I said.

"Well, go get them! I don't want to be the only one dressed up. Here, take my car." To my surprise, my mom put the keys in Emma's hands. Of course, I didn't have my license, so she certainly wasn't going to let me drive.

"Awesome," Emma said, pulling at me. "Let's go get our costumes. See you later, Andrea."

As we were walking back to the parking lot, we spotted Derek coming our way in his own costume.

"You guys are leaving already?" he joked as he approached us.

"We're just going to get our costumes," Emma answered, "but we might not be back for a while."

"Okay. I'll keep you updated."

As soon as we walked away from Derek, I saw a tall girl with dark hair and wings trailing behind her. She was coming toward us.

"Do you have it?" Justine asked when she was close enough.

"We're going to get it right now," I answered, excited that this was all working out.

"That's great. I can't wait." Then to my surprise, Justine bent down— she was a lot taller than me, especially with her heels on—to embrace me. "I'd come with you, but I promised I'd help run the kissing booth for the first shift." She pulled away. "And Crystal, I'm really sorry about black-mailing you. I wasn't actually going to tell anyone your secret. I just really needed your help."

I smiled in forgiveness and thanked her, but her last words echoed in my mind. "Justine, if you have psychics in your family, why didn't you go to them about this? Why me?"

Justine gave me a look of apology like she was sorry she dragged me into this. "From everything I know about my family's gift, it's not very strong. And my aunt is only an empath, after all. It just sounded like you had a gift that could honestly help in this situation." She paused. "I was right, wasn't I?"

I smiled and realized that yes, I think she was right.

Emma and I said goodbye and made it to the car. Emma climbed in behind the wheel while I found my place in my usual seat. I pulled out my phone from my pocket and texted Derek.

Have you spotted her yet?

No. Someone said she was picking up a few last-minute things at home.

Crap. Okay. Thanks.

"We can't go get it yet. Tammy's at home," I told Emma.

"Okay, so we'll stake out by her house."

I shook my head. "I don't know. I think she'll notice and suspect something. She knows my mom's car, which is supposed to be at the park."

"You're right. Maybe we should just go get our costumes first."

"Yeah, I guess we can do that."

So we went to my house instead and slipped on our red onesies, which were surprisingly comfortable.

"I think we can leave these in the car when we rob Tammy Owen's house," I suggested, rolling my blue pompon wig in my hand.

"Crystal, it's not robbing," Emma said as she adjusted her own wig. "It's Olivia's camera, and she wants us to have it."

I thought about that for a moment. "Yeah, I guess you're right." The familiar chime of my phone sent me reaching for it.

I've spotted her. You're good to go.

Awesome. Thank you, Derek.

BTW, I thought I was supposed to be texting Emma.

She's my driver.

Lol. Ok. Good luck.

"Okay, we're good to go," I told Emma.

"Sounds good. Ready for your first criminal act?"

I rolled my eyes at her. "According to you and Derek, we're not breaking and entering or stealing, so I think we're good."

Emma laughed as we headed back to the car. The sun had fallen low in the sky, but it still wasn't dark.

"Do you think anyone's going to suspect anything?" I asked warily.

"No. First, a lot of people are at the festival. Second, we'd just look like we were sent to pick up supplies or something. No one is going to see us. We'll be fine."

"Even in these?" I gestured toward our costumes.

"People will just think we've been downtown." She had a point.

It didn't take long to make it to Tammy's house. We parked across the street and looked around to make sure no one was watching. We couldn't see anyone, but the hairs on the back of my neck still stood as if someone *was* watching us.

I scanned the street again. No one. *I'm just nervous*, I told myself until I believed it.

"Okay, I think we're set to go." My heart pounded as I took off my seat belt and opened my door. Even though the air was cool, I felt almost too warm in my costume, which made me sweat all over.

"Well, *are* you ready?" Emma stared at me as I simply stood there, but when I nodded, she took my arm and led me across the street.

I wasn't even surprised when the back door opened easily. We walked onto a landing where one set of stairs led to the main floor and the other to the basement. I climbed the stairs and found myself in a pristine kitchen. I led the way, although I wasn't entirely sure the layout of the house.

"Her bedroom is upstairs," I whispered, even though I was sure we were alone. "Stay quiet."

"Why?" Emma asked, mirroring my volume.

"I don't know. I just feel better about it. The stairs are over here." I rounded a corner and went down a hallway before I crept up the stairs. I was careful not to make a sound. When we came around the banister, the door I was looking for was already open.

And then I heard it, which only made me creep back down the stairs and hide. I gripped the owl pendant that hung around my neck and rubbed it for good luck. I peeked up to the floor's level to try to see into the room, but I couldn't tell what was going on.

"Text Derek," I mouthed to Emma. I handed her my phone after making sure it was on silent.

I watched intently, trying to detect what was happening in the room. It sounded like someone was shuffling through boxes. I heard footsteps, and then objects shifted as they bounced against each other in their containers. I listened closely and heard rapid breathing and then a sob.

"Derek says she's still there," Emma whispered so quietly that even I could hardly hear her. Then who was digging through boxes in Olivia's room?

I snuck back up the stairs, intent on finding out who was screwing up our operation. My pulse quickened as I thought about the possibility of getting caught. I pressed my body against the wall as I slowly and quietly stepped closer to the room. Then even slower, I peeked around the open door. I could feel Emma right behind me.

A young woman about my age with blonde hair was facing away from me and shuffling through boxes. She was dressed in a baby blue dress, white tights, and black flats.

"Where is it?" she mumbled, lightly kicking one of the boxes in frustration. I knew who it was immediately.

Without thinking, I emerged from my hiding spot and entered the room. "Kelli, what are you doing here?"

CHAPTER 26

*K*elli Taylor whirled around to face me. "Me? What are *you* doing here? And in your pajamas?"

My pajamas? I looked down at my costume. I liked our Cat in the Hat idea. I liked her Alice in Wonderland costume, too, but this was no time to admire costumes.

"Um... Tammy sent Emma and me to get something for the Halloween festival." At the mention of her name, Emma came into the room. "We heard something up here and thought you were a burglar or something." I could feel my eyebrow twitching.

I was never good at lying, so I was shocked when Kelli bought it. I released the tension in my shoulders.

"Me?" she said. "No, not a burglar. I'm just looking for something."

Emma, knowing I'd never been a good liar, took over for me. "Tammy sent us for something in the boxes, too, so do you mind if we look with you, do you?"

Kelli scowled. I wasn't entirely sure she believed us anymore. "But this is all Olivia's stuff."

"And apparently yours," Emma said casually as she went over to a box and flipped it open to peer inside.

Kelli had shifted boxes all over the room so that it didn't look quite the same as when Olivia showed me where the camera was. Yet somehow, I still knew where it was as if its energy drew me closer. Suddenly, I understood what energy I was feeling.

Olivia's spirit sat above the boxes and peered down at me. I thought I'd helped her cross over, but she wasn't gone yet. I briefly wondered how she'd appeared so easily and why I wasn't feeling as woozy as I normally did when she appeared. As I thought this, she glanced over at Kelli, and I realized why. Her connection with Kelli was strong enough to ground her here if she was close enough.

"Tell her," Olivia said from her perch, although only I could hear her.

"What?" I asked. Both Kelli and Emma stared at me.

"Crystal, are you okay?" Emma asked.

"Tell her where it is," Olivia repeated.

"Yeah, I'm okay Emma, but why?"

Kelli and Emma both gave me a weird look again.

"Look," Kelli said. "I don't know what you guys want, but you're not going to find it here. These boxes are all full of Olivia's stuff."

"You have to show it to her," Olivia told me.

As much as I didn't think that was a good idea, I figured Olivia knew better than me. I sighed and moved aside several boxes until I found the one I was looking for. I pulled it free, set it on the floor, and opened it.

Inside was the same camera case Olivia was carrying in her memory along with her tripod and other belongings I didn't recognize. I pulled the bag from the box and stood up.

"Is this what you're looking for?" I asked, holding it out to Kelli.

"Oh, my god, yes!" she exclaimed while reaching out for it.

"Crystal," Emma scolded in the same moment. "What are you doing?"

"No!" Olivia cried, which made me recoil. I pulled the camera bag back to my chest. "Don't give it to her. Show her the video. She has to see it."

"Just hold on," I said, trying to calm everyone, including myself. I unzipped the bag, and Kelli watched wide-eyed.

"That's mine! You can't do that." Kelli lunged toward me, but Emma stepped in between us to stop her.

"Actually," I said, "I know for a fact this was Olivia's." I pulled the camera from the case. It was a large digital camera, clearly made for a photography lover. I pushed the power button, but it didn't turn on.

"There's a fresh battery in the front pocket," Olivia told me.

I continued talking to keep Kelli at a safe distance while I retrieved and changed the battery. "For one, Olivia was the photographer, not you. Only she would own a camera this expensive." I didn't know how I knew it. The words simply flowed from my mouth. I wasn't sure whether they were true or not, but I suspected they were by the way Kelli simply stood there and listened. "Not to mention that the strap has her initials on it. But the real proof is on the camera, isn't it, Kelli?"

I had the batteries changed by now. This time when I pressed the power button, it turned on. The battery wasn't full, but it was enough to do what I needed.

"And what do you think is on it?" Kelli asked accusingly.

"I don't know," I replied innocently, even though I did know. "Why don't we see?"

I pressed the playback button. The video I was looking for was the first image to appear. I pressed the play button, initiating the sound.

"You don't know what you're doing! Give that here!" Kelli dove for me again, but Emma came to my rescue for a second time and caught her before she could get very far. They were both stronger than they looked, but Emma was bigger and could hold Kelli back.

"Kelli, we're only here to help you," I said evenly, hoping my tone would calm her down. The video was playing through her serves. I knew we didn't have much time until Nate would walk into the gym and slap her. "Kelli, your friends are worried about you, both Justine and Olivia, and they asked us to help. Now, I want you to take a look at this. If you can honestly tell me that you're okay with what Nate has been doing to you, we'll let you go, and I won't intervene anymore."

"What is it with you?" Kelli asked. "You and Justine really are plotting against me, aren't you? Nate's not a bad guy."

"Really?" I asked, knowing full well the video was almost at the point where he came in. "This doesn't look that bad?"

I turned the camera so that she could watch the video play back. I listened as Olivia's memory replayed itself on the screen. I watched Kelli's face fall as she stared at it.

"You better have a damned good excuse," I heard Nate say through the speaker, but I was watching Kelli. Tears sprang to her eyes. Her bottom lip quivered as she watched. And then the sound of skin on skin, Nate slapping Kelli, came through the small speaker on the side of the camera, which only caused Kelli to fall to the ground. I wanted to pull the camera away, but when I looked toward Olivia for guidance, her eyes told me to keep the video playing. I didn't drop the camera, and Kelli didn't avert her gaze. She continued watching until the thud came, the one when Nate shoved Olivia into the wall.

"Okay, okay. Stop it!" she shouted in tears.

I felt awful, like I was the one torturing Kelli now. I turned the camera around and stopped the video. I removed the memory card and placed the camera back in the bag.

Kelli curled up on the floor, knees to her chest and face in her hands. Nobody said anything for a long time until Kelli's croaked voice broke the silence. "I—I never thought it was that bad, but seeing it from a different angle... Oh, my god. He hurt my friend, my best friend."

"I know, Kelli." I aimed for a comforting tone as I bent down to her level.

"I was going to destroy the video. When Justine said she had proof to help me, that she was going to get a video tonight, I knew the video she was talking about, only I didn't think it still existed. I thought it'd burned in the fire."

That explained why she was here now and why she was in costume. She must have just found out after we told Justine we were going to get the video now, only since we'd waited for Tammy to leave, Kelli got here first.

Kelli sobbed again. "I—I never intended to watch it, but... it's just so horrible. I thought I loved him, you know. I mean, I do. I do love him, but he can just be horrible sometimes."

"I know, Kelli. That's why you have to turn him in. You shouldn't have to live with this, and neither should your friends." I took a gamble and rubbed her shoulder. To my surprise, she didn't pull away.

"No, they shouldn't, but what if he hurts me if I turn him in? He'll come after me." She looked up at me, her eyes glistening with tears. "I was lucky enough to get away from him tonight for the festival. He didn't want to come. If I had ditched him there, he'd have my head on a silver platter. But it'd be my fault, you know. It always is. I shouldn't be here without him." Kelli started to get up. "I should go to him. We should destroy the video. That's what Nate would want. "

"Kelli," I said kindly. "You can make your own choices. Nate doesn't have to dictate everything you do." I found myself repeating Justine's words and feeling a deep sense of truth to them.

She shook her head. "You don't understand."

"There are people who can protect you, Kelli," Emma said. "Besides, you have friends to help you."

"I know. Nate is good to me most of the time, though." She paused. "I have Justine, but Olivia was always my true best friend, and—and when she died, I was so screwed up. Nate was there for me through it, you know? How could I leave him then? And now—now how can I leave him?" She lowered her voice to a whisper. "I've been so terrified the past year that if I leave him, he'll not just go after me, but he'll go after my family and friends. I mean, look what he did to Olivia over something so stupid."

She took a deep breath. "I thought about leaving him this summer," she admitted. "I found out I was pregnant, only when I told him, he freaked. I lost the baby."

Emma and I both drew in a quick breath. I was reminded about something Justine said. *It's like something happened between them last summer.*

124

"I don't know why I'm even telling you this. I never told anyone. But I can't just *leave* him. I love him and hate him at the same time. You two wouldn't understand."

"Kelli," I tried. "You're not in this alone. You have to admit it to your family and friends, and they can help you. Maybe one of them will understand better than us."

She nodded and sank to the floor again. After a few breaths, she looked at us. "How did you guys get roped into this? I mean, why didn't Justine just do it herself?"

I exchanged a glance with Emma. "Justine doesn't exactly know what happened yet," I admitted.

"Then how do you?"

I contemplated this for a moment, wondering if I should tell her. I glanced back at Olivia on her perch, but she wasn't there anymore. I turned my head back toward Kelli and nearly jumped out of my skin when I saw Olivia standing behind her. Olivia nodded as if to say it was okay to tell Kelli.

"I know because Olivia told me."

"She told you? But you hardly ever talked to her."

"You're right. I didn't really talk to her when she was alive."

Kelli's eyes skimmed over me. They still sparkled with tears. "What are you getting at?"

"Kelli, I've talked to Olivia recently. She's the one who told me that the video was still here."

"What?" she gasped. "Like, you talked to her ghost?"

I took a deep breath. "Yes, and she's here right now."

Kelli's sorrow turned to rage. "Whatever sick joke you're playing, it's not funny. Olivia is dead."

"I'm not joking," I defended.

"Well, if she's really here, then ask her what gift I got her the Christmas before she died."

"She can hear you," I assured her.

Olivia began speaking. I relayed the message to Kelli. "She says you made her a picture frame with shells glued on from your trip to Florida a few summers ago. She said she loved it so much because she collected shells. She loved the pictures of you two from when she went on your family's vacation to California before that."

Kelli's jaw dropped in disbelief. "I don't know how you knew that."

"I told you. Olivia's here."

"Then ask her about our childhood," she insisted. "When we were in sixth grade, what did we promise we would grow up together and do?"

"She says you wanted to write poetry and publish song lyrics and that your pen names would be your childhood nicknames for each other, Kel-Kel and Livie."

She eyed me again like she still wasn't sure what to believe. "What did we do on her 13th birthday that we never told anyone about?"

"You went to the movies to celebrate, but when you got there, you realized you'd dropped your money somewhere along the way. You snuck into the movie without paying."

Kelli's lips curled up to hold back her tears, and her brows came together in sorrow. "Olivia?" She turned her head toward the ceiling and closed her eyes. "Livie, you're really here. God, I've missed you so much. I know you would have told me to stay away from Nate, to do something about it, and even though I had Justine by my side, I didn't have *you*. I needed you so badly." Her voice cracked. "There's so much I wanted to say over the past year. I wish you would have been here."

"She was," I said, translating. This only made Kelli cry harder.

"Tell her about the candle," Olivia said.

"What?" I replied, confused.

"Tell her I lit the candle to pray for her."

I nodded and took a deep breath in preparation to translate. "Kelli, Olivia wants you to know that the candle she lit, it was for you. She was praying for you."

With this, Kelli broke, sobbing uncontrollably and curling deeper into her ball.

I rubbed her arm for comfort again, continuing to relay Olivia's message. "And she says she hopes that you'll let your friends and family help you so that you can return to your old self. She doesn't want to see Nate hurt you anymore."

Kelli didn't speak for a few moments. Then she nodded slowly. "Okay. I promise. You've been my best friend forever, Olivia, but can you promise me that he won't hurt me anymore?"

"She says she'll be watching over you, like a guardian angel."

"Thank you," Kelli said. I wasn't sure if she was thanking me or Olivia.

I watched Olivia from behind Kelli. "Thank you so much for everything you've done, Crystal," Olivia said.

"I'm glad I could help," I replied out loud.

"Um, Crystal," Emma said. "I think we should go. I have a weird feeling."

"We will in a minute," I promised. *Put more faith in your friends. They might surprise you*, a thought surfaced in the back of my mind. *Is Emma being paranoid, or have her psychic exercises paid off?* I wondered.

Olivia jerked her head and looked at something behind her that even I couldn't see. "Emma's right. You have to leave," she told me. "Go. Go now. Tell Kelli I'll always be watching."

"I will," I promised as she faded. "She's gone."

"Gone?" Kelli asked softly.

"She said she'd always be watching, but we have to leave."

"Thank you," Kelli said one last time, her eyes sparkling. "What do we do now?"

"We keep you safe," Emma replied.

CHAPTER 27

*W*hen we exited the Owen's house, "safe" was not the first word that came to mind. Completely and utterly vulnerable was more like it. I nearly tumbled over a tall figure as I left the house. I stumbled backward in surprise.

"You," the figure snarled accusingly.

"Nate," I spat back.

He caught a glimpse of Kelli trailing behind me, and then his eyes fixated on me again. "I thought it was you I saw following Kelli here." His voice was anything but friendly. "I told you this ain't none of your business. I waited, but when you never came back, I came to make sure you weren't filling my girl's head with crazy ideas."

"You—you followed me?" Kelli asked in disbelief.

"Of course I did. I didn't want to go to that stupid festival, but I had to keep tabs on my girl."

Kelli shied back.

Stand up to him, Kelli, I thought. *Olivia once gave me courage. Let her do the same for you.*

With that thought, my prayer was answered. Kelli's posture changed, her eyes brightened, and she took a step forward. Kelli spoke in a tone that didn't seem like her own. "Kelli is not your *girl* anymore. You don't get to push people around like you do and expect something in return. You're a meaningless piece of crap that doesn't deserve someone as amazing as Kelli."

Olivia? I thought.

Nate shrank back in surprise. He took a second to digest what she'd just said, and then he reached for her. "Come on. We're leaving."

Kelli pulled away. "I'm not going anywhere with you!" This time it sounded like she was speaking for herself.

"Come on." The anger in his voice rose. "You can't be serious."

There were so many emotions thick in the air.

Kelli took a stand. "Oh, I am. Olivia showed me just how much of a jerk you are. If it wasn't for you, she might still be alive!" Something in her tone told me this was the key to everything.

"Olivia?" he practically shouted in confusion.

With that, Olivia appeared again, only this time she seemed more solid, more real. When I heard a gasp from everyone around me, I knew I wasn't the only one who could see her.

"What the—?" Nate's eyes widened. He took a few steps back and tripped over his own feet. He lay on the ground in terror. "No. It can't be. You're... you're... What the *hell*?"

Olivia advanced. A swirling wind consumed her, and I swore her eyes glowed red. "Leave my friend alone," she warned.

Nate raised his hands to shield himself.

Olivia continued moving toward him. "If you so much as touch her again, I will make your life a *living hell*. Every step you take. Every corner you turn. I will be there waiting."

Nate whimpered.

My mouth was open in awe. *You go girl!*

"You come near my friend again—any of my friends, and that includes Crystal—you will regret it. For. The. Rest. Of. Your. Life."

Olivia's apparition charged at him again. He didn't waste another second. Nate scampered to his feet and ran off toward the street.

"Okay, okay," I heard him yelling back. "I swear it. I'll leave her alone."

Olivia turned to us and laughed. "That was fun."

Kelli's eyes fixated on Olivia. "Is that really you?" she asked slowly.

Olivia nodded.

"But... how?" Kelli asked.

"I don't know, to be honest. I've always been watching you, Kelli. I've always been here trying to help, but I think Crystal's the one to thank. I wouldn't be here like this without her here." Her gaze turned to me. "You have a really unusual gift, Crystal."

Tears sprung to Kelli's eyes. "Thank you. Thank you both for everything."

"My pleasure," Olivia responded. Then she turned as if she saw something the rest of us couldn't. "I think this is it for real this time."

"You have to go?" Kelli asked sadly.

Olivia nodded. "I can finally see the light. I don't think Nate is going to hurt you again. I think in all honesty he pissed his pants."

We all gave a chuckle.

"Will I see you again?" Kelli asked.

"I'll be here like always," Olivia promised.

~

Kelli didn't want to wait to go to the police station. She said she needed to talk about it while she still had the courage. I suggested that she bring someone with her, and because of how much I knew Justine cared, I convinced her to talk to Justine. She asked us to come along for the extra support, too.

I held onto the memory card on the way back to the park. There, we all went searched for Justine together.

I texted Derek.

We're done. You're off duty. We'll explain what happened later.

When we got to the kissing booth, though, Justine wasn't there. We walked up and down the rows of tents and booths looking for her.

"I'd text her," Kelli said, "but I know her phone doesn't fit in her costume."

We continued searching. As I was looking around, I spotted my mom.

"Hey," she waved. "I haven't seen you girls all night. Where are your wigs?"

"Um, they got itchy," Emma lied.

"Aren't you supposed to be fortune telling?" I asked.

"I took a 15 minute break. Why don't you come in, and I'll tell your fortune?"

"That's okay, Mom. Maybe another time."

"I'd like my fortune read," Kelli interjected, pushing her way past me toward my mom.

"Okay," my mom said. "You can go wait by my booth, and I'll be back in a few minutes."

"Sounds good." A small smile twitched at the edge of Kelli's lips.

Emma and I followed Kelli to the booth just to make sure we didn't lose each other in the throng of people. There was a "Back in 15 minutes" sign on the tent flap, so no one was waiting in line. My mom was back in a matter of minutes welcoming Kelli into the tent in a fake mystical voice.

In the bit of privacy we had, Emma's excitement finally burst. "I saw a ghost. A real ghost! I know it wasn't under the best of conditions, but it still happened." She beamed as if it was the coolest thing in the world.

I was about to tell her to calm down when I heard a familiar voice calling out to us. I turned to see a Cat in the Hat hat bouncing above the crowd. "How'd it go?" Derek asked once he reached us.

"Not as expected," I admitted.

"But pretty well," Emma finished. "Justine told Kelli about the video, and she showed up before us. I think we've convinced her to move on, and we're going to help her. Kelli's getting a reading right now, though." She gestured toward the tent.

"You know," Derek lowered his voice. "I've been wondering. Is your mom's fortune-telling booth, you know, real?"

Emma and I exchanged a glance. We giggled and nodded.

Derek raised his eyes. "Then I have some pretty good prospects for my future."

"You got your fortune read?" I asked.

"Yep."

"What'd she tell you?" I prodded curiously.

"You're the psychic. Figure it out."

I rolled my eyes at him. "It doesn't—"

"Work that way," he finished. "I know. I was just teasing." He nudged me. I was happy to have my problems solved and be back with my best friends, although we still had to find Justine and make it to the police station.

"So what'd you find out?" Emma asked Derek again, curious about his fortune.

Derek shrugged. "Just some good things about my romantic future."

Emma and I giggled together. "Your romantic future?" I asked. "You've never been romantic with anyone."

"Maybe I've just been waiting around for the right girl," he said, but he wouldn't meet either of our eyes.

Emma started to say something, but before she could, Kelli emerged from the tent with a smile. "Your mom says everything is going to be okay. Thank you."

To my surprise, Kelli pulled me into an embrace.

"No problem," I said. "Now let's go find Justine."

"I just saw her over by the apple bobbing booth," Derek announced, so we all took off together to look for her. Luckily, she'd stayed put since Derek last saw her. We waved her over from the end of the line.

She noticed Kelli first. "Kelli, are you okay?"

"Yeah, I'm..." She paused in search of the right word. "Fine. We found it, and they helped me." She pushed a strand of hair behind her ear nervously. "I'd like your support when I go to turn him in. You know, if you're not super mad at me for pushing you away."

Justine hugged Kelli. "That's great. I don't want to wait another minute. I'm so glad you've come to your senses."

We all piled into my mom's car again. With the memory card still securely hidden in my hand, Emma drove us to the police station.

"Thank you all so much for supporting me," Kelli said in the car. "I'm still scared to death, but after what you guys did and what your mom said, I think everything will be okay. I haven't felt this confident in a long time."

I felt prideful of her transformation, knowing full well that it was my translation of Olivia's words that had changed Kelli's mind.

We walked into the police station, and people were staring at us, probably perplexed by our costumes.

"Can I help you?" an officer who was walking through the main hall asked.

"We're just looking for Teddy," I said. "He's my mom's boyfr—I mean, fiancé."

"Oh, right," the guy said, pointing his finger at me in recognition. "You're the girl who started his nick name around here. Teddy Bear. Classic! He's at his desk." The officer turned and continued on his way.

When we reached Teddy's desk, he looked up from his paperwork, and his eyes filled with shock. "Crystal. Are you all okay?" His eyes shifted between each of us, searching for something that would indicate why we were here.

I set the small memory card down on his desk. I didn't know if he could actually use the video in a case since we obtained it illegally, but I wasn't sure that was the point of it anymore. Justine believed it was evidence, but Olivia wanted us to get the video to convince Kelli to get out of her relationship with Nate. I handed the card over anyway. "Um... this is evidence, and my friend Kelli would really like to talk to you about something. I need you to promise to keep her safe."

"I can do that," he promised. "What exactly is this about?"

"My boyfriend, sir," Kelli said.

Teddy nodded in understanding. "Kelli, do you mind having a seat over there?" Teddy pointed her toward some nearby chairs.

"I'd like Justine to stay with me," Kelli told him.

"Okay," he agreed kindly. "And you two," he pointed toward Emma and Derek, "do you mind if I have a word with my future step-daughter?"

Everyone left, leaving me to wonder what Teddy was planning to ask me. Was I in trouble? I took a seat across from him. He crossed his hands.

"Crystal, how did you get involved in this? You aren't friends with those girls, are you?"

I was momentarily stung by the accusation, as if I wasn't cool enough to hang out with popular girls, but I reminded myself how well he knew me and my friends.

I hung my head guiltily. "Justine asked me to help because she found out I was... you know." I lowered my voice even though everyone within ear shot already knew my secret. "Psychic."

"And did you use those abilities to help Kelli?"

I nodded. "I found the memory card."

He didn't ask where I'd found it like I'd expected but instead shifted through the folders piled on his desk.

I glanced back toward my best friends, who were waiting for me by the door.

Teddy opened one of the folders and pulled a photo from it, looking at it as he spoke.

"This girl went missing from her home recently. Her name is Hope Ross. Of course, we're working with some larger departments on the case, but no one has made much leeway. The first 48 hours are crucial in an investigation like this, and we've already hit that time limit, but we still don't know much. We don't even know if she's still alive, but we're hopeful. I was wondering if maybe you could help us crack the case."

He handed me the photo. When I took it, my heart fell to the floor because I recognized the girl. It was a school photo, probably taken at the beginning of the school year, of a young girl around six years old with brown hair, freckles across her nose, and big chocolate eyes.

An image of her face as it was at that very moment flashed through my head. Her cheeks were full of color, but her eyes drooped in sadness. It was just a flash of her face telling me she was alive, and then it was gone. Unfortunately, it wasn't enough to give me any clue as to where she was.

My hands trembled as I set the photo back on the desk. My heart threatened to beat out of my chest.

"What?" Teddy asked. "What is it?"

I couldn't answer him at first. "You mean, you believe me?" I asked, my voice wavering. I knew he had accepted the idea, but I didn't think he actually *believed* it.

He paused for a moment as if pondering what to say. "Do you know why I'm a police officer, Crystal?"

I shook my head. He'd never told me why he entered the police force.

"I seem to have this strong sense of..." He paused in search of the right word. "Intuition. I'm good at solving cases. When I met your mother, I always suspected she had that same sense of intuition. It's what drew me to her. That, among other things."

I took in a sharp breath. Could Teddy have psychic abilities, too? My mom had said that the area had a rich history of psychics. I could hardly believe it, but that explained why he'd taken it so well.

"Unfortunately," he said, "my intuition is failing me on Hope's case. Do you think you can help?"

I paused for a moment, unsure. Then I nodded slowly. "I hope so. You'll have to give me some time, but I can tell you that I know she's still alive."

CHAPTER 28

*T*eddy thanked me, told me to enjoy the remaining few hours of the Halloween festival while he talked with Kelli, and sent me back to my friends. I asked Kelli if she wanted us to stay, but she told us we'd helped enough and that we should go enjoy ourselves.

Now that I had the issue of saving Kelli and Olivia off my chest, I felt like I deserved a good night out with my friends. I glanced back at Justine and Kelli as I exited the building, and I knew Kelli was going to be okay.

Emma drove us back to the park, and I worried about Hope the whole way. Emma noticed my nerves and encouraged me to just enjoy myself for one night. She was right. There wasn't anything I could do to help Hope right now anyway.

We walked up and down the aisles playing games and listening to the band play. We even took a walk down the haunted trail while Emma and I clung to Derek for protection, which honestly made me feel a bit safer even though the zombies were just volunteers in costume.

Sometime during the night, I cracked a real smile as I realized how much I'd accomplished in the last few hours. Kelli was okay and free from Nate, and Olivia had crossed over, which I hoped meant that her mom could move on, too.

I veered off from my best friends for a few minutes to visit my mom in her tent. She was standing outside waiting for her next victim.

"Maybe I could get a reading," I suggested.

"Or maybe I could get a reading from you," she joked, pulling back her tent flap and inviting me in. I walked into the small makeshift room, which was lit by electric candles since the coordinators agreed real candles could be potentially hazardous. There was a round table placed in the middle of the tent, one chair at the far end and one chair close to me. The table was covered with an appropriate table cloth, and her tarot cards and a crystal ball were sitting on top of it.

"Are you going to tell me where you really were all night?" she asked.

Of course, I thought. *She knows me far too well.*

"Just, um, some detective work," I managed to answer. It wasn't a lie, at least.

My mother looked at me like she didn't believe me.

I caved. "Okay, we didn't actually end up with the video last night. We went and got it today."

"You broke into Tammy's house to steal it?" She was disappointed.

A wave of guilt fell over me.

"Well, Derek says that since the door was unlocked, we didn't break in, and Emma says that since Olivia wanted us to have it, it wasn't stealing," I rationalized.

The look of disappointment was still painted on my mother's face. "Crystal, you may have fantastic abilities, but you have to learn how to use them responsibly. Being psychic doesn't mean you're entitled to things other people aren't."

She was right.

"Okay," I agreed. "I understand, but I can't say I'm sorry. I may have saved Kelli's life."

My mother sighed. I wasn't sure if it was a sigh of defeat or because she couldn't accept my excuse.

I dropped my head in guilt, and my eyes fixated on the crystal ball as it called out to me.

"Mom!" I scolded. "Is that my crystal ball?"

"Yeah," she admitted as she took a seat across from me.

"But, why?" My face fell, hurt that she'd taken it from my room without asking.

She shrugged like it was no big deal. "I'm sorry. I figured that we owned one now, so I didn't have to borrow one from the shop."

"But it's mine," I said possessively, picking it up from its stand and pulling it close to me. It began glowing in my hands. I didn't look up to see if my mother noticed it, too; I was too consumed by the swirling colors pulling me in. I studied it intensely as its energy wrapped around me. I never knew what I saw in it, but after a moment, I quickly returned it to its stand.

"What?" my mom asked. "What did you see?"

"I—I don't know."

I didn't. All I knew was that it was about the little girl, the one with big chocolate eyes. I knew she needed help, and I knew she would be the focus of my next psychic adventure.

"Crystal, with everything I've seen you do, you have amazing abilities, which is surprising since just a few weeks ago I didn't think you had *any*. You're going to be a really amazing psychic."

Yeah, I thought, but I knew that being psychic wasn't ever going to be easy. I knew that from this moment on, I would never stop using my abilities to help people.

DESIRE IN FROST

ALICIA RADES

CHAPTER 1

I knew the nightmare was coming before I closed my eyes. The same vision had been haunting my dreams for nearly a month, but as the weeks passed, I only witnessed it more frequently. By now, I was seeing Hope's abduction in my mind almost every night. I didn't want to face him again. I didn't want to feel Hope's terror as she was taken away. But I couldn't fight the fatigue any longer. I let my eyes droop, and then I drifted.

～

A hand clamped around my mouth, and my eyes shot open. My heart skipped a terrifying beat, and I began sweating under my covers. I wanted to open my mouth to scream, but the shadowed figure pressed down too hard against my face. Nothing came out.

An index finger hovered over the assailant's mouth, warning me that if I didn't stay quiet, there would be trouble. The room was eerily dark, but the moonlight outside my window illuminated a strip of his face. All I saw were green eyes staring back at me and the faint outline of his form cloaked in a black hoodie.

He picked me up gently from my bed, wrapping his arms around me, but he managed to keep one hand pressed against my mouth. It wasn't the comforting kind of hug my mother shared with me but the unfamiliar and terrifying kind I wanted to squirm away from. My six-year-old body was light, and I knew I couldn't fight my way out of this. I thought about screaming again so my mother would come to rescue me, but I was too petrified to make a sound. I didn't know what else to do. All I knew was that I couldn't fight him off. My body shook in fear, and a tear fell down my cheek. I prayed the stranger wouldn't hurt me.

The man cradled me in his arms and crawled back through my window the way he came. The pink lace curtains brushed against the top of my head as he pushed us both through the narrow space. He paused for a moment and released his grip on my mouth, but I was too frightened to make a peep. What was going to happen to me if I did? I didn't want to know the answer to that.

He quickly but quietly hurried across my yard toward the street, placing me in the front seat of a car I didn't recognize and shutting the door behind me. I caught a glimpse of myself in the side mirror. My young freckled face stared back at me with big chocolate eyes.

~

My blue eyes shot open. I breathed a sigh of relief, glad the nightmare was over again. My body was drenched in sweat, my heart was racing, and my covers were kicked to the foot of the bed. That's how it always was when I woke from this nightmare.

Like every morning this happened, I found myself wondering why. Why did I keep having the same dream about Hope without any new information to find her? This was one of the first dreams I'd had since I found out I was psychic a few weeks ago. If I had known what was happening then, I may have been able to save her. But the fact of the matter was that I didn't know what was happening then, and I was still confused, especially now that I was seeing something that happened weeks ago. My powers were supposed to help me find Hope, weren't they? So why weren't they giving me anything new to work with? All I saw was everything the police already knew.

I recalled the night of the Peyton Springs Halloween Festival when I visited my mom's fiancé, Teddy, at the police station. He knew my secret, so he asked if I could help find Hope. I remembered the way I felt and how my heart fell inside my chest when I looked at her picture. I recognized her.

"This girl went missing from her home recently," Teddy had told me. "Her name is Hope Ross. Of course, we're working with some larger departments on the case, but no one has made much leeway. The first 48 hours are crucial in an investigation like this, and we've already hit that time limit, but we still don't know much. We don't even know if she's still alive, but we're hopeful. I was wondering if maybe you could help us crack the case."

"I hope so," I remember telling him. "You'll have to give me some time, but I can tell you that I know she's still alive." I didn't know how I knew, but a flash of her face told me she was still breathing. Even weeks later, I still believed that wholeheartedly.

But I've spent too much time searching for her in my dreams! I cursed the universe. I kept seeing the same scene over and over with no new information that could lead me to her whereabouts. Since the police still hadn't found her, I was her only hope.

I curled into a ball on my bed and let a tear fall from my eye. I'd already helped people by using my newfound abilities, but I couldn't control them well yet. I could see minor things about people when I tried, but I could never see what I really wanted to see. With Hope, I didn't even know where to begin.

I'd tried different techniques, like looking into my crystal ball. Teddy even managed to snag one of Hope's beanie babies from her room—totally illegal, I know—so that I could touch something of Hope's and find her. So far, my gift of psychometry—finding things—was limited to lost books, CDs, and games of hide and seek. I didn't think I'd ever be able to find a person with this method.

Even when Teddy and I turned to Mom and her business partners, Sophie and Diane, who were also psychic, they hadn't seen anything. For some reason, my gift was stronger than all three of theirs put together. None of us knew why, but I had a theory. See, I'd only found out that I was psychic a few weeks ago, thanks to my mom hiding it from me for 15 years in hopes that I'd end up normal, but my abilities manifested on their own anyway. Looking back on it, I knew I had it in me all along. Maybe all the time I spent suppressing it and not knowing about it made it build up inside of me or something.

Without any concrete help from my mom and her friends, it was like everything that Hope was—and is—was frozen in time the night of her abduction.

A knock rapped at my bedroom door. "Crystal," my mom said gently. Without waiting for an answer, she opened my door a crack. "Are you awake?"

I quickly dashed the tear away before she could see me crying. I had told her I'd embraced my abilities. I didn't want her thinking I couldn't handle them.

"If you don't get up soon, you're going to be—sweetheart, what's wrong?"

I was never good at hiding my emotions, especially from my mother or my best friend Emma. I hated bothering my mom with my troubles. I mean, I knew she would help me and all, and she'd be more than supportive, but on some level, I felt like it was *my* responsibility.

I shrugged. Lying was out of the question. She knew me far too well, so I simply didn't say anything.

"Crystal, sweetie," my mom said. She crossed my room and sat at the end of my bed.

I rose to sit beside her. She took me in her arms and stroked my long dirty blonde hair. This only encouraged my emotions to run, and I sobbed into her arms. It felt like we had done this too many times since I'd discovered my powers, but I was glad she understood and could relate since she was psychic, too. The problem was that her abilities never seemed to give insight into the same situations as mine did, so she couldn't exactly help me on that end.

She didn't say anything; instead, she let me have my moment. When I was ready, I took a deep breath.

"It's Hope again, isn't it?" she asked.

I nodded. "I just can't figure it out." My voice cracked. "Like, what's the point of having this gift if it isn't leading me anywhere? I feel like I should have found her by now, but she just feels so far away."

"Crystal," my mother said with a tone of reassurance. "Our abilities aren't perfect. We're often shown what we need to see."

"But that's just it, Mom. I've seen the same thing night after night, and I'm not seeing anything new!"

My mother sighed. "Maybe you're just not looking hard enough." She gave me a look as if to say, *That's a good point, you know.*

At first, I didn't believe her, but the more I thought about it, the more I realized she was right. I was always looking at the facts that were staring me in the face. I never took a chance to forget Hope's fears and really look at the peripheral of the scene. Maybe it was a good idea to open up to my mom more often so she could give me more insight like this. I thought about her suggestion—to look deeper—and wanted to try it, to see if I could pinpoint exactly what I was missing, but I didn't have a chance to investigate right now. I was going to be late for school if I didn't get my butt in gear.

I thanked my mother for her support and suggestion and then shooed her out of my room. I quickly got ready for school without bothering with makeup. I added my owl necklace—the one Teddy had given me when he proposed to my mom a couple of weeks ago—as a final touch.

At lunch that day, I found my seat next to Emma and Derek. I caught a glimpse of Kelli and Justine one table over and waved to them. After I used my psychic gift to rescue Kelli from an abusive relationship—with Justine's help—I'd grown close enough to them that I wasn't just an underclassman anymore. I was, on some level, a friend. Kelli smiled back at me. She seemed so happy now that Nate was gone. His mom didn't pull strings at the courthouse like we thought she would. She sent him to live with his dad instead so Kelli would be safe from him during his probation period, and hopefully long after. I could see it in her eyes that she was doing a lot better.

"You are so lucky," Emma raved.

I thought she was going to say something about how cool my abilities were again, something I had only told the people close to me. Sure, they seemed pretty awesome at times, but with the mystery of Hope Ross's abduction hanging over my head, I still had my uncertainties.

"How am I lucky?" I asked.

Derek looked at me like I'd just asked the dumbest question in the world. "You're kidding, right?" he asked. "You're leaving for Florida in the morning and get the whole week of Thanksgiving off. We only get two measly days off."

I must have lost track of the days because I hadn't realized it was already Friday. I hadn't even started packing yet. Sure, I was really looking forward to lazing on the sand at my future step-grandparents' beachside home, but I was afraid the trip would only complicate things with the responsibilities I felt toward Hope.

"Oh, yeah," I said flatly. I couldn't help it when a hint of uncertainty leaked into my tone. "Lucky."

CHAPTER 2

"*E*mma," I complained. "I don't need this many outfits for just one week."

Emma was digging through my closet after school and tossing everything she thought I "needed" for my Thanksgiving vacation into a pile on my bed. Derek sat in my desk chair and laughed at us.

"Besides," I said, "we'll be in the car for most of the trip, so I should pack, like, athletic shorts or something comfortable, not all three of my swimsuits." I picked up my one piece and held it out to her as if that would explain my irritation.

"Oh, come on," Emma insisted. "You're going to be lying on the beach. You need a swimsuit so you can come back all tan. Why not this one?" Emma reached into my closet and held up the bright pink bikini she made me buy when we were shopping together last summer.

"A bikini? I've never even worn that thing. You're the one who made me buy it."

Emma rolled her eyes and tossed it back into my closet. "Yeah, so you could wear it for something like a trip to Florida."

"Why not this one?" I asked, holding up my tankini. "It's still a two-piece but a little more *appropriate*."

"Fine," Emma said. "Bring that one along, but I'm going to sneak your bikini in your bag anyway. You can leave your one-piece here." Emma shifted through some more clothes. "You might as well wear a sun dress while you're down there, too."

I sighed. "Okay. *One* sundress. I don't need four of them!" I didn't even know I had four sundresses. I reached for one of the dresses and placed it back on its hanger.

"Are you guys hungry?" Derek asked, running his fingers through his brown hair. "I'm hungry. Mind if I make us some sandwiches or something?"

My friends never had to ask to raid my kitchen. I nodded. "Sure. Sounds great."

Derek left the room.

I gazed at Emma as she watched him leave. Her eyes fixed on him, and her lips parted slightly and curled up at the ends, almost forming into a smile. When she turned back toward me, I was grinning in a teasing manner.

"What?" she asked defensively.

"Oh, don't think I didn't see that. You are so hot for him. I don't think I should ever leave you two alone," I laughed.

"Whatever," Emma said a little too high pitched. "I am not."

I kept my eyes fixed on her.

Emma crinkled her nose. Whenever she did that, it made her look like a chipmunk. "Is he cute? Okay, maybe a little. Is he, like, super nice? Yeah. But do I *like* him?" She paused. "But it's not me we should be talking about, Crystal. Are you okay?"

Emma caught me off guard.

I quickly dropped to my closet and pulled my duffel bag from the corner. "Yeah, I'm fine. Why?" My eyebrow began twitching. Emma knew that happened when I lied, so I always tried to turn away from her when I did. But I was a terrible liar. She could hear the dishonesty in my voice. I was sure of it.

"Crystal, we've known each other our whole lives. I can tell when something is bothering you." She paused for my response, but when I didn't say anything, she continued. "It's Hope again, isn't it?"

I finally turned to her and bit my lip. I'd confided with Emma about my dreams, but I never thought she'd be able to help me. Emma was thrilled about my abilities, and even though she wasn't born with the same gift, she'd been practicing "getting in touch with her inner psychic," as she called it. She came over almost every day for our "psychic exercises," her words, not mine, which consisted mostly of yoga and meditation.

As my mom explained, everyone is born with a sort of psychic ability, and all it took was practice—unless you were born with a stronger connection to the other side, like me.

Sometimes Emma would tell me more about things she read up on regarding the supernatural. I wasn't always sure what information to trust, so I'd spent some time with my mom at her Halloween-themed shop recently to learn more about being psychic. Even so, I didn't feel like I was getting anywhere new with my powers. Surprisingly, however, Emma had made quite a bit of progress in the last month. She was pretty accurate when she got feelings about a situation, which only made it harder for me to lie to her.

"Okay," I admitted. "Yeah, it's about Hope. It's just... I keep having this nightmare, and each time, I think it will continue and show me where she is or something, but it just stops when she gets in the car, and I don't know how to find her."

"Well, maybe if you tell me more about it, I can help," Emma offered.

"Come on, Emma. I can't tell you about the case." I wasn't actually supposed to know anything other than what was released by the media. I'm pretty sure Teddy had broken some laws by telling me what he knew, but he was convinced I could help him find Hope. At first, I thought I could, too, especially because I saw her in my dreams before she was even taken, but it had been weeks, and I still had nothing. In fact, no one had anything. Most everyone on the case had already given up.

Emma stared at me with her big brown eyes and played with a strand of curly dark hair. "Crystal, you know I've been getting better at this stuff. I just want to help."

She had a point. I mean, I knew she wouldn't tell anyone, and Teddy hadn't exactly made me promise anything.

"Okay," I caved.

We both took a seat on my bed, and I told her everything I knew. "Teddy says Hope's dad died right before she was abducted. It was a motorcycle accident." My voice caught in my throat for a second. I coughed to clear it.

Emma rested a hand on my shoulder. She understood far too well. My dad had died when I was around Hope's age, and to this day, the thought of death still got to me.

"Anyway," I continued, "the police have been on the guy's brother because of a mental history and a criminal background—I think it was just drugs and stuff like that—but Teddy doesn't think it's him. Well, they haven't actually found anything to tie the brother to Hope's abduction, but I'm thinking that maybe he was working with someone else or something."

"Why would he even take her?" Emma asked. "I mean, what's the point?"

"I asked the same thing. I guess the brother—Jeff, Teddy said his name was—has this thing against Hope's mom. When his brother Scott died, he thought he would be better for Hope than her mom was or something. I don't know… none of this really makes any sense to me. That was just the police's theory."

I paused to collect my breath. "Jeff does sound like a logical suspect, but Teddy said there was no ransom note and that after Scott's funeral, Jeff went back home somewhere south. They've checked all his credit card records and everything. But, I mean, it had to have been someone from the funeral, right? It was that same day, so it only makes sense."

Emma's lips pressed together in thought. "Why even treat it like a kidnapping, then? Couldn't she have run away?"

"Abduction," I corrected her. "I don't know, really. I imagine they looked into that possibility, but where would she go? If she was anywhere around town, they would have found her weeks ago. Her mom sent her to bed, and then she was just gone in the morning. Abduction makes sense. Plus, there's my vision that clearly shows she was abducted."

Emma rolled her eyes like that was obvious. "Yeah, well, the *police* don't know that. For all they know, she could have run away and slipped in the river."

"You're right, and I think some of them are giving up because they're so clueless. I mean, Teddy won't say that to my face, but I get that feeling from him. It doesn't help that I'm not learning anything new about her, either."

"Didn't they dust for fingerprints or something?" Emma asked.

"I don't know. It's not like I was there with the police. If they did, they didn't find anything."

Just then, the doorbell rang. I had learned over the past few weeks to stay put whenever this happened. Emma would always stop me and say, "It's the perfect opportunity to practice your abilities!" She'd make me sit there and guess who it was, not that we had a lot of visitors. We did the same thing with phone calls and texts, too.

"I'll get it," Derek shouted from the kitchen.

Emma and I stayed put on my bed and both closed our eyes, trying to summon an image of the person at the door. When I saw his face in my mind, I groaned.

I still wasn't sure if Emma could actually do this or if she just guessed most of the time. "Who's the hunk?" Emma asked.

That's when I knew she was just guessing. "Hunk? Robin is *not* a hunk."

"Oh, it's *Robin*."

I wanted to slap the cheesy grin off her face.

"The hot musician who's going to be your step-cousin in a couple of months? You'll have plenty of time to 'get to know each other' on your trip." Emma wiggled her eyebrows suggestively.

I swatted at her lightly. "Shut up. For one, Robin is not hot. Two, he's hardly a musician. He just plays in a really dumb garage band. And three, ew! He's Teddy's nephew. Once Teddy marries my mom, that'd be, like, incest or something."

"Not really since you aren't blood related," Emma pointed out.

Robin lived in the city about an hour from Peyton Springs, but since he was coming with us to Florida, he came today so we could get on the road extra early the following morning.

I heard Derek and Robin shuffling down the hall. I rolled my eyes at Emma and took the opportunity to escape her teasing. I hopped up from the bed and exited my room.

Robin was taller than I remembered. He had short blonde hair that stood up in every direction and a little bit of stubble that, okay, I had to admit was a bit attractive. His blue eyes shone bright, and his features seemed to come together flawlessly.

But I didn't like him. He was always making some stupid joke at my expense. When Teddy first introduced us, I honestly had to ask, "Robin, as in Robin Hood?" because I didn't hear him right.

And then he spat back, "And you're Crystal, as in crystal meth?" And he was always picking on me for playing sports. Emma may have been right saying he was attractive, but the guy was a jerk.

"Um, you can stay in here," I told Robin, gesturing to the room next to mine. It was usually an office, but we added the fold up cot for him to sleep on that night.

He smiled at me, which was weird because, like I said, the guy was a jerk. "Hi, Crystal," he said.

"Um, yeah. Hi." I didn't know how else to greet him. "Did your parents drop you off?"

Robin's parents weren't coming because neither of them could get off work, but Teddy had invited Robin along anyway to come see his grand-parents with us.

He pushed his way into the guest room and dropped his bag. Then he turned and jingled his keys at me. "I can drive, you know."

"Oh," is all I could say. Right. Robin was 17. I was briefly reminded that I was the only one in the house who still couldn't drive.

Robin slipped off his jacket. Underneath it, he was wearing a short sleeve shirt that gave me a nice glimpse of his muscles.

I looked him up and down for a moment and then realized what I was doing. "Uh… make yourself comfortable," I said with a half-hearted smile before fleeing the room.

CHAPTER 3

*T*he next morning, I woke with relief that I hadn't dreamt the previous night. Even so, it was a restless sleep, so I was tired. I slumped down the hallway with my duffel bag and purse and loaded them into the car.

I settled in my spot behind the driver's seat and fitted a pillow between my head and the door. Everyone else piled into the car quietly since it was early and we were still sleepy, but soon enough, we were on our way to Florida.

I didn't like the idea of facing Hope's abduction in my dreams, but I figured I was safe to rest my eyes. I must have drifted off because when my eyes flung open, I was in Hope's bed again, being silenced by her abductor's grip and then carried out through the window and placed in the car like normal.

Somewhere in the back of my conscious mind, I remembered what my mom had said. I had to look deeper, to forget the fright I was feeling and to seek further clues. The Crystal part of me struggled to break through the barrier that made me feel like Crystal on one side and Hope on the other. Was I Crystal, or was I Hope? While in the dream, I could never tell.

But then, for a brief moment, the Crystal part of me did break through. It didn't last long, and it wasn't enough to notice anything particular, but for a second, I knew who I really was.

My body gave a start, and I woke back in the car with my family. We had already made it from southern Minnesota to the flat terrain of Iowa. I slowed my breathing and stared out the window at the passing corn fields. It wasn't much to look at. Since it was the end of November, all the greenery I enjoyed about the area was replaced with a dull brown pallet. A light layer of snow dusted the corn fields. It was still early morning. I couldn't spot the sun, but I knew it was hiding somewhere behind the clouds.

It made me feel the way Hope was feeling right now. I didn't know how, but I could feel her sometimes. I knew when she was lonely and when she was hungry and when she was sad. Right now, Hope was feeling sorrowful, and the gray November sky seemed to mirror her emotions.

My stomach sank in response, and guilt consumed me. I still hadn't found her, and I was running away from the place where she had been taken when I knew she needed me. But what more could I do? I couldn't just put my life completely on hold and refuse the trip in hopes that I'd find something new in the next week that I hadn't seen in the past month. Besides, both Mom and Emma kept telling me I needed to relax. It's not that they weren't concerned about Hope. It's just that my gift worked better when I wasn't constantly worrying.

From next to me on the back seat, Robin pulled his earbuds from his ears. He looked at me with an expression I couldn't quite read. Disgust, maybe?

"Are you okay?" he asked.

I blinked a few times. Did Robin just show concern for me? Maybe he had matured a bit since I last met him. I almost cracked a smile at the thought that he might be a decent guy.

Normally I would tell people I was fine, but I found myself saying, "Just a nightmare that's been bothering me. Why?" I wasn't good at lying, but I had a way of bending the truth so I didn't feel so bad about misguiding people. Yet it surprised me that the full truth was coming out of my mouth, especially since I was speaking to Robin.

"Well, it's just, you kind of look like you're miserable, and it's bringing the whole mood in the car down. Let's try not to suffer through this trip, okay?"

My jaw almost dropped. Okay. There goes the idea that Robin might be nice for a change.

We rode in silence, and everyone attended to their own devices or watched the scenery to kill time. I spent most of the day with my nose in a book. I wasn't usually one for reading, but it helped take my mind off things. I texted Emma and Derek a bit, but I had only been gone for a few hours, so there wasn't anything new to talk about. I glanced over at Robin a few times. Each time I did, he had his earbuds in and was texting someone. I wondered if maybe it was his girlfriend.

Looking at Robin, I found myself curious to know if he had some sort of ability like I did. I was thrilled that I had my mom by my side, and it was cool to know that Teddy was intuitive, something I had learned last Halloween. I loved the support Emma gave me, too. But what if Teddy's strong intuition came from somewhere in his family's lineage? What if Robin inherited that, too? It would be different with him. I'd have someone my age who understood the awkward stage I was going through.

Sure, I had Emma, but she wasn't born with an ability like I was. She was preparing herself and practicing her intuition whereas my gift was sprung on me from out of nowhere. Would Robin understand that feeling? I knew I couldn't just *ask* him straight out, so I turned back to my book.

In the late afternoon, Teddy decided it was time to stop for the night. I thought it was a little early for turning in, but I was glad to stretch my legs.

Teddy pulled off an exit and into the parking lot of a rundown motel. The paint on the side of the building was peeling, and the parking lot was riddled with cracks that weeds had started growing through. Each room had a door that led straight onto the sidewalk.

"*This* is where we're staying for the night?" I asked in disbelief. I mean, our budget wasn't *that* low for this vacation, and I knew Teddy's parents were helping us cover some of the costs.

My mother looked at me with a disapproving glare. "Crystal," was all she said, but it was enough of a reprimand to get me to shut up.

"I think it looks cozy," Robin said as he got out of the car and looked around.

Teddy opened his door and walked toward the front office to check in.

"Mom," I said once we were alone. "What is this? This looks like the kind of place where they don't wash the sheets and people get bed bugs and stuff."

My mom shifted in her seat to look at me. She was a gentle woman who was more like a friend to me than a mother. It seemed that since the engagement, however, she had been taking sides with Teddy more and more. It's not that I argued with either of them often, though. We actually all got along great.

My mom just looked at me and said, "Well, don't let them bite." Then she turned back toward the front of the car and laughed at her own joke.

I wanted to give her a look of disapproval behind her back, but her light mood made even me giggle at her dumb joke.

I scanned the streets. I still wasn't sure about the place. It just didn't sit well with me. Everything around here looked run down. There was a gas station across the street closer to the highway and a fast food place up the road. A small family diner sat next to the motel, but I didn't see many people around, as if this was a dying town despite its proximity to the highway. My gaze wandered farther down the landscape.

That's when my eyes fell on Teddy through the windows that led to the motel's office. I noticed motion as he slid something into his pocket. *That wasn't his wallet,* I thought. *It was—oh, my gosh. Did Teddy just flash his badge?*

"I'm going to—um—stretch my legs," I told my mom, which wasn't a complete lie.

I opened my door and began walking to no place in particular. I stole a glance at my mother, who was reading her book while she waited for Teddy. Robin was facing away from me studying the scenery, which wasn't much to see in this tiny little town.

I slunk around the building and stayed low so Teddy wouldn't see me. I pressed my body against the side of the motel and peeked in a window. My heart pounded in my chest. I'd never been very good at or confident in sneaking around. I was always too afraid I'd get caught, but I challenged the situation anyway and kept my eyes fixed on the scene before me.

I was close to Teddy now, so close that I saw him slide a photograph across the counter toward the attendant. The man picked it up, looked at it, and then handed it back to Teddy. I caught a glimpse of the image when Teddy took it back. It was a photograph of a man with short hair, cut almost to his scalp, and dark brows that a pair of menacing eyes looked up from under.

What is Teddy doing? I wondered. *He's not supposed to be investigating a case. He's supposed to be on vacation!*

The man behind the counter shook his head and then pointed to a high spot in the corner of the room. I followed Teddy's gaze and noticed a security camera attached to that spot on the ceiling. I was shocked a place like this even had a security system.

They exchanged a few more words I couldn't hear, and then I watched Teddy slide his credit card across the counter, thanking the attendant. He started to leave.

I circled around the building the opposite way I'd come so it wouldn't look like I was roaming around near the office. It was clear along the length of the building, so I took off running to get blood flowing to my legs. It felt fantastic after spending all day cooped up in the car. When I arrived back at our vehicle, I was huffing.

"Where did you run off to, Kiddo?" Teddy asked kindly.

I shrugged. "Just needed to stretch my legs."

Robin scowled at me, although I wasn't entirely sure why.

I didn't know how long I stayed awake that night in our motel room afraid to face Hope's abduction again. When I finally fell asleep next to my mother, I was extra tired as I felt Hope's and my own fatigue stronger than ever.

CHAPTER 4

I woke to the familiar chime of my cell phone. I was sweating again and had relived Hope's abduction one more time, yet I hadn't seen anything new. I had tried, but I hadn't broken through that barrier that distinguished Hope from me. I knew I would get it with more practice, but that still meant waking up terrified each morning.

Sometime during the night, I had thrown the covers off me, so they were now doubled up in a heap on my mother's sleeping body. I fumbled around for my phone on the nightstand and prayed it hadn't woken anyone else. Robin stirred from the bed next to mine. I looked over at my mother on my own bed. She was still sound asleep.

I turned the volume on my phone to silent so I wouldn't wake anyone and then checked the text I'd just received.

Rise and shine! It was from Emma.

What? I replied. I looked around the room. It was still dark. The only light seeped in through the curtains from a nearby street lamp.

It's yoga time. You promised we'd keep up while you were gone.

Oh. Right. I guess I hadn't realized she'd want to do it at the break of dawn. I sighed. She had really thought this through. I mean, we couldn't exactly share a yoga session while I was in the car the rest of the day.

I swung my feet over the edge of the rather uncomfortable bed and stretched my arms above my head, careful not to make too much noise. I tiptoed to my bag, pulled out my laptop, and unrolled my yoga mat—the one with an owl design on it that I had bought just weeks ago when we started these sessions—near the bathroom. The room we were staying in had a wall separating the sink area from the rest of the room, so I tried to get a little privacy behind it.

I fired up my computer and immediately received a video chat call from Emma. Her face glitched across the screen, an indication of the poor Internet connection.

"So?" Emma asked, her tone full of anticipation. About what, I didn't know.

"So, what?" I asked quietly.

"Duh." She rolled her eyes. "How's Robin? You can't go on a vacation with a guy like that without something interesting happening."

"Emma, he's practically my cousin," I whispered. "That would be so gross. Besides, I think he might have a girlfriend. He was texting her all day in the car yesterday."

Emma crinkled her nose in disappointment.

"So," I said, mirroring her tone in hopes that we could get off the subject of me and Robin. "What about you and Derek?"

"What?" Emma squeaked a little too loud.

I peeked my head around the corner to make sure she hadn't woken anyone. Everyone else was still asleep.

"There's nothing going on between me and Derek," she insisted, but I swore I could see her blushing, even if the video quality was poor. "Um... why don't we start our yoga session?"

I laughed a little inside at how she so quickly changed the subject.

Emma seemed to know what she was doing, so she was my guide for the day. I tried to make my legs bend in the right direction as she showed me new positions. The quiet, tranquil music she was playing through my speakers helped calm me, so I was relaxed when we finally said goodbye.

Emma had lectured me constantly the past few weeks about how important relaxation exercises could be when getting in touch with your "inner psychic." Although I was a bit reluctant to try them, I believed her. Now that I was relaxed, I figured it would be easier to get in touch with Hope.

I thought about tiptoeing back across the room to get my crystal ball from my bag, but I didn't want to affect the "zone" I was in, so I just crossed my legs on my mat and set my mind on Hope. I felt like I sat there for quite some time, but after a while, I started to feel something. I never knew how I knew it, but I could feel exactly what Hope was feeling. I knew she missed her mom. This was the feeling I always got when I focused on Hope. But this time, something was different. The feeling was stronger. I wasn't sure if it was because Hope missed her mom more now than ever or if I was developing a stronger connection with her.

I sat there for another few minutes without feeling anything new except for a chill spreading out from my spine toward my fingertips. All my sweat had evaporated and left me cold. I longed to crawl under the covers next to my mother's warm body. I knew people would start waking up soon, so I ended my session by opening my eyes and pulling myself from the floor.

I glanced in the mirror as I stood and almost screamed. My heart jumped when I saw not only my face, which was fixed with terror, but a man with green eyes standing behind me. His expression wasn't one of malice, but he wasn't supposed to be there, and that made my pulse quicken at a threatening rate. I whirled around, ready to defend myself, but the man in the mirror was gone.

I gripped the edge of the sink countertop to steady myself as I slowed my breathing and frantically scanned the room. I nearly dropped to the floor when I realized I had just seen my third ghost.

CHAPTER 5

*A*fter everyone woke, we piled in the car again and hit the road. It was just starting to get light out. I eyed Teddy from the backseat and wondered again what exactly he said to the desk attendant at our motel. Was the man in the photograph a suspect in one of his cases? Why would he have to ask someone so far away about a suspect in a case? Does Teddy even have *suspects*? Peyton Springs is pretty small, so I can't imagine he does much more than write parking tickets and respond to domestic disturbance calls.

I thought about taking a nap because I was bored, but I didn't want to face Hope's abduction again, especially when I was prone to thrashing around in my sleep while experiencing it. I didn't want Robin, who was sitting next to me in the back seat, to see that. It was embarrassing enough when my mother came into my room during the night to quiet me down.

The longer we drove, the more bored I became. My eyes fell on Robin, and I wondered if we could maybe do something together to ease my boredom, like actually have a decent conversation. But his earbuds were in, and he was texting again. I didn't want to bother him. I just opened my book and continued reading.

I was glad when we stopped at a gas station to stretch our legs. Mom and Teddy suggested each of us grab a snack to hold us over until we reached his parents'. I browsed the aisles and chose a package of trail mix and then met Mom and Teddy at the register.

"Did you use the bathroom?" my mom asked.

"Mom!" I glanced around.

"Well, I don't want to stop in an hour because you have to use the bathroom."

I sighed and handed her my bag of trail mix before heading to the bathroom.

A few minutes later, I stepped back into the main part of the gas station. I scanned the room, but my mom, Teddy, and Robin had already checked out. I caught a glimpse of them through the window. Robin was climbing into the car, and my mom was arranging herself in the front seat. Teddy was reaching in his pocket in search of the keys.

I began toward the exit doors to meet them at our vehicle. Then I saw something out of the corner of my eye that frightened me. My breath left my chest for a moment, and I had to do a double take down the aisle. There were two men standing there. One was a large man close to me browsing the chips. The other stood at the end of the aisle and stared back at me with green eyes.

I couldn't move for what felt like several long seconds. I only heard the pounding of my own heartbeat in my ears. My head spun, and I rested a hand against the store shelf to hold myself up. A shiver ran down my spine the same time my palms began sweating, throwing off the equilibrium in my body and making me feel faint.

The large man turned and crossed the aisle, blocking my view from the guy with green eyes, the one I was sure I'd seen earlier this morning in the mirror. *Green eyes just like the abductor*, I thought.

When my breath finally returned, I didn't wait another second. I wasn't quite sure what I was doing when I pushed past the large man in pursuit of the man in the mirror, but it didn't matter because he was gone.

The large man grunted and gave me a look that said, *What's wrong with you?*

"Sorry," I said, looking around the store again. And then I saw him. He had his back to me, but I watched him duck his head into a silver car.

I bolted. I wasn't thinking about what I was doing. All I knew was that if I was seeing this man, there were some questions—although I didn't know what they were yet—that needed answering. I prayed that those answers would lead me to Hope, wherever she was.

The man's car pulled out of the parking lot the same time I pushed my way out the door. I only stopped for a split second, and then I raced to my side of our car. My family met me with confused expressions.

"Him!" I shouted, pointing at the car that was getting away. "Teddy, follow him."

Everyone stared back at me blankly. Teddy and my mom exchanged a quick glance as if to say, *Do you know what she's talking about?*

"I saw him. Teddy, it's *him*." My eyes widened in urgency.

Suddenly, Teddy's expression shifted, and I knew he understood. He turned the key quickly and whipped out of the parking lot.

"Where'd he go?" Teddy practically shouted.

I didn't know. My heart pounded, and my breath quickened as I scanned the area for the gray car. We couldn't lose him! Then I spotted it. Desperation overcame me, clouding any other feelings, including rationality. "There!" I pointed.

Teddy stepped on the gas, whipping me back into my seat. He took the corner to the onramp a little too fast, and I slid into Robin. I caught my breath and looked up at him for a moment. His brow was furrowed, but he was surprisingly calm. I regained my composure—well, as much as I could muster—and slid across the seat and fumbled with my seat belt. Teddy weaved around a few cars until we were right on the guy's tail.

"Uh... Crap!" Teddy said under his breath.

I knew exactly how he felt. Now that we caught up with the guy, what were we going to do? I didn't have any time to think this through. All I knew was that this man was important and that I needed to get to him somehow.

Teddy whipped his body around to check his blind spot, and then he moved into the left lane. He stepped on the gas again until we were side by side with the gray car. Teddy honked his horn. He and my mom made frantic gestures from the front seat to get the guy to pull over.

I craned my head to look at him, but when I saw the man's confused expression and his brown eyes looking back at us, my heart sank to the deepest depths of my body.

Teddy honked the horn again.

I could hardly breathe. How could I have been so wrong about something like this? What was I thinking? Hadn't I said the guy I saw was a ghost? How could I think he could just get into a car and drive away?

"Teddy," I finally managed to choke out, only he was still honking the horn. "Teddy," I said a little louder.

He had his badge out and was holding it up to the window on my Mom's side of the car.

"Teddy!" I shouted as loud as I could. I wasn't one to shout, so I knew it surprised him.

The car went completely silent for a split second.

"It's not him."

CHAPTER 6

"*W*hat?"
My eyes brimmed with tears, and my throat closed up in embarrassment. "It's not him," I repeated, but my voice was so quiet that it felt like the words were sinking back into my chest.

Teddy dropped the hand that was holding his badge. He glanced at me in the mirror, and I could see his face tightening. Was he confused, or was he mad at me? I couldn't tell.

"What do you mean?"

I didn't like the sound of his voice. It was quick, deep, and critical.

Robin's and my mother's eyes bore into me. Teddy's were shifting between the road, the man in the car next to us, and me. I wanted to curl up in a ball that would swallow me and my disappointment whole. Maybe then I would be as small as I felt at that moment.

"I mean I made a mistake." My voice was just loud enough for them to hear, but I was too ashamed to raise it any louder. My throat closed up around my own words.

The car slowed as Teddy realized what I was saying. I caught a glimpse of his eyes in the rearview mirror. He looked mad. I mean, really mad. I'd never seen Teddy mad before, so I wasn't sure how to handle the situation. Teddy put on his blinker and merged into the right lane before taking the next exit. Nobody said a thing until Teddy stopped the car at another gas station.

My nose tingled as I fought back the tears I knew were coming. How could I have been so stupid? I tried to put the pieces together in my head. The abductor had green eyes. The man in the mirror had green eyes. The man in the gas station was the same man I saw in the mirror. I thought I saw him getting into a silver car, except I only saw the guy from the back. I was sure the man in the mirror was a ghost, what with him disappearing and the shiver I got both times I saw him. That means he couldn't have been the person I saw getting into the gray car. But he could be Hope's abductor... And that would mean—

"Crystal, *what* is going on?" Teddy demanded in a loud voice that pulled me from my thoughts.

A tear fell from my eye, and I quickly dashed it away. "I—I don't know." My voice cracked. "I saw him. I was sure of it." I paused. All eyes were on me. Another tear rolled down my cheek. "I just—I'm sorry." I didn't know what else to say.

Teddy's mouth curled down in disappointment. He took a breath to calm himself. "Do you have any idea how embarrassing that was for me to flash my badge at someone who *wasn't* a suspect?"

Embarrassing for him? I was mortified for getting it all wrong. It was *my* fault. I couldn't tell if I was crying because I was mad at myself or because I feared Teddy's reaction. Either way, showing weakness like this in front of everyone in the car pulled at my self-esteem and made me only want to cry more.

"Next time, you better be 100 percent positive," Teddy warned.

A sob caught in my chest. I stared up at the ceiling in hopes that my tears subside, but I knew the tears were already written all over my face.

My mom touched Teddy's shoulder lightly to calm him down. He turned from me and exited the car. I watched him pace back and forth in the parking lot and then start walking toward the building.

I turned to face my mom and Robin. Robin's expression twisted into a cross of confusion and disappointment.

"What?" I snapped without intending to sound so bitter.

He looked at me for a few more seconds and then said, "I don't know what that was all about, but it sure sounds like you have issues." Then he unbuckled his seat belt and followed his uncle into the gas station.

I let the tears fall down my face. I didn't want to cry in front of Teddy and Robin, but right now, I wasn't shy about holding my tears back in front of my mom. She was the only one who would understand me. As much as I didn't want to show weakness, I knew she wouldn't chastise me for crying.

I couldn't quite explain what I was feeling. I was embarrassed for making Teddy chase after the wrong guy. I was furious that my abilities had failed me. I was frightened by the way Teddy reacted. And I was unsure if Teddy would ever trust me and my gift again. I knew Teddy didn't understand my mother's and my abilities—not to mention whatever mild intuition he had—but at least he trusted us. He trusted me enough to run after someone without a single explanation, and I had it wrong. What did that say about my powers and my judgment?

Most of all, little pins stung at my heart because I wasn't entirely sure how much *I* trusted my gift. That was what hurt the most.

My mother squeezed my hand to comfort me. "It's okay, sweetheart," she assured me.

I knew she understood on some level, but I had to wonder if her abilities had ever caused her to make such an utter fool out of herself. She'd told me that people had hurt her because of it and called her a witch, and that's why she never explained to me about psychics. If it skipped a generation with me, then I wouldn't have to face the ridicule, she'd said.

But did she ever feel this way about herself? Did she really know how a mistake like this bit at my self-esteem and ached my heart? I honestly didn't know the answer to that question.

"I just don't get it, Mom," I said. "I mean, I thought I saw the guy."

We both didn't speak for what seemed like forever. She just stared at me with a sympathetic expression in her eyes.

I took this time to again review the situation in my head. If the guy in the mirror was, in fact, Hope's abductor, that would mean that he was dead. That would mean that he couldn't have physically driven a car and that I mistook another man for him. But the fact that I saw the man with the green eyes in the first place means that he was trying to contact me about something. I knew that the farther south we traveled, the more I could feel Hope's emotions, yet I didn't know what that meant. I didn't know what any of it meant yet.

And then something small clicked in my mind. Finally, I broke the silence. "Mom, I'm starting to get the feeling that this trip isn't about Thanksgiving anymore." I met her gaze. "I think everything from here on out is going to be all about Hope."

CHAPTER 7

*T*eddy and Robin returned. I could see Teddy stealing glances at me in the rearview mirror every so often as we drove. All I could see were his eyes, but I could still tell he was frowning. Each time I looked at Robin, he met my gaze with a scowl. At first, I almost thought he was mad at me, too, but it was so hard to tell with Robin.

Emma and I texted for a while, but I didn't tell her about what had happened. I felt reserved about the whole situation mostly because I was mad at myself about being misguided by my abilities. For the most part, texting Emma helped take my mind off it even though we didn't talk about anything important—and I liked it that way. It was an easy way to escape my worries. After a while, she had to go, and I was once again left alone with my thoughts.

Relief overcame me when we finally arrived at Teddy's parents' that evening. I could get out of the confined car and away from the scrutinizing glances—and perhaps clear my mind.

Teddy's parents' house was a quaint one-story home with the sand literally at their back door. A woman with salt and pepper hair and a big smile emerged from the house. She rushed toward us with her arms wide open as we all piled out of the car. Teddy embraced the woman and gave her a kiss on the cheek.

"Teddy," she smiled. "I'm so happy to see you!" She turned to me since I was closest to her. "You must be Crystal," she said. I expected her to shake my hand or something, but instead, she pulled me into a hug. "You can call me Gail. Oh, and Robin!" She circled around to the other side of the car to greet her grandson, leaving me a mere split second to react.

A half smile formed across my face. Gail's upbeat emotions and cheerful grin felt like a refreshing shift to my otherwise depressing day.

"Crystal," Teddy said, pulling me to full attention. His voice was soft again, but I could still hear a hint of something in it that told me he wasn't over what had happened earlier. I turned back toward him and found an older man standing next to him. "This is my dad, Wayne."

I forced a smile. "Hi."

And then he hugged me, too. Wayne and Gail greeted my mother for the first time, and then they led us into their home for the grand tour, which wasn't much because it was only a two bedroom house. Mom and Teddy were going to stay in the guest room while Robin would sleep on the couch, Gail explained.

"Where do I stay?" I asked.

Gail led me to an enclosed porch at the rear of the house. "I hope this will do," she said kindly.

I looked around. The porch was small, but it was decorated tastefully with shell picture frames and a matching clock. The air was warm, and I could hear the waves crashing against the shore just out the window. There was an air mattress set up for me, which practically took up the whole porch, but I was happy to have my privacy.

"I love it," I told her in all honestly.

After we unpacked the car, Gail called us to the kitchen for dinner. I sat next to Robin and breathed in the sweet aroma of freshly baked dinner rolls.

Once we were all settled in our spots and we'd said grace, Teddy cleared his throat. "Mom, Dad," he addressed. All eyes turned to him in anticipation. I watched his face twist into a nervous expression just like the night he asked my mom to marry him. "I have some big news." He paused. He wrapped an arm around my mother and looked deep into her eyes.

Her gaze met his, and they locked onto each other. I loved seeing them together like that. It made me feel warm inside knowing that this was a part of my family. Teddy's soft expression made it seem like he was less worried about what had happened earlier, and that helped calm me down, if only slightly.

The room went quiet for several long moments while Mom and Teddy exchanged a silent conversation—the kind I still wasn't completely able to decipher myself.

My mother finally broke their stare and shouted in excitement, "We're getting married!" Then she extended her left hand and showed her ring to Gail and Wayne. I noticed Robin sneak a glance at it, too.

Gail leapt from her chair and said something in such a high pitch that

I couldn't quite understand her. She hugged both of them. Excitement emanated from the room as each face around the table filled in with a smile. I smiled at the announcement, too, even though I was there when Teddy proposed.

I twisted the owl pendant he had given me at the time around my fingers and thought back to that night. I liked how things could be so simple at times. Wayne and Gail asked a lot of questions of my mom, and she told them about her shop, Divination, only she left out the part about some of the things being useful to real psychics. We then talked about the wedding as we ate, and I let the happiness of the moment sink into my heart, hoping to keep this moment in my mind as I faced the inevitable trials of my psychic powers.

~

After we cleared our dishes, I finally found a moment alone with my mother. "Do you want to walk down to the beach with me?" I asked, hoping she would get the hint and accept my offer.

She smiled in reply.

My mother followed me down the stairs that led to the beach. I sat beside her in the sand and dug my exposed toes into it. Neither of us spoke for a long time. I grabbed a handful of sand and watched it fall through my fingers and back to the earth. Silence stretched between us as I mentally worked up the courage to confide in her.

"Mom," I finally spoke, but I didn't meet her gaze. "Have you ever used your abilities to help someone? I mean, to really help someone, like I did with Kelli and Olivia?"

"Oh, sweetheart," she said sympathetically, running a hand down through my blonde hair. "Is this about Hope? You're afraid you're not doing enough to help her, right?"

I knew my mother was intuitive, but she'd also told me that her psychic visions and feelings didn't work with her family members. That's how I knew she was speaking out of her motherly instinct, the one that taught her to understand me so well and to pick up on my emotions in a snap. I didn't always like when people could read my moods because it made it hard to lie, but at times like this, I was grateful my mother knew me well enough to understand me.

I lifted my head to look into her eyes. "That's just it, Mom. I haven't done *anything* to help her. I mean, I know I should use my gift to help people and everything, but it's just, sometimes I don't know what I'm doing."

"I know, sweetie." She ran a hand down my head again the way she

167

always does when she's trying to comfort me. "Believe it or not, I do know how you feel. I've been called on to help people in the past, too."

I breathed a sigh of relief. At least I wasn't in this alone. "Really?" I asked, almost in admiration. My mom had been helping me over the past few weeks alongside Emma as I discovered more about my abilities, but only now did I realize that I didn't know that much about hers. I knew she could see pieces of the future and that she could find things through touch, but she hadn't told me much about her past as a psychic. Suddenly, I wanted to know.

"Who have you helped?" I asked.

"A few people," she answered vaguely.

Now I only felt like she was making me beg for information. "Like who? And how did you help them?" Maybe if I knew more about the people she'd helped, I could understand better how to help Hope and anyone else who came along.

"There was this guy once," she explained. "I had a dream—a vision—that he was going to die. For the longest time, I never knew what my dream meant. I didn't even know the guy at the time. In the end, my dream helped save his life."

I smiled at the thought that my mom was a real hero. Maybe I could be a real hero to Hope, too.

"Was it hard for you, you know, when you found out you were psychic?" I asked.

"That's where I have some regrets," she admitted. "You know my mom didn't have the gift but my grandma did. My grandma had always spoken to me about it, so when I started realizing that I had it, it wasn't completely confusing. My mom hated my grandma. I think she felt left out that my grandma and I were both psychic and she wasn't."

She sighed and then continued. "So I always thought it had skipped you like it skipped my mom. I didn't want to have an awful relationship with you like my mom and grandma did, and I wanted you to live a normal life. But now that I know you have the gift, I regret never telling you about it."

She'd mentioned this to me before, but she'd never delved into so much detail.

"I'm trying to be there for you as much as I can, sweetheart, but if there's one thing I remember when I was growing up, it's that I needed my space a lot of the time to think things through, so I'm trying to give that to you." Her hand came to grip mine in comfort. "But to answer your initial question, yes, it was hard for me, too."

I let this information sit in my mind for a minute, and then I moved onto a new question. "Have you ever saved someone who was abducted or kidnapped?" I asked, hoping her insight could help me here.

"Kidnapped? No, I haven't." She paused for a moment. "But with my experience, I've learned that psychic abilities can work in mysterious ways. You'll see what you need to see when you need to see it."

I thought about this for a second. "I don't know, Mom. Like you said before, maybe I'm just missing something. Maybe I'm supposed to be seeing something, but I'm just not. It gets really hard sometimes. Like tonight around the dinner table, everything was so happy and simple, and then the happy moment ended and my thoughts drifted back to Hope. And I feel I'm working myself up over something I have no control over, but at the same time, I feel guilty if I'm not worrying about her."

"Sweetie, I know you're scared, but the best advice I can give you is to stop worrying so much, face your abilities head-on, and wait for the answers to come. You can't control when or how you'll get answers, but you can control how you interpret them and use the information."

With that, my mother kissed me on the forehead and left me sitting on the beach alone. I could tell she left me so her last statement could sink in. So I let it.

CHAPTER 8

top worrying so much. I repeated my mother's advice in my head while I walked back up the stairs to the house. I decided I needed something to take my mind off everything psychic related to actually make this possible. Just then, I spotted Robin exiting the back porch and coming my way. I figured a little criticism and snarky comments from him might do the trick. Or maybe there'd be enough human left in him that we could actually enjoy each other's company.

"Hey," I greeted.

To my surprise, Robin actually smiled at me in response.

"Where are you headed?" I asked.

"Actually," he said, running his hand through his hair, "I came out here looking for you. I don't really know what happened earlier today, but you seemed pretty upset about it. I just wanted to make sure you were still okay."

I almost fell back down the stairs I'd just walked up. Robin was concerned about me?

"I am okay," I assured him. "Want to... I don't know... walk down the beach or something?" I didn't understand why I couldn't formulate my words correctly or why I wouldn't meet his gaze.

"Sure," he said, once again taking me off guard.

"So," I started when we finally reached the sand. "I, uh, saw you texting a lot on our way down here. Is that, like, your girlfriend or something?" Why was I asking him this? I wasn't actually interested if he was single or not, was I? Or maybe I was just wondering because if I found out he was single, it would probably give him an excuse for being so bitter because, you know, he didn't have anyone to keep him company.

He laughed. "Or something."

Oh. So he did have a love interest.

"And you?" he asked. "You've been texting your boyfriend, too?"

I laughed so loud it was almost embarrassing. I quickly snapped my jaw tight. "Me? A boyfriend? No. That's just Emma and Derek. They're my best friends."

"Derek, huh?" Robin said in thought. "So you two aren't — "

"No!" I practically shouted. "I mean, I think he kind of has a thing for me, but I know Emma likes him. I could never date a guy my best friend likes." I tucked a strand of stray hair behind my ear.

We both went silent for a few moments until I spoke. "Don't you think the ocean is really pretty here?" The sun was already setting, but there was just enough light to enjoy the scenery.

He gazed out on the water. "Yeah, it is really pretty."

"I kind of want to stick my toes in it. Do you think it's cold?" I crossed ahead of him and approached the water. A small wave crashed at my feet. I squealed. "Yes, it's cold!"

Robin laughed from behind me.

"Aren't you going to stick your feet in?" I asked.

I glanced back at him only to notice that he was wearing long pants and still had his socks and shoes on. His sweatshirt hung unzipped around his shoulders. He shook his head. "No, I'm okay."

"You don't like the feeling of sand in your toes?" I asked, playfully digging my feet into the white powder that lined the beach.

Robin shrugged. "It's okay, I guess. Just not for me."

We walked along the beach until we couldn't quite see Wayne and Gail's house anymore. We eventually hit a pier next to a park, and lights from nearby houses illuminated our way until we made it to the end. We dangled our feet off the side and sat mostly in silence as we watched lights glitter off the water.

"This is nice," Robin said. Something about his tone seemed awkward, like he was forcing himself to be kind to me.

"Yeah," I agreed because I didn't know how else to respond. The hairs on my arms rose in response to the chilly air. I hadn't realized how cold it would get as soon as the sun set. I was still dressed in the shorts and t-shirt I wore on our way down here.

"You look cold," Robin pointed out.

I nodded. "I'll be fine, though."

"Are you sure? Because you can have my sweatshirt if you want it." He was already shrugging it off his shoulders before I could refuse.

I eyed him as he held it out to me, not daring to touch it.

"What?" he asked.

"Why are you being so nice? You've, like, never been nice to me."

He sighed. "I'm not being nice. Just put the sweatshirt on."

I didn't know where in his world he thought sharing his sweatshirt with me didn't constitute as "nice," but I couldn't reject his insistence. I took it and wrapped it around my shoulders, comforted slightly by its fresh smell.

We didn't talk about anything important while we sat there, and I was surprised that he hadn't asked more about what happened earlier. Eventually, we figured we should head back. At the house, we went our separate ways. It was only when I was crawling into bed that I realized Robin *had* taken my mind off Hope, if only briefly.

~

I opened my eyes to a room full of people. I wasn't sure how I got there. Practically everyone was dressed in black, and a few people were crying. I spun around to take in the scene. Chairs were lined up in rows on each side of the room, and I was standing along the center aisle. Almost every chair was taken. My eyes moved toward the front of the room, and that's when I saw a casket sitting there. It was closed and had a flower wreathe sitting on top of it.

For a moment, my breath caught in my chest as I thought about my father. And then I saw the picture of *him*, the man with green eyes who I saw in the mirror earlier that day. It was positioned near the casket and nearly took my breath away.

Oh. My. God, I thought, fixing my eyes on the photo. A strange vibe called to me from behind, willing me to look away. I turned slowly to investigate what exactly was tingling my senses. A woman with tears in her eyes sat in the back row. Her large red bun and black hat seemed to conceal the source of my feeling until she shifted and I spotted the man I was sure the strange vibe was coming from. His eyes were dark under his brows, and his hair was cropped short. My breath actually left my chest this time when I realized he was the same man in the picture Teddy had shown to the desk attendant at our motel.

His eyes shifted and focused on something toward the front of the room. I followed his gaze, and I had to swallow a lump in my throat before I could start breathing again. My eyes fell upon a little girl with short brown hair and big chocolate eyes who was fidgeting at the front of the room. For a moment, I was dumbfounded, completely paralyzed.

I regained as much composure as I could—which honestly wasn't much given the circumstances. "Hope!" I tried to say to get her attention, only nothing came out.

Suddenly, I understood what was going on. This was Hope's dad's funeral. The ghost I saw in the mirror and at the gas station was her dad, Scott, not Hope's abductor. And the man in the back was her uncle Jeff. I looked back at him again, studying his face. His eyes were still fixed on Hope.

"What did you do to her?" I wanted to shout, only there still wasn't any sound. No one reacted to my being there, but I already knew they wouldn't since I was looking into the past. But I didn't care. I was too overcome with anger and frustration. I clenched my hands into fists, and my body shook in rage. All I wanted to do was find Hope, and now I was staring into the eyes of her abductor. I was sure of it. That must have been what Scott came to warn me about—about his brother.

But I still needed answers. "Where is she?" I said, quietly at first to myself. Then, even though I knew no one would respond in a dream, I gritted my teeth and shouted the question at the top of my lungs.

A blood curdling scream tore me from my vision and jolted me awake. The scream continued, and only then did I realize it was my own.

My mom and Teddy rushed into the room.

I covered my face in embarrassment. I had never awoke from one of my nightmares screaming so loud and terrified like that before. Or was it anger? I couldn't fight it. A sob broke from my chest, and then suddenly, I was bawling into my hands. I curled my knees to my chest. My mother knelt beside my air mattress and wrapped her arms around me. Footsteps echoed outside the room just before Wayne and Gail hurried in to see what was wrong.

"Is she okay?" Gail asked.

"She'll be fine." I could still somehow hear Teddy's whispers over my sobs. "She just gets nightmares. It's fine. You can go back to bed. We'll handle it."

"Poor thing," Wayne said before he left.

Teddy closed the door to give the three of us privacy. I felt the mattress shift when he sat down and rubbed my shoulder for comfort. Even though I was crying, I was glad he was back to his sympathetic self.

My breath came in shallow heaves at first, but when I regained control of my body, I inhaled a deep breath to calm myself. "He took her," I finally said.

"Who, sweetie?" my mother asked. "Who took her?"

"Jeff," I said. "At the funeral, he was watching her. He was planning something. I just know it." I couldn't be wrong again. I just *couldn't*.

"Well," Teddy said, "he *was* our main suspect." I could hear it in his tone that he was forcing himself not to add, *But he's already been cleared.*

I took another few deep breaths to ease my cries. "I'm sorry to worry you guys."

"No, it's okay. We don't mind, Kiddo," Teddy assured me. "When you feel you have something you need to talk about, you know you can come to either of us, right?"

I met his gaze and nodded. I knew he was being honest with me, but I still wasn't sure how much he trusted my latest instinct. "Yeah, I know that. I just—there's no reason to worry you. The vision wasn't all that scary anyway. I think I was more angry than anything."

Mom and Teddy stayed to console me for quite some time, and then they said their goodnights and headed back toward their bedroom. I knew they were going to discuss the incident in private. Knowing they were just on the other side of the wall from me, I took advantage of this. I pressed my ear to the wall. Through muffled whispers, the only thing I could make out was Teddy saying, "My gut is still telling me it wasn't Jeff."

I wasn't sure if I was supposed to trust my own intuition or his.

CHAPTER 9

I was grateful when I woke and hadn't had another dream. Even so, I couldn't fight the knot in my chest that was full of concern for Hope. I had to find her. I just had to. I lay in bed for what must have been 20 minutes trying to sort through everything. I replayed the dream of the funeral in my mind, and suddenly, something occurred to me. I was aware it was a vision the whole time. Why could I see the peripheral details in that vision but not in the one of Hope's abduction?

I thought this through for several long minutes and realized that in Hope's abduction scenario, I was always in her head. At the funeral, I was a disembodied person looking down on the scene as if it were playing on a television. I knew I couldn't fall asleep and dream now because I wasn't tired, but I did know that when the opportunity presented itself, I had to look deeper into Hope's abduction and discover what I was missing.

After what felt like lying in bed forever, I decided there wasn't anything more I could do by staying under the covers. I threw on a pair of shorts and a t-shirt and listened to the ocean waves out the window. I checked my phone. Emma had already sent several texts reminding me about our morning stress relief session.

Sorry, I replied. *I just woke up.*

It was Monday morning, which meant Emma was already at school and I couldn't expect a text back for a few hours. I felt kind of bad for sleeping in through her texts. Emma was only trying to do me well.

I heard voices from the next room, but the ocean air called out to me. I decided to head down to the water instead of greeting my family immediately. I figured it would give me a chance to do some relaxation exercises like I'd promised Emma I would. Maybe it would even help me get in touch with Hope. I honestly didn't have a better option.

I sat along the bank with my legs crossed and my eyes closed. I tried to clear my mind, but thoughts of Hope, my friends back home, and even Robin kept creeping into my consciousness. I shifted to get more comfortable and then focused on the sound of the water and my own slowing breath while I let my mind drift in a realm that wasn't quite my own. It took several times of catching my mind wander before I finally let my body relax. I felt like I was floating, and my mind drifted on its own accord.

I miss my mommy, I thought. I didn't quite feel right. Nothing felt right, and I just wanted to go home.

"You hungry?" A voice whipped me out of my trance.

Hope, I thought. *She wants to go home.*

I looked up to find Robin standing above me. Even though it was morning, it was still hot out, much hotter than anything you'd feel in Minnesota at this time of year, so I was surprised to find him covered in long jeans. Didn't he get hot? It might be nice if he showed a little more skin every now and then.

Wait. What am I thinking?

"Huh?" I asked.

"Breakfast is ready." Instead of turning to head inside like I expected him to do, he lowered himself to sit next to me in the sand. "What were you doing?" His eyes locked on mine for a second.

I pushed a strand of dirty blonde hair behind my ear and stared at my feet in embarrassment. "I was, uh, meditating?" The statement came out sounding like a question.

"Mediating? You're not, like, a crazy wellness nut or something, are you?"

I should have known he'd have something rude to say, even if he didn't exactly hit it on the nose. "Uh, no. Not exactly. It just helps me relax."

"So, about what happened yesterday. I still don't really know why we were chasing that guy. I figure you know something about one of Teddy's cases that I don't, given that he was flashing his badge and all."

Whoa. I didn't realize he'd put the pieces together. I thought I had just come off looking insane.

"But," he continued, "whatever it was, I really respect you for following your intuition. Not a lot of people would do that."

My heart leapt in my chest. Did Robin just give me a compliment? That was a rare occurrence.

He ran his hands through the sand and looked down at the patterns he was making. "And I'm sorry for whatever I said to you about it before in the car. I don't even remember what I said. I do that a lot. I guess it's a defense mechanism or something."

My jaw dropped. I was speechless. Robin not only gave me a compliment, but he was also apologizing to me.

"Wow," I said with a hit of sarcasm and amazement. "Is Robin Simmons actually admitting that he's sorry for something he said? Who are you and what have you done with Robin?" I gave a little giggle.

But Robin didn't laugh back like I thought he would. Apparently we didn't share the same type of humor. Instead, he fixed his eyes on me and held an unamused expression on his face. "Stop being immature."

I immediately stopped laughing.

Okay, he was back to his old self. So much for thinking he might be a real human being.

He ran his fingers through his hair. "Did you not hear a thing I just said? Crystal, I'm insecure. I use my wit as a defense mechanism, but I don't take it well. It's hard enough sharing my feelings, especially around pretty girls, so just be glad that I apologized. Don't make fun of me for it."

Stunned, I didn't move for several long moments. I just stared after him while he retreated up the stairs slowly. My thoughts hung on the word "insecure." How could a guy like *that* be insecure? He was clever, and, okay, he was hot. What did he have to be insecure about? Only when he disappeared into the house did I rise from the sand and join my family for breakfast.

After breakfast, Mom, Gail, and I talked wedding plans, and Mom showed some ideas for the cake on her phone. I almost started thinking about Hope, but then I remembered that things were easier for everyone and I had a better chance of finding her when she was not at the forefront of my mind. I again basked in the simplicity of the wedding planning and offered my opinions when necessary.

Later, Wayne suggested we all go down to the tennis courts nearby and play a game. I thought this was a great idea until I realized that if everyone else was gone, I would have time to try connecting with Hope. I knew I had said it was best to keep my mind off her, but I really wanted some privacy with my crystal ball since I hadn't had a chance to use it yet after everything that happened. I kindly said I didn't want to go and excused myself to my guest room.

Once I heard the front door shut and a car pull out of the driveway, I pulled my crystal ball from my bag and set it on the floor in front of me. I took several long deep breaths to calm myself, and I held the owl pendant around my neck close to my heart for good luck. I stared deep into the ball. I had been able to make it work in the past, but I still struggled with it. I had an especially hard time clearing my mind.

No expectations, I reminded myself.

I used the sounds of the waves coming in my window as an anchor so I'd have something to focus on besides my racing thoughts. The minutes ticked by, and after a long time, colors began swirling in the ball. They became the center of my focus as I fell deeper into the unknown. A faint figure formed in the crystal ball. I almost thought I saw Hope's face, but then the image washed away as a chill settled over the room.

"Help!" A voice startled me. My eyes jerked up to find a young girl standing in the room.

My head began spinning. I was glad I was sitting down so I didn't have to find an extra support to keep myself upright. I was starting to understand this feeling all too well.

The girl had long dark hair and big beautiful eyes. For a second, I almost thought she was Hope. My heart sank at the thought that I'd failed her, but the girl standing in front of me was a lot older than Hope, just a few years younger than me.

I wanted to smile at her, to let her know that I wasn't a threat, that I could help her even. I didn't when I saw that the ghostly girl had an expression of urgency fixed to her face. My expression transformed to mirror hers when I realized that someone was likely in danger. I couldn't think of any other excuse for why this ghostly girl would show herself to me.

"You have to help her," she said. "She's been scared for so long. I just want to see her happy."

Now I knew for sure someone was in danger. *Calm down*, I told myself, but that was always difficult when a ghost was asking for help.

"Who?" I asked, a little bit louder than I intended. "Who do you need me to help?"

The girl looked around the room as if trying to take in her surroundings, and then her eyes fell back on me.

"My sister."

CHAPTER 10

$\mathcal{A}$ knock at my door startled me.

"Crystal, are you okay?" asked a deep voice.

Robin.

My eyes jerked toward the door in surprise then back at the girl, but she was already gone. The chill that filled my body each time I saw a ghost subsided. I quickly shoved my crystal ball back into my bag and covered it up with a shirt just as Robin opened the door a crack.

"Can I come in?" he asked without looking.

I plopped onto my mattress to make it look like I was just relaxing. If he could hear my racing heartbeat—and I was almost paranoid that he could—it would undoubtedly give me away. "Yeah," I answered in a fairly normal tone. "I'm fine. I thought you went with everyone to play tennis." I picked at my fingernails so I wouldn't have to meet his gaze. I'd never been a good liar. At the same time, it would be far too difficult to explain to him what I had just been doing. No way would he believe I'd just encountered a ghost.

He scoffed, pushing his way farther onto the porch. "I've told you before, I don't play sports."

I looked him up and down. "Really? Because you're really—"

Wait. What was I just about to say?

Robin took a seat next to me on the air mattress. My heart sped up, and I realized how uncomfortable I was being so close to a guy. I'd never really had a boyfriend before, and I only ever hung out with Derek when Emma was around, so being alone with a male of any sort was out of the ordinary for me.

Robin smiled and raised his eyebrows. "I'm really what?"

I wanted to lie to him, but I couldn't come up with an alternative excuse. His stare encouraged me to explain. I spoke slowly, but my voice wavered. At least he would attribute that to my embarrassment instead of my anxiety over the ghost girl. "Uh… I was going to say muscular, but now that doesn't feel very appropriate." I added a slight teasing tone to my words, but I could still feel a blush rise to the surface of my cheeks when I spoke. It surprised me that I was able to admit something like this to him.

"Oh, you think I'm muscular?" he said, flexing his bicep and looking down at it.

The gesture was in humor, but it only made me think, *Um, yes!*

"So," I said, hoping to change the subject. "If you don't play sports, what *do* you do?"

"I do weight lift a little, but nothing where I have to run around a court. Mostly, though, I play music."

"Oh, so you're in band? I play the clarinet."

Robin gave a sort of laugh that made me feel insecure about my choice of instrument. "I'm not in *the* band, Crystal. I am in *a* band."

"I knew that, but you're, like, not in band in school?"

He shook his head.

"So, are you in any extracurricular activities?"

"For me, it's just basically school and my band."

"And your girlfriend, right?" I said, only I regretted it immediately. Why did I have to say such stupid things sometimes? I ran my fingers through my hair and twisted it at the ends.

Robin simply laughed, but he didn't say anything about his girlfriend.

"So, what? You're just going to play music the rest of your life and hope you make it big?" I asked in an attempt to break the awkward silence stretching between us.

"Well, it's holding me over for now. We've had a few well-paying gigs. It's not much since we've bought some new equipment and I have to split the profit between four other guys, but it's helping me save up for college. I want to go into occupational therapy and help people who have been in accidents and stuff."

"Oh," is all I said, even though I wanted to tell him how noble that sounded.

"And you?"

It took me a few moments to realize what he was talking about. I was only 15 for goodness sakes. I hadn't really thought about what I wanted to do with my life. Maybe I could turn my psychic skills into some sort of practice, but I wasn't sure how I would make a living that way. I couldn't *charge* people to have me help them.

I played with the ends of my hair and said, "I want to help people. Kind of like a counselor or something." I shrugged like it wasn't a big deal, but I knew it kind of was. I hadn't thought about how my abilities were going to affect the rest of my life. I was still trying to make it through my sophomore year alive. "Anything else I should know about you?" I asked, wondering if he was going to show more of his human side.

He didn't. He just said nope and exited the room, leaving me to stare after him. I had a feeling he was hiding something from me. I wondered again if he inherited some of the intuition Teddy had and if that was what he was hiding from me.

Only when he was out of the room did I have a chance to think back to the girl who had come to me. Suddenly, it felt like all my responsibilities related to my gift were piling up again. I had to somehow find Hope, and God only knew I wasn't making any progress on that end. I probably had to talk with Scott's ghost again. After all, he had to be trying to contact me for a reason. And now I had a new ghost who wanted me to help someone else who I knew absolutely nothing about.

I fell back down on the air mattress and closed my eyes in an attempt to relieve my anxiety. I didn't fall asleep. Instead, I figured I should stop worrying about everything like my mom had suggested.

I spent most of the rest of the day lying on the beach in the sundress Emma insisted I bring along while enjoying the weather and reading a book. Diving into a different world was the best way I could think of to take my mind off everything. I had already finished the first two books in the series in the car, and I was onto the third. It was about a psychic girl, much like myself, named Sabine. We could do different things with our abilities, but I had a lot to learn from her character. At the same time, I found it easier to focus on her problems instead of my own since I wasn't getting anywhere by worrying.

At one point, I looked up toward the house to see if my mom and everyone else was home yet. I could have sworn I saw Robin looking out the window. I wasn't sure if he was watching me or if he was just enjoying the scenery.

After I finished my book, I walked back up to the house. Robin was still the only one home. It felt awkward with only us two in the house, like I was obligated to do something with him. When I entered the kitchen, he was sitting at the table shuffling through a deck of cards. A part of me wanted to talk to him, but another part of me felt like he didn't want me around. I was about to turn back toward the porch when he spoke.

"Want to play something?"

I almost looked around the room to make sure he was talking to me, but I already knew I was the only one there. I blinked a few times, shocked by his offer, before I found my voice. "I'm not very good at cards."

"Do you know how to play rummy?" He finally tore his gaze from the deck and looked up at me.

"Yeah," I said, slowly inching for the chair across from him.

"Play you to 500 points?"

I shrugged. "Why not?"

"We need something to keep score with," he pointed out.

I felt like a fool rummaging around the kitchen looking for a notepad and a pencil, but I eventually found both and took a seat across from him, sliding the pad and pencil his way. At the top, I watched him write Crystal Frost on one side and Robin on the other. Then he separated the sides into two columns.

"Why'd you write out my full name and only your first name?" I asked, pointing to the paper.

He shrugged. "I think your full name is really cool. It's like your first name is an adjective and your last name is a noun."

I had never thought of it that way before.

"I might just call you by your full name from now on," he said.

"Please don't," I begged. When I noticed he was smiling, I realized he was kidding. He stared across the table at me, and my cheeks flamed in response. Was he *flirting* with me? No. Not Robin. He wouldn't.

"Just deal the cards," I insisted.

We played for a long time, although it wasn't as great of a game with just two people, until eventually Robin won. Only after the game ended did I realize that I was smiling and laughing with him. I could hardly believe it.

Robin gathered the cards into a pile and started shuffling. "Rematch?"

"But you already won. Why would you need a rematch?"

His eyes bore into mine. "Maybe I don't want the game to end." Something about it sounded like a challenge, so I accepted.

Robin handed me the note pad and told me to keep score this time. I started by ripping the top sheet off and crumpling it into a ball. I scrawled my name first on a clean sheet, making a point to write just my first name, and then I added Robin's alongside mine. I could see him peeking at my writing from out of the corner of my eye.

"What is that?" he asked.

"Huh?" I looked up to meet his gaze.

"My name has an 'i' in it."

I glanced back down at my handwriting. I knew my handwriting had always been poor, and now Robin knew it, too. That meant he had something to make fun of me for. But I wouldn't let him use it against me.

I scowled at him. "I did put an 'i' in it!" I dug the pencil into the paper to accent the dot over the 'i.' "Yes, I have chicken scratch handwriting. Now, can we start the game?"

Robin called rummy on a card I placed in the discard pile on accident, but then I caught him doing the same thing later. We both grabbed a can of pop from the fridge and sipped on them and laughed at ourselves as the game continued. When I had a moment to really evaluate the situation, I was shocked at how much I was enjoying myself. I knew there was nothing particularly fantastic about the game, but something about playing with Robin made me loosen up a bit.

Robin won a second round just as everyone else arrived home. They were carrying in shopping bags, and I noticed Teddy had a box of leftover food from a restaurant. Clearly they'd spent the day doing more than playing tennis. A part of me didn't care that I wasn't included when I looked across the table at Robin and realized I'd actually had fun with him.

That night, I called Emma via video chat. I was a little surprised to see Derek in her room with her. Of course, her door was open and her little sister Kate was in there with them. I could see Kate in the background coloring on something on the floor. Still, it was either always just Emma and me or all three of us together. It made me feel kind of left out.

"How are you liking Florida?" Emma asked.

"The weather here is so nice," I raved.

"And the boys, too?" Emma asked.

"Emma!" I scolded at the same time Derek did. We all giggled.

"Crystal," Derek said. "You'll never believe what happened."

"Yeah," Emma agreed. "It's really pretty sad."

"What?" I asked, alarmed.

Emma looked at Derek. "You tell her."

Derek's eyes drooped in sadness. "My dog, Milo, ran away."

"Oh, no, Derek. That is really sad. I wish I could help."

"No, it's okay," he told me. "We've got it covered. Kate is drawing fliers for us to put around town so we can find out if anyone has seen him. The thing is, he slipped out of his collar, which is how he got away, so anyone who finds him won't know he belongs to us." I thought I could hear a sob cut at his tone.

I felt bad for Derek, and I told him so. He eventually turned away and crouched next to Kate on the floor to help her with the fliers.

"Is he going to be okay?" I asked Emma.

She looked back at him. "Yeah, I'm sure he will be. If you were here, maybe you could work some of your magic."

I laughed a little because of the way she said it, but she was probably right. I had become quite good at finding things, but I had to have something to touch, like the dog's collar, to tell where he was.

"I'll work on it, but I probably won't find anything," I told her.

"Well, I've been trying my best, too," Emma said, "but I've never had experience with finding things. The best thing I can come up with is that I have a good feeling about a penny. Like, a lucky penny or something." She shrugged. "Except I don't think that it's about Derek's dog. I think it has to do with you."

CHAPTER 11

*T*hat night, I dreamt about Hope. I was again in her body, being carried out her window by a man I still couldn't get full features of. I knew I had to become aware of my surroundings. I had to somehow find what I was missing, but when the Crystal part of me broke through, all I could do was scream in my own mind at the assailant.

"Where is she?" I cried, only I was watching a scene that happened weeks ago, and the man couldn't hear me.

I woke once again with a start. I was getting too used to this. I pulled my covers up from the foot of the bed and wrapped them around my body for comfort. I stayed in bed, closed my eyes, and controlled my breathing to calm myself.

"Oh, Hope," I whispered. "I wish I could help you. Where are you?" A tear fell down my cheek. "Why am I seeing you if I can't help you?" I wanted to shout it, but I didn't want anyone else to hear, so I kept my voice low.

A sob broke within me. I didn't fight it. All I wanted was to use my gift to help people, and I couldn't control it well enough to do so. My head ached. I pressed my face into my pillow and screamed.

"I just wish I could help you," I said again, squeezing my eyes shut to get all the tears out.

"Crystal," a voice called out.

My eyes shot open in surprise the same moment I bolted up in bed. My gaze fell upon the ghostly girl standing next to my air mattress. It was the same girl who had visited me yesterday. I wiped my eyes as my racing heart slowed. I couldn't refuse helping the girl, and I knew it, even if that did take me further from Hope.

I composed myself in a quick moment. "Can I help you?" I asked quietly but in a friendly tone.

She looked back at me with urgency. Her eyes weren't quite the same color as Hope's, but something in them reminded me of her.

"I just want to see my sister happy," she said.

I was getting fed up with the way ghosts spoke to me. They never seemed to give me a clear cut answer to the information I needed. But I stayed calm. "How can I help her? What's wrong with her?"

"I don't think she's safe. My mom has kind of... gone crazy. She's not herself."

Oh no, I thought. I didn't like the sound of someone being in danger. It broke my heart. "Who are you?" After I asked it, I knew it wasn't the best question to ask since the girl probably didn't have much time here.

"I'm Penny."

"You're—" My breath caught.

I have a good feeling about a penny, Emma had said.

Not *a* penny. Just Penny.

"Penny?" I whispered.

If Emma was giving me clues about this girl before even *I* knew her name, there was something really important about her. I mean, I knew she was important because she'd shown herself to me, but something about the whole situation made her seem significant in a different way that I initially thought.

"You have to find hope," she said.

I almost broke out crying again. "Hope? I haven't had much of that lately."

"No," Penny said. "Not 'hope' as in faith. I mean Hope. My sister."

Suddenly, my vision blurred. Instead of sitting on Wayne and Gail's porch, I found myself in front of a small blue home. As soon as I saw it, the vision was gone. I was back on the porch again, but Penny was nowhere in sight.

~

My head spun. Penny had shown me where Hope was, and then she disappeared. I still couldn't believe that all this time I *was* getting closer to Hope. She was only about four hours north of here, and even though I didn't have an address, something inside of me knew exactly where to go.

When I could finally move again, I made my way to the kitchen. I found my mom and Teddy sitting at the table and Gail standing over the stove.

"Mom," I said quickly.

She and Teddy both looked up at me in alarm. "What's wrong, sweetheart?" she asked. "Are you okay?"

"No, not really," I admitted, taking a seat across from her. I kept my voice low, hoping Gail wasn't paying too much attention. "I know where Hope is. It's only about four hours away. We have to go find her."

Mom and Teddy both stared at me, but I couldn't quite read their expressions. I thought my mom's was one of sympathy and Teddy's was one of disbelief, but I wasn't entirely sure. Silence loomed over us for several long seconds as they stared back at me. It was like they hadn't even heard what I'd said.

"What are we waiting for? I finally have something!"

I wanted them to leap up in excitement and follow me to the place Penny had shown me. Instead, all they did was exchange a glance.

"Kiddo," Teddy said, setting down his newspaper and folding his hands on top of it. He looked at me with all seriousness. "Are you sure about this?"

I nodded eagerly. "I'm positive."

Teddy twisted his face into an expression that could only be described as skepticism. "You can't just go chasing after a kidnapper."

I gaped at him. "But I have to."

Teddy shook his head lightly. "You don't. We can have someone else check it out. Someone who is trained and armed."

I furrowed my brow. "I—I don't know how to tell them where to go."

"What do you mean?" Teddy asked with a hint of annoyance in his voice. "You just said you knew where she was."

"I do. I can't explain it, though. It's like I'm drawn to the place, but I won't know how to get there until I'm there."

"Well, you said it's four hours away, so you know the general area. We can have someone in the county look into possible leads."

"And that could take days!" I exclaimed.

Teddy pursed his lips and went silent for several moments. When he finally lifted his gaze to meet mine, he spoke. "I don't think now is the time."

"What?" I practically shouted.

Gail turned to me from the stove, but I could tell by her expression that she didn't want to be a part of this argument. She tended to her food again to give us a minor amount of privacy.

"Teddy, I'm telling you I've found Hope, the girl you've been searching for for weeks, and all you can say is, 'It's not the time?'" My chest tightened when it hit me that I was right about Teddy. He wasn't going to trust me again.

"The thing is, Crystal, you were wrong last time, and I don't want to be sent on a wild goose chase. And we still don't have anything on Jeff. I think we should just enjoy our time here. We're on vacation. Enjoy yourself. Stop worrying."

There it was again. Everyone, it seemed, was telling me to stop worrying, but I didn't have the heart to do that without guilt pulling me down. Everything he'd just said made it feel like he'd reached into my chest and ripped my heart out. I could hardly breathe. My nose tingled at the threat of tears.

"What are you saying?" My voice cracked in response to my crushed heart. "That you don't believe me?"

He sighed. I'd never thought Teddy would treat me like this. He'd told me things about the case because he thought I could help him. Was he giving up on me? If he didn't believe me, how was I supposed to believe in myself?

"Crystal," he said through gritted teeth. "I'm just saying that I can't go barging into someone's house without probably cause. Right now, I have no evidence."

Something—I'm not sure if it was my psychic powers or if it was something in his eyes—told me that wasn't the real reason he didn't want to listen to me. The truth was that Teddy didn't trust me anymore.

I stood in rage. "You're the one who came down here looking for her! I saw you asking questions about Jeff at our motel. So why won't you follow me to Hope now?"

Teddy's voice rose slightly to mirror my own. "Crystal, I haven't given up on Hope. What you saw—I'm still trying to find her even though pretty much everyone else believes she's dead. The reason we stopped there was because we have credit card records showing that's where Jeff stayed after he left the funeral. *That* kind of evidence I can manage, but you're asking me to spend all day following a lead that makes no sense in the realm of science!"

This time, his words cut even deeper, which I didn't think was possible. Tension formed in my head, and it felt like a boa constrictor was wrapping its body around my skull and trying to crush it. I clutched at my stomach because in that moment, it felt completely empty. I thought Teddy believed in me. How could he say that about my gift?

My breath returned to my body. "She had an older sister! Did you know that?" I was shouting now. It was the only thing I could do after the way he was making me feel, like the biggest part of me didn't matter to him at all, like I was stupid and untrustworthy, like he didn't want to listen to anything I had to say.

"What? Hope? See, Crystal, that's why I can't go chasing after her. You were wrong about the man earlier, and you're wrong about Hope now. She was an only child."

I was momentarily struck dumb by this information. I knew I couldn't be wrong about this again, yet something in the back of my mind left me worried that I was. I managed to find my voice again. "She's dead, Teddy. Penny is dead, and she told me where to find Hope." I didn't even care at this point that Gail was hearing all about my abilities. All I knew was that I had to find Hope.

"I assure you that Hope was Melinda and Scott's only child."

I took a step back. I couldn't believe he was treating me like this. He didn't believe a word I'd said.

It brought worries to the forefront of my mind and made me wonder myself. *Their only child? That can't be right. Was Penny having me run after a different girl named Hope?* I blinked a few times as I processed this information.

My tone finally returned to its normal volume, but I spoke through gritted teeth. "Either way, there's a girl named Hope four hours from here who needs rescuing."

Teddy stared at me with an apologetic expression on his face, and then he spoke quietly. "Crystal, I'm sorry."

I knew that was the end of our conversation, although I wasn't entirely convinced that he *was* sorry. I stormed back through the enclosed porch and down the steps toward the beach. I took a seat in the sand and curled my knees to my chest while I sobbed into my arms. I tucked my head in close to my body, trying my best to make myself as small as I could to reflect the way I was feeling.

How could Teddy not believe me? He was the one who had asked for my help. I had assumed he believed in me. He'd said he had some heightened intuition of his own, so why was he pushing everything we both believed in away? Or was that the problem? Had my mistake made him so afraid of his own intuition that he no longer wanted to accept it as truth?

Several long minutes later, a hand touched my shoulder. I jerked up in surprise, ready to retaliate. I let my body relax when I saw that it was only my mother. She sat by me on the sand and pulled me into an embrace. I sobbed in her arms. I tried not to since it seemed like I'd been doing so much of that lately, but I couldn't help it. Someone was out there who needed my help, and I was only going to fail again.

"I'm sorry, sweetie," my mom said after a few moments.

"Why didn't you back me up?" I asked, pulling away from her and looking into her eyes. I wiped at my tears in an attempt to calm down.

My mother's mouth opened like she was going to say something, but then she shut it. "I'm always here for you," she finally said. "I don't know exactly what you've seen, but I want to encourage you to go wherever your gift takes you. I don't usually get feelings about family members and people close to me, but I know that wherever you go, your abilities will keep you safe."

My tears nearly subsided in response. She was actually taking my side.

She tucked a strand of hair behind my ear. "Look, I talked to Teddy and suggested that you get some time away from the house today to think things over. I thought maybe you and Robin could go shopping or to the movies or something. He said he'd gladly take you. So, um, here are the keys to the car, and here's my credit card if you find something you think you need."

She dropped the card and keys into my hand. I met her gaze to thank her and tell her at the same time that I didn't need this. A shopping trip wasn't going to make me feel better. And then I realized something in her eyes. She was inviting me to follow my gift.

I sprang toward her and gave her a tight hug. "Thank you, Mom! Thank you so much."

"Be careful, okay?"

I nodded. "I will."

Minutes later, Robin and I were in the car. I handed him the keys.

"Your mom told me to take you wherever you wanted to go," he said.

I took a deep breath and then told him where to take me.

*M*y heart sped up before we even made it to the freeway. I was finally on my way to rescuing Hope. Well, maybe not. All I knew was that I was on my way to finding someone, whoever Penny's sister happened to be.

"So, uh," Robin started. "Where exactly are we going?"

"I already told you," I said.

"No, I know. I just mean, why so far away? I mean, there are malls and movie theaters all over the place here. Is this, like, a special mall where they have only one pair of the shoes you need in stock?"

I was momentarily taken aback. He thought I was *that* kind of girl? Not even close!

Apparently he noticed my expression. He stole a glance at me from out of the corner of his eye, and then a sideways smile formed across his face. It was the type of smile that made my heart flutter.

Wait. What was I thinking? I forced my pulse to slow.

"I'm just kidding, Crystal. Can't you take a joke every now and then?"

I pushed a long strand of hair out of my face but didn't meet his gaze. "I guess not," I said, but what I was really thinking was that it was harder for me to take a joke from Robin than from the average person. Something about him struck a nerve every time he spoke. It was like I wanted him to think good things about me, but every joke he made just cut at my heart and made me realize that I was no different from any other girl.

He has a girlfriend, I reminded myself. And then I realized what I was thinking. I shouldn't care if he had a girlfriend or not.

"So, what exactly are we doing?" he asked again.

"Oh, uh." How did I answer this? I wasn't quick on my feet like Emma was, and when I lied, the dishonesty was written all over my face. I turned to stare out the window so he wouldn't see my eyebrow twitch, which was what happened when I lied. "Just to meet a friend." When my eyebrow didn't move, I wondered if I'd gotten better at lying or if I was putting more truth into that lie than I thought.

He didn't push the subject further, although I had expected him to ask how I had a friend way down in Florida.

"Do you mind if I listen to some tunes?" Robin finally broke the silence that had been hanging between us for the last several minutes.

"Go ahead."

Robin connected his phone to the speakers, and an upbeat modern song began playing. I'd never heard it before. He sang along quietly. I couldn't help but notice that he had a pretty decent voice. Okay. That was a bit of an understatement. Although he was trying to stay quiet, Robin's voice filled the car with the most beautiful sound I'd ever heard. His voice somehow synced up with the singer's perfectly.

After a few songs, I found myself bobbing my head and even trying to hum along to the chorus that already played through once. I was a terrible singer, so I didn't let my voice get too loud.

Robin reached for the controls and turned the sound down until I could hardly hear it anymore. I looked up at him.

"You like it?" he asked.

I nodded. "Yeah, I really do. Who is this?"

He smiled that sideways smile again. My heart fell deep into my chest in a good way, but I quickly composed myself.

"It's Echo Score," he answered.

My face must have been plastered with a blank expression. I'd never heard of them.

His smile only spread wider. "Crystal, it's my band. Echo Score is the band I'm in."

"Oh." I didn't know what else to say. That made sense why he sounded so much like the singer. I hadn't ever realized he sang lead vocals. I always thought he sat in the background and played drums or something.

"You, uh, have a really great voice," I told him shyly, and then I turned back toward the window so he wouldn't see my cheeks flame.

"You have a gift, too," he said.

Suddenly, everything inside of my body froze. Oh. My. God. How did he know? This wasn't something I shared with a lot of people. But if he was psychic, too, then he would have picked up on it, right? Was Teddy mad enough at me to explain my gift to Robin? Would Robin actually believe me?

All these questions raced around in my mind, but all I could manage to say was, "Please don't tell anyone." The words came out sounding like I was begging him, which honestly, I kind of was.

"Why not? Your voice is great. We could use a female voice in the band."

Wait. What? "My voice?" I asked warily. So, he wasn't talking about being psychic?

"Yeah. I heard you humming over there. What did you think I meant?"

I breathed a sigh of relief then hesitated. "No, uh, that's what I thought you meant." I could feel my eyebrow twitching now, but luckily Robin was watching the road. "I just don't agree with you."

"Maybe if we put on something you know," he offered, changing the settings on the dash to play the radio.

My mouth dropped open. "You want me to *sing?*"

"Come on," he encouraged. "It will be fun. It's just us two in the car."

I stared at him in disbelief.

He looked over at me for a moment before fixing his eyes back on the road.

"You can't be serious," I objected.

"I am."

I recalled a time when Derek, Emma, and I tried to sing karaoke. Emma was the one with a voice, but we couldn't stop laughing at ourselves long enough to sing decently. I hadn't sang in front of anyone but my two best friends practically my whole life. I wasn't about to start embarrassing myself now, especially not in front of Robin.

"You'll just make fun of me, like you always do," I told him.

Robin sighed. "No, I won't. And I do not always make fun of you. I've been known to give you a few compliments every now and then. Seriously, Crystal. You need to lighten up and have some fun. You're always so serious." He poked me while he said this. Part of me wanted to retaliate and slap him in the face, but I actually found myself laughing.

The song on the radio changed. After a moment, I noticed my favorite song was playing. It was the kind of song with an upbeat tempo that you simply couldn't listen to without dancing.

"Come on," Robin pleaded. "You have to know this song." He reached over and turned it up. He smiled and began dancing and singing in his seat. His head bobbed to the beat while one arm moved along with it.

I couldn't help it when a smiled formed across my own face while watching him. When the song hit the chorus, I reluctantly joined in. I was quiet at first and sat unmoving in my seat. Robin looked over at me, a smile still fixed on his face while he sang and danced. The look he gave encouraged me.

I closed my eyes and let my head fall back as I laughed. If Robin could act this weird in front of me, he surely wouldn't judge me to do the same. So I raised my voice and sang along. When it got to the part in the third verse where the artist was speaking instead of singing, Robin let me take it away. I even added motions and facial expressions as I sang. And then the singer belted out a really high note. I was shocked to hear the same note coming out of my own body. And it wasn't half bad!

When the song ended, Robin and I were both still laughing.

I watched him from where I sat and was completely stunned when I noticed I was having fun with him again. Robin, the guy who always had a criticism on the tip of his tongue. Robin, who I had absolutely nothing in common with except his uncle. Robin, who seemed so cool on the outside but admitted to having some dark interior I still hadn't cracked. Then again, I hadn't been worrying about the secret I was sure he was hiding because I was too worried about—

Hope. Oh, my god. How could I be having so much fun when Hope was still out there and needed my help? A wave of guilt rushed over me.

Robin was still singing along to the next song when he glanced over and noticed me looking out the window again. "Crystal, are you okay? I thought we were having fun."

"Yeah. No. I mean, it was fun. It's just..." I didn't know how to finish. Just then, my phone rang, saving me from an explanation. The caller ID told me it was Derek.

"Hi," I greeted. "Did you find your dog yet?"

"No," Derek said, a hint of sadness to his voice. I felt sorry for him. "That's why I'm calling. I was wondering if maybe you could... I don't know... Use your powers or something."

I remembered the way Emma and I talked about the same thing earlier, but I knew I couldn't do it. I had to have something to touch if I was going to find Derek's dog. Besides, I'd never found a living being before.

"I'm sorry, Derek. I don't think I can." I lowered my voice. "Besides, I thought you didn't even believe me." It was true. After I'd told Derek I was psychic, he'd been having a tough time accepting it as truth.

"I want to, Crystal, and right now, you're my only hope."

"Derek, I'm literally across the country. Why don't you have Emma try to find him? She's been making a lot of progress lately." I quickly realized what I was saying in front of Robin. "Just suggest it to her, okay?"

"Yeah, okay. Thanks, Crystal."

"Derek, aren't you supposed to be in class?"

He gave a bit of a laugh. "It's lunch time, Crystal." I looked at the clock. I had forgotten about the time difference. "I'll see you later, Crystal. Bye."

I hung up.

"Was that your boyfriend?" Robin asked.

"Well, he's a boy, and he's a friend," I replied.

We sat in silence most of the rest of the way there apart from me telling Robin where to go. When we drove up to the house I knew Hope was staying in, all the nerves in my body went into overdrive.

CHAPTER 13

*M*y palms grew clammy, and my pulse quickened. I could hardly breathe as I prepared to face the man who had haunted my dreams for weeks. And then the obvious hit me. I couldn't just walk up to his door and demand he give me Hope. Why had I even come here? Couldn't I just call the cops now that I knew where the house was?

No. I knew I couldn't do that. They would never believe in a psychic vision, and if I could somehow explain how I knew Hope was here, it would look like I was somehow involved.

"Well," Robin said. "Are you going to go meet your friend?"

My head reeled as I considered the consequences of my actions. What would happen when I went up to that door? How would I help Hope get back home? What was I even doing here? Still, we couldn't leave now. I wouldn't be able to explain what was going on to Robin, and I couldn't possibly abandon Hope.

I closed my eyes and took a deep breath. "I just need a minute, okay?"

"That nervous? Is this an old boyfriend or something?" I wasn't in the right mindset to place Robin's tone.

"No," I answered. "Nothing like that. Just a girl who used to live in my town."

But is she actually here? I wondered. The whole time we'd been driving down to Florida, I felt like I was getting closer to Hope, but now sitting in front of the house I was led to, I didn't feel her presence. And there were a lot of other things that didn't add up, like how Penny told me to help her sister, Hope, only Teddy said he knew Hope didn't have a sister, not to mention that I couldn't make sense of who would bring Hope all the way down to Florida. Could I be misinterpreting everything and headed down the wrong path once again? I shuttered at the possibility.

I needed to know if Hope Ross was in that house one way or another. If it wasn't Hope Ross, then I needed to know who else needed help and why I was sent here.

I stared at the house in front of me. It looked like a normal house, albeit small. It was a light shade of blue, complete with a small deck attached to the front and a decent sized lawn. Nothing about the house screamed danger. In fact, the house looked like a peaceful place to raise a family, but I knew that something dark lurked behind those walls.

A lump formed in my throat when I thought about knocking on the door. I swallowed to force it back down. My voice quivered when I spoke, but I didn't take my eyes off the door. "Will you come with me?" I asked Robin because I wasn't sure I could do this alone.

I knew I had to do it nonetheless. The front door called out to me, taunting me for coming this far but not having the courage to investigate. I had to do this. I had to prove to myself—and to Teddy—that my abilities were leading me down the right path, that they weren't flawed.

"Sure," Robin agreed, opening his door and stepping out of the car.

I had no choice but to follow him. My hand shook when I reached for the door handle, and I nearly missed it as my extremities came to life in a nervous shutter.

I stepped out of the car into the bright sun. My knees locked in place. Was Hope in there? Was this going to work? Why couldn't I just see the future and see what would happen if I knocked on that door? All these thoughts kept me from pushing my legs forward.

"Crystal." Robin's voice called me to attention.

I looked up at him in a daze.

"Are we going to do this or not?" Robin's eyes ran over my face, and then he stepped closer and gripped my shoulders in support. I caught a whiff of his scent and almost crumbled into his arms. His eyes were full of seriousness, an emotion I'd rarely seen in him. "Are you okay? You look pale."

I felt like I was going to hurl, but I took a deep breath instead and pushed all my nerves down my throat until they gathered at the pit of my stomach. "I'm fine," I assured him. "I'm always pale." I faked a smile to show him I was okay, but I didn't think any confidence showed through.

To my surprise, Robin grabbed my hand and led me up the walkway toward the door. I was nervous enough that Robin's touch hardly had an effect on me. I caught my breath once again as we neared the steps. When we reached the door and Robin released my hand, much of my anxiety fled away. *I can do this*, I thought. *I'm the only one who can do this.*

Robin looked at me expectantly. I raised a hand and knocked on the door. We both listened for footsteps but didn't hear any. I let out a sigh of relief, but at the same time, a wave of disappointment washed over me. I wasn't any closer to Hope than I was this morning. We waited another few long seconds. Nothing. I knocked again, louder this time.

"Sorry you came all this way," Robin said, "but I don't think your friend is home."

I wanted to be relieved since this would allow me more time to come up with a plan of attack, but I couldn't think straight. The thought of losing Hope once again consumed me. Why was I here if there was nothing to find?

"No," I insisted. "That can't be right. She has to be here somewhere."

Someone has to be here. Otherwise, why am I here? All the nerves drained out of me when I thought this, and suddenly, all I felt was a burning desire to find Hope. I gripped the door knob and twisted. It didn't budge.

I turned from the door and looked around in exasperation, hoping there would be an answer nearby. There wasn't much for activity. A few children were playing in a yard nearby, and a maroon car slowed along the street and then continued on its way. Then I noticed an elderly man sitting on a porch swing at the house next to the one I stood at. I started toward him.

"Crystal, what are you doing?" Robin asked.

Without looking back at him, I told him, "To get some answers. Just give me a minute alone, okay?"

"Okay," he agreed. His footsteps drift away as he headed back toward the car.

A faint sensation washed over me as I made my way over to the man. *Nerves, again*, I told myself.

The man smiled at me when I approached his porch steps. He was slightly plump with gray thinning hair and wrinkles around his eyes and mouth as if he smiled a lot. He was swinging back and forth on his porch swing to the rhythm of the light breeze. The air was cold against my nervous skin, which sent a chill down my spine.

"Can I help you with something?" the man asked.

I couldn't help but hold onto the porch's support beam when I made it to the top of the stairs. It was all I could do to not topple over in anticipation of answers.

"Hi," I greeted him with a smile. "Uh, my name is Crystal, and I'm just wondering if you know when your neighbors will be home. I came a long way to visit them, but they aren't there."

He looked over at the blue house. "You're looking for Lauren? She left this morning, and I haven't seen her since."

Lauren? I thought. *No, I'm not looking for Lauren. I'm looking for Hope.*

My stomach twisted at the thought of being wrong once again. How could my visions be so inaccurate? Why would I be here if the abductor didn't take Hope here? The sickening feeling returned, and I once again felt a stab of anger and frustration when it hit me that I'd made another huge mistake. I thought I had a decent grasp on my abilities, but it turns out I didn't, and that sent my self-esteem crumbling down.

I took a deep breath anyway to calm myself. I wanted desperately to be right about something. "Does Lauren have a boyfriend or something?" I asked, wondering if the abductor took Hope here at some point. Maybe Lauren was Jeff's girlfriend and he'd taken her here. Maybe she was a relative of his. "A brother or someone who has been hanging around?" I added.

The man thought about this for a second. "Not as far as I've noticed. Just her."

"What about a child?" I asked desperately. "She doesn't have a little girl with her?"

"A little girl?" The man seemed taken aback. "No. Not since..." He paused for a second. "No, I haven't seen a child around lately."

I thanked the man and walked back to the car. I bit the inside of my lip hard to hold back the tears and mask my utter disappointment in front of Robin.

"What was that all about?" Robin asked once I slid into the passenger seat.

"I was just asking the guy a few questions."

"What guy?" Robin craned his neck to get a good look at the house I'd just been at.

I didn't say anything. Instead, I sat there frozen, realizing what his words meant. The man I just spoke with was a ghost, and the nerves I felt when I walked up to his porch were the effects of his presence.

CHAPTER 14

*R*obin suggested we get something to eat. I couldn't do anything but agree. I thought it best to have something that would settle my stomach. As we drove back to a commercial part of town to find a restaurant, I once again tried sorting through my thoughts. *Why had Penny led me here? Who was I supposed to find? Why did I find a girl named Lauren instead? Was I supposed to help Lauren in some way?* I wasn't sure I was capable of taking on another challenge since the ones I was already tackling were kicking my butt. *Why does it seem like every move I make is in the wrong direction?* I wondered.

Robin pulled into the parking lot of a small family diner and managed to find a shaded parking spot behind the building. When we entered the diner, most of the tables were empty. We slid into a booth across from each other and ordered right away.

"So, what do we do now that your friend wasn't home?" he asked. "Can you text her and see where she is? I hate to have come all this way for nothing."

Robin leaned forward across the table. His eyes bore into mine in a way I couldn't describe. It was like he was daring me to look away first. For a few moments, I completely forgot about his question and instead let myself fall into the eyes staring at me from across the table. My breath all but ceased, but my heart sped up until my fingers quivered. Without taking his eyes off me, Robin sipped on his ice water. I bit my tongue ever so slightly without realizing it.

"So?" Robin snapped me back out of my daze.

What was his question again? "What?" I asked, blinking a few times.

"I said I hate to have come all this way for nothing. Didn't she know you were coming?"

"Uh, I kind of wanted it to be a surprise."

"Can you text her, see where she is?"

"Oh, uh, yeah. Can you give me a minute?" I didn't wait for an answer. I stood up and nearly raced to the bathroom.

Once safely in a stall, I rested my head against the stall wall, closed my eyes, and took a deep breath. *I cannot be thinking about Robin right now,* I scolded myself. *Hope is my main priority. Anything regarding my abilities is my main priority.*

I took a few more calming breaths and was thankful when I sank to the ground and the stall was big enough for me to sit cross legged in.

Hope. I need to find Hope.

As I let this desire consume me, I put all the practice Emma and I had been doing to work. I struggled to clear my mind and find something that would tell me where to go next. I only hoped it would lead me to the right place this time. Maybe Teddy was right. Maybe I was embarking on a wild goose chase.

I knew time was passing, but I didn't know how long I sat there. Gradually, I became completely oblivious to my surroundings. I wasn't in the bathroom anymore. I was floating in a different realm where I reached out to Hope. I could feel her slightly, and when I did, I pushed harder. She was lonely, but she wasn't alone. She wasn't hurt. I knew that much, and that was somewhat comforting to me. But it wasn't enough. I put every ounce of power I knew I had into connecting with her. I *had* to find her. I wouldn't accept any other alternative.

I just want to go home, Hope's thoughts said in my mind. *I want to go home where I'm with my real mommy. I want my mommy to hug me again, to call me Hope. I just want to go home.*

My eyes shot open. I was close. I was really close to Hope, but that's all I knew. I couldn't go back to Gail and Wayne's right now. I had to stick around until I knew more.

I closed my eyes again to get Hope's location, but nothing came to me. I shook off an odd feeling as I stepped out of the stall, but I nearly jumped out of my skin when I saw a man with green eyes staring back at me. My first instinct was to scream because there was a man in the girl's bathroom, but I recognized those eyes. I quickly regained my composure and swallowed the lump in my throat. My mouth went dry, but I somehow still managed to croak out, "Scott?"

He stared back at me, and I nearly broke down. My gaze locked on his in desperation. "You have to help me! I know I'm close, but I don't know where Hope is. Why are you here? Can you tell me where she is?"

"I didn't know," he said.

Why is he here if he doesn't know where she is? I thought. *I need the answer, and being psychic isn't doing anything for me!*

Just as I opened my mouth to speak, a knock rapped on the door. My eyes darted to the door for a second then back to Scott, but he was gone. The door creaked open, and I heard Robin's voice through the crack.

"Crystal, are you okay in there?"

I couldn't answer for a moment. I didn't know how long I'd been gone. I didn't know if I *was* alright. I looked back toward the spot where Scott had been standing, but I found myself staring into thin air. "Yeah," I answered. "I'll be right out."

When I got back to our table, our food was already there. I was glad because it meant we wouldn't have to talk. My mind was still racing with questions. What was Scott trying to tell me? What would he have said if Robin hadn't interrupted?

I was nearing the end of my meal, contemplating these ideas all the way through it, when Scott's words came back to me and I realized something. I had asked where Hope was. Scott said, "I didn't know." Not *I don't know.* I didn't know. What could that possibly mean?

As I was finishing up my meal, Robin started speaking. "So, what do you want to do now? Should we go find your friend again?"

The thought scared me. I didn't actually know where Hope was. We'd gone to the wrong house to begin with, but I knew I was close. What *could* I do now? I couldn't talk to Robin about this. He'd either think I was crazy, or if he believed me, he'd find some way to criticize how terrible a psychic I was for getting everything about Hope's abduction wrong. I thought about calling Emma and discussing the situation with her, but I didn't want to run off from Robin again. He'd know something was up, and he probably suspected something already. But I couldn't tell *him.* He wouldn't understand. Unless he was hiding an ability, too.

"I don't know yet," I answered. "Can we go somewhere to relax? Like a park or something? I just need to clear my mind."

He shrugged. "Okay."

We paid for our food and exited the diner. Robin was telling me a funny story about one of his band members while we walked. I knew he was just trying to cheer me up, and it was almost working. I had just cracked a smile when we rounded the side of the restaurant and I watched Robin's face fall. I followed his gaze and nearly crumpled to my knees. Robin rushed to the vehicle before I could truly react.

It took me a moment to digest the scene in front of me. I managed to compose myself in a brief instant and chase after him. It was all I could do not to crumble into the pit forming in my stomach.

Robin was frantic. His fingers ran viciously through his hair as he paced beside the car and cursed.

When I reached the car, I let myself finally fall to my knees. I couldn't believe what I was seeing. The tires on Teddy's car were slashed, the front window was caved in, and the passenger side window was smashed. Scratches ran up and down the side as if someone dug their key into it.

"This can't be happening," Robin said in disbelief. "Uncle Teddy is going to kill me."

It's not your fault, Robin, I wanted to say, but I couldn't move from the ball I was curled into. I stuck my face in my hands.

"What kind of person would do this?" Robin ranted. "It must have been a random hit, but why us? Why now? Why here? Teddy is going to be furious."

I squeezed my eyes shut in frustration, and then suddenly, I wasn't in the parking lot at the restaurant anymore. I found myself behind the wheel of another car. I drove along a street in a neighborhood I recognized and slowed the car as I neared a blue house. I almost pulled into the driveway until I noticed two people standing on the deck.

Who are these people, and what are they doing at my house? I thought. *I can't let them see me. Not with her.*

I sped away.

The scene shifted until a new one played in my mind. All I saw was a baseball bat connecting with the car window. In slow motion, the glass shattered in my mind.

Just like that, I was back in my own body, and I knew without a doubt that this wasn't a random hit. This was a *warning*.

CHAPTER 15

*A*ll the stress I'd been feeling lately caught up with me in one big wave at that very moment. I couldn't breathe. Someone was out there, someone who wanted to hurt me. I gasped for breath.

"Crystal." Robin rushed to my side. Suddenly, his anxiety about telling Teddy left him and was replaced with sympathy for me.

I couldn't let Robin see me like this, but that thought only made me gasp harder. Robin's arms wrapped around me, and he pulled me into his chest. I wanted to enjoy this, to take in his scent and let his embrace envelop me in a serene encounter, but I couldn't get past the fact that someone had just vandalized our car and it was all because of me. What would they do if I pursued my visions any further? Would they hurt me? Would someone else get hurt because of me? I trembled with fear, wondering if the perpetrator was still nearby. I couldn't help but sob into Robin's shoulders.

"Crystal, shh. It will be okay. I was overreacting. Teddy will understand."

I shook my head. Robin didn't comprehend my true fear.

"We'll figure things out, Crystal. It will be fine."

Robin pulled me in closer. I took this opportunity to bury my face in his chest. He smelled good, like a fresh spring morning. I inhaled his scent to soothe myself. He gently kissed the top of my head, and I almost pulled away in surprise, but then his arms came around me tighter, and I let myself melt into him.

When my sobs ceased, I finally pulled away. I wiped at the tears on my face. "I'm sorry," I said with a nervous giggle. "That was really embarrassing." I hated that I'd been crying so much lately.

"No," he insisted. "It's fine. I understand."

I expected him to say something witty, but he didn't. I finally nodded in agreement. Only, he didn't understand how terrible the situation truly was. What if the person who did this was still hanging around? What measures would he take the next time I tried to pursue a path in which my abilities led me? I couldn't just ignore my abilities and the messages they sent me, even if I did go on the wrong path. Would the vandal come after me?

Robin was standing up now and had his phone to his ear. My heart pounded in anticipation of Teddy's reaction.

I heard a muffled voice on the other end of the line, but for the most part, I could only hear Robin's side of the conversation.

"Uh, hi, Uncle Ted," Robin greeted nervously. He laughed, probably his way of leading Teddy into bad news. "What would you say if something bad happened to your car?" Pause. "No, I was driving safely. We're both fine. It's just... well, here's the thing. We went out to eat, and when we came back, your car was kind of damaged." Pause. "Well, not kind of. I mean, the tires are slashed and everything. Looks like someone thought we were an ex-boyfriend or something." Robin laughed again to ease the tension, but we both knew this wasn't a laughing matter.

I finally got to my feet while Robin spoke and walked to the front of the car to inspect the damage. That's when I saw it. I glanced over at Robin briefly, but he wasn't paying any attention to me. I reached in through the smashed passenger side window and snatched the letter from my seat. I stared at it through blurred eyes for a few moments before focusing on the words. My hands quivered, so I gripped the piece of paper with two hands to steady it.

"STAY AWAY!" was all it said, sprawled in surprisingly smooth letters.

I heard Robin's voice grow louder as he turned back toward me. I quickly balled the note up and shoved it in my pocket, trying desperately not to let my quickened pulse show through in my expression. I couldn't let Robin believe someone had targeted us. That only meant I would have to tell him I was psychic, and I still didn't want to do that. I was sure he wouldn't believe me and would only push me away.

"No!" Robin practically shouted into the phone. "I mean, coming here doesn't really make sense. We can find someone to fix the car."

"Where exactly are you!?" I heard Teddy shout from the other end of the line.

Robin looked around nervously. "Like, four hours north or something. Look, Teddy, really, there's no reason for you to come here. That's just another eight hours of driving for you, and you'll have to get the car fixed somewhere around here anyway. We'll be fine."

My jaw nearly dropped to the pavement when Teddy agreed. When Robin finally hung up, I stared at him wide eyed. "Teddy's just going to let us handle this ourselves?" I asked.

Robin ran his fingers through his hair. "I know. I can hardly believe it either, but I guess my logic made sense to him. I don't think I could handle him seeing this. We'll have it fixed soon and be back on the road in no time."

"He didn't say anything about us being here?" At this point, I was certain he'd be more upset about me disobeying him than he would be about his car.

Robin just shrugged, which left me to believe Teddy was upset at me and Robin wasn't about to repeat what he said.

Robin searched his phone for a nearby garage and towing service. When he finally found someone, he told me they wouldn't have the right tires in until tomorrow and that we'd have to wait. Robin called a few other places nearby, but tomorrow was the best any of them could do.

I shook with nerves when Robin called Teddy back to give him the news. I was shocked when Teddy said we had no other choice but to stay the night and wait for the tires to come in. He made us promise to call the police and get a report filed before we had the car towed.

I was mostly calmed down until I saw the squad car drive into the parking lot. Luckily, the parking lot was secluded enough that we didn't have any onlookers. The note felt hot against my thigh, but I knew I couldn't tell the officer about what really happened here. My family and friends had been supportive when I found out I was psychic, but I didn't think a stranger would be. I didn't know how to explain my situation in any other way no matter how much I wanted to tell the officer this was a targeted attack.

I watched nervously as the officer stepped out of his vehicle and approached us. "Officer Brown," he introduced himself, sticking out a hand toward us. Robin shook it firmly, but I think my nerves showed through in my grip.

Robin immediately jumped into an explanation of what had happened. "We just came out of the restaurant and saw it like this. We're not even from around here. I figured it was a random hit. I've been looking around, and it doesn't look like the restaurant has any security cameras." He pointed to the areas where security cameras would be. The officer's eyes followed Robin's gaze. Mine did, too, but I didn't spot any security cameras anywhere. I was shocked that Robin was calm enough to notice this.

A sickening sensation overcame me the more I thought of the attack, which gave me a good excuse to not really pay attention to anything the officer was saying. I didn't feel like I could talk to him about what really happened, so I let Robin answer most of the questions.

Soon enough, pictures were taken and the officer had our witness report before he was on his way. I purposely left out a few details, like that I had a vague idea of who the vandal was.

Maybe I should just stop pursuing this, I thought briefly, but at the same time, I knew I couldn't just let this go.

Shortly after the police officer left, someone came to transport our car to the garage. "You two need a lift somewhere?" the guy asked. I hadn't even thought of that. What were we going to do while we waited for the car to get fixed?

"No," Robin said. "I saw a hotel down a couple of blocks. We'll stay there and then get a bus or something to bring us to the garage when you're done with it tomorrow."

A hotel? Like, I was going to be sleeping in the same room all alone with Robin? In almost any other situation, two teenagers in the same hotel room alone at night would be completely inappropriate. Then I had to remind myself that we were practically cousins. *Although not blood related*, a voice in the back of my mind—which sounded a lot like Emma's—reminded me.

Robin shared his feelings about the vandalism with me on our walk to the hotel. "Bad luck, I guess," he kept saying. We arrived at the hotel before I even realized it. It wasn't super fancy by any means, but it was a step up from the run down motel we stayed at on our way to Florida.

I briefly wondered how we were going to book a hotel room as two young teens, but somehow Robin wooed the desk attendant into letting us stay. I was grateful for my mom's credit card when I handed it over to pay for the room.

I looked around the lobby while I waited for Robin to finish talking to the desk attendant. There was an area for a continental breakfast, a sitting area with a TV mounted against the wall, and a payphone around the corner. Before I knew it, Robin was getting my attention and leading me toward our room.

"How did you do that?" I asked once we reached the second level.

"Do what?" he responded, only I heard a hint of smugness to his voice that told me he knew exactly what I was talking about.

"Get us a room. I thought you had to be at least 18 or something."

He quickly flashed me an object in his hand, but it disappeared too quickly for me to process what it was.

"Is that a…" I paused in realization. "You have a fake I.D.?" I hissed.

We reached our room, and Robin slid the key card in the door. "A guy can have a bit of fun, can't he?" He smiled a sideways smile before pushing into the room.

I fell onto the bed closest to the door. Everything that had happened earlier came crashing down on me all at once. Completely exhausted, I let the fatigue overcome me, and I drifted off in no time.

CHAPTER 16

*I*t felt like only minutes later that Robin was lightly shaking me awake, but when I opened my eyes, I noticed it was getting dark outside. I was calmed by the fact that I'd had a nightmare-free sleep but also slightly disappointed that I hadn't learned anything new to point me in the right direction.

"How was your nap?" Robin asked with a smile.

"Surprisingly good," I answered honestly. "What's up?" I sat in bed and rubbed my eyes, forcing my body to wake.

"Hear that?" Robin pressed a finger to his hear. We both paused for a moment, and I strained to hear whatever he was talking about. I did hear it. A deep bass pulsed through the walls of our hotel room.

I stared up at him. "Music. So what?"

"Not just music. A party."

I didn't take my eyes off him. "And?" I paused. Oh. "You want to go?"

He shrugged and then walked over to the other bed and sat on it. "You've just been so down lately. I've noticed you've been crying a lot."

I almost cringed at the thought that he'd noticed.

"It's just," he continued, "this is supposed to be our vacation. It's supposed to be fun. I thought it might get your mind off of things for a while."

I recalled how I had gotten my mind off things before and it led to the vision of the funeral. Maybe if I did it again, I could finally figure out the missing piece to the puzzle. But I couldn't go to a party. Apparently my expression gave away that thought.

"Come on," Robin insisted.

"Robin, look at me." I gestured toward myself. "No one is going to let me into a party." I glanced over at my reflection in the mirror on the wall. I was too skinny with small boobs and no hips to speak of. My face was that of a 12-year-old's, not a 15-year-old's, and certainly not any older.

Robin leaned across the space between the beds and gently touched a finger to my cheek. He was so close now that I could feel his breath on my face. My cheek flamed in the spot where he was touching it. He stared deep into my eyes, but I couldn't bring myself to look directly at him. I glanced anywhere but his eyes: the clock on the nightstand, the lamp in the corner of the room, and his lips. I was suddenly overcome with a desire to kiss him just to see what it would taste like. It would be my first real kiss.

My mind fought the thought as the rational part of me remembered we were almost related. But what would it be like?

"Crystal, you underestimate your beauty." That was all he said, and then he pulled away. The place on my cheek where he'd touched it grew cold in disappointment.

Why was he being so nice to me? He seemed so rude and cocky before. What had changed? I couldn't seem to sort this guy out the same way nothing else about this trip made sense in my mind. I swallowed, forcing the butterflies further down my stomach.

Robin stood and ran his hand through his hair again. "I just thought maybe you'd want to get your mind off things for a night." He shrugged again like it was no big deal, but the look on his face told me that it was.

My heart dropped. My rejection for his invitation was only breaking his heart, and I couldn't stand the thought of that. Somehow, I managed to put on a smile. "I'll go. It will be fun."

Robin beamed for a second before he realized how much emotion he was showing, and then his face fell back to its normal expression.

"Give me a minute," I told him. I dug around in my purse and found some makeup. Although I usually went light on it, I tried making it darker so I would look older. A night out with Robin could end up being really fun, I thought. Besides, what else could we accomplish by sitting in our hotel room the rest of the night?

"How do I look?" I asked, not really expecting much of a response. Robin took me by surprise when he looked up at me. He didn't answer for several long seconds. A smile formed across his face, and then he said, "Honestly, you look really good."

My heart fluttered. That was the second time he'd called me beautiful today. It wasn't something I heard often from guys, so it immediately boosted my confidence. I pushed my hair out of my face and nervously thanked him.

While shoving my makeup back in my purse, I noticed a new notification on my phone. I quickly checked it and saw that I had a missed call from my mom along with a text.

Just checking in. Hope you two are alright.

Even without my abilities tingling my senses, I knew my mom wasn't just concerned for my physical wellbeing. She was wondering how I was doing emotionally with my gift.

I swallowed nervously, unsure of what to say to her.

We're okay, I texted. *No need to worry. Love you.*

Almost immediately, my phone vibrated in my hand.

I know, and I trust you. But I'm your mom, and it's my job to worry. Love you, too. Stay safe.

I smiled at my mom's encouragement before slipping my phone back in my purse.

"Ready?" Robin asked.

Soon, we were following the sounds of the pumping bass and I was leaving my troubles behind in the hotel room. The music grew louder as we walked. Eventually, we met up with a crowd of people swarming a grassy area. A band was playing on a stage, and some people were dancing near it. Others were seated on benches simply bobbing their heads to the beat. My confidence grew even more when I noticed that the majority of the audience was teenagers.

A gate lined the perimeter of the park. A few people stood near the entrance in matching red t-shirts that read "Autumn Fest Battle of the Bands." Their shirts had the dates of the competition on them, and I noticed the event lasted all week—every night through Thanksgiving. We paid our admission fee and entered the premises to explore. Food vendors sat along the peripheral of the lot along with booths housing band tees and CDs.

I almost smiled when I caught Robin bobbing his head out of the corner of my eye.

"These guys are pretty good," he said. "Almost as good as Echo Score."

I was about to ask him who Echo Score was before I remembered that it was his band. *Almost as good,* I thought. *Of course he would say something like that.* I listened to the music coming out of the speakers, and I decided that he was right. Echo Score *was* better.

"What do we do now?" I asked.

"What?" he shouted over the music while moving his body to the beat.

I leaned into him so he could hear. I could feel heat radiating off his body and was suddenly overcome with a desire to touch him, but I resisted. "What do we do now?" I repeated loudly.

Robin smiled that sideways smile that made my heart do flips. "We dance!"

I wanted to pull away from him and refuse his offer when he grabbed my hand and pulled me toward the stage. His touch sent an electric current through my hand and toward the rest of my body. Suddenly, I didn't want to let go. I couldn't do anything but follow him.

A voice in the back of my mind scolded me. What was I doing thinking about Robin like that? I didn't like him, and we were going to be related soon. Shouldn't this be weirder than it is? Besides, what would happen if it didn't work out between us? Every Thanksgiving and Christmas would be super awkward once Mom and Teddy got married.

Robin and I reached the space in front of the stage that people were using as a dance floor. The beat was great, and I chuckled when Robin swung his body to the beat. It wasn't exactly spectacular dancing, but I could see his confidence shine through, which made him look even better at it. I'd never really danced much before. I didn't know how. I smiled up nervously at him, half enjoying his outgoing nature and half trying to reassure myself that a night away from my worries was what I needed.

Robin leaned in close to shout in my ear. "What's wrong?" His hot breath touched my skin, melting my insides.

"I don't know how to dance," I admitted.

He rolled his eyes at me, not in a condescending manner, but in amusement. "It's easy. Just jump up and down. Sway your hips."

I glanced around nervously and watched the girls around me for inspiration. I awkwardly tried to sway my body in the right direction, but it felt too weird.

Suddenly, Robin's hands were gripping my hips and guiding them. "Like this," he said, but I could barely hear him or the music over my own pulse pumping loudly in my ears. For a second, it felt like my heart was floating in my chest as it flipped anxiously. Then it was back, pounding against my rib cage.

I couldn't take my eyes off Robin until he released me. I caught a glimpse of a circle of teens behind him who were jumping up and down to the music. I figured that was the best way to dance without embarrassing myself, so that's what I did. Robin didn't jump along with me, just sort of banged his head to the beat and added arm motions that surprisingly didn't look half bad. As Robin and I moved more, I became more confident in my dancing. I was actually having fun! I jumped and giggled, and he stared back at me. The song ended then, and I stopped, unsure of what to do next.

"See? You're having fun, aren't you?" Robin asked.

"Yeah," I admitted. "This was a really good idea."

The band on stage said a few words and then began playing their next song. It was a slow, romantic song in complete contrast to their last one. People began moving off the dance floor, thinning the crowd. The few who stayed grabbed a partner and swayed slowly in a circle. I looked around nervously. *What do I do next?*

I was about to find a bench to sit on when Robin's hands settled on my waist. My breath caught, and I looked up at him in shock. Something about his expression sent my body immediately melting into the situation. I reached up slowly to test his reaction and then wrapped my arms around his neck. Should I be doing this? His hands gripped tighter around my waist, and he pulled me in. I briefly wondered what his girlfriend would think of this, but I couldn't think far enough past his touch to worry too much about it. Besides, I knew I didn't have a shot with him. I was practically his cousin, and I was too young for him anyway.

I blinked a few times, wondering what I was doing. When Robin's arms held me in an embrace, I took it as in invitation to rest my head on his chest. I could smell the fresh spring scent again, and it made every sensor in my body come to life. I didn't want the song to end.

What am I doing here? I thought. *How did I go from hating Robin so much to being filled with this desire to never let him go?* I shuffled through my memories of the past few days. *When did things change?* I remembered when he opened up to me and told me he was insecure. He hadn't been mean to me since. Did that conversation perhaps mean a lot more to him than I thought it did?

Actually, I recalled, he'd been nice to me since I made us chase after the wrong guy. Was he taking pity on me for embarrassing myself, or did he actually admire me for following my intuition like he said he did?

My head spun along with our movements as we slowly shifted to the melody. I closed my eyes to relish in the glory of his sweet embrace. When I opened them, I wasn't on the dance floor anymore.

CHAPTER 17

*G*reen eyes stared back at me. I wanted to move in surprise, but my body stayed put, fixed on the green eyes peering up from behind the sink I was standing next to. I pushed myself away from the countertop, and so did the man I recognized as Scott, only he looked younger. I wanted to open my mouth to ask him why he was here, but my body wasn't moving on my own accord. When each step Scott made mirrored my own, I realized I *was* Scott and that he was looking in a mirror. I had somehow stepped into one of Scott's memories.

I—or rather, Scott—finished washing my hands and turned to the paper towel dispenser. The Crystal part of me could feel the discomfort of being in someone else's body. It wasn't quite the same as when I had visions while I was asleep. I was more aware of things now, like that I was actually Crystal and this wasn't real. At the same time, I struggled to pinpoint my own thoughts while experiencing Scott's memory. I took in what I could about the situation. Scott looked younger than he had when I met him. He was wearing a Florida University hoodie, so I figured I was in a memory from when he went to college. But *why*?

Scott exited the bathroom, and I heard music booming down the hall of the campus building. He showed his student I.D. to the attendants at the door where the music was echoing into the hallway. Scott's memory told me he was joining an end-of-semester party hosted on campus. The attendant stamped his hand before he entered the vast room. The music grew louder, and almost immediately, his body began rocking out to the beat. His eyes scanned the dance floor and struggled to make out each figure. He was looking for someone, but the Crystal part of me didn't know who.

His gaze locked on a woman who was facing away from him near the middle of the dance floor. In his memory, everything else around her faded—the lights, the music, the room—until it was just a woman with red curly hair dancing alone. When Scott began pushing through the crowd and making his way toward her, the music and lights returned to his memory.

"There you are," he said once he reached the girl.

She turned, her beautiful red curls flying around her face gracefully. My heart nearly dropped out of my chest when I—Crystal—realized that I recognized the girl. Who could miss red fiery hair like that? I knew I had seen her at Scott's funeral.

The memory continued, even though I had no idea what it meant.

The girl beamed up at him. "Scott. You made it!"

He smiled back at her. "I wouldn't miss it for the world."

She reached for him and pulled him into a hug. He never pulled away from her but rather wrapped his hands around her waist.

"I was really hoping you'd make it tonight so we could talk later," she shouted over the music.

"Oh? What do you want to talk about?"

The girl wouldn't meet his eyes. "I think it's best if we talk about it later. Not here."

Scott put a hand to her face and guided her green eyes back to his. "Look, I'm sorry I'm leaving, but my family needs me back home." The words should have come out quietly, but Scott couldn't tell her how sorry he was with his tone over the pumping bass. "Dad's sick, and Mom can't handle it alone. We all know Jeff isn't going to help. My parents don't even want him around anyway after all the crap he's pulled. Let's just enjoy our last night together. How does that sound, Lauren?"

Shock riveted through my conscious mind.

Lauren smiled back at him, and then Scott pulled her in closer and slowly brought his lips to hers.

The scene shifted around me. I felt woozy for a second, and then my sense of balance returned. But something was different. There were still lips locked on mine. I opened my eyes to see Robin's face not even inches from my own. And then the realization of what was happening hit me. I was *kissing* Robin. His lips were soft on mine, and I couldn't help but go faint at the encounter. He tasted *so* good.

Suddenly, the rational part of my mind broke through the confusion. I found enough strength to push away. All I could do was stare at him in shock. Did I just have my first kiss? My first kiss was the result of a ghostly encounter? That just didn't seem right.

"What?" Robin asked, stepping closer to me.

I took a step back.

"What's wrong, Crystal? It wasn't good?"

It took me a few seconds to process his words. Hold on. Was he saying he was kissing me back? But what about his girlfriend? My head couldn't take all the confusion right now. I had visions and pieces of the puzzle to sort through. I had to figure out why Robin was kissing me. Did he *want* to kiss me?

I couldn't breathe. I gasped for air.

Robin immediately rushed to my side. "Crystal, are you okay? What's wrong?"

I blinked a few times, trying to regain my strength. "I just—I want to go back to the hotel," I managed to say, although my head was spinning so fast that I could hardly understand him. My balance seemed slightly off, and I wasn't entirely sure if it was because I'd just had a vision or if it was some reaction to my first kiss. I didn't have time to decide the cause of it. I gripped Robin's arm for support and waited until my sense of balance returned.

"Crystal, are you sure you're okay?"

"I am. I just think I'm getting sick." My eyebrow didn't even twitch when I said this, which told me that I believed my own words. "I don't mean because of you. Sorry. I just... Can we please go back?"

Robin led me back to our room, insisting that he support me the whole way so I wouldn't pass out. I assured him several times that I was fine, and he finally quieted.

Once things went silent on our walk back, I attempted to sort through what I knew. Scott knew a woman named Lauren. That just happened to be the name of the woman's house Penny sent me to. Lauren was at Scott's funeral just before Hope was taken. Scott went to school somewhere down here, which is where he met Lauren, which would mean that Lauren was probably from around here. That's why Hope was here. *Because Lauren was the abductor.*

My mouth literally dropped open when this hit me. I know I should have had a much different reaction, but I couldn't help it when a giant smile came to form across my face. I wasn't wrong! I was actually getting somewhere. My abilities weren't failing me. Suddenly, I felt a restored level of faith in myself. I knew what I had to do. I had to go to sleep and hope that my dreams would tell me where Lauren and Hope were, not to mention that it would help if I knew *why* Lauren took Hope.

Although I'd napped not long ago, I fell asleep almost instantly when we returned to the room.

I woke to the feeling of a hand gripping hard around my mouth. Like every night I encountered this, I wanted to scream, but nothing came out. The Crystal part of me that was watching the scene through Hope's eyes struggled to think straight. *I am not Hope,* I told myself. *I am not being abducted. Think. What's here that you've never seen before?*

Even as I thought this, my mind was still caught in confusion. A part of me felt like I was Hope, yet I still knew I was Crystal. The Crystal part of me fought to push through the barrier that muddled everything. I needed to let go of Hope's fears and think objectively. I needed the Crystal part of me to *see* something. I pushed harder. *Come on.* Suddenly, the Crystal part of me broke through.

And then it hit me. Just like that, the obvious washed over me, and what I hadn't ever seen before—what Hope hadn't seen that night— became crystal clear. A red curl peeked out from behind the assailant's hood. I always thought the perpetrator was male, but now that I looked closer, I realized that the figure was slim.

Suddenly, a lot more about what had happened made sense, like how when I'd tried connecting with Hope, I felt like she didn't like her *new* mommy.

Hold on, Hope, I said in my mind. *I'm coming for you.*

Once the car door slammed shut and I saw Hope's freckles and big chocolate eyes in the car mirror, the scene shifted around me as if someone smeared paint across a canvas only to uncover another image underneath.

I stood in a room filled with chairs with an aisle running down the middle. A casket sat at the front of the room, and a photograph of Scott stared back at me. I was back at his funeral. *But what am I doing here?* I thought. I spun around the room to take in my surroundings.

A strange feeling once again called to me from the back of the room. My eyes followed the source, and they fell upon Jeff. Next to him sat a woman with a fiery red bun and black hat.

I drew in a sharp breath. *Lauren.*

Her eyes were fixed on something the same way Jeff's were when I first encountered this scenario. I followed her gaze to the front of the room. Hope was in her same chair, fidgeting the same way she had the first time I saw her in this same scene. Jeff wasn't the only one watching her.

My heart beat wildly against my chest as all the pieces of the puzzle began falling into place. *But why? Why had she taken her? Were Jeff and Lauren working together? Where is Hope right now?*

Before I had a chance to draw in another breath, the scene shifted around me once again. I heard the beeping of the machines before my eyes adjusted. A white curtain separated the room I was in, and voices whispered behind it.

"You'll be okay, honey. I promise," a woman said. I recognized Lauren's voice.

I took a step closer to the curtain. For a moment, I was afraid she would catch me spying on her, but then I remembered I was seeing into the past. It was always easier to recognize a vision when I wasn't seeing it through someone else's eyes.

I crept around the corner of the curtain in the hospital room to view the scene. Lauren sat next to the bed and had her hands wrapped around those of a little girl's. For a second, I thought I saw Hope lying there, but then I realize that this girl was older and had lighter eyes.

Penny.

Of course! I thought. I remembered something Penny had said to me. *I don't think she's safe. My mom has kind of... gone crazy. She's not herself.* I scolded myself for not seeing the connection sooner.

"I'm scared, Mama," Penny said from the hospital bed. Tears rose to her eyes, which only made my heart sting. The way mother and daughter looked at each other was almost too sad to bear. I knew how this story ended. I knew Penny wasn't going to make it.

"Honey, the doctors perform surgeries every day," Lauren assured her. "They know what they're doing."

Penny sniffled. "I just…" She trailed off, unsure of what to say.

Lauren ran a hand through Penny's brown hair. "You've had heart surgery before, and look how strong you came through. We can't accept anything less than you making it through this time." I had a suspicion that Lauren was saying these words more for her own sake than for Penny's.

"Colette and Abby will be here in the morning to wish you good luck," Lauren told her. Fear held strong in her eyes when she stared at her daughter.

I couldn't take it anymore. Even though Lauren had taken Hope, I felt bad that she'd lost Penny. A sob caught in my throat the same time I was whisked away from the dream.

I sprung straight up in bed. My sheets were damp with sweat, and my mind was reeling. It took a few seconds for my eyes to focus, and when they did, I found two figures standing at the end of my hotel bed.

CHAPTER 18

"You have to help her," Penny pleaded.

My hand came up to support my pounding headache. It was early, so little light was seeping in through the windows. I looked back and forth between the two figures. Scott and Penny stood at the foot of my bed, side by side. Their eyes were the same color of green, and their facial features were strikingly similar. How could I not have noticed this before? Everything was starting to make sense now. I was overcome with relief knowing that I wasn't wrong about everything and that my abilities were still leading me in the right direction.

"You didn't know," I whispered so quietly that even if he was awake, Robin wouldn't have heard me.

They both looked back at me with a quizzical expression.

"That's what you said to me," I explained to Scott. I heard a stir from the other bed and looked over at Robin. He was still asleep, but I lowered my voice anyway. "I thought you misspoke when I asked you where Hope was. You said, 'I didn't know.' You meant you didn't know about Penny, didn't you?"

I could see it in his eyes. That's what Lauren wanted to tell him that night they were dancing together. That's what he never knew.

"Look," Scott said. "Lauren isn't dangerous. She's just... not herself. You need to get Hope back to her mom for everyone's sake. Lauren needs help."

Everything was making sense to me now, but I still had so many questions. Why did Lauren take Hope in the first place? Why didn't anyone suspect her? Where was Hope now?

"Where is she?" I asked, but before I could get an answer, both figures disappeared the same moment a voice cut through the momentary silence.

"Who are you talking to?"

My head jerked toward Robin in surprise. My heart sped up, and my breathing quickened. I'd just been caught, and I couldn't meet his gaze. "Um... myself," was all I could say. I could already feel my eyebrow twitching before I said it.

Robin narrowed his eyes at me. It was that same look everyone else gave me when I told them I was psychic, like they didn't quite believe me.

I could feel my face flush. I wasn't sure if it was because I'd been caught talking to ghosts or because seeing him made me think about our kiss last night.

"You were talking to yourself?" Robin asked skeptically.

I still couldn't meet his gaze. Since I'd learned about my powers, I'd been wary about telling anyone. My mother warned me about telling people, but as my eyes lifted to meet Robin's stare, I saw a glimmer of something in them. For a moment, I thought he might actually believe me. I again wondered if Robin had a gift like Teddy did, a heightened intuition. If he did, I couldn't pass up a chance to share this with someone my own age.

I sighed, preparing myself to divulge my secret. It felt like the right thing to do. "Okay," I started slowly. "I wasn't talking to myself. I was..." I didn't know if I could say it, yet Robin had been so nice to me after I thought I saw the abductor in the gas station. Maybe he had realized I was psychic and took a liking to me because of it. I wrung my hands in my lap. It all made sense, so he'd have to believe me, right?

I took another deep breath and forced down any uncertainties I had about telling him. "I was talking to a ghost," I told him slowly. "Well, two, actually." I couldn't look at him when I said this. I was always afraid of people's reactions after I told them. For some reason, though, telling Robin brought even more fear and nerves to my body. In all fairness, I didn't know him that well. I used that as justification for why I was feeling so weird telling him my secret.

I waited for what seemed like forever, but it must have only been a split second. Robin didn't react the way I thought he would. I was expecting one of two things. Either he would excitedly admit he was psychic, too, or he would scoff and make fun of me. Either way, I would know if he was psychic or not.

But neither of those things happened. He just sat in his bed and looked at me expressionless. It was impossible to tell what he was thinking.

"Robin?" I finally broke the silence.

His expression shifted. My heart sank deep into my chest when he said, "Are you trying to tell me our hotel room is haunted? I'm not going to fall for that."

I held my breath in an attempt to think straight. What did that even mean? Was he saying he didn't believe me?

"Robin," I scolded. "Be serious for a second. I'm trying to tell you a very important secret, and it's really hard for me." I forced myself to meet his gaze to gauge his reaction.

A smile formed across his face, and for a second, I thought this was it. I thought that he was going to tell me he was psychic. Instead, he just sarcastically said, "Yeah, okay."

"Wait, you mean, you're not psychic?" I thought I had put the pieces together and that I had figured him out. I could feel he had a secret, and being psychic seemed logical seeing as Teddy had some sort of gift, too.

He laughed. A hole formed at the pit of my stomach, and my eyes burned. I couldn't believe I'd just divulged my deepest secret to someone who didn't understand. Mom had told me people would use it against me. She had warned me about telling too many people. Suddenly, Robin felt like one too many, and that made my heart ache on a deeper level than I thought possible.

Disappointment washed over me when I realized my suspicions about him were completely off. If he wasn't psychic, then what secret was he hiding? I asked the question in my mind, and suddenly, the answer came to me. Certain things about him started making sense, like how he always wore long pants, how he wouldn't go swimming with me or touch the water on the beach, and how he wouldn't jump up and down at the concert. That's why he'd scowled at me when I ran around the motel and made fun of me because I played sports. It's why he wanted to go into occupational therapy.

"I am psychic!" I insisted. I couldn't stand the thought of him not believing me. He just had to. "I'll prove it. If I'm not psychic, how do I know about your prosthetic leg?"

Robin recoiled in shock.

"Your 'defense mechanism?' You're self-conscious because of your leg."

Anger flickered across Robin's face, but then his expression shifted. "That doesn't prove anything."

"How else would I have known?" I challenged.

"My uncle," he said as if the answer was obvious. And it was. Why hadn't the universe given me something good to convince him with?

"Let's stop playing games," Robin insisted. "I know you're just trying to get out of talking about what happened last night."

I was momentarily confused, thinking he was talking about my vision on the dance floor, but how could he know about that? An instant later, the rest came back to me.

"Oh. Right. Our kiss." I could hardly say the words myself, as if saying it was admitting it happened. My voice came out as a whisper. "I'm sorry about that. I, uh, wasn't myself."

"Sorry? Crystal, if I remember right, I was the one who kissed you."

CHAPTER 19

I gaped at him for a second before composing myself. I had assumed the kiss was my body acting on the motion in the vision. Nothing about this seemed to make sense right now.

Most of all, I couldn't figure out why he would kiss me. Especially not when he had a... I interrupted my own thoughts so I could speak. "But, you have a girlfriend! I won't help you cheat on someone."

His brow furrowed in confusion. "A girlfriend? Where'd you get that idea?"

"That girl you're always texting. I asked you if she was your girlfriend, and you said she was."

Robin looked confused for a moment and then threw his head back and laughed. "Sage? I may have said something, but I never said she was my girlfriend. You assumed that all by yourself. She's just my lab partner. We were talking about our homework project. And I wasn't just texting *her.*"

Something about this newfound knowledge left me with a sense of relief. It meant that Robin was available that we could... Wait. "But we're, like, cousins," I pointed out.

Robin shifted and came to sit on the edge of his bed just a few feet from my own. His body was so close to mine now, and it felt like as each second passed, he closed the gap another inch. He was still wearing his jeans, but he didn't have a shirt on. I couldn't help but notice the fantastic curves of his abs. I looked away quickly before he would notice, and I discovered I was biting my lip. I stopped instantly.

"Crystal, it's not like it's incest. We're not actually cousins." The way he said it sounded like an invitation, which only made my desire to touch his polished skin burn brighter.

"And what if it doesn't work out?" I asked. "Wouldn't things be weird between us?"

Robin shrugged. "And what if it does work out? You wouldn't want to miss that chance, would you?"

Silence stretched between us as if the questions didn't actually need answering.

"So, what?" I finally asked in a quiet voice. "You like me?" I couldn't believe I was asking him that, nor could I contain my heart in anticipation of his response.

He smiled that sideways smile that made me go faint. I longed to kiss him again. "What's not to like? You have a strong personality, you're a lot of fun to be around, and you're really pretty."

I could hardly focus on his words. All I could pay attention to right now was his fingers caressing my face when he said I was pretty.

"Plus, I really feel like I can talk to you," Robin said. "All that stuff I said on the beach—about my insecurities. I wouldn't admit that to just anyone. I haven't been able to stop thinking about you since. About... doing this."

The next few moments passed in slow motion. My heart thumped quicker in my chest, yet the sound of my pulse slowed in my ears as if time altogether decelerated. Robin's hands came to cradle my face as he leaned across the space between the beds and pressed his lips to mine. I met his lips in return. I was too overcome with a need for him to even wonder if I was doing it right.

The last few moments disappeared to the back of my mind as a greater sensation overcame me. I completely forgot my anxiety about telling him my secret. His reaction didn't even register in my mind as my lips crushed into his for a second time.

His hand moved into my hair and then trailed across the back of my neck. His tongue lightly grazed my lips. I wanted to grab and claw at him and press my body tight against his.

Instead, I pulled away. Part of my mind scolded my actions, but I thanked another for being rational. We both breathed deeply as we came up for air. I couldn't help but marvel at Robin's smile, and when I couldn't take it anymore, my face broke into a full on grin. I'd never imagined a first kiss—or rather, a second kiss—would feel like that. But as much as I didn't want it to ever end, it didn't feel right with everything else happening right now that needed my immediate attention.

I didn't have to say anything. Robin nodded his head in understanding. "Thank you," he said.

"For what?"

"Pulling me off of you."

I laughed.

"I mean, Uncle Teddy and your mom trust us. It just wouldn't be right to do it here."

My eyes widened.

He caught a glimpse of my face and quickly corrected himself. "No! I didn't mean that! I respect you. I mean... Let's just take it easy."

A part of me didn't want to. A part of me wanted to jump on him and lock my lips to his and never stop. But I knew exactly what he was saying.

"It's just that I really like you is all I'm saying," Robin explained.

My heart fluttered at the compliment, but I also knew I needed to put some distance between us. He was right. It wouldn't be right to break Mom and Teddy's trust.

"Well, uh, I'm going to go to the bathroom," I announced, my anxiety showing through in my tone.

Once I had a chance to get away from him for a few moments, Robin suddenly became less important in my mind. I desperately wanted him to believe me, but the fact that he still liked me even if he didn't accept my abilities left me with a sense of comfort.

Still, I had bigger things on my plate. I hopped in the shower and let the mystery of Hope's abduction consume me. Now I had most of the pieces to the puzzle, although it should have been obvious to begin with. I still had one problem, though. I had to rescue Hope. But what could I do? Lauren already knew my face. She knew what car we drove. She would never open the door to us. Besides, what would happen if she *did*? How would that actually help anyone?

When I exited the shower and was pulling on my clothes from the day before, a knock sounded at the bathroom door. "Do you want to go downstairs to get some breakfast?" Robin asked through the door.

"Why don't you go on without me? I'll be down in a few minutes."

I heard the door to our room click behind him. I quickly reached into my purse and grabbed a handful of change and turned to make my way down to the lobby.

Just then, my phone rang. The caller I.D. said it was Emma, so I answered right away. "Hello?"

"Hey, Crystal. Are you ready for our yoga session? I texted you but you haven't answered yet."

I pulled my phone away from my face. Sure enough, there was a message notification. "Sorry. There's just been a lot going on lately. I don't think I can join you this morning."

"Why not?" Emma's voice filled with disappointment.

"I don't have my computer with me, so we can't video chat."

"Use your phone," Emma suggested.

"Now's not a good time," I admitted. "My yoga mat isn't even here."

"What? Where are you?"

I wanted to tell Emma about Robin so badly, but I knew she'd just rub it in my face that she was right. My heart flipped at the thought as I replayed Robin's kiss in my mind. I was glad she was right, yet I had so much more to tell her. "Well, uh, how much time do you have?"

"I still have time before I have to leave for school."

Right. It was only Wednesday, so classes were still going on.

Emma's tone shifted and rose a few notes. "Are there juicy details?"

I couldn't help but smile. *Yes!* I wanted to shout, but I kept my cool. "Well, let's just say you were right about Robin."

Her voice rose about two octaves as she squealed into the receiver. I had to pull the phone away from my ear to avoid hearing loss. I could feel my face flame in response to her excitement.

"What happened?" Emma asked once she calmed herself down. "And where are you?"

"We kind of got stuck in a hotel room together," I confessed.

"Like, overnight? Did anything happen?" I could practically hear her raising her eyebrows suggestively through the phone.

The idea of teasing her with fake juicy details crossed my mind, but I was too excited about what *did* happen between us that I told Emma the truth.

There was a brief silence, and in that moment, I remembered the change in my hand. I knew there were more important matters to attend to than spilling details about my love life, no matter how much I wanted to talk about it.

"Speaking about love," Emma started, but I cut her off.

"Look, Emma, I have to go. I'll tell you everything later about me and Robin and everything else that's happened, okay?"

"Okay, I guess." Disappointment held heavy in her voice. "Well, have fun! Bye."

I hung up the phone and plugged it in to charge—luckily I had my charger in my purse—before leaving the hotel room. When I reached the first floor, I hung around the corner near the payphone and peeked toward the breakfast area to check on Robin. He was facing away from me and trying to choose a muffin flavor.

I turned toward the payphone and slipped a quarter in. I didn't know if I actually needed one to dial 911, but I put it in anyway. When a voice picked up on the other end, I lowered my tone and gave her Lauren's address and told her that's where Hope Ross was.

"Can you please tell me your name?" the woman on the other end of the line asked.

I hesitated. I couldn't. They'd ask too many questions, and they wouldn't believe me. I hung up. Just because I was paranoid, I used the bottom of my shirt to wipe the phone of any prints, even though they didn't have my prints on file and that didn't make a whole lot of sense.

My heart beat wildly against the walls of my chest at the same time I breathed a sigh of relief. This was all over for me now. The police would find Hope, Lauren would get the mental help she needed, and Penny and Scott could cross over.

My nerves eased, and I smiled as I basked in the glory of completing another psychic mission. I finally rounded the corner to meet Robin for breakfast. Now that I knew Hope would be safe, I let myself focus on Robin. I filled my plate with free food—they even had bagels, my favorite —and went back to sit by him. He smiled across the table at me, and I couldn't help but get lost in his eyes.

I took a gamble and asked him about his leg about halfway through our breakfast. "So, what happened?"

Robin shifted, and I could tell the subject was uncomfortable for him.

"I'm sorry. I didn't mean to prod or anything. I'm just curious."

"No, it's okay," he assured me. "It was a bad car accident a couple of years ago. All I lost was a leg. It could have been worse."

All he lost was a leg? He seemed a little too optimistic about the situation, but something about his positive attitude made me like him a little bit more.

"And you can still drive?" I asked.

"Oh, sure. No problem."

I wasn't sure how much the subject bothered him, so I dropped it, and we talked about happier things like his music. He told me a little more about his friends who were in his band, and I shared a few of the less embarrassing stories about Emma, Derek, and me. We went back and forth like this for what seemed like hours but probably wasn't. I laughed at his stories and was honestly enjoying myself.

In the middle of our lighthearted chat, a strange but all too familiar sensation suddenly overcame me. My joy came to a screeching halt when I looked up and saw a girl with dark brown hair and green eyes standing at the other end of the room. Penny stared back at me with an expression that told me this wasn't over yet.

CHAPTER 20

I excused myself and dropped my paper plate in the trashcan Penny was standing next to.

"What is it?" I hissed more sharply than I intended. I was sure this was all over and Hope would be returned safely home, but the look in Penny's eyes told me I wasn't even close to done with this mission.

"They're gone!"

"What?" I kept my voice low and glanced around to make sure no one heard me. Robin was rising from his chair and would be next to me in a matter of moments. I threw Penny a glance to make it quick.

"They're not at my house anymore. You still have to find her."

I could feel Robin's heat radiating off his body as he came in close to me, almost touching, and threw his own dishes in the garbage.

"Ready?" Robin asked.

I wanted to smile up at him and never let go of the mood I was in just moments ago, but the high I was feeling plummeted to the ground as I processed what Penny had said. I didn't think about what I was doing when I wrapped my arms around Robin's waist and rested my head on his chest. I just needed a bit of emotional support. His fresh spring scent soothed me.

"You okay?" Robin asked, running a hand through my hair.

I pulled away from him and forced a smile onto my face. "Yeah, I'm fine." I turned away quickly when my eyebrow started twitching.

We spent the next few hours in our hotel room listening to music until the garage called and told us our car was ready for pick up.

I tried my best not to worry about Hope in those few hours. Part of me was really enjoying Robin's company and wanted to bask in the glory of it. Another part of me trusted that wherever Lauren took Hope, the police would use my anonymous tip and somehow track them down. I also reminded myself that I still didn't know where Hope was and that the best thing I could do was forget about her and enjoy myself so that another vision would come and show me where to find her. Yet my heart knotted while I guiltily enjoyed myself instead of focusing on Hope.

The hotel graciously let us ride their shuttle to the garage. When we got there, the car looked good as new apart from the few scratches that remained. It was hard to believe that just yesterday the tires were slashed and the windows were smashed.

Soon enough, we were on the road. Being in the car again only made me think back to what the vehicle looked like the day before when we walked out of the restaurant. I remembered the note still shoved in my pocket. I couldn't look at it, but it made me think of how serious Lauren was about Hope. I still didn't quite understand what drove her to take her away from her mother. In fact, there were a lot of things I still didn't understand, but I knew there was nothing I could do about it right now. I'd already tipped off the cops, and that was the best solution I could think of.

The series of events that had transpired over the last few days once again ran through my mind, and I thought back to when I had tried to tell Robin I was psychic, only he didn't believe me. But he still liked me. I didn't get it, but I knew that above all else, I wanted—no, I needed—him to believe me.

My hands knotted in my lap, trying to work up the courage to talk about it. I'd only told people close to me, people who had known me for years. None of them seemed to flat out reject the idea as much as Robin had, yet right now, he was the one I wanted to believe me the most.

For the longest time, I didn't think I could bring up the subject again. To ease my shaky hands, I knew I needed to give them something to do, so I dug my phone out of my purse and texted Emma. I noticed she'd already left me a text asking about the details between Robin and me, so I told her as much as I could. I wasn't expecting her to respond because I knew she was in class, but she must have snuck her phone in because she texted me back right away. *Sounds romantic!*

Yeah, but there's more, I texted back. And then I went on to tell her as much as I could through text about what had happened with Hope over the past few days. *But Robin doesn't believe me*, I complained. *I really want him to.*

Have you told him about Hope?

Not yet.

Well, maybe you should.

I really wanted to take Emma's advice, but it was hard enough for me to tell him in the first place. I didn't want to get rejected again, especially now that I knew he didn't share my gift in any capacity.

Did you find Derek's dog? I asked when Emma didn't text for a while.

Not yet, she texted back with a sad face.

Are you using your, I paused typing, trying to come up with the right word, *abilities?*

I've already told you I don't have psychometry.

But you get feelings. Go around town and see which direction feels right, I suggested. *Maybe get Sophie and Diane to help.*

That's a good point. Now go convince Robin what you can do.

I smiled at Emma's last text. It was so like her. I sat in my seat quietly for several long minutes, stealing glances Robin's way to try gauging what would convince him. I rolled my owl necklace between my fingers for good luck and took a deep breath. I opened my mouth to cut through the music playing in the car, but my jaw snapped tight before I could get a sound out. I must have done this two or three more times as I contemplated what to say to him, until I finally managed to squeak out his name.

Robin looked at me and turned the radio down. "Something bothering you?" His eyes shifted between me and the road.

My gaze fell to my hands. "I'm fine." I didn't even bother hiding my twitching face this time. The lie showed through in my tone.

Robin glanced at me again and then turned his eyes back to the road. "No, you're not. Is it about us? Because we don't have to kiss again if it's too weird."

"No!" I practically shouted. I didn't want to think about ending things with him, even though we weren't anything official yet.

"I mean, it's not that. It's..." I didn't speak for several long seconds, and Robin let me have a moment to collect my thoughts. "It's about what I told you earlier. I know you think I'm crazy, but it's the truth."

A look of confusion fell over Robin's face like he didn't know what I was talking about. "Oh," he finally said. "You mean about the hotel being haunted?"

"Robin, I'm serious. I never said the hotel was haunted. I said that I saw ghosts. They aren't attached to the hotel. They're attached to... me, I guess."

When Robin didn't say anything, I continued. "They came to me for help. The girl I went to meet, she's not exactly my friend. I wasn't lying when I said she was from my town. It's just that she's six years old. Her sister and dad came to me asking me to help her because she was abducted."

I waited for Robin's response. Yet again, he didn't react how I expected him to. I was sure he would cut me off at some point and tell me I was crazy, but he didn't. He simply narrowed his eyes in thought while I spoke. I gave him a few moments to digest this, and then his words cut through the silence.

"Crystal, I can tell that you believe every word you're saying." His tone had a hint of something to it I couldn't quite pinpoint.

"What do you mean by that?" My voice came off sounding more offended and accusatory than I intended.

He sighed and glanced at me. "I mean I can tell when you're lying. Your eyebrow twitches every time you do."

My hand flew up to my face. "What? It does..." I trailed off. I couldn't even try lying about that now. How did he know? Did Emma tell him?

"I noticed," he said, answering my unspoken question. It only made me blush at the realization of how much he'd been paying attention to me.

"Well, then you should know I'm not lying about being psychic," I insisted.

"Like I said, I think you believe it. It's not hard to lie about something you believe as truth. But how am I supposed to believe in something like that?"

His words cut deep, but I still understood on some level where he was coming from. *Now, how do I convince him?*

"The car," I blurted without really thinking about where I was going with this.

Robin shot me a confused expression.

"It wasn't a random hit," I explained. "I knew when it happened that it wasn't. It was Lauren."

His blank expression reminded me that he didn't yet know who Lauren was. I quickly told him everything I knew about the case before he could interrupt me. When I recounted the part about the car, even though he clearly knew this part, I finally told him about the note left in the passenger seat. I dug into my jeans pocket and pulled it out.

"And how do I know you didn't write that yourself?" he asked skeptically.

I looked at him in disbelief for a few moments. "Robin, look at the handwriting. You've seen my handwriting. I write in chicken scratches. You know I can't write this well."

He took a long look at the paper before turning his eyes back to the road. Then he glanced at me a few more times. "You are serious, aren't you?"

I breathed a sigh of relief. "That's what I've been telling you this whole time!"

"Well, that explains a lot, I guess." He paused, and I could tell he had more to say, so I didn't interrupt him despite the anticipation that was killing me. "Okay," he said. "I believe you. But you know what that means?"

"What?" I asked, a little afraid of the answer at the same time my heart flipped.

"It means we're going to have to find that little girl with or without Teddy's help."

I beamed. Robin was on my side.

$\mathcal{W}$hen we made it back to Wayne and Gail's and entered the front door, everyone flooded us with questions.

"Are you two okay?" my mom and Gail said at the same time.

"How's the car?" Teddy asked.

"What exactly happened?" said Wayne.

Robin and I both exchanged a glance because we didn't know which question to answer first. After a moment of silence, Teddy stood from the couch and asked Robin to show him the car. Teddy stuck his hands in his pockets and remained surprisingly calm. He followed Robin outside, leaving me to answer everyone else's questions. I quickly peeked out the front window. Teddy was assessing damages and running a finger along one of the scratches that the garage hadn't buffed out.

I answered everyone's questions the best I could without revealing to Wayne and Gail why Robin and I were there in the first place. I assured them we were both alright, and eventually, they were satisfied with my answers.

I stole another glance out the front window. Teddy had his arms folded across his chest and was leaning against the vehicle, staring seriously at Robin. I couldn't tell what they were discussing, but I thought I saw a hint of a smile cross Robin's face.

I excused myself and exited to the back porch so I could put on some clean clothes. A quiet knock came at the door just as I was slipping on a fresh t-shirt. "Come in."

"Sweetie," my mom said kindly, poking her head onto the enclosed porch. She slowly moved her way into the room and then closed the door behind her.

I smiled to let her know I was fine, but I wasn't sure the smile reached my eyes. "Yeah?"

She reached out to me and pulled me close. It felt good to be in my mother's arms. She was warm and familiar, and for a second, it felt like the events of the past few days hadn't happened. Then she pulled away and broke the spell that made me forget about my troubles.

"How'd it go?" she asked. Even though she never explicitly admitted to helping me out, I could tell by her tone that she was wondering about Hope.

"Not well," I admitted. "I learned a lot more about things, but she's still missing." And then I explained to my mom everything I knew so far. I excitedly told her that she was right about there being something more to my dream that I needed to pay attention to, but then my voice fell flat in disappointment when I recounted the rest of the story.

We were seated side by side on the air mattress, which needed pumping up again, when she wrapped a single arm around me. "You'll find her. I know you will."

I smiled at her encouragement. "I hope so. I just wish the answers came easier, you know?"

"Just give it time. Be patient. I'm sure things will work out."

I wanted to believe her, but every step I took toward Hope seemed to push her further away from my grasp. I wanted Penny or Scott to show up again and to just give me all the answers, but I already knew it had been tough for them to show themselves to me in the first place. Maybe we could hold a séance. It had worked for us in the past, but the more I thought about it, the more I figured it probably wouldn't work with just two people. I decided to take my mom's advice and be patient. That's what seemed to be working best for me lately.

"Did anything else happen on your trip?" she asked.

"No, not real—what?" I cut off.

My mother raised her eyebrows and twisted her lips up.

"What?" I asked again. Heat rose to my cheeks.

"You think I can't see what's going on?" she asked. I could tell by the look she was giving me that she knew exactly what was going on, but how?

"I thought you didn't get feelings about your family members," I pointed out.

"Sweetie, this is not a psychic feeling. It's a mother's intuition. I saw the way you looked at him when you two came in the door."

I wasn't about to lie to my mother. I didn't even have a desire to lie. A smile formed across my face, and I could feel the blood rise in my cheeks. "I know it's kind of weird with you and Teddy getting married and all, but I really like Robin."

"Did you two…" Her voice trailed off.

It took me a few seconds to realize where she was going. I recoiled in shock. "What? No! Robin's not like that," I told her. "And neither am I," I added. "It was just a kiss. Or two. But Mom, it was my first kiss!" My body shivered with excitement. I knew some girls wouldn't be comfortable telling their mothers this, but my mom was different. She was like a best friend to me.

She smiled back. "As long as you're happy."

I returned her smile. "I am."

Silence stretched between us for a few long moments until I finally broke it. "You don't think it's weird, do you?"

"Why would it be?"

"Well, because after you and Teddy get married, we'll kind of be cousins."

My mom laughed. "I guess so, but I think you two are mature enough to make your own decisions."

She quickly kissed me on the side of the head and left the room. I was sure she intended to leave at that moment to let the statement sink in. She always did that. I took a few seconds to really think about it, and I decided I was proud my mom thought I was mature.

Robin entered the porch a few minutes later while I was pumping up the air mattress. "So, uh, everyone done freaking out?"

I chuckled. A joke like one he would make in this situation danced on the tip of my tongue, but I couldn't quite think of the right way to word it, so instead I just said, "Yeah. I seemed to convince them we were fine." When he didn't say anything, I spoke again. "So, how'd it go with Teddy? Was he really mad?"

Robin stared at me seriously. "I think that if he wasn't a cop, he probably would have murdered me on the front lawn."

My eyes widened. "He's that mad?"

Robin laughed, and my body relaxed. "Nah, I'm just kidding. He took it surprisingly well. I think he's just glad we're safe."

"Did he get mad about us taking the trip even though he didn't know about it?"

"We didn't really talk much about that."

"Oh," I said flatly. "What did you talk about?" I pushed down on the mattress to test its firmness and then turned off the air pump.

Robin sat on the mattress and shrugged his shoulders casually. "You."

"What?" I squeaked. I swallowed, returning my voice to normal. "Only good things, I imagine."

That sideways smile that made my heart flutter crept across Robin's face. "I told him about what a terrible, horrible person you are." His tone didn't reflect his words, and he still had a smile fixed on his face when he slowly leaned in toward me.

My heart thumped. Oh, my god. Was he coming in for a kiss? My brain could hardly process what was going on as a fire rose within my chest and spread out through my face and my extremities. Robin paused just inches from my face, his gaze seductively shifting between my lips and my eyes. I hardly noticed when my lower lip curled into my mouth and my teeth came to clamp down around it.

"Food!" Gail shouted from the kitchen, pulling me out of my trance. Apparently Robin felt the same way because, like me, he instantly recoiled.

I finally had a chance to catch my breath and realized what was just about to happen. Then Robin's fingers grazed over mine and held onto them for a moment until he rose and walked out of the room. He looked back at me for a second before leaving. Something gleamed in his eyes, and he raised his brows a bit. I silently cursed at him when I realized he was teasing me the whole time. I wanted now more than ever to kiss him. Instead, I was forced to follow him out into the kitchen and try not to let the thought of him overcome me during our meal.

The rest of the day I spent purposely getting my mind off Hope, waiting patiently for something to come to me. A part of me felt guilty for not worrying about her, but another part of me knew that I'd done all I could up to this point. Yet another part of me wanted to be consumed by thoughts of Robin. We didn't get another chance alone since Mom, Gail, and I spent time chatting and playing cards while Robin, Teddy, and Wayne enjoyed their own guy talk in the living room.

I fell asleep that night dreaming of Robin. In my dream, Emma and I were singing as part of his band. There was another girl there, too, someone who my mind told me I was friends with but, when I woke up, I was sure I'd never seen before. It was a comforting dream that made me feel like I could be a real part of Robin's life.

CHAPTER 22

I woke Thanksgiving morning feeling utterly guilty. No visions of Hope surfaced in my dreams. I still didn't know where she was, and I wasn't sure if my anonymous tip led to her safety.

After showering and getting dressed, I found my way into the living room. Everyone was awake except Robin. He was stretched out across the pullout couch shirtless. My eyes lingered, and I consciously let them stay fixed to his abs. I nearly drooled at the sight of him.

After several long moments, I snapped myself out of it and reminded myself why I came in here in the first place. I didn't want to wake him, but I turned the TV on anyway and kept the volume low. I sat in the chair on the other side of the room and flipped through channels until I found the news. My eyes fixed on the screen for several long minutes without hearing a single thing about Hope. I wasn't sure if that confirmed anything or not. I didn't know how far the news would travel or which stations would pick it up.

Robin's voice pulled me from the TV. "Hey," he greeted in a tired tone.

I smiled wide at him without trying to. "Good morning."

He looked at the TV and didn't say anything, but I could tell he knew why I was watching it. He smiled back at me. "Good morning to you, too." He yawned and stretched his arms above his head.

My eyes danced around his chest again, but they lingered a bit too long when he came down from his yawn and noticed me staring. His smile spread wide as if he was teasing me. I blushed. I was grateful that Teddy walked into the room just then to keep Robin from saying something that would make me turn pure crimson.

"Put some clothes on," Teddy teased, tossing one of the throw pillows at Robin. It hit him in the face, but he just laughed and pitched it back. I was glad they were getting along and that Teddy wasn't too upset about everything.

Robin groaned at the thought of getting out of bed, but he finally stood, grabbed a shirt that was slung over the side of the couch, and walked out of the room toward the bathroom as he slipped the shirt over his head.

"Does he sleep with his leg?" I asked absentmindedly.

Teddy rolled his eyes. "He probably shouldn't, but he's self-conscious about it. I'm surprised he even told you. He gets upset when anyone even mentions it, and he made half his family promise not to tell anyone else. I can't say I understand why, though maybe he doesn't want people to take pity on him."

I shrugged nonchalantly.

Teddy took a seat at the end of the pull-out bed and stared at the TV for several long seconds. The look in his eyes told me he wanted to say something more. I did him a favor and broke the silence first.

"Look, Teddy," I started.

He tore his gaze from the TV and stared at me. He offered a half a smile that told me he was sorry for the other day. I was happy to have the old Teddy back. My hand clamped around my owl pendant, the one he had given me, in hopes of finding a bit more courage to speak to him about everything that had happened recently.

"I'm really sorry about running off like that," I said, staring down at my hands. "She was there. She really was, but now she's not, and I don't know where Lauren has taken her." After I said it, I almost expected him to ask who Lauren was, but then I figured my mom passed on the information I had told her.

"I'm really sorry I didn't believe you," he admitted. "I just," he cleared his throat, "just wanted to let you know that my team is looking into things further now. We've notified the larger departments we've been working with and labeled it an anonymous tip. No clue as to where she's taken Hope, though." He wouldn't meet my gaze when he apologized. "I just want to thank you for your help."

"Teddy, did Mom tell you I called in an anonymous tip? You should probably get in contact with the area police department to see what they've found. Maybe they found something at the house."

Teddy nodded. "I'll look into it, Kiddo." He stood and exited the room.

My heart softened. Teddy was starting to trust me again, and that filled me with more confidence than I'd had this whole trip.

Almost immediately, Robin reentered the living room freshly dressed. "What was that about?"

"What? Oh, Teddy. He was just apologizing."

"Yeah, I told him to," Robin said casually while he cleaned up his blankets and folded the bed away.

"What do you mean?" I sat up a little straighter in my chair.

Robin shrugged. "I just think that if he asked for your help, he shouldn't have been so quick to dismiss it, so I kind of scolded him and told him to apologize."

"You scolded him?" I raised my eyebrows.

He nodded as he moved about the room. "I kind of have that effect on my uncle."

I gave a light chuckle, but Robin's words had me wondering. Was it because of Robin that Teddy was putting a bit more trust into me again? I had no doubt my mom talked to him, too. Even if I didn't have Teddy's full trust, I did have my mom and Robin on my side. Realizing this made me feel like all my troubles and responsibilities with my gift were vanishing, if only for a moment.

For most of the rest of the day, I helped my mom and Gail in the kitchen. They put me in charge of the apple pie. My mom joked that since it wasn't a salty dish, there was no fear of me over salting it. I joked back and told Gail to put my mom in charge of the salad so she couldn't burn anything.

My mind wandered back to Hope every so often, praying that the police would find her. There simply wasn't anything more I could do at this point.

Just as I finished washing my hands after cutting apples, my phone rang. I quickly dried my hands and answered Emma's call.

"Hello?" I quietly excused myself from the kitchen and entered the enclosed porch for a bit of privacy.

"Hi, Crystal! How's your Thanksgiving going?"

"It's okay. We're just cooking and watching the Macy's Thanksgiving Day Parade. You?"

"Well, with my parents' divorce, things are kind of weird. Mom was going to cook, but my dad thought he deserved to have me for the holidays since, you know, I live with my mom. So I just said screw it to both of them, and I'm having dinner with Derek's family. His twin sisters are so cute!"

I felt a stab of emotion—one I couldn't quite pinpoint—when I thought about her and Derek hanging out and having fun without me. I wished for a second that I could be there with my two best friends.

"I can't believe you ditched your parents like that," I told her, but the truth was that it was something I could totally see Emma doing. She was always more bold than I ever was, and with her parents going through a divorce, they were both probably quick to give her whatever she wanted.

"Eh, I couldn't take their bickering," Emma continued. "Someone has to show them that there are consequences to fighting. But that's not why I called. I have some great news!"

Emma paused, and I knew she was waiting for my response, so I played along and prompted her. "What is it?"

"I found Derek's dog!" She screamed with excitement.

"That's great!"

"I did just what you said. Derek and I walked around town, and I could just *tell* when things felt right and when they didn't. We ended up finding Milo across town. This little kid, like 10 years old, convinced his parents to take him in. Since he didn't have a collar on, they didn't know what else to do. But Milo was excited to see Derek, so it wasn't hard to convince the kid that Milo was Derek's dog."

When Emma found out I was psychic, my mom told her that normal people can have mild psychic abilities if they work hard enough at them. For a long time, I thought maybe she was crazy. I didn't think Emma would develop psychic powers, but the truth was that Emma put a lot of work and practice into strengthening her intuition, and she was getting really good at it. So when Emma told me her news, I smiled, honestly happy with her progress.

"That's really cool to hear. When I get back, we should do some more practice together."

"Yeah, I'd like that," Emma agreed.

Emma and I talked for another few minutes, and I filled her in on the latest details of Hope. I wanted to talk with Emma longer and maybe even get some insight from her, but after a while, she told me she had to go. I could hear laughter in the background and again thought about how I missed my friends.

When I stepped out of my guest room and saw Robin across the kitchen, though, my mood lifted. I only hoped that after this trip was over, he would somehow find a place in my group of friends so I wouldn't have to choose between them.

Robin laughed at something Gail said, and then his gaze met mine. His smile touched his eyes and somehow found its way into my heart and made me beam back at him. I joined my family in the kitchen, and Robin and I finished preparing the apple pie together as we all talked and laughed.

Eventually, we gathered around the table and said grace. Robin's chair was pushed so close to mine that I could feel the heat radiating off his body. It was driving me nuts, and I could tell by the sideway glances and smirk he was throwing me that he knew it. He was such a tease.

"Andrea, Crystal," Gail addressed my mother and me. "There's a little tradition our family does every year at Thanksgiving. During our meal, we go around the table and say one thing we're thankful for. I'll start it off this year." Gail's eyes trailed around the table at each of our faces. "I'm thankful you were all able to make it this Thanksgiving, and I'm thankful I got to meet you two," she said, looking from my mother to me. "I'm very happy for Teddy and glad to hear about the engagement." She smiled. "I know that was more than one thing, but I have so much to be thankful for."

It was Teddy's turn next. His eyes fell on my mother, and he had that same expression as the night he proposed. "I couldn't be more thankful that Andrea said yes to my proposal."

My mother smiled and kissed Teddy lightly on the lips. Then it was her turn. She looked at me. "I'm thankful that my daughter has grown into a strong young woman."

I blinked in shock. I knew my mom was proud of me, but I was sure she would say something about Teddy before she'd say something about me. Something about her words and the way she looked at me held a deeper meaning. I was pretty sure she was telling me she was proud of my abilities. I was trying to figure out what exactly she meant that I missed what Wayne had said. I may not have heard Robin if he hadn't said my name.

"I'm thankful for Crystal," he said, looking at me.

Wait. What?

I could feel my face flaming. Out of all the things in the world that he could be thankful for—that he survived the accident that took his leg or that he had an amazing singing voice and a band to help express that—he chose to be thankful for me. My pulse quickened, and I blushed in flattery.

Something in Robin's eyes held a hint of romance, the same type of look Teddy had just given my mother. From under the table, he took my hand and squeezed it tight. My stomach flipped in response.

"I know we only just got to know each other," he said, "but I'm thankful we had the chance to."

For a moment, it seemed like we were the only two people in the world. Everything else in the room faded into nonexistence until the only thing in my vision was Robin's face. Then I suddenly became aware of all the eyes staring at us. A part of me shivered with nerves, especially because Robin and I would be step-cousins in a few months and I still found that a little weird. But when all I saw were smiles staring back at me, I realized the happiness on everyone's faces doubled as a look of approval.

I beamed back at Robin. "I'm thankful for you, too."

"Your turn," Gail told me.

"I just went. I said I was thankful for Robin."

"You can't choose the same thing as him," she teased.

My mind raced. There were many more things I felt ungrateful for than those I felt grateful for. If they asked me to spout off that list, I could do it in a heartbeat. I was ungrateful for the fact that I still hadn't found Hope. I was ungrateful for the feelings of guilt and disappointment that the situation brought me. I was ungrateful that no matter how many questions I asked regarding my powers, only more inquiries arose. I was ungrateful that I had to keep it such a secret—something that I tried to do for my mother's sake since she'd warned me to keep it quiet.

But another part of me had so much to be thankful for, like the way my gift brought my mom and me closer together since we shared it, or the way it made me feel like I had a sense of purpose bigger than myself. Or how I could tell my friends about my gift and no one had pushed me away because of it.

All these ideas went through my head in a split second, and then I knew what to say. "I'm thankful for my talents and abilities." Little did Wayne and Gail understand just exactly what I was capable of.

Dinner seemed to end too soon, and I'd shoved myself so full of stuffing and potatoes that I didn't have any room left for desert. Everyone else apparently felt the same way. Wayne suggested that we wait an hour or two before dessert, and we all agreed that was a good idea.

"Want to take a walk down to the water with me?" Robin asked.

I was more than happy to accept his offer despite feeling like I could hardly move. His fingers intertwined with mine, and he led me down the staircase to the sand. I could hardly stand up straight as my body came alive with butterflies. We sat next to the water with my hand still in his.

"So," I started. Robin's eyes met mine, and the glow of the setting sun only enhanced his blue irises. I tucked a loose strand of blonde hair behind my ear. "What are we exactly? Am I, like, your girlfriend?"

Robin chuckled. "If you want to put a label on it."

"I don't mean to pressure you," I cut him off. "I mean, we don't need labels if you don't want them."

"No," Robin said. "I think it's good. I'd like to be someone's boyfriend for once."

I stared back at him, hardly able to believe what that statement meant, like he hadn't had many girlfriends before. I was too afraid to ask about that, though. I just smiled instead, happy to realize that one issue seemed to be resolved. But something in my face must have given away my anxiety about other issues, yet Robin didn't seem to read my expression correctly.

"You don't want labels?" Robin asked.

"No. I mean, yes. Yes, I do. That's not the problem."

"Oh? What is?"

"It's just..." I stared down at the sand, attempting to pick out patterns in it. "It's nothing about you. I'm really nervous about Hope. I haven't heard anything, and I'm still afraid for her, you know?"

My eyes were still locked on the sand when Robin spoke. "Maybe this will help ease your nerves." And then he pulled me in close and touched his soft lips to mine. The kiss wasn't too soft, but it wasn't smothering, either. His lips parted ever so slightly, and his tongue grazed against my lower lip. My hand came up to cradle his face as his lips crushed into mine. A feeling of warmth consumed my chest, making me want to melt into the sand below me. I became so lost in Robin's touch that for those few moments, everything seemed to disappear except for him.

Eventually, we both pulled away. It was silent for a long time until I finally spoke. "Why are you thankful for me?" I blurted. I immediately wanted to take it back, but the question was already out in the open.

"What do you mean?" Robin asked.

"I—uh... Nothing. Forget about it."

"No," Robin insisted, but his voice was still soft and kind. "Tell me."

"At dinner you said you were thankful for me. There are so many other things you can be thankful for. Why me? I mean, if we're being honest, we still hardly know each other."

"Hardly know each other? Crystal, I've been able to open up to you more than I have to anyone in practically my whole life. Shutting people out, it's what I do, but not with you. These past few days, you've made me feel like I finally have someone I can share myself with. And what about you? How many people have you told about your abilities?"

I mentally ticked off the people in my head. I'd told Mom and Teddy, and of course both Emma and Derek knew. Justine and Kelli only knew because I'd used my powers to rescue Kelli from an abusive relationship, and Justine was helping me. And then there was Sophie and Diane, Mom's business partners who were also psychic. I reviewed the list in my head and realized that all these people had one thing in common: I trusted them. And now there was Robin, and I'd told him, so that must have meant I trusted him.

"See?" Robin asked rhetorically. "I opened up to you. You opened up to me. It's not something I experience often, and I kind of like being able to talk to at least one person. *That's* why I'm thankful for you."

"Oh," was all I could say because his answer was so simple. It made complete sense. "Well, there's still a lot I don't know about you, like what your favorite color is or what your relationship is like with your parents or what your friends are like."

Robin thought about this for a moment. "You know the real me, and that's what matters." For a second, I thought he was going to leave it at that as he put an arm around me and pulled me closer, but then he continued speaking. "But just so you know, my favorite color is blue, my parents and I don't spend a lot of time together—my dad is kind of a hard ass—but we get along, and my best friends are basically idiots." He rolled his eyes and laughed at his last comment.

He went on to tell me about his friends, and we ended up talking until after dark about the simple things in life. I nearly forgot all my troubles.

Eventually, my eyes began drooping, and I took in a deep yawn.

"Tired?" Robin asked. "Am I boring you that badly?"

"No!" I nearly shouted because he wasn't. Then I looked at him and realized he was just teasing.

Robin and I walked back to the house together and went our separate ways.

When I crawled into bed that night, I fell asleep almost immediately. That night, I dreamt about Hope's abduction again, only this time, I saw it from a different angle.

CHAPTER 23

*L*auren's thoughts played in my mind.

I didn't plan this. It's not something I came to Minnesota to do. All I wanted was to pay my respects to the father of my child. I wasn't even supposed to be here. It was practically sheer luck that the obituary made its rounds on social media and far enough through my connections that I even heard about Scott's death. I wasn't invited to the funeral, but I found my way in anyway. I hid myself in the back of the room where the family wouldn't notice me.

Only after I sat down did I realize the guy I'd sat next to was Scott's brother, Jeff. I wasn't quite sure because I'd never met him, but he fit the description. I noticed he was sitting alone, which made sense based on everything Scott had told me over the years. I shifted nervously at first, but if Jeff was anything like Scott talked about him years ago, then he wasn't exactly on speaking terms with the rest of the family, so I knew he wouldn't rat me out, not that he had any idea who I was.

I tried not to cry during the funeral. I'd done enough crying over the past few months. But then I saw her.

Penny, I thought.

Somewhere in the back of my mind, a voice was telling me that the little girl sitting at the front of the room wasn't my daughter, but I couldn't fight the feeling that she needed me just as much as Penny did. And I had failed Penny.

Was this the second chance I'd been praying for?

The little girl turned around in her seat. I caught a glimpse of her profile, and my breath caught in my throat. Her eyes were darker than Penny's, a deep chocolate brown instead of hazel. Her hair was shorter, too, but it fell to her shoulders in the same shade that Penny's did. Those freckles. I could swear they were set in the exact same pattern as Penny's were.

I couldn't help but watch her while the funeral service continued. Tears pricked at my eyes when I thought about Scott's death, but they started falling—and I quickly dashed them away—when I saw the little girl who reminded me so much of my own daughter. When the service was over, my eyes were still fixed on her. I noticed the woman she'd been sitting next to was talking with a few other guests. She didn't even acknowledge the little girl.

I could do so much better, I thought. This time, I won't let Penny die.

The thought only crossed my mind for a second. I knew there was something off about the idea, but I still couldn't take my eyes off the little girl. The more I looked at her, the more she morphed into Penny in my mind. Penny had been gone for so long. All I knew was that I had to get her back and keep her safe this time. Something shifted inside of me—something I couldn't quite pinpoint—when I made this decision. Penny was always at the forefront of my mind, but now she became the sole focus of everything that I almost forgot why I was here.

When I found myself parked in front of a house I didn't recognize, I was dazed. It was dark outside, so I knew time had passed since the funeral, but I couldn't place where I'd been or what had happened in the past few hours. I didn't know how I got there or what I was doing. I looked around frantically as my body adjusted to the situation. I knew I was sitting in my own vehicle. The driver's seat was familiar, and the moon glowed off the maroon hood.

I looked further past my vehicle and noticed that I was in a residential area, but I didn't recognize the place. My eyes fixed upon the house I was parked in front of. It had orange lights strung around the doorway and lit jack-o-lanterns on the stoop. It didn't look familiar in the slightest. I took in the details of all the other houses along the street. At first, my gaze shifted past the house across the street, but then I noticed a black vehicle sitting in the driveway. I knew I'd seen it before, but I wasn't sure where. A quick memory flashed back in my mind, and a little part of me knew I'd followed it here.

I continued to eye the house and wondered why I was here. That's when I saw her again. The young girl passed in front of the window, and my breath all but ceased.

"Penny," I said out loud.

I opened my car door and stood on the pavement. When I looked back, I saw a woman pass by the window, too. She never noticed me sitting outside her house.

I can't go in there now, I thought.

I sat back in my car, wondering what I was going to do to save my little girl. I had to get Penny back. She'd been away for so long. Is that why I was here? To get my daughter back? It felt too much like fate to turn back now.

The air was chill in the car after opening the door. I grabbed my hoodie from beside me on the seat and slipped it on. I didn't know exactly what I was doing. I *wasn't even thinking. I stayed in the car for another hour watching the house. The light in the living room turned off, and another one flipped on at the other side of the house. I watched the woman pass by the window a few times in her nightgown, and then she shut the light off again.*

I waited another hour to make sure she was asleep. I knew I had to get to Penny as soon as I could, but if I was going to get away with her and bring her back home to Florida, I had to be patient.

I flipped my hood up when I got out of the car to shield my body from the chilly night air. The sleeves fell to my fingertips, so I balled them into my fists. I walked around the corner of the house and peeked in the windows. It wasn't easy to see inside, but there was enough moonlight that I could make out each room.

I stopped when I came across a room I was sure was Penny's. A nightlight enveloped the room in a soft hue. The walls were pink, and there was a collection of teddy bears in one corner.

Of course, *I thought.* Penny always loved her teddy bears.

I noticed a small lump on the bed.

Penny! *I almost shouted, but I kept my mouth shut.*

I pressed my cloaked hands against the window and stared into the room. All I knew was that I had to get to her, but I wasn't completely sure how. I could try the front door. I could break the window.

I pushed away from the glass in exasperation, and to my surprise, the window moved. It was only so slightly, but it was enough to tell me that it wasn't locked. I had found my way to Penny. I fit through the window easily. For a moment, I just looked around the room again, and then I stared at the girl.

What am I doing? *a voice in the back of my mind asked. But then I looked at her face. I really looked at it, and I knew she needed me. Knowing there was another woman in the next room, I figured it best not make any noise.*

A moment later, I had my hand clamped down around Penny's mouth. I pressed a finger to my lips to let her know to be quiet. I knew she would. After all, she was my *little girl. I hugged her close to me, and she wrapped her arms around my neck. I finally had my little girl back.*

I crawled back through the window I came in from and used one hand—still shoved in my hoodie for warmth—to pull it down and press it shut. I set Penny in the passenger seat of my vehicle and then crossed around to my side of the car. I was so happy to have my daughter back.

My dream appeared to fast forward though the events of the next few weeks, and I caught glimpses of Lauren and Hope in my mind. The images slowed when Hope asked to play at the park and Lauren reluctantly agreed. A few hours passed through my mind in a second and then slowed again when I saw myself through Lauren's eyes standing on her front deck. Days flew by in a few short moments, and then the images regressed to normal speed and fell upon a yellow house just as small as Lauren's.

~

I sat up straight in bed and gasped for air. I was partially relieved to know why Lauren took Hope and that it wasn't in malice that she did so. I knew she hadn't, and didn't intend to, hurt her. Most of my relief, however, came from the fact that I now knew where Lauren took Hope. I didn't know who the yellow house belonged to, but I somehow knew this was where Lauren took Hope after she destroyed our car.

Light gently seeped in the porch windows, and I could hear voices in the kitchen. I leapt from my bed and excitedly entered the kitchen. "Teddy," I practically shouted.

He looked up expectantly from the newspaper he was reading.

My eyes shifted from Teddy to my mom and then to Gail, who was tending to breakfast by the stove. "Can I, uh, talk to you two in private?" I asked, looking between my mom and Teddy.

They exchanged a glance and then rose from the table and followed me onto the porch that served as my guest room. "Did you find out anything about Hope?" I asked Teddy once my mom shut the door behind us.

Teddy's face fell. "I'm sorry, Crystal. We haven't found anything more, but it turns out that Lauren was a good lead. After getting her description out, some witnesses recalled seeing her at the funeral. She wasn't on the guest list, and Melinda didn't remember seeing her, which is why we didn't know to look into her to begin with," he explained. "There wasn't anything else to connect her to this initially. She hadn't been in contact with Scott for years. The problem is that the local police have searched her house but didn't find anything. There's no indication of where she took Hope or if she's hurting her or anything. There haven't been any reports matching her license plate number, either."

"That's great!" I said, but I didn't mean it in that way. Both my mom and Teddy fixed a look of confusion on their faces. "I mean, I know where she is now. I don't know how, but I do. And it's on our way home!"

Like the last time, I couldn't pinpoint an address. I had to physically go there if I was to find it.

"We have to go get her," I told them. "I mean, we're headed home today anyway." I wanted to hate Lauren for taking Hope, but a part of me felt her pain. "And we have to help Lauren," I added.

I never knew how I knew it, but I was able to tell Teddy where to go. Within a few hours, we were pulling up in front of a small yellow house along a one-way street.

Who lives here? I wondered. *And why would Lauren bring Hope here?*

Teddy stopped the car in front of the house but on the opposite side of the street. He looked back at me from the driver's seat. "Remember, we do this my way. Andrea and I will ask questions. You stay here."

I knew Teddy had already mentioned this, but my jaw still dropped in disbelief. My mother got to go with him, but I didn't? But this was *my* responsibility. *I* was the one who was supposed to rescue Hope. My heart dropped knowing I wasn't going to be a part of it, but the rational part of me was just glad Hope would be safe whether I was in the midst of the action or not. Teddy gave me a serious look, and I quickly agreed that I would stay put.

"I hope you have your hand cuffs," I said before he exited the car. I was only half joking, but he shot back a knowing smile that told me that he had them on him. I didn't even know if he could arrest someone here, but that didn't matter to me when Hope needed rescuing.

Teddy and my mom exited the car together. I glanced over at Robin. His eyes were closed, and his chest rose and fell slowly. I almost thought about waking him and telling him we were here, but he looked so peaceful. I didn't want to disturb him.

I watched out Robin's window and hardly noticed I was holding my breath as Teddy knocked on the door. It felt like time stood still, waiting for something to happen. Teddy pounded on the door again. The anticipation was killing me, but after several long minutes—or at least what felt like it—the door swung open, and a woman with dark hair and olive skin stood behind it. She must have been in her 30s, but I didn't recognize a thing about her. I didn't know what I was expecting—maybe Lauren or someone who looked enough like her to be her relative, or perhaps a male who could have been her boyfriend—but when I caught a glimpse of the woman, the pieces of the puzzle just didn't fit right.

My heart sank in my chest. Was this another mistake? Why was it that every time I felt close to Hope, something happened that only pushed me further away? I was sure Teddy was going to be furious that I'd led him on the wrong path again. Never again would I hear him say he trusted my judgement.

Just as I watched Teddy flash his badge, my phone vibrated in my pocket. I didn't want to respond, but the vibrations continued. The only person who ever called me was Emma, so I answered it.

"Hello?" I answered quietly, careful not to wake Robin. My gaze never shifted from the front door of the yellow house.

"Crystal," Emma breathed a sigh of relief as if she had been holding her breath. Something in her tone hinted at urgency, leaving my body frozen in fear.

"Emma, are you okay?"

"Yeah, I'm okay. Are *you?*"

"What do you mean? Of course I'm okay. Why do you sound so terrified?"

"I just—I guess it's nothing. I just got a really bad feeling. I wanted to make sure you were okay."

"A bad feeling? About me?"

"Yeah. You're not near a white garage, are you?"

"What?" I didn't quite understand where she was going with this. I glanced up and down the street. The houses were all so colorful here. "No, no white garage."

"Good. I'm just getting a bad feeling about a white garage. Just don't go into it, okay?"

"Uh… okay. I don't imagine that I will, but thanks for the warning." My eyes stayed locked on the woman's porch. She stepped out onto it and closed the door behind her. I saw lips moving but didn't know what they were saying—probably Teddy just asking routine questions. I needed to pay closer attention. I needed to know what was going on, to see if there was any hint in the woman's words that told me why I was sent here. "I have to go, Emma. I'm kind of in the middle of something really important."

"Okay. Just be careful."

"I'll be fine, Emma. You don't have to worry about me."

We said goodbye and hung up. I really wanted to know what was happening on the porch. I slowly climbed over the middle console and crawled into the passenger seat. I knew my mom had an extra key to Teddy's car, so I quickly dug it out of her purse and stuck the key in the ignition just enough to roll my window down a crack in hopes of making out some of the conversation on the porch.

When I turned back to look at the house, I saw it. The corner of a white garage peeked out from the side of the yellow house. It was tucked far back from the street, but it was the only white garage I noticed. I could hear the voices on the porch now, but I couldn't make out what they were saying. My pulse quickened, and my eyes locked on the white building situated behind the woman's house.

Emma knew it was going to be there. She warned me about it. That meant it was important somehow. And I knew exactly how. Hope was in that garage. Those long moments the woman took getting to the door must have been spent sneaking Hope out of the house. I may not have believed it myself if I didn't feel it in my bones. I knew Hope was close, and something about the garage called out to me.

I didn't process what I was doing when I slid out of the vehicle. The promise I'd just made to Emma moments before didn't even register in my mind while I moved. Teddy's and my mom's eyes were on the woman while her own gaze stared in the opposite direction down the street from me. Nobody saw me slink around the side of the house next door and double back through that person's back yard. I couldn't explain what possessed me to sneak to the garage on my own. It was as if my abilities were drawing me in and the rational part of me all but ceased to exist.

I stayed low as I approached a window on the side of the garage. My heart pounded against my chest in preparation to face the unknown. I pressed my back against the side of the garage and peeked into the window. For a brief moment, everything within my body froze. A small figure was curled up in a chair near the far side of the garage. Her knees were pulled to her chest and held tightly by her arms.

My nervous system went into overdrive. I recoiled from the window and rested my head on the side of the building, forcing my heart to slow and my breathing to normalize. I had found her. I'd finally found Hope, and she was sitting mere feet away from me with nothing but a wall to separate us.

I glanced back into the window, careful to keep my face as hidden as possible. I knew for sure that the girl sitting there was Hope. I scanned the room but didn't see anyone else. My eyes darted toward the porch, but no one could see me from here. I was clear. If I took my chance now, I could get Hope out of there and away from the situation quickly, and Teddy would be able to handle the rest.

I didn't give it another thought. I knew it was something I had to do. It was now or never. I held my breath and scanned the area cautiously while I circled around to the side door. As I passed another window, I quickly checked again that Hope was alone. The best I could tell, she was. A mixture of emotions overcame me, sending my heart pounding and my hands shaking.

I nervously gripped the door handle but couldn't wait another moment. I rushed into the room and immediately over to Hope. She saw me instantly, and her eyes lit up.

"Hope!" I called, hurriedly crossing the garage to her corner. Her arms reached out toward me, and I swooped her up, cradling her in my embrace. I was ready to explain to her who I was and that I was there to save her, but I didn't have a chance before she spoke.

"Crystal!" she exclaimed excitedly.

My whole body tensed for a brief moment, but there wasn't time to ask her how she knew my name. All I knew was that I had to get out of there and back to the car before anyone realized I was missing from it. It hadn't even occurred to me to worry about where Lauren was right now. For all I knew, she had dropped Hope off here and left. The desire to get Hope to safety consumed me.

Hope and I pulled away from our embrace and gripped each other's hands. I didn't even get a chance to turn around before witnessing the terror fixed in Hope's eyes. Before she could shout a warning, something hard cracked into my skull. I crashed to the ground, and my vision went black in response to the ache pulsing through my head. The world swayed around me, and I couldn't make sense of which way was up and which way was down.

Objects across the floor blurred. Even after a few seconds when my vision returned, I couldn't understand what was going on. I quickly realized I was no longer holding Hope's hand. I knew I had to get up, but I still couldn't find my balance. I braced my palms against the concrete and strained to push myself from the cold surface. The room spun around me, and a high-pitched ringing assaulted my ears.

I finally found my way to a sitting position and cradled the area of impact with my left hand. My head reeled in a terrifying struggle to figure out what had just happened to me. I blinked a few times, and when my vision began to normalize, I looked around the room. A wooden board sat a few feet from me, and I instantly knew it was what hit me.

Then my eyes adjusted to find two figures standing in front of me. A woman with wild red hair held Hope against her body with one hand clamped down around her mouth.

Lauren, I thought, my mind full of spite for the woman. Every ounce of empathy I'd ever felt for her drifted away and was replaced with rage. I wouldn't stand by and let her beat me to a pulp, and there was no way I was going to let her hold onto Hope the way she was, not with the terror fixed in Hope's chocolate eyes.

"Stop it, Lauren," I demanded with every ounce of courage I could muster. I finally found enough sense of equilibrium that I stood from the floor. The task was harder than it sounded with the pounding headache and impaired sense of balance the blow had given me.

Lauren took a step back. Her eyes went wide, and it made me realize how crazy she actually looked. There was no doubt about it; Lauren needed some serious help. Unfortunately, I didn't have it in me to worry about helping her when Hope was shaking in terror. All I could think was that I hoped her mental state was stable enough that she wouldn't hurt Hope.

"How do you know my name?" Lauren demanded. "Who are you?"

"Just let her go," I insisted, taking a gentle step forward. Lauren only distanced herself from me, dragging Hope with her. "It's not worth it, Lauren."

"She's my little girl! I'd do anything for her." Lauren pulled in quick, shallow breaths with each step she took away from me. Just a few more feet and she'd be trapped against the back wall. She glanced around frantically until her eyes fell upon an object on the shelf behind her. She quickly grabbed for it and held the screwdriver out at me as if it were a sword. "Stay away from us," she threatened with a shaky voice.

"Just calm down," I tried as kindly as I could. "You know she's not your little girl. You know she's not Penny."

Lauren's face twisted into a cross between fear and anger. "How do you know about Penny?"

"I just do." I inched closer to her. "Now, let Hope go."

"Shut up. Just shut up!" Her eyes darted around the room, but she still held the screwdriver out at me. Her gaze fell upon me again as she spoke. "I don't know who you are, but you're not taking my little girl away from me again."

I kept her talking, hoping this might calm her down and she'd eventually release Hope. Frankly, I didn't have any other strength in this situation and didn't know what more to do. If I dove quickly, I might be able to grab ahold of the board she had used to hit me with, but I didn't think I had it in me to inflict physical pain on her, even as worry for Hope's sake washed over me.

"Why didn't you ever tell Scott about Penny?" I asked, partially to keep Lauren talking and partially out of my own curiosity. I knew she had tried to tell him the night before he left, but she never did. Maybe things would have turned out differently if she had told him and he'd been a part of their lives.

She narrowed her eyes at me like she couldn't quite place how I knew about her and Scott. Still, something about her demeanor changed as she reflected back on this time in her life. I almost thought I saw tears in her eyes, and she even dropped the screwdriver slightly when she spoke.

"He *left* me. I was going to tell him, but at the last minute, I decided I didn't want to make him choose between me and his father. So I let him worry about his dad for a while. After his dad died and he was done grieving, I was going to tell him, only *she* was already a part of his life, and they were getting *married*. Do you know how that made me feel?"

She didn't wait for an answer. "It's like he reached into my chest and ripped my heart out. The one man I ever loved was gone thanks to another woman. But how could I tell him then? I couldn't break apart a family like that, so I kept my distance."

"You didn't even tell him Penny died," I said to keep her talking.

"He didn't know about Penny at all. How could I tell him his daughter died when he didn't even know she existed?" Lauren's expression grew more sour as she talked. "What do you care anyway? And who are you?"

Her eyes narrowed at me the same time I opened my mouth to give her some lame excuse, but she spoke again before I could. "And why were you at my house?"

"Why did you destroy my car?" I retorted.

"It's because of you and your boyfriend that I had to bring her here. Your Minnesota license plate gave you away. We were fine before you came around looking for her."

Even as I spoke, I knew I should have been more afraid of Lauren. For some reason, I thought her wild eyes and disheveled look made her appear weak and scared even though she still held the screwdriver in front of her like it were a weapon.

"You can't keep running away, Lauren. There's a policeman here, and he's going to help get Hope home safely and get you the help you need."

"The police?" The hand holding the screwdriver came up to brush the hair out of her face, but the crazy look in her eyes remained. Suddenly, her eyes locked on me, and her entire stance shifted so that she was no longer rocking nervously. The screwdriver came out in front of her body again defensively when she realized what I was saying. "No, the police can't take her," she practically shouted. Her face twisted into an evil snarl. "I'll be damned if someone is going to take my little girl again!"

In one quick motion, she spun Hope to the side to clear a path to me and twisted the screwdriver in her hand so she was holding it like a knife. And then she lunged.

CHAPTER 25

A shriek escaped my lungs and reverberated off the walls of the garage as the screwdriver ripped through the skin on my left shoulder and Lauren's weight sent me crashing to the ground. I heard the crack of my phone as it crushed in my back pocket. Everything happened so fast that it was difficult to process.

Lauren gripped so tight onto the screwdriver that her knuckles turned white. She raised her arm above her head and thrust it down on me again. I tried to roll out of the way, but her body bore too much weight on my own. I squeezed my eyes shut, bracing myself for the second blow.

A second later, the blow still hadn't come, and then suddenly, Lauren's weight was lifted off me. I heard shuffling and opened my eyes just in time to see Robin's fist connect with Lauren's face. A little part of me rooted for him. He lunged for her again and pried the screwdriver—which she was now trying to assault him with—from her fingers. For a moment, I forgot how to move.

"Go," Robin shouted at me the same time he pinned down Lauren's flailing body.

I didn't waste another second. I quickly got to my feet and rushed over to Hope, who was crouched in the corner with tears streaming down her face.

"Come on," I prompted in a low voice.

Hope rushed to me immediately. I gripped her small hand, and together, we ran out of the garage toward the front of the house.

Teddy was already sprinting our way, no doubt in response to my scream. He slowed as he met up with us, and his eyes shifted from Hope to me then to my bloody shoulder. "Are you okay?" he asked frantically. Both of his hands came to grip my biceps, and his eyes stared seriously into mine.

"The garage," I said breathlessly, pointing behind the house with my good arm. Teddy immediately understood what I was saying and didn't waste another second. He ran off toward the garage.

Hope and I took off in the other direction at the same time. When we rounded the side of the house, the woman standing next to my mother finally processed what had happened in the last few seconds. I watched her fist come back, and I made a noise to warn my mother, but my mom was already shifting her weight. She dodged the punch and, in one swift movement, gripped the woman's wrist and twisted it around before pushing the woman's body up against the side of the house. The woman couldn't fight my mom off no matter how much she squirmed.

I came to a halt in witnessing this and stared in disbelief at my mother. I hadn't realized she was capable of that.

She caught a glimpse of my expression. "I took a self-defense class once," she explained. She cocked her head toward the car, and I understood immediately what she was trying to say.

I held on tight to Hope's hand and ran across the road, opening the door for her and helping her crawl into the passenger seat. I rounded the car and slid into the driver's seat. The keys I'd stuck in the ignition were still there, and even though I still didn't have my license, I was ready to make a quick getaway if needed.

"Are you okay?" I asked Hope. My chest rose and fell in time with my racing heartbeat.

Hope closed the gap between us and flung her arms around my neck. "I knew you'd save me. I just knew it! Thank you so much."

"Wait. What?" I asked as I pulled away from her. "How did you know? And how do you know my name?"

"I see you sometimes," Hope admitted slowly. "In my dreams. You're always there when I have nightmares about that night—the night she took me—and you're telling me that everything is going to be okay and that you're coming to get me. I knew you wouldn't let me down."

I couldn't move for several long seconds as I processed what she was saying. Every night that I'd dreamt about her abduction, she was reliving it, too. Only somehow, I was there with her. That phenomenon amazed me, but I didn't have the time to dwell on it for long. We were still in the middle of a crisis.

"It's not like she hurt me," Hope was saying. "I mean, she never tried to, but I was so scared. I miss my mom." Hope sniffled, wiping tears away from her face. "I hate it when she calls me Penny. I tell her that's not my name. She never believes me. Is it all over yet?"

I gazed past Hope to see if I could tell what was going on toward the house. I couldn't see anything but my mom holding the woman's body in place.

"Not yet," I told Hope. I reached into my pants pocket and pulled out my phone, desperately hoping it was still functional. I breathed a sigh of relief when the backlight came on. A crack ran the width of the screen, but I was still able to make a 911 call.

I never took my eyes off the yellow house while I spoke to the woman on the other end of the line. I had calmed down enough that I could make coherent sentences, but based on the woman's questions, I knew I wasn't quite making sense. I gave her the address I was at and said the word abduction enough times that I think she understood me. She assured me help was on the way and had me stay on the line until they arrived. When she asked if we needed an ambulance, I almost said no, but then the pain in my shoulder prompted me to answer yes. Besides, I had no idea how beat up everyone else was. Before I knew it, I could already hear the sirens.

"Are they coming to take me home?" Hope asked quietly.

I nodded. "Yes."

"Can't you take me home?"

I met her eyes. "I'm sorry. I don't think I can." Her face fell in a way that stung at my heart. "But I'll be back in Peyton Springs, and maybe if your mom lets us, we can spend some time together."

Hope's face lit up at my suggestion, but that only made me feel bad because I wasn't sure what would happen next. Her mom may choose to move away from where so much tragedy had happened recently, or maybe she simply wouldn't let anyone near Hope again. That's probably what I would do if my child was abducted.

I took a moment to examine my shoulder. My shirt was ripped, and a deep scratch ran up the front side of my deltoid. The screwdriver hadn't penetrated as deep as it could have but instead skidded along my skin. I didn't think I needed stitches, but the injury still stung and was lightly dripping with blood. I grabbed some tissues from the middle console and pressed them into my raw skin, biting back a cry of pain in the process.

I wrapped my good arm around Hope, glad this would soon be over for real. We both watched the police cars approach the house and shook nervously when they emerged from their vehicles. None of them noticed us right away. They first ran to my mother and the woman she was holding. I couldn't hear what was going on, even with the window cracked open, but I saw my mother release the woman, and her hands came up in a surrender stance. Her mouth moved, and then some officers raced around to the back of the house on their way to the garage.

A knock rapped at my window, and I nearly jumped out of my skin. I turned to find an officer standing above me. I hadn't even noticed him making his way over here. I quickly opened my door for him.

"Are you two okay?" he asked.

"I think so," I answered.

His eyes shifted to my injured shoulder and widened. "Our EMTs should take a look at that."

I nodded in agreement. The officer led me to the back of the ambulance, and an EMT tended to my shoulder while other officials questioned Hope.

I watched several officers lead a handcuffed Lauren around the side of the house. "She needs help," I said to no one in particular. My eyes remained locked on her.

The EMT followed my gaze. "Is she hurt?" she asked.

"I don't think so. Not physically. Ouch." I winced in pain when the EMT touched my shoulder. I could see a dark purple bruise forming now that some of the blood was gone. "She's sick. Mentally. That's why she took Hope. She needs to get psychiatric treatment."

The EMT nodded, but I didn't really think she was listening. She said I didn't need stitches but wrapped me up in gauze and tape instead. She also inspected the lump that was now forming on my head and questioned me about dizziness or nausea to be sure I didn't have a concussion. The pain had already passed except for a lingering headache, so I answered her honestly and assured her my head would be fine. She gave me an ice pack anyway. The whole time the EMT questioned me, I never shifted my gaze from Lauren until after they drove away with her.

Soon after I was properly bandaged, an officer came to ask me about what I had witnessed. I told as much of the truth as I could, bending it only so slightly. I explained how this was Teddy's case and that we'd been on vacation. Due to new information he'd received while on vacation— which I feigned ignorance to—he was compelled to check it out on his way back home. I told the officer that while Teddy left Robin and me in the car, I noticed motion behind the house, and, stupid little girl that I am, I went to check it out and found Hope and Lauren there.

I sounded innocent enough that I was positive he bought it. The rest of the events were the truth, only I left out the part about Hope telling me she knew me. I figured that would sound too suspicious, and I wasn't about to tell the officer about my abilities when I already knew he wouldn't believe that kind of story. So I stuck to what was most believable.

When I was finally free to go, I started toward Robin, except something in my peripheral vision caught my eye. Two figures stood on one side of the house, only they didn't quite fit the picture. Everyone else here was living, and I was the only one who could see them. I casually strolled toward Scott and Penny and leaned myself up against the house to make it look like I was still trying to recover, which in truth, I was.

I angled my body away from the crowd so people wouldn't see me talking to myself. "Is it all over, then?" I asked them.

They both smiled back at me. "I think so," Scott replied. "We can't thank you enough for rescuing Hope."

I offered a shy smile in return. "I couldn't have done it without either of you. You both led me to her. That's why I kept seeing you, Scott, wasn't it? In the hotel, gas station, and restaurant? You were trying to tell me I was getting closer to her, weren't you?"

Scott nodded.

"And you, Penny. You showed me where to go even though it seemed silly at the time."

Her smile widened in pride. "I couldn't cross over until I knew my mom was going to get the help she needed. I learned about Hope shortly before finding you. I'm glad we could help them both."

I looked between both of them. They really did look like father and daughter. It was painful to know they'd never had a chance to get to know each other and that Hope wouldn't grow to know her sister.

"It's okay," Penny said like she could read my thoughts, which I wasn't entirely sure was completely off from reality. "We get a chance to be together now, and someday, Hope will be with us, too."

They both shifted their gaze and looked at something I couldn't see.

"The light?" I asked.

Scott nodded while Penny smiled. "It looks like it," she said. "Thanks for helping my sister and my mom. I'm pretty sure she'll get the help she needs now."

"Always a pleasure," I replied. "Only, if you decide to ask for my help again," I joked, "could you not be all mysterious?"

"Will do," Scott agreed. Then he lifted his daughter onto his shoulders, waved goodbye, and walked into a light I couldn't see. They faded into nothing.

I smiled after them, happy that I could help them cross over and better their—for lack of a better word—lives. Unsure what to do next, I glanced around the lawn and locked eyes with my mother. She hugged me as soon as I was close enough.

"I thought we told you to stay in the car," she scolded, but I could hear relief in her voice.

"I'm sorry," I said guiltily, still locked in her embrace. "I couldn't just sit around."

"I know, sweetie. I know you're hurt, but I'm glad you took the initiative."

I pulled away from her in surprise. "You mean, you're not mad that I went to face Lauren alone?"

She shook her head. "I know mothers should be concerned about their child's safety, but I'm not your typical mother. You're a strong girl, Crystal, and I know that no matter what paths your abilities lead you on, you'll come away from each situation stronger than ever."

I didn't quite understand what had changed my mother's mind. A few weeks ago, she was scolding me for breaking into Tammy Owen's house to help my friend Kelli. Now she was praising me for breaking into someone's garage? I guess I proved to her that sometimes I had to break the rules to save people.

My mother paused for a moment and then continued. "We weren't getting much out of Colette—that was the girl's name who Teddy was questioning. It looked like Teddy was wondering if you made another mistake because it didn't make sense why Lauren would bring Hope here."

I still didn't understand it myself. "Why *did* she bring her here?"

"You can thank me for the answer to that," she told me proudly. "I asked Colette that same thing. Turns out Colette's daughter, Abby, and Penny were in the hospital at the same time, both for a heart condition, so Colette and Lauren got to know each other. I guess she was just a friend who understood her pain and was willing to take her in when she had nowhere else to go. Colette told me she'd lost Abby, too."

I dropped my head. A part of me still felt for Lauren's loss even though she'd attacked me. I couldn't imagine everything she'd been through with her daughter and her daughter's father dying around the same time.

I thought back to the funeral that I'd seen in a dream. "So, Jeff didn't have anything to do with this?" I asked.

"It doesn't look like it," my mom answered.

I looked over my mother's shoulder and caught a glimpse of Robin. I excused myself and made my way over to him.

His left eye was a dark shade of purple. He noticed me staring right away. "She got in one good punch," he explained.

"I'm so glad you're okay!" I exclaimed.

Robin pulled me into a gentle embrace. "Forget about me. What about you? How's your shoulder?"

"I'm fine," I answered, but the truth was that I was still a little shaken up.

"Fine enough that I can punch you?" He playfully punched my good shoulder.

"What was that for?" I asked, my voice rising a few notes above normal.

"For thinking you could handle something like that. Why didn't you wake me up? You may not have that nasty gash in your shoulder if you did."

My mouth twisted up guiltily. "I'm sorry." There was a brief moment of silence. "Hey, how did you know to save me anyway?"

"I didn't. I woke up and saw you were gone, only I could see you weren't with Teddy or Andrea, either. They didn't even notice when I went around the side of the house to look for you. I caught a glimpse of motion in the garage window, and then I heard you scream. When I went to check it out, you were getting your ass kicked."

"Hey," I defended playfully. "I ended up being fine."

"Only because I was there!" His arms came to wrap tighter around me again, pulling me to his chest. "I can't imagine what would have happened if I wasn't. She could have killed you, you know."

I hadn't thought about that, but I still wasn't entirely sure what lengths Lauren would go through to continue convincing herself that Hope was her daughter. Perhaps Robin was right. I was more thankful for him now than I'd ever been before.

"Thank you," I said softly, and then his lips came down to meet mine.

CHAPTER 26

ears streamed down my face. "Stop it, Robin!" My words were separated between my giggles. Robin's hands were clamped around my midsection, and he'd just found out how incredibly ticklish I am. I wriggled beneath him on my living room floor after we arrived home from our trip, but my attempts to flee were rendered useless.

"Teddy and I are leaving soon," I told him between giggles. "I have to get ready to go."

I screamed a high pitched yelp when his fingers found my most ticklish spot and dug in. I watched upside down as my mother entered the room and looked at us with an amused smile fixed on her face.

"Mom," I cried between laughs. "Tell him to stop."

"Robin," my mom scolded with a laugh.

Suddenly, his hands stopped moving, and I was finally able to catch my breath again.

"Sorry, Andrea," Robin said.

"Sorry? I was just going to say that you're doing it wrong." And then my mom bent to my level and tickled me under the arm pits. I screamed in laughter. Part of me wanted to kick each one of them in the face while another part of me was enjoying the fun.

The doorbell rang just then, and the hands tickling me pulled away. My mother leapt up from her crouch and headed toward the door while Robin and I dragged ourselves to the couch.

We still hadn't stopped laughing when I heard a familiar voice behind the door. "Emma!" I exclaimed, springing up to greet her.

My mother held the door open as Emma came into the house and crushed her body into mine in an embrace. I winced when she pressed against my bad shoulder, but I tried not to let the pain show through because I was too excited to see her. Besides, it wasn't as bad as it had been a few days ago. Derek followed behind Emma and gave me a light hug.

Emma bounced on the balls of her feet. "We missed you."

"I missed you guys, too."

"So, did you have fun on your vacation?" Derek asked.

"It was pretty good," I answered, unable to hide the bit of blush that was brewing in my cheeks as I thought about how close Robin and I had become in the last few days. I glanced at him quickly and realized how awkward this must be for all of them. "Uh, guys, this is Robin," I introduced.

"We met before," Derek pointed out, which made me feel a bit like a fool.

"Right," I said.

I watched my mom exit to the kitchen, and then I looked back to Emma. She was giving me a wide eyed look like she was trying to tell me something, only I didn't know what. I furrowed my brow in confusion.

"We need to talk," she whispered even though everyone else in the room could hear her. She gripped my arm and pulled me toward my bedroom. "You two get to know each other or something," she called back. "We'll be right back."

I could hear Derek behind us. "Must be a girl thing."

"What is it, Emma?" I asked once she shut the door to my bedroom.

"I have something to tell you, but you have to promise you won't get mad at me."

I narrowed my eyes suspiciously. What could she say that I would be mad about? "Um, okay. I won't get mad."

"Promise?"

I wasn't entirely sure because my psychic radar wasn't picking up on what she was about to say, so I didn't know if it was something I should be mad about or not. "I promise," I said anyway.

Emma pressed her lips together as if stifling a smile, and her cheeks flushed. I could even see the blush beneath her tan complexion. "Derek kissed me."

I smiled at her, partially out of happiness and partially because it was my duty as a best friend to tease her. I raised my eyebrows a little. "Ooh," I said, elongating the sound.

"You're not mad?"

"No, why would I be mad?"

Emma shrugged. "I don't know. I mean, I knew he kind of liked you for a while, and I still wasn't sure if you felt the same way about him."

"Derek? No."

"It's just," she continued, "we kind of had time to get to know each other on a personal level with you gone, and I don't mean that in a bad way—that you being gone was a good thing, but it kind of was." Emma bit her lip and didn't meet my gaze. "Finding his dog, spending Thanksgiving with him, it was all just so—"

"Emma," I stopped her. "It's fine. I'm with Robin now anyway, remember?"

She nodded. "I don't want you to feel like a third wheel or something."

"Emma," I put a hand on her shoulder and stared seriously into her eyes. "I'm fine with it."

A giant smile formed on Emma's face. "Thank you so much, Crystal." Emma surprised me with a hug so tight I could barely breathe.

"Calm yourself," I teased.

Emma rushed out of my room and back down the hallway. I followed. She raised both her thumbs in excitement. "She said yes!"

Derek's smile grew, and he hugged Emma. "That's great!"

It was a little weird to see them together like that, but if Emma was going to be with any guy, I was glad it was Derek.

Just then, Teddy entered the room. "Ready, Kiddo?" he asked.

"Ready," I said, grabbing my purse off the side of the couch. "Sorry, guys, but I have somewhere I have to be," I told Emma and Derek. "We can hang out later, okay?"

A few minutes later, Teddy and I arrived at the police station. Hope's mom, Melinda, said she wanted to thank me personally for helping rescue Hope, and Teddy agreed to mediate a session—not that we needed a mediator, but I felt more confident facing Hope's mom with Teddy there, especially since a part of me still felt guilty for not finding her sooner.

Happiness washed over me when I spotted Hope standing by her mother's side. It gave me extra reassurance that I really had rescued her and it wasn't all in my head. Hope looked mostly like her dad, but I could see now that she had Melinda's eyes.

Teddy introduced us. Immediately, Melinda's arms enveloped me. I grimaced as she squeezed my injured shoulder tight, but I knew she probably didn't know I'd been hurt, and if she did, she was probably too overcome with emotion to remember.

"Thank you so much." Her voice cracked, and I didn't need to look at her to see that tears were falling down her face. She pulled away and looked me in the eyes. "Hope tells me you were the one who found her.

That's what the news has been saying, too, although they never mentioned you by name because you're a minor."

I nodded and gave her a reassuring smile. "Yeah, I did."

"I can't imagine. And what are the chances that you're from Peyton Springs, too?"

I shrugged because I didn't know what else to say. Surely I couldn't tell her it was all because of my abilities.

"Lucky, I guess. But I mean, Teddy was there, too, and he's been working on the case, so it's not that much of a coincidence." I was babbling, but I didn't want to have to explain myself, so I babbled instead.

Melinda wiped at her eyes. I looked down at Hope to see her smiling up at me and her hand held firmly against her mother's. It wouldn't surprise me if Melinda didn't let Hope go for a long time, which is why I was shocked with the next words that came out of her mouth.

"Hope won't stop talking about you. I'm looking for a babysitter who I can trust. My previous one is scared after what happened. I know I shouldn't let Hope out of my sight, but with Scott gone, I can't give up any extra work. Hope seems to really like you, so I thought maybe you'd be interested."

My jaw dropped in disbelief. I'd never imagined she would ask me this, and the thing was that I really liked Hope, too, and I knew we would have a blast together.

Melinda took my silence as a negative response. "It will only be a few hours every day after school. You would just have to pick her up from school and stay with her for two hours or so until I got home. You can have the weekends free."

"Please, Crystal," Hope begged. Her chocolate eyes widened until she looked like a sad puppy dog.

My shock only lasted another split second until I finally composed myself. "Yes!" I practically shouted. "I'd love to!"

Hope beamed at me, and I smiled back. After all the stress I went through to bring Hope home, I was glad I'd made a friend out of all of it. I could only wonder what I would gain from my next physic adventure.

INSPIRED BY FROST

ALICIA RADES

CHAPTER 1

$\mathcal{M}$y fingers quivered as I reached for the dress's zipper and a wave of nausea hit me. I closed my eyes and took a deep breath, hoping the dizziness would pass. The dressing room spun around me, and I braced myself against the bench in the corner for support. I opened my eyes and fixed them on a spot on the floor. Then the realization of what was happening hit me.

Not again, I thought. *Not now.*

The last few months had been fairly passive as far as my psychic abilities went. I had been practicing how to use them in case something like this happened again, but to have it happen now of all times was a bit of a shock. I was becoming a better psychic, and I had almost fully mastered the little things, but I still didn't know how to control my body when a ghost came around.

I lowered myself to the bench. The lavender dress still hung loose around my shoulders. I took a deep breath to steady myself, and when I looked up, there she was.

I could tell she was dead, partly due to the feeling I was getting. The other reason I knew she was dead was because I could see straight through her like she wasn't entirely there. Judging by how transparent she was, I knew she didn't have much time.

She had long brown hair, but nothing about her was particularly striking. I probably wouldn't remember her if I saw her on the street.

"Crystal?" she asked.

I didn't know how, but whenever a ghost came to me for help, he or she always knew my name and could tell that I could see them.

I wanted to help her. I always wanted to help anyone who came to me, but I was hoping I could enjoy a day of shopping with my mom for my maid of honor dress without any interruptions. Now that she was here, though, I couldn't push her away, not when she needed my help.

"What?" I managed breathlessly in almost a whisper so no one else would hear.

"My name is Melissa," the girl said. "And I need your help."

I swallowed. "How? How can I help you?" I tried to keep my tone as friendly as I could, but it came out sounding more urgent than I wanted it to.

"You need to save her."

"Save who?" Ghosts always had this way of telling me what to do without actually telling me what to do.

"Sage."

Sage? I didn't know any Sage. How could I help someone I didn't even know? I knew that fact alone would make this mission difficult.

"Sage Anderson," Melissa clarified.

"How? How can I save her? What's wrong with her?" I kept my voice to a low whisper.

Melissa blinked and shook her head in sadness. "She's too young. I don't want her to suffer the same fate."

"Huh?" was all I could say.

Then Melissa's eyes locked on mine. "If you can't save Sage, she's going to die. She'll take her last breath the next time you wear that dress. That is, unless you can save her."

My breath caught in my chest the same moment Melissa vanished. Something about her words, the way they seemed so final, told me she wasn't coming back. That was the first and last time I would see her.

A million questions raced through my head. *Who is Sage? How is she going to die? How can I save her? Will I be able to save her?*

A knock at the dressing room door startled me from my thoughts.

"Crystal, are you okay? What's taking so long?" my mother asked.

"Yeah," I called back, my voice wavering. I took a quick breath to calm my nerves. "I'm fine. I just... I can't reach the zipper." I unlocked the dressing room door and held it open a crack. "Can you help me?"

My mom pushed her way into the dressing room. It was a tight fit, but we were both small people. She was dressed in her regular jeans and tee since she'd already picked out her dress weeks ago. Now, with only four weeks left until the wedding, it felt like we were getting down to crunch time. It's not like the wedding was going to be huge or anything. It was just going to be family and close friends at one of the hotels here in the city.

My body shook slightly as my mom zipped up my dress and I thought about a girl whose life supposedly depended on me. I tried not to let it show, and even though I was always bad at hiding things, I didn't think my mother noticed my unease.

"How does that feel?" she asked once she had my zipper up.

I smoothed down the fabric and took a look at myself in the mirror. The dress had a tank-style lace top with a ribbon around the waist. The skirt fell just above my knees. It looked so good on me that I hardly noticed my nonexistent hips and flat chest. Best of all, the lace top complemented my mother's gown.

"I love it," I told her, but Melissa's words still echoed in my head. *She'll take her last breath the next time you wear that dress.* That meant that if we went with this one, I had until the wedding to save a girl I didn't even know. A mere month's time didn't seem like enough. "But, I don't know," I added. "Maybe we should keep looking." It didn't seem right to wear this dress and seal in Sage's fate.

"Well, come on," I heard Sophie's voice from outside the dressing room. "Let's see it on you!"

My mom and I emerged from the changing room. I glanced through the shop windows. The sun hung low in the sky. Since Mom ran a business with Sophie and Diane, her two best friends and bridesmaids, we had to go shopping when their shop was closed and everyone could get together away from work. On a normal day, the setting sun might bring thoughts of Robin to my mind and make me wonder how much time I would have to spend with him tonight before my curfew. But today, the setting sun only made me feel like time was already running out to save a girl I didn't even know.

Sophie and Diane were wearing the same dress I was. I eyed them and couldn't help but wonder if they could somehow assist me before it was too late for Sage. Like me, mom and her friends were all psychic. It's how they became friends in college and ended up opening their Halloween-themed shop, Divination, in my hometown.

Maybe, I thought, *they can help me figure out what Melissa meant and who she was talking about.* The thing was that in the past when they'd tried to help—like when I'd found a little girl named Hope who'd been abducted—they couldn't see anything about the situation. It was like the universe wanted me to do it all on my own.

"I like them," Diane said, twirling around in her own dress. She was a bigger woman, but the dress still looked great on her. In fact, it looked fantastic on all of us.

"It looks like we've found the one," Sophie agreed.

They both admired their new wedding attire in the full-length mirrors on the dressing room doors. I followed their gazes and noticed my fallen face. We couldn't choose this one, could we?

She'll take her last breath the next time you wear that dress.

If I never wore this dress again, that would mean she wouldn't die, right? I tried to put on a smile, but I wasn't sure how successful I was at it. *Should I tell them? Is it worth ruining this special day?*

Sophie turned to me. "Crystal, are you okay?"

I was never good at hiding my emotions with anyone, but it was impossible to hide behind a smile in front of Sophie. She was an empath, which meant she could feel other people's emotions and influence them.

I felt the tears stinging at my eyes already. I bit my lip to hold them back, but I couldn't help it. I flung myself into Sophie's arms and let a tear fall down my cheek. I shook my head. "No," I answered. "I'm not okay."

Suddenly, everyone was at my side. I didn't know where the lady who was helping us earlier went, but right now, it was just me, Mom, Sophie, and Diane, and I was grateful for that. I needed the privacy.

"Sweetie, what's wrong?" my mom asked.

Everyone went quiet for a beat while I composed myself. After I released Sophie, she led me over to one of the nearby chairs and sat me down.

I took a deep breath. "It's happening again. I—I saw someone in the dressing room."

They all exchanged glances, looking for something to say. My mother knelt beside me and took my hand. "It's okay. You can tell us."

I nodded. I knew that much. It was a secret we all shared together. The thing was that I was the only one of all of us who could see ghosts. It felt like an overwhelming responsibility.

"She said her name was Melissa. She warned me that someone was going to die and that I needed to help her. I really don't want to see someone die if there's something I can do about it." I didn't add what I really wanted to say: *I'm terrified.*

"Sweetie, you know we're always here for you, right?" my mom said.

I nodded again, but I knew there was meaning behind those words that she wouldn't voice aloud. They were there for me emotionally, but their abilities couldn't help me.

"Did she say anything else?" Diane asked.

I nodded again and spoke so softly that even if someone was close by, they wouldn't overhear. "She said that the girl who needed help was named—"

"How are you ladies liking that dress?" a voice interrupted. The woman who was helping us before returned.

We all shifted to look at her. A girl a little older than me with dark red hair, pale skin, and freckles across her nose stood next to her.

"I'm terribly sorry," the lady said, "but I have a family emergency. If you need anything, you can ask Sage." The lady gestured to the young woman beside her.

My heart stopped.

CHAPTER 2

I forced down the lump in my throat. This had to be the girl Melissa was talking about. I mean, how common is the name Sage, and why would I meet this girl here immediately after I received a warning if it wasn't her? I knew it was her and that if I didn't do anything, she was going to die.

Sage put on a friendly smile and introduced herself to each of us. I wasn't as good as Sophie was at it, but I could get feelings about people's emotions if I touched them. When Sage held out her hand to me, I rose from my seat and put on my best smile. I shook her hand, hoping to learn something from it.

I must have thought I would get all my answers right away, like how she was going to die, but all I got was a feeling of terror—her terror—when I touched her. She was afraid of something or someone, only I didn't know what or who.

How are you going to die, Sage? I wondered. *How can I help?*

But what was I supposed to do? I couldn't tell her she was going to die and hope she'd let me know how. Surely, she wouldn't believe me, and it would only make things worse as far as my involvement went. I had to find some way to get close to her so I could investigate her impending death, except I had no idea how to do that.

Sage complimented our dress choice and made a few suggestions for accessories before I had a chance to fully process the situation. Diane seemed suddenly interested in what Sage had to say and led her over to a rack of sashes while asking questions. Diane shot us back a glance that said she was giving us privacy.

I returned to my chair, and my mom and Sophie stood on either side of me. "That's her," I whispered, stealing a glance at Sage. "The girl in the dressing room said Sage was going to die. That has to be her."

Sophie nodded in understanding. "I can feel her fear. She's afraid of something."

"I know," I agreed. "Only, I don't know what."

Sophie bit her lip. "Me, either."

My mother rubbed my shoulder sympathetically. "I'm sorry, but maybe I can give a bit of advice. She's about your age. Why not try making friends with her? You might find out a bit more."

"Yeah, but I don't know what to say to her." I pressed my lips together nervously and peered at Diane and Sage again. Diane was successfully keeping her preoccupied.

"Mom, Melissa—the ghost girl in the dressing room—said I have until the wedding to save Sage. Well, what she said is that I have until the next time I wear this dress. I don't think we should get these ones. Then maybe Melissa's prophecy won't come true."

Sophie shook her head. "I don't think it works that way. I don't think it will matter what dresses we get. The good news is that you have a clear timeline."

"*And* you know who the girl is," my mom added. "We'll try to help you the best we can, but when it comes to interfering with another psychic's mission, the rest of us are just normal people."

I understood all too well what she was saying. Each time the universe had picked me for a mission, none of them saw what I saw. Sure, they'd been helpful, and I'd learned a lot about my abilities from them, but I knew any new piece to the puzzle would have to come from me.

Then I realized something. They had all helped me with a séance before, and it had worked. What if we tried contacting Melissa to get more answers?

That seemed like a good idea, so I mentioned it to them. They both agreed that we could try contacting her when we returned home. I smiled, mostly to reassure myself I could do this but also because I was glad to have their support.

"Why not try to get some answers from Sage first?" my mom suggested.

"Okay," I agreed. "Just give me a few minutes."

I took a deep breath and rose from my seat. I casually strolled over to the jewelry and tried to make it look like I was interested in the earrings. What I was really doing was stealing glances at Sage and Diane. When it seemed like they were finally done talking about accessories, I cleared my throat.

"Um, Sage?" I asked.

"Yeah?" She smiled, but it didn't quite reach her eyes.

"I'm curious if you have any suggestions for jewelry." My voice wavered a little, but she didn't seem to notice.

"Oh, sure."

"I'm Crystal, by the way."

"Crystal. That's a pretty name."

I tucked a long strand of blonde hair behind my ear. "My boyfriend says my name is really special because it's like my first name is an adjective and my last name is a noun. Crystal Frost is my full name."

Sage tilted her head slightly. "He's right. That is really cool." She held out a pair of earrings to me. They dangled and were adorned with a purple gem atop a pearl. "These would look great with your dress. We also sell a matching necklace."

I lightly touched the owl necklace hanging around my neck. It was the one Teddy had given me when he proposed to my mom. I rarely took it off. I knew it was kind of dumb, but I felt like it gave me good luck.

"I already have a necklace in mind for the wedding," I told her, "but I really like the earrings."

"Do you want to see them on you?" she offered.

"Really?"

"Sure." She held them up to me.

I placed them in my ears and looked into the mirror next to the jewelry. "I really like them."

Hopefully I was connecting with her on some level. I wanted to see some indication of how I was going to save her, but I knew I couldn't push it. The universe had a way of showing things to me when it thought I was ready. Still, I couldn't help but want the answers right away.

"So, uh, this must be a pretty cool job, huh?" I asked. "You help women pick out dresses and accessories. It's like every girl's fashion dream."

Sage gave a light laugh. "Not really. I'm just saving up money for after high school. It's kind of tough since I only work on the weekends, but it's something."

"Well, you're lucky your job probably pays well," I said. "All I have is a babysitting job that pays only a few dollars an hour." I didn't bother mentioning that I loved babysitting Hope and would probably do it for free, but I was mostly aiming to find a common element between us. Perhaps that would give me a reason to talk with her more and learn more about her predicted death. When she didn't say anything, I tried another route. "Apart from that, I'm usually busy with extracurricular activities. Do you do anything fun at school?"

She shook her head. "No, not really."

"I play volleyball in the fall, and I'm in the band. I play clarinet. You don't play anything?"

She shook her head again. "I, uh, used to, but not anymore. But I still like music."

Disappointment washed over me. How much more could I say before I only pushed her away? Maybe I could fake a dress emergency during the week and come back here. Wait. That wouldn't work because she said she only worked on weekends.

But music... I might be able to work with that. "My boyfriend is in a band. Not the school band like me. They're more into pop, but they write their own songs. You should check them out sometime. They're actually going to be playing at my mom's reception."

Sage shrugged. "There are some local bands I've been meaning to check out, but I don't know. I don't really have the time." She bit her lip nervously like she wasn't telling me the whole truth. I got the feeling it was about whatever she was afraid of.

"Maybe you could give me your number and I could text you when their next performance is," I suggested.

"Oh, uh, I don't mean to be rude, but I don't really give out my number."

"I understand," I said as kindly as I could, but I was actually disappointed.

"But you seem really nice," she said with a shy smile. "I guess it wouldn't hurt to actually get out once in a while."

I grinned, perhaps too excitedly. I would be able to see her again and maybe get some more answers! At the same time I got excited about getting her number, I realized that it was too easy. I could only wonder what would go wrong later.

CHAPTER 3

$\mathcal{M}$y first indication that something was wrong happened when we got in the car. We had purchased our dresses, and Mom had even bought me the pearl earrings. I slipped my phone out of my pocket and opened the Facebook app, hoping to learn more about Sage on her profile. I found a few other Sage Andersons online, but based on the profile pictures, none of them were her. I tried Twitter, Pinterest, and Instagram but didn't find a single profile matching the girl I'd met in the bridal shop. I even turned to Googling her name, but all I came up with was the social profiles of other girls whose pages I already looked at.

How could a girl about my age *not* have a Facebook account? Or maybe her profile was buried beneath all the other results. I hadn't realized Sage was a common name, let alone that there was more than one Sage Anderson in the world. I tried narrowing my search but still couldn't find her.

Then a thought hit me. What if the Sage I met at the bridal shop wasn't the girl I was supposed to save? What if her last name wasn't Anderson and I was focusing on the wrong person? What if one of the Sage Andersons showing up in my search was the girl Melissa warned me about?

No, that didn't seem right. It had to be the girl in the bridal shop. No matter how long I thought about it, I couldn't come up with a clear answer.

Robin and I had planned to hang out after my shopping trip since I was already in the city and that's where he lived, but I called him disappointedly and told him I couldn't make it. I didn't tell him about Sage yet because I hoped I would have more answers after we tried contacting Melissa.

Robin and I had been dating since our trip to Florida last Thanksgiving when I rescued Hope and learned about Robin's car accident that led to his prosthetic leg. Our relationship was somewhat odd because his uncle Teddy was engaged to my mom, so in a few short weeks we'd technically be step-cousins, but we'd long gotten over that fact, and no one else seemed to mind since we weren't blood related.

But I couldn't hang out with him right now, not when a girl's life depended on me. He didn't ask me why I couldn't come over, but he did ask if I was alright.

"I'm fine," I told him honestly. "After we finished shopping, we realized we had something else to do, and it's not something that can wait until the wedding."

He seemed to understand even though I wasn't telling him the whole truth. I wasn't exactly lying to him either, but I didn't want to worry him.

After I ended my call with him, I found Emma's number in my contacts. She was my best friend and knew about my abilities, too. Emma had even been trying to channel her inner psychic over the past few months and was getting really good at it. The way my mom put it, Emma didn't have a natural connection to the other side like I did, but since everyone is mildly psychic, the work she'd put into practicing had made her a bit more psychic than the average person. I told her briefly about Melissa and Sage and that we were holding another séance.

"That's so cool," Emma raved. She was always excited when I brought up anything related to the paranormal, and she had taken it upon herself to research the crap out of anything supernatural. We even had regular practice sessions together. I knew Emma probably wanted Derek to join us, but even after all this time, he was still a bit of a skeptic.

When we arrived home, the house was empty. Teddy had said that since we'd be gone anyway, he might as well work the weekend at the station. Even though Mom and Teddy weren't married yet, he'd completely moved in a few months ago.

I hung up my lavender dress in my closet, which felt oddly depressing thanks to Melissa's warning. It wasn't supposed to be like this. Picking out my maid of honor dress was supposed to be fun. I lingered at my closet door for a few seconds, staring at the dress. *But it will be worth it*, I thought, *if I can save her.*

I forced my gaze off the dress and headed back to the living room. On my way out of my room, I caught a glimpse of my crystal ball on my dresser. I made a mental note to try that later if the séance didn't work.

Sadly, crystal ball gazing was one of the skills I still couldn't quite get down.

Mom already had candles placed around the kitchen table. When I walked into the room, I made a note of how there were six chairs around the table but there would only be five of us conducting the séance. I wondered briefly what it would be like if Teddy filled that empty chair.

When I first found out about my—and my mom's—abilities, Teddy didn't know either. I'd helped Mom tell him, and he seemed accepting of it. Only later did I find out that he had a heightened sense of intuition, a type of psychic power, although it wasn't as strong as the rest of ours. I wasn't entirely sure what Teddy was capable of, but the way I understood it, he and Emma were at about the same level. They were both believers with mild abilities.

I still couldn't pinpoint why there were so many psychic people in my life. Part of me wondered if it was just more common than I thought and that everyone who was psychic thought they were a freak and tried to hide it. Another part of me wondered if maybe it was the universe's way of helping me learn to accept my abilities.

Emma came in the door just as my mom lit the first candle. She was my best friend, so there was no need for her to knock. She dropped her duffel bag and pulled me into a hug that sizzled with excitement.

"I know hosting a séance usually means bad news for someone," Emma said, "but it's so cool to be a part of it again."

I smiled. Her enthusiasm lifted my mood slightly. "I'm glad you're here."

Sophie and Diane shuffled around the house to shut the shades. We definitely didn't want anyone to see what we were up to. We still didn't know how the community would react if they found out the town's Halloween and herbal gurus had real powers.

I eyed Diane as she lowered the shade above the sink, and I wondered something out loud. "Do you think we'll ever tell people?"

"What?" my mom asked in confusion.

I pulled my eyes off Diane and looked at my mother. Drawing out a chair at the table, I sat down as I spoke. "I was just wondering what would happen if the community knew about us. Do you think they'd accept us?"

My mother shook her head in amusement. "Crystal, I don't think you realize how lucky you are. We weren't lucky enough to have a network of psychics at our fingertips when we were growing up. My grandma was psychic, but that was it for me. Sophie did have a big family of psychics. But even so, we've all learned that not everyone is so accepting of the paranormal. I think it's best if the town went on believing Divination was based off the make believe. The ones who understand the true nature of some of our products will seek us out. Other people don't always understand."

I let her words sink in for a moment. Maybe I had been too lucky lately.

"Okay," I nodded and left it at that, but her words only made me wonder when the time would come for a friend to turn away from me because of my gift.

My mom flipped off the lights, and everyone situated themselves around the table. Emma and I had only been to one séance before, the one we held to contact Olivia Owen's ghost, which ended in me rescuing a classmate from an abusive relationship. Even though I was fairly inexperienced in séances, I was confident that if we could contact Melissa, I had the best team of people to do it sitting in my kitchen.

"Last time, we all held hands," I said, "so I think that's what we should do now." I gripped onto Emma's hand to my left and my mom's to my right.

"Remember, Crystal," my mom said, "this is your ghost, so you'll have to lead the séance."

I nodded. Even though I'd been doing my best over the past few months to confront my abilities and get better at them, I wasn't entirely sure about doing this. *Is there another Sage out there I'm supposed to meet? Will Melissa make contact?*

I took a deep breath to calm my nerves. My mind told me to rush through this to get the answers that might save a girl's life, but I also knew that nothing would come if I hurried.

I spoke softly and gave a gentle reminder to everyone to clear their minds. I tried to let go of any uncertainties I had. When I met Melissa in the dressing room and she faded, it seemed like she wasn't coming back. Would a séance work, then? I didn't know.

I also couldn't help but notice that none of us knew anything about Melissa. All I knew was her face and her name. I didn't even have a last name. How could the rest of them focus on someone they couldn't even put a face to? Last time, we had something that belonged to the ghost: Olivia's volleyball jersey. This time, we had nothing.

Luckily, I'd practiced enough over the past few months that I was able to push these thoughts aside and clear my head. I opened my mind to the other side and encouraged everyone else to do the same. I could feel a heightened energy in the room, one that told me we were doing everything right, but I couldn't feel a spirit anywhere nearby.

"Melissa," I called out after a few minutes. I wished I had gotten her last name so I had more to go by. "You told me to help Sage. I need more answers. I need more so that I can help her."

We sat in silence for several long minutes. Nobody moved or spoke. We were all so concentrated on the spiritual realm that if someone was listening in on us, they wouldn't hear a thing. Even the breathing around the table had slowed to hardly make a sound.

"Melissa," I called out several minutes later. Nothing. Absolutely nothing.

Was it my uncertainty in this task that made it impossible? Was it because I had very little to go on to get her to come to me? All I could do was call her name.

So that's what I did. Another half hour must have passed. Every few minutes, I called Melissa's name. I periodically reminded everyone to clear their minds. Even with all the thoughts racing around in my own head, I felt confident in my connection with the other side. I knew I had cleared my mind enough that I should come up with *something*, but nothing happened.

After what must have been 45 minutes of silence, I finally broke the circle. "She's not going to show," I told everyone. Hadn't I already known that since she disappeared in the dressing room? I knew she wasn't coming back to help me, and that fact scared me, like I was all alone on this. Then I gazed around the table and remembered I wasn't alone.

"Even though Melissa probably isn't going to show up again, we can still save Sage," I told them with confidence. "We have until the wedding." A shiver traveled down my spine when I realized how little time that truly was.

CHAPTER 4

I slumped to my bed in disappointment. "I can't let her die," I told Emma.

"Crystal, she's not going to die. She has you on her side." Emma sat next to me on my bed.

I gave a smile at her compliment, but I wasn't quite sure. In the past, it seemed like I'd never paid enough attention to my visions. This time, I wasn't going to make that mistake. Still, no one's life had depended on me before. Sure, I'd helped people who were in danger, but I'd never had to save someone from *death*.

The questions that sprang to my head only seemed to create a bigger problem. How was I going to prevent it? What could I do? How was she even going to die?

"I feel like I just wasted an hour. Trying to contact Melissa was useless, and now Sage is another hour closer to dying."

"Don't beat yourself up over it, Crystal," Emma said. "I have a good feeling about this. You're going to save her."

With Emma's practice, she'd become talented at assessing situations and determining if they were good or bad. At first, I didn't believe in her abilities, but I've started trusting them more and more. So when Emma said she had a good feeling about my involvement, it really did lift my spirits.

"I hope you're not lying to me," I told her, but I didn't think she was.

"Cross my heart and hope to die." Emma drew an imaginary X over her heart.

I paused for a moment and swallowed deeply. "You probably shouldn't say things like that."

She frowned. "Yeah, you're right. I'm sorry."

I stood from the bed and paced around the room to ease my nerves. "I don't want to waste any time trying to figure out how Sage is going to die and how I'm going to help her, but I don't know what else to do. I already tried to learn more about her online, but it's like she doesn't exist on the Internet. Don't you think that's weird?"

Emma nodded and shifted on the bed. "That is really weird. Doesn't she at least have a Facebook account?"

I shook my head. "Not that I could find. I'm wondering if the girl from the bridal shop is the same girl Melissa warned me about. I mean, why else would a ghost warn me about a girl named Sage if I was only going to meet a girl with that very same name minutes later? This doesn't make sense."

Before Emma could offer her opinion, my phone began buzzing in my pocket. "Hello?" I answered, sliding back down onto the bed.

"Crystal," Robin greeted.

Emma raised her eyebrows. "Is it Robin?" she whispered, leaning in until I could feel her breath on the side of my face.

I swatted her away but couldn't help but smile at Robin's voice despite the troubles I was having. "Yeah?"

"I just wanted to call and see how your thing went. Did you get everything figured out?"

"Not really," I answered honestly. "But I'm glad you called because I just remembered something. I was wondering when your next gig was. There's a girl I met today when we were shopping who said she wanted to check you guys out." I only hoped I wasn't wasting time on the wrong girl.

"We're playing this coming weekend at Bradshaw Park. I already told you about that. It's for Asher's brother's birthday party, remember?"

"Yeah, I guess I forgot that was this weekend. You don't mind if I invite someone?"

"Nah, Troy won't care if more people come. He'll probably just feel more popular or something."

"Thanks." I wanted to steer the conversation toward Sage and her death so I could confide in Robin. To hell with him worrying. I knew if I wanted this relationship to last, I couldn't hide anything from him, not even things related to my abilities. "Um, about the girl I'm bringing. I have something to tell you about her."

"Uh, okay."

"When we were shopping for my dress, I saw this ghost." I paused to gauge his reaction.

Emma shifted on the bed and picked at her fingernails like she wasn't listening, even though I knew she was invested in every detail of the conversation.

"Okay," Robin said slowly as if he didn't know where I was going with this.

I stood again and paced a few steps around the room before flashing a glance at Emma, looking for some way to help explain it all. "She gave me a warning and told me a girl named Sage was going to die soon. I'm still not sure—"

"Wait," Robin interrupted. "Sage who?"

"Anderson. Well, that's what the ghost said."

"You're kidding."

"No, I'm not."

"You're telling me a ghost told you that Sage Anderson is going to die?"

"Yeah. What?" I paused for a second, and then realization sank in. "Do you know her?"

"She goes to my school. I mean, we're not exactly best friends, but she's my lab partner. Crystal, if Sage is going to die, we have to save her."

My knees rapidly grew weak. I sank back down onto the bed to steady myself.

"Crystal, what's wrong?" Emma asked.

I stuck a hand up to tell her to give me a minute. "Does the Sage you know work at Special Day Bridal?"

"I think so."

Suddenly, I became very excited. Perhaps the emotion was a bit unwarranted, but at least that meant the girl I met today was the girl I was supposed to save. Granted, she was in danger, but I wasn't completely lost and wondering whose death I could prevent.

"Robin," I said breathlessly into the receiver. "You're my connection!" I had been looking for something that would connect us earlier, and now Sage and I had something in common: Robin.

"What do you mean?" he asked.

"Are you at least close enough that she might hang out with you?"

I could practically hear Robin shrug on the other end of the line. "I guess so. She doesn't really hang out with anyone, but maybe if I asked her..."

I mentally added that bit of information to the weirdness surrounding Sage. I mean, it wasn't like she was socially awkward or super ugly or anything. How could she be a loner?

"You guys are practicing at Asher's on Tuesday night, right? What if you invited her to come watch you practice? Then Emma and I can come over, too." I was happy the end of basketball season a few weeks ago also marked the end of pep band for the school year, so I was finally free to watch them practice. "I don't think I can wait a whole week to learn more about her," I added.

"I guess I can try, but I don't know if she'll say yes."

"Thank you, Robin! Asher's parents won't mind?"

"No, they're pretty cool."

"Okay. Do you know much about Sage? I mean, does it seem like she's in danger?"

"Not that I've picked up on," he admitted. "We talk a little in class, but she mostly keeps to herself. I'll let you know if I notice anything, though."

"Thank you, Robin."

I hung up only for Emma to immediately jump into her inquisition. "What was that about? It sounded like he knows Sage? Did he say 'I love you?' Why didn't you say it back?"

I shoved her lightheartedly, mostly to hide the blush rising to my cheeks. "No, he didn't because neither of us have said it yet. It's not like you and Derek have, either."

"I'm waiting for him to say it first," she defended.

"Maybe I'm doing the same thing."

We both immediately dropped the subject because neither of us wanted to discuss the fact that even after five months, for both of our relationships, the "L" word still hadn't come up once.

"Anyway," I said, "Robin *does* know Sage. He's going to ask her to come to his practice on Tuesday."

"And I suppose you want me to drive you there," Emma said.

Emma had her driver's license, and I had only recently got my learner's permit. I nodded.

"Okay," she answered. "Derek's invited, too, right?"

"Yeah. As long as Asher's parents are okay with so many people coming along."

When I asked Mom about going to Asher's on Tuesday, she insisted I call to make sure his parents would be home. Mom was always more like a best friend to me than a mother, but ever since I started dating, she'd been getting more protective. The rule was that I couldn't hang out with Robin unless an adult was present or we were in public. I explained to her about Sage and her connection with Robin, and then she seemed more accepting of letting me go. She still made me call as a courtesy.

I wasn't exactly great friends with Asher yet, but we'd met a few months back after Robin and I started dating, so I had his number programmed into my phone. The good news was that Asher didn't care if we tagged along, and his mom was going to be there. Apparently, his family had this "the more, the merrier" policy.

I couldn't wait. That night, I lay in bed wide awake as Emma snored lightly on the fold-up cot next to me. I could usually get little bits of information about people just by focusing on them, but it never seemed to work when I was sent to save them. It's like the universe didn't think the little things were important when I knew fully well that they were.

I fell asleep without learning anything new about Sage Anderson.

$\mathcal{I}$ woke Sunday morning to Emma's ringtone. She shifted on the cot and reached for her phone in her overnight bag on the floor. The sunlight seeped through my curtains, casting a sliver of light across my bed. I checked my clock and found it was already 8:00. I stretched, thinking about how well I'd slept, and then the memory of everything that happened the day before came flooding back to me. Suddenly, I felt guilty for sleeping so well when a girl's life depended on me. But honestly, I had no idea what to do next.

"Derek wants us to hang out with him after he comes home from church," Emma told me.

What I really wanted to do was talk with Sage. I reached for my own phone on my nightstand and spun it around in my hands. I didn't even realize what I was doing until Emma spoke again.

"You're thinking about Sage, aren't you?"

"What?" I jerked my eyes up at her. How did she know?

"It's written all over your face. You're like an open book, Crystal."

I sighed. She was right about that.

"Be careful," Emma warned. "You don't want to come across too pushy. You want her to trust you."

I nodded and looked down in disappointment at my phone again. It felt like any moment I wasn't learning more about Sage was time wasted, but at the same time, I understood where Emma was coming from.

"So, Derek's?" I asked. "Sounds fun."

While we waited for Derek to get home, Emma insisted we have one of our psychic practice sessions. Normally we practiced after I was done babysitting Hope, but Emma said that since we'd be at Asher's later this week, doing it now would make up for our Tuesday practice.

With a reluctant eye roll, I agreed. She was right. Even with the progress we'd both made, I still needed to practice my abilities.

I unrolled my owl yoga mat across my carpet while Emma reached into her bag and pulled out her own mat. My room wasn't exactly the cleanest place on earth, but most of the mess was piled in front of my dresser where a heap of clean clothes sat unfolded and a drawer was open. That left enough room for the both of us to stretch out.

"How did you know?" I asked accusingly, eyeing Emma's yoga mat.

"What?" she asked innocently as she situated her mat on my floor.

"You were just using Tuesday as a convenient excuse, weren't you? You would have come up with anything to make us practice."

Emma shrugged as a smile crept across her lips. "You know me well."

I twisted my mouth up at her in discontent. Still, I couldn't help but be grateful for her persistence. Without it, I wasn't sure how good my abilities would be at this point. Plus, I was itching to make a psychic connection with Sage.

But, of course, I couldn't let Emma know I was happy about this practice session. There'd be too much pride in it for her.

"After our warm-up exercises, I thought we could practice more with your crystal ball," Emma said. "I mean, *you* should practice, but I'll be here to help if I can. I'm not nearly ready for crystal ball gazing yet."

I nodded. Maybe it would give me a glimpse into Sage's near future, like how she was going to die. Then I'd have a better idea of how I could save her. Unfortunately, I didn't have a way of controlling the information that came to me.

"Ready?" Emma asked, stretching her arms above her head to loosen them up.

"Yep."

She fiddled with her phone for a few seconds until a soothing melody began playing out of it. Our first 10 to 15 minutes or so of each session was spent clearing our minds and relaxing our bodies. When we started these sessions, Emma would tell me what to do, but now we just gave each other time to do whatever our bodies felt was needed to clear our minds.

I took a few deep breaths and forced the muscles in my face to relax. I could hear Emma's deep breathing next to me. She let out a soft hum.

I breathed in and out slowly and deeply as I concentrated on different points in my shoulders and back to relieve any tension. The task proved difficult as I worried about my newfound responsibility toward Sage. *How can I save her when I don't know what danger she's really in?*

I rolled my head to the side to stretch my neck.

I tried my best not to think; I attempted to clear my mind, but it was to no avail. As time passed and I worked my way through my yoga poses, my thoughts ran in a web of connections that eventually took me to a memory of my father before he died.

I was all of four years old when our next door neighbor, Mrs. James, fell in her kitchen. In the winter, Dad was always there to shovel Mrs. James's driveway. In the summer, he'd even cut her grass without asking for anything in return. So when she fell and managed to reach a phone, my dad was the first person she called. He ran over to her house immediately and called an ambulance.

"Daddy," I remember asking, "why did you have to help Mrs. James? Why did she call you?" What I was really trying to ask is why she hadn't called the ambulance herself, but I don't think I ever quite worded it right because what my father said next stuck with me.

"Crystal," he had said, "sometimes we're called on to help other people. Sometimes it's because people trust us. Other times it's just sheer luck. And you know what? It's our duty to rise to the challenge and help them. If we don't help each other, that's when we stop being human."

I heard Emma shift on her mat, and I took this reminder to make my own body move. I folded my legs under me and positioned myself onto all fours, my head turned up and my belly sunk toward the floor in cow pose.

I wasn't entirely sure if I was remembering my father's words correctly, but as I looked back on them, I had to wonder if he was trying to tell me something more important than I ever imagined.

I pulled my chin and tailbone into my body and stretched my spine upward into cat pose.

Was he trying to tell me that someday I would be called on to help people? Because of my abilities?

Cow pose.

He knew my mom was psychic, so maybe he thought I was, too, which turned out to be the truth.

Cat pose.

Was that why I was always so desperate to help anyone who crossed my path? Was it because of what my dad said to me when I was four?

I curled my toes into the mat, lifted my knees from the floor, and pushed my butt toward the sky to position myself into downward facing dog.

What would things be like if I hadn't been psychic like Mom had thought for so many years? No one would have come to me for help, and I wouldn't have a responsibility toward anyone.

I slowly lowered my entire body to the mat and then lifted my chest up into cobra pose.

A normal life. That sounded pretty nice. It'd be like it was before last Halloween.

I paused back in downward facing dog.

I'd be able to hang out with my friends care-free and enjoy my teenage years without abuse, abductions, and death on my mind.

I shifted my body weight between each of my legs, pressing my heels into the mat to stretch my calves.

But wait. That would mean that my mom would still be hiding her secret and that we wouldn't have this bond anymore. That would mean that Kelli might still be in an abusive relationship and that, after everyone but me gave up on her, Hope would still be in Lauren's hands. That would mean that Robin and I would have never taken that side trip last Thanksgiving and gotten to know each other and started dating.

That would mean that Sage wouldn't have a chance.

A loud clap snapped me out of my thoughts. I fell to my knees and jerked my eyes up toward the sound.

"I'm sorry," Emma said. "I didn't mean to clap that loud. Ready to move on?"

With me, Sage has a chance, I thought, which filled me with a sense of hope.

Emma and I continued through our exercises. We started by writing down three predictions for tomorrow. Mine were really dumb, like what was going to be on the lunch menu. We had done this exercise so many times that I could see little things like that with ease. What I really wanted was to see something about Sage, but even as I focused on her, I couldn't see even the tiniest bit of detail.

Next, Emma made me leave the room while she hid an object for me to find. I was gifted with psychometry like my mom. When I reentered the room, I knew exactly what she'd hidden before I even touched anything. That's because the one thing in the room that was always in its proper position was missing. Emma had hid my stuffed owl, Luna. I immediately unzipped Emma's duffel bag and found Luna sitting on top.

"Whoa." Emma took a step back in shock.

"What?" I asked with a shrug. "I didn't do anything different, did I?"

Emma nodded slowly, like she was unsure of what I'd just done. "You didn't even touch my hand to find out what was missing."

Oh. She was right. Normally I needed something to touch that had recently been around the hidden object.

"Well," I said, "I noticed Luna had moved as soon as I entered the room, so maybe since I already knew what was missing, I knew where it was."

"Or maybe you're just getting better," Emma theorized. "Or maybe it's because you're so attached to Luna."

"What?" I practically squeaked. "I am not."

That was such a lie, and Emma knew it. Still, I turned my face and put Luna back on her shelf so Emma wouldn't notice how blatantly I was lying—since my eyebrow twitched every time I lied. The truth was, I was attached to Luna. After all, my father had given her to me.

"Okay, your turn," I told Emma.

Emma didn't have psychometry. She could never tell what I hid, but she could get feelings about situations. It was like she could tell when she was hot or cold because of which decision felt better to her.

Once she left the room, I searched for something to hide. I couldn't make it too hard for her, but I also couldn't make it too easy. I stood in the middle of my room for several long moments wondering what I should hide for her. When my wandering eyes fell to my feet, I was reminded of the first time we played this game and Emma hid her sock. I decided to do the same. I slipped off the other sock just so she wouldn't notice I was missing one.

"Okay, you can come back in," I called.

She stood by my open door with her eyes closed for what seemed like forever. I knew she was trying to get "in the zone," as she put it, but her silence left me wondering if I had made it too hard for her. I sat on the end of my bed and simply observed.

After a while, she began moving around my room. She'd go one way and then turn around and pace a few steps the other way. She did this several times, inching closer and closer to the sock each time. Several long minutes passed. Finally, she stood over her duffel bag and opened her eyes.

"You hid it in the same place, you dirty little cheat!" she exclaimed.

"Well, I didn't think you'd look there."

She opened her bag and threw my sock at my face. We both laughed.

"Okay. Are you ready for crystal ball gazing?" Emma asked.

I sighed. "I guess." This was one thing I still wasn't good at, and it always made me nervous. I crossed the room and picked up my crystal ball from where it stood on my dresser. Every time I touched the ball, it called out to me somehow. Colors swirled in it, and I felt nothing but tranquility.

Suddenly, Emma's ringtone cut through the silence. I jumped, and the ball slipped out of my fingers. It fell with a thud onto the clothes in my open dresser drawer.

"I'm sorry!" Emma said. "It's just Derek. He says he's back from church."

"I guess our practice is cut a little short today." I knew that even as much as Emma loved practicing her psychic abilities, she wanted to get to her boyfriend's house as soon as possible.

"I guess so," she agreed.

I glanced back at my crystal ball and lazily decided to let it lay where it was. Besides, it looked kind of cozy tucked in a cradle made of my tees.

CHAPTER 6

*W*hen we reached Derek's, we entered his house without knocking. I still found it weird, like I was intruding, but ever since Emma and Derek started dating, things had shifted slightly in our group of three. It wasn't so bad that I felt left out or like a third wheel or anything, but even after a few months, it was still awkward to witness their peck when they greeted each other. The good news was that Derek's parents adored Emma.

"Do you guys want to see it?" Derek asked excitedly.

"See what?" I replied.

"My driver's license. That's why I left school early on Friday. Remember? I texted you about it."

Derek handed over his license, and Emma and I gazed at it with enthusiasm. Milo—Derek's dog—sniffed at me while I tried to get a good look, so I petted him softly to calm him down.

"That's great that you passed the first time, Derek," I said, momentarily reminding myself that now everyone I knew could drive and I was still the youngest one around. At least it gave me a chance to hang out with my friends when I needed a ride, though.

We said hello to his parents and twin sisters and then followed Derek to his bedroom—but had to leave the door open per his parents' rules. He eagerly told us about his driving test.

I sat in his desk chair while Emma and Derek claimed a seat on his bed.

"I know you haven't talked about it a lot, Derek," Emma started, "but this just reminds me of your birth parents. Did your mom and dad ever really tell you more about them?"

Derek had found out he was adopted when he got his learner's permit and he caught a glimpse of his birth certificate. When he finally admitted his secret—well, not so much admitted it as much as I found out because of my psychic abilities—he said he didn't care because his birth parents were dead and it didn't change that his adoptive parents were still his parents.

He shrugged in response to Emma's question. "I guess my mom and dad have always felt like my mom and dad. I don't really feel any need to search for information about my birth parents."

Emma ran her fingers through her curly dark hair. "Wouldn't it at least be nice to kind of know where you came from?"

"It's not like I'm having an identity crisis," Derek said lightheartedly, like he didn't care to know what happened to them. I couldn't bring myself to believe he wasn't at least curious.

"I know." Emma shifted on the bed. "I guess I just feel like if I found out I was adopted, I would at least do a Google search and try to figure out more about my birth parents."

Derek shrugged again. "I guess."

"Well, why not?" She stood from the bed and shooed me from my spot by Derek's computer. "What were their names?"

"Uh, Thomas and Sharon Woods. I got the Johnson last name from my mom and dad," he explained, meaning his adoptive parents.

Emma typed his dad's name into the search bar.

Meanwhile, I turned to Derek. "Want to hear about the crazy stuff that happened to me this weekend?"

"Psychic related?" he guessed.

I nodded.

Derek still had a hint of doubt about my abilities, but he'd been supportive about it the entire time. He said he wanted to believe it, and I found comfort in confiding in him. I told him about the warning and about meeting Sage at the bridal shop. I also told him about how I couldn't find anything online about Sage. He agreed that her online absence was odd.

"Dang it," Emma complained, interrupting us. "Derek, why didn't your birth parents have less common names?" She didn't even look up when she said this, which led me to believe it was a rhetorical question.

"Anyway," I continued, "Robin knows Sage and is going to try to get her to come watch his band practice on Tuesday. Emma is driving me, and you're invited, too."

"I bet Emma is dying to go," he teased. "She drools over musicians."

I laughed because it was so true, but Emma remained glued to the screen like she didn't hear us. Derek wasn't in the school band like Emma and I were, but he had conveniently began learning guitar since they started dating.

I caught a glimpse of the guitar in the corner of his room and raised my eyebrows. "You know, you don't need to learn guitar for Emma to drool over you. That just comes naturally to her."

He tried to hide it, but I could see him blushing. "I'm not learning for her," he lied.

"Yeah, right," I teased.

"This is useless." Emma swiveled the chair back toward us. "There are too many people named Thomas and Sharon Woods in the world."

"Emma, you've only been looking for a few minutes," I pointed out.

"It's fine," Derek said. "I'll search more information about them later if it means that much to you. Who wants to play Xbox?"

CHAPTER 7

onday couldn't pass by any slower. I did my best to focus my energy on Sage when I had a spare moment, but the little things still wouldn't come to me. I wasn't sure if it was because I was so anxious waiting in anticipation for Tuesday night or if that was just the way the universe worked. I was 99 percent sure it was a combination of both.

At lunch, Robin texted me. *Sage said yes! See you tomorrow.*

That's great! I texted back, which lifted my mood.

I still have a few weeks left, I reminded myself.

After school, I picked up Hope from the elementary school and walked her home. We played games for a couple of hours until her mom came home from work. Hope was a surprisingly smart and insightful first grader. Since I'd found her after she'd been abducted last year, she knew I was psychic. I almost considered telling her about Sage because I felt, despite her young age, she would understand.

But I didn't tell her. Her dad had died last year, and I really didn't want to bring up the topic of death. Although that was something we had in common—that both of our dads died—I did my best to avoid the subject, and Hope never brought it up, either.

I arrived home just in time for supper. I took my seat at the table after greeting my mom and Teddy.

"Your mom says something happened on Saturday, Kiddo," Teddy told me once we started eating. "She said you might want to tell me yourself and that I might be able to help."

"That would be great!"

Teddy was a police officer, so whatever danger Sage was in, he might be able to find out what that was. I didn't mention that I wished I could find that out myself through my abilities, but having the answer through Teddy was better than no answer at all.

I immediately delved into the story of what happened with Melissa's warning, and I even told him how I couldn't find anything about Sage online. By the time I was done, my first bite of lasagna was lukewarm.

"Hmm..." Teddy mused. "It is really weird that she isn't online. These days, teens post so much that it's easy to bust them for drug abuse and things like that."

"I know. Weird, right? Do you think you can find anything out about her?"

"I'm technically not supposed to access police records for things like this, but I will look into it. Anderson, right?"

"Yep." I turned to my mother. "No one else has seen anything that can help?"

She shook her head as she bit into her food. "Sorry, sweetie. If I could give her a reading, see her in person, maybe..."

"That's actually a really good idea," I admitted, "but I hardly know her. I can't just text her and be like, 'Hey, my mom wants to read your future. Can you come over?'"

Mom and Teddy laughed, but I didn't think it was that funny. Just then, the front door opened, and I watched Emma enter the living room.

"I'll just be a minute, Emma," I told her as she came farther into the house. I shoveled my lasagna into my mouth and chugged my milk.

"Do you want some food?" Teddy asked.

He was a great cook, so it was tough to refuse dinner from him, but Emma politely declined and told him she already ate.

Emma and I escaped to my room for our psychic practice. We started with our normal yoga routine and then wrote down a few predictions. So far, I hadn't missed one in over a month, but it was still only little things like what the gas price would be tomorrow. I didn't consider many of these predictions accomplishments, although I congratulated Emma on each one she got right. She only had about a 15 percent success rate, so it meant a lot more to her when she was accurate.

"Maybe you could predict how Derek's birth parents died," Emma suggested.

I wasn't sure that was something I could just *see*. "I don't know, but I can try. Honestly, though, I doubt I'll see anything about that. Why are you so interested anyway?"

Emma's eyes darted down to the paper in her hand, and she nervously pushed dark curls out of her face without meeting my eyes. "I'm not that interested. I was just curious."

Normally, Emma wasn't such a bad liar. I eyed her, wondering where her curiosity was coming from. After a few moments of silence, I realized what it was. I didn't have to be psychic to figure it out; I simply knew Emma well. Her parents had just finalized their divorce. She was either using Derek's birth parents' issue as a distraction from that, or she was looking for reassurance that her own family matters weren't that bad. It was probably a combination of both.

I turned back to my piece of paper and closed my eyes to clear my mind. Sometimes I knew what I was writing. Other times, my subconscious took over and I didn't even realize I was making predictions. That's what it was like now, and although I wasn't completely aware of it, I knew that something was different about this time. My mind cleared so much that I wasn't even aware of my surroundings. It was like I was lost in a different dimension where tranquility ruled the world.

Slowly, the hum of my laptop and the noises of the TV in the living room came back to life. I blinked a few times until my room focused, and then I gazed down at my sheet of paper. The handwriting was crooked as usual, but something about the prediction riled me. I had no idea what to make of it.

Tomorrow you will find the answers to the questions you never asked. Be prepared to listen carefully.

"Great," I complained to Emma, who was already watching me expectantly from her spot next to my desk. "I got another fortune cookie prediction."

"What does it say?" she asked with a hint of excitement in her voice.

I handed her my sheet of paper. "How do I know what questions are being answered if I haven't asked them yet?"

Emma pressed her lips together. "At least you finally have something about Sage."

"What do you mean?" I asked as she handed the sheet of paper back.

"Well, it says 'tomorrow.' Tomorrow is the day we're going to meet Sage so you can learn more about her. It must be about her, right? I mean, it only makes sense."

She had a point, but I wasn't entirely convinced.

CHAPTER 8

*E*mma picked me up straight from Hope's house on Tuesday. I climbed in the back seat behind Derek, and we all rode to Asher's together. I silently stared out the window at the passing scenery, which was still recovering from the last snow we had and was slowly turning green. Emma and Derek were talking in the front seat, and she was asking him about his birth parents again. Derek said he didn't find anything online and was going to ask his adoptive parents more about them if it meant that much to Emma. Something in his tone told me he didn't like poking into this mystery, but Emma didn't seem to notice his reluctance.

Later, they were discussing Emma's extensive music collection while the radio played in the background, but I was so nervous about meeting Sage again that I didn't say much.

When we made it to Asher's house, his mom told us everyone else was already in the basement, which she kindly explained was soundproofed as not to disturb the neighbors. They weren't playing yet, and there were a few other people I didn't know gathered around to listen. Sage wasn't there, which made my palms sweat nervously. Would she make it? Or was this night wasted?

When I spotted Robin, I knew that even if Sage didn't show, coming here wasn't for nothing. I fell into his arms immediately. It'd been over two weeks since we'd seen each other, and I missed him terribly. He placed a soft kiss on my lips, which earned us a few whistles from his band members. Robin grabbed a pillow from the couch and threw it at Tyler, who played the drums.

He introduced Emma and Derek to his band members. There was Tyler on percussion, Logan on keyboard, Skip on bass guitar, and Asher on lead guitar. Robin, of course, sang lead vocals.

Asher introduced us to the other people in the room, including Troy —Asher's younger brother—Troy's girlfriend Faith, and Faith's brother Andrew.

"Well, we're going to get started soon," Robin announced. "I will warn you that it's going to get kind of loud. Feel free to take a seat. Oh, and there's some pop upstairs in the fridge if anyone wants some." Robin left a kiss on the top of my head before turning to situate his microphone.

Luckily, there were two huge couches set up in the basement, so there was enough room for all of us. Asher strummed a few chords on his guitar, and then he adjusted his amp volume. Everyone else tinkered around and did the same thing with their instruments.

Movement by the stairs caught my eye. My heart fluttered excitedly at the sight of auburn hair. It hung loose around Sage's body, and she tucked a strand of it behind her ear while scanning the room uncertainly. My first opportunity to learn more about Sage had finally arrived.

"Sage," Robin greeted, heading over to her. "I'm glad you could make it. Let me introduce you to everyone."

As Robin started the second round of introductions, Sage's eyes fell on me. They widened a bit in surprise and recognition. I smiled back as friendly as I could. After Robin finished introducing everyone, Sage finally made her way over to me.

"That band you were talking about... It's them?"

"Yep," I answered proudly.

"Which one is your boyfriend?"

"Robin."

"Good choice." Almost immediately, a blush rose to her cheeks. "I didn't mean it like that. I don't like him like that. I just mean he's a good guy."

I gave a lighthearted laugh in hopes of making her feel better, but it was tough to force a laugh when I was face-to-face with a girl I knew was going to die soon. "Yeah, he is. Do you need somewhere to sit?" I offered her the spot next to me, and she sat down.

The band started playing, and I listened the best I could, but my mind was so overcome with worries about Sage that the blaring noise from the amps seemed almost nonexistent. How was I going to work up the courage to talk to her? And how could I talk to her over the music?

Robin stopped the band and had them rework the verse they were on.

I turned to Sage. "They're pretty good, right?"

She nodded.

How was I going to get through to her? I had to know what type of danger she was in, yet I knew I couldn't just blurt it out.

"Do you want a pop?" I asked over the music.

"What?" Sage shouted back.

"Do you want a pop?" I repeated. I gestured for her to follow me. When we entered the kitchen, the music from downstairs was surprisingly faint. "Robin said there was pop in the fridge if we wanted some."

"Hi, girls." Asher's mom greeted us as she entered the kitchen. "I'm making cookies, and they'll be done in a few minutes. You can grab a soda out of the fridge if you want one."

"Thank you." I opened the door to the refrigerator, which was huge compared to mine. There had to be a dozen different types of drinks. I grabbed a Sprite for myself.

"How was the rest of your weekend?" I asked Sage as she grabbed a diet Mountain Dew. "I mean, after my mom and her crazy wedding party left the bridal shop."

She laughed lightheartedly. "If you think you guys are crazy, you should see the groups that come in there. Compared to some, your wedding party is pretty normal."

If only she knew…

Sage slid into one of the chairs around the kitchen table and opened her pop can. I pulled out a seat next to her.

"You know, you should come again, to Robin's band practice, I mean." As soon as I said it, I realized my invitation sounded a bit premature since the practice had barely started, but I couldn't think of anything else to say.

Sage smiled at me. "Yeah, I think I might. It was really sweet of him to invite me. Not a lot of people are so nice, especially entering a new school as a senior. Most people already have their group of friends and don't want to hang out with the new girl."

"I didn't realize you were new here. Where are you from?"

She stared down at her can. "Oh, uh, I'm from… around. It's just a new school."

Her tone told me that it wasn't something she wanted to talk about, so I didn't push it, but I did make a mental note to figure out where she lived before she moved to the city and why she moved. Something about it felt important to me.

I did my best to keep her talking. "Robin says the band is looking to add a female voice to the group. Is that something you might be interested in?"

She shook her head lightly. "I'd rather not be in front of big crowds."

I nodded in understanding. I wasn't thrilled about being in front of crowds, either, unless I was playing a solo on my clarinet in band. "You never even played in front of crowds when you played an instrument?" I remembered her telling me she used to play, but I couldn't recall the details.

"Oh, I did. I just... don't anymore."

"What did you play?"

She set her Mountain Dew down on the table and tugged at her long sleeves. "Saxophone. It was good for a while, but I had to give it up. So, how did you and Robin meet?"

She was obviously trying to change the subject, and as much as I wanted to know whatever secrets she was hiding, I definitely didn't want to push it and risk my chance at her trusting me. I knew I didn't have a lot of time with her, but I also understood that patience was a virtue.

I told Sage about how Robin and I met because his uncle was getting married to my mom. The whole time, questions raced through my head. *What can I say to pinpoint what type of danger Sage is in? I can see that she's trying to hide something from me, but what is it?*

I remembered my prediction from the day before and wondered what I was supposed to be listening for. It sounded like Sage was hiding something, but nothing she'd said seemed very significant, except for maybe that she transferred schools. Did something bad happen at her last one that she had to leave? What if there was someone dangerous at her last school?

"Your mom doesn't think that's weird?" Sage asked about Robin and me.

"No, everyone is pretty cool with it."

"Well, I guess. You're not blood related."

A stillness settled over the room as we both struggled to come up with something to say. Sage finally broke the silence. "Do you want to go back down and listen to them again?"

I honestly didn't want to. I wanted to learn more about her and the danger she was in, but telling her she was going to die would only make me look crazy. If only I was better at being subtle.

I followed Sage down the stairs and took my spot back on the couch, but sadly, I didn't get another chance to talk with her privately.

After Echo Score finished practicing, Robin and I finally had a moment alone. Sage had already gone home, which left me a little disappointed, but I was happy to have a second with Robin. Everyone was finishing up the cookies in the kitchen when he pulled me aside into the hallway that led to the bedrooms.

He wrapped his arms around my waist and pressed his lips gently to mine. For a moment, I completely forgot about Sage, as if Robin had some power that could magically melt all my troubles away.

He drew away from me and smiled. "So, how'd it go with Sage? Anything?"

I shook my head in disappointment. "I wish I could say there was."

Robin held me close to his chest, and I wrapped my arms around his body for comfort. "It will work out," he assured me. "I've seen you save people before. You're the kind of girl who can't *not* save someone when they're in trouble."

"So, I'm, like, the opposite of a damsel in distress?"

Robin laughed. "I guess you could say that."

I buried my face in his chest and inhaled his fresh spring scent. It made everything seem okay for a few seconds until I pulled away and Sage's face flashed through my mind. How could I be enjoying myself when she was going to die soon and I was the only one who could do anything about it? It didn't seem fair.

"Come on, Crystal," Robin insisted. "I hate to see you like this. Things are going to work out. We'll figure this out together, okay?"

I shyly met his gaze. How could he know that for certain?

He didn't say another word but instead pulled me close again and crushed his lips to mine. That gave me reassurance even after we parted. After all, I still had a few weeks to save her.

On the way home, I relayed everything Sage had said back to my friends in hopes that they'd help me make sense of it all. The whole time, I wondered if there was anything significant in her words, but nothing jumped out at me except for her transferring schools. Was that the piece of information I needed to solve this mystery?

When I arrived home, I slumped to bed and fell asleep almost instantly. I only hoped my dreams would give me something good.

CHAPTER 9

*T*hat night, I dreamt about death.

A red sedan drove through the thick rain. The tires sprayed water up as the car pushed through puddles that gathered on the road and ran down into the ditch. A bright glow filled the scene as if it was still daytime, but the clouds were so thick, and the rain was coming down so hard that visibility was near non-existent.

The car approached another corner, and before I knew what was happening, it hydroplaned until one of its wheels slipped into the ditch. The car's gathered momentum sent it off the road and down the slight dip neighboring it.

My heart beat wildly in my chest. I wanted to scream for the people in the car, to give some sort of warning, but I already knew it was too late for them.

The vehicle flipped twice before it landed on its top, its wheels spinning toward the sky.

~

I woke with a start and found myself lying in a puddle of my own sweat. I knew it was a vision of some sort, but what did it mean? Someone had died. But who?

I thought about it for several long moments before it hit me. Of course! Derek's birth parents. Emma had asked me to figure out how they died, and now I knew.

That Wednesday morning, Emma and I walked to school together like normal. I didn't think it was fair to tell her about Derek's parents before I told Derek what I had seen, so I kept quiet, intending to tell them both about my dream later. Emma and I entered the doors to the school a little early.

It was typical of Derek to get to school just in time for the first period warning bell, so I wasn't worried until I heard him call out my name just as I reached my locker.

"Crystal!" Derek rushed up to me. He seemed out of breath.

"Are you okay?" I asked.

Emma's eyes widened in surprise a few lockers down from mine. She immediately pushed through the crowd of students on their way to their own lockers.

Derek nodded and then sucked in another long breath.

"Were you running?" I asked. I tried to stay calm, but my palms began sweating. What had happened? Was he okay?

"Derek, what's wrong?" Emma put a gentle hand on his shoulder, but he didn't tear his gaze from me.

"Last night when I got home, I did a little more digging on my birth parents. I tried out a whole bunch of different key terms, like the city I was born in and stuff like that. I asked my mom about it. At first, she wouldn't tell me anything, but then she told me she thought my birth dad was an accountant and my birth mom was a nurse, so I used those search terms, too. Anyway, I kind of went crazy with keywords and eventually found all this information on them."

"Do you know how your parents died?" Emma asked the same time I breathed a sigh of relief knowing that he was okay.

"It was a car crash, wasn't it?" I guessed. "They died in the rain."

Emma and Derek both stared at me wide eyed.

"No, but how did you—?" Derek started. "Hold on. I'll get to that in a minute. This morning, I was thinking about what you said about Sage not being online. So, I thought I could do the same thing with her, you know, narrow the search a little bit. Anyway, I remember what you said about her playing saxophone. I found this."

Derek handed me a printout image of a paused video. In it, Sage was standing on a stage in the center of a concert band with her saxophone to her lips. Everyone else was sitting down, most of them hidden behind the stands. The director was facing directly at her. It was clear she was playing a solo.

If she was good enough to play solos, why did she quit? I wondered. I didn't say anything; I simply studied the image, amazed that Derek actually found something on her. *And why did she tell me she didn't like being in front of crowds? This photograph proves otherwise.*

"I can show you the video later. She's *really* good. But that's not all."

I tore my gaze from the photo and looked back up at Derek. What else had he found?

"What you said about the car crash in the rain…" Derek paused for a moment. "It wasn't my parents. It was Sage's."

I drew in a sharp breath. Part of me was surprised that I'd seen something related to Sage. Another part of me was shocked that Derek had dug up this information. The biggest part of me, however, was stunned to hear that Sage was an orphan. I could only partially relate because my dad had died, but I couldn't imagine losing both of my parents.

He handed me a news article, and all I could do was stare dumbfounded at it. Emma peeked over my shoulder.

"How did you find this?" I asked him in amazement.

"See, that's the funny thing. I was trying out this search term that I thought wasn't going to go anywhere. I just did it on a whim, and then this came up."

"What was the search term?" Emma asked.

My mouth went dry, and I tried to swallow, but I couldn't. As my eyes scanned the news article, I already knew what term he'd searched.

"Well, Crystal said the ghost's name was Melissa. I searched for Sage and Melissa Anderson and found the article about Melissa's death."

∾

I spent all of first period reading and rereading the article about how Melissa and her parents died. It said that the family was driving to their daughter's concert performance. It was last summer, so I figured she was part of a traveling music group or maybe she went to band camp like I had a few summers back. The article didn't say. It didn't actually name Sage because she was still a minor, but some people who knew the family had left comments with her name in it.

Now I knew why she had stopped playing. Now I knew who Melissa really was.

But questions still nagged at me. What does that mean for Sage's death? How was she in danger? How could I save her?

I wanted to hurl when I realized that I only had three and a half weeks to figure it out.

CHAPTER 10

$\mathcal{A}$ nticipation taunted me as I waited to talk with Teddy about what he found out about Sage, if he found out anything. With school, babysitting, and Robin's band practice, I hadn't had a chance to talk with Teddy since Monday night. I was so out of it at Hope's house that she won every game of checkers we played.

She eventually noticed my mood and asked me what was wrong.

"It's just... teenage stuff," I told her. I knew Hope was smart for her age and had an idea about my abilities, but I still wasn't completely open to telling her about Sage.

"Boyfriend troubles?" she asked in the most casual tone that I laughed out loud at her. What would a seven-year-old know about boyfriend troubles?

"How about we watch a movie?" She kindly placed her hand on mine for comfort.

I smiled. "Sounds great."

Hope's mom returned home the same time the movie ended. I said goodbye and walked back to my own house at a quicker pace than normal. When I reached home, I immediately rushed to the kitchen where I knew Teddy was already preparing supper.

"Did you find out anything?" I blurted.

"You mean about Sage?" Teddy asked, turning to the sink to fill a pot of water.

"I can't help but worry about her," I admitted.

"I did find a few things out."

"Well?" I asked expectantly.

He paused, shutting off the water. Something in his demeanor made me suspect he was reluctant to tell me what he knew. "Her parents died," he said with a hint of sorrow to his voice.

"I know. A car accident."

Teddy's eyes locked on mine, and he looked momentarily shocked. Then, as if he remembered I was psychic, he relaxed a little bit. "She's living with her aunt and uncle on her mom's side."

Okay, so the switching schools thing was starting to come together, but something in Teddy's tone told me there was more.

"What else?" I gripped onto my owl necklace, hoping the news wouldn't be all bad.

Just then, my mom entered the kitchen. I glanced at her and then back at Teddy.

"Come on, Teddy," I insisted. "You can tell me anything. I swear I can handle it."

He leaned up against the counter and took a deep breath. He exchanged a glance with my mom like he wasn't sure if he should tell me or not.

"Just tell me," I demanded with almost too much volume.

Teddy set his pot on the stove and shoved his hands in his pockets but didn't meet my eyes. "Sage's paternal uncle has been missing for the last five years," he finally said.

Silence filled the kitchen for a few moments as I absorbed this information.

"Okay. How does that put her in danger?" I asked.

"There's a warrant out for his arrest."

"So, he's on the run from something. Is Sage in danger from him?"

Teddy shrugged. "It's possible, but I doubt it."

"Why? What did he do?" I felt my mom's hands touch my shoulders for comfort, but I was too annoyed at how Teddy was beating around the bush. I shook her off. "Teddy, just tell me. I have to protect her."

He took a long breath before finally answering. "Child abuse. He's wanted for abusing Sage, and I don't mean hitting her and stuff. It was a lot worse than that."

My breath caught, and I stared at Teddy in horror. How could someone do that to a little girl? How could that happen to someone I knew?

I balled my hands into fists. "Anything else?"

He shook his head.

"Then I'm not hungry." I turned and raced to my bedroom.

I fell down on my bed and buried my head in my pillow. I hoped it would help stifle the lump forming in my throat. My face grew hot, and I squeezed my eyes shut as if that would help my problems go away. I didn't want to imagine what Sage had been through, and I was terrified of what I had just been put up against.

If all I had to do was prevent Sage from getting in a car that would cause a death like her family's, that would be simple. There wouldn't be anyone working against me. But instead of saving Sage from a car crash or some natural accident, I had to save her from someone dangerous.

But what if her uncle is irrelevant? I wondered. *What if it is a car crash or something like that that's going to kill her? I need to find some way to be certain before I start jumping to conclusions.*

A knock rapped at my door.

"Crystal," my mom called, "can I come in?"

I forced down the lump in my throat and sat up in my bed. "Yeah. Come in."

My mom took a seat next to me. "Sweetie, I know that kind of information is tough to swallow."

You have no idea, I thought as the lump in my throat began rising again.

"It's harder when you know the person," she continued. "But look, sweetie. We're going to figure this out." She ran a hand through my hair like she always did to comfort me. "Have your abilities ever failed you before?"

I didn't meet her gaze, but I did put some real thought into her question, and she was right. They hadn't. But I hadn't even been using them for a year. Surely I was bound to make a mistake at some point.

"That doesn't mean they won't fail me this time," I told her.

"Why would they when you're so determined to help her?"

"Maybe I'm too determined," I said a little too aggressively. I took a breath and adjusted my tone. "I mean, I'm so focused on Sage that I don't actually see anything about her. The only thing I've seen is the car crash that killed her parents."

"Remember when you had this same problem with Hope?" my mom asked.

I nodded.

"Remember how spending time with Robin helped you get your mind off things and you started seeing more?"

I nodded again.

"Maybe that's what you need to do, then. You need to get your mind off Sage first."

"Easier said than done."

"You could spend some time with your friends this weekend to try clearing your mind," she suggested.

"I guess Robin and I could do a double date with Emma and Derek." I shrugged. "I don't know. That just makes me feel like I'm abandoning Sage or something." But if it was the only way I would get the answers I needed... I had to know what danger she was in. How else was I going to prevent her death?

"Sweetie, you won't be abandoning her. The point is to make progress."

"I know." I stared down at my hands.

"Hey," my mom said, forcing me to look at her. "You're not the only one who cares about Sage. None of us want to see her get hurt. I may not be able to use my abilities to help her, but I will do whatever I can to make sure your abilities do. I'm not going to just leave you hanging, okay?"

I nodded.

A silence stretched between us for several long seconds. "Mom," I finally said. "You told me once that you had to save someone's life. How did you handle it?"

My mom shifted on my bed and inched closer to me. "I guess I never told you about that, huh? Did I ever tell you anything about how Teddy and I met?"

"Mom, don't change the subject."

Her eyes bore into mine seriously.

I blinked a few times before finally realizing what she was saying. "No!" I practically shouted in surprise. "You don't mean—Teddy was going to die?"

My mom nodded, but a smile played at the corner of her lips like she was proud of saving him.

"How?" My voice came out in almost a whisper this time. All she'd ever told me before was that they met while she was out on a walk. There was never anything paranormal about the story as far as I knew.

"It was right around the time he got the job on the force here in Peyton Springs. I kept dreaming about his face, only I'd never met him. I didn't even know his name, so I had no idea how I was going to save him."

Her expression fell, and she stared at a spot on the floor like she was remembering something horrible. "I kept watching him die night after night, and I was sure there wasn't anything I could do about it. I didn't know when he was going to die. I couldn't pinpoint the place in my dream. I didn't even know who he was."

"What happened?" I leaned in closer, engrossed in her story.

"You'd think being a police officer, Teddy would have been in danger while on duty. It wasn't that at all. In my dream, I kept seeing this big brown dog chase this orange tabby cat. I'd watch them tear through the streets until the cat raced underneath a ladder. Each night, the dog followed the cat underneath the ladder, and each night, he'd send it off balance. Every night, Teddy was at the top of that ladder. Every night, he fell. In my dreams, he always died. He was supposed to break his neck."

"How did you save him if you didn't know how?"

"It's funny how the universe works. Earlier that day, one of our clients called and put in an order for some herbs and candles—the kind we use for contacting spirits and things like that. She called later and said that she was sorry, but she wouldn't be able to make it to pick them up. She said she'd come another day, but I offered to drop them off. It was on the other side of town, but you were staying over at Emma's that night, so I didn't mind walking over there."

My mother paused for a moment to take a breath. "After I dropped off her order, I was walking back home, and I saw this orange tabby cat come tearing down the street. I knew... I just knew it was the same one I saw in my dreams. I didn't even think about it. I ran after the cat, but I wasn't as quick as it was, and just as I started following it, the brown dog appeared. I kept running.

"As they disappeared around the side of a building, I caught a glimpse of the ladder in my peripheral vision. The cat and dog were still weaving through the streets. In a split second, I decided to head to the ladder, hoping to cut them off."

She shook her head but smiled in humor. "Teddy didn't even realize I was there. I gripped onto the ladder just as the cat and dog were coming around that side of the building. That's the first time Teddy looked down and noticed me there. The dog managed to hit the ladder the same way it always had when I saw it in my dreams, but since I was holding on, it didn't knock it off balance."

"Seriously?" I asked. "That's how you two met?"

She nodded.

"It sounds more like you made that up," I said with a small laugh.

"It's true!" she defended, but it was clear she didn't think I was serious. "I had a tough time explaining why I was holding onto his ladder, but he even joked that if I wasn't there, he may have broken his neck. Of course, I couldn't tell him how right he was about that. And how could I? He was up there cleaning the gutters for his elderly landlord just because he's nice like that. You don't tell someone that a good deed is going to kill them."

"Have you ever told him he was going to die that day?" I was partially curious because it was my mom and Teddy, but I was also nervous about the answer. What if I had to tell Sage one day about her pending death? How would she handle it? How would *I* handle it, for that matter?

"I didn't even think to explicitly tell him," my mom admitted. "I don't think about it a lot, but I'm sure he's figured it out." She ran her fingers through my hair again. "But you see what I mean? You wouldn't get these warnings and visions if the universe thought you couldn't do something about them. It works in funny ways, but it manages to *work*."

I nodded in understanding. Part of me believed her wholeheartedly, but part of me still worried. "What exactly is the universe? The 'other side,' I mean. Why do we have these visions? Are they all from spirits and things like that?"

"That's something that has always been a mystery to all of us. Most of us believe it's our ancestors and other spirits who are able to see these things and then communicate with us from the other side."

"And what do you believe?"

"Honestly? I think a lot of it has to do with the universe making things right. I think there are times when cause and effect get out of control, and we're sent to balance it out. I'm not sure if all our visions come from spirits, but I definitely won't argue that there are spirits on the other side helping us out."

"How is it that we've never had this conversation?" I asked with a small laugh.

My mom looked at me seriously for a moment, and then she broke the silence. "Because I don't want to tell you what to believe. How can I put that on you when I'm not entirely sure myself?"

I blinked a few times as I absorbed her words. "I guess I never thought about it enough to decide what's worth believing in. After all these months, I still don't know how it all works."

"I'm sorry."

"For what?"

"That I can't explain to you how it all works. I know I'm your mom and I'm supposed to know everything, but I don't. I shouldn't be admitting this to you, but your abilities intimidate me a little bit."

My gaze flew to hers in shock.

"I mean, at first I thought I had so much I could teach you, but now after everything that's happened, I think you have more to teach *me*. Your abilities are truly amazing, Crystal. I've tried to teach you what I know about it all, but I don't know how much more I can help, especially when you're so reluctant to learn."

I twisted my face at her. "What's that supposed to mean?" The words didn't come out spiteful, but I was a little offended by her statement. I'd been working hard to practice my abilities.

"You have this 'let's get it over with' attitude. If you'd just relax and welcome your abilities with open arms, it may not be as difficult for you."

Now I was starting to get upset. What was with her picking on me like this? "I am trying!" I defended.

"I'm sorry, sweetie. I didn't mean to offend you. I'm only trying to help."

"I know, but it's tough to hear something like that when I'm already trying so hard."

"I'm sorry." My mom pulled me close into an embrace. "Let me know if you need any more help, okay?"

Then my mom left the room.

CHAPTER 11

*J*ust as my mom's footsteps faded down the hall, I heard Emma's coming toward my room. I quickly took a breath to compose myself; I didn't want my mood over my mother's accusations to show. I stole a quick glance in my mirror and put on a smile.

A second later, Emma burst into my room. "I am *so* sorry I'm late."

"Late?" I glanced at my clock. She was only a few minutes later than normal, and it's not like our practice sessions were set in stone. "It's fine, Emma," I assured her, and I really meant it. If she had come earlier, my mom and I wouldn't have finished our conversation. Sure, I was hurt that my mom felt I wasn't trying with my abilities, but I was also glad she told me the story about Teddy and opened up to me about her opinions.

"Derek and I lost track of time," Emma started.

"Seriously, Emma," I cut her off, "it's okay. You can be late for our psychic sessions. They don't have to start on the dot." I smiled at her teasingly.

Emma placed a hand on her hip and narrowed her eyes at me. "You just want to get out of it, don't you?"

I knew she was just poking fun at me, but I couldn't help but realize how much truth there was to her words. She was right, and my mom was, too. I was always reluctant to practice, and I wasn't doing my best to understand my abilities.

I sighed and rose from my bed. I didn't know what else to do, so I began arranging a few things on my desk. "Actually, not tonight. I do want to practice." I didn't let my gaze meet Emma's. Something about admitting this felt so out of character to me that I was afraid of what Emma would think. But she didn't say anything.

I broke the silence. "Dinner won't be ready for a while. Do you want to maybe do some research until it's done?"

"Research?" she asked with surprise. "Since when are you into research?"

I shrugged, but her words cut at my heart a little. "I just thought it'd be a good way to kill time." I turned away from her and reached for my phone on my bedside table so she wouldn't see my expression. Emma could read me like a book, and I knew there was self-doubt written all over my face. If she noticed, though, she didn't mention it.

"What do you want to research?" she asked as she took a seat on my bed.

"I don't know, actually." I set my phone back down—there wasn't anything on it to check—and took a seat next to her. "Is there anything fun you've come across lately?"

"Oh, there are tons of fun things." Her eyes brightened. "I try to focus my research on your abilities, but there are other things we can learn about."

"Like what?"

"There are things like astrology and tarot card reading we haven't really looked into, but I know you aren't really interested in all that."

She was right. I wasn't terribly interested, but who's to say I couldn't give it a shot? After all, my mom was a great tarot card reader.

"And there are things like telekinesis," she continued.

"You think that's a real thing?" I asked skeptically.

Emma shrugged. "It's not really any more unbelievable than seeing the future, is it?"

I stared at her for a minute because I wasn't sure if it was. I also wasn't sure if she was looking for a real answer.

"We could also research astral travel," she suggested.

"That's, like, seeing things outside your body, right?"

She nodded excitedly. "Yeah. It's like an out of body experience. It's where your spirit leaves your body and travels on the astral plane."

"That one sounds interesting," I admitted, "even though I don't have that ability."

"Maybe it's something you can achieve, kind of like how I've been learning to be psychic but wasn't born with it."

I nodded, although I wasn't sure if I would be leaving my body any time soon. "Okay," I agreed. "Let's do some research on that one, then."

Emma and I read about astral travel for a while until she reminded me to look up the video of Sage playing the saxophone. I pulled out the sheet of paper Derek had given me earlier and used that to quickly find it through an Internet search. Emma and I sat silently as we listened to the crisp tone and melodic tune coming from Sage's saxophone.

Emma's mouth hung open in shock. "Wow. She's really talented."

I nodded in agreement. "I know. It's sad that she doesn't play anymore."

"There's no one in our band who can play that well."

"Except maybe a first chair clarinet player," I teased, but then I realized how insensitive that suggestion was. No way could I ever compete with Sage's talent. I quietly turned back to the screen.

"Why do you think she stopped playing?" Emma asked.

"The article on her parents death. Remember?" I handed her the sheet of paper. "They died coming to watch her play. I'm not saying I would quit playing, but I can see where she's coming from, I guess."

Emma stared at the news clipping. "Do you notice how she's all reserved?"

I knew exactly what she meant.

She finally looked up to meet my eyes. "Maybe if she played again, it would help. It could be like therapy or something."

"It would be cool to hear her play in person," I admitted, looking back at the screen.

"Oh, my god!" Emma exclaimed.

"What?" I asked in a quick breath.

"Look!" she said, pointing to my computer screen. "The date that video was uploaded is the same day her family died."

I looked back and forth between the article in Emma's hands and the video on my laptop. "Oh, my gosh. This is the concert performance her family was driving to see. She didn't even know. In this video, she probably thought her family was out in the audience, but they were already dead."

"That's so sad," Emma agreed quietly.

"Dinner," my mom called from down the hall, pulling Emma and me from the article and the beautiful tunes of one Sage Anderson.

～

After supper, Emma and I went through our normal routine, and I filled her in on what Teddy had told me. As much as I was motivated to learn more and start doing better with my abilities, it didn't feel like anything had changed.

You can't expect things to get better at the snap of a finger, I told myself after Emma left. *If only*, I thought, *then I'd be closer to figuring out this whole thing with Sage.*

It was getting late, but watching Sage play saxophone earlier had me itching to break out my own instrument. I rarely practiced—it's not like anyone else in our school band did—but our conductor made us bring our instruments home every night. I pulled my clarinet from my backpack and assembled it. I played through a few of the songs we were practicing for our spring concert, which helped me relax slightly before crawling into bed.

That night, I snuggled with my stuffed owl Luna for comfort and reached for my phone on my bedside table. I sent Robin a quick text—nothing special—and we stayed up texting for a while. I wanted to talk more about Sage, but I didn't know what to say. Nothing could be said that we hadn't already discussed. Eventually, Robin's texts stopped coming, and I assumed he'd fallen asleep.

Despite the late hour, I still couldn't bring myself to close my eyes and drift off to sleep. Too many worries raced through my mind. I thought about all the work I'd put into my abilities, but it didn't seem like I'd come very far. I replayed my mother's words in my head and pondered what they meant for my past and my future.

I didn't know how much time passed, but I still couldn't fall asleep. I thought long and hard about the other side and considered what was there. Did I get visions because of spirits, or was it something else? If it were spirits, who were they? Could it be possible that my dad was sending me messages?

I gripped onto my owl necklace and held onto that thought for some time as I wondered what it would be like if he was the one communicating with me. I pondered it so hard until I nearly believed it. A single tear ran down my cheek. I pulled Luna in close to my body in hopes of making my chest feel whole again. I couldn't help it. Whenever I thought about my father, a feeling of emptiness consumed me as if physically reminding me of the years he hadn't been here.

But what if he was here all along? I thought. *What if he's here now?*

"Daddy," I whispered into the darkness. I couldn't feel a spirit there. I had no way of knowing if my father could even hear me, but a little part of me wanted to believe it was possible, that if I spoke to him, he might actually help. After all, he had to be on the other side somewhere, right?

"Daddy, I feel so lost," I admitted to thin air in a quiet whisper. "I guess I'm ashamed of myself a little bit. Mom's right. I haven't put enough effort into my abilities, and it could cost a girl her life. If you're out there, Dad, will you help me save her? It's been days since my warning, and I haven't figured much out. I don't know how she's going to die. I don't know how to save her. Is her uncle coming for her? How can I fight against a full-grown man? You must know, right? Someone over there on the other side must know how to save her."

I took in a deep yawn as my eyes began to droop. "I don't have a whole lot of time left—just until the wedding—but I hope you'll be there for me when I need you, Dad."

After I let a few more thoughts go out to my father, I drifted off to sleep soundlessly.

CHAPTER 12

I was restless at school on Thursday as I thought about what I might say to Sage if she came to Asher's again that night. I texted Robin to make sure he'd invite her again. He said he would, but all I could do was cross my fingers all day.

That night, Emma drove Derek and me to Asher's like before. I felt more comfortable this time as I settled into the now familiar basement.

"Is she coming?" I asked Robin quietly when I greeted him with a hug.

"She said she would." I could see the hint of sorrow in Robin's eyes. It was like he was already grieving for her. I knew he had faith in me, but at the same time, I understood how hard it was to talk about someone who you knew was likely to die soon.

Robin gave me a peck on the lips before he turned to tweak some of the equipment settings. I could see him stealing glances at me as he poked at things. I couldn't help but smile back at him.

"Troy." Emma positioned herself near Asher's younger brother on one of the couches. "Why aren't you in their band? Don't you play music?"

Faith, Troy's girlfriend, nearly choked on her laugh.

I took a seat on the opposite couch as I listened to the group talk. I was still waiting on Sage, but I didn't want to feel left out, either.

"Nah," Troy answered. "I love to hear them play, but I don't have that kind of talent. Imagine me playing guitar." He curled up his hand like he was holding an imaginary guitar. "My fingers just don't bend that way."

"And he can't keep a beat or sing in tune to save his life," Faith added.

"I'm more a visual artist, I guess," Troy said as he put an arm around Faith and pulled her close.

"What about you, Andrew?" Emma asked.

"Huh?" Faith's brother muttered, looking up from his phone. "Oh, yeah. I don't do this kind of stuff, but I play sax in the jazz band at school. It sounds nerdy, but it gets pretty intense there."

We all talked for a while to get to know each other. Eventually, we exchanged Facebook friend requests. Just as I accepted Andrew's friend request on my phone, I caught a glimpse of movement on the stairs.

"Sage!" I exclaimed a little too excitedly as I shot up from my spot on the couch. I quickly calmed my voice. "We saved a spot for you," I said dumbly, gesturing to the cushion next to me.

She smiled back sweetly. "So, uh, what are you guys doing?"

We all had our phones out and were huddled around the couches in a semi-circle, all except Robin and Asher, who were trying to fix a tuning problem on Asher's guitar.

Tyler twirled his drum sticks around his fingers. "Just falling victim to social media addiction," he joked. "Want to join?"

"It's okay," Sage declined, taking a seat next to me.

"What?" Tyler teased. "You don't use social media or something?"

Sage didn't say anything for a moment, and then she spoke softly. "No, I don't."

Even though Sage tried to stay casual, everyone but Emma, Derek, and me froze and stared at Sage like she'd just grown two heads.

"What?" Faith exclaimed. "How can you not use social media? My grandma is the only person I know who doesn't use social media, and that's because she's in a nursing home."

"Even our cat has a Facebook page," Andrew added.

I could see where this was going, and all I wanted to do was jump in and save Sage the trouble of explaining. I still didn't understand it completely, but I was sure it was something she didn't want to tell the whole room about. As if he could hear my prayer, Robin's eyes locked on mine from across the room. I tried my best to communicate a warning with my expression.

"Okay, guys," Robin announced.

I breathed a sigh of relief.

"We got the tuning problem fixed. Time to get started."

"What takes you guys so long to set up anyway?" Troy complained.

That started a whole string of snarky remarks from the band members until Robin got them to calm down again. Soon, they came together in harmony to play their songs to near perfection. Since I had downloaded their songs, I knew most of what they were playing. Some of them were new and weren't on iTunes yet. It was pretty clear since they weren't as good on those.

When they began playing a song I knew again, I couldn't help but sing along. I was pleased when I glanced over at Sage and she was moving her body to the music. That was the happiest I'd seen her since I'd met her. I almost turned away, but then I noticed her lips moving to the words.

"You know this song?" I asked above the music.

Sage pressed her lips together shyly. "They're on YouTube," she explained.

I smiled as I went back to singing the chorus.

Emma's voice rang loud above my own, even almost louder than Robin's. She had also downloaded their songs a while back and had memorized them all in under a week. I admired her ambition and courage to be heard in front of everyone.

"Hold on," Robin said into the microphone, stopping the music in its tracks.

Tyler was so surprised at the abrupt halt that he dropped his drum sticks.

Robin's eyes locked on mine almost aggressively. Had I done something wrong? What happened? "Crystal," Robin said, "you're in big trouble."

"What?" I asked in a way that came off sounding horrified.

"Why didn't you ever tell me Emma could sing?"

All the muscles in my body relaxed.

"We've been looking for female vocals, and here we knew a great singer all along. And it looks like she knows our songs."

"What?" Emma asked, enunciating the word. "Are you serious?" She made the question come off sounding like she wasn't up for it, but I knew Emma far too well. Inside, she was surely jumping at the chance to be part of a group like this.

"Yes, I'm serious." Robin held out his hand to her. "Come up to the microphone."

Emma glanced at Derek as if asking if she should.

Derek pushed at her. "Go on. It's only, like, your dream to sing in a rock band."

Emma smiled excitedly and hopped up from the couch. "What do I do?"

"Sing background vocals, of course," Robin instructed as he positioned her in front of a second microphone. He fiddled with it for a moment before it turned on. "You obviously know this song, right?"

Emma nodded. She tried to stay casual, but she was bouncing up and down slightly. A smile played at the corner of her lips.

"Think you can improvise a harmony?" Robin asked.

"I play harmony in band a lot, so I'm sure it can't be that hard."

Tyler interjected. "Those two look like they know what they're doing, too." He pointed a drum stick at Sage and me.

Sage and I exchanged a glance.

Robin smiled at us in a way that made my heart swoon. "You girls want to try it out, too? Just for fun?"

Sage and I looked at each other again. Her eyes lit up slightly.

"What the heck?" I shrugged, hopping up from the couch.

Sage planted a look of uncertainty on her face, but a part of her expression told me she was having fun. She finally rose from the couch, and we stood around Emma's microphone together.

"Okay," Robin said. "From the top."

Tyler beat on his drums, and suddenly the rest of the basement came to life. I stood there stupidly for the first verse like I was unsure of myself. Honestly, though. Me? Singing? I wasn't much of a singer, but as Emma's voice grew louder, I couldn't help but let go of my insecurities and simply enjoy the beat.

Something about the moment gave me déjà vu. A memory played back through my mind, and I was pretty sure I had dreamt of this moment before. Was it possible that I was connected to Sage even before Melissa's warning?

I caught Sage's eyes opposite me, and she broke out into a full-on grin. I'd never seen Sage look so happy. The moment I realized this, nerves twisted in my stomach. Sage didn't have long. How many more happy moments would she have like this? Was I wasting her time with this whole band practice thing, or was it best that I let her be happy while she could?

"That was fun!" Emma exclaimed when the song ended. "Now go sit back down so I can try by myself," she teased, poking at me.

"Actually, I could really use something to drink," I said. It was true, but I was hoping for a moment alone with Sage again. "What about you, Sage?"

She smiled and tugged on her sleeves, balling them in her fists. "Yeah, sure. I'm pretty thirsty, too."

We escaped upstairs while the band began playing again. I pulled a cup from the dish rack and filled it with water, all the while wondering what I could say to her. I wanted to somehow ask if she was in danger—maybe from her uncle—but I didn't know how to bring the subject up lightly. The question of *how* she was going to die still nagged at me. I felt like if I knew that, I'd know how to save her, but then again, I knew *she* obviously didn't have that answer.

"Sage," I started, hoping this would work. "I've been wondering about something."

She took a seat at the kitchen table and popped open her soda can. "Yeah?"

I gently pulled out a chair next to her and sat down. "That thing you said earlier about not having social media profiles... Is there a reason for that? I mean..." I paused, looking down at my glass for a moment. "Are you in any danger or something?"

"What?" Sage laughed, but it sounded forced. "What would give you that idea?"

I shrugged. What was I supposed to tell her? That it was her dead sister who gave me that idea? I didn't have that sort of trust from her yet. As much support as I'd received from my family and friends, I knew telling a near stranger about my abilities probably wouldn't go over well.

"Nothing, I guess. I just wanted to make sure. I wouldn't want to miss a chance to help you if you were in trouble. Not that I think you are," I lied. My eyebrow twitched slightly. At least she wasn't aware that this was a clear indication of my dishonesty. "I just want to make sure because sometimes you do seem okay, but other times, it's like..." Now I was just babbling.

"Crystal," Sage said, stopping me. "I'm fine. Really. If I gave the impression that I was in any trouble, I'm sorry. I've just been really stressed lately."

I couldn't help but remember how it felt when I shook her hand that first day. She was scared of something. Was she still scared of it?

"Okay," I answered. I casually placed my fingertips on her exposed hand. "If you ever need anything, though, I am willing to listen."

I pulled my hand away, partially because I knew it was weird to touch her in the first place and partially because in the few seconds I was in contact with her, I didn't see a single thing. If there was something there, I should have seen it. At least that's what I told myself.

Sage sipped her Mountain Dew and then smiled at me. "Thank you, but I'm fine."

Even after Sage left, I still didn't believe her.

CHAPTER 13

"*I* feel like I'm getting nowhere," I complained to Robin after Sage went home. Faith and Andrew were gone, too, and everyone else was up in the kitchen snacking on Asher's mom's home-made cookies. Robin and I sat together on one of the couches in the basement, his arm slung around me casually.

"Maybe you need to be more direct with her," he suggested.

"You mean, tell her that her dead sister warned me of her impending death? Tell her that her uncle might be coming for her? She'll call me crazy!"

"Has anyone called you crazy because of your abilities before, Crystal?" Robin brushed my blonde hair out of my face and looked me in the eyes as he asked this.

He was right. I'd told a good dozen people or more, and none of them had called me crazy. "In all fairness, I actually know everyone I told," I pointed out. "I don't really *know* Sage yet." Even as I said this, a small part of me believed Robin was right, so why was I so afraid to tell Sage when it could save her life?

"It may be worth a shot," Robin insisted. "I mean, I believed you, and we ended up saving Hope because of it."

I took a deep breath. "That's because I was able to prove it to you. What am I supposed to say to Sage? You can't just tell people they're going to die, Robin. Then it'd be like it was my fault."

"And if you didn't tell her and it happened anyway, would you regret it?"

I sighed in defeat. "You're right. I have to tell her. Beating around the bush isn't doing me any good."

"You know I'm here for you, right?" He kissed the top of the head. "No matter what happens. I care about Sage, too, so you don't have to feel like you're in this alone."

I nodded and pressed my head into his shoulder for comfort.

Robin gripped the bottom of my chin lightly and guided my face up to his. "I mean it," he said seriously before he pressed his lips to mine. I let myself fall deeper into the kiss until both our lips parted slightly.

Emma's footsteps on the stairs moments later made me pull away from Robin. I pressed my lips together in embarrassment, hoping that might stifle the blush rising to my cheeks.

"Crystal," Emma asked, bending from a higher step to get a good look at me, "are you almost ready to go?"

I nodded again and rose from my seat, still gripping onto Robin's hand. "So, I'll see you on Saturday at the park for Troy's birthday, then."

Robin stood up with me and stayed close. I could feel his breath on the top of my forehead as he looked down at me. It made the butterflies in my stomach spring to life.

"Will you invite Sage?" I asked. "Maybe I could talk to her more then. You know, about what we just talked about."

"Yeah," Robin said, closing the small gap between us. "I'll convince her to come. Have a safe ride home, okay?" He bent to my level again, pulling me into a passionate kiss.

"My eyes!" Emma exclaimed jokingly. When I turned to look at her to let her know I wasn't amused, one hand was covering her eyes. "My virgin eyes!"

"As far as I heard, there's nothing virgin about them," Robin joked back.

Emma froze for a second and looked at me with wide eyes as if to ask, *What did you say to him?* Not that Emma ever told me a secret on that topic.

Robin laughed. "I'm *kidding*, Emma. Chill."

She stood and pulled at the bottom of her shirt casually. "Well, yeah. I knew that."

I followed Emma upstairs and grabbed a cookie. "Oh, before I forget." I turned back to Robin, who had trailed behind me. "Do you guys want to do a double date sometime soon?" I remembered what my mom had said and figured I should follow her advice.

"Sure," Robin said with a cookie in his mouth. "Does Saturday night work for you?" He looked toward Derek and Emma, who both agreed.

"I'll be ready in a minute," Derek told us as he grabbed a few more cookies.

"Okay." Emma pulled at me. A look of *let's talk in private* crossed her eyes. On our way out the door, Emma spoke again. "So, still no 'I love you?'"

Thanks for reminding me, Emma, I thought. "It's not like you and Derek have said it, either."

"Actually," Emma announced proudly, "we have said it."

"What?" I practically choked on my surprise. "When?" I climbed into the back seat of Emma's car as she pulled open the driver's side door.

"Earlier this week."

"Why didn't you tell me?"

She shrugged. "I didn't really think about it until I realized you and Robin still haven't said it. It's not like you tell me everything."

"What are you talking about?" I asked, momentarily stung by the accusation. "I do tell you everything!"

"'About that thing we just talked about.' It's like you didn't want me to hear whatever it was you and Robin were saying in private."

"No, it's not that," I insisted, feeling hurt that she'd think I would hide something from her. "He was just saying I should tell Sage about my abilities. Then there might actually be a chance at saving her."

Emma pressed her lips together in thought. "I don't know, Crystal. You don't really know her..."

"That's what I said, but I think he's right."

Derek's passenger side door opened with a click, and he climbed in. Emma and I both looked at him and went silent.

"Telling secrets, are we?" Derek joked.

I sighed because this whole decision about whether to tell Sage or not was stressing me out. "I was just getting Emma's opinion. What do you think, Derek? Should I tell Sage about my abilities or not?"

Derek shrugged. "I guess it's up to you, but it could just push her away."

"I know, but Robin thinks I should, and I trust him."

Emma started the car and pulled out of the driveway. "We're not going to tell you what to do, Crystal, but I *am* going to tell you I don't think it's a good idea."

I gazed out the window in thought. "But I'm not getting *anything* out of her otherwise. I have no idea what to ask or how to ask it. Everything I've found out is what Derek and Teddy told me. Fat lot of good my abilities are doing me."

Emma made a noise from the front seat. "Crystal, your abilities are really awesome. Don't say that."

I spent most of the rest of the car ride staring out the window wondering how Sage was going to die. Melissa had said that she didn't want Sage to "suffer the same fate." Did that just mean her death, or did it mean Sage was going to be in a car accident? And what was this whole thing with her uncle?

That thought reminded me to tell Derek about it. When he suggested we do a Google search on her uncle, I realized Teddy had never given me a name.

～

I took my time between Thursday and Saturday to think about what my friends had said, but even Friday afternoon at Hope's, I still felt completely lost. At least I'd gotten a name from Teddy, but I was unable to find anything on the right Alan Anderson. Why did Sage have to come from a family with such a common surname?

"Crystal." Hope snapped her fingers in front of my face.

"Huh?" My eyes refocused, pulling me from my thoughts. I gazed down at the Life board only to find that Hope already had another set of twins. I hadn't even gotten married yet.

"You seem out of it," she said.

I sighed. "That's because I am." I spun the Life wheel before looking back up to meet Hope's eyes. "It's just one of my friends," I started to explain, but I trailed off, wondering whether I should open up to Hope about this or not. I wasn't sure if she'd understand.

"Is she okay?" Hope asked, pulling a miniature husband out of the Life box for me.

"Not really," I admitted.

"Is it because you can see the future?"

I tensed. "What do you mean?"

"You found me because you can see the future, right?"

I relaxed and nodded. "I'm supposed to help this girl, but I don't know if I should tell her about my gift or not."

"If she's like me, she'll believe you."

"What do you mean?"

Hope straightened up and put a mature expression on her face. "The whole time I was missing, I dreamt about you. I knew who you were before you ever came to save me. Maybe your friend knows you're going to save her, too."

I thought about this for a moment, but it didn't make any sense that Sage knew. After all, when I helped my friend Kelli, she didn't know. "I don't think she's like you," I finally said.

"Well, I think you should tell her," Hope said, spinning for her turn.

Great. Now there was just one more opinion to add to the confusion, especially since I was leaning toward not telling her.

On my walk home, I swung by Divination to get my mom's opinion since I knew she was working late and I might not get a chance to talk to her later. She always kept the shop open a little later on Friday nights, but there weren't any customers around when I entered.

As soon as I brought the subject up, my mom's entire demeanor changed. Her body tensed, and she wouldn't meet my gaze. She crouched down to a bottom shelf and reached into a box nearby to restock a few items.

"Mom," I prodded.

She sighed, stalling. "I've told you before what I think about you telling people." Her gaze finally reached mine.

I crossed my arms over my chest. *Not the answer I was looking for.*

She stood and pushed past me with her empty box. I followed her to the back of the shop.

"I'm not saying you can't tell her. It's not my job to tell you that, but you asked for my advice." She pushed open the door to the storage room. I followed, and the door clicked shut behind me.

"It's one thing to tell your best friends," she continued. "Even telling Robin made sense." She finally turned to me. "But if you start telling so many people, you're going to get too comfortable with it. Someday, you're going to tell the wrong person."

I wanted to roll my eyes at her, but with her next sentence, a sense of empathy washed over me.

"Believe me. I know."

I sighed and spoke softly. "So your vote is that I shouldn't tell her, then?"

"I can't tell you what to do, sweetie."

I gritted my teeth in exasperation. Aren't mothers supposed to have all the answers? She was really starting to sound like the mysterious gypsy she pretended to be every year for Halloween. "Well, if you were in the same situation, you wouldn't tell her, right?"

"I guess I'd have to be in that situation to tell. I don't know Sage well enough. The best thing I can tell you to do is to follow your instinct."

"Mom, I have no instinct. That's why I'm asking you. You're supposed to be my instinct."

She threw her head back and laughed. I couldn't help but let out a giggle with her.

She finally composed herself. "Once you're in the situation, you'll know what to do."

Why was she making this harder for me? "What would Sophie and Diane say?"

"Probably the same thing as me."

"Well, you guys are no help," I complained. My mom pulled me into a hug to calm my nerves.

"I can teach you about your abilities, Crystal. I can advise you against sharing your secret. But I can't tell you how you should feel. I won't tell you what to do. You know Sage better than I do. Do you think she'll believe you?"

Just then, the bells on the front door jingled, indicating a customer had just entered the shop. I let my mom tend to them, said goodbye, and headed home.

CHAPTER 14

*I*t was here: the moment of truth. I still didn't know what I was going to say to Sage, which only made me nervous on the car ride to the city.

"Crystal." Derek's voice brought me back to the present inside the car.

"What?" I asked, pulling my eyes from the scenery to meet his.

"What's wrong?"

"Nothing," I said as casually as I could. My eyebrow didn't even twitch this time. "What would make you think that?"

"Because you're chewing your nails like you're nervous."

I gazed down at my hands and realized he was right. The nail on my right ring finger was chewed raw. "It's just…" I paused for a second. "Life," I finally said confidently. "It sucks being a teenage girl."

Emma and Derek both laughed from the front seat.

"I hear ya," Emma said, raising her hand in agreement.

I couldn't lie to them. "I'm still worried about Sage," I admitted. "I have a feeling the whole thing about her uncle being on the run is important, but given that the police don't know where he is, Teddy doesn't know anything else."

"Maybe Derek could work some of his detective magic," Emma suggested.

"Yeah," I agreed. "I tried finding him online, but Alan Anderson is a common name."

"I guess I could try," Derek offered.

"So, Emma," I started, trying to get back into casual conversation so they wouldn't worry about me. "Will you be up on stage today?"

She rolled her eyes. "I don't even know if I'm an official band member yet, and I haven't practiced with them enough."

"You'd love it, though," I told her.

"Maybe we could start our own band," Derek suggested with a laugh. The sad thing was that he sounded half-serious, and my only guess was that he didn't want to share Emma with a group of four other guys.

It was sunny with a light breeze when we reached the park. The last of the snow was gone, replaced with bits of spring greenery. I stepped out of the car and tugged slightly at the bottom of my hoodie as I looked around. There was a playground on one end of the park and a walking trail that went across a river and through the trees on the other side. I scanned the area for Robin but didn't see him anywhere.

"Where do you suppose they are?" Derek asked.

"Over there." Emma pointed. I followed her gaze and saw Asher's brother, Troy, under one of the pavilions. As we neared the shelter, I started to make out people I recognized, like Faith, Andrew, and Skip.

"Crystal," Robin greeted, embracing me and giving me a peck on the lips. Then he turned to Derek. "We're still getting some of the equipment out of the van. We could use another man if you're up for moving stuff."

Derek just shrugged and joined Robin to help. There weren't a lot of people there yet since we were technically early for Troy's birthday party, so Emma and I decided to take a stroll on part of the trail.

We talked as we walked, but the conversation remained casual. Eventually, we could hear Echo Score's beat coming from the pavilion the same time we met a fork in the path.

"It looks like if we go that way," Emma pointed to the left path, "it will take us back to the pavilion."

"Okay," I agreed, following her lead.

Just as we cleared the trees and spotted the pavilion again, I noticed a familiar figure making her way toward the music.

Sage.

"I'll catch up with you later, Emma."

She nodded and followed my gaze to Sage. "Are you going to tell her?"

I twisted my lips up in thought. "I don't know yet."

"Do you want someone there with you in case you do? I could, like, back you up."

I shook my head. "It's okay. Really. I don't even think I'll tell her, and no offense, but I think I have a better chance of learning more about her if I'm alone with her."

"It's okay. I understand." Emma gave me a cheerful wave as she broke away from me to go find Derek.

"Sage," I called as I caught up with her.

She smiled back at me. "I was looking for you. I don't really know anyone else here except Robin, but he's singing up there."

"It's kind of a relief hearing them out of the basement isn't it?" I joked. "It's not as deafening."

Sage chuckled. "So, uh, should we go meet some of Troy's friends, or will we just be those girls who sit in the corner?"

I let out a light laugh. "I'm okay with sitting in the corner, although that cake looks pretty tasty."

"Well, I won't say no to free food."

Sage and I grabbed some food and found our way next to Emma and Derek on one of the picnic tables. We all talked, laughed, and listened to the music for a while. When I stood to throw away my paper plate, I noticed that a small group of people had gathered on the side of the pavilion to listen.

"You know what we should do, Crystal?" Emma asked, grabbing my arm excitedly. She didn't wait for an answer. "We should dance to the music. It'd be good publicity for the band." She raised her eyebrows, pleading for me to join her.

"Seriously, Emma?"

"I know this line dance that would actually work really well with this song."

"Aren't line dances for country music?" I asked.

Emma shook her head. "Not all of them. Come on. It will be fun."

"Sounds fun," Faith cut in as she neared the trash can with her empty plate.

"What?" I asked.

"I'll help you, Emma," Faith said.

Emma jumped up and down excitedly. "Okay. I'll show you how to do it." She positioned herself near the front of the pavilion away from the picnic tables. "Hold on. Let me get the beat." She bobbed her head a couple of times before starting a grape vine.

After a few moments, Faith jumped in. "Oh, I know this one. You're right. It does work well with this song."

Dancing honestly *did* look like fun.

"I know this one, too," Sage said to me. "These guys taught it to me last summer at band camp."

I watched Emma and Faith hopelessly. "Well, I don't, so you'll have to teach me."

By now, another girl who I didn't recognize, but who seemed to know Faith, had joined in.

Sage slowly showed me how the dance went. After a few demonstrations, I told her to do it to the beat and I'd catch up. I didn't do so great as I watched Sage's feet move quickly, but I eventually started to get the hang of it.

When the song ended, we were all giggling while the onlookers actually gave us a round of applause.

"What now?" Sage asked when we sat back down at our picnic table. She tugged at her long sleeves and balled them into fists like she always did. I figured it was something she did in uncomfortable situations, and I was willing to bail her out of this one.

"Emma and I went for a walk earlier," I offered. "It was really pretty back in the trees. Want to go for a walk?"

"Sure," she agreed.

Once we neared the trees, Sage spoke again. "I actually walk through this park a lot, so I know how pretty it can get back here. But like I said, I haven't lived in the city long, so I haven't really seen it in full bloom yet."

"Why did you move to the city?" I asked. Even though I knew the answer, I figured a simple question like this would help her open up to me more.

She glanced at me for a moment and then locked her eyes back on the path. "I don't tell a lot of people this, but I feel like I can trust you. I can, can't I?"

"You can," I assured her.

"Okay, well…" She paused like she wasn't sure she wanted to tell me yet.

I looked at her for a moment and noticed her eyes turning red like she was holding back tears. Her voice cracked slightly when she spoke. "I moved here to live with my aunt and uncle."

"What about your other family?" I prodded. Was I doing this right, or was I overstepping?

Sage shook her head. "My family isn't around." She paused briefly. "Sometimes I feel like I'm all alone. My grandparents are all dead, and it just wouldn't work out to live with other relatives."

Her uncle, I thought. I only knew a small piece of that story, but I couldn't help but wonder what the rest of the pieces would tell me about her.

"You're not completely alone, though," I pointed out. "Your aunt and uncle must be pretty nice to take you in. And you have friends."

Sage gave an uncomfortable laugh. "They've been fine, but I don't think they understand what I'm going through." She didn't care to explain what she meant, but I already knew she was referring to her family's death.

She continued. "Brian—my uncle—just tells me to suck it up all the time. They don't have any kids yet—my mom was a lot older than her sister—so I don't think he really knows what it's like to be a dad yet. It's okay living with them, but I'm really glad Robin has been inviting me to these things. It's really sweet of you guys to include me."

A silence stretched between us because I didn't know what to say to that. You're welcome?

I was just about to answer when Sage tucked a strand of auburn hair behind her ear and spoke. "Can I ask you something?"

"Sure. Anything."

She tugged at her sleeves again. "Robin. Do you think he asks me to come to these things because he feels sorry for me?"

"No," I answered honestly.

"I guess I can't figure it out. He's known me all year and hardly said anything, and now he's constantly inviting me to these things. I mean, he practically begged me to take off work today to come. I just can't tell if he honestly thinks of me as a friend or not."

I bit my cheek nervously and thought about telling her the truth. Just then, we reached the fork in the path.

Sage pointed to the right this time. "If we go this way, there's a really pretty bridge. I could show you if you want."

"Okay. I haven't gone this way before."

My heart beat fast in my chest, telling me this was the moment. I knew I needed to tell her, but all the nerves twisting inside my belly made me want to chicken out.

"Actually..." I took a deep breath to help work up the courage to say something. "About Robin. He invited you because I asked him to."

Sage stared at me in surprise, but we didn't break our pace. "What? You didn't even know me. We met that one time."

"I know, but... I guess you just seemed like someone I could get along with."

I expected Sage to respond to that, but instead she said, "We're almost there."

The trees thinned slightly as we reached the bridge, which hovered over a small river with a steep bank. The greenery came to life around it with little pops of yellow and red along the water. I figured this river was a branch of the stream I spotted closer to the pavilion.

"You're right. This is really pretty."

"Oh, this isn't what I wanted to show you." She crossed the bridge and began making her way down the bank.

"Where are you going?" I looked toward the water nervously, afraid I'd slip and fall if I tried to make my way down there.

"It's okay. You won't fall," Sage assured me as she disappeared under the bridge.

I followed behind her. When I broke through the weeds and made it under the bridge, I found myself standing on a sort of sand bar that created a flat, dry platform.

Sage untied her shoes and dug her feet into the sand at the same time she plopped down onto it. "I come down here a lot to think. Something about it makes me feel safe, like no one could find me down here. As far as I can tell, I'm the only one who ever comes here. There's some graffiti and stuff," she pointed up to the bridge, "but I've never run into anyone down here."

I took a seat beside her. "It is kind of peaceful, like a little hiding space. Well, a spacious hiding place."

"Yeah," Sage agreed. "But just so you know, if you tell anyone, I'm going to have to kill you." She faked a serious face, but she couldn't hide her smile.

"Cross my heart and hope to die." My heart sank at that thought. I should definitely not be making death jokes. The idea of it only brought a lump to my throat as I again tried to work up the courage to say something to her.

"You know what's funny?" Sage started before I could say anything. She leaned back on her hands and crossed her ankles to stretch out.

All I could do was pick at the bits of grass growing up through the sand. I didn't meet her eyes. "What's that?"

"I just told you one of my biggest secrets. Well, two actually. There's this place," she gestured around, "and then the fact that I live with my aunt and uncle."

I nodded for her to continue.

"Yet when I told you I was living with my aunt and uncle, you didn't ask why. It's all part of a bigger secret."

I froze for a moment. I knew how her parents died. Did that make me look suspicious? "That's private, isn't it?"

"I really would have thought the first time I told someone my own age that, they'd want to know why."

"Well…" I could hardly get the words out. My throat felt like it was closing up, and my brain was racing with questions about whether I should tell her the truth or not. My mother's voice echoed in my mind. Once I'm in the situation, I'll know what to do, she had said. I *wanted* to tell Sage. I swallowed and held my breath for a moment. It was now or never. "I actually do know," I finally admitted.

Sage's expression transformed into one of confusion. "How could you know?"

I continued picking apart the blade of grass in my hands, but it disappeared too soon. When that was gone, I pulled a small red blossom from the edge of the weeds and began plucking at its pedals. My voice wavered nervously as I spoke. "I wanted to add you on Facebook, but when I couldn't find you there, I turned to Google. I found the article about the accident." It wasn't the whole truth, but I didn't see a point in telling her my friends were involved, too.

"Oh," she said in understanding. "I didn't think they put my name in the article."

"They didn't, but some people from your hometown put it in the comment section."

"Oh. I guess I didn't really intend for anyone around here to find out."

"Why not?"

Sage shrugged. "I guess I don't want people feeling sorry for me. They've done that for years, and I just thought I'd kind of get a new start with all of that when I moved here. After all, it's hours away from where I grew up, so it was kind of a relief that no one knew who I was or what happened to me. I like my aunt and uncle on one level because they kind of make me feel safe, and I need that while I'm finishing up high school. But I'm only with them until I graduate next month—I'm not 18 yet—and then I can go anywhere I want." She stared into the distance. "There are so many possibilities. That's why I work at Special Day Bridal. I'm saving up so I can get far away from here."

"What's wrong with Minnesota?" I asked.

Her eyes focused, and then she looked at me, but she didn't answer. Instead, she began picking apart her own blade of grass. After a long silence, she spoke again. "It was my fault."

"What?"

"The accident. My family wouldn't have died if it wasn't because of me."

"You can't blame yourself, Sage. The weather—"

"No. It was. You have to remember all that flooding we had last summer. Maybe you didn't have it around here. Anyway, I was at band camp, and my parents almost weren't going to come. But they couldn't reschedule the final performance, so I begged my family to come. I could have sworn I saw them in the audience, so I played my best for them, only afterward, I found out they never made it…"

Another silence settled under the bridge until I finally spoke. "If you think about it, they could have been there."

"What do you mean?"

I shrugged in an attempt to force nonchalance. "Like, in spirit, I mean."

Sage let out a breath of air that sounded a lot like a laugh to me. "You think that moments after their death, my family would have nothing better to do than to watch me play music? I'm sure if they were out there somewhere, they wouldn't be worrying about me."

Here's my chance, I thought. My pulse quickened as if in warning, but in the moment, I felt like something needed to be said. "But they are worried about you."

Sage went silent for a beat, and then she looked at me sideways. "You say that like you're sure of it."

My hands shook slightly, and the red blossom fell out of them. I closed my eyes for a few seconds to compose myself. "That's because I am." I forced down the lump rising in my throat. *This. Is. It.* "The first day I met you, I also met your sister."

There. I said it. Would she believe me? Would it save her? The following split second felt more like minutes. For a moment, I wasn't sure if admitting this was a victory or a mistake. I held my breath until Sage spoke.

"What are you talking about?"

"Melissa was there with me in the dressing room at Special Day Bridal," I confessed. "She told me that I needed to help you." I swallowed again, but the task was becoming more difficult as Sage stared at me in skepticism and my confidence in the situation plummeted. I locked my eyes on a rock near my toes.

"You mean to tell me…" Sage started slowly.

I wanted to take what I'd just said back because I could tell it was freaking Sage out, but the implication of my words was already out there.

"That I'm psychic? Yeah," I finished for her. "I know you probably don't believe me, but I can see ghosts and predict things about the future. I can even find things that people have lost or hidden, and sometimes when I touch people's skin, I can feel what they're feeling. You? You're scared of something." I finally lifted my eyes to meet her gaze, although I was terrified of her reaction.

The moments it took Sage to respond seemed to stretch into eternity. *Please believe me. Please believe me*, I chanted in my head. The seconds ticked by, taunting me and leaving me far too much time to wonder if this was the right choice or not. At first, I was sure it was bad, but then a glimmer of hope washed over me when she met my eyes.

"Oh, my god. You're crazy," she finally said.

My heart sank as I witnessed my worst fear come true.

"You actually believe that?" Sage asked, pushing herself to her feet. "I —I can't believe I brought you down here." She paused for a second, just long enough for tears to sting at my eyes. "I have to go."

"Sage, wait," I said, grabbing for her wrist to stop her. In that moment, fear consumed me. Fear. Sage was afraid of something, and this time, I knew what it was. *Me*. She was afraid of me.

"Please," Sage said, pulling away from me. The look in her eyes begged me to let her go, so I did.

CHAPTER 15

I tried to hold back the tears, but the force at which they hit felt like a dam had broken inside of me. Sage's words cut into me like a knife, making me feel rejected.

You're crazy.

You're crazy.

You're crazy.

Can I really blame her for saying that, though? I thought the same thing when I learned about my abilities.

But the one thing that really ripped me apart was the thought that I'd failed. Sage wasn't going to talk to me again, so how was I supposed to save her?

I didn't know how long I stayed there, but I eventually calmed down enough, swallowed my pride, and crawled out from beneath the bridge. I wanted nothing more than to fall into Robin's arms and tell him what happened, about how I'd failed. He'd surely have something to say that would lift my spirits.

Luckily by the time I got back, the band was already packing up their equipment. The moment Robin saw my face, he ran toward me. "Where have you been, Crystal?"

Tears pricked at my eyes again.

"And where is Sage?"

"She left a while ago." I wrapped my arms around Robin's muscular frame for comfort. "I couldn't do it, Robin." My voice cracked. "I failed. I can't save her."

"Crystal," he said, pushing my hair out of my eyes to look into them. "What are you talking about? What happened?"

I took a deep breath and finally composed myself. My voice came out surprisingly even given the circumstances. "I told her like you said I should. I told her I was psychic. Robin, she called me crazy and said she didn't believe me."

He pulled me into a deeper hug. "I'm sorry I encouraged you to tell her. So, she knows she's going to die, then? Or at least that you think she is?"

I ran the conversation back through my head and realized I'd never mentioned that. "Actually, no. I told her about her sister and that I saw her." I paused for a moment. "I get where she's coming from, but I just—I wish it would have gone better."

Even as I said it, I wasn't sure how much I did understand where Sage was coming from. After all, I hadn't been through what she had. Sure, I'd lost my dad, but there was always someone there to support me 100 percent. The more I thought about it, the more I realized that the overwhelming amount of support I had in my life had clouded my judgement. Everyone I had told about my abilities had accepted them, but with the pain of rejection coursing through my veins now, I finally understood—if only slightly—why my mother insisted I be careful about who I tell.

"Maybe I took it too far," I admitted to Robin.

He didn't say anything. He just took my hand and led me back to the vehicles next to the pavilion. At the same time, Emma was already making her way toward us.

"Crystal, are you okay?" she asked once we met up. She rested a hand on my shoulder for comfort. "It didn't go well, huh?"

All I could do was shake my head. We reached the vehicles, and I leaned against the band's van for support.

"Sage didn't believe her," Robin explained in a low voice.

Emma opened her mouth like she was going to speak, but then she closed it. I figured she was ready to gloat about being right until she noticed how much it was really bothering me.

Derek showed up next to Emma a second later and placed his arm around her shoulder. "What's wrong?" he whispered to Robin, who promptly explained the situation.

I kept my gaze locked on a pebble in the parking lot. Sage's words played over and over in my head, and for several long minutes, it was the only thing I could focus on. Even my vision blurred as symphonies of *You're crazy* played through my mind. Next to me, I was sure my friends were discussing Sage, but I didn't process anything they said.

"Crystal." The sound of my name pulled me back into focus. I looked up to meet Emma's gaze. "So, how about that date?"

I forced a half smile. Would that solve anything? Was it fair to enjoy myself when I still didn't know how Sage was going to die? It felt like in the last hour I'd just taken ten steps backward. I didn't respond, but my thoughts were clearly written all over my face like normal.

"You realize you don't need her to believe you in order to save her, right?" Derek pointed out.

"What do you mean?" I asked.

Robin was the one to explain. "Just keep using your abilities, and then be there when it's going to happen."

I blinked a few times, absorbing this idea. "Robin, she's supposed to die on my mom's wedding day." I didn't know why I felt the need to point this out. On one level, I felt like I couldn't abandon my mom. On another, I knew I wouldn't abandon Sage when her life depended on me.

"You're right," I said after a long silence. "I don't need her to believe me. I just have to figure out what's going to happen, and then I'll know how to stop it. At least I know when. I still need to know where and how."

Robin smiled at me encouragingly. "That's what I like to hear," he said, leaning in and kissing the top of my head. "Remember we'll always be here to help. We're all concerned about Sage, but unlike you, *we* believe in your abilities."

I smiled back at him. He was right. Maybe I didn't need Sage to believe in me, but as long as my friends believed in me and I was just as confident, anything was possible.

"Like Robin said, we're all just as worried about Sage as you are." Somehow I doubted that, but Emma continued. "We're going to help you save her, but I think you need to take your mind off Sage for a few hours." Emma sounded strangely like my mom.

Taking my mind off Sage wasn't easy, especially because it felt like I'd just pulled a knife out of my heart, but when I snuggled into Robin's arms in the back seat of Emma's car, I found the task much easier. I was grateful for all the psychic practice I'd done in the last few months in learning how to control my thoughts and body. It allowed me to put Sage out of my head the way my mom told me I needed to do.

"So, do we know what we're doing?" Emma asked as she pulled out of the parking lot.

"Well, we all just ate," Derek pointed out, "so I'm not hungry or anything."

"Crystal," Robin asked, "what do you want to do?"

"Hmm..." I thought. "Something fun?"

"Well, duh," Emma said from the front seat.

"A movie?" Derek suggested.

Robin crinkled his nose. "I don't know of anything good out right now. We could go bowling or something like that."

Emma weaved through the city streets. "Well, I'm going to just keep driving around until someone tells me what to do."

Everyone fell silent for a minute as we all pondered ideas. "What about something like laser tag? Or maybe paintball?" I suggested.

Emma drew in an excited breath. "That sounds like a lot of fun! Is there a place like that around here?"

"Yeah." Robin resituated himself closer to Emma to give her directions.

We drove past the city limits and out to a secluded paintball arena. There was a forest on one side and the familiar flat cornfield of southern Minnesota on the other. The arena itself was spread across an enormous field and dotted with inflatable bunkers. Before I knew it, I was suited up, an employee was handing me equipment, and we were being ushered into the arena. We were up against what must have been a 12-year-old's birthday party.

"This is a game of elimination," the employee explained to us. "Each team will start at their respective bases. From there, you're free to roam the arena. Once you've been hit, you'll go to the elimination zone," the guy gestured to a section off the field, "and wait for the next round to start. Everybody good?"

When no one had anything to say, we entered the field and took our bases. When the employee announced it, the game was on. I stood there like a fool, trying to take in my surroundings. Emma and Derek were already gone, and our enemies had scattered.

"Crystal," Robin said in a low voice, "what are you waiting for?"

I scanned the area again and immediately spotted one of the boys aiming his gun straight for my chest a few bunkers away.

"Run," Robin shouted, pulling me after him. He never was one for physical activity because of his leg, but he managed to react quickly enough to dodge the kid's paintballs.

The paintball flew past me as I dove for cover behind a second bunker. I couldn't help but laugh in relief.

"What's so funny?" Robin asked.

I shrugged. "I don't know what I'm doing."

"It's all about strategy. Follow me."

Robin stayed low as he peeked around the corner. I could hear the boys running around the arena and yelling at each other. One was barking orders while the others laughed in exhilaration.

"This should be easy." I grinned mischievously. It was only a minute into the fight, and I was already starting to relax. It was easier to put Sage out of my mind when I could channel my feelings in a game of war.

"I hear one coming," Robin whispered. "Are you ready?"

I nodded.

On his signal, Robin and I jumped from behind our wall of safety.

Pop, pop, pop.

Each of Robin's paintballs hit the boy square in the chest. One of mine managed to catch him in the leg.

The boy fell to his knees and dropped his gun. "I've been shot!" he exclaimed dramatically as he clutched his chest and fell to the ground. In a struggling whisper, he managed to say, "Tell my mother I love her."

Robin and I exchanged a glance. Was the kid just taking this thing too seriously, or did we actually hurt him?

"Dude," Robin said, standing above him. "Are you okay?"

The kid opened one eye. In one swift motion, he grabbed his gun, sprung up from the ground, and shot Robin twice in the shoulder.

"I'm fine, sucker," the kid shouted before running away.

I couldn't help but let out a laugh.

Robin rolled his eyes at me. "Okay, I'm not falling for that one again." Then he turned to yell at the kid. "That doesn't count. You were already eliminated!"

"Awe, but it was funny," I laughed.

"Keep laughing and you're getting one of these," he wiggled his gun, "straight to the chest."

I shut my mouth immediately but couldn't hide my smile.

"Come on. Let's go kick some butt." Robin took my arm again and led me behind another inflatable bunker. He put his finger to his face to tell me to be quiet.

At the same moment, I heard footsteps behind me. I whirled around and brought my gun to my shoulder but relaxed when I realized it was just Derek. He was already covered in blotches of paint.

"You look dead," I joked.

"Ha ha," Derek said sarcastically as he continued on his way to the elimination zone. "Let me know how it feels once you've been eliminated."

Robin peeked around the side of the bunker to get a good look while I crouched down low, waiting for him to tell me what to do. After what seemed like several minutes, he cocked his finger at me, and I followed behind him. We quickly shuffled across the field and ducked behind another bunker.

I spotted movement from one of the other team members and fixed my eye on the bunker I thought I saw him dive behind. The next thing I knew, the kid emerged from his hiding spot and began racing straight toward me. I fired a few shots, but they all exploded helplessly in the grass around the kid's feet.

"Run." I pushed at Robin, and we both took off.

He positioned himself behind a smaller bunker and shot at the boy to cover me while I headed for my own hiding spot. I'd always been a fit person, but as I closed the distance to my target bunker, my breathing quickened and became shallow, like my lungs were closing up.

Suddenly, the scene shifted around me. The green of the grass faded into the pale gray of concrete, and the bunkers surrounding me transformed into tall buildings. People milled around me, but I pushed through the busy crowd, never slowing. My mind completely detached from the paintball arena. All I knew on this busy street—one I didn't even recognize—was that if I didn't keep running, something bad was going to happen to me. I glanced behind me to make sure I wasn't being followed, but I didn't see anyone. Still, I sprinted forward to save myself, dodging people the entire way.

I rounded a corner and finally emerged from the crowd. With a free stretch down the secluded street, I sprinted as fast as I could. It felt like I'd never run so fast in my life the way my legs protested and burned. I took a huge gulp of air, but it felt like a weight was crushing down on my lungs. I couldn't stop now. I spotted an area of trees and ran for cover.

A moment later, I found myself back in my paintball gear complete with a gun in my hand, but the arena was gone. I removed my helmet and looked around frantically. What had just happened? Trees surrounded me in a thick forest, but through them, I caught a glimpse of the blue and red bunkers.

Leaves crunched next to me, and I immediately brought my gun up to my shoulder. I recognized the figure making its way toward me.

"Robin?" I asked, lowering my weapon. "What happened?"

"I don't know," he said, slowing his pace until he was standing right next to me. "You just took off, but you were running so fast, I couldn't catch up. Are you okay?"

The look on my face must have answered his question because in the next moment, he dropped his gun and pulled me into his arms.

"Crystal, what's wrong?"

I blinked a few times to hold back the tears. "I have no idea. I—I think I just had a vision. I was being chased."

"Well, you were being chased," Robin told me, although there was a hint of sympathy to his voice. "That kid was chasing you down, and then you left the boundaries of the arena, so I came after you."

I shook my head. "I don't mean it like that, Robin. I wasn't... here. I was in the city somewhere, but I didn't recognize it."

"Do you think it has to do with Sage?"

That hadn't even occurred to me. "What? I—I don't know. Why do you think that?"

"Because your visions always mean something. If not about Sage, then what?"

I remained silent in his arms for what seemed like several minutes while digesting this and playing the vision back through my head. Maybe if I could talk with Sage again, I could figure out what it meant, but would she talk to me?

"Maybe it's, like, a metaphor," I suggested. "Like, Sage is trying to run away from something, but I mean, I already knew that. She's clearly trying to escape the memory of her family's death, and she says she wants to get out of the city once she graduates. But the thing is that she probably won't talk to me again."

"Maybe I could try talking to her."

I hugged Robin tighter. "Would you? I mean, I just don't want her to see me as a freak. She doesn't have to believe me, but I still feel like I need to be around her to protect her."

Robin pushed my hair out of my face. "I'll try to get her to come around." Then he took my hand. "Come on. Let's get back to the arena, and we can turn our stuff in."

When we made it back, Emma and Derek were both splattered with paint. Since the kid shot Robin in the shoulder, I was the only one paint-free.

"Crystal, what's wrong?" Emma asked immediately.

"I'll tell you about it in the car. Can we just go?"

As we rode home, I realized that my mom was right. Taking the time to relax *did* help me with my abilities, but I still didn't know what the vision meant. That sent a nervous shutter throughout my body.

CHAPTER 16

On Sunday, I spent my time helping my mom with last-minute wedding plans in hopes of taking my mind off Sage again so I'd see something worthwhile, but it didn't get me anywhere. Mom, Sophie, Diane, and I sat around the kitchen table putting together the center-pieces for the wedding.

"Sophie? Diane?" They both looked up at me expectantly. "Have either of you two seen anything about Sage?" I kept my gaze on the ribbon I was measuring out.

Out of the corner of my eye, I watched Sophie set down her center-piece. "I'm sorry, Crystal, but I haven't seen anything except what I felt that first day."

"I've been trying, too," Diane said, "but there's nothing."

"And Teddy doesn't have any more insight?" I asked, although I knew he would have told me if he did.

My mom shook her head.

"Maybe we could postpone the wedding," I joked with a nervous laugh. Would that even work? Melissa said Sage would die when I wore the dress. If we postponed it, all that would do was postpone Sage's death, and by that point, I may still not have any more answers. My heart sank at the joke. "I didn't mean that. I'm sorry. But maybe we could hire her a body guard." I suggested half-seriously. "Or talk to the police."

My mom shook her head again. "What would we say? 'Officer, my daughter and I are psychic, and we need you to protect a girl we know because her dead sister told us to.'"

I knew how silly it sounded. If we lived in a world of logic, there'd be no real reason to worry about her. No one would believe us if we told them she was in danger.

"Sweetie." Sophie inched closer to me, and I raised my head to meet her gaze. "Being psychic is a lot harder than how Hollywood portrays it. With things like this, it's usually a one-girl mission, which is a shame, and rarely will you be able to control anything you see. But you should know that if you have any questions, we are *always* here to answer them."

"Okay." I set my project down. "I don't understand why I can control some things and not others. Like, if I want to find lost keys, I can do it like *that*." I snapped my fingers. "If I want to feel someone's emotions, I can usually do it just by touching them. I can even tell when it's going to rain. But things like seeing the past and the future, or even ghosts, is totally out of my control. Is there any way *to* control it?"

"Crystal," my mom said, "remember that you've only been at this for a few months. I mean, we're all surprised at how far you've come in such a short amount of time." They all exchanged a glance in agreement. "But it will take you years to be remotely close to controlling things like that. Finding things doesn't take a lot of energy, but looking into the past and the future is harder."

"Just keep practicing," Diane encouraged, "and things will get easier."

I nodded. "Yeah, I know you guys are right, but with everything the universe has thrown at me in the last few months, with Kelli, Hope, and Sage, it would just make more sense if it'd show me more at one time."

"Maybe it's trying," my mom pointed out. "You just have to make sure you're listening." There it was again. That accusation, like I didn't *care* enough about my abilities. Her voice was soft and kind, but her words cut into me like a razor blade.

I didn't say another thing. We finished the centerpieces, and then I shut myself in my room. I couldn't believe my mom didn't think I cared about my abilities. Was she *serious*? I gritted my teeth in frustration.

Setting out to prove her wrong, I spread my yoga mat out at the foot of my bed. Hours passed as I let go of expectation and connected with the other side. I knew I wanted to see something, but I gave myself permission to not care if a vision came or not. Even after darkness enveloped my room and I finally opened my eyes, I still hadn't seen anything, but the fact that I was doing something to improve my abilities by getting in tune with them left me with a sense of comfort as I crawled into bed.

∽

On Monday, Derek, Emma, and I chatted quietly in geometry as Mr. Bailey left us to our own devices.

"So I did some research," Derek said.

"About your parents?" Emma asked excitedly. "Do you know how they died yet?"

Derek shook his head and kept his voice low. "No, I'm talking about Sage."

I leaned in closer to the center of our little triangle in intrigue.

"You guys were talking about her uncle before, Alan Anderson. I spent pretty much all day yesterday looking for him online. I tried out different spellings of the name, narrowed the geographical area, and all that."

"And?" I prodded.

"I honestly didn't come up with much. I found some public records, but that's basically things we already know, like that he's a fugitive. Other than that, I found that he used to work construction, and the best I can tell, he's never been married." Derek pulled a sheet of paper from between the pages of his notebook. "This was the only picture I could find of him online, but it has to be pretty old."

Alan didn't look all that scary, with soft brown eyes and a sweet demeanor. Except I knew what he had done, and that frightened me. I handed the photo back to Derek. "Okay, so we don't know anything more about him really, but do you guys think he's important in some way? I mean, do you think I should waste any time caring about him? He's probably long gone."

Emma shook her head lightly like she wasn't sure. "I don't know... I think it has to mean something. I mean, at least it explains why Sage is so reserved and kind of shy."

Derek twisted his mouth in thought but didn't say anything.

I recalled the way my mom said that sometimes the universe is trying to tell me something but I just don't listen. What if this was one of those times? "Actually, Derek. Can I keep that photo?"

"Sure," he said, handing it over.

I folded it up and slipped it into my backpack after class.

~

That afternoon, I picked Hope up from school and walked her home like normal. Today, she wanted to play Go Fish.

"Crystal," she said in a scolding tone after she dealt. "You're distracted. Is it your friend again?"

I finally met her gaze and realized I hadn't even picked up my cards yet. I didn't even know what I was thinking about, but she was right. I was distracted. "It's—yeah. It is my friend. It's—" I couldn't decide if I should tell Hope or not. I mean, she knew about me and everything, but she was still so young. "I'm kind of on a time limit to figure something out, and I'm running out of time. Not to mention that my friend won't talk to me anymore."

"You could always, like, peer into your crystal ball to see what to do," Hope suggested jokingly. That immediately brought up an idea I couldn't believe I hadn't thought of before.

As soon as I entered my house, I rushed to my room. I had intended to use my crystal ball a week ago, but it had gotten buried under my pile of clothes in my messy room. I threw shirts out of the way until my hands clamped around a rock-hard object. My heart beat madly in excitement as I set the ball back on its stand. I wanted to get started right away, but I knew nothing would come of it. I needed to calm down first. I took a deep breath but was still twitching in anticipation. I needed a quick break before I tackled this. Emma would be here soon, and we'd "get in the zone," so I figured I could try the crystal ball after Emma left. I needed the privacy.

I made my way to the kitchen to find that Teddy was almost done preparing food. I took a seat on one of the stools along the counter. My mom wasn't anywhere in sight, so I figured she was still at the shop. Since she owned it, it was always somewhat unpredictable when she'd be home.

"Teddy?"

He looked at me expectantly. "Yeah? Is something wrong, Crystal?"

What would give him that idea? As soon as I asked myself the question, I realized I was biting the corner of my lip and clutching the owl pendant around my neck. I relaxed.

"I guess I was just kind of wondering if you knew anything else. You know, about Sage."

Teddy stirred the soup he was making. "I wish I could say I did, but you already know everything I know. As far as Sage's uncle, the police have been looking for him for nearly five years, and nothing's come of it. If it's not in the records, I don't know anything."

"What about..." I trailed off.

"What about what?" he asked curiously.

"I mean, you don't have a feeling about any of this or anything?"

"You mean, like, a supernatural feeling?"

I nodded.

He gave a slight laugh. "Crystal, I don't know how much my 'feelings' would help in a situation like this. I've always been intuitive, but nothing like you and your mother."

I nodded in understanding. "You don't think Sage's uncle has anything to do with my warning, do you?" I didn't even know if *I* thought that, but it was information connected to Sage nonetheless.

"Do you want my professional opinion?" Teddy didn't wait for an answer. "I really don't think Sage is in any danger from him right now. A guy like that wouldn't come out of hiding after so many years for risk of being caught, unless he felt guilty about what he'd done. But in that case, he wouldn't hurt Sage. The truth is, he's probably changed his name and face and is long gone."

I thought about this for a moment and knew Teddy was probably right. "I guess that makes a lot of sense. If you come up with anything else, you'll tell me right away, right?"

"You bet," he said before he turned back to the soup.

A few minutes later, Emma arrived. I ate my soup and then joined her in my bedroom. My thoughts were on my crystal ball, but I knew I had to get through the relaxation part of everything before that would even work.

Today, it was the same thing as normal, except Emma stayed a while longer so we could finish up our geometry homework together. When she left, I felt ready to connect with my crystal ball.

I situated myself at my desk and took several long, deep breaths then hovered my hands over my crystal ball.

I couldn't tell how much time passed as I sat there focusing on my breathing.

In.

Out.

No expectations.

In.

Out.

No expectations.

I repeated this mantra in my head. My shoulders relaxed, and my eyelids fell into a comfortable, closed position.

In.

Out.

No expectations.

Soon, the mantra lost all meaning, and my mind cleared completely. A feeling of tranquility overcame me so much that I felt I wasn't even conscious, like I was peacefully dreaming. At some point, though, a voice in the back of my head told me to open my eyes. When I did, my crystal ball was glowing. A wave of beautiful colors emanated from the ball, dancing in a serene motion that pulled me in. I leaned toward it, magnetized.

My nose hovered inches above the ball as an image began to take shape. At first, it was all just a cloudy mess, but then the cloud transformed into flames. Each flame rippled in the image, like fingers trying to claw their way out of the glass. As soon as I saw them, the flames took the shape of solid fingers. The bright orange glow darkened to a deep red. Crimson liquid pooled in the hand and ran off it in drips.

No, I thought, horrified. The moment the terror consumed me and an intense fear rippled throughout my body, the swirling colors in the crystal ball disappeared. It returned to normal, like it was just an ordinary decoration.

I quickly pushed myself away from my desk to put distance between myself and the ball, nearly toppling over in the process. I buried my face in my hands, and my body heaved with dry sobs.

No, no, no, I thought.

The reality of the situation hit me hard and stayed there, like a weight was pulling me down. My breath ceased to the point where I had to remind myself I needed air. My breathing wavered as I swallowed the lump in my throat and faced the dire truth of the situation.

Unless I did something to save her, Sage was going to die a gruesome death.

CHAPTER 17

*E*ach sunrise over the next few days felt like a countdown in a ticking time bomb. It was less than three weeks until the wedding, and a sickening feeling consumed me as each preparation we made for it felt synonymous to a step closer to Sage's death. The question of *how* she was going to die still aggravated me.

Most of my time was spent trying to come up with a way I could save Sage when she wouldn't hear what I had to say. The least I could do was try to get her to come around, so that Tuesday morning, I tried calling her in hopes of getting her to come back to the band practice that night. She didn't answer, so I called Robin.

"Hello?"

"Hey, Robin. I was just curious how it went with Sage yesterday at school. Did you talk to her?"

"I tried, but she didn't say much," he admitted.

I sighed, and then I jumped into the explanation about what I saw in my crystal ball.

"That's really freaky. I will definitely try to talk her into coming tonight, but I mean, I can't make any promises."

"I know."

"But you know what?" Robin said. "Even if she doesn't want to talk to you, you're still going to save her. You know that, right?"

I didn't answer because in all honesty, I *didn't* know that. Was it going to be a car crash? Was her uncle coming for her? Was it something else entirely?

I still didn't know her all that well. If I could warn her... But how could I warn her when I didn't know what to warn her about? She wouldn't listen to me anyhow, would she?

"I hope you're right," I finally said. "I—" I stopped, realizing for a moment that I almost told him I loved him. It was the truth, wasn't it? But I couldn't bring myself to say it first. "I'll see you tonight."

～

"She'll be okay," Robin promised after his band practice. "She has you on her side."

Sage hadn't shown up for practice, and I was positive it was because she was scared of me.

"But how exactly do I help her? What, am I supposed to stalk her on my mom's wedding day?"

Robin's eyes shifted in thought.

"I can't miss my mom's wedding. Am I supposed to tell her to cancel? It's not like I can get Sage to come to the wedding, not when she won't even come to your band practice anymore."

Robin rubbed my arms for comfort. "You don't know she didn't come because of you."

"Did she tell you why she wouldn't come?"

"She just said she was busy."

"That's textbook translation for, 'Your girlfriend is a freak, and I don't want to be around her.'"

"Hey," Robin said softly, kissing me lightly on the lips. "She might still come around."

I wanted to believe Robin's words, but when Thursday came and Sage still wasn't there, I knew he was completely wrong about that. Even so, I found myself half-believing his idea that I could still save Sage despite her need to avoid me. I wasn't entirely convinced, but at least there was a glimmer of hope.

"What do you guys think I should do?" I asked Emma and Derek when we piled into the car Thursday night. My social studies homework was spread across my lap in the back seat, but I couldn't pay attention to it while this question rattled around in my brain.

"About what?" Derek asked, twisting in his seat to look at me.

"Sage clearly doesn't want to talk to me, but I still have to save her. I don't know how she's going to die—even with that freaky thing I saw in my crystal ball. So, how do I make sure she's safe on my mom's wedding day?"

"You could tell her not to leave the house," Derek suggested.

I slammed my textbook closed in annoyance. "I just said she won't talk to me, and even if she would, she wouldn't believe something like that."

Derek held his hands up in defense. "Hey, you asked for suggestions…"

I sighed deeply. "Yeah, I know. I'm sorry. That wasn't a personal attack, Derek. It just seems like nothing is going to work."

"I'd say you should invite her to the wedding," Emma said, "so she would be safe, but like you said, she may not agree to it."

A brief silence filled the car as we all worked to come up with a solution, but I couldn't stand the silence.

"It's not just that that's annoying me. I mean, all of this… I still don't know how she's going to die. I mean, if I did, I could prevent her from, say, crossing the street, or getting into a car, or doing whatever freaky thing is supposedly going to kill her. But it's not even just that, either." I reached for my backpack and unzipped the front pocket. "I still can't figure out what Sage's uncle has to do with all of this."

I unfolded the paper and studied the man's face, using the headlights of the car behind us to illuminate his features. "And there's so much left unanswered with him. Like, I get why he's on the run, but what prompted it? And how far did he run? And is Sage in danger from *him*? And if she is, what do I do about it?"

Neither Emma nor Derek said anything. They both just shrugged their shoulders like they didn't know what to say.

When the car went silent again, I rested my head against the window and stared at the photograph of Alan. His involvement was shrouded in so much mystery. The longer I looked at him, the drowsier I became, and at some point on our way back home, the exhaustion overtook me.

∾

The day I told my mother was the most terrifying day of my life. I didn't want to tell her because I knew he would kill me if I did.

"You won't tell anyone, will you, Sage?" he had said the first time.

All I could do was look up at him in terror and shake my head in agreement.

"Good. Because you know what will happen if you do?"

The fright I felt for my uncle caused my throat to close up. I could hardly breathe, let alone speak. I shook my head.

"I'll kill you." He said it like it was a joke, but I was in no state of mind to take the words lightheartedly. "You understand, then, right?"

I nodded as bile rose to my throat. I forced it down, along with my disgust for my uncle, because that was the only way I figured I'd survive.

But even though I'd never said anything, my mom somehow knew. I lied to her at first, but at 12, I could read her expression well enough that I knew she'd caught on and wouldn't accept my refusal.

My mother sat me down in her bedroom and spoke to me lightly. "Sage, I need you to tell me the truth. It's really, really important. Is Uncle Alan hurting you?"

Tears rose to my eyes. "No," I said without meeting her gaze.

"Are you sure?" My mother's eyes bore into mine in a way I'd never seen before.

I nodded.

"You'd tell me if he was, wouldn't you?" she asked.

I thought about this for a moment. How long could I keep lying to her? It was only a matter of time before someone witnessed something. I blinked a few times, considering telling her the truth. If I did, my uncle had promised he'd kill me, but was that any worse than what he was already doing to me? Was it worth keeping up this lie just to save my own life? Wouldn't it hurt less once all this was over? In that moment, I decided that I'd rather die than continue lying about it.

Slowly, like I was still thinking about the decision to give up the lie, I shook my head at my mother. She pressed her lips into a thin line, and her eyes grew red like she was going to cry.

That night, my mother told Melissa and me she was taking us to the movies. I wasn't stupid. I knew it was just a way to get us out of the house. But we didn't make it out the door before my uncle came home and I heard my father's confrontation with him.

"What the hell were you thinking, Alan?" I heard him say. "They're my daughters. You're a sick bastard. And after everything we've done for you? We put a roof over your head! You're no longer welcome in this house. Not now. Not ever!"

I heard the thud as my father's fist connected with my uncle's jaw. I exchanged a horrified glance with Melissa the same time my mother pulled us both into a hug. Tears ran down all of our cheeks.

Six more thuds reverberated through the walls before I heard the roar of my uncle's pick-up truck spring to life.

My uncle never came back to our house, but every time I closed my eyes, he was there in my nightmares.

~

My eyes shot open, and I gasped for air.

"Crystal?" I heard Derek's voice say.

I swung my head around, trying to figure out where I was. It was dark, and I was moving. After a moment, I realized I was still in the car. I clutched my hand over my chest as my heartrate slowed.

"What was that? Are you okay?" Derek asked.

"I—" I thought about it for a second.

On one level, I was freaking out at the terror I felt in Sage's memories. On another level, I'd *seen* something, and although it wasn't directly connected to Sage's death, it left me feeling one step closer to helping her.

"I'm fine," I answered truthfully.

CHAPTER 18

*T*he weekend passed like any other—uneventful—although a sense of worry taunted me as Saturday marked just two weeks until Sage's death. As guilty as it made me feel, I didn't know what else to do but wait and hope for the best.

Monday came with good news.

Talked to Sage, Robin's text said during lunch. *Says she's not mad at you.*

I had to wonder exactly what that meant. Did it just mean she was trying to get rid of Robin and stop his inquisition, or did it mean she was interested in talking to me again? All I could do was cross my fingers and hope she would show up to Robin's band practice on Tuesday. I wasn't keeping my hopes up too high. That's why I was shocked when my phone rang on Tuesday on our way to the band practice and Sage's name came up on the caller ID.

"Hello," I greeted, almost too quickly.

"Crystal?" Sage's voice came across the line.

"Yeah."

"Hi." She paused for a moment like she didn't know what to say. I heard her take a deep breath. "Let me start by saying I'm really sorry."

"About what?" I asked, feigning ignorance. It came across sounding fake, even to me.

"You know exactly what I mean. I shouldn't have called you crazy. Anyway, I just wanted to let you know I was sorry."

"So, you're coming to the band practice?" I asked, almost with too much enthusiasm.

"Actually," Sage said, her voice coming off a little shy like usual. "I was hoping you'd accept my apology over dinner or something, if you haven't eaten yet. We could meet at the food court in the mall. I'm more in the mood for a girls' night instead of hanging out with all of Robin's friends. Not that there's anything wrong with them. But only if you don't mind."

"No!" I nearly shouted. "I don't mind. I'm almost to the city. I can be there in about 15 minutes. Does that work for you?"

"Yeah! I'll see you soon."

I hung up. "Emma, is it okay if you drop me off at the mall? Sage wants to meet up with me there. You guys don't think it will be weird being at Asher's without me, do you?"

"Of course not!" Emma said. "Besides, I'm practically in the band now."

"You've only practiced with them three times," Derek pointed out.

Emma frowned at him but let the statement slide. "Yes, I'll drop you off, Crystal. It's kind of exciting that she's talking to you again. Do you want us to come with you?"

"No." I shook my head. "It sounded like she wanted it to be just me and her."

"Okay," Emma agreed with a look of worry in her eyes. "You can text or call me when you're done, and I'll come get you."

When I exited the car, I nervously shifted my backpack on my shoulder and took a deep breath as I entered the mall. I was excited to talk to Sage again, but I was scared of what she had to say to me. I was sure she still didn't believe me, so warning her about her death was off the table.

I scanned the tables and restaurant lines for Sage, but I didn't see her. Maybe she wasn't there yet. I was headed toward an empty table and about to sit down when I caught a glimpse of auburn hair the color of Sage's. She looked up to meet my eyes as I made my way over to her.

"Hey," I greeted, slinging my backpack strap over the chair across from her.

Sage offered a smile, but it was the nervous type she always had. "So, uh, what type of food are you in the mood for?"

I scanned the restaurant signs. "Chinese?"

I put my backpack back on as we made our way into the line, thankful that I had a few dollars from babysitting stashed away in it. I knew there had to be a reason Sage invited me here, like she wanted to talk about something, but all we could do was make small talk—like what kind of chicken we should order—until we got back to our table. I suspected she was too nervous to start talking, and I was already covered in a thin sheen of sweat anticipating what it could be about.

After a few bites and complete silence, I finally set my chopsticks down. "Did you want to talk about something?"

"Huh?" Sage looked up from her food.

"I guess I can't figure out why you invited me here," I admitted.

Sage gave a long sigh, the kind of sigh you make when you're trying to calm your nerves. She set down her own chopsticks and tugged on her sleeves until they were balled into her fists. She wiped at her nose with the back of her hand. "You're right. I do want to talk to you about something, but it's just really hard for me."

"You can tell me anything."

"Isn't that weird?" Sage said, catching me off guard. What did she mean? "The thing is, I know I can talk to you about anything, and that's crazy. We've only known each other for two weeks. I've been to therapist after therapist, and I couldn't talk to any of them. And then you... But then you said those things about my family..."

"Sage," I interrupted. "I'm sorry about that. I—"

"No, it's okay. It really is." She picked up her chopsticks again and poked at her rice. "I should be the one apologizing about the way I treated you." She bit into a piece of chicken.

"Thank you," I said, twisting some noodles around my chopsticks.

Sage swallowed. "Who's to say you're not telling the truth?"

I nearly choked, but I forced the noodles down my throat without a problem. "Are you saying you believe me?"

Sage shrugged as she shifted the rice around on her plate. "I'm not saying that. I don't know what to believe. Remember how I told you I thought I saw my family after they died?"

I nodded.

"Well, I've been thinking a lot about it, and what if I *did* see them?" Sage paused for a moment. "You didn't call me crazy when I said that, so I just feel pretty terrible about calling you crazy. Besides, Robin's been talking some sense into me." She gave a bit of forced laugh.

"Yeah, he's pretty good at knowing what to say."

An awkward silence filled the air between us while we each dug into our food.

"So," I finally said. "What was it you really wanted to talk to me about?"

Sage gave an exhale through her mouth as if preparing herself. "So, I thought a lot about what you said. At first, I was really scared."

"Of what?" I asked when she paused.

"I—I guess I was scared you knew too much about me. I'm really good at shutting people out." Sage rubbed at her eye nervously. "You probably picked up on that."

I nodded and offered a sheepish smile.

"But like I said," she continued, "I have this weird feeling that I can trust you. My therapist says that if I can't open up to her, I should at least talk to someone. She tried to get me to write in a journal, but I just couldn't do it. Like, what if someone found it?" She sniffled and took another bite of rice. When she swallowed, she spoke again. "So, I figured I'd take a stab at talking to you."

A little part of my heart fluttered, touched that she trusted me enough to talk to me. I listened quietly and chewed slowly as she spoke.

"There are a few things you should probably know about me. You already know that my parents and sister died. But that's just one of my issues. When I was little, my uncle used to live with us." She pressed her lips together and looked around to make sure no one was listening. She lowered her voice. "He used to... do stuff to me." Her eyes shifted nervously but wouldn't look at me.

It took me a few moments to realize that I wasn't supposed to know this already. "I'm so sorry," I told her honestly.

"No, it's okay. Really. I was doing fine until my parents died. I mean, my dad always made me feel safe. But now that he's gone..." Sage twisted her sleeves nervously in her hands. She finally looked into my eyes, her own brimming with tears that threatened to pour over the threshold. "I don't feel safe anymore."

"Oh, Sage," I said quietly. This time when I reached over to touch her hand that now rested on the table, it wasn't awkward. But the moment I touched her, something changed. A sickening feeling overcame me. It felt like my insides were twisting and my guts were trying to force their way out of my throat. A tightening sensation rose to my eyes, and my nose tingled. Hairs stood up on the back of my neck.

I pulled away from Sage, almost too quickly. "I know how you feel," I told her, but I knew she had no idea how much truth there was to that statement.

Sage forced a smile, returning her hands back into her lap. "That's sweet, but I know you're just trying to make me feel better." She took another deep breath. "After my dad died, the nightmares of my uncle came back. That's why I didn't fight living with Anna and Brian—my mom's sister and her husband. I actually *wanted* to live with them because I felt I needed someone there to protect me. My therapist already knows all this, but what she doesn't know is something that terrifies me more than anything else."

"What is it?" I asked in a near whisper.

"I—" Sage paused like she wasn't sure whether to tell me or not. She stole another nervous glance around the food court.

"You can tell me," I assured her.

She bit her lip as if it was the only way to stifle the tears. Finally, her eyes locked on mine. "Sometimes I think I see him."

I drew in a sharp breath.

"Sometimes I think I'm going crazy," Sage admitted, rubbing the back of her hand at her eyes to wipe away tears she was trying so hard to hold back. "I don't know—maybe I am going crazy. Other times, I'm scared he's come back. Like, now that my dad's gone, he's coming to get his revenge, like he's still mad that I told my parents about him."

I didn't know what to make of this. If she was seeing her uncle—if he was stalking her—then that would definitely mean she was in danger from him.

"Where have you seen him?" I asked.

She shrugged. "Just around. I don't know. Once I thought I saw him when I was at the grocery store with my aunt. Once I thought I saw him driving down our street." She paused for a second and tilted her head in thought. "Actually, the day I met you, I thought I saw him on the bus on the way to work. But I don't know. I could be imagining things."

My heart sank, and I tried to picture what she was going through. Then something clicked. *That's* what she was scared of the first day. I took just a split second to absorb this, and then worry filled my mind. If her uncle was stalking her, could he be out for blood?

"I believe you, Sage."

"Really?" she asked, raising her head and wiping her eye for the last time.

"I really do, but Sage, why haven't you told anyone? You should at least call the police."

She shook her head. "I would, but..." She hesitated like she had more secrets to tell and wasn't sure about whether to share them or not. "I'm not sure yet if I'm actually seeing him or if I'm just crazy."

If she wasn't willing to call the police, and I was still pretty sure I couldn't tell her when she was going to die, then what could I do? Maybe if I could change the course of the future...

"You know what I think you need?" I asked her.

"What's that?"

"I think you need to relax. That way, you'll be able to think more clearly, and you'll really know if you're imagining it or not. Why not hang out with us again? We can keep you safe." I smiled at her, hoping she'd believe me. I tried convincing myself of this at the same time. Could I really keep her safe?

"You, Robin, Emma, all you guys? You really think you can keep me safe?"

"It's better than being alone, isn't it?"

Sage shook her head. "I don't think any of you understand how messed up I am."

"Well, we're willing to help. We could go back to Asher's and listen to them finish up practice. And you know what? They're playing again in two weeks at my mom's wedding. You should come to that, too."

"Really?" Sage said with a half-smile. "You're inviting me to your mom's wedding?"

"Why not? There will be a buffet and dancing," I added, hoping these extra perks might convince her.

"But you already have it all planned."

"Sage, it's fine. We're not super formal people. So, will you come?"

She sighed. "I'd have to take off work again, and I don't know what my boss will say since I already took a day off to go to Troy's birthday party."

"You could call it research," I quickly suggested. "Tell your boss you were invited to a client's wedding and you thought it would be a great opportunity to see how successful it was and to market the bridal shop."

Please say yes, I chanted in my head. If she said yes, it'd be my ticket to helping her. Then she'd be far away from her uncle or whatever it was that was supposed to cause her death. Plus, she'd be by my side all day, and I wouldn't have to miss my mom's wedding. *Please say yes.*

Sage's half-smile grew wider. "You don't realize how sweet you are, Crystal. I honestly would love to be there. I'll do my best to get off work."

I was so excited that I actually jumped out of my chair and gave her a hug.

Sage laughed. "What are you so excited about?"

That you're going to survive! I thought. Instead, I shrugged. "I'm just happy we're friends."

Sage's smile was a genuine one this time. "Yeah, we really are, aren't we?" After a pause, she spoke again. "You won't tell anyone, will you?"

I tensed for a moment. My friends already knew most of it. But they didn't know about Sage thinking she saw her uncle, and she trusted me enough not to tell. I couldn't betray her trust.

I shook my head. "I won't say anything."

~

After Sage agreed to come my mom's wedding, I finally felt like I could relax. We caught a bus from the mall and walked the few blocks from the bus stop to Asher's.

"This is it," I told Robin after the band finished practicing and Sage had left.

"What do you mean?" he asked.

"She agreed to come to the wedding. This is how I save her, isn't it? I changed the course of the future. She'll be safe now." I took a breath. "Right?" I added.

Honestly, I wasn't entirely sure. What if it was some type of self-fulfilling prophecy and I was somehow going to *cause* it? No. That couldn't be right. There wouldn't be anything dangerous at the wedding.

Robin answered my question with a smile. "I think there's a good chance of it. You just have fun at the wedding, okay? I'll keep an eye on Sage."

"Really? Thank you so much!" I threw my arms around his neck and placed a kiss on his lips. My nerves were finally beginning to ease.

"Crystal," Emma interrupted, "are you ready to go?"

"Yep!" I bounced up the stairs excitedly. "I'll see you Thursday, Robin. Bye!"

"What are you so excited about?" Emma asked as we headed toward the car.

I didn't answer for a moment as I thought about it. "I just have a feeling that everything's going to be alright."

Emma narrowed her eyes at me in thought.

"What?"

She sighed. "Just don't get too excited. It may not turn out to be all rainbows and butterflies."

Emma's words put a halt to my excitement. Did she know something I didn't?

CHAPTER 19

$\mathcal{T}$he week passed by almost normally. I didn't have any prophetic visions, but Emma and I kept up with our regular psychic sessions. We continued visiting Robin's band, thanks to Emma being a part of it now. I almost didn't even worry about Sage since she was showing up to band practices, and I finally felt like I'd sorted things out with her. Now it was just a waiting game. Homework, babysitting, and studying my psychic abilities took up most of my time, but as the wedding day neared, I spent more time talking to Mom about last-minute details.

The night before the wedding had me more nervous than I'd been the previous week. The rehearsal dinner went well without a single hiccup, so I wasn't scared about walking down the aisle or anything. What I was scared about was whether or not my plan was going to work.

I stripped off the dress I'd worn to the rehearsal dinner I'd just returned from, took a shower, and changed into my pajamas. The hot water did little to soothe my worry.

"Mom?" I asked, knocking on her door.

She emerged a moment later dressed in a bath robe. "Yes?"

"Can I talk to you in my room for a moment?" I asked, spotting Teddy behind her. He was propped up on the bed reading a book.

"Sure."

Mom and I crossed the hall to my bedroom and both took a seat on my bed.

"What is it, sweetie? You look worried."

I forced a smile that came off genuine. "No, I'm fine. I just don't really know what to expect tomorrow. Part of me is sure Sage is going to be okay. But then there's a part of me that says it's all going down in flames tomorrow. I don't know which part is the psychic part."

My mom laughed. "That's always tough."

"Anyway," I sighed, "I just wanted to tell you that no matter what happens, I don't want you to worry."

My mom eyed me. "Do you know something I don't?"

The truth was, I did, but I'd promised to keep Sage's confession about her uncle secret. I wanted to open up to my mom about it because I still wasn't entirely sure if Sage was just being paranoid or not, but I promised Sage I wouldn't tell.

"No," I lied. I managed to keep a completely serious face without a single twitch of my eyebrow. "I'm just saying that this is your *wedding* day. If something *did* go wrong, I wouldn't want you postponing something or doing anything that would make you miss out on your special day."

My mom took a strand of my long blonde hair and tucked it behind my ear. "Maybe we *should* have rescheduled."

"No!" I said almost too quickly. "That's what I'm talking about. I don't want my abilities to get in the way of things like this. Besides, how much would that have mattered?"

My mom twisted her lips in thought. "You realize that I'm going to worry about you whether something happens to Sage or not."

I smiled and nodded. "Yeah, you probably are."

"I'll be worrying about her, too, but cancelling it won't change your prophecy."

"Are you sure?" I asked half-jokingly, even though I agreed with her. There simply wasn't anything she could do.

"If it's what you want, I'll give you some space," she told me.

"Promise?" I didn't know why I was asking her this. I didn't even expect something bad to happen, but now that we were discussing it, it made the possibility a reality in my head.

"I'll try." She smiled.

"Okay. Now go get your beauty rest." I pushed at her playfully.

She headed toward the door, but right before she shut it, she said, "I love you, Crystal." Her tone conveyed true worry, as if she thought this was the last time she was going to see me. But I was going to be fine, wasn't I?

"I love you, too, Mom."

Are you going to be alright, Sage? I wondered after my mom shut my bedroom door. I took a deep breath. *Only time will tell.* Just to be sure I wasn't missing anything, I stretched out on my yoga mat and channeled my energy. *Sage is going to be safe, right? I mean she has to be. I can't fail her.*

I took deep, long breaths as I focused my energy on my fingertips to clear my mind. I couldn't help it when my mind raced with the possibilities.

Was inviting Sage to my mom's wedding the best idea? What if I'm wrong about the entire prophecy? What if this isn't when Sage is supposed to die? But if her uncle is stalking her, he might come to the wedding. What if her uncle finds her?

The idea of Sage's uncle finding her played through my mind, almost like the thought was mocking me. Had I been ignoring his involvement for too long? Alan was the one thing in all this that felt completely out of my control. I didn't even know much about him. Should I have told Teddy? He may have been able to help make sure Sage wasn't being stalked. But Sage told me not to tell. Was that a mistake?

So many worries flooded my mind.

"Daddy," I called out, my eyes still closed and my legs crossed on the mat. While I didn't know if he could even hear me, it eased my nerves a little to believe he could. "I need help," I whispered. "I need to know that Sage is going to be safe tomorrow. If her uncle is somewhere nearby... Well, I just need to know that I'll be able to save her. Please send me some sort of sign so I know what to look out for, so I can save her like Melissa asked."

It was already super late, but I sat silent for another hour or so. Much of my anxiety subsided, but nothing profound came to me. I decided to have a go at my crystal ball, hoping it would show me something that would help guide me in the day ahead.

I situated myself at my desk and relaxed enough that glowing colors swirled within the ball almost instantly. I only had to remind myself once to go into it with no expectations.

The swirling colors turned to fire like they had last time. Just like last time, the flames transformed into a deep red and took the shape of fingers. A hand lay limp in the crystal ball, floating there without a backdrop or surroundings to tell me *where* this would happen. Even as the image faded, I managed to keep most of my anxiety from rising back up in my chest. I closed my eyes and took a deep breath, letting the rest of my nerves fall away.

I can do this, I told myself.

I wasn't entirely sure what the image meant. Did it mean Sage was still going to die? Or was the ball just trying to deliver my still unanswered question: *how* was Sage supposed to die?

I wasn't sure. The best I could do was crawl into bed and hope that the next day would run smoothly. Before I slipped under the covers, I dug around in my book bag and pulled out the picture of Alan.

Are you dangerous? I pondered. I studied his face and wondered about him until I fell asleep.

~

A man balanced on a rooftop, arranging new shingles before nailing them in place. Sweat glistened off his back, and his brown hair—that shone slightly red in the sunlight—stuck to the back of his neck. A few other guys milled around atop the roof.

"Carl," a man called from the ground, but Carl couldn't hear him over the noise of his nail gun. "Carl," the man called louder.

Carl stopped and turned to the man on the ground. His waterfall of hair fell to his chin and concealed his face.

The man on the ground motioned for Carl to come down, and he did as he was told.

"What is it, boss?" Carl asked with annoyance.

"You're supposed to be on break."

"And?" Carl challenged.

"I can't afford to pay you guys overtime. Besides," his boss said, gesturing to him, "you look like you could use a drink. I can't have guys passing out up on that roof."

"I'll be fine, boss." One could practically hear Carl gritting his teeth.

"Carl," his boss said sternly. "Take your break."

Carl let out a puff of air. "Fine."

He stalked off toward a white van and reached inside for a water bottle. After slamming the door, he leaned up against the side of the company vehicle. The big red logo advertised Sorensen Construction based out of Woodmont, Indiana.

Instead of drinking his water, Carl poured half the bottle over his head. Only when he pushed the hair out of his face did his appearance become clear.

~

I woke with a start. Even though his hair was longer and his eyes had become cold over the years, I still recognized him. I threw the covers off instantly without even bothering to see what time it was. I burst into my mom's room without thinking to knock.

"Teddy," I said breathlessly, although his room was only across the hall, so I wasn't sure why I was out of breath. All I could think was that I was *relieved*, and I knew I needed to act upon my dream quickly.

Teddy groaned and rubbed his eyes. I looked at the clock on my mom's nightstand. It was 5:30 in the morning.

"Crystal? What is it?" Teddy asked with a tired voice.

"I know where he is! I found him!"

My mother cleared her throat and sat up in bed. "Found who, sweetie?"

"I found Alan! He goes by the name Carl now, but it's him." I couldn't help but smile at my victory. I made my way fully into the room and plopped down on my mom's bed. "He's in Indiana, and he's working for this place called Sorensen Construction."

Teddy was already reaching for a pen and paper out of his bedside table. "Are you sure?"

"I'm sure," I answered confidently.

"Okay." Teddy dragged out the word as he wrote down the information. "I'll call Roger and have him contact the police down there and get this figured out. After all," Teddy said, turning to my mom with a smile, "I shouldn't be working today. It's my wedding day." He leaned in for a kiss.

"Yuck," I groaned. "Get a room."

My mom blushed and threw her pillow at my head. I ducked just in time, and it hit the wall behind me.

"Well, I guess there's no point in going back to bed," my mom said. "I'm too excited!" She bounced up and headed to the bathroom.

"You know what this means?" I asked Teddy since he was the only one around.

"What?"

"That everything's going to be okay! Since Sage's uncle is in Indiana, she's safe. No one is going to hurt her. It's going to be a beautiful day and an amazing wedding!" I headed back toward my bedroom. Just as I was about to close my mom's bedroom door, I turned back. "Teddy?"

"Yeah?"

"Will you let me know what happens with Sage's uncle?"

He nodded. "I will."

"Okay, thanks."

CHAPTER 20

"Crystal, has anyone told you how beautiful you look?" Diane raved.

I sat in front of a mirror at the salon, and the stylist had just finished curling my hair.

"I hope Robin tells her that all the time," Sophie said as another stylist twisted her curls into a bun. "Otherwise, you should ditch him, Crystal."

I laughed. "He does tell me that, and I'm not going to ditch him."

A sense of happiness filled my heart. My mom's marriage became more of a reality as the day wore on. There was the added perk that I'd texted Sage earlier and she told me she was still coming to the wedding. Everything was going great.

Mom, Sophie, Diane, and I laughed and joked until we were in full hair and makeup. Once we were done, we drove to the hotel and piled the last of our supplies into a small event space. We were the only ones there so far, and we took this time to arrange last-minute decorations that we hadn't finished setting up after the rehearsal dinner last night. Since it wasn't a big wedding—and the hotel we were at didn't even have wedding planning services—it was all up to us to set everything up. Everything, that is, except the catered food and the music, which Robin's band was providing.

I stayed with my mom in the smaller of the two conference spaces where we were holding the actual ceremony. Diane and Sophie were taking care of decorations for the reception in the other event room.

Just as I was helping adjust the last of the tulle, Robin popped his head in the door.

"Hey," he said. "We're here to set up the band equipment."

I smiled and hopped down from the chair I was standing on. I greeted him with a hug and a small kiss.

"Eww. Get a room," my mom joked.

I rolled my eyes at her. It was the best I could do since I didn't have a pillow to throw at her head.

"Come on," I said, taking Robin's hand and exiting the room. "I'll show you where the other event space is."

"I've been texting Sage," Robin told me in the hallway. "She says she still plans on coming. Are you still feeling good about this?"

I nodded excitedly. "I," I started, looking around to make sure no one was listening. "I have to tell you something." I pulled Robin down a secluded hallway and told him about my dream.

"Teddy didn't say yet if they caught the guy?"

I shook my head. "It's only been a few hours, and I haven't seen Teddy since this morning."

"Okay. Can you show me where to set up?"

"Oh, yeah. It's this way."

Emma and Derek showed up a few minutes later to help us. I carried in band equipment and set things up for a while until Diane told me it was time to get dressed. Mom, Sophie, Diane, and I piled into a private hotel room to finish getting ready.

A few people came and went from the room to congratulate my mom in private, including Teddy's mom, Gail, along with some of my mom's cousins who I didn't even know. After the greetings died down, I helped my mom into her dress, and Sophie attached her veil.

"Wow." I stood back from my mom to get a good look.

She gave me a grin that bordered somewhere between excited and nervous.

"I can't believe you're doing this again," Diane said.

I pulled my mom into a hug. "I'm so glad I get to be a part of it."

Just then, a knock rapped at the door. Sophie hopped up from the bed to answer it. My Grandma Ellen—my mom's mom—stood on the other side of it.

"Grandma!" I rushed over to give her a hug. I hadn't seen her in ages.

Grandma Ellen adjusted her glasses. "Crystal, is that you? You've gotten so big."

I rolled my eyes at her.

"Oh, Mom. Come here." My mom crossed the room to hug Grandma Ellen. Tears of happiness pricked at both their eyes, but they did their best to hold them back.

"You guys can't cry, because then I'll start crying," I complained.

"Well, why don't you go put your dress on?" Sophie suggested.

I locked myself in the bathroom for privacy, but when I pulled my dress off the hanger, a lump formed in my throat.

She'll take her last breath the next time you wear that dress.

This can't be it, I thought. *Sage is going to be alright.*

But how did I know? A sickening feeling hit my stomach, and I sat on the toilet for support. I held the lavender dress out in front of me. I didn't move for nearly a minute as Melissa's words echoed in my mind. After what seemed like several minutes of holding my breath, I stood and put the dress back on the hanger.

"Why aren't you dressed yet?" Sophie asked when I emerged from the bathroom. "What were you doing in there?"

"I'll be right back. I just don't want anyone seeing me in my dress yet. One of you can get dressed first." And then I left the room.

I made my way down the hall to the room I knew the groomsmen were getting ready in. After I knocked, Robin answered.

"Can I talk to Teddy real quick?" I asked.

"Yeah, sure." Robin pulled the door open wider to invite me in. "Why aren't you dressed yet?"

Teddy turned from the mirror as he finished adjusting his tie. "Crystal, I'm glad you're here. I wanted to let you know that Roger called me back. Your anonymous tip was right. They picked Alan up this morning."

I let out a breath I didn't know I was holding. "That's great!" I threw my arms around Teddy's neck in excitement. "Sage really isn't in any danger, then." I had the confirmation I needed, and I knew now that Sage had just been paranoid about seeing her uncle. She was never in any true danger from him. "Oh," I said, turning back to Teddy. "Congratulations."

Moments later, I was back in the ladies' hotel room and was pulling my dress off the hanger again. Each time I saw it, those words repeated in my head.

She'll take her last breath the next time you wear that dress.

What if she was never in danger from her uncle? What if it was something else all along? I wondered.

I pulled my cell phone from my back pocket.

"Hello?" Sage's voice answered.

"Sage," I said with a breath of relief. How could I think she wasn't going to be safe? After all, I'd invited her to the wedding and changed the course of the future. When she came, I'd be able to keep an eye on her all day. "Are you okay?" I found myself asking.

"Yeah, I'm fine. Why?"

"You're still coming, right?"

"Yeah. Actually, I was just headed out the door. Your hotel is only a couple of bus stops away, so I'll be there soon."

A smile formed across my face. I *was* right. I did change the future. She was going to be okay. "Okay. I will see you soon."

"Okay. Bye."

Once I hung up, I finally relaxed. I slunk down onto the closed toilet lid and took a few deep breaths.

A knock at the door pulled me to full attention. "Crystal," Diane said through the door, "you should be dressed already. Guests are arriving!"

I pulled the door open with my dress still in my hands. By now, my grandma was already gone, so it was just my mom and her bridesmaids in the room.

"This dress," I said, holding it out as if that explained everything I wanted to say.

They all looked at me quizzically.

"You guys think Sage is going to be okay, right?" Why was I bringing this up, anyway? I mentally scolded myself. It was my mom's special day. She shouldn't be worrying about things like this.

My mom made her way over to me and gave me a hug. "Honestly? Yes, I do think she's going to be okay. She has you on her side. Shall I also add that you changed things? Without you, she wouldn't be coming to the wedding. Without you, she'd be on a different course. And now, she's on one that leads to you. You've already changed her destiny by becoming her friend."

I closed my eyes and took a deep breath, absorbing my mother's confidence the best I could.

Sophie squeezed my hand for encouragement.

"Okay. I'll go get dressed now." I locked the bathroom door behind me for a third time and stripped down. I pulled the dress up over my hips and managed to reach the zipper this time. It hugged my body the same way it had the first time.

I emerged from the bathroom to find my mom and her best friends smiling at me.

"You look great, Crystal," my mom said, pulling me into a hug. Jeez. There were so many hugs going around today. After a moment, Sophie and Diane joined us, and we ended up in a group hug.

The ceremony grew closer, and we finished up last-minute preparations. Just as I was placing my pearl earrings in my ears, another knock came at the door.

This time, Grandpa Ed came in. "Are you ready to walk down the aisle?" he asked.

My mom nodded, though she appeared at a loss for words.

Grandpa kissed her on the cheek. "I'm so proud of you."

She wiped at her eye carefully as to not mess up her makeup. "I know, Dad."

Grandpa checked his watch. "It's just about time."

My mom gave another one of those nervous but excited grins.

"Crystal, don't forget your shoes." Diane handed me my sparkly flats and my bouquet. This was it.

After a few more minutes of talking with my Grandpa and waiting for the ceremony start time to approach, we made our way downstairs. I gripped onto my owl necklace the whole way down.

"Crystal," Robin said when he saw me. He spoke in a near whisper so that only the two of us could hear. "I don't mean to freak you out, but I haven't seen Sage yet."

"What?" I nearly shouted.

Robin's dad gave me a stern look as if to tell me to be quiet.

My heart nearly fell out of my chest. The ceremony was about to start. Sage should be here by now.

"Are you sure?" I asked.

Robin nodded nervously. "I've been keeping an eye out for her, and I tried to text and call her, but she isn't answering anymore."

My face grew hot as I thought about the possibilities. *This can't be happening. I had to put on the damn dress.*

I stepped around the corner and peeked into the ceremony room.

"Crystal," Diane scolded. "What are you doing?"

Robin quietly explained to her as my eyes scanned the crowd. With Sage's auburn hair, it should be easy to pick her out of such a small crowd, but not a single strand of red hair stuck out. Robin was right. Sage was missing.

CHAPTER 21

"*D*o you have your phone on you?" I asked Robin.

"Yeah." He handed it to me.

His father gave another look of disapproval.

"It's on silent," Robin explained, like that would make his dad approve of him having it during the ceremony.

I found Sage's number in Robin's contacts and pressed the call button. My pulse increased with every ring. *Pick up, Sage,* I thought. When it went to voicemail, I felt like my entire world was collapsing around me. This was it. My worst nightmare. I'd failed her.

I froze so still that the phone dropped from my hand. I didn't even remember to breathe until Robin gripped my shoulders. I was sure it was the only thing keeping me from sinking to my knees.

"Crystal." Robin's voice made me feel stable again.

When the wooziness in my head finally cleared, I knew I had no other choice. I grabbed Robin's hand.

"Crystal, what's going on?" Sophie asked.

I turned back without slowing my step. "It's Sage."

"Crystal," Sophie stopped me. She quickly closed the distance between us and grabbed my wrist. "You can't go by yourself. We should come with you."

"No," I insisted without really thinking about it. "You guys told me this was *my* mission."

"That doesn't mean you should go alone."

My gaze shifted between Sophie's eyes. "Everyone keeps saying that I need to put more faith in my abilities. If *you* believe in my abilities, you'll let me do this myself, and you won't worry about me."

Sophie's eyes softened in defeat. "We do believe in you."

"Then you have nothing to worry about."

She finally released her grip on my wrist.

My mom was still hiding around the corner with my grandpa so that no one would see her before the ceremony. I called back to Sophie. "When Mom asks, tell her that she promised, okay?"

"Promised what?" Sophie raised her voice as I distanced myself from her.

"She'll know. Don't wait around or worry about me. Have fun."

Robin and I escaped into the sunlight and raced toward his car. He didn't waste a second and already had his keys out and the door unlocked before my hand even touched the handle.

"Where to?" Robin asked quickly with a wavering tone.

"I have no idea," I admitted. Robin was already pulling out of the parking lot. "Last she told me, she was headed out the door. What if she never made it that far?"

"You think something happened while she was at home?"

"I don't know, but that's my best bet right now. Do you know where she lives?"

"Luckily, yes. I had to drop off a homework assignment one time when she was sick from school. It's not far."

I couldn't sit still on the short ride to her house. Robin was right. It wasn't far, but the slow traffic made it feel like the car ride stretched into eternity.

"I could walk faster than this," I complained nervously, but when I looked out the window at the people on the sidewalk, it was clear we were traveling faster than any other method. The seconds ticked by, and my mind raced with the possibilities.

What happened to her? Is she still okay? Why did I have to put on the dress? I was right. It sealed in her fate. It was self-fulfilling. How could I have been so wrong about this? Is it her uncle? Has he come for revenge? No. That doesn't even make sense. He was caught this morning, and even if he did escape custody somehow, he couldn't have made it here in time.

We finally pulled up to Sage's house. Robin was driving so fast that when he slammed on the brakes, I had to brace myself against the dashboard. I was already out of the car before he shut off the engine.

I raced up the walkway and pounded on the door. Sage's aunt—I assumed—answered the door. "Sage," I said breathlessly because that was all I could manage to spit out. I took a deep breath. "Is she here?"

The woman's eyebrows furrowed in confusion. "She left quite a while ago. She told us she was spending time with Robin again." Her eyes moved past me and locked on Robin. "Robin," she said in surprise. "Isn't Sage with you? We wouldn't have let her go out if she was going somewhere else."

Robin reached the door and stood next to me. "That's why we're here, Anna. Sage *was* supposed to meet up with us at my uncle's wedding, but she's not there. We were worried and came to check on her."

A man came up behind Anna. "I knew she was up to no good," he mumbled. This must have been Sage's uncle Brian. I remembered her telling me he had a "suck-it-up" attitude.

"Hey," I defended. I was surprised when my voice came out loud, but I was too scared for Sage to lower my tone. "Sage isn't *trouble*. She's *in* trouble. She's staying with you so that she feels *safe*, and now she's not. She's not safe." I covered my face with my hands because it was all just too much. A wary breath escaped my lips. Everyone else was too stunned to say anything. "Oh, god, Robin. It's my fault." I dropped my hands and looked up at him.

"What are you talking about?" Sage's uncle asked. He stepped forward in a defensive stance. "Did you get Sage into trouble?"

"No," I answered honestly. "I—I think—I mean—I couldn't get her *out* of it."

"Crystal," Robin said in a tone I knew was supposed to soothe my nerves but didn't work. "Calm down." He turned to Anna. His voice was surprisingly even, something I couldn't imagine doing with the rate my heart was racing and my fingers were trembling. "Can you give us a minute?"

Anna and her husband eyed us.

"I'm sure Sage is okay," Robin told them. "It's just a stressful day for Crystal, and she's overreacting. Sage is probably already there and we just didn't see her." I could hear the lie in Robin's tone.

"Should we call the police?" Anna asked warily.

"She should be fine," Robin assured her. "Can you just give us a moment?"

Anna let the door fall shut as I turned and sank down onto the steps. I buried my face in my hands. Robin sat down next to me and pulled me into his arms. Tears were already falling down my cheeks.

"I've failed her," I managed to whisper.

"It's not over yet," Robin promised. "Let's think rationally for a minute."

I nearly laughed at the thought that I would be able to think rationally at a time like this.

"Thanks to your abilities, we knew Sage was in danger. What if we can use them now to find her?"

"How?" I asked hopelessly.

"Well, let's see. What can you do? You can see ghosts."

"I can't control who I see or when."

"Okay. You can see the past."

"I don't know how that's going to help us." I finally pulled away from Robin and wiped the tears from my eyes with a sniffle. "I can see the future, too. Maybe if I could concentrate hard enough, I could see something about the future and hopefully change it."

Robin nodded. "That's a good idea, but do you know how to control those visions?"

I dropped my shoulders and shook my head. "I can also feel people's emotions, but I have to touch them. I guess I could feel Hope while she was in trouble even though she was far away, but I've never felt Sage like that. I don't think that will help us find her."

"Wait," Robin said excitedly. "Finding her." He looked at me like I should know exactly what he was talking about. "You can find things."

I gave him a look of disbelief. "Yeah, I find things like CDs and old books and socks and stuffed animals. I've never found a person."

"You found Sage's uncle," Robin pointed out.

I thought about this for a moment. "That could have just been a vision of the past or future."

"And you found Hope."

"That's because a ghost told me where to find her."

"But it worked. Both times."

I pressed my lips together in thought. "I usually need something to touch. Like, when Emma and I practice, I have to touch her hand to know where she hid the object."

"Okay, then we'll do that." Robin stood up.

"What do you mean?" I asked, but he was already knocking on the door again.

I could hear the voices behind it stop abruptly. No doubt they were discussing whether or not to call the cops. Anna answered after a few moments.

"Can we see Sage's room?" Robin asked.

Anna and her husband both looked at each other warily. "Brian?" she addressed him.

"Why do you need to see her room?" he asked.

"To see if there's something that could tell us if she was headed somewhere else." Everyone went silent for a few moments until Robin spoke again. "Look, I don't mean to offend anyone, but I've probably spent more time with Sage than anyone else here. I know her best. If there's something wrong, I should be able to find it in her room."

After another long silence, Brian finally nodded. I knew Robin hadn't talked to Sage often, but as Anna opened the door wider to invite us in, I felt it was an indication of how little her aunt and uncle knew about her.

Robin and I stepped into Sage's bedroom. It was small with an untidy twin bed against one wall and a dresser against another. The walls were bare as if the owner had only come to stay the night.

"We'll let you know if we find anything," Robin told Anna and Brian. His tone was one that asked for privacy once again.

"They seem to trust you," I said, but my heart sped up with the feeling that we were wasting time.

"I think I'm the only one of Sage's friends they've ever met," Robin admitted. "It was just that one time when I came to drop off her science homework, but I don't think she gets a lot of visitors. I thought they were her parents, though. She never mentioned her family's death to me."

I took a few deep breaths to calm my heartrate. I pushed farther into the room, hoping something would call out to me.

Robin was already opening and closing drawers. "What type of thing do you think you need?"

"It has to be something she touched recently and was probably special to her." I opened the top drawer of her dresser but found nothing except clothes.

Robin flipped through the dresses in her closet.

"A few weeks ago, Emma and I were practicing, and I did better when she hid something that was really special to me."

"Luna?" Robin guessed. He closed the closet door and headed toward the bed.

I blushed because the idea of still sleeping with a stuffed animal sounded childish. "Yeah," I admitted as I pulled the third drawer open. Nothing.

"So, do you think something like this would work?"

I turned around to face Robin, who was holding up a teddy bear.

"It was under the covers," he explained.

I shrugged. "I don't know if this is going to work at all, but I don't see anything else very personal lying around. We might as well try this." I grabbed the bear from his hands.

I again took one of my calming breaths as I situated myself on the bed and leaned my head against the wall. I closed my eyes and stroked the bear's soft fur. The bed shifted when Robin sat down, but he didn't say anything.

No expectations, I reminded myself. *Just breathe, stay calm.*

The task proved quite difficult, but I managed to slow my breathing enough that my hands stopped trembling. After what felt like a few minutes, I pulled the teddy bear to my face and inhaled its scent. It was weird that I recognized the fragrance, but it smelled like Sage. As soon as the aroma hit my nose, an image flashed behind my lids—a bloody image.

I sucked in a sharp breath and opened my eyes.

"What?" Robin asked. "What did you see?"

I shook my head. "Nothing useful yet, but I think this might work. Give me another minute." I closed my eyes again and brought the bear back up to my face. In that moment, I took everything I'd learned in practice sessions with Emma and applied it to relaxing my body, relieving my anxiety, and letting go of expectations. I became so relaxed to the point where every nerve in my body went numb.

A floating sensation overcame me, and I had to open my eyes to make sure I was still in Sage's room. Oh, I was in her room alright, but it was all different. When I opened my eyes, I was looking down on my own body that sat on Sage's bed and clutched her teddy bear.

CHAPTER 22

I gave myself a mere moment to take in the scene. I knew if I reacted badly, I'd be instantly snapped back into my body. Instead, I filled my mind with thoughts of Sage. I thought back to the first time I saw her at Special Day Bridal. I pictured us singing together with Emma in Asher's basement. I let her genuine smile and freckled nose fill my mind, and I pictured her pulling at her sleeves in the nervous manner she always did. And then I pulled up the memory of her playing saxophone.

I let the melody and the memory of her gorgeous tone play in my head. As the song continued, I began floating high above the house until I was taken above rooftops and guided over office buildings.

After the last notes of her solo played in my head, I restarted the memory, and it kept me pushing forward. A forest of trees up ahead looked awkward butted up against man-made structures, but the melody pulled me closer, like what I sought was hidden in the trees. The tune grew louder, and the melody slowed as I descended toward a path.

In an instant, all the scenes I'd just passed whirled by me in a blur. My eyes shot open.

"What?" Robin asked, rushing to reach for my hand. "Did you find her?"

I stared wide-eyed at Robin because I couldn't believe what had just happened. Did I *astral travel*?

"I—I..." I stammered. "I don't know if she's alright, but I think she's in the trees. They're just that way." I pointed. "It's in the city. Not far."

Robin and I both sprang up from the bed. I let the teddy bear fall to the floor, and we rushed out of the room.

"What is it?" Anna called as we hurried to the car.

"It's fine," Robin assured her. "We'll let you know what happens. Sage is going to be alright."

"Are you sure?" I asked as soon as Robin drove off.

"What?" He glanced at me.

"Are you sure she's going to be alright?"

He squeezed my hand and nodded. "I told you that weeks ago. She has you on her side, remember?"

Anxiety built inside me. Were we too late? Robin turned a corner onto a busy street, slowing us down. I eyed the scene. Something about it seemed strangely familiar. Tall buildings lined the street, and groups of people milled along the sidewalk. A bus up ahead pulled to a stop, and people piled out.

I caught my breath, and I knew where I'd seen this street before. "Stop!"

"What?" Robin looked around and slowed the vehicle. "Do you see her?"

"No, but this is it!"

"What do you mean? I thought you said the park. That's where I'm going."

"She was running." I closed my eyes. Behind them, a scene played through my mind, and I found myself in Sage's body, as if I *was* her.

I climbed onto the bus and kept my head low. I didn't meet anyone's eyes as I took my seat and adjusted the strap on my purse nervously. I tugged at my cardigan's long sleeves and balled them into my fists. Hairs rose on the back of my neck. I swallowed, forcing down the lump rising in my throat. I situated closer to the window and angled myself toward it. Hopefully no one would want to sit by me.

The feeling that someone was watching me grew stronger as the bus ride grew longer. I glanced around nervously to the man in the seat next to me. He was fiddling with his phone and didn't even notice me. I subtly glanced to the back of the bus. Soft brown eyes met mine. I quickly turned away from him. Fear knotted in my chest.

That's not him, I told myself. But what if it is?

I stole another glance toward the back of the bus. His head was down now and hidden behind the chair in front of him, but the hair was the same shade of brown that had haunted my dreams for years. I trapped my lip in my teeth to bite back the bile rising in my throat. How did he find me? How long had he been following me? What would happen when he finally caught me?

I can't do it, I told myself. He can't catch me.

The bus pulled to a halt at the next stop. I couldn't waste another second. I slipped off the bus as quickly as I could and took off running. I glanced behind me to make sure he wasn't following. For a second, I was sure I saw his brown eyes through the crowd. I pushed forward harder, dodging people as I went.

When I rounded a corner, I broke free from the crowd. Up ahead stood a wall of trees offering me a hiding place.

He can't get to me. I can't face my nightmare in person. He's haunted me for too long. I won't give him that satisfaction.

I sprinted as fast as I could. Even as I found cover in the canopy, I still pushed forward.

My eyes sprung open. "The day at the paintball arena. It was warning me of *this*."

"What do you mean?"

"She's there." I pointed to the road that had taken her to the trees.

Robin turned down the road and found a parking space alongside the curb. I kicked my door open before he even stopped, and I ran toward the trees the same way Sage had in my vision. My dress flew out around my legs, but I pressed forward. Robin didn't run much thanks to his leg, but I knew he was following me as quickly as he could.

As soon as I broke into the trees, I slowed. "I—I don't know where I am," I spoke to thin air. I scanned the ground for any sign of footprints or broken twigs, but I had no experience tracking someone. My heart sank, and I fell to my knees.

Robin was at my side as soon as he caught up. "Crystal."

"I—I don't know what to do next. The trees are all I saw, but I don't know where she is in the trees."

Robin knelt down next to me, but he kept his eyes on the forest, no doubt searching for a sign of Sage.

"Where are we, anyway?" I asked. "What's a forest doing in the middle of the city?"

"Don't you know where we are?" he asked.

I looked at him stupidly.

"This is Bradshaw Park. That's what you were describing before. I thought you knew where we were going."

A feeling of confusion overcame me, but it only lasted for a moment. This is where Troy held his birthday party. It's where Sage and I took a walk together and where she called me crazy.

But it's also where Sage told me…

"I know where she is!" I exclaimed, rising so quickly that I got a head rush. I took off again after the dizziness passed. I didn't know where I was exactly since I'd never been on this edge of the park, but I knew Sage was somewhere in here, and if I could find the path, I knew exactly where she would be.

"Where? How?" Robin called behind me and spoke between breaths.

"It's where Sage told me she comes to think." I breathed heavily. Since it'd been a while since volleyball season, I wasn't exactly in the best of shape. "It's where she feels safest."

We finally hit a path, and I started toward the center of the park.

"How do you know where you're going?" Robin asked.

"I don't," I admitted, but I pressed on. After only a few moments on the path, I saw the bridge up ahead. I sprinted faster, leaving Robin in my wake. *Please be okay, Sage.*

I dodged the bridge and headed to the edge of the water. I didn't calculate my momentum and ended up sliding down the steep bank. My wrist caught my fall, and it ached. Dirt coated my lavender dress, and my right foot fell into the water.

But I didn't care. That's because the sight I saw in front of me was more horrifying than anything I'd ever seen before. I'd seen things like this on TV before. I'd even seen flashes of blood in my mind. But none of it could prepare me for witnessing it in person with my own two eyes. Not even the sight of my father's casket when I was little could measure up to this gruesome moment. I immediately wanted to hurl.

Sage's body lay unmoving on the sandy platform. A bracelet of red liquid wound around her wrist and dispersed into her palm and off her fingers. The bloody image from my crystal ball came to life right before my eyes.

I rushed to Sage and fell into the sand next to her unmoving form. *We're too late*, was my first thought. My breathing grew heavy, and I took a split second to assess the scene. Sage's red cardigan was pulled up past her elbow. All along her right arm lay red marks, some fresh while others were already healing.

I could hardly believe what I was seeing. I'd always noticed how she nervously tugged at her sleeves, but what I didn't notice about it was that she was *always* wearing long sleeves. Now I knew why. She was hiding something beneath them.

Robin appeared next to me and pulled his suit coat off. He wrapped one of the sleeves around Sage's bloody wrist. Neither of us cared that it was a rental. Sage's life was all that mattered right now.

"Is she…" I couldn't finish my sentence. All I could do was stare at her pale, lifeless body and hold my breath.

Robin leaned down to her face. "No. She's still breathing."

"Should I call an ambulance?" I cried.

Robin shook his head and shifted, pulling Sage into his arms. Sage groaned slightly as Robin lifted her body. I breathed a sigh of relief. At least she was still with us, if only slightly.

"There's a hospital a block away," Robin told me. "It'll be faster if we took her there ourselves."

After Robin swooped Sage into his arms, I spotted a silver object in the sand. I snatched it up, along with her purse, and trailed behind him. "Are you sure you can carry her that far?" My throat felt like it was closing up, causing my voice to come out a few notes higher than normal. "What about your leg?"

"I can carry her, Crystal. She hardly weighs 110 pounds. We'll make it there. It's just a matter of getting there in time." Robin's words sent a nauseating sensation through my gut. He quickened his pace when he reached the path.

"Is she going to be okay? How far is the hospital? Do you need any help?" I couldn't stop babbling like a fool. Had I failed her?

Although we were walking as quickly as we could with Sage in Robin's arms, the stretch to the hospital seemed to drag on forever. As Robin said, it was only a block away, but every step we took closer to the hospital made it feel another mile away. Tears fell down my cheeks in fear for Sage.

I placed a hand on her head as we walked in hopes of comforting her if she was even mildly conscious. What I saw—or rather felt—twisted my gut.

Even as I touched her, I didn't think I understood what she was going through. I could feel her fear, and for a moment, I was able to see her uncle's face from her perspective, as a nightmare. The revolting feeling that hit me was nothing compared to the chronic fear Sage faced every day. In the moment my hand made contact with her head, I understood why she wanted to kill herself, why she wanted the nightmare to end.

The feeling was too overwhelming. I jerked my hand away almost immediately, like I'd just touched a hot stove.

Thoughts played through my mind as we neared the hospital. Why didn't I send someone to pick her up? Why didn't I mention her uncle and his arrest sooner? Then she wouldn't have been so scared.

Finally, we reached the door to the emergency room. The lady behind the counter noticed us immediately and came rushing to our aid with a wheelchair. As Robin set Sage down and helped balance her semi-conscious body in an upright position, I finally got a good look at her face. Her lips were drained of color, and her normally bright freckles seemed faded.

"What happened?" the lady asked.

"She lost a lot of blood," Robin said breathlessly.

The lady gazed down at the coat tied tightly around Sage's wrist. "How long ago?"

Robin and I exchanged a glance, but it was Robin whose head was clear enough to speak. "We don't know. We found her like this 10 minutes ago. Maybe sooner."

Another nurse was already by our side trying to calm us down. "Are either of you family?"

"No," Robin said, but his breathing sounded labored. I wasn't sure if it was from carrying Sage or because he was just as scared as I was.

Sage moaned, and I was instantly at her side.

An unfamiliar hand, undoubtedly the second nurse, grabbed at me. "Ma'am, we need to get her to a doctor."

I shook her off and gripped onto the wheelchair. "Sage?"

Sage forced her eyes open halfway and spoke my name in a hoarse whisper. "Crystal?"

Robin's hands were the ones that gripped onto my shoulder next. I managed to relax my hold on the wheelchair, and the first lady wheeled Sage away.

"I'm her friend," I cried after her, but the second nurse was pushing me back. "No," I struggled, raising my voice. "Sage needs me. Melissa said I was supposed to save her!"

Robin entwined his fingers through mine and pulled me into a one-armed hug. I nuzzled against his shoulder, and tears fell from my eyes.

"You already saved her," he told me, leading me to one of the chairs in the waiting room.

"You think that's it?" I finally asked after a brief silence, lifting my head to meet his gaze. "You think that's all I needed to do?"

"We've done all we can. What I don't understand is why she did it."

I went silent for a moment. Sage had confided in me about thinking she was seeing her uncle. I told her I believed her, but I could see now that she really was being paranoid. Still, I *did* promise not to tell anyone about that.

"She was just scared," I finally said. I shook my head during the silence that followed. "The stupid thing about all this is that if I hadn't invited her to the wedding, it may have not happened at all."

Robin pressed his lips together in thought. "I don't know about that."

"But then she never would have been on that bus, and she never would have run to the park, and never would have..." I couldn't finish over my sobs.

Robin hugged me tighter. "This could have happened at any time. The difference is that because it happened like *this*, today, you were able to stop it."

After a long silence, I spoke again in a small voice. "I saw her thoughts, Robin. She wasn't even thinking about the wedding. On some level, I think she forgot where she was headed and was so caught up in her fear. She just wanted out."

"Where'd she get it, though?" he asked.

I looked at him. It took me a moment to realize he was talking about her weapon of choice. I still had her bag slung over my shoulder. I reached into it and pulled out the blade, twisting it around in my fingers. A string of blood ran along the length of it. Thank goodness I was sitting down because when I spotted the blood, I grew queasy.

An image flashed through my mind. Sage sat in the bath tub, and I watched the scene from her eyes as she spread soap across her leg. She reached for the razor and ran it across her skin. On the third stroke, it caught the end of her ankle. A single drop of blood fell into the water and dispersed in an almost artistic display.

The scene only lasted a second before my eyes focused on the room once again.

"Look at it." I held the blade out toward Robin. "It's from a bathroom razor. She tore it apart a few months ago."

"How do you know that?" He looked at me, but a moment later, his face softened as if to say, *Well, of course because you're psychic.*

"I just do."

Robin handed the blade back to me, and I slid it back safely into Sage's purse. The thought to bury it later and put the memories of Sage's attempt in the ground crossed my mind.

I excused myself briefly to go clean up. Luckily, I'd only accumulated a bit of dirt, so it wasn't too hard to dust off, although I had to wipe down my wet shoe since sand had gathered on the sole and sides. When I emerged from the bathroom, I was as good as new—at least, I looked that way; I couldn't say the same about my aching heart.

As soon as I sat down, a man behind us cleared his throat. The second nurse from earlier stood beside him.

"Hi," he said with a smile. It didn't do much to cheer me up, but I knew it was supposed to be welcoming.

"Hello," I managed to croak out. I knew a series of questions was about to ensue.

Robin and I stood to meet the man's outstretched hand.

"I'm Cole DuBois, and I'm a social worker here at the hospital. I understand that you just came in with a female patient. In order to provide the proper care, I was wondering if I could ask you two a few questions about her before you leave."

"I don't want to leave," I told him. I glanced at Robin to make sure this was an appropriate response. He gave me a slight head nod. "I want to stay until I can talk to her." I *had* to. She had to know her uncle wasn't a threat. Maybe then she wouldn't be so scared.

After we answered Cole's questions—like how we knew Sage and what her home life was like—we remained in the waiting room.

Robin checked his cell while we waited. Apparently Emma had already called four times, so Robin called her back. He explained most of the story to her, leaving out the part about me astral traveling in case anyone else overheard. Then he handed the phone to me.

I stared at it questioningly.

"She wants to talk to you," he explained, shoving the phone in my direction.

I took it warily before putting it to my face. "Hello?"

"Oh, good," Emma said with a breath of relief. "Your mom wants to talk to you."

Before I could say anything else, my mom's voice came over the line. "Crystal?"

"Hi, Mom. How was the ceremony?"

"We didn't start yet," she admitted.

"Mom! I told you to go ahead without me. You promised."

"That wouldn't be fair."

"You're wrong. It's unfair to you that Robin and I are keeping you and your guests waiting." Of course I wanted to be with my mom on her wedding day, but I couldn't leave now, not until I knew Sage was alright, and that could be hours from now. I also didn't want my mom rescheduling her wedding because of me. "Mom, seriously, don't worry about me."

"How can I not worry about you?" she asked.

I sighed. "Look, Mom, I can't leave Sage right now, but it's only fair that you get married today, so will you please stop keeping your guests waiting and walk down the aisle already?"

"Snarky, are we?"

"Well, it's the only way you'll get married today."

My mother sighed in defeat. "Okay, I'll get married. You're fine, though, right?"

I loved how much my mom cared. "I really am. I love you."

"I love you, too, sweetie," she told me before we said goodbye.

"I better call her aunt and uncle," Robin said after I handed his phone back to him.

"It looks like the hospital beat you to it." I pointed to a man seated away from us. Brian and Anna must have come while we were talking to Cole.

Robin rose from his seat and cleared his throat. Brian turned toward us.

"Hello," Brian greeted quietly, sorrow full in his voice. "I—" His voice cracked, and he swallowed to clear his throat. "I'm sorry. I'm just so mad at that girl right now." Brian said he was mad, but his demeanor showed he was more sad than anything. "I just don't get it. We take her in, put a roof over her head, and then she goes and pulls this stunt."

I wasn't even about to explain it to him. I knew he wouldn't get it.

"Anna is in there with Sage's therapist."

"Can we see her?" I asked, but I knew it was probably a dumb question. Of course I couldn't go in there while she was talking to her therapist, if, in fact, she was actually awake and talking.

We sat in the waiting room for another long while. The only thing I could do was worry about Sage.

"I feel like I could have done more," I told Robin when Brian stood and went to the restroom. "I should have sent you to go pick her up or something."

"Crystal, there's no point in worrying about what you should have done. Take a look at what you *did* do. You knew where to find her. You—and your abilities—saved her life. Do you have any idea how incredible you were today?"

I managed to crack a half a smile. He was right. I had *astral traveled* and managed to get to Sage before it was too late. A sense of pride washed over me at the thought that my abilities saved her, just like Robin had said I'd do all along.

I closed my eyes right there in the waiting room and whispered a short prayer to my father. I still wasn't sure if he was the one who had helped me, but it soothed my nerves nonetheless. "Thank you, Daddy," I said in such a low voice that even I could hardly hear it. I only hoped my words would find him.

Several hours had passed since we'd found Sage, but eventually, Anna and Sage's therapist approached us in the waiting room. Anna came to our side immediately. Her eyes were red like she'd been crying. Before I knew what was happening, she was pulling us both into a hug. "I just wanted to let you two know how thankful I am that you were there today. Your instinct was right, and if it wasn't for you, we may have lost her. I've always known Sage had issues, but I didn't realize how bad. I'm just so happy to see she has friends like you."

All I could do was force a friendly smile in return. After we exchanged thank yous and you're welcomes, a nurse led us to Sage's room.

As soon as I walked in, I immediately rushed to her bedside. Her face was gaining its color back, but her expression was stone cold.

"You should have let me die," Sage whispered.

I looked toward Robin for help and then back to Sage. I grabbed onto her good hand for encouragement. "No, I couldn't do that."

Sage closed her eyes and went quiet for a moment. "I'm sorry I ruined your big day," she finally said. "My aunt and uncle, and my therapist, are really disappointed in me. I can't imagine how mad you are."

"I'm not mad."

She threw me a sideways glance. "If I had died, none of you would be bothered by me."

"You're not a bother, Sage," Robin assured her. He stood at the foot of her bed.

"I'm not trying to gain your sympathies. I just—sometimes I feel like I don't want to face things anymore. Sometimes I just want it all to go away."

I shifted and squeezed her hand tighter. "Sage, there's something I need to tell you, and I hope once I do, you'll change your mind."

She looked at me with an expression of confusion.

"Your uncle—not Brian, but Alan—they found him this morning. He was living under an alias, but he was arrested in Indiana earlier today."

Sage's eyes widened. "No. That's not possible. Remember what I told you?"

I glanced toward Robin nervously since he didn't know what she was talking about, but he remained calm.

"I've seen him. He was stalking me. That's why—why I had to do it. I had to get away."

"No, Sage. My mom's boyfriend—well, my step-dad—is a cop. He told me about the arrest. You're safe now."

Sage's body seemed to relax when I said this. She looked from me to Robin then back at me. "Really?" Tears welled up in her eyes. "You really mean it? I didn't see him on the bus?"

I shook my head. "No. You've always been safe with your aunt and uncle. You don't need to be afraid anymore. Besides," I glanced at Robin, "you have us."

A single tear fell down Sage's cheek. She spoke slowly and quietly like she was drained. "Oh, my god. I can't believe it. If what you're saying is true... That's such a relief." Sage gave a half-hearted laugh, but it came out sounding more like a grunt. "Now I feel like a total ass for dragging everyone into this." She paused for a moment. "How did the two of you know, anyway? They said you found me."

Robin and I exchanged a glance. Should I tell her the whole truth?

"We noticed you weren't at the wedding," I started.

"Right," Sage interrupted. "I'm really sorry. When this all happened, it's like I forgot where I was going. I just ran. I sat under the bridge for a while, and then... well, you know the rest of the story. How'd you know I'd be there?"

"Well, when you weren't at the wedding, Robin and I went to find you. We stopped at your aunt's and uncle's, but then I remembered what you told me about the bridge, that it's the one place you felt safe."

Sage nodded in understanding. I guess I didn't have to scare her off with psychic stuff again.

"So, I guess you'll have to kill me now," I said playfully.

Sage's eyebrows came together in confusion, but after a moment, her face softened.

"I feel like I missed something," Robin said from the foot of the bed.

Sage explained. "I told her if she showed anyone the bridge, I'd have to kill her. But I'll give you a pass this time. I already attempted to take one life today."

Sage's last statement hung in the air uncomfortably, but I felt better that she was able to joke about it. After a while, Sage yawned and complained about being tired. I could tell it was her way of encouraging us to attend the rest of the reception.

"How long are they keeping you here?" I asked.

"They want to keep me overnight and make sure I'm not going to harm myself again."

"Okay. We'll be back tomorrow to see how you're doing. Sleep well."

Robin and I walked back to his car and drove to the hotel. The whole while, I stared out the window with an inadvertent smile on my face. All my friends were right. With me on Sage's side, she'd always be safe.

CHAPTER 24

*W*hen we entered the reception hall, Emma was singing into the microphone, and the floor was crowded with people dancing. Emma's eyes lit up, and she waved to us without missing a beat. I immediately found my way to my mom and her bridesmaids.

My mom squeezed me so tight I could barely breathe. "I was so worried about you."

"You said you wouldn't worry."

"I know. That was the only thing keeping me from calling the party off and going after you."

"It sounds like you almost did call it off. I'm glad you didn't," I told her.

"She made us stay back, too," Diane explained. "She told us she needed us more than you did. Given your talents, she was probably right." I knew Diane was just poking fun of my mom.

"That's not what I meant," my mom defended. "I have faith in you, Crystal."

"It was tough, but I managed. I'm sure Emma filled you in."

They all nodded.

"We'll be back to visit Sage tomorrow. For now, she's doing fine, so I guess I can finally relax."

The song ended and then shifted to a slow melody. I felt someone grab my hand and turned to find Robin. "Aren't you supposed to be singing?" I asked.

"I requested one more song so we could dance." Robin wrapped one arm around my waist and took the other in his hand. "Did I tell you yet how brave you were today?"

"This is only the fourteenth time," I joked.

Robin raised his eyebrows. "So, you've been keeping count?"

I laughed and waved goodbye to my mom and her friends as Robin pulled me across the dancefloor. It felt so good to laugh and be close to him like this, all the while knowing Sage was still breathing thanks to my abilities.

Derek approached us as we danced. "Hey, I heard what happened. I hope everything is alright."

"I think it is for now," I told him. "We're going to see Sage in the morning again."

"So, it appears all your mysteries are solved." Derek waved his hands in front of his face in a mystical manner.

I twisted my lips up in thought. "Not all of them."

He dropped his hands. "I'm not sure if I can help, then."

"Actually, you can. We still don't know anything about your birth parents."

Derek laughed but quickly relaxed. "You mean, Emma didn't tell you?"

I narrowed my eyes playfully at the band where Emma was singing. "No, she didn't tell me."

Derek sighed. "To be honest, I didn't want to know because I was scared of what I would find. I guess I just didn't want to ruin the image of my birth parents that I had in my head."

Just as I suspected, I thought to myself. *He really did care after all.*

"But I did it for Emma, you know. She's too curious. After convincing my mom I had a right to know, she finally told me. I felt kind of bad because she thought that since I'd found out I was adopted, I didn't think of her as my mom anymore." Derek shook his head like it was a ridiculous idea. "When I told her Emma was the one who wanted to know, she relaxed a little."

"So, what's the answer to the mystery?"

"As strange as it sounds, they died in a tornado. Apparently I was with my biological grandma when it happened, but my mom says it was a love story; they were found under a pile of rubble holding each other's hands."

"That's so sad."

Derek nodded. "I know, but it's romantic on one level, too, and knowing that, it kind of makes me feel better about it." He paused for a second. "Anyway, I'll let you guys dance. Then maybe Robin can get up there and give me a chance to dance with Emma."

Robin twirled me in circles, and we swayed to a slow melody. When I finally got a chance to listen to the tune, I realized it was familiar, but I couldn't place it until... "Oh, my gosh. Your band *learned* this song?"

When Robin and I were getting to know each other, we went to a Battle of the Bands concert. This was the song playing when we shared our first kiss. Granted, it was the result of a freaky psychic vision that led to our kissing, but still. "But this was that band's original song. How did you even remember?"

Robin shrugged. "I found the song on Youtube and sent it to everyone to practice, including Emma. We perform major pop songs. Why can't we play another band's songs as long as we don't claim it as our own?"

"Honestly? I don't care about copyright laws. This is downright romantic!"

"As romantic as dying holding hands?"

I pretended like I needed to think about it. "Almost."

Robin released my hand and wrapped both arms around my waist, pulling me in until our bodies were pressed together. He leaned his forehead down and rested it on mine. "You know what would be romantic?" he whispered in a seductive voice.

I could smell his sweet spring scent and feel the warmth of his breath as it rushed across my face. It left my insides fluttering with anticipation. "What?" I whispered back.

And then Robin swooped down and pressed his lips to mine. He pulled my feet from the ground and twirled me around. Only when he set me down and released me did he speak again. "That."

I gripped onto his arms to steady myself and then wrapped my hands around his neck again.

One last time he came down to brush his lips across mine, and then the words I'd been waiting to hear for so long escaped his lips. "I love you, Crystal."

Happiness surged through me. "I love you, too, Robin."

~

That night, I stayed at Emma's house while Teddy and my mom got a hotel room before they flew out on their honeymoon in the morning. After sleeping in—thanks to a long night—I woke to realize I was so tired on the car ride home the night before that I'd forgotten to tell Emma all the details.

Emma yawned from her bed as I shifted from my spot on her floor.

"Emma, about yesterday, I realized I forgot to tell you something."

She rubbed her eyes and spoke with a yawn. "What do you mean?"

"After we went to Sage's aunt's and uncle's, I never told you how we actually found Sage."

Emma twisted her face in confusion. "Yeah, I was kind of wondering about that, but you were half asleep on the car ride home." Her demeanor instantly shifted, and she bounced onto her knees fully alert. Her eyes shined brightly, but she spoke at a million miles per hour. "How did you do it? Did you see the future? Did you find her with psychometry? Did you—"

I bit my lip to keep from letting a huge grin form across my face.

"What?" Emma asked. "Did you, like... I don't know. What else can you do?"

A blush rose to my cheeks, and I smiled proudly. "You're not going to believe me."

Emma shifted her gaze as if wondering what I could have possibly done. I expected her to continue guessing, but when she didn't say anything—thanks to being deep in thought—I spilled the beans.

"I astral traveled!"

Her jaw legitimately dropped. She didn't even blink. She just locked her eyes on mine, stunned. At some point, she realized that she had to actually *breathe*, so she shut her mouth and swallowed. "Are you sure?"

I nodded. "Well, we did all that research on it. It definitely felt like I was out of my body."

"Whoa. What did it feel like?"

"Kind of like I was flying."

"I knew I had a good feeling about astral travel."

"What?" I asked, but when I looked up at her, a cheesy grin spread across her face. I grabbed my pillow and threw it at her playfully. "You're good, but you're not that good."

Emma tossed her dark curls over her shoulder dramatically. "Oh, I'm *that* good."

All I could do was roll my eyes at her.

An hour later, Derek met up with us so we could go visit Sage together. Derek sat in the passenger seat silently as I filled him in on the details.

"That's all just so... unbelievable."

I bit my lip nervously. Did he really mean that?

"I mean, it's amazing." Derek finally shifted to look back at me. "I hate to abandon my whole belief system, Crystal, but unless you're lying to me, I can't think of any other explanation. And you obviously weren't lying." He pointed to my face. "Your eyebrow wasn't twitching the whole time."

My hand immediately flew up to my eyebrow. While he was right—I wasn't lying—I had gotten better about the whole eyebrow twitching thing lately.

Derek noticed my reaction and burst out laughing.

Once the laugher in the car died down, Emma spoke. "You know, maybe you don't have to change your belief system. I mean, you believe in an afterlife, Derek. Given that Crystal has seen ghosts and helped them cross over, she *knows* there's an afterlife."

This gave us all something to think about, and the car filled with silence.

"Do you think we should bring her a gift?" Derek asked as we neared the city. "Maybe a get-well card or a stuffed animal or something."

Emma gave Derek a look of disapproval. "She's not going to want a stuffed animal. Maybe we should have brought some of the leftover cake Sophie took home."

"I don't know," I said from the back seat. "I think a stuffed animal and a get-well card is a good idea."

"Crystal, she nearly died," Emma pointed out. "It's not like she's a kid with strep throat."

"Well, what do you suggest? Besides cake."

Derek and Emma went back and forth with ideas as we drove, but after a while, I figured I should call Robin and let him know we were on our way. I opened up my contact list, and there on the top sat a name pulled from my Facebook friends' list. Something he'd said a while back surfaced in my memory, and I instantly had the perfect idea on what to bring Sage. Even Emma had suggested the same thing weeks ago.

Maybe if she played again it would help. It could be like therapy or something, Emma had said.

I pulled up Andrew's profile on my phone and sent him a quick message, praying that he'd see it soon. Not even a minute later, he sent a message back agreeing to help me.

We stopped at Andrew's and Faith's house on the way to the hospital and then swung by to pick up Robin. I talked to one of the nurses before she led us to Sage's room. She was wary of my plan at first, but Robin managed to work a bit of his charm and convince her.

When we walked into Sage's room, it seemed smaller with Emma and Derek along, but Sage looked to be doing a lot better. She was sitting upright in her bed and staring at the TV. She greeted us with a nearly genuine smile and pressed a button on the remote. The TV went silent.

"So, how was your mom's wedding?" Sage asked in a light tone that told me she was feeling better. "You know, after I ruined it."

"You didn't ruin it," I assured her. I blushed and looked over to Robin, remembering the way he'd told me he loved me the night before.

"What's that?" Sage asked, pointing to the case in my hand, the one I'd borrowed from Andrew.

I pulled it close to my chest despite it being a bit big. "Well, we wanted to bring you something, and we thought this might help you feel better."

"Is that what I think it is?"

I set the suitcase-sized case next to her on the bed and clicked it open. "If you think it's a saxophone, then you're right."

Sage's eyes lit up when she saw the horn. It was like watching a small child peering into a treasure chest. Her hand reached for it, but she pulled away at the last second as if she'd realized what she was doing.

"I can't," she said, shaking her head. "The hospital wouldn't allow it."

Just then, Sage's nurse stepped into the room. "Actually, I just talked with the other patients in the hallway, and they'd be delighted to hear you play. Your friends say you're quite good."

Sage looked at each of us warily. "How did you even—I mean—where did you get it?"

"Remember Andrew?" I asked.

Sage nodded.

"Well, I remembered he said he played saxophone in the jazz band. I messaged him on the way here. He let us borrow it for you."

Sage looked down at the horn in wonder and then back to her nurse. "Are you sure?"

Her nurse nodded kindly.

Sage took a deep breath and then reached into the case to assemble the saxophone. "I don't even know what I'd play."

"Play your solo," Emma suggested.

Sage looked at her in confusion.

Emma sighed like the answer was obvious. "We watched a video of you playing a solo last year. Your eyes were on the director, so you obviously had it memorized."

Sage situated the saxophone in her hands. "I don't know if I remember it anymore."

"I still remember my last solo and ensemble piece on clarinet," I said. "You probably practiced a lot more than I did."

Sage placed the mouth piece to her lips but pulled it back out. A tear pricked at the side of one eye. "I can't believe you did this for me." Then she brought the horn back to her lips and breathed into it. Her hands moved across the keys, and the most beautiful tune I'd ever heard filled the room and echoed down the hallway.

As she played, I lifted my eyes to the ceiling and whispered a silent prayer to my father. "Thank you for helping me save her." A feeling of serenity washed over me, and I knew at that moment that even though I couldn't see the spirits helping me from the other side, they were always watching over me. "And thank you for helping me find the courage to face my own demons," I added.

Sage kept her eyes closed the entire time, concentrating on the notes. After just a few bars, a small crowd had formed outside her room. The intensity of the solo grew to near fierce proportions but then softened into a relaxing tune. Sage held out the last note with perfect tone. Applause filled the room, and Sage opened her eyes for the first time since starting the solo. More tears fell down her cheeks when she realized how many people had been listening.

"I forgot how much I loved it."

EPILOGUE

The summer heat left my mom and me fanning ourselves in the living room. I'd asked Teddy earlier if he wanted help fixing the air conditioning unit, but he insisted he could do it himself. It was a Saturday morning, and my mom and I had nothing better to do than fold up paper fans and blow air each other's way. It was actually fun since she'd brought her craft box out and we'd glued lace and other fun things to our fans.

"It's going to be a girl," I told my mom confidently.

She rolled her eyes at me but continued fanning my face. "How many times do we have to go over this? It's going to be a boy." She laid one hand on her still flat belly.

"I thought you couldn't see the future if it had to do with friends or family," I accused.

My mom just laughed. "I don't have to see the future. I'm a mother. Women know these things."

"So you knew I was going to be a girl?"

She nodded proudly.

Just then, the doorbell rang. We both exchanged a look of confusion since we weren't expecting anyone. Maybe Teddy finally decided to call a professional.

I rose from the couch and pulled the door open. Bright eyes and a freckled face stared back at me. The redhead wore a flattering green tank top that exposed her arms.

"Sage!" I cried in excitement, pulling her into an embrace. We'd stayed in touch since she was released from the hospital, but I hadn't seen her in a few weeks. "Come in. It's not any nicer in here, though." I opened the door wider so she could step inside.

"Sage," my mom greeted from the couch. "Want a fan?"

Sage eyed the fan, and an amused smile played at her lips. "No, I'm okay. I actually just came to give you this." She held out an envelope made of fine stationery.

"What's this?" I asked warily, taking it from her hands.

"Well, after everything that happened a few months back, my therapist and I got to talking seriously. I asked her if there were any music therapy programs around, and she said she hadn't heard of one in the area."

I peeled open the envelope as she spoke.

"So, she suggested we start one. We have a huge group of teens who come together once a week for music group therapy, and we're putting on a concert in a few weeks. I was really hoping you'd come. After everything you did for me, I just wanted to show you how much I appreciated it."

"That's so nice of you," I said, pulling the invitation out of the envelope.

"We've been working on winter-themed songs."

"Why winter?" I asked. "It's not even autumn yet."

Sage only smiled at me. That's when I finally looked down at the invite and noticed the title of the concert:

Inspired by Frost

VISIONS AMONG FROST

ALICIA RADES

VISIONS AMONG FROST

A shriek echoed throughout the house, and my body tensed.

Emma clapped her hands over her ears for show. "Geez. Betsy really needs to take it down a notch."

"Yeah," I agreed. "If she keeps that up, the neighbors are going to think we're filming a horror movie."

"Or worse," Katie joked from across the room. She sat in Betsy's recliner and scrolled through her phone while Emma and I waited on the couch for the rest of our volleyball teammates to arrive.

A flash of blue flew by the entrance to the living room as Betsy ran down the hall to answer the front door. "Jenna!" Betsy cried in excitement. The two exchanged words in such high-pitched voices that I couldn't understand what either of them said. I guessed it to be some sort of best friends' code language.

I raised my eyebrows at Emma. "We're not that bad, are we?"

She crinkled her nose, which made her look like a chipmunk. "*Nobody* is as bad as those two, Crystal."

I breathed a fake sigh of relief. "Thank God."

Almost as soon as Betsy welcomed Jenna inside, the doorbell rang again, setting off another round of excited shrieks from girls across the house. Almost our entire volleyball team was coming for our end-of-summer sleepover. Even the new girl, Alyssa, had agreed to come.

The moment Alyssa crossed my mind, she peeked her head into the living room and gave a shy smile. We'd only met her the first day of practice a few weeks ago, but she was already morphing into a vital member

405

of our team. She'd played volleyball at her old school and was better than everyone in the junior class—all except Emma.

"Come on in!" Emma said, scooting closer to me and patting the cushion at the end of the couch.

"Thanks." Alyssa's smile grew wider, but it still read uncertainty. She dropped her purple backpack next to the couch and sat beside Emma. She opened her mouth to say more, but before she could, Jenna hurried into the room, a look of excitement on her face.

"Who wants Jell-O shots?" Jenna asked in a sing-song voice, wiggling a transparent container in my direction. The red Jell-O jiggled but maintained its shape.

I gaped at her, but Emma was the one to speak. "You're kidding, right?"

Jenna rolled her eyes before plopping down on the carpet and opening the container. "Of course I'm kidding. They're just Jell-O Jigglers. My mom made them." She popped one of the red squares into her mouth and shoved the container toward Emma. With a full mouth, she asked, "Want one?"

Emma twisted up her nose again, but she took one anyway.

"Hey, Jenna," Katie called, straightening up in her chair. "Ever heard of a thing called manners?"

Jenna narrowed her eyes in Katie's direction. "I'll shove one of these down your throat, and then we can talk about manners."

Katie held up her palms in surrender. "Whoa. You sure those aren't spiked with anything?"

The two continued their friendly banter, and I pressed my lips together, afraid that if I laughed they'd try to get me involved.

More and more girls filtered into the house, some heading to the kitchen right away to drop off the snacks they brought along, while others set their bags in the living room. We chose Betsy's house for the sleepover because hers had the biggest living room, but once we crammed eighteen JV and Varsity players into it, it didn't seem so big anymore.

"Okay, okay," Betsy called once everyone had arrived. Slowly, the chatter in the room faded, but it was only after three more attempts by Betsy that everyone heard her. "Simmer down," she scolded in the silence, as if she hadn't been the obnoxious one earlier. "There are snacks in the kitchen. Feel free to gorge yourselves. The bathroom is down the hall and to your right. Please avoid going upstairs because my parents are up there. If it's an *emergency*, there's a bathroom at the top of the stairs. Capiche?"

Everyone nodded. Laughter played out from a few girls in the opposite corner of the room.

"Okay. Who wants to kick off the night with a game?" Betsy asked.

Jenna hopped up from her spot on the floor and headed over to a cabinet set against the far wall.

"Truth or dare?" someone suggested.

"Maybe later," Betsy said with a sly smile. "But first, Jenna and I had something better in mind."

Conversations rose again as Jenna shuffled through the cabinet. She pulled out a box, presumably a board game, but when she turned and I caught a glimpse of the game's title, the sense of comfort I'd felt moments ago shattered. My eyes grew wide, and my breath left my chest.

"No!" The word slipped out of my mouth before I could stop myself.

Jenna shot me a questioning look. "It's just for fun, Crystal. You of all people should know that."

My jaw hung slack. What could she possibly mean by that?

"Yeah," Betsy agreed. "Doesn't your mom sell these in her shop? There's nothing to be afraid of."

A few girls across the room rose to their knees to get a better look while Jenna pulled the contents out of the box.

"What is it?" someone whispered.

"A Ouija board," another answered in a quiet voice.

Those words sent a shiver down my spine. I didn't have the focus to make out who'd said them.

Betsy was wrong. Though my mom ran a shop filled with paranormal trinkets, she'd never put a Ouija board on her shelves. There had to be a reason for that. When I was younger—when I still believed my mom's shop was built on the make-believe—she'd told me never to use a Ouija board. I didn't understand why at the time, but now I knew they could invite evil spirits into your home. With everything I'd learned about the paranormal since discovering I could see ghosts and predict the future, it wouldn't feel right not to heed my mother's warning.

"No, you guys," I pleaded. "This could be dangerous."

"Yeah," Alyssa agreed in a shy voice, shifting on the couch. "Maybe we shouldn't."

Jenna rolled her eyes. "It's just for fun. You know it's not real."

I swallowed deeply and glanced around at my teammates. They'd all gone silent. I couldn't say I *believed* in it, not when the whole town accepted my mom's shop as "just for fun." Besides, what would I say to them? *I'm Crystal Frost, the girl who sees ghosts and has visions. In fact, I helped one of our deceased team members cross into the light a year ago.* Yeah, I didn't think that would go over well, whether they thought I was playing a trick on them or not.

Emma grabbed my wrist tightly and pulled me out of the room. I stumbled along behind her, rendered speechless in surprise. She stopped in the hall near the bathroom and turned to me.

"What's the big deal?" she whispered. Her tone read a cross between curiosity and concern.

"I—" I wasn't sure I had an answer, but if I did, Emma was the only person here I could tell. She'd known I was psychic almost as long as I had. "I don't know. I just remember my mom saying they were bad news. We could actually summon a spirit."

"And?" She stretched out the word and raised a dark eyebrow. "It's not any different than the séances you've done, is it?"

"But my mom knows more about this stuff than I do," I tried to rationalize with her. "I trust her, and if she doesn't think these things are safe, then maybe we shouldn't be playing around with them."

"You don't feel any spirits around, do you?"

I glanced around the hall as if expecting one to spontaneously appear. "No," I admitted, dropping my shoulders.

"Then there's nothing to worry about, is there?"

Maybe she was right.

"Why are you so interested?" I accused. "You don't *want* us to summon a dark spirit, do you?"

The corners of Emma's mouth twitched like she thought that might be cool. "No. I just want to see everyone else freak. It will be fun."

I pursed my lips and crossed my arms over my chest. The light from the living room went dim. They were already setting up to play, and it was me against the rest of my teammates—except maybe Alyssa, who seemed almost as wary as I was. I sighed heavily. I wasn't going to win this one without telling them why I was so against it, and even then, who knew how many would believe I could see ghosts?

"Fine," I agreed reluctantly.

Emma smiled and hurried back to the living room, her dark curls swaying behind her. I took the walk down the hall slowly, feeling sick to my stomach for letting this madness continue. But maybe Emma was right. Maybe this wasn't any more dangerous than the séances we'd done before.

When I entered the living room, everyone had gathered around the Ouija board in a big circle. The room once again buzzed in conversation. Two girls had claimed the spots on the couch where Emma and I had been sitting, and I had to climb over three others to reach an empty area of carpet between Emma and Alyssa.

I reached for Alyssa's backpack to tuck it closer to the wall so I could sit. When my hand gripped around the top, an image flicked across my vision. A woman's frail hands slipped a piece of paper and a golden heart-shaped necklace into a small pocket at the top of the bag. That was all I saw before my eyes refocused on the dim living room, lit only by the setting sun filtering in through the thin curtains. The image caught me off guard, sending me stumbling a bit. I caught my fall on the edge of the couch and casually slid all the way to the floor, setting Alyssa's backpack down on my way.

"You okay?" Emma asked quietly. Her question was almost drowned out by the rest of the chatter.

"Yeah." I settled into my spot. "That was weird. I just...saw something. But usually that doesn't happen unless I'm looking for it. And even then, it's usually hard to see."

Emma tilted her head in question. "Saw something?"

"Yeah. I don't think it meant anything."

Before Emma could ask me exactly what I saw, Betsy rose her voice again to get everyone to settle down. "Everyone needs to be quiet," she insisted. It took another few tries before the girls quieted and silence settled over the room. "Jenna and I will place our hands on the pointer. Everyone else needs to stay quiet or you might scare the spirit away."

A couple of girls laughed at how serious she was being. Surely Betsy didn't actually believe a spirit would show, did she?

Even in the darkness, I couldn't miss the daggers Betsy shot the other girls. "Let's be serious about this or it won't work."

They quickly quieted. In the silence, I heard Alyssa draw in a deep breath from beside me. I had to do the same to calm myself. *It's fine*, I told myself. *Like Emma said, there aren't any spirits around. It's harmless.* But just because I didn't see anyone now didn't mean they wouldn't show. I swallowed hard, hoping that wouldn't happen. Then I'd be left to clean up Betsy and Jenna's mess because I could talk to the spirit.

After several long moments of silence, Betsy spoke. "Is anyone there?"

The planchette didn't move, and I slowly let out my breath, releasing the tension from my shoulders. These girls didn't know what they were doing. It wasn't going to work.

Betsy drew in another long, deep breath and tried again. "Is anyone there?"

The planchette twitched, and my breath ceased once again. Several girls murmured incoherent words, each voice blending into the next. Was that something supernatural, or was it one of the girls' hand moving?

"Shh," Betsy warned. "Is anyone there?"

Slowly, the planchette slid across the board and landed above the answer: "Yes."

Alyssa's breathing rate increased, and I noticed her hand squeeze tightly around the sofa's arm rest. I could feel the horror fill my face, but in the dim room, no one else noticed. My gaze darted from girl to girl in search of someone who wasn't supposed to be there. With so many girls here, a ghost could easily blend in, and who knew if that ghost would be nice like the others I'd encountered before?

Emma leaned into me and whispered so quietly that no one else could hear. "Do you feel anything?"

Her question made me focus on my body. Usually when a ghost was around, a chill would spread out from my spine and to my fingertips. That wasn't the case now. Was the Ouija board stronger than I was? Was it somehow messing with my abilities?

I shook my head.

"Are you good or evil?" Betsy asked the spirit.

I held my breath as the planchette slid over to the middle of the board. *Keep moving. Keep moving*, I chanted in my head. To my horror, the planchette crossed over the E and stopped. Everyone in the room took in a collective breath, but it didn't slow the planchette's motion as it continued to spell out the word "evil."

"Guys, you should stop," I urged, still glancing around the room for any signs of a ghost.

"Relax, Crystal," Katie said. "I want to see what else it says."

A chorus of agreement traveled around the room. The only other person besides me who didn't agree was Alyssa. Emma shot me a look that I couldn't quite read. It was like she was both excited and nervous about this.

I sat back, giving in once again. It didn't matter what I said. Everyone else was having fun and wouldn't listen to me. The best thing I could do was stay and keep an eye out for the spirit, but if there really was one here, why couldn't I sense it? Could the spirit somehow hide itself from me?

Betsy spoke again after the word "evil" was complete. "Do you have a message for someone in the room?"

The planchette slid over to the word "Yes." In that moment, I felt the energy in the room shift. A negative energy settled around us all, but I was the only one who noticed.

No, no, no, no, no. I'd never had to deal with an evil spirit before. I didn't know what to do or how to help.

"Who?" Betsy prodded the spirit.

The planchette hovered over the letter A before moving toward the other end of the board. Several girls let out sounds of shock in unison. Everyone glanced between Alyssa and Aya since they were the only two on the team whose names started with A. We all held our breath in anticipation of the next letter. At least, I held my breath. The pulsing in my head drowned out any other sounds.

The planchette stopped at the letter L, and every eye in the room fell on Alyssa. She glanced back at them all for a moment before jumping up from the couch and rushing out of the room, stepping over several girls on her way. I didn't question for even a second that I had to go after her. I rose from my spot on the floor and followed her down the hall.

I knew I'd be the one to clean up their mess, I thought in frustration. I half expected Katie to come after Alyssa as well since she'd been the one to befriend her during practice, but only laughter followed us.

Betsy shouted over the laughter. "It was only a joke!"

It wasn't a very nice one, I wanted to bite back, but I wasn't about to waste my energy chewing Betsy out right now. I needed to make sure Alyssa was okay.

She stopped in the kitchen, bracing herself up against the edge of the counter and inhaling a deep breath.

"You okay?" I approached her and placed a comforting hand on her back. As soon as I touched her, a wave of emotions flooded through me. Fear, loss, and embarrassment all hit me at once. I could have told Alyssa I knew exactly how she felt, but she would never know how much truth there was to that sentiment.

She whipped her gaze toward me, her brown French braid swinging over her shoulder. The first thing I noticed was her red, swollen eyes. She sniffled and wiped the tears off her cheeks.

I dropped my hand to my side. "You lost someone." It wasn't a question. I didn't need my empathic abilities to tell me that, but they helped confirm it.

Alyssa could barely get the words out. "My mom." She tore her gaze off my shocked face and focused on a spot on the counter.

"That wasn't cool what they did in there," I told her.

After a moment to compose herself, Alyssa turned to me with puffy eyes and rested her hip up against the counter. "That was my mom in there."

I knew now for certain it wasn't. The girls were only being cruel, and the negative energy I'd felt had been Alyssa's, not an evil spirit.

"Why would you think that?" I asked. "Your mom wasn't evil, was she?"

Alyssa's lips turned down at the corners, and she glanced to the floor.

"Well, no, but...who else would want to leave a message for me?" Her voice cracked, and she rubbed the back of her hand across her eyes again.

"No one," I said simply. How could I possibly explain to her how I knew there wasn't a spirit in the room without telling her about my abilities? The last semi-stranger I'd told had called me crazy. "Those girls were just goofing around. I'm sure they didn't mean anything by it, but it wasn't your mom in there. Trust me."

She blinked a few times. "You really think so?"

I nodded reassuringly.

"Why would they do that? I thought we were all getting along." She sniffled again, though the tears had subsided.

"Have you told anyone in Peyton Springs about your mom?" I did my best to keep my voice calm and reassuring. I wanted her to know she could trust me.

Alyssa shook her head. "Just my dad's family, but it's a small town. I'm sure it's gotten around by now."

"Well, I didn't know. I'm sure they didn't either. If they did, they wouldn't have done that. They're really nice girls."

Alyssa swallowed deeply and went silent. I hoped my words were comforting to her. At the very least, the negative energy I'd felt coming from her before had faded. I wanted to reach out and touch her to see what she was feeling now, but I knew touching her again would only be awkward for both of us.

"My parents were separated," Alyssa said, offering me information even though I didn't ask. "My mom died of cancer last June, and I came here to live with my dad. I thought joining the volleyball team would help take my mind off it." She gave an uncertain laugh. "Guess that didn't work. Maybe I should just quit." Her gaze dropped to the floor again.

"No! You can't quit." I almost stepped toward her to comfort her again, but I paused. I didn't know her well enough for that. "You're one of the best on our team."

At least that got her to look at me. She almost smiled. "You're just saying that because you feel bad for me."

"No, I'm not. I mean it." I said the words with so much conviction that I was sure she had to believe me. "Do you think you're going to be okay?"

She remained silent for several long seconds as if mulling over the question. "From tonight? I guess." She shrugged. "From my mom's death? Probably never."

"Well, that's not true."

Her lips turned down again. "You can't know that."

"I can. I lost my dad, too, about ten years ago." This time, I was the one who turned my gaze away.

"I'm sorry," Alyssa said slowly and quietly like she thought it wouldn't be right to break the silence.

"It's okay." My voice had more confidence to it this time. "We all move on eventually."

She took two deep breaths before speaking again. "What if they don't, though?"

I shifted so I could lean against the counter opposite her. "What do you mean?"

"Like, what if my mom didn't move on after she died?"

I crossed my arms over my chest casually. "You think she had unfinished business?"

"Of sorts, I guess." She shrugged and shifted her weight between her feet.

"Oh?"

Alyssa shook her head. "It's silly, really."

"I won't judge."

She eyed me as if gauging whether I was trustworthy or not. She must have decided I was because she relaxed and let the story slip past her lips effortlessly. "My mom had this locket that she used to wear all the time. I always thought that if she died, keeping it would be like keeping a part of her with me. We even talked about it, and she promised me that once she was gone, I could have it. I think she didn't give it to me right away because she didn't want to give up. As long as she was still wearing it, it was a sign of hope for both of us, you know?"

Alyssa cleared her throat and continued. "But after she died, the hospital staff couldn't find the necklace. It was like losing two parts of her that day. I mean, don't get me wrong. I'd choose my mother over the locket in a heartbeat, but at least that was supposed to be a sure thing. It was supposed to help me get through it all, and now it's gone. Sometimes I dream that she'll come back and tell me where it is, like that will be enough for me to know she's okay and that I will be, too."

Her voice cracked, and she coughed to clear it. "Like I said, it's silly. I don't even know why I'm telling you this. Maybe you'll understand since you lost your dad."

My jaw hung slack, and I had to make a conscious effort to snap it back shut. Even though Alyssa's mom hadn't communicated through the Ouija board, maybe she had come back in some way. Perhaps sending me that vision was the only way she could communicate after crossing over.

"Was the locket heart shaped and golden?" I asked, the image I'd seen earlier flashing through my memory.

She tilted her head in question. "How'd you know?"

I shrugged. "Lucky guess."

Alyssa sighed like it didn't matter. "It's not like I'm going to find it now anyway."

I spoke quickly before she could give up completely. "Maybe the reason the hospital staff didn't find it was because your mom already left it to you." I pictured the pale hands I'd seen in my vision. She must have slipped the locket and letter into Alyssa's backpack on one of her last days.

"Well, she didn't."

"One thing my mom used to do for me was leave little notes in the top pocket of my backpack. You know, the little pocket by the handle that's kind of hidden." It was a total lie. Emma would be able to tell in a split second that I was making it up, but Alyssa didn't know me well enough for that. "Maybe she slipped it in there when you weren't looking."

"How would she even—" Alyssa cut off, mulling over the idea. "I did spend a lot of time with her at the hospital. Maybe she...No. She would have said something."

It made sense that she hadn't told Alyssa where she'd left it, perhaps hoping she'd find it on her own. She wouldn't have wanted Alyssa to know she'd given up. I hated to think about it.

I shrugged nonchalantly. "It's worth checking."

Alyssa's mouth hung open, but a second later, she hurried down the hall to the living room. I followed behind her. As soon as she entered, the conversations quieted, and several girls mumbled an apology. Alyssa ignored them and slung her bag over her shoulder before escaping back down the hall again.

I remained in the doorway, glaring at Betsy and Jenna with my arms crossed over my chest. The lights were back on, and they'd already cleaned up the board, but the tension in the room remained. Emma glanced at me from across the room with a look that said, *Let's talk about this later.*

Betsy caught my glare. "It was just a harmless prank. We all pick on each other. Anyone else would have thought it was funny."

"She lost her mom," I stated flatly.

The few people still talking or laughing immediately went silent, and every face in the room dropped, including Betsy's and Jenna's. It was so quiet that the only sound I could hear was the buzz of the ceiling fan.

"We had no idea," Jenna said in a regretful whisper.

The guilt was clearly written across Betsy's face. "Yeah. If we'd known, we would have never..." She seemed at a loss for words.

I glanced down the hall toward Alyssa. She'd taken a seat on the stairs. She held the heart-shaped locket out in front of her, letting it swing like a pendulum while she stared at it in awe. Tearing her gaze off the locket, she shifted her attention to the note her mom had left, unfolding it carefully like she was afraid it might crumble in her hands. Her eyes visibly filled with tears as she scanned the page.

I turned back to Betsy and Jenna. "Just give her a minute alone, and then you two should go apologize."

"We will," Jenna assured me with an eager nod. "We're *so* sorry."

"Don't apologize to *me*," I bit almost too sharply. "She's part of our team now, and she deserves to feel like it."

Betsy turned her gaze down in guilt. "We didn't mean to single her out. It was just supposed to be for laughs."

I raised my eyebrows, about to point out that no one was laughing now, but I didn't want to drag it all out. The girls could clearly see that what they'd done was wrong. I glanced back down the hall to Alyssa on the steps. She folded up the note and slipped it into her bag before clasping the locket around her neck and wiping her eyes.

I dropped my arms from my chest. "You can go apologize now."

Jenna and Betsy sprang up from their spots on the floor and practically raced each other down the hall. "We're so *sorry*, Alyssa," they cried in unison.

I crossed the living room to sit beside Emma on the floor. The whispers around the room slowly grew to full conversation, giving Emma and me a chance to talk.

"Is Alyssa okay?" she asked, biting her lip in uncertainty.

I nodded. "I think she'll be fine. Turns out that thing I saw earlier meant something."

"Yeah? What'd you see?"

I lowered my voice and leaned toward her to fill her in on the details. When I drew away, her eyebrows were practically touching her hairline.

"Wow. Well, at least it all worked out for the better, you know?"

I nodded again, but I wasn't sure it was all worth getting the Ouija board out for. At least Alyssa now had something to comfort her after her mother's death, but knowing the Ouija board was only a few feet away from me in the cabinet kept my nerves alive.

Betsy, Jenna, and Alyssa returned a few minutes later. I didn't know what they'd said to her, but Alyssa's tears had dried. She crossed over to her spot on the couch—which no one had been rude enough to claim—and set her backpack next to me. She caught my eyes as she sat and mouthed, "Thank you." Her hand came up to clamp around the locket.

"You're welcome," I mouthed back.

When no one else was looking, she slid her fingernail between the creases of the locket and popped it open. I couldn't see what sort of pictures were inside, but she breathed a sigh and relaxed into the couch before securing it shut again.

I quickly took my eyes off her so she wouldn't notice I was watching.

"Hey, Alyssa," Katie called from across the room. "Why don't you come sit over here by us?"

It was a nice gesture, and I was glad to see my teammates acting like their usual welcoming selves again. Before Alyssa could agree or disagree, Betsy suggested everyone head to the kitchen to get food. Everyone stood and shuffled down the hall, not one person but me wondering how we were all going to fit into the kitchen at once.

Emma was the last one out of the room besides me. She turned back in the doorway. "Crystal, are you coming?"

I stood planted in place. "Yeah, just a minute."

Emma headed down the hall with everyone else, giving me privacy. I glanced around the room, focusing on its energy to confirm there hadn't been any spirits at play earlier that night. After verifying that everything felt normal, I finally let myself relax. But as I exited the room to join my teammates in the kitchen, a sense of wariness settled over me. Though there hadn't been any evil spirits here tonight, I couldn't shake the feeling that the evil spirits would eventually find me—and soon.

FADING FROST

ALICIA RADES

CHAPTER 1

$\mathcal{I}$t's easier to accept death when you know there's an afterlife. I was certain of this fact because I'd seen ghosts and watched them cross over into the light before. Even so, I wasn't prepared to go.

As the car jerked to the right and I slammed on the brakes, all I could think was that I wasn't ready. Robin and I still had so much to experience together, and I knew Emma would be devastated if I was gone. What would happen when Mom's baby came? I would never get to know my little brother or sister. If I died right now, I wouldn't have even made a dent in my junior year of high school. No finishing up my first Varsity volleyball season. No junior prom. I'd die a virgin!

All of this went through my head in a split second. The car jolted when it passed over the edge of the road and into the ditch. I couldn't do anything to slow its momentum. Before I could process what was truly happening, the world tumbled around me, and my head smashed into something hard.

It took me several seconds to realize the car had come to a halt. A pain pounded through my head, and my vision blurred. I struggled to keep hold of my consciousness, like if I let my guard down for one moment, I'd fade. At least I was conscious enough to rejoice in the fact that I wasn't dead—even if the moment of joy lasted but a millisecond. I didn't know how long it took me to finally raise my head, but when I managed to blink the world back into focus, one thing was clear: for the first time in a long time, I had no idea what was going to happen next.

Shock overcame me, and I couldn't bring myself to cry even though I wanted to. I gulped down the terror rising to my throat, but that didn't slow my racing heart. When I finally managed to glance around the vehicle, I realized I had somehow lost control of the car, and when I hit the ditch, it had flipped. The side of my skull had connected with the driver's side window. I was lucky enough that the car had landed upright, and I didn't appear to have a broken bone or anything.

Slowly, I reached across the middle console toward my purse sprawled at the foot of the passenger seat. Something caught my body before my fingers touched the strap. I straightened up and tried again. This time, the seat belt stretched far enough so I could reach the purse and pull it onto my lap. I fumbled in search of my phone, ignoring the other contents that had flown from my purse just moments ago. The other line began ringing, and I put the phone to my ear.

"Hello?" my mom answered.

I pressed my free hand to my forehead, partially to ease the ache pulsing through my skull and partially to get myself to *think* about what to say to her. I must have remained silent for too long because my mother began speaking with a worried tone.

"Crystal, sweetie, are you okay?"

What could I say to that? Sure, my head was throbbing, but overall, I *was* physically fine. What about emotionally? I hardly had my license for two months, and already I was in an accident. As if that wasn't humiliating enough, my sixth sense immediately felt hazy. Although I'd only known about my psychic abilities for a year, I suddenly didn't feel like myself anymore.

"I'm okay," I half-lied, forcing down the bile in my throat. The truth was, I was riled enough to puke the entire contents of my dinner onto Teddy's steering wheel. I decided to focus on my physical state so I wouldn't worry my mother. Who knew what stress would do to my little brother or sister?

"But something's wrong," she concluded based on my minimal words and croaky voice.

I pressed my hand harder against my face like that would ease my headache and help me figure out what to say to her. I remembered the time Robin had called Teddy and told him about the car when a stranger slashed our tires. I decided to ease into it slowly by taking his approach.

I forced a painfully fake laugh. "Um... What if I told you something bad happened to the car?"

"Oh, my gosh, Crystal. What happened? Are you hurt?" At least she was less concerned about the damage I'd done to the car and more concerned about me.

"I'm not. It's just a headache." I lightly grazed my fingers across the goose egg-sized lump I already felt forming along my hairline. It immediately stung. I pulled my fingers away from the injury and saw they were covered in a layer of blood. The blow against the window must have split my skin open. "And a minor scratch," I added, though I wasn't sure how honest those words were. Truth be told, it hurt like *hell*. I quickly glanced into the rearview mirror and noticed it looked as bad as it felt. I was pretty sure I'd be alright, but that didn't stop a wave of hysteria from overcoming me.

"Tell me what happened," my mother insisted. "Were you speeding?"

I couldn't stop the words from tumbling out of my mouth. "What? No. Mom, I'm a good driver. I swear. It's just—I don't know. I lost control somehow. One second I was on the road, and then the next—"

"Crystal," my mother stopped me before I could hyperventilate. "It's going to be okay. We'll call an ambulance." I heard a shuffling in the background and my mother's muffled voice as she spoke to Teddy.

"No, Mom," I tried to tell her, but she didn't hear me. The phone shook in my hand.

A second later, she was talking into the phone again. "I'm going to keep you on the line while we call an ambulance with Teddy's phone, okay? Where are you? How long ago did you leave Robin's?"

"Mom," I stated sternly so she'd listen to me. "I'm only five minutes from Peyton Springs. It will be faster if you or Teddy come and get me." Our town was so small that our ambulance service came from the next town over.

"That doesn't change the fact that I'm still calling an ambulance. We'll be there soon. Stay put."

Where else would I go? the snarky 16-year-old in me wondered, but I kept quiet.

Mom kept me talking as she and Teddy rushed out to meet me on the secluded highway. I pressed some tissues to my gash as I waited, but it stung and didn't seem to help the bleeding. During a brief silence when my mom turned her attention to Teddy, I couldn't hold it in any longer. The pain in my head and the fright I'd felt when it happened all caught up to me. Tears sprang to my eyes and rolled down my cheeks.

My mom's vehicle was the first I saw after the car had flipped. When I spotted it, I finally hung up the phone. I hadn't moved and was still buckled in my seat.

"Crystal!" my mother exclaimed when she exited the car. She rushed across the road to the vehicle I sat in and pulled on the door, only it didn't budge. "It's locked, sweetie." She gestured to the lock on the door.

Still slightly dazed, I unlocked the door. She opened it, but my stepdad was the one who knelt next to me, cupping my face in his hands.

"Are you okay?" he asked calmly. I didn't know how he remained so calm; it probably had to do with his police training.

Tears welled in my eyes again, and all I could do was nod.

Teddy reached up to take the tissues from my hand. "Here, let me help with that." He pulled the wad away from my face to inspect the wound before dabbing it against my forehead again.

I winced.

"That's a nasty gash," he said, stating the obvious.

I sniffled. "Can we go home?"

Teddy shook his head as a look of apology settled over his face. "We need to get you to the hospital first. You could have a concussion."

"No, I want to go home," I argued, but my voice came out sounding like a whisper.

"You're going to the hospital. Andrea?" he addressed my mother.

"He's right, sweetie," she agreed.

My gaze flickered between each of their eyes. "Okay," I agreed, but only because I loved them so much, not because I thought I actually needed to go.

We'd settled that argument, but nobody moved for several minutes as we waited for emergency responders to arrive. The chilly night air rushed in through the open driver's side door and filled the car.

Teddy finally stood and let my mom kneel beside me. He rested his hands on his hips and eyed the car. It was crumpled on all sides, though I was grateful there weren't any trees nearby that could have signed my death warrant. I was lucky enough to miss the telephone poles lining the road, too. He rounded the car to assess the damage before he spoke. "Looks like you blew a tire. I can't think of why, though. These tires aren't that old."

I pondered his statement for a moment, and that's when I realized it was all my fault. "Uh, I blew that tire up at a gas station before leaving the city. Robin said it looked low."

Teddy gazed at me. "Did you check the pressure?"

I shook my head guiltily. I didn't know anything about cars. I didn't even know if Teddy had a pressure gage in the car or, if he did, where to find it.

"It's okay," he finally said. "I'm just glad you're alright." Just then, his eyes locked on something in the distance, and that's when I noticed the emergency responders approaching in the rearview mirror. "I'll stay here while you two go to the hospital," he offered.

We all agreed that was a good idea. The rest of the night was a blur, but I remembered they let Mom ride with me in the ambulance.

"Don't fall asleep," she demanded when I lolled my head to the side. "You could have a concussion."

"I'm not sleeping," I told her truthfully.

"You need to keep talking so we know you're okay." She exchanged a glance with the EMT as if to ask whether she was right or not.

"I'm okay, Mom," I insisted. "I just need to collect my thoughts."

She seemed to accept this and gave me several minutes to digest what had happened. When she noticed I was crying, she attempted to comfort me.

"It's okay, sweetie. I know Teddy loved his car, but we're just glad you're okay."

Little did she know, I wasn't crying about the damage I'd done to the car. The real reason I was crying was for a pain that was practically eating me whole. Something I couldn't quite pinpoint felt *off* about my abilities, and that terrified me to the depths of my soul.

CHAPTER 2

*T*he doctors gave me stitches and bandaged my wound. They said there was a good chance I had a mild concussion, but there wasn't really anything they could do but send me home with instructions to get plenty of rest.

"You don't have to go to school tomorrow if you don't want to," my mom offered on the way home after Teddy had picked us up with her car.

"I'm fine," I told her half-honestly. "I don't want to miss volleyball practice."

"Are you sure that's a good idea?" She eyed me from the passenger seat.

"It will be fine. If I miss it, I'll have to make it up. But if I feel dizzy or anything, Coach Kathy should let me sit out, or I can help Derek and be co-manager for the day."

She looked to Teddy in the driver's seat as if he might be able to reason with me. When he didn't say anything, she turned back toward me. "Do you still want to take that campus tour on Wednesday?"

"Mom," I practically snapped, "you're worrying too much. I'll be fine. Besides, I promised Kelli and Justine I'd be there. We were going to meet up and have lunch."

The campus tour Mom mentioned was a field trip to Southern Minnesota University for all interested seniors. The only problem was that they didn't have enough people interested, and they needed two more to get approval to take the bus. Our guidance counselor, Mrs. Blake, suggested Emma and I come along even though we were only juniors. Mrs. Blake knew my mom attended SMU and thought I might be inter-

424

ested, and she was right. Although I didn't know what I wanted to do for a career, I wanted to go to college, and it made sense to go there. It was only an hour away, so I could visit my family often. It was actually a closer drive to Robin's college than my current drive was, too. Plus, a lot of the kids from our school went there, so I would know some people, especially if Emma decided to enroll at SMU. We could even be roommates.

"Mom," I wondered aloud, "why did you choose SMU?"

She glanced back at me. "What do you mean?"

"I'm just thinking about how Mrs. Blake asked me to go on the tour. She thought I might want to attend SMU because you did. I haven't really thought about my options and was just curious if SMU is the right choice for me. And I'm interested in why you didn't choose a college closer to your home so you could visit your family."

My mom let out a puff of air that sounded like a laugh. "Crystal, I know you and I get along, but your Grandma Ellen wasn't the easiest person to get along with at the time. Besides, I was young and interested in getting out on my own. I chose SMU because they had a good psychology program."

"Why'd you choose psychology? You don't even use your degree."

She pressed her lips together. "I wanted to do more with my degree at the time. I thought majoring in psychology would help me understand my abilities better and that maybe I could use them to help people—as a counselor or something. But then I met Sophie and Diane, and my ideas about my future changed. Diane was majoring in business, and so we came up with the idea of Divination together. We moved to Peyton Springs because it's where Sophie grew up, and there's a long line of psychics in the area. They help keep our business running even though everyone else just thinks we sell magic sets, Halloween costumes, and chocolate. Starting a business with my best friends was one of the best decisions I've ever made."

"So, do you think SMU is right for me?"

She shrugged. "I can't say I would be against you going there. I'd like you to be able to visit every now and then, but I don't want you to feel pressured if there's somewhere else you'd like to go."

I didn't even know what I would major in, but it was encouraging to know my mom had a good college experience there. "I guess we'll see how I feel about it on Wednesday," I finally said as we pulled into the driveway.

∾

I fell onto my bed and shoved my face into my pillow. I immediately recoiled when a pain shot through my head. Not the smartest idea, although it didn't hurt as badly now as when the accident happened. I rolled over to my back and pulled the covers over my body. Before I had a moment to even *think* about crying, my mom knocked on my door and opened it a crack.

"Crystal, do you need anything before bed?"

I was about to tell her she was fussing too much, but I appreciated the sentiment. "No, Mom. I'll be fine. Thanks for asking." I could have told her about what was really going on—that my sixth sense felt off—but I didn't want to worry her, not with a baby on the way.

"Hey, Mom," I called before she shut the door completely.

"Yeah?" She opened it again, casting a strip of light from the hallway onto my bed.

"How's the baby?"

We'd only discovered in August that Mom was pregnant, though she and Teddy had been trying since their wedding last spring. Honestly, they were surprised to have gotten pregnant so quickly since they were both in their late 30s. They wouldn't be able to learn the sex of the baby for another few weeks, but Mom and Teddy decided they didn't want to know anything unless something was wrong. They wanted to be surprised when it came.

My mother's silhouette shifted in the doorway. "Why do you ask?"

I went silent for a few seconds before answering. "I just—I know tonight was really stressful, and I don't want the stress to affect the baby or anything."

She pushed into the room and sat on the edge of my bed. She rested a hand on her belly, which was still pretty flat. I shifted and placed my hand next to hers, even though there wasn't actually anything to feel.

"There's no reason to worry," my mother assured me.

I tore my gaze from her belly and looked up at her. "It's just..." I paused and then swallowed. "I already love her." I had bet on it being a girl, but my mom thought it'd be a boy. "Or him," I added, pressing my ear to her belly.

She jumped slightly in surprise before relaxing.

"I really love her—him," I said against her belly before pulling away. "You just worry about my little brother or sister. I'll be fine."

She smiled at that and then kissed my forehead. I took it as an agreement, but then she twisted her mouth in amusement and said, "Fat chance of that. I'm your mom. It's my job to worry about you."

"It's just a *scratch*," I lied. Luckily, the room was fairly shadowed so she couldn't see the worry written all over my face.

"I know." She smoothed down my hair. "But right now, it sounds like you're more worried about me being worried than I am worried about you."

I started to nod and then replayed what she'd just said in my mind. "Wait... what? That was confusing."

"Don't worry about it," she teased with a smile.

"You just worry about growing me a healthy brother or sister," I told her before kissing her belly and telling her goodnight.

"I love you, Crystal," she said before shutting my bedroom door and leaving me in darkness.

While my mother's company helped take my mind off the accident, I couldn't help it when I replayed it in my head as soon as she left. I pulled my stuffed owl Luna down from her shelf like I did every night and snuggled her close to me. Tonight, I needed the extra comfort.

I wasn't even that upset about the accident itself. If everything had happened like it did but I still felt my abilities inside me—if I felt like myself—I'd be fine. But the fact was that something was *wrong*. I couldn't explain it. I couldn't put it into words, but I knew it was happening to me nonetheless.

I should have called my boyfriend, Robin, or my best friend, Emma, right away. I knew one of them would make me feel better, but somehow, I felt like I couldn't explain *this*. So instead, I called out to the darkness.

"Daddy?" I said in a whisper. I clung to the stuffed animal he'd given me as a gift before he died. I had no way of knowing if he could hear me from the other side. Even when I had my gift, I'd never made contact with my father or felt him there with me. Still, I'd been talking to him—in a way—for the last few months whenever I felt I couldn't talk to a living person.

I fell asleep after asking my father for protection.

CHAPTER 3

"$\mathcal{F}$eel free to take notes and pictures once we reach campus," Mrs. Blake announced as we neared SMU on Wednesday.

Emma sat next to me on the bus, and I twisted my hands nervously in my lap. I had been excited about visiting SMU earlier this week, but the closer we got, the more anxious I became. It was like the idea of growing up had finally hit me, and I wasn't ready to think about college yet.

"You'll have the chance to talk to our tour guides as well as other students about their experiences," Mrs. Blake continued. "Take advantage of these opportunities, but don't forget that for most of you, this is your first campus tour. The school will host a couple more field trips throughout the year; however, most of you will also attend other tours with your parents."

"Crystal," Emma said in a low voice while Mrs. Blake continued talking toward the front of the bus. "What's up?"

My eyes flew to hers. "What do you mean?"

"You're practically strangling your sweatshirt," she pointed out, gesturing down to the sleeve I'd been twisting around in my hand. "You've been acting weird all week, ever since your car accident."

I relaxed my grip on my shirt and swallowed. I still hadn't told Emma —or anyone, for that matter—about what really happened to me, about how after I hit my head, my sixth sense had gone hazy. I hadn't been able to predict the lunch menu all week, something I'd once had a 100 percent success rate with. Every time I subtly tested my skills over the last three days, I hadn't been able to feel anyone else's emotions through touch. On one level, it left me feeling empty and alone. I'd become so used to being in tune with the people around me that it was strange to go back to normal—the way I'd been before puberty hit and my abilities manifested. On another level, I felt frightened, as if I would never get my abilities back. I wasn't quite sure why I hadn't mentioned it to anyone. Maybe I didn't want to admit it, like that would make the situation more real. A year ago, I may have rejoiced in this news, but now it only left me worried.

Luckily, Emma and I had been so busy with volleyball, homework, and boyfriends that our psychic practice sessions had slowed down. So far this week, I hadn't had to show my weakness in front of her. I knew she'd find out sooner or later, but I was hoping I'd feel better at the "later" point and my abilities would be back to normal.

Robin had freaked out when I told him about the accident. I could only imagine how scared he was to hear I'd crashed. He'd been in a bad accident a few years ago and lost his left leg from the knee down. I assured him on the phone I was okay. That seemed to calm him down, but even after a few days, I hadn't called him back to tell him about my gift fading.

"It's not the accident," I lied to Emma. I glanced her way quickly before fixing my eyes back on my hands. She didn't seem to notice my dishonesty, which was a victory for me. "I've just been nervous about this campus tour." Okay, that wasn't a complete lie.

"I know. Me, too," she agreed.

I let out an inaudible sigh of relief.

"I was excited at first," she continued. "I mean, we're only juniors, and already we're being all responsible and thinking about college, but now it's kind of scary. I mean, it's *college*. I have no idea what to expect."

"Yeah," I agreed. In all honesty, I added, "Me, either." The resounding truth of that statement sent a shiver down my spine.

∼

Kelli and Justine waved to us from across the dining hall. Our field trip group was halfway through our tour, and we each received a meal voucher at the campus's buffet. Emma and I made our way over to them after we filled our plates.

"Hi," I greeted cheerfully.

They both stood, and we all exchanged hugs. After I'd helped rescue Kelli from an abusive relationship a year ago—with Justine's help—we'd become friends. Thanks to my abilities, I saw their friend Olivia's ghost, who held the key to saving Kelli. When they graduated, Kelli and Justine both headed off to college at SMU. I sat, wondering if more of our classmates would join us since they all knew Kelli and Justine, too, but no one did.

"What happened to you, Crystal?" Kelli gestured to the stitches on my head.

My hand came up to graze them lightly. "I, uh, had an accident."

"She blew a tire and flipped her car," Emma clarified.

"Oh, I'm sorry," Kelli told me.

"No, it's okay. My head hit the window, and that split the skin open. It's okay, really."

"Well, it kind of sucks," Justine said slowly.

I nodded. "So, how's your freshman year going?" I remembered Mrs. Blake's instructions to ask students about their experiences.

"It's great," Kelli beamed. Her voice was so full of happiness, completely opposite of the Kelli Taylor I'd known just a year ago. And then there was her new look. She'd dyed her hair a dark blond—closer to her natural color—and a small diamond stud now adorned her nose. It suited her well.

"It's okay," Justine shrugged.

"Just okay?" Emma asked skeptically. "That's not encouraging."

Justine laughed. "No, it's great, but…"

"But what?" I prodded curiously.

Justine glanced around the room. "Honestly? The campus gives me the heebie jeebies."

Kelli burst into a fit of laughter, and Justine joined in. I suspected there was some sort of inside joke I was missing.

"What do you mean?" Emma asked.

"Oh, it's nothing, really," Justine assured us.

Kelli laughed again. "Justine has a stalker."

I tensed for a moment. "A stalker?"

"No, I don't," Justine defended, swatting lightly at Kelli.

"She says she feels like she's being watched," Kelli teased. "I think it's that kid who sits behind us in psych. He's a creep."

My nerves subsided when I realized Justine wasn't in any real danger from a stalker. It really was just an inside joke I was missing out on.

"So," I said once I swallowed my potatoes, "Mrs. Blake says we're supposed to ask students about their experience at SMU. Why'd you guys choose this school?"

Justine gave a light eye roll. "Ha! Mrs. Blake. She's great but so serious. I remember doing campus tours with her. It's so different in college."

"How many colleges did you tour before choosing SMU?" Emma asked.

"Honestly," Justine said, "not many. I always knew I was going to go to

SMU. It's close to home, and the tuition is decent. My mom and my aunt —you know, my aunt Sophie—both went here, so I've known my whole life that I'd end up here, too."

I nodded. It made sense. "And you, Kelli?" I asked before biting into more potatoes.

She shrugged. "Same reason, I guess—location and tuition. And I got lucky that my best friend came with me. We get to be roommates for the next four years!"

I glanced over at Emma, and she was eyeing me with a smile. I didn't have to be psychic to read my best friend's mind, which was saying, *We could be roommates here, too!*

"So, do you think you two will apply here your senior year?" Justine asked.

Emma nodded enthusiastically. She'd been in a state of pure glory all day during the tour.

"Yeah, maybe," I answered. "I think it's either going to be this or where Robin goes."

"That's right," Kelli said. "What's your boyfriend doing now? Still playing music?"

"Not as much as he did in high school. He's majoring in occupational therapy."

"And your boyfriend, Emma?" Justine asked. "You two are still dating?"

Emma straightened in her chair. "Me and Derek? We've never been better! He bought me flowers and took me to a concert for my birthday last month. It was so sweet!"

"Aww," Kelli and Justine sang together.

"You two are cute together," Justine said. "I always saw you watching him at volleyball practice last year when he was catching balls. I'm surprised it took you two so long to get together."

Emma smiled. "Yeah, well, it was worth it."

I didn't say anything as they talked about the cute boys in their classes and student organizations. Eventually, their conversation faded into the background until it felt like I was secluded in my own little bubble and the rest of the cafeteria ceased to exist. My sixth sense tingled, a sensation that spread through to my fingertips. Joy overcame me when I realized what this meant. My abilities hadn't been destroyed in the accident!

I glanced around the dining hall, searching for the source of my feeling. It was only when I scanned the room for a second time that I noticed him. My eyes locked on a dark figure standing across the cafeteria, causing the sensation in my body to intensify. I knew immediately that no one else could see him because I was the only person I knew who could see ghosts.

Something about him was different, though. I couldn't make full features of him. Instead of looking like the other people milling about the hall, he appeared as just a shadow, dark with a hazy outline. Even though I couldn't see definite eyes, I knew he was looking my way.

~

I remained quiet on the bus ride back to the high school, the whole time contemplating what it meant to see a ghost but not being able to see what he really looked like. After thinking about it for some time, I came to the conclusion that he appeared fuzzy because my accident caused my abilities to work inefficiently. At the very least, seeing a ghost on campus meant my abilities weren't completely lost to me. I might actually be able to keep this minor hiccup a secret before I had to admit my newfound weakness to anyone.

But why had I seen a ghost in the first place? Did he need my help? How could I help him when my abilities weren't working well?

I decided I'd try a few psychic exercises at home after volleyball practice in hopes of connecting with the ghost. Then Emma's voice pulled me from my thoughts.

"So, what do you think? Still want to go to SMU?" Her tone was full of excitement.

What could I say to that? If I said I still wasn't sure, it would break her heart, but if I told her I wanted to go there and decided against it later, that'd be even more heart breaking.

"Well, we both still have a lot of schools to look at. Are *you* sure you want to go to SMU?"

The question was silly. Emma had purchased a butt load of SMU-branded goods from their campus store while we were there—a hoodie, a t-shirt, even a notebook. Though she said she was nervous about the campus tour, I could tell that if she had the choice, she'd graduate early and start classes next semester. She'd already pegged SMU as her school. I'm not sure why, maybe because she already had it figured in her mind that I was going to go there and she didn't want to leave her life-long best friend.

Emma nodded enthusiastically in response to my question.

"Do you even know what you'll major in?" I asked.

Her face fell. "I don't, but I have a lot of time to figure it out. Maybe music? Do you have any idea what you'd major in?"

I took a deep breath. I didn't know. I didn't have the slightest clue. For the last year, I'd wanted to do something with my abilities—maybe go into the police force or something, in which case I wouldn't have to go to SMU, which is why I wasn't ready to make that decision. *Now that it looks like my abilities might be failing me, maybe I should study something else,* I thought.

I averted my gaze from Emma's watchful eye and began to scan the rest of the bus in search of some sort of answer to give her. I was spared the hassle of answering when I looked to my right and came face-to-face with a black shadowy figure. His face didn't have any features, but it was hovering just inches from my own.

My heart leapt in fright, and I screamed.

CHAPTER 4

*E*ven if my abilities were in peak condition, I couldn't have anticipated what happened next. My scream of terror hardly had a chance to fill the bus before I felt my body lurch and I went flying across the center aisle. If the shadowy ghost was still there, I would have fallen straight through him. I flung my hands out to catch myself against the seat across the aisle. I managed to prevent myself from sliding into a senior named Jackie Smith, but I couldn't keep my right knee from smashing into the seat's metal frame. Emma's weight slid into me, and Jackie's head smacked against the window. An intense pain throbbed in my knee.

A moment later, the initial shock had subsided and everyone was rubbing at their aches and pains. A few people stood to piece together what had just happened. I couldn't manage to move for a few seconds. All I could do was remain frozen with my hands on Jackie's seat and my body situated in the center of the aisle.

Did I cause that with my scream? I wondered.

Then, the bus broke out in a buzz of voices.

"What was that?"

"What happened?"

"Is everyone okay?"

"Crystal," Emma said, resting a hand on my back and leaning in to view my face. "Are you okay?"

I finally shifted to look at her. "I—I'm not hurt." It wasn't actually an answer to her question, and it was a complete lie because my knee was burning in pain. For a second, I was scared that I actually shattered my knee cap, but when I shifted to sit back next to Emma in our seat, I knew it wasn't that bad. "I just hit my knee. Are you okay?"

Emma nodded. She didn't appear to have hurt anything.

"Jackie?" I asked, looking over at her.

She nodded, too, although she was rubbing her head. "I'm fine."

Once I was sure everyone around me was okay, I finally looked toward the front of the bus to see if I could understand what had just happened. Gazing out the windows, I could see that the bus had swerved and now sat unmoving across both lanes of traffic. Although we had been driving along a rural highway, one car coming from the opposite way had already stopped, and another was slowing down behind it. Between the bus and the first car, I saw what had really happened.

My scream hadn't caused the bus to swerve. A huge tree lay crossways in the road just in front of us. It had pulled the power lines down around it. The top of the dead tree lay sprawled in the field to our left while the rotten stump appeared mangled to our right.

"Is everyone okay?" Mrs. Blake repeated.

By now, everyone appeared to be back in their seats, although some were standing and assessing the damage to the power lines. Our bus driver turned around in her seat and brushed the hair out of her face. Mrs. Blake was already beginning her way down the aisle to make sure everyone was okay. Then our bus driver, Mrs. Peterson, spoke up.

"Who was the one who screamed?" she asked sternly.

My heart dropped in my chest. Could I really be blamed for this? I mean, it's not like I had super powers where I could tip a tree with my voice. I bit my lip and looked at Emma nervously.

"Who screamed?" she asked again just as Mrs. Blake passed by our seat and headed further to the back of the bus.

I raised my hand nervously. "It—it was me." My voice came out so quiet that it sounded like a whisper.

"Crystal Frost, right?" she asked, making her way toward me.

I nodded sheepishly.

Then Mrs. Peterson stuck her hand out. I eyed it. What was I supposed to do with her hand?

"Thank you," she said, completely taking me off guard.

Oh. She wanted me to shake it. But why?

"If you hadn't seen the tree tipping and screamed, I wouldn't have noticed."

My mouth hung open. I shyly took her hand, not daring to admit that wasn't the reason I had screamed.

∾

435

The rest of the day passed by in a haze. We sat around for a while to make sure everyone was okay and that the school knew what was going on. I called my mom's cell, but she didn't answer since she was at work. I left a message assuring her I was alright.

Our miracle of a bus driver managed to turn the bus around and get us headed back to the school on an alternate route. School had already let out by the time we got back.

"Ready for volleyball practice?" Emma asked with little confidence when we stepped off the bus.

"I don't think I'll be ready for practice until next season," I said half seriously.

Emma and I hurried to the locker room. Luckily, there were still a few girls getting into their practice gear, which meant we weren't late. Already this week, Coach Kathy had made me take it easy because she didn't want my head wound getting ripped open by a flying ball. I was grateful for that because I didn't want to have to dive for the ball with a bruised knee, even if I was wearing knee pads.

Once all the girls cleared out of the locker room, Emma spoke. "Are you going to be okay?"

I pulled on my shoe and began tying it. "What? Me?"

"Yes, you." She swatted at me with the t-shirt she was holding before pulling it over her head. "Is there anyone else here?" She looked around nervously when she realized what she'd just said. "Wait, there isn't, is there?"

I looked up to meet her gaze, but she was still scanning the locker room like she expected a ghost to reveal itself from behind the lockers.

"No, there's not, but—" I stopped mid-sentence. I hadn't wanted to tell anyone about losing my abilities for the better part of the week, so should I even bother telling her about the shadowy ghost I saw?

"But what?" Emma eyed me suspiciously. "Oh," she said slowly, realization dawning. "I was wondering how you saw the tree falling from where we were sitting. That's not why you screamed, was it?"

Boy, she caught on quickly. I shook my head.

"Who was it? What did they say?"

I shook my head again. "I have no idea, and he didn't say anything. I saw him on campus first, and then when I saw him on the bus, it kind of scared me." I didn't have to tell her he looked hazy and like a shadow, did I?

"'Kind of?' Crystal, that was the scream of 'bloody murder.' You don't know what this ghost wants?"

I shook my head for a third time and pressed my lips together. "I have no idea."

"Well," Emma said while tying her shoe, "you'll figure it out, like always. Let's get out there before Coach Kathy makes us run extra laps."

I quickly double knotted my second shoe and jumped up from the locker room bench to follow her into the gym. I split off in a different direction and found my way to Coach Kathy. All the other players were just getting started with stretches. "Coach?" I asked.

She looked at me expectantly.

"I, uh, don't know if you heard, but some of us on the field trip today were in a minor accident. I hit my knee," I peeled back my knee pad to show her the bruise that was forming, "and I was just wondering if I could help Derek again."

Coach nodded. "That's fine, Crystal. I don't want you getting into it too much until you get your stitches out next week anyway. Just don't cross the court when we're practicing serves. I don't want any balls hitting your stiches."

I nodded and then joined my team for stretches—at least those were safe enough. As soon as balls began flying, I headed over to Derek. Derek was one of my best friends and Emma's boyfriend. He was also our team manager, which meant he helped keep track of stats during the games and helped run drills during practice.

"Hey, Derek," I greeted. "I guess it's back to co-manager duties for me again today."

"Sounds good." He smiled. "Hey, I heard what happened to you guys after the campus tour. Are you both alright?"

"I hit my knee, but we're fine."

"I haven't had a chance to talk to Emma. She's okay? You're sure?"

It was cute how he seemed so worried about her. I knew Robin would act the same way, like he did when I'd told him about my first accident, but I still had to tell him about what happened today on the bus. "Derek, she's fine."

"Okay. Thanks for letting me know. I'll catch the balls along the edge of the court if you get the ones that go across the gym. I'd hate to see your stitches get ripped open."

"But if they did, maybe I could keep them until Halloween," I joked. "I'd make a great Frankenstein—or maybe a zombie."

Derek let out a laugh before heading to throw some balls back onto the court for the girls who were practicing their serves.

Last year, Emma, Derek, and I had dressed up in a trio costume for the Peyton Springs Halloween Festival. Derek was the Cat in the Hat and Emma and I were Thing 1 and Thing 2. Now the festival was just a few weeks away again, and I still didn't know what I was going to be. I could drag out my costume again from last year, but Emma had already talked about doing a couple's thing with Derek. Maybe Robin and I could do something together. If I was smart, I'd go as the same thing every year like my mom did so I wouldn't have to worry about choosing a new costume every Halloween. She always went as a gypsy and hosted a tarot card reading booth—and no one had figured out yet that it was the real deal!

I threw a couple of balls at my teammates as they practiced their spikes but sat out when they played a scrimmage at the end of practice.

Normally, I would walk home with Emma, but she headed in the opposite direction with Derek after practice to work on homework for their government class—a class I wasn't taking this semester. At least, that was her excuse. In reality, "homework" was probably code for "making out," but I didn't say anything.

I walked home from practice alone, the hairs on the back of my neck standing straight up the entire way.

CHAPTER 5

"I'm fine," I assured Robin when I called him that evening. For some reason, I couldn't bring myself to tell him I saw a ghost on the bus. I told Emma—even if I didn't tell her the whole truth—but I felt if I mentioned any of it to Robin, he would worry too much. His first semester of college was putting enough stress on him already, so I just told him about my bruised knee.

"Two car accidents in one week? Are you sure you're okay?" Something about the way he said it made it sound like he was suggesting it was more than a coincidence, but honestly, I couldn't think of an alternative.

I plopped down onto my bed. "I knew you would worry."

"Worry? Me? Never," he feigned before his tone returned to normal. "Of course I'm worried about you, Crystal. I love you."

My heart fluttered even though I'd heard him say that a million times since last spring. "I love you, too, Robin."

"Maybe you should just take it easy," he suggested.

"I am. I haven't even been participating in drills during volleyball practice. Coach didn't even put me in the game on Tuesday."

"You have a game tomorrow, right?"

"Every Tuesday and Thursday."

"Do you think your coach will put you in tomorrow?"

I shook my head even though he couldn't see me. "Not a chance, not until I get my stitches out next week."

"Maybe you should skip," he suggested. "I think you should take the day off and get some rest. You've been acting... I just think you could use a day off."

I didn't bother prodding him for what he was going to say. I knew it. I'd been acting *off*, and even though we'd only talked on the phone since my accident, I wasn't surprised that he'd picked up on it.

"It's a home game," I pointed out. "We don't need to travel or anything. It should be fine."

"Crystal." Robin's tone became more serious. "Why can't you just give yourself a break every now and then? You deserve it."

"I do?"

"Of course. I have a big break between classes in the middle of the day tomorrow. I could come over and help you feel better."

What is he suggesting? "You mean, skip out of school? Mom and Teddy would never go for it."

"It's not skipping out of school if you're sick."

"I'm not sick," I defended, curling up beneath my blanket.

"That's not what I mean exactly, but you've been through a lot this week. You could use some rest."

I sighed in defeat. Sleeping in *did* sound nice, and if I said I was sick, I could easily get out of school and volleyball for a day. At least my babysitting job had been put on hold during volleyball season, so I didn't have to worry about that.

"I'll talk to Teddy," Robin assured me. Robin was Teddy's nephew—though we'd been dating before Mom and Teddy got married—so they were pretty close. "Besides, I miss you, and I don't want to miss you visiting this weekend. You could end up stressing yourself to death."

I giggled lightly. "I doubt that."

Robin and I talked for a while longer until he said he had to go for some sort of get-together at his dorm. Although he was only going to school a few minutes from his parents', he'd decided to live in the dorms "for the college experience," he'd said.

"Okay, I'll talk to you later," I promised. "I love you."

"I love you, too, Crystal."

As soon as I hung up, an eerie silence fell over my bedroom. Mom was still at the shop since we were getting into Halloween season, and they always stayed open later in October because of that. Teddy had said he was getting Roger to drive him to the dealership today to pick up our new car. His, he said, was old enough that it wasn't worth fixing anymore. To be honest, I think he was glad my accident gave him an excuse to buy a new—well, new to us—car, not that he wasn't worried about me. Anyway, because my mom and Teddy were busy, I was home alone.

I slipped a hoodie over my head and headed toward the kitchen to find something to eat, all the while contemplating what Robin had suggested. He was right. I *had* had a tough week. It wasn't just the pain in my head and knee, either. I had been living my week in a daze, going to bed early and not really paying attention in class. Maybe I could use a day away from school and volleyball practice. At least then I might have the time to sit down and figure out where exactly I was with my abilities.

A chill spread over me as I made my way to the kitchen, so I adjusted the thermostat as I passed the controls. I shuffled through cupboards, but I wasn't the best cook in the world, so I didn't know what to make. I wasn't even that hungry, but I knew I needed to eat *something*. Finally, I found bagels and popped one in the toaster.

While waiting for my bagel to toast, I settled into a chair at the table and balled my sleeves into my hands. Jeez. Did no one notice the temperature outside had dropped recently and it was time to kick on the heater?

I chewed on my nails, again mulling over Robin's suggestion. It *would* be nice to see him, but would Mom and Teddy really let him come over with no one else here? No. The idea was absurd. The whole concept of skipping school and the volleyball game made me feel like I'd already broken the rules.

My bagel popped, and I jumped, looking up from my nails for the first time in the last few minutes. When I finally raised my gaze, I nearly fell out of my chair. A shadowy figure stood between where I sat and the front door. I squealed the same split second the door opened and my mother stepped through it. The figure whipped around and stared at her for a moment before disappearing.

My heart rate slowed, and I suddenly realized what the chill I'd felt was. It was because the ghost had been there. Both fear and relief flooded through me at the same time. Fear because the chill indicated the ghost had been there for several minutes. It was like he'd been watching me that whole time. Relief because it was another sign that my abilities hadn't been completely lost. I released my firm grip on the side of my chair as my mother stepped closer to me.

"What was that all about?" she asked.

I swallowed. "I—you just scared me. My bagel popped when you came in the door, and it made me jump is all." I didn't know why I didn't tell her about the ghost—probably because I still couldn't work up the courage to tell anyone that my abilities had been failing me lately, and I didn't want to explain how the ghost appeared hazy. She didn't seem to notice I wasn't telling her the whole truth.

"Yum, bagels. Can you toast me one?" She retreated down the hall to drop her purse in her room.

My hand shook lightly as I spread cream cheese on my bagel and then popped my mom's in the toaster. I shouldn't have been so frightened. I mean, it was only a ghost, and I'd communicated with several in the past year. Unlike what people tended to think about ghosts, all the ones I'd seen had been friendly. At the same time, most of them wanted something from me, like my help to solve some mystery or communicate with their loved ones they'd left behind. I'd helped them because, well, I was the only one who could.

I knew seeing this ghost meant I had to help him, too, that he wanted something from me, but I hadn't actually spoken to him yet, so how could I know what he wanted? With my hazy abilities, that task could prove quite difficult.

My mom returned to the kitchen with her phone in hand. She didn't look up from the screen as she spoke. "You left me a voicemail? What about?"

I shrugged like it was nothing. "The field trip."

"Was it fun?"

I swallowed my bite of bagel and leaned against the counter. "It was... eventful."

"Oh, my gosh." She finally glanced up from her phone. "The school left me a message, too. Crystal, what happened today?"

Then I told her everything I could—everything except the bit about the ghost because I knew that would only worry her. Normally, I was more than willing to open up to the people I loved, but I couldn't bring myself to let them all worry before I even knew what was happening myself.

After my mom finished listening to her voicemail messages, I spoke again. "Robin thinks I should take the day off from school tomorrow. He says I've been through enough this week."

My mother set her phone on the counter and began spreading cream cheese over her own bagel. "I can't say that's a bad idea. You probably should have stayed home Monday, too."

I gaped at her. She liked the idea? "But I'm not actually sick."

"After what happened today, I think you deserve to relax."

"Mom, where's this coming from?"

She bit into her bagel and spoke between chews. "You keep telling me to stop worrying, and you're doing enough worrying for the both of us. Have you seen yourself lately? Two car accidents in one week is a lot to take in, and maybe you should just take tomorrow to sleep it off."

I wasn't about to argue with my mom if she was willing to give me permission. I finished up my bagel and escaped to my room to work on the homework I had to make up after going on the field trip that day. While finishing it up, I eyed the crystal ball sitting on my desk a couple of times, wondering if my abilities were strong enough to try that out and see if I could gather a clue to what the mystery ghost wanted from me. I fell asleep before working up the energy to try it out.

CHAPTER 6

J woke Thursday to the feeling of strong hands lightly shaking me. When my eyes shot open, I found Robin's smiling face standing above me.

"Rise and shine, beautiful."

"Wh—what?" I asked, dazed. I knew I was staying home from school today, but I didn't expect Robin to be in my bedroom so early in the morning. Was I dreaming? "What are you doing?" I pushed myself to a seated position. I made a point to keep most of my body covered because my pajamas were rather skimpy—short shorts and a tank top, not that Robin would mind. "I thought you had class."

"Already done," he smiled.

"What? What time is it?"

"It's past 10." He twisted away from me to grab a plate I hadn't noticed was resting on my desk. "Breakfast?"

I stared down at the plate of eggs, toast, and bacon curiously. "I slept in that long?" was all I could say.

"I told you that you needed the sleep." He shoved the plate toward me, insisting I take it, so I did.

"Where are Mom and Teddy?" I asked after swallowing a bite of eggs. I noticed immediately how great of a cook Robin was. I'd never tasted Robin's cooking before, but I guess he took after his uncle.

Robin shrugged. "At work."

"So, Teddy actually let you come over with no one else here? Seems to me like you're pushing your luck. I'm shocked enough that they let me visit you at school on the weekends."

444

"That's because they met my roommate, and he never leaves the room. Even if we *wanted* to do anything, it's not like we'd be able to find a private place short of sneaking into one of the bathroom stalls."

It's not like I didn't *want* to do anything with Robin, but it just hadn't happened yet. I shrugged. "I guess Mom and Teddy do trust us. It's not like we've given them a reason not to."

"And I don't intend to," Robin said, finally taking a seat on my bed.

"But still… It's hard to believe Mom and Teddy let you come over unsupervised."

"Oh, they didn't," Robin said casually.

I immediately stopped chewing. "What do you mean? I thought you said you'd talk to Teddy."

"I did. I just didn't tell him I'd be coming over."

"Well, that's a great way to earn his trust," I said sarcastically. I couldn't believe he lied to my parents. "What *did* you talk to him about?" The question came out a bit too sharply.

"I talked to him about how you'd had a rough week and convinced him you should take it easy for a day. They don't have to know about my visit."

"Oh. I already talked to my mom last night about staying home."

Robin shrugged like it wasn't a big deal. "Well, it looks like I was right. You've been sleeping for hours."

"Then why'd you wake me up?" I teased.

"I couldn't let the food go cold." He smiled.

Convinced I needed my rest but not wanting to waste a moment of my company, Robin made me stay in bed while he brought out his laptop and pulled a movie up on Netflix.

"One of my favorites," he said, peeling back the covers to cuddle next to me. He didn't bother to kick off his shoes first. I suspected it was because of his leg. Even after all this time, he was still self-conscious about it. I had to wonder if that was one of the reasons we hadn't made our relationship physical yet—not that I was 100 percent ready to take it to the next level, either. But then again, he did manage to get me alone…

"Robin," I pushed away lightly before he hit play on his laptop. I twisted to look him straight in the eye. "What are we doing? Why did you make me stay home from school? Is this… Are we…" I couldn't finish that sentence. "I'm not quite ready yet," I finally said.

Robin let out a light laugh. "Crystal, that's not what this is. Honestly, I'm just concerned about you and thought you could use some comfort."

"Well, with everything, it just seems like—"

Robin cut me off by placing an index finger to my lips. "When the time is right, it's going to be better than watching some lame movie in your bedroom."

"I thought you said this was one of your favorite movies," I said behind his finger.

He laughed again. "I didn't mean the lame movie thing like that. For real, I just—" His expression shifted to become more serious. "I just got scared, okay? It was bad enough hearing about your first accident this week, and then you told me about what happened yesterday. I just wanted to spend time with you."

I swear I saw a hint of tears welling up in his eyes. It was a side of Robin I rarely saw, so I knew everything he was saying was genuine.

"I was just scared, okay?" he repeated.

I nodded. "It's okay. I'm not going anywhere. I love you." Then I planted a long, passionate kiss on his lips before turning toward the laptop and snuggling up in his arms. After the movie ended, Robin and I lay there in silence long enough that we both fell asleep. We woke to the sound of Robin's phone.

"Sorry," he said, pulling away from me while wiping drool off his lower lip. "I set an alarm for when I had to head back to class." He shifted to turn the alarm off. "I should go, even though I don't want to."

I yawned. "It's fine. You have to get back to class. You really did make me feel better."

A grin formed across his face. "I'm glad to hear that. Now, you keep getting better so you feel well enough to come visit me this weekend, okay?"

"I will," I promised.

Once Robin left, I felt at a loss of what to do. At first, all I *could* do was replay the day in my head and think about how comforting it was to nap in Robin's arms. I still couldn't believe the guy had the guts to come over while my parents were at work. I'm sure he knew that if he had told me to begin with that he'd be coming over secretly, I would have never allowed it. Once he was here, though, I didn't want him to leave. I wanted him right back here in my arms, but I couldn't be the type of girlfriend who made him skip class for her.

I crawled out of bed for the first time that day to use the bathroom. When I returned to my room, I noticed the plate Robin had brought me for breakfast was still sitting on my desk next to my crystal ball. I decided to take a shot at using the ball, although I didn't think it would do any good considering I'd never been very good at using it. Now with my abilities going haywire, I wasn't sure it would work at all.

After taking my breakfast plate to the kitchen, I situated myself in my desk chair next to the ball and hovered my hands over it. I was already calm enough from my earlier nap that I didn't think I needed to do any more relaxing.

I breathed in a deep breath and then let it out slowly, further relaxing the muscles in my shoulders and face. In and out. In and out. My mind fought to forget about the mysterious ghost and go into my crystal ball gazing with no expectations. Eventually, I managed to clear my head enough that my troubles seemed nonexistent at the moment. When I stared deep into the crystal ball, it appeared as if faint colors were swirling in it—so faint that I may not have noticed them if I hadn't been practicing and knew exactly what the ball looked like normally. A complete sense of serenity fell over me, but as the minutes passed, the colors failed to take shape. I didn't let my frustrations get to me.

The sound of the doorbell snapped me out of my trance.

I pushed away from my desk. Even though I couldn't make out any shapes in the ball, the fact that I'd made some connection with it left me feeling hopeful—hopeful that my abilities would return to normal at some point.

I didn't rise from my chair right away. Instead, I closed my eyes and attempted to form a mental image of the visitor at the door. It was a game Emma liked to play. It was supposed to help me practice my abilities and make them stronger. Normally, it was a simple task, but now, I could use the practice in hopes of rehabilitating my gift. I couldn't conjure a mental image of the visitor before the doorbell rang again and a voice called to me from the living room.

"Crystal, are you home?" It was Emma.

I sighed, feeling down that the simple exercise hadn't worked, but I stood and exited my room to meet her anyway.

CHAPTER 7

*W*hen I made it into the living room, I immediately noticed that Derek was with Emma. I blushed lightly before quickly rushing back to my room to slip on sweat pants and a t-shirt over my pajamas.

"I'll be right back," I called. I noticed the clock next to my bed read 3:28. My friends must have come over right after school let out. "What's up?" I asked once I emerged back into the living room.

Emma dropped her backpack on the couch. "You were sick from school today, so we thought we'd come over and take care of you before the game."

"I don't need taking care of," I told them, but I did appreciate that they were worried about me.

Emma headed to the kitchen while she spoke, and Derek and I followed her. "It's no problem. After what happened yesterday and last weekend, I get that you may be a little shook up." She pulled a pot from the cupboard as if she owned the place, but I didn't mind. She'd spent enough nights at my house over the years that it was like a second home to her. She set the pot on the stove and pulled Derek into her arms before speaking again. "Besides," she joked, "Derek and I could use the parenting practice."

I knew her words were only in jest, but Derek immediately pushed away. "Whoa, I am not ready to hear that."

Emma poked him. "I'm just teasing."

At least he was able to laugh along.

"You don't look sick," Derek pointed out when Emma turned back to the cupboards.

"I'm not," I answered honestly, sinking into one of the kitchen chairs as I spoke. "At least not physically. I really needed the mental break with everything that happened this week."

Derek took a seat across from me and nodded like he understood. "Is it…" he paused for a second, trying to come up with the right words. "Is it psychic related?"

I eyed him curiously. "Did Emma tell you?"

Emma's voice piped up from across the room without even turning toward us. "No, she did not."

I gazed down at my fingernails, which had been chewed down to nearly nothing—apparently a new habit I was forming. "Is it that obvious?"

Derek shrugged. "Not *that* obvious. It's just that I've seen you go through this psychic stuff before, and you've been acting weird, like something is bothering you—something more than your car accident."

Derek had never admitted to believing I was psychic, but with everything he'd seen, I knew his skepticism had declined over the past year. As Emma pointed out not too long ago, even though Derek was somewhat religious, he didn't have to abandon his belief system to believe me. After all, we both believed in the afterlife.

My gaze shifted between Emma and Derek, although Emma wasn't paying any attention. Should I open up to Derek? I mean, he was one of the first people I told about being psychic because I love him like a brother, but this whole losing my abilities thing made me wary to admit any of my recent encounters out loud. What else was I supposed to do, though? It was obvious—at least to my best friends—that something was going on.

I chewed the inside of my lip. "I've been seeing another ghost."

Derek gave a slow nod as if absorbing the information. "So, uh, what does the spirit—ghost—want?"

I shrugged. "I have no idea. He never said anything to me."

"I have an idea!" Emma practically shouted, flicking her mixing spoon into the air, which sent splatters of soup across the room. She ignored it and rushed over to the table and slid into the chair on the end between Derek and me. "We could…" she paused for suspense. "We could hold a séance."

I swallowed. Were my abilities up to that? Derek and I exchanged a wary glance, but Emma continued.

"If we contacted him, you could see what he wants and help him!"

"I—" I started to say, but Derek's voice cut me off.

"That might actually work," he agreed.

Wait. What? Derek was willing to be in on this? So he *did* actually believe me now?

My best friends stared at me expectantly. If I refused, that would look suspicious. I had to comply.

"I don't know if it'll work." I sighed. "Remember when we tried contacting Sage's sister, Melissa? She didn't appear that time." At least it wouldn't seem so bad if this time didn't work, either.

"It's worth a shot," Emma pointed out.

"Okay," I decided cautiously. "We'll try, but after soup."

"After soup," Emma agreed.

~

My friends and I formed a triangle on my bedroom floor. I had lit a few tea candles to set the mood.

"So for this to work," I explained, "we all have to be in the right mind-set, which means you need to be relaxed and open to any possibilities, even if we end up contacting someone who isn't the ghost I've been seeing." My eyes bore into Derek's.

"What?" he asked innocently.

"You have to *believe*," Emma told him.

"Come on," Derek said, "you guys think after everything I've seen Crystal do I'd still question that psychics are real? She found Sage bleeding to death and saved her life at the *exact* time she said it was going to happen. If that's not a miracle…"

"It's not a miracle, you dummy." Emma swatted at him lightly. "It's paranormal—supernatural—whatever you want to call it."

"Okay." Derek held his hands up defensively. "All I'm saying is that I believe it now."

"Okay," I agreed. "Now that we have that out of the way, let's focus on our ghost." I filled my voice with confidence, but the truth was, I was anything but confident. In fact, I was *sure* this wouldn't work. "The thing is that we don't have anything that belonged to the ghost. We don't even know his name or anything, so we'll have to focus harder than normal."

Emma's smile widened, and I knew she was fully enjoying this.

"Let's start by linking hands and doing some breathing exercises to clear our minds," I instructed.

Emma and Derek followed my lead while I guided them through relaxation exercises and continued to remind them to clear their minds of nothing but our ghost. I didn't know how much time passed. It could have been 10 minutes or half an hour. It wasn't long enough for me to give up, but then I felt something tingling my senses. I sucked in a sharp breath, and without consciously realizing it, I squeezed my friends' hands tighter.

"Something's happening," I whispered, focusing my mind even more on the mysterious ghost. What could I do to help him? What did he need?

The tingling in my fingers grew more intense, though not to the level I was used to when I saw a ghost. I took in another long breath and let it out slowly, picturing the silhouette of the shadowy ghost in my mind. A chill spread throughout my skin, raising the hairs on my arms.

Focus. Focus. I repeated this in my head, locking onto an image of the man's outline. He was almost here, almost ready to tell me what he needed my help with. The tingling sensation grew stronger, and then swiftly, my eyes sprung open. The shadow ghost hovered only inches from my nose, but I didn't have even a moment to take in the scene before the energy in the room exploded.

There wasn't a noise or a light as one might expect from an explosion. Instead, it was as if a strong, silent wind had blown through the room to whip my body back. My shoulder blade slammed into the sharp corner of my desk. I cried out in pain. When I managed to focus on the room, I saw in the dim light—thanks only to daylight behind my curtains since the candles had blown out—that my friends had been forced back from the circle as well. Emma was rubbing her head after hitting the wall, and Derek's body was pressed up against my closet door. He looked around in a daze.

"Is everyone alright?" I asked immediately, rubbing my aching shoulder. Add that to the list of aches and pains I'd accumulated this week.

"What happened?" Emma's eyes went wide. "That was *wicked!*"

I wasn't sure how far off she was with that statement.

"Derek?" I asked.

He looked at me with an expression like he couldn't really recall where he was.

"Derek?" I repeated. "Are you okay?"

He pushed himself up to a more comfortable position. "I'm—yeah." He looked down at his hands, flexing them, making me wonder if he'd gotten hurt as well.

"Are you sure you're okay?" Emma asked worriedly. She touched him lightly.

"I'm good," he assured us.

I pulled myself from the floor and flipped the light back on. "I—I don't know what happened, but I don't think I want to try that again."

Emma looked at me warily. She was still crouched next to Derek.

"Yeah," he said. "Best not."

"I think we really freaked him out," I told Emma after Derek left to use the bathroom.

"To be honest, it freaked *me* out," she admitted. "But at the same time, it was *really* cool, whatever it was."

"I couldn't tell you what it was." Even if my abilities were working properly, I may not have been able to explain it. It was like a surge of paranormal power, only I had no idea what it meant.

CHAPTER 8

*A*fter a while, Emma announced it was time to head to the game. She asked if I wanted to come, but I insisted I still needed my "sick" day. Emma dragged Derek from my house and went to the game without me. I was slightly disappointed that I wouldn't be there to watch it, but I wouldn't be playing anyway.

I lay down on the couch knowing Mom and Teddy wouldn't be home for a while. Mom was at her shop, and Teddy had said he'd be over at Roger's working on the baby crib they were making in Roger's workshop. I flipped on the TV to kill time. I needed something to take my mind off everything, although I really should have been working to solve the mystery of the shadow ghost. I must have fallen asleep because I jolted awake to the sound of someone entering the door.

"How was your day?" my mom asked. "Did you just watch TV all day?"

I shrugged, pushing myself up. "I watched a few things." It wasn't a lie. No way could I tell her about Robin popping in for a visit, and that sent a guilty sensation to form in my stomach. I still hadn't decided if I'd tell her about the other thing that happened. I'd been hiding enough lately. What was one more thing?

"What is it?" My mother sat beside me on the couch.

"Nothing," I told her, but she didn't buy it.

"Your face says otherwise."

I had to give her something, so I spit out the first thing I could think of. "I've just been thinking."

"About?"

"I know what I'm capable of, but I was curious what kind of powers ghosts have." Hopefully I made it sound like a simple enough question so it wouldn't prompt her to ask about the creepy encounter from earlier. I still wasn't ready to talk about it.

"Well, you're the one who sees ghosts."

"Yeah, but you know more about all this than I do."

"From what I do know, ghosts can't do much but communicate with us. That's how we get visions. The longer they've been dead, the more power they have."

I recalled the time when a ghost I knew, Olivia Owen, was able to push over a guy with the power of the wind. She'd been dead for a year at the time.

I nodded. "That makes sense. Thanks for satisfying my curiosity."

"Are you hungry?" my mom asked as she rose from the couch and finally slipped her jacket off.

"No, I—oh, my gosh! What happened?"

A strip of gauze wound its way around her forearm. A thin line of blood was visible under the bandage.

She inspected her arm. "Dang, it's still bleeding."

"What happened?"

"I was unpacking some inventory, and I was stupid and put the box cutter on top of a pile of unstable boxes. When I bent down, I knocked the pile over. The box cutter fell on me and sliced my arm open."

"I'm glad you're okay. Now you have a wound to match mine," I teased, pointing to my head.

"It's not a perfect match, but we can grieve together. Let's do ice cream for supper."

Ice cream for supper? My mom was awesome.

~

My day off didn't seem long enough. When my alarm buzzed Friday morning, I audibly groaned as I pulled my butt out of bed and sluggishly prepared for the day. I thought about asking my mom if I could stay home again, but I needed to collect my homework from the day before and didn't want to fall even further behind in class.

I met up with Emma at our usual corner and walked with her to school. We arrived just before the bell rang that released students from the commons and to their lockers. Everything about the day felt positively normal, like the last week hadn't even happened. I wasn't even surprised when Derek met up with us at our lockers and had to ask Emma for his combination again. He'd misplaced his class schedule for the second time in the few weeks since school had started and had to pick up another copy from the office. It was so typical that it almost felt strange to me with everything that had been happening lately. The pulse of my headache, however, reminded me that everything that had happened this past week was, in fact, real.

Luckily, my headache subsided as the day went on, but it returned at lunch. I pushed my chicken patty away from me, suddenly losing my appetite. The sad thing was, I really liked the school's chicken patties.

"You okay, Crystal?" Emma asked from across the table. She giggled and shifted in her chair like she'd already forgotten the question. Her eyes darted to Derek's, who had a blank expression on his face and didn't seem to notice. It was obvious she was trying to play footsy with him under the table. I didn't mind so much since I was used to it.

"I'm just not hungry," I told her. "My headache is back. Want my chicken?"

"Crystal Frost is turning down her chicken patty?" Emma teased.

I nodded.

"Mm." She smiled down at my sandwich like she'd just won a pot of gold. "After I finish mine."

"Want my tater tots, Derek?" I offered since they were his favorite.

An emotion I couldn't read flickered across his face, but he didn't say anything.

"Derek?" I asked a second time.

He blinked a few times before answering. "Uh, no."

"What?" Emma asked exaggeratedly. "Since when does Derek Johnson turn down tater tots?"

Derek's eyes shifted between mine and Emma's. After a brief pause, he spoke. "I just think she should eat, is all." He gestured toward me when he said "she."

"Well, yeah, but you never turn down tots." Emma leaned into Derek and clung to his arm. She looked up at him with big brown eyes. "Are you okay? You're not getting sick, too, are you?"

Derek shrugged her off. "I'm fine," he assured her before his expression changed to a more cheerful one and he fixed his gaze on me. "Do you want to hang out after school? Maybe at your house?"

"That's a good idea." I smiled. It might actually make me feel better. "I don't know what we'll do, but if your guys' parents are okay with it, we can walk home together after volleyball practice."

"Right. After volleyball," Derek said. "Sounds good."

∽

Practice resumed like it had the last few days with me playing co-manager with Derek. We didn't really talk much, and I didn't mind since I still wasn't feeling well. We just ran around trying to keep the balls on the court. I was happy to see Emma kill her jump serve since it was something she'd been working on.

"Did you see how well I did at practice today?" Emma asked on the walk back to my place. She held Derek's hand and leaned into him.

"I did. It was awesome. I'm falling behind, though, thanks to my stitches," I complained.

"Oh, don't say things like that," Emma encouraged. "You had an awesome jump serve last week."

"Yeah, *one*. Most of the time, I can't make it over the net. I'm thinking I'll just practice my normal serves. I'm not sure I'll ever get a jump serve down."

Emma wrinkled her nose in thought, which made her look like a chipmunk. "I don't know. I guess do whatever works for you. You're pretty good at serving either way."

We reached my house, and I pushed inside only for the smell of Teddy's delicious cooking to hit my nose. "You're not at Roger's?" I asked as I stepped into the kitchen. The smell of garlic bread filled my senses.

"Nah, his wife's out of town for the weekend, and he had to watch the kids. We didn't want to do wood working with little ones running around."

"I hope you don't mind if Emma and Derek stay for supper." I glanced back at both of them while I spoke.

"It's fine. I'll just put in some more garlic bread. There's enough spaghetti to go around."

"Thanks," I told him before turning back to the living room.

"Where's your mom at?" Derek asked as he and Emma trailed behind me.

"It's mid-October," I pointed out. "Everyone's getting ready for Halloween, so the shop's staying open later. I never know when she'll be home this time of year."

"Hey," Emma said as she took a seat on the couch. "Maybe we should decide on a time to go shopping again for our Halloween costumes. Derek and I are thinking about going to the festival as Pikachu and Ash." Emma cuddled into him when he took his seat.

I settled into the other chair. "I don't know what I'll go as yet."

"Well, keep thinking on it," Emma smiled. "It's going to be a blast!"

My mom arrived home a few minutes later while Emma and I were discussing my costume ideas. All of Emma's ideas were so not my style, like being a belly dancer or a cheerleader.

"I'm not going as a half-naked mermaid," I insisted about her latest suggestion. "It sounds like food is ready anyway."

Emma bounced up from the couch. "Oh, good. I'm hungry."

We all gathered around and dug into Teddy's delicious spaghetti and garlic bread.

"Mrs. Frost," Derek broke the silence.

My mother's eyes brightened when she looked up. "It's Simmons now, but yeah?"

"Oh, right. I keep forgetting."

"No problem. What is it?"

Derek looked like he had something important to ask, but then he relaxed. "Do you have any ideas for Halloween costumes?"

My mother immediately launched into the list of costumes they carried in the shop this year. I'd already heard the list, but I listened anyway in case it sparked any ideas. I liked the thought of dressing up as an over-the-top psychic, kind of in the same style of gypsy my mom dressed up as. It intrigued me, like I had one night a year to truly show off who I was, but I was also scared it would only upset me since my gift had been fading recently. Who knew if I'd even be feeling well enough in the next few weeks to go anyway? My headache still hadn't eased.

I reached for another slice of garlic bread and noticed my friends' expressions. They were both staring at my mom, completely engrossed with her costume ideas. I locked my eyes on Derek as I pulled back from the tray of bread. It had sounded like he had something important to ask my mom before, like he had changed his mind at the last second. If my abilities were working, I may have been able to scrape by with a hint as to what was on his mind, but my powers seemed pretty much useless at this point. Still, I couldn't help but wonder what was bothering him.

Derek and Emma both called it a night at the same time. Emma hadn't brought any overnight stuff, so I figured we weren't having a sleepover.

Derek cleared his throat. "Uh, Emma? Will you walk me home?"

Emma's eyes lit up. "Of course." Then she turned to me. "We'll see you on Monday. Have a good weekend with Robin and all of that."

"See you guys," I called as they left my house.

That night, I retreated to my bedroom—my headache easing slightly —and thought about how normal my day seemed. After the last week, it was relaxing for things to be back to normal, although I knew deep down that they weren't, not really. I still had the mystery of the shadow ghost to figure out. What did he want, anyway?

I sent out a short plea to my father that night, asking him to help me find answers. Then I crawled into bed and fell asleep.

CHAPTER 9

On Saturday morning, I borrowed my mom's car and drove to the city to visit Robin. Even though I'd seen him on Sunday and Thursday, I missed him terribly. I wanted him to wrap me in his arms and tell me everything would be okay.

To some degree, I wanted to believe that it would be, but on the hour drive to Robin's, I couldn't put the shadow ghost out of my mind. Since Emma, Derek, and I held that séance, I hadn't felt that tingling sensation anymore, the one that made it feel like someone was watching me. Granted, my headache had persisted afterward, but at least today I felt fine, which probably meant my headache was just from stress and not a ghost.

But I still couldn't stop wondering what the ghost wanted and why he wasn't interested in contacting me anymore. Had that surge of energy at the séance somehow prevented him from coming back?

I was thinking too hard. I reached over to the radio to turn it on, and then I cranked up the volume to drown out my thoughts.

I had blasted music long enough and loud enough that I was able to nearly forget my troubles by the time I reached Robin's dorm. He met me in the commons area, and I flung my arms around him the second I saw him.

"Miss me?" he asked with an amused laugh.

"Yes!" I told him without pulling away.

"How are you feeling?" He drew away from me and brushed my blond hair out of my face to inspect the stitches along my hairline. "It looks like it's healing well."

"Mom's taking me to get the stitches out tomorrow."

"And your headache?"

I shrugged. "It comes and goes. I feel fine right now."

Robin smiled and placed a kiss on my forehead. "That's good to hear."

Then he took my hand and led me to his dorm room. His roommate, Joe, sat in the corner at his desk and clicked through items on his computer. He mumbled a half-hearted greeting as we entered the room. I didn't know Joe very well and didn't know what exactly he did on his computer, whether he was studying or gaming, but I did know he was attached to the thing and hardly ever left the room except for class. I'm sure that was the only reason Mom and Teddy let me visit Robin.

We didn't stay in the room long since there wasn't much to do there. We started with a walk around the wildlife reserve next to campus before we found our way to the basement of Robin's dorm where they had a pool table.

"You suck," Robin teased before sinking his pool ball in a corner pocket.

"I'm trying to let you win," I joked back.

His brows shot up. "Is that what you're doing? You're looking into the future to see how to set up my shot perfectly?"

I forced a laugh, but inside, my heart sank. An unexpected thought made its way into my mind. I pushed it away as soon as I realized what I was thinking, but it came back just as quickly. *What if my abilities never return?* I wasn't sure I wanted them when I first found out I was psychic. Was my accident perhaps a blessing? Could this be my ticket to leading a normal life, the life my mother wanted for me?

Except, I still had a mission with the ghost. Could I abandon that? It didn't matter how much I worried or how many questions I asked right now anyway. There was nothing I could do about it. This shadow ghost was just going to have to find another psychic to help him. I didn't let myself visibly react when I realized how painfully selfish that sounded, but what other choice did I have than to let this mystery go?

Robin missed a shot, and he gestured for me to take my turn.

He'd lined up my next shot perfectly. I situated myself behind the ball and lowered my body to the pool table for a better perspective. I wet my lower lip in concentration and then thrust the pool stick forward. The ball sank into the pocket perfectly. I jumped in excitement and couldn't help the grin that spread across my face.

"That was awesome!" Robin cheered.

Though we'd played pool several times together already, something about sinking that ball felt so *normal*. Maybe losing my abilities wouldn't be so bad after all...

~

Mom and Teddy drove me to get my stitches out on Sunday morning.

"So," I teased from the back seat. "When do we get to make your next medical run?"

My mother twisted around in her seat. "You mean for the baby?"

I nodded. "For my little sister."

"You mean your little brother." A mischievous grin spread across my mother's face, and I knew she was only teasing me. "It's next week, but you know, I'm not sure I want to know anything unless there's something wrong." She turned to Teddy in the driver's seat.

"If that's what you want," he agreed, squeezing her hand. "I don't mind being surprised."

"It's going to be a girl," I said, ruining the surprise for him, although I knew at this point I was only guessing.

I returned home afterward with a new scar along my hairline. Luckily, it was easy to hide behind my hair.

Emma noticed straight away on Monday. "Oh, yay! You got your stitches out."

I fell into step beside her at our corner on the way to school. "How bad is the scar?"

"Not bad at all. At least now you can get back to volleyball practice! We can see how good your jump serve is."

"Probably not very," I admitted. "I'll just be glad to be on the court again."

"You're feeling well enough to play again, right? How have your headaches been?"

I shrugged. "On and off. I haven't had one in a few days." We reached the school just then and headed to our lockers.

Lunch was quiet on Monday between our group of three. My headache had returned mildly, and Derek seemed oddly quiet. After a few attempts at starting conversation, Emma gave in to the silence.

At volleyball practice, I was so excited to get back into things that I was the first one out of the locker room. After stretching and running a couple of laps, Emma found her way to me to team up for other warmup exercises.

"Have you seen Derek?" she asked, gazing around the room in hopes of spotting him.

I followed her shifting eyes. "No. He's not here?"

"I haven't seen him. He seemed awfully quiet at lunch today, too. I mean, you're normally quiet, but Derek and I never run out of things to talk about. He didn't text me much this weekend, either. Do you think he's sick or something?"

"I don't know. He'd tell you if he was, wouldn't he?"

"Yeah, that's what I thought." Emma twisted her mouth in uncertainty. "I'll text him after practice."

"I'm sure he's fine," I told her, but unfortunately, I had no way of truly knowing that.

~

I returned home that night to find Teddy in the kitchen. No surprise there.

"How was work?" I asked, dropping my backpack onto one of the kitchen chairs. I only asked to make small talk.

Teddy turned from the stove and shrugged. "It was everyday police work."

"Sounds boring." I pushed my way around the counter. "Mind if I help?" I didn't typically ask to help Teddy with dinner—I guess I was afraid of ruining it—but I honestly didn't have anything better to do.

"Sure, Kiddo."

I inched closer to the stove. "What are you making?"

"Baked chicken and mashed potatoes."

"Oh? What can I help with?"

"Mm," Teddy thought. "Can you peel and cut the potatoes?"

"Sure."

I spent the next several minutes scrubbing, peeling, and cutting up potatoes. Just when I placed the pot on the stove, the doorbell rang. Teddy's hands were dirty from the chicken, so I offered to get the door. When I opened it, I found Emma standing behind it, only something was wrong. Her eyes were red and bloodshot like she'd been crying. An indescribable pain shot through my heart when I saw the expression on her face.

"Emma, what's wrong?"

She swallowed, and her bottom lip quivered. Her silence lasted only a split second before she broke down crying and flung herself at me into a hug. "Derek br—broke up wi—with me."

I held onto her tighter once I decoded her words through her sobs. "Oh, my god. What happened?"

Emma drew away and buried her hands in her face. She didn't respond.

"Come on. Let's go to my room and talk."

I led Emma to my room, but it was like she didn't really know what was happening. I sat her on my bed, and her shoulders shook along with her sobs. I wasn't sure if she realized I'd moved her.

I took a seat at my desk chair next to her. "Emma, what happened between you two?"

"I don't know," she wailed, throwing her body onto my bed and burying her face in my pillow.

I didn't say anything for a long time and figured it best if I just let her cry it out. Finally, she lifted her head and wiped the tears away.

"After practice, I texted him, but he didn't text back, so I went over to his house to see what was up. I thought maybe I could make him some soup or something if he was sick." She paused for a second and began picking at the ends of her dark curls. "He was like, 'What are you doing here?' I was like, 'Well, you weren't at practice. I wanted to make sure you were okay.' Then—you're not going to believe this—but he said I was too *clingy*."

Well, okay, I didn't expect Derek to come out and say something like that, but truthfully, Emma was pretty clingy.

"He's like, 'Why would you need to check up on me? You're so clingy.' I was like, 'I was just worried,' and the next thing I know, he's like, 'You're so annoying. I don't know why I'm with you. Let's break up.'"

My mouth hung open in shock. Derek called Emma annoying? But I thought he loved her!

"Wow," I finally said. "Emma, I'm sorry."

"It's awful," she cried, falling back down onto my pillow. "We've always been best friends, all three of us. Now what's going to happen? We'll never be able to hang out just the three of us again. You'll have to choose between us!"

That thought made it feel like a brick had fallen on my stomach. *Uh oh*. I was going to be right in the middle of this, and I didn't even know what had happened!

"Emma, it's okay," I assured her. "You're still my best friend."

She looked up at me. "I am?"

"Of course you are."

"Maybe you can talk to Derek for me," she suggested, sitting up in the bed. "Maybe ask him where I went wrong. When I tried to ask, he just slammed the door in my face."

I bit my lower lip nervously. I didn't want to be thrust into the middle of their relationship battles. I didn't know what was going on in Derek's head, but he *had* been acting unusual lately. Maybe he'd been thinking about breaking up with her for a while. Perhaps that joke about them having kids scared him.

"Please," Emma pleaded with puppy dog eyes. "Maybe if I know why he broke up with me, I can change. We can be together again."

A voice in my head was telling me I shouldn't do it, that I shouldn't get in the middle of this, but they were my best friends. I wanted to see them happy, to see them together.

"Fine," I agreed. "I'll talk to Derek for you."

"Thank you, Crystal."

CHAPTER 10

For the next few hours, Emma and I talked about her and Derek. Well, it was more like Emma talking and me adding in a few sounds where I could. Teddy didn't bother us about dinner. I figured he sensed something emotional was going on here—and not just because he was intuitive.

Emma wiped at her cheeks after her tears had dried. "I'm sorry. I've been going on and on about me and Derek. How are you?"

"It's okay, Emma," I assured her. "You need to let it all out."

She took a deep breath before speaking. "I think I've said all I can right now. I just don't want to talk about it anymore. Can we talk about something else to take my mind off it?"

"Sure."

"How's your ghost?"

My heart sank. I'd hardly thought about the shadow ghost in the past two days, and it made me feel incredibly selfish. "I haven't seen him."

"Oh? Do you think he found what he wanted?"

I shrugged slowly while mulling over her question. "I have no idea what he wanted, and he never actually got to speak to me, so I don't think so." My best theory was that the surge of energy from the séance somehow slammed the door on our connection.

"Maybe we should try contacting him again. Only this time, we should get your mom, Sophie, and Diane involved. I'm sure the energy will be stronger if we have more psychics there."

I pressed my lips together in thought. That was a good idea. I mean, I'd been saying there wasn't anything I could do about the ghost and his problems, but Emma's suggestion might actually work. At the very least, it would ease the guilt knotting in my stomach after not even *trying* to help him.

"Yeah, I'll mention it," I finally said.

Emma and I moved on to more trivial conversation. It seemed to cheer us both up, but eventually, she headed home.

"What was that?" my mother questioned from the couch after I'd led Emma out the door. She turned the volume down on the TV. Dishes clinked around in the kitchen, where Teddy was washing them.

I crossed the room to sit beside my mother, a somber expression fixed on my face. "Emma and Derek broke up."

My mother's intake of breath was audible. "Oh, no. What happened?"

I shrugged. "I don't know. Derek's been acting strange lately." I paused for a second. "He was acting weird even before they broke up. I wonder if something else is going on with him."

"Something at home, you mean?" my mom asked.

I thought about it for a moment before answering. "I guess so." That's when I realized how truly self-absorbed I'd been lately. I hadn't even realized that one of my best friends may need my help. Something was clearly bothering Derek, and even though he broke my best friend's heart, he was still my friend. Surely he needed my comfort as much as Emma did.

"I was wondering about him," my mother said, her voice cutting through my thoughts.

My brow furrowed. "What do you mean?"

She shifted on the couch to sit up a little straighter. "Well, he came into the shop today after school. I didn't ask him about it, but I thought it was weird that he wasn't at volleyball practice."

"He did? What was he doing at the shop?"

"Well, at first, he was just browsing through the costumes. I asked him if he needed some more costume ideas. He said he didn't, but he did have questions about colleges. He wanted to know more about where I went, what I majored in, if I was part of any clubs, and all that."

"I don't get it. Why would he care?"

My mother shrugged. "It sounded like he was looking for advice on where to go. I know Emma's dying to go to SMU. Maybe he was wondering if that's where he should go, too."

"That can't be why he broke up with Emma," I said with certainty, only it made a bit of sense. If he was trying to convince himself to go to SMU but didn't think he actually wanted to, maybe he broke up with her to ease the heartache of having to do it when we graduated. Except, they more than a year left together. "Why is he worrying about colleges now? We're only juniors."

"Well, you and Emma went on the college campus tour. Maybe it scared him about his future."

"Maybe," I agreed, pressing my lips together in thought. "I guess that means he doesn't want to go to SMU. What'd you tell him about it?"

"I said I loved it. I told him about how I had great professors and learned a lot, and that there were always fun things to do on campus. I told him how Sophie and I started The Sensitive Society and found Diane. We've been life-long friends ever since."

Intrigue got the better of me. "How'd you come up with that club anyway?"

My mother smiled like she was happy I was interested. "It wasn't a true club that the school endorsed or anything. It started my freshman year. I was in one of my first psychology lectures when I asked the professor about people with abilities—a sort of sixth sense. I asked if he, as a psychologist, believed in that sort of thing and if so, if there was a way to explain it with science. He told me to talk to him after class. You have no idea how excited I was to learn more about my abilities. Thankfully, my grandma had taught me a lot about how to use it, but I wanted to know more about why it happened in the first place. Unfortunately, my professor couldn't give me an answer, and to this day, I still don't have a clue how it works."

"So, what'd he say to you after class?" I asked.

"He said he knew of this girl on campus who had been interested in doing some research on extrasensory perception. She was an upperclassman in the psychology department, and he thought I might be interested in talking to her."

"What'd you find out?"

The expression that crossed her face told me she had her own little secret. "Well, I learned that there were more people with abilities than just me and my grandma."

"So, the girl you met was psychic, too?"

Her eyes brightened. "She was Sophie."

A smile broke out across my face. My mother had never told me this story in so much detail before. All I knew was that she'd met her business partners in college and they formed this group called The Sensitive Society.

"After we discovered what each other could do—that I could see bits of the future and find things and that she could read and influence people's emotions—we became interested in meeting other psychics. So we put posters up for our 'club.' That's when we met Diane."

"And she was majoring in business," I confirmed. "She was the brains behind you opening your shop."

My mother smiled like she was glad I remembered. "Exactly." In the next moment, her face fell like she was remembering something terrible. Her gaze dropped to her hands in her lap. "Unfortunately, Diane was the only person who understood what our group was about. Other people defiled our posters and wrote things like 'witches' on them."

I gasped. "Oh, my gosh. Did anyone hurt you guys?"

My mother's gaze flew to mine, and then she relaxed. "Thankfully, no, but they weren't very nice about it, especially the people who found out we were the ones in the club. We took the posters down and mostly kept quiet. People eventually seemed to forget about it."

"So, you three were the only members?" I asked curiously.

She nodded. "Well," she changed her mind. "I guess Sophie's sister, Theresa, tried to be a part of it, but she never had the gift. She left the group shortly after we started it." My mother swallowed and looked past me across the room. It was like there was more to that part of the story that she wasn't going to share with me.

I didn't manage to get a second to focus on it when I realized something. "Wait. Theresa, Sophie's sister. That's Justine's mom, right?"

She nodded.

"I remember Justine saying her mom went to SMU, too. So, you guys were all there at the same time?"

"Theresa was in my class, but she dropped out halfway through when she met Justine's dad and got pregnant."

That made sense since Justine was two years older than me and my mom had me just out of college.

"So, if Sophie was older than you, did you start the business when she graduated or when you did?"

"It was an ongoing process after Sophie graduated. I would travel the hour drive from here to SMU. I wasn't a huge part of the business in the first few years, especially since your dad was trying to get me to go on dates every Friday night."

I smiled at the thought of my dad courting my mom. I only wish I had gotten the chance to know him better. At least I remembered him well enough to know I loved him.

"Anyway," my mom said, steering the conversation back on course. "I hope Derek figures everything out."

"Me, too."

My mother patted my knee before standing. I watched her take a few steps and noticed a limp to her gait.

"Mom," I stopped her.

She turned back toward me.

"What happened?"

She looked down at her foot like she'd just noticed the ache in it for the first time. "Oh, it's not a big deal. At the shop earlier, a crystal ball fell from one of the top display shelves, and it smashed a couple of my toes. It's no big deal."

"No big deal?" I asked breathlessly. "Mom, you could have broken toes. One of those things could have crushed your skull! You have to be more careful in the shop, especially with the baby." I rose from my seat and crossed over to her to caress her belly.

"Oh, stop fussing," she said, casually shooing me away. "I didn't break anything. I almost caught the ball, so I slowed it down. I think I'll go take a hot bath to soothe it."

"Okay," I said, but at the last second, I remembered that Emma requested I ask her about a séance. If I had any chance at helping the ghost, it was with my mom and her friends. "Oh, Mom?"

She paused and turned back to me.

I rested on the arm of the couch. "I didn't tell you because I didn't want you to worry, but I saw this ghost last week."

She twisted her lips at me like she was disappointed I didn't tell her.

"I don't know what he wants, though. Emma suggested we hold a séance to contact him." I didn't tell her that we'd tried one on our own because I knew it would make me sound irresponsible.

"I guess we can do that," she finally said. "You have a game tomorrow night, so why don't we try Wednesday night after we close the shop?"

I nodded. "Thanks."

I retreated into my bedroom, where I texted Derek.

You around?

He didn't text back. I wasn't sure if that was because he was honestly busy or if he just sensed I wanted to talk about Emma and he didn't want to talk to me.

Eventually, I crawled into bed that night after whispering to my father, asking him to help me find strength to help out the shadow ghost and help Derek through whatever trials he was currently facing.

CHAPTER 11

J wanted to find Derek and talk to him on Tuesday, but I didn't get a chance to before the final bell to first period rang. It was no surprise that he hadn't shown up before the warning bell since he usually didn't, but I unfortunately didn't have any classes with him until after lunch this semester. I wished I could text him as the morning announcements read over the loudspeaker, but I was never one to sneak my phone into class, so I didn't have it on me.

Knowing there was nothing I could do for Derek until lunch, I set my mind on my other problem: the shadow ghost. I attempted to formulate theories in my mind as to who he was and what he wanted from me, but I came up completely blank. I replayed everything I remembered about him in my mind, how I noticed him on the SMU campus, how I saw him on the bus, and how he had been in my house afterward. I thought back to the séance Emma, Derek, and I held and how I saw his figure in the middle of our circle before the energy exploded in the room. None of it gave me a single clue as to what he could possibly want.

In fourth period, something finally clicked. I had first seen him on the SMU campus, and then it was like he'd been following me since, like he knew I could see him and was trying to get my attention. Could it be that he was a student, or maybe a professor, and had been wandering the campus before noticing me? It was the best theory I had. Actually, it was the *only* theory I had. I should have made the connection sooner. I made a mental note to research deaths at SMU over the past few years to see if there was any clue as to who this guy was. I gave up with formulating any further theories as soon as the bell after fifth hour rang. Now it was time to talk to Derek.

I spotted him in the hall near his locker. "Derek," I called. When he didn't look up or acknowledge me, I called again as I approached him. Finally, he noticed me. I couldn't read the expression on his face. "Are you okay?" I asked once I stopped next to his locker. "I tried to text you last night, but you didn't reply."

He opened his locker and shoved his textbook inside. "I—uh—was asleep."

"Do you want to talk about it?"

"About what?" His eyes met mine before he slammed his locker, which was the only way to get it to shut with all the crap spilling out of it. He wasn't exactly one for keeping his locker clean.

"You can't pretend that nothing happened between you and Emma. Clearly, you need a friend right now. Do you want to talk?"

Derek simply stared at me without answering, and I wasn't sure if that meant yes or no.

"Oh, right," I finally realized. "You guys probably don't want to sit by each other at lunch." I bit my lip in thought, searching for a solution. "We could go off campus to talk."

Derek's eyes lit up slightly before regressing to normal. "Where would we go? Could we stop by your mom's shop and pick up some chocolates?"

I had to admit, that did sound good. Chocolates were part of what kept my mom's shop, Divination, going when it wasn't Halloween season.

"After we pick up some lunch," I agreed. "We can walk down to the gas station and grab some sandwiches or something."

I wanted to go tell Emma that I wouldn't be around for lunch, but I suspected there'd be tension if Derek followed me to the lunchroom. Instead, I stopped by my locker to ditch my textbook. I picked up my phone while there and texted Emma on our way out of the school.

Oh, she texted back. *Will you talk to him for me?*

Yes, I told her.

"So," I started as we emerged from the school into the October air. I tucked a long blond strand of hair that had escaped in the breeze behind my ear. "Are you ready to talk about what happened between you and Emma?"

Derek sighed like he didn't really want to talk about it. "She's just annoying."

My gaze flew to his face, but he showed almost no emotion. How could he say that about her? Okay, I guess I could see it on some level, but she was our *best friend*. You get over a person's annoying tendencies after being friends with them as long as Derek, Emma, and I had been a group. But maybe it was different actually *dating* her.

"Derek, she doesn't understand why you broke up with her. Was it that comment she made a few days ago about having kids? You know that was just a joke, right?"

Derek glanced at me quickly. "Yeah, it was that."

Except I could tell that wasn't the whole story, like he was saying it just to get me to stop asking. "Okay, so that bothered you, but it has to be more than that. Was it about college?"

"What do you mean?" He didn't tear his gaze from the sidewalk in front of him this time.

"I mean, you know you and Emma probably won't end up at the same school, and you're trying to break things off before you two completely fall so hard that you can't follow your own dreams."

"What would make you say that?" he asked, his tone so even that he almost didn't sound like himself.

"My mom said you came in to talk to her about colleges."

I noticed a slight change in Derek's pace. "I guess you caught me."

I knew it! Even without my sixth sense, I was still a good detective. A sense of pride washed over me, but I quickly shooed the emotion away because I knew Derek still needed to talk to me.

"Derek," I tried to reason, "you and Emma have almost two years left to spend together. Why give up those two years just because you might not be together in college?"

He didn't speak for a long time. "I can't explain it."

I could tell he wasn't going to let me push it, but I tried to get him to talk anyway. "Nothing else is going on at home?" I asked with worry in my tone.

"What? No." This time, Derek did look at me. "It's just the college thing."

"Don't you want to talk about it?"

"No, actually, I don't," he told me in a clipped tone.

Luckily for him, we reached the gas station just then. I picked up a turkey sandwich, and Derek grabbed some chips and a burger. He didn't have money on him, so I paid for his lunch with a bit of babysitting cash I had with me. We didn't talk much as we made our way to Divination. We simply chewed on our food. At this point, I didn't know what else to say.

By the time we reached Divination, I had finished my sandwich. I balled up the wrapper and shoved it in my pocket. The bell on the door dinged when we walked in.

"Crystal. Derek. It's great to see you," Diane greeted when she noticed us.

I smiled and gave her a hug. When I pulled away, I noticed the expression on her face. It was almost a wince. "Are you okay, Diane?"

She shook her head slightly, as if trying to rid her mind of a strange feeling. "I'm fine. I just have a bit of a headache. Nothing to worry about."

Her hands were still touching me, and although I wasn't as good at assessing emotions recently as I should have been, something told me she was masking the severity of the situation.

"I've been getting headaches, too," I told her. "I even have one now."

She gave an encouraging smile. "See? Nothing to worry about."

"Is Andrea around?" Derek asked.

Diane's eyes finally met his. "No. She and Sophie went out to pick us up some lunch."

Derek pressed his lips together. "Oh. We just came by for some chocolates." He pushed his way into the store and past the costumes to eye the candy by the counter.

"Diane," I whispered. "What's going on? Your headache?"

She looked at me with concern in her eyes. Then she grabbed my arm and led me into the second room in the shop, the one that used to be another business until they'd expanded and punched a doorway in the wall.

My heart pounded against my chest in worry. "What's wrong?"

"I don't know." Her voice came out as a low whisper. "I just suddenly got these flashes. It made me go kind of woozy."

"Flashes?" I asked cautiously. "What do you mean?"

Diane could see into the past—that was her psychic superpower—but I'd never actually seen her powers in action. She fell silent like she didn't want to tell me. Finally, as if realizing she couldn't hide it from me, she spoke. "It was just flashes of memories, honestly. But it was like I was seeing them through someone else's eyes."

"Does this happen a lot?"

Diane shook her head.

"How does it work? Your gift?"

She pressed her lips together. "It's like seeing memories, but I know they're not my own."

I had a good idea of what she meant. It was the sort of feeling I got when I tried to find things by touch. I just *knew* where to find them.

"And now?" I asked.

"It's nothing really. I wouldn't worry about it." And she left it at that.

We returned to the main room. Derek's face was still glued to the chocolates in front of him. It was like he hadn't even noticed we'd left. I passed by the rows of costumes on my way to him, fingering a few as I went.

"Do you know what you're going to be for Halloween?" Diane asked.

I shook my head. "I should get on that, though. The festival is only a week and a half away."

"Do you know what you want to be, Derek?" she asked, finally getting him to look up from the chocolate.

He shrugged. "I don't even know if I'll go."

"What?" I practically screeched. "How could you not?" Only a moment later did I realize it was probably because Emma would be there. If he was trying to avoid her, he wouldn't really have anyone else to hang out with. "Never mind. What kind of chocolate are you thinking about getting?"

"Truffles sound good."

Derek and I returned to the school, but I hadn't managed to cheer him up or learn more about what was bothering him. I didn't get another chance to talk to him, and he didn't show up for our volleyball game.

"He just quit when we only had two games left?" Coach Kathy asked in disbelief before the game started.

I shrugged. "I guess so."

A muscle popped in her jaw. "He should have come to me and told me."

All I could do was apologize, not that I really had anything to apologize for, but I hated to see Coach Kathy so upset.

CHAPTER 12

That night after the game, I locked myself in my room and opened my laptop. I hoped to learn something more about the shadow ghost before we tried contacting him tomorrow. I started with an Internet search to find out more about recent deaths at SMU. The most recent death was of a young man, who was said to have died of natural causes, but his frame was too small to be my shadow ghost.

The second most recent death I found was of a young woman. I paused for a second, wondering if my shadow ghost could be female, but when I pictured the outline in my mind, I knew for sure it was a man. The shoulders were too broad and hips too narrow to be a woman.

I skipped over the following women's deaths and focused on the males. The school seemed to average about two deaths per year—both faculty and students—which I didn't think sounded too odd considering the thousands of people who attended the school.

After what felt like hours of searching, I came across at least two dozen articles about different male students' deaths, but none of their photos seemed to match the outline of the ghost I saw.

How much further back do I go? I wondered. I'd never seen his clothing, and his hair seemed a timeless close cut, so I had no way of knowing if he had died within the past few years or if he'd been haunting the school for a century.

I noticed how most of the deaths I ran across hadn't actually occurred on campus. Some, I assumed, were due to illnesses while others mentioned car accidents. The only one I found that mentioned an on-campus death was about a professor who'd had a heart attack in his office. Only, he didn't seem to fit the profile, either.

Could the ghost I'd been seeing perhaps have died somewhere else? But then, what was he doing on campus? I only hoped that by some miracle I would learn more about him when we tried contacting him.

～

"So, tell us more about this ghost, Crystal," Sophie said on Wednesday night after we'd situated ourselves around my kitchen table for the séance.

I glanced around at the four women at the table: my mom, Emma, Sophie, and Diane. Teddy was back at Roger's working on the crib. Quickly realizing how nervous I must have appeared, I forced myself to relax.

"I don't know that much," I admitted. I knew so little about this ghost that I thought for sure this séance wouldn't work. "I saw him on the SMU campus when we visited, and I thought I might be able to help."

"What did he look like?" Diane asked.

I chewed the dry skin on my lip. "Does that matter? Will it help?"

She shrugged. "It might help us focus on him better."

What could I say? "Um... He was kind of tall, short hair, an athletic build, I guess. He was pretty normal." *Except that he was just a shadow!* I held my breath, hoping they wouldn't ask any more questions about his appearance. Luckily, they didn't. "Uh, this is probably going to be tough. I don't know his name or what happened to him."

"Well, we could all try focusing on the university," my mom suggested. "If he's attached to it, it might help create a more familiar atmosphere in the room for him."

That sounded like our only option, but I wasn't getting my hopes up too high. I mean, sure, I wanted to help him. I just didn't think I could. We linked hands around the table, and I instructed everyone to relax.

"Um... ghost?" I called out. I didn't know how else to address him. "We can help you."

Nothing.

I forced uncertainty out of my mind and allowed the muscles in my neck to relax. I reminded everyone to do the same. This went on for quite some time. *Deep breath in, and out. Relax. Think of the SMU campus. Remind everyone to do the same. Think of the ghost's silhouette. Deep breath in, and out. Relax.*

"We can help you," I repeated again.

Again and again we went through this cycle. *We can do this*, I thought to myself. *Deep breath in, and out. Relax.*

A tingling sensation, though small, made its way into my body. It was hardly noticeable at first. Normally, my psychic feelings were much stronger, but I was relaxed enough that I recognized the sensation. I didn't let myself get too excited just yet. I needed more energy.

Deep breath in, and out. Relax.

"What do you want? We can help," I called out again. My eyes were closed to help me relax, but in my next deep breath, they shot open as a wave of energy coursed through me.

A man stood across the table from me. He had short dirty blond hair and striking blue eyes. His body was surrounded in a bright glow that illuminated his features. Now that I saw his eyes, they looked familiar. Only a split second later did I fully register where I knew him from, and suddenly, all my memories of this man came rushing back. My mouth fell open in shock, but I couldn't manage to speak, to ask him what he was doing here.

"I don't have much time, Crystal," he said.

Tears began to well in my eyes.

"I've already crossed over, so it takes an incredible amount of energy to appear here tonight."

Is that why I saw him as a shadow? I wondered. *Because he wasn't earthbound?*

"I need to warn you," he continued. "It won't be long before you have to make a choice. You are going to have to save three of the people you love most."

My breath caught in my chest. What could he possibly mean?

His next words sent my world tumbling down.

"Soon, you'll have to die to save the ones you love."

My hands flew to my mouth, breaking the circle. I hadn't been thinking. One moment he was there, and the next, he was gone. By breaking the circle, I'd weakened the energy in the room, and he instantly disappeared.

No! Come back! I wanted to shout, but I couldn't get the words out.

"Uh, Crystal?" Emma's voice seemed far off. "What happened?"

I blinked a few times and finally swallowed the lump in my throat. When I looked around the table, everyone's eyes were fixed on me.

"You didn't see him?" I asked.

They all shook their heads. Of course they didn't. They never saw ghosts.

"I felt something," my mother admitted. "There was some sort of energy, but I couldn't hear him, and you didn't talk to him. What happened?"

I have to die to save the people I love. That's what he had said. My life for those of the three people I loved most. I didn't have enough time to consider the concept as eight eyes stared back at me, waiting for an answer.

"I was so shocked when he showed up that I accidentally broke the circle," I lied. "I'm sorry. I just didn't think he'd show."

"We can try again," Sophie suggested.

"I'm actually really tired. That took a lot out of me." At least that wasn't a lie.

"Maybe some other time," Diane said. "You have had a rough couple of weeks."

"Thanks," I told her. I opened my mouth to speak again. I had to tell them who I'd just seen, only I couldn't manage to find the right words. I fell silent.

After we'd given up, I found my way to my room as soon as I could. I pulled Luna down from her shelf and cuddled her closer to my chest than I ever had before. I pressed my nose into the stuffed owl's head and inhaled her scent. It helped soothe my anxiety slightly so that when I raised my head, I was finally able to absorb what had just happened.

For the first time since the car accident that killed him a decade ago, I'd seen my father.

CHAPTER 13

ours later, I still hadn't fallen asleep. I couldn't believe my father had spoken to me. All these months that I'd been talking to him—never knowing if he was there or not—he'd been listening.

Except, what could I possibly make out of the warning of my own death? When I got the warning about Sage's death, it was because I was supposed to save her. Was that what I was supposed to do here? Only, if I survived, did that mean the three people I loved most would die? That'd be my mom, Emma, and Robin. What was supposed to happen to them? When? How? If only I hadn't broken the circle, I may have gotten my answers to those questions.

My chest compressed, and my head grew increasingly sore from the tension I couldn't hold back. I'd already cried out all the tears I could manage. Now, my sobs only came in dry heaves. I buried my head into my pillow so no one would hear me.

"Daddy, come back. Please, I need answers." I called out to him again and again, but he never appeared. I'm not sure he could. He told me it wasn't easy for him to show himself. If he could hardly manage it with a room full of psychics, then he wasn't going to show when it was just me —and a broken me at that.

Even though he couldn't appear to me, I suspected he could somehow hear me. That brought me a slight sense of comfort until I realized I didn't know what to say to him except beg for answers I was unlikely to get. I broke out into sobs again. This time, a single tear traveled down my cheek. I watched it fall to my pillow and soak into the fabric.

"Daddy," I whispered again to the darkness. "I don't want to die."
My last words drifted off, and finally, exhaustion overtook me.

∾

The next morning, a sense of dread hit me when I woke. All I wanted to do was crawl back under the covers and forget about the warning my father sent me, but it had already consumed me. I could think of nothing else as I pulled myself out of bed and headed to the shower. Even in the soothing hot water, I couldn't escape my worry. The simple math wasn't lost on me. My life for the lives of the three people I loved most. It seemed like a fair trade. Besides, it's not like dying would be all that bad. My father would be there, and I knew that once I crossed into the light, I'd find peace.

So why did it seem so difficult to accept?

A knock at my bathroom door startled me out of my thoughts. My heart skipped a beat at the unexpected noise. Mom and Teddy had their own bathroom; they never knocked on mine.

"Yeah?" I shouted over the sound of the running water.

"Crystal, do you have any idea what time it is?" my mother's voice called through the door.

"No," I told her honestly. It was only in that moment that I realized how lukewarm my shower water had become.

"You have less than 10 minutes before you have to leave for school. Didn't your alarm go off?"

It had. "Sorry. I'll be quick!"

I quickly rinsed off and hurried to my room, where I threw on the first pair of jeans and a t-shirt I found at the top of the mound of clean clothes in front of my dresser. There wasn't time to dry my hair, so I threw the wet strands into a messy bun and rushed out of my bedroom.

My mom caught up with me in the living room. "Crystal?"

I paused and turned to her, forcing my face into a placated expression. "Yeah?"

"Is something wrong?" She drew me into a hug, and I melted into it.

For a second, I didn't say anything, but then I realized she might interpret my silence as an answer. "No, Mom," I lied. "Everything's fine. I'll see you tonight. Love you. Bye." I placed a kiss on her cheek before heading out the door.

On my walk to meet up with Emma, I questioned why I hadn't mentioned the warning to my mom or told her I'd seen my father. Surely she would help me make sense of it. Fear settled in my gut at that thought. If I told her, she'd want to take my place. That would mean I'd lose my loved ones. It was either me or them, and they'd all willingly die for me. I couldn't let them do that, which meant they couldn't know.

In that moment, I knew I would sacrifice myself for them. Pain knotted in my chest, but I didn't have any other choice. I took a long, deep breath, accepting this as my reality. Now the only thing I could do was make the most out of the time I had left.

CHAPTER 14

$\mathcal{I}$ played my hardest at our volleyball game on Thursday, not just because it was our last game of the season, but because I knew it was the last game I'd ever play. I killed three jump serves in a row before the opposing team sent it back over the net and my teammate Betsy returned it but it landed out of bounds.

"You were awesome tonight, Crystal," Emma raved after the game in the locker room.

I wanted to smile, but it wasn't genuine. I did well, yes, but my heart broke a little knowing it was all over. Assuming my father's warning meant my death was just around the corner, I'd never play volleyball again.

"Just think about how awesome we'll be next year," she said.

I couldn't help it. Something broke inside of me, and I pulled her into a tight hug right there in the locker room.

She tensed in surprise. "Whoa. Calm down, Crystal. You okay?"

I pasted a fake smile on my face and drew away from her. "I'm just glad we won," I lied, something I'd become increasingly good at over the past year. She didn't notice my dishonesty.

"Me, too."

"Want to stay the night?" I practically begged. I needed more time with her. I didn't want to leave her just yet.

"On a Thursday night?" she asked.

"Why not?" I shrugged.

Emma agreed, but my mother didn't approve when I called to ask permission. "Emma can stay the night tomorrow, but you have school in the morning. I don't want you staying up all night," she'd said.

"Fine." I gritted my teeth and hung up angrily before turning back to Emma. "Tomorrow night, okay?"

She nodded. "Sounds like fun."

Friday after school was our annual pizza party to celebrate the end of volleyball season. It also doubled as our "turn in equipment" day. Derek wasn't there like he should have been if he hadn't quit. My heart dropped thinking about him. I hadn't talked to him in the last couple of days. In fact, I hadn't even seen him in school. But I felt a need to help him through whatever he was going through. I had a feeling he'd never told me the whole truth about what was bothering him, but at the very least, I had to say goodbye.

I started by saying goodbye to Emma at our sleepover that night. I never actually said goodbye or breathed a word of the prophecy to her. I simply enjoyed her company, taking in every bit of joy I could from her laugh, focusing on the way she crinkled her nose and how that made her look like a chipmunk, and reveling in all the memories of our years of friendship.

Emma snorted and threw her head back in laughter. We were both sitting on my bed and couldn't stop laughing as we recounted stories from our past. "And remember that time when you fell face first into the mud on our first grade fieldtrip to that farm?" She giggled uncontrollably. "Oh, my gosh. Your face was *covered* in crap—literally."

"Hey," I defended. "It was really wet that day, and I slipped in the mud. At least it's not as bad as the time you peed your pants on our second grade field trip to that nature center."

Emma covered her face with her hands. "Oh, god. Don't remind me!"

I wanted to tell her about how much I would miss our sleepovers and our walks to school. I wanted her to know that I'd miss our volleyball practices and band performances. I wanted to tell her not to worry about me when I was gone, that I'd be with my dad on the other side. But I didn't. I couldn't risk telling anyone, or they'd try to get me to change my mind. I would save them no matter what.

The following morning, Emma and I made chocolate chip pancakes, just one more thing I'd miss about our sleepovers. She didn't stay long because it was her dad's weekend, and she had to drive herself and her little sister, Kate, over to his house to visit.

As soon as she left, I borrowed my mom's car and drove to the city to visit Robin like I did almost every weekend. He hugged me tight when he came downstairs to meet me in his dorm's common room.

I squeezed him back and nuzzled into his shoulder, never wanting to let him go. I inhaled his fresh spring scent and went weak in the knees. I didn't want to say goodbye.

"Crystal." Robin drew away and stared me in the eyes. "What's wrong?"

Apparently I'd been squeezing him too tight. "Wrong? Nothing. I just missed you."

He pulled me back into his body. "I missed you, too. Do you want to drop your purse off in my room, and then we can take a walk or something?"

"Sure," I agreed. I had put some thought into what I wanted to do with him on possibly one of my last days. I wanted our time to count for something, but I had yet to come up with a good idea.

When we arrived in his room, his roommate was surprisingly gone.

"Where's Joe?" I asked.

"Oh, he went home for the weekend. Said he needed to beg for some money from his parents. You know, the whole 'poor college kid' scenario?"

I shrugged, but a moment later, I realized something. "So, that means we have this room all to ourselves?" I raised my eyebrows suggestively and closed the distance between us.

Robin rested his forehead on mine, and his hot breath warmed my face. I couldn't waste another second, not when I didn't know how much time I had. I wrapped my arms around his neck and planted a kiss on his lips.

He kissed me back and entwined his fingers in my hair. I pressed my body against his, wanting nothing more than to get closer to him, to melt right into him as if we could become one. I parted my mouth slightly, letting my tongue graze across his lower lip. He mimicked my movements in reply. When I was confident he was getting into it as much as I was, I pushed at his body until the back of his knees butted against the edge of the futon under his bunk, and we tumbled down. His hands moved down over my back and then settled on my hips. I ran my fingers through his hair and parted my lips even further. My heart hammered against my rib cage, and my skin grew hot in anticipation.

Without warning, Robin tensed and gently pushed me away.

"What's wrong?" I asked.

He struggled to work his way to a seated position. Noticing his discomfort, I reluctantly pealed myself off of him, and we sat next to each other on the futon.

"I'm sorry," he said. "We—we can't do this."

My mouth hung open in disbelief. All I wanted was to say goodbye to him.

He gripped onto the legs of his jeans and pulled them down to adjust them. "It just—it wouldn't be right."

"What's not right about it?" I demanded. A fire burned within me, one that longed desperately for him. "What do we have to lose?"

He eyed me sideways before averting his gaze. "A lot, actually."

"Robin." I scooted closer to him and kissed his cheek. "It's just us. Right here, right now. All I want is to show you how much I love you."

"There are other ways to do it than this." He still wouldn't look at me.

I blinked a few times. He was turning me down? Did he understand what I was offering him? "Robin..." I couldn't find the words to finish my thought. "Why, not?" I finally asked in a whisper.

"It's just..." He scratched the side of his face. Apparently he couldn't come up with the right words, either. "You're too young," he finally said.

"I am not. The age of consent is 16 in our state."

Robin sighed. "Well, it's just... there are other reasons that it wouldn't be right."

"It's your leg, isn't it?" I asked. I knew he was self-conscious of it, but this badly?

He finally looked at me. "No. Well, uh, yeah. You're right. It is my leg, and I'm just not ready."

I kissed the side of his face again. "Robin, you don't have to worry about that. I'm not bothered by it at all. I *love* you. And that's all that matters."

"I love you, too, Crystal, but there are other ways to show it."

"Not compared to this, Robin." I reached up to place my hand on his cheek and pulled his lips to mine. He almost gave into it, but he caught himself before he could fully surrender to my kiss.

"Crystal!" His voice filled the room as his arms came up to shove me away from him.

I fell back into the bunk bed's metal bars. Tears welled in my eyes, but I didn't make a noise. He still wasn't looking at me.

"Just stop pressuring me," he demanded.

I held my breath to keep from crying. I wasn't even sure what I was feeling at the moment. Guilt because I'd been pushing it? Hurt because he'd shoved me into the bars? Anger because I knew I'd die without ever showing him how much I truly loved him?

"I should go." My voice cracked, but I kept my face turned away from him as I reached into my purse for my keys and situated the strap on my shoulder.

"Wait, Crystal," he insisted, but I was already out the door. "Crystal!" he called down the hall. His voice barely reached my ears as I raced away from him.

In the car, I let go, and the waterfall of tears struck almost immediately. I drove out of the parking lot and headed straight for home. I didn't stop crying the entire way, thinking about how that was the worst possible way to say goodbye to him. I bawled even harder when I realized it may be the last time I saw him.

When I arrived home, I thought about hopping right back in the car and driving to Robin's dorm to apologize, but a little voice in the back of my head kept telling me he wouldn't appreciate that, that he didn't want to see me. And as much as I didn't want to listen to that voice, I let it consume me.

CHAPTER 15

$\mathcal{A}$lthough my farewell to Robin hadn't ended the way I would have hoped, I knew there were more people I had to say goodbye to. On Monday after school, I walked the short distance to the elementary school. I spotted Hope as soon as she exited the building. She ran over to a girl I recognized from school. She was a freshman named Bethany and was Hope's temporary babysitter while I was in volleyball.

I caught up to them quickly. "Hope," I called from behind her.

She turned and smiled at me, her big chocolate eyes bright. "Crystal!" She released her babysitter's hand and ran to me. The impact of her body startled me as she smashed into my middle and squeezed me tight. "I missed you," she said into my belly.

I laughed. "I missed you, too."

Bethany eyed me.

"Hi," I greeted her. "I'm Hope's other babysitter. Do you mind if I talk to her for a couple of minutes?"

"Uh." Bethany looked between the two of us. Apparently she figured I wasn't a threat because a moment later, she agreed.

I led Hope to the stairs in front of the school and sat her down. We were far enough out of Bethany's earshot, and the other students had already fled to the busses or their parents' cars.

"What are you doing here?" Hope asked me.

"I just wanted to see you." *And say goodbye.*

"Are you going to be my babysitter again?" she asked hopefully.

"I—" I glanced toward Bethany. I'm not sure why, maybe so I wouldn't have to look Hope in the eyes. "I really want to."

Hope hugged me again.

I squeezed her back. "I just wanted to tell you how much I enjoyed being your babysitter."

"Uh oh." Hope pulled away from me. "Is something wrong?"

She had always been pretty smart for her age, and I mentally kicked myself for forgetting how quickly she caught on to my emotions.

"Wrong?" I asked. "No, of course not. Why would you say that?"

Hope shrugged. "You're acting like you aren't going to be my babysitter anymore." Suddenly, her expression shifted, and her lower lip quivered. "You are still going to be my babysitter, aren't you? You said you'd come back in November."

I pressed my lips together in thought. How was it that she could always pick up on what I was feeling? "Hope?" I locked eyes with her in a serious gaze. "Can you feel me?"

"What—what do you mean?"

"Can you feel my emotions? The way we used to connect when— when you were with Lauren?"

She shook her head. "No. I don't see you in my dreams anymore."

Why were we ever connected in the first place? I wondered. "You don't feel what I'm feeling right now?"

"Not since you saved me," she admitted.

I hadn't felt her either, but then again, she was the only person whose emotions I'd ever felt when I wasn't touching them. "Why are we connected?" I wondered aloud. I narrowed my eyes into the distance like there was someone out there who could give me the answer. I didn't expect Hope to respond.

"Connected?" Hope asked and then shrugged. "At first, I thought you were an angel or something. I prayed for someone to help me, and then there you were in my dreams, telling me everything was going to be alright."

And then it clicked. Just like that, it made complete sense. Hope had asked the other side for my help, and they'd answered her prayers. That's why I could feel her when I was searching for her last November. I'd never felt anyone else like that because they'd never *asked* for help. When I rescued Kelli, she didn't want help. It was Olivia and Justine who'd asked me to help her. When I saved Sage from her suicide attempt, it was her sister Melissa who had asked me to help her. Sage never prayed for my help.

The tension in my heart eased. "I get it now," I said aloud. I looked back down at Hope again. "I guess in some sense, I really was your guardian angel. I will always watch over you," I promised. "I love you, Hope."

She hugged me for one last time before I said goodbye. "I love you, too, Crystal."

As I watched her walk away with Bethany, a comforting sensation overcame me when I realized this wouldn't be the last time I saw her. When I moved on, I'd still be watching over her.

~

On Tuesday, I drove to the city again after school. I didn't come to see Robin. I had another friend to say goodbye to. I nervously walked into a room full of chairs and music stands with my clarinet case in my hand. Several kids about my age were milling around before practice. Some were blowing into their horns while others were goofing off in the back near the percussion instruments.

The director stood at the front of the room next to a red-headed girl with freckles across her nose. She wore a flattering white short sleeved shirt, something I would have never caught her in just a few months ago. I forced myself not to look at the scars that ran along the inner side of her forearm. The two had their eyes locked on the director's score on his stand.

"I think we should run through this part," the girl said, pointing to the sheet music. "The percussion said they were having trouble with it."

I cleared my throat lightly, and the red-headed girl looked up. Her eyes brightened as soon as she saw me.

"Oh, my gosh! Crystal!" She rushed over to me and pulled me into a hug.

I smiled but wanted to cry at the same time. I hadn't seen her in so long. "Sage."

She pulled back and looked me up and down with a smile on her face. "What are you doing here?"

I gestured to the clarinet case in my hand. "I thought I would join your therapy group for the night, if that's okay."

"That's totally fine. You aren't looking to play in our next concert, are you? Because we could use the extra musicians."

I shook my head, but I couldn't tell her that I probably wouldn't be around to make it. "No. I just wanted to visit you."

"Well, I'm glad you did."

Sage turned to her friends and introduced us. Most of them were younger than her, in the middle to high school range. They were all a part of her weekly music therapy group she'd started with the help of her therapist a few months back. They practiced after school in one of the local high school's band room, where the school's music teacher had agreed to be their director. It was supposed to help people like her cope with their emotions. The group wasn't huge, but so far she'd helped at least half a dozen kids recover from cutting, anorexia, bulimia, drug abuse, and similar issues. They'd held a concert a few weeks back, which Sage dedicated to me after I helped save her life.

"You can sit by Kristie," Sage told me, guiding me into a chair next to another clarinet player. I guessed the girl to be about 14, but her tiny frame made her look younger.

"I'm Crystal," I introduced.

"Oh, cool," she said sincerely. "Kind of like my name. Kristie. So, what are you in for?"

I furrowed my brow. "In for?"

"They say I have an eating disorder." She pushed brown stick-straight bangs out of her face and tucked them behind her headband. "My foster parents put me in the program."

I was momentarily dumbstruck by her willingness to share. I was about to tell her nothing was wrong with me, that I was just friends with Sage, but the truth was, there was so much wrong right now. My ability had faded to the point where I hardly felt like myself these past few weeks, and now I was here because I needed one last moment with a friend before I died—something my own deceased father warned me about. It sounded crazy. Maybe it was. Maybe the entire last year of my life had just been one big dream that I'd finally wake up from soon.

I swallowed. "You'd think I was crazy."

One of her dark brows shot up. "Crazier than compulsively starving yourself for no good reason?"

I went silent.

"Hey," Kristie said. "If you don't wanna tell, you don't have to. We all have our secrets." For some reason, her words comforted me.

I stayed after the practice for at least an hour with Sage. We sight read music together. The beautiful tone of her saxophone filled the room, sending shivers down my spine.

"You okay?" Sage asked, dropping her saxophone to her lap.

"Yeah. It's just your music. It gives me shivers."

She blushed. "Oh, stop."

"I mean it. You should do it professionally."

She shrugged. "I don't know. I like helping out the kids. When I'm finished with my degree in music, I think I just want to keep up the therapy thing. It's been really good for them."

Sage was currently living with her aunt and uncle and working at a bridal shop while she went to school. A couple of months ago, all she wanted was to get away, but after what she went through, she'd settled into her life and devoted it to helping others.

"I'm glad you've found your calling," I told her.

"You haven't found yours yet?" she asked.

I'd once told Sage I was psychic, but after she'd rejected my abilities, I hadn't spoke of it again to her. I wasn't sure what she thought about that part of me. Ever since I discovered my abilities, I knew I wanted to use them to help people. Now I wouldn't have any more chances to do that.

In that moment, I realized I *had* found my calling. My abilities had given me the warning I needed to save my loved ones—and I would. That's what my fate was.

"You know, I think I have found it," I told her, answering her question.

"Oh?" she asked curiously.

"It's… something I'm preparing for."

She didn't prod. It was like she'd worked with enough reserved kids to know when to let people and their secrets be. She began disassembling her horn. "Well, it's really time to lock up the band room. It was great seeing you. When do you think we can hang out again?"

I tensed for a moment. I didn't want to answer that question, not when I couldn't follow through with any promises I made. I wasn't sure how much time I had left.

"We could meet up for Halloween or something," she suggested.

"The Peyton Springs Halloween Festival is this weekend," I told her, though I wasn't sure I'd last that long.

"Oh, awesome." She stood with her saxophone case in her hand. "I'll see what kind of costume I can come up with, and I'll try to make it."

I gave her a friendly smile, never once promising that I'd be there.

After visiting Sage, I swung by Robin's dorm. We had made up over text the past few days, but it just wasn't the same as apologizing in person. He gave me the biggest hug when I arrived in the common room.

He spoke into my hair. "I'm so sorry, Crystal."

"I'm sorry, too. I shouldn't have left like that."

"No, it was my fault."

I drew away from him. "No. It was me. I shouldn't have tried to pressure you."

"Really, it was my fault. I wasn't honest with you."

I tilted my head in confusion.

He gestured to a set of chairs nearby. The only other person around was a student desk attendant, but he had earbuds in his ears and was listening to music while his eyes focused on a textbook.

I sat in the chair and fixed my eyes on Robin. "What are you talking about?"

He took a deep breath and rubbed a hand over his face. "I lied to you about why I don't want our relationship to get physical."

I narrowed my eyes in thought. Where could he possibly be going with this? "I thought it was because of your leg."

He shook his head. "Not with you, Crystal. I'm not self-conscious about that with you. The thing is..." He shifted in his seat. "I want to show you how much I love you, too. I just... I don't want to risk it."

I blinked a few times, still confused. "Risk what?"

Robin pressed his lips together like it was almost painful to say. "Crystal, I don't want to get you pregnant."

I let out a laugh that was almost too loud for my own liking. "Robin, didn't you have health class in high school? There's such thing as protection."

An unidentified emotion flickered across his face. Pain, perhaps? "That doesn't always work," he pointed out.

"Well, it's pretty effective."

He shook his head. "Not enough." That emotion flashed across his face for a second time, and then something clicked in my mind.

"Robin." I held my gaze on his. "This isn't about us, is it? It's about something bigger. Did something happen to you?"

He pulled away from me abruptly. "What? No. Not—not me. I'm like you. I haven't... But there *is* a reason."

I sat silently, waiting for him to explain.

"I never told you about what really happened with my leg."

"It was a car accident." At least, that's what he'd told me.

He nodded. "It was. But my leg wasn't all that was lost that day." He paused like he couldn't finish, but finally, he spoke. "Crystal, I killed someone that day."

*M*y chest compressed. I shot up from my seat and paced a few steps away from him before turning back. "No," I said sternly. "I distinctly remember you saying, 'All I lost was a leg,' because I remember how silly it sounded."

His gaze fell shamefully. "I lied. I didn't want to talk about it."

I still didn't understand where this was going. What had really happened in that accident? I knelt down beside him, forcing his gaze to mine. "Robin, *tell* me."

He took a deep breath, stretching out the moment of silence. It fell so quiet in the room that I could hear the muffled music coming from the desk attendant's earbuds. I let Robin take his time, and neither of us spoke for nearly a minute.

Once he worked up the courage to open up to me, the words tumbled out of his mouth. "My best friend at the time had gotten pregnant at 16. Her name was Vanessa. They had used protection, but as soon as her boyfriend found out, he left her to raise the baby on her own. Her parents weren't much help, either. I was there for her through it all. I drove her to ultrasound appointments and let her cry on my shoulder when she needed to. I bought her chocolate every time she asked. I was the first one to feel the baby kick. It was a boy. She named him Jackson."

An ache opened in my chest when he talked about Vanessa, and I knew why he never told me about her. "You loved her," I stated. There was no question about it.

He nodded, and tears glistened in his eyes. "I thought I could take care of her, you know?" His breath caught in his throat. "She found this lady online who was selling tons of baby clothes for really cheap, and she needed a ride. The baby was due in a couple of weeks, and she didn't have much for him. I agreed to take her. Well, on the way to this lady's house, Vanessa went into labor right there on the highway. I freaked out and didn't know what to do. She was telling me how much it hurt, and I was trying to console her, and I just stopped watching where I was going. I drifted into oncoming traffic and..." A sob broke in his chest.

"She died?"

Robin shook his head somberly. "No, but Jackson did."

It took a few seconds for me to absorb all of this. I blinked several times to keep the tears at bay. "Robin. I. Am. So. Sorry."

He went silent for several long moments before speaking again. "She blamed me. I just—I don't want there to be a chance that I'd lose someone like that again."

"Robin, that would never happen to us." Except he was going to lose me. I still couldn't tell him, especially when he was sobbing like he was.

"Now you know all my secrets," he whispered so quietly that I barely heard him. "You know why I've always been so guarded."

I'd always thought it was because of his leg, but now I knew better. I hugged him as hard as I could and told him for one of the last times that I loved him.

~

I returned home that night determined to find a way around my father's prophecy. I couldn't leave Robin.

"Mom?" I asked in a small voice. I leaned against the door frame of the master bath, where she was brushing her teeth and getting ready for bed. Teddy was in the kitchen washing the dishes after our late supper.

"Yeah?" She spoke as soon as she spit her toothpaste into the sink.

"Can I ask you something about our abilities?"

She turned the faucet on and leaned down to the sink to spit again. "Anything, sweetheart."

"Okay, so you can see the future. Have your visions ever been *wrong?*"

She wiped a towel across her lips. "Well, sure. Remember the time I told you about how Teddy and I met?"

Some of the tension I'd been holding in my shoulders over the past few days eased. I should have thought of that story on my own. If my mother was able to save Teddy from his death, and I saved Sage, that meant I could save myself, right?

"Have you seen something?" she asked, suddenly concerned.

I shook my head in honesty. I didn't *see* anything. "No. It's just something I was wondering about." I paused for a moment. "Have you ever *not* been able to save someone?"

She stared into the mirror while brushing her hair. "Crystal, are you sure there's nothing going on?"

I stiffened, but she didn't notice. "No. I swear. So, you've always been able to use your gift to help people?"

"Oh, my god!" My mother's left hand flew to her stomach, and her right hand holding the hairbrush fell to her side. Her eyes lit up when she looked back at me in the doorway. "I think the baby just kicked!"

"What?" I shouted in excitement. I stood up straighter and immediately closed the distance between us. "Let me feel." I pressed my hand against the soft plush of her robe and waited for movement, but it never came.

"Sorry, sweetie," she apologized. "It's still pretty early, so you may not be able to feel it." She pushed out of the bathroom and shut the light off on her way. My mother let out a long yawn before crawling into bed. "Sleep well, sweetheart. Goodnight."

"Goodnight, Mom," I told her before escaping to my own bathroom to get ready for bed. Only when I lay down that night did I realize she'd never actually answered my question.

∽

"Want to go out for lunch again?" I asked Derek at his locker on Wednesday before he could make it to the lunch line. I needed some time alone with him to say goodbye.

He turned to me with a hard expression on his face like he was angry about something. "I don't know. I guess. Can we stop for chocolates again?" I could sense the tension in his voice.

"That's not a problem. Are you okay, though?"

We fell into step side-by-side.

"I'm fine," he said, but I didn't believe him. Something was definitely up, something much bigger than Emma's joke about kids and his choice of colleges.

We broke out into the autumn sun, and I stopped him. "Derek, you *have* to tell me what's up. I can help you."

He clenched his jaw as he stared at me. His blue eyes seemed a darker shade than normal. "Believe me. You can't help me with this."

He began walking briskly, and I hurried to catch up with him. "You don't know that. You can at least tell me." If it wasn't about Emma, and it wasn't about colleges, what could it be? Was it the séance? Had we freaked him out that badly that he was forever changed by it?

"Derek," I begged. "I'm your best friend. You know you can tell me anything."

He stopped in his tracks and faced me, his expression stone cold. "It's beyond frustrating, alright?"

"What is? Derek, please tell me. I want to help." Tears began to well in my eyes. I was supposed to be enjoying my time with him before saying goodbye, but I couldn't do that when he was suffering and I didn't know how to help.

"It's not something you could possibly understand."

"I understand a lot, Derek."

"Not this." He began walking again.

For each step he took, I had to take two to keep up with him. I racked my brain wondering what this could possibly be about. Something was definitely going on at home, but what? His parents were awesome, and so were his twin sisters.

"Derek," I tried one last time.

"God, just stop it, okay? You're getting to be as annoying as your friend Emma." He didn't slow his step.

"She used to be a friend to both of us," I pointed out, becoming increasingly angry at the way he was keeping secrets. "I just want to help."

"Don't worry. Soon, this will all be over."

When we reached the gas station, I slipped into the women's restroom for a couple of minutes to clear my mind. My face burned in anger, and my headache was flaring up again in response to my stress level. Derek needed help right now, and prodding him for his secret wasn't going to do any good. Being upset at him wasn't going to help anything, either. I took several long deep breaths to calm myself. *If Derek doesn't want to open up to me, he has that right*, I told myself. What I needed right now was to simply enjoy what little time I had left with him, even if he wasn't acting like himself lately.

When I exited the rest room, I was feeling better. I grabbed a sandwich and paid for our lunch.

"Derek, I'm sorry," I tried one last time, but he didn't say anything back. We walked in silence and munched on our sandwiches on our way to Divination. It was probably better that way.

When we arrived, my mom was sitting behind the counter flipping through a catalog.

"Slow day?" I asked.

She shrugged. "It's lunch time. Everyone's out eating."

"And Sophie and Diane?"

"They're in the break room having lunch, too."

"Okay. We just came for some chocolates."

495

My mother smiled. "Well, I can help with that. How are you, Derek?"

He just shrugged, but that darkness in his eyes returned as he stared at my mother.

"Well," she said awkwardly. "You both like the truffles. Is that what you want today?"

"Sounds good," I agreed.

Derek turned up his nose. "I'll have peanut butter."

Jeez, he was really being cranky today. I wish I knew what his problem was. I pulled my sweatshirt sleeves over my hands and gripped onto the ends in my fists. I wasn't sure if it was because I was getting more annoyed at Derek or because I suddenly felt chilly.

My mother bent to the glass case where they displayed their small selection of chocolates. She placed three small truffles into a bag for me and three peanut butter truffles into a bag for Derek before standing and shutting the display case window behind her. In the few steps it took her to walk from the chocolates to the cash register, she somehow managed to trip. I watched in what felt like slow motion as her arms flailed and a terrified expression crossed her face. The bags of chocolates flew out of her hands, and then she was gone behind the counter.

"Mom!" I exclaimed, immediately rushing to the other side to help her up.

"I'm fine," she insisted from where she lay on the ground, but I could already see the bruise forming on the bottom of her chin where she'd clipped it against the stool they kept behind the counter.

"Mom." I reached out my hands for support and quickly glanced at Derek as if hoping he could help as well.

He stared at my mother, his jaw still clenched. He wasn't even trying to rescue the chocolates that had escaped. I was about ready to snap at him for his terrible behavior, but I refrained. Instead, I turned back to my mother, who'd made her way to a standing position.

"You have to be more careful," I warned. "You've been really clumsy lately."

She sighed. "I know. It was just this dumb rug. It caught my foot." She kicked at it to settle it back into place before brushing her blond bangs out of her eyes.

I didn't take my gaze off her as I made my way back to the other side of the counter. What was wrong with her? Had the pregnancy been affecting her, maybe making her dizzy?

"Are you sure you're okay?" I asked again, handing her the few chocolates I'd picked up from the ground.

She touched her bruise and winced. "I swear one of these days I'm going to throw this rug in the dumpster."

"That'd be too easy," I teased. "You need to hang it outside with a sign that says, 'This rug tried to kill me.'"

My mother laughed. "Are you telling me to publically shame my rug?"

I smiled playfully. "It's the only way to make it pay for the bruise on your chin."

Her laughter grew. "I'll think about that one. Sorry about your chocolates. I'll get you some new ones."

Several minutes later, Derek and I were on our way back to school with our chocolates in hand. He didn't say anything the whole way back, but he again increased his pace like he was frustrated about something. I didn't try to push it because I knew he wouldn't tell me anything anyway. His silence brought my mood down as we walked. I slumped to my locker disappointedly because I wasn't able to give Derek a proper good-bye, and I wasn't sure I ever would.

"You okay?" Emma asked at our lockers.

I bent to my textbooks and let my hair conceal my face. "I'm fine," I tried confidently in an attempt to convince more than just her. Even though she bought it, I couldn't bring myself to believe I was okay, not when I knew that nothing about my life had been "fine" in the past month.

CHAPTER 17

That night, I eagerly waited for my mother to arrive home from work. I lay on the couch and poked at my phone in anticipation of the sound of her car, but I wasn't really processing anything I saw or read on the screen. Instead, I was consumed with thoughts about my death. What was going to happen? And could I prevent it? At least with Sage, I had a timeline to work with. I had known when she was going to die. This time, I had nothing. All I knew was that I had to die to save the three people I loved most.

My mother arrived home late, but I needed to finally say goodbye to her the way I had with the rest of my friends. I didn't know when my death would come, but I needed one more night with her and Teddy.

"Mm," my mother said when she walked in the door. "It smells good. What's on the menu tonight?"

I sat up on the couch. "Teddy made chicken noodle soup. It was really good."

"Well, it certainly *smells* good."

I followed her to the kitchen. "Are you okay?"

She dropped her purse on the counter and turned to me. "Of course I'm okay."

My gaze locked on the bruise on her chin. "What about your fall? Doesn't it hurt?"

"Oh, it's nothing."

"Mom," I said sternly. "Stop brushing this stuff off. Is it the baby? What if something's wrong with my little sister?"

"No, sweetheart." She reached in the cupboard for a bowl. "What would make you say that?"

"Things keep happening to you, and I'm concerned. You've been so clumsy lately." I didn't want to leave her if something was wrong.

"I'm fine, really." She opened the lid on the pot that was still warm on the stove and scooped some soup into her bowl. "So, have you decided on a costume for the festival yet?"

I knew she was only trying to change the subject, but I figured it best to enjoy what little time I had left with her instead of fighting about whether she was okay or not.

"I don't know yet," I told her. I wasn't even sure if I'd make it until Saturday. "Mom, can we..." I trailed off because I wasn't sure how to finish that sentence. I wanted to do something with her, to make my time with her count, but I didn't know what to do.

She leaned against the counter and took a spoonful of soup. "Can we, what?" she asked once she swallowed.

I relaxed. "Can we make brownies?"

She smiled back at me.

Teddy joined us after my mom finished her soup, and he guided us through the recipe for homemade brownies. They weren't the kind my mom always made from a box. We had to use cocoa powder and flour and everything. We chatted and laughed, and thanks to Teddy's skill, the brownies came out without crusty edges like my mom normally made them.

All the fun I had with them nearly made me forget about how little time I had left. At least, I could only assume I didn't have much time left. Otherwise, why would the warning have come now? I contemplated this as I lay in bed that night. If I made it until Saturday, I'd have at least one more night to say goodbye to everyone since they'd all be at the festival.

And that's when it hit me. Everyone would be there, everyone I loved. It was supposed to happen then. My heart sank, and though I'd been full on brownies just moments ago, an empty feeling opened up in the pit of my stomach. On Saturday night, I was going to die.

The following day at school passed by hazily as I contemplated what it all meant. The three people I love most—my mom, Emma, and Robin—would all be at the festival on Saturday, and I was supposed to die to save them from... from what? The most dangerous thing at the festival would be tripping on a root along the haunted trail. What could possibly happen to them?

By the time lunch rolled around, I still hadn't come up with any good ideas. I sat by Emma, but Derek was nowhere to be seen. Emma and I chatted, and I put on a smile in hopes of making one of my last lunches with her a bit more memorable. She didn't talk about Derek, and I didn't bring him up. I only hoped they would work it all out when I was gone.

When I was gone... Why did I have to go? I only thought about it more and more as the day wore on. If I had to die to save three people, then it would be safe to assume they'd all be in the same place at once. Maybe if I could keep them all apart, nothing bad would happen to them.

~

"Hi, Sophie," I greeted when I entered Divination after school. A couple of younger kids were browsing through costumes nearby, but there weren't many left since it was so close to Halloween.

She looked up from behind the counter. "Hi, Crystal."

"Where's my mom at?"

"She and Diane are in the back organizing some stuff that Tammy and Sheryl asked us to bring for the festival. Need help with anything?"

I smiled reassuringly. "No, I'm good." I passed by the front counter and headed toward the storage room.

"Oh, I can use that in my tent," my mom said to Diane, grabbing the table cloth from her hands. She looked up and noticed me. "Crystal."

"Hi, Mom."

"What's up?" She pulled herself from the floor and dusted off.

I shrugged. "I just wanted to talk to you. Is that okay?"

"Sure, sweetheart. What is it?"

I glanced at Diane on the floor. "Diane looks busy. Can we talk in the break room?"

"Sure." My mom followed me across the hall to the small room where they kept their purses and snacks. A table with four chairs around it sat in the middle of the room.

I turned back to my mom and crossed my arms over my chest when the door clicked shut. "Mom, I need to know something, and I don't want you to lie to me this time."

"Lie to you?" she asked innocently. "I wouldn't lie to you, sweetie."

I chewed the dry skin on my lip because I wasn't sure exactly how to confront her about this. "Mom, the last time I asked you this, you completely diverted the question, so please be honest with me." I took a deep breath. "Have you ever *not* been able to help someone?"

Her brows shot up. "You want me to be honest with you? Then you're going to have to be honest with me." Her tone softened. "Crystal, what is this about?"

I swallowed hard, but it felt like trying to force needles down my throat. I had to lie to her. If I told her the truth, she'd want to take my place. Everyone I loved would die for me, and I couldn't let them do that. "Mom, I need you to trust me when I say that I can't tell you, okay?"

She bit the inside of her cheek. I wasn't sure if it was because she was disappointed or because she was thinking hard. "I don't like this." She crossed her arms over her chest and pursed her lips. "Can't you trust me enough to tell me?"

"It's not like that, Mom. I *do* trust you."

Her voice rose slightly. "Then why can't you tell me what's wrong with you? You're my daughter, and I'm supposed to protect you. How can I do that when I don't know what's wrong?"

And how can I save myself when I don't know how I'm going to die?

"Please believe me, Mom," I begged. "It will put people in danger if I tell you."

Her nostrils flared, and her breaths grew shallow. She took a deep breath to calm herself. "Okay. You really want to know if I could save everyone? The answer is no, I couldn't. Please, take a seat." She gestured to the break table, and I slid down in the chair farthest from the door. "Excuse me for a minute."

I didn't ask why she had to leave the room, but she came back a couple of minutes later with Sophie and Diane in tow.

"Uh, don't you have customers out in the shop?" I asked. My heart thumped in my chest nervously. What was so important that they all needed to be in here at once?

"We closed up early," my mother answered.

"But it's so close to Halloween! You can't close up."

"This seemed more important," my mom said.

She took the seat across from me while Sophie and Diane sat in the chairs on either side.

My mother shifted in her chair. "I asked Sophie and Diane in here to help me tell the story."

I blinked a few times. "Uh, okay. Why?"

They all exchanged a glance, but my mother was the one who spoke. "Because the story has to do with all of us. We were all there. We all watched Sam Marshall die."

CHAPTER 18

"Who's Sam Marshall?" I shifted my gaze between all of them. They swallowed in unison like they had all suddenly formed a lump in their throats. My pulse quickened in response.

"We knew him in college," Diane explained.

"He was a friend of your father's. He was also my sister Theresa's boyfriend," Sophie clarified.

I drew in a sharp breath. "Oh, my gosh. Justine's mom's boyfriend?" It took me a second to absorb the information. Did that make Sam Marshall Justine's father? I'd never met her dad, but I thought her parents were still together. Plus, Justine's last name was Hanson, not Marshall. Apparently my question was written in my expression because Sophie quickly clarified.

"He was her boyfriend at the time. Justine's dad came into the picture later."

I hadn't realized how quick my pulse had become, but it returned to normal once Sophie explained. "Is that why she dropped out of college? Because her boyfriend died?"

Sophie shook her head. "No. This happened about a year before she dropped out."

My mother spoke next. "I met Sam shortly after I met Sophie and then her sister, Theresa. It wasn't long after we formed our Sensitive Society group. Ever since I met him, I kept having visions of his death, how he was going to get hit by a bus while on his bike."

My eyes widened. That must have been terrible for her.

"I couldn't feel anything strange from him," Sophie said, "and Diane couldn't see anything from his past out of the ordinary. Your mom was the one who could see his future, but we were there to support her 100 percent."

I drew closer to the table, completely engrossed in their story.

Diane took over. "We invited him to my dorm room one night to warn him about it. We thought maybe if he didn't ride his bike around anymore, it wouldn't ever happen."

"But it did," I finished for her.

My mother nodded. "The hardest part wasn't telling him that we were psychic. It was warning him of his death."

Sophie rested her elbows on the table and leaned closer to me. "At first when we told him we were psychic, he just kind of scoffed. He said he saw the posters around campus and thought our 'little joke' was kind of funny."

"We tried to tell him we were serious," Diane continued, "but he didn't believe us. I remember him asking, 'And why should I care?'"

My mother swallowed hard. "And that's when I told him about his death. I told him I'd seen it and that if he didn't trust us, he was going to die."

The surface of my skin began to heat. My mother had told me about how people had rejected her and her abilities before. A boyfriend in high school had told everyone she was a witch, and she had to transfer schools. This was another one of those stories, I knew, and she was finally giving me the details. I couldn't bear to think about all the people who had rejected her throughout the years.

"Then what?" I asked.

"He freaked," Diane answered. "He told us it was true what everyone was saying, that we were all witches."

My breath caught in my throat. I couldn't believe what they'd been through.

Sophie spoke. "I think he was more scared than anything. I'm not sure if he really believed we were witches, but we certainly freaked him out."

"He just kind of ran after that," my mom told me. "We chased after him. I remember calling out to him and asking him to trust me, but he just kept running down the hall and out of the building. When we made it out of the dorm hall, he had already grabbed his bike from the bike rack next to Diane's dorm, and he was riding away. We chased after him, and that's when it happened."

Her eyes glistened with tears. When I glanced around the table, I realized they were all on the brink of crying.

Sophie stared into the distance, not really looking at anything. "He was so scared. He wasn't watching where he was going. He crossed the street just as the city bus was coming down it. We rushed over to him, but it was too late to do anything."

Silence settled over the room until my mother's whisper cut through it. "I watched him take his last breath. I held his hand while he died."

I wanted to cry, but nothing came out. How did my mother handle her abilities after that? Everything I'd gone through over the past few weeks now seemed trivial in the grand scheme of things. Except, if they couldn't save Sam, then would I be able to save myself?

"I don't get it," I said. "If Sam only died because he was running away from you, wouldn't that make it a self-fulfilling prophecy?"

My mom shook her head and gazed down at her hands. "It wasn't like that, exactly. In my visions, it always happened a different way. He was wearing a different shirt, and the bus number was different. I remember thinking the same thing, but after looking at it all closer, I realized his real death wasn't the same one I was seeing in my visions."

"It's like he was always meant to die that way," Diane told me. "It almost didn't matter if we told him or not because he'd always end up getting hit by a bus one way or another."

My head hurt thinking about it. I didn't understand how I could save Sage from her death but they couldn't save Sam. If Sage was supposed to die from suicide several months ago, did that mean she would die from suicide later? If I didn't die this Saturday, would I end up dying later on to save the people I loved?

I voiced my thoughts. "Why can we save some people from death and not others?"

They all sighed in unison as if collectively agreeing this was a difficult question to answer.

Sophie was the first to compose herself. "Sometimes we're *supposed* to save them."

"I don't get it," I complained again. "If we're supposed to save the people we're led to, then why would Mom have a vision of Sam in the first place? Doesn't that mean she was supposed to save him?"

"Not necessarily," my mother pointed out. "Sometimes the things we see don't mean anything at all. Maybe my visions of Sam weren't even meant for me."

Though it was difficult to wrap my head around, I understood on some level. Sometimes I knew people's secrets without even caring about the answer, but I'd never seen something so *huge* without being able to help.

"Or maybe it wasn't even about his death," Diane said.

I cocked my head. "What do you mean?"

"Maybe it wasn't about saving him. Maybe it was about teaching *us* something. We all became very close after that day. We learned a lot about keeping our secrets... well, secret."

My mother reached across the table and rested a hand on mine. She spoke soothingly. "Crystal, I'm sorry if that's not the story you wanted to hear."

I wiped a stray tear from my eye. "No, it's okay. I think that's exactly what I needed to hear."

I left the break room mulling over their story again. My dad's warning wasn't about my death and how I could prevent it. It was about my loved ones' deaths and how I could *save* them. I had around 48 hours left of my life—if I was right about this all happening at the festival—and I was going to make it count.

I passed by the costumes on my way out, and one caught my eye. I finally knew what I was going to dress as for Halloween.

CHAPTER 19

"*C*rystal, can I be honest with you?" Emma asked at lunch on Friday.

I looked up from my pizza. At least we were having something tasty on one of my last days. "Sure." Though I was dreading what was to come, I spoke confidently. There was no point in making my last few hours miserable or causing others to worry about me.

Emma shifted in her chair. "I've been feeling... strange."

I stopped chewing. "Strange? What do you mean?"

She shrugged. "I'm not sure I can explain it. We haven't done our psychic practice sessions in a while, so maybe I'm getting rusty, but I think I'm feeling something. Maybe it's a bad omen?"

Through Emma's practice, she'd become talented at feeling good or bad about a situation since everyone had some intuition. My abilities had been so weak lately that I'd almost forgotten there was a chance she could pick up on my bad vibes.

"I'm sure it's nothing," I lied to her. It was the only option I had. "It's probably just about your breakup with Derek. Are you second guessing going to the festival?"

"You think he'll be there?"

I forced a look of uncertainty on my face, even though I knew he said he probably wouldn't come. It was the best way to distract her from trying to weed the truth of my prophecy out of me. "He might be."

She looked down at her food. "Maybe I can just avoid him, unless you were planning to hang out with him."

"Don't be silly," I told her. I still felt bad that I hadn't been able to give

Derek a proper goodbye and figure out what was wrong with him, but I didn't know what else to do when he wouldn't talk to me about it. "If you come, then I'll hang out with you."

If you come...

The words echoed in my mind. What if there was a chance she didn't come? Then the three people I loved most wouldn't be in the same place at the same time, and I might have a chance of preventing whatever was supposed to happen. Unless whatever it was wasn't supposed to happen tomorrow night...

Make up your mind, Crystal, I scolded myself. *Are you going to die for them or not?*

I would. I would die for them *if* I had to. But what if it never came to that? What if keeping them apart was how I saved them?

"Maybe you're getting sick," I suggested. "If you're getting sick, you probably shouldn't come to the festival. You don't even have a costume, do you?"

Emma's face fell. "You're right. It's probably just a mixture of heartbreak and the flu or something."

"I think maybe you should go home and get some rest over the weekend."

"I *do* feel kind of sick," she admitted.

Except I knew it wasn't the flu. She could tell something bad was coming. She just didn't know what her intuition was telling her.

"Well, go ahead and rest over the weekend, okay?" I said.

~

After school, I returned home and killed time by completing my homework. I wasn't sure if it would matter, though. After Teddy arrived home, I told him I was going on a walk, and I strolled the few blocks to Divination. I knew my mom wouldn't be around, but I double checked anyway.

"Is my mom here?" I asked Sophie after waiting for her to check out a couple of customers.

"I'm afraid not. She's attending a last-minute festival meeting for us." Sophie checked the clock on the wall. "She should be back in under an hour if you're looking for her."

"No. It's okay. I was just wondering." I glanced over at Diane, who was helping a young boy pick out costume makeup. My heart sank. If something was going to happen, I still had to say goodbye to Sophie and Diane, but I didn't know how. I turned back to Sophie. "I still don't have a costume."

"Oh, that's no problem. Let's see what we have." She came around the side of the counter.

There weren't many costumes left on the racks since the Halloween festival was tomorrow, but the costume I had my eye on yesterday was still there.

"Let's see," Sophie mused. "What do we have that will fit you? I think there's still a pumpkin costume."

I wrinkled my nose as she held it up. "Do I have to stuff it?"

She laughed back at me. "I suppose you could. Balled up newspaper works well, and there's a string at the bottom where you can pull it tight so the stuffing doesn't fall out."

I reached for the costume. It might at least be fun to try it on, even if I didn't want it. "Well, let's see what it looks like."

I hurried into a dressing room and pulled it on over my head. When I emerged, Diane was done attending to the customer, and I had both of their attention. When they spotted me, they both burst out laughing.

"This is why it's still on the rack," Diane joked. "No one wants to be caught dead in that thing."

"So, why'd you stock it?" I teased back.

"You'll have to ask your mother," she responded. "That one was her idea."

I twirled around, showing off the awful costume. "Let's try the next one."

Diane and Sophie put me in a banana costume next, followed by a dress designed to look like a Skittles bag.

"What's with all the food?" I asked with a laugh.

"That's all we have left!" Sophie defended. "All the good ones are gone."

I knew that wasn't true, but I was enjoying dressing up for them. We made it through another half dozen costumes and another half hour of laughing together before I finally mentioned the costume I had my eye on.

"Oh, I didn't realize we still had that one," Diane said. She strolled down the aisle and pulled it off the rack. "It looks about your size. Go ahead and try it on."

I did, and it hugged me perfectly in all the right places as if it was tailor made for my body. When I stepped out of the dressing room, Diane and Sophie both whistled at me.

"You like it?" I asked.

"It's perfect," Diane raved.

"It looks great," Sophie agreed.

I checked the price tag and breathed a sigh of relief that I had enough cash to buy it. "Thanks. I like it, too."

I retreated into the dressing room and placed the costume back on its hanger. When I exited the dressing room, I walked over to the checkout counter, and Sophie rang up my total. I left Divination that night both happy about my costume and comforted by the fun time I'd just had with the two women who were like the aunts I never had.

∼

After I arrived home, I called Robin. I'd already convinced Emma to take it easy and skip the festival, but just as reassurance, I didn't want Robin there, either. If I was right and this was when it was supposed to happen, I didn't want any of the three people I loved the most to be near each other.

"What are your plans tomorrow?" I asked him.

"I was going to come over early and head to the festival with you. You're going to love my costume."

He still hadn't told me what he was going to be, and I hadn't bothered mentioning my costume idea, either. My eyes fell on it in my open closet, but I tore my gaze away so I could focus on the conversation Robin and I were having.

"It's not even going to be that fun," I lied.

"What do you mean? It's Halloween. Of course it'll be fun."

"Well, I'm going to be helping out with some of the booths, so you won't even see me much." It was a lie. I was going to help with the setup, but other than that, I'd be free to enjoy the rest of the night with him. But keeping everyone apart was the best option. Then nothing bad would happen to all of them at once.

"What booths are you helping with?" he asked. "Maybe I can volunteer, too."

I tried to think of a booth that would be half believable. I couldn't tell him I was working the kissing booth, but maybe he'd believe I was helping at the apple bobbing booth. "I'll be all over the place," I finally said. "I'm going to be pretty busy."

"Well, maybe I can meet up with Emma and Derek while you're working. Surely you can take a break and spend some time with us for a bit."

I swallowed hard. This wasn't working. "Emma and Derek broke up, remember?"

"Right. Well, I mean, I'll find someone to hang out with while you're busy. And if all else fails, I'll just listen to the band they're getting to play."

I could only see one way out of this. It was the only way to be *sure* nothing would happen tomorrow.

"Robin," I said sternly. The tears were already rising to my eyes, but I kept my voice steady. I couldn't risk him knowing how much the words would hurt me. I paused for a moment because I knew what I was going to say next would tear me apart, but I quickly worked up the courage. It was my only option to ensuring we'd all be safe, at least for now. "I don't want you to come."

The words sounded like they were coming from someone else's mouth. How could I possibly say something like that to him? Before he had a chance to speak, I reminded myself that if I could get past Saturday without anyone getting hurt, Robin and I would have plenty of time to make up.

"You don't want me to come?"

His words felt like a punch to the gut, but I didn't let my voice waver. "Please don't come."

"Why not?" His voice was so small, so injured. "Is this about the fight we had recently? I thought we made up."

I pressed my lips together, hoping to hold back the tears. I couldn't believe what I was saying to him, but I had to stick to my lie. "I'm not over it yet."

"I don't get it. What happened since we last saw each other? Why are you mad at me again?" He spoke slowly, each word ripping open my heart even more.

"I never stopped being mad at you." My voice almost cracked, but I forced it to remain strong. I reminded myself that hurting him now was better than walking to my own death and leaving him. It would tear him apart, and maybe, just maybe, I could spare him the heartbreak while saving myself in the process.

"Oh," he said softly. "I didn't realize. I guess I'll give you your space."

I hung up without even saying goodbye and then threw myself into my pillow. My shoulders heaved as I drowned the pillow in sobs. At least it muffled the noise so my mom and Teddy wouldn't hear.

After getting ready for bed, I whispered to thin air, hoping my father would hear. If he had heard me before, I had faith that he'd hear me now. I asked him for a sign so I'd know if I was making the right choice. Was it supposed to happen at the festival anyway, or was I focusing on the wrong event? Did I do the right thing by convincing Emma and Robin to stay away, or was I only ruining my relationships with them?

By the time I fell asleep, I still had no idea if I had made the right choice.

CHAPTER 20

$\mathcal{T}$he day of the festival arrived, and I couldn't quite tell what I was feeling. It was neither good nor bad. I didn't know what else to do about it all, so I figured I'd just take the situation as it came. To keep myself busy, I headed down to the park with my mom to help them set up. Volunteers hustled around the area, setting up the booths they were running while others headed into the neighboring woods to finish up the last touches on the haunted trail. A large stage stood as the highlight of it all, where a band would be playing later on in the night.

I started by helping my mom set up her booth. It wasn't much. We put up her tent together and then carried in her table, chairs, and props. I situated her tablecloth and electric candles on the table before adding her final center piece, a crystal ball. My mom didn't do real crystal ball readings at the festival—that was just for show—but she did give real tarot card readings.

"Is that it?" I asked, looking around the tent to see if we'd missed anything.

"It looks like it," she replied. "The only thing left is for me to get into my costume, but we have plenty of time. There are lots more booths we can help set up." She pulled the tent flap aside for me.

We spent the rest of the morning helping where we could. I spent some time assisting Sophie for a while before helping Diane. After lunch, which was provided for the volunteers, Mom and I took a short break to head home and get into our costumes.

I didn't apply any more makeup than normal, but when I looked into the mirror after putting on my costume, complete with black tights and

511

Mary Jane heels, it felt like I'd been transformed. I never really thought black was my color, but in this outfit, with its blue accents that complemented my eyes, it suited me. The top was modest, but the tutu skirt supplied just enough of a sexy flare. I let my long hair fall over my shoulders and added the final touch: a black pointed hat.

When I stepped into the doorway of my mom's bathroom, where she was applying her makeup, she gasped. She paused and caught my eye in the mirror. "Where'd you get that costume?"

I twirled around to show it off. "Sophie sold it to me. I think it suits me." I also knew exactly what my mom thought about it, and she wasn't pleased.

She pressed her lips together and turned to me. "Why would you want to be a witch for Halloween?"

I didn't let her discomfort bother me. "I know you've been hurt by the term before, but I guess this is my way of embracing who I am."

"Crystal, you're not a witch. You're a psychic."

A shred of guilt eased its way into my heart. I didn't choose the costume to hurt her. "But if this is the way other people see me, I don't want it to bother me. I can do things that no one can explain. In some ways, it does seem like magic. And this," I gestured to my costume, "is me telling the world that it doesn't matter what they say. I love myself for who I am." *Even if I may never get my abilities back*, I thought to myself.

My mother didn't say anything as she pulled me into a hug. I stiffened in surprise before relaxing into it.

After about a moment, she finally spoke. "Crystal, I am *so* proud of you." She drew away to look me in the eyes. "I would have never acted the way you do when I was your age. You're beyond your years. Don't ever change."

I smiled at her in response.

～

When we returned to the park, there weren't many cars around since the festival hadn't officially started yet.

"Well, I'm going to go get situated in my tent," my mother announced. "Things will get bustling here pretty quickly."

I glanced around. I didn't have any volunteer ideas in mind, and it's not like I had anyone to hang out with when I'd convinced my friends not to come.

"I guess I'll just wait around until I see someone I know," I told her.

"Okay, have fun." She waved and then headed off toward her tent.

I scanned the area for a moment and then decided to sit at the picnic tables by the food. On my way there, I spotted Teddy in his police uniform. He had just said goodbye to one of the volunteers he was talking to when I approached him from behind.

"You're not working at the station this year?" I asked to get his attention.

He turned to me, a smile on his face. "Nope. Most of the town is going to be here tonight, and they wanted two of us patrolling the festival."

"So you got stuck on duty?"

He shrugged. "I don't mind."

"Well, have fun," I told him before making my way to the picnic tables. He headed in the opposite direction.

I took a seat and again glanced around. Without my friends here, it was going to be a boring night, but at least no one would get hurt. Since I didn't have anything else to do, I pulled out my phone and scrolled through it mindlessly. After nearly 20 minutes of sitting there bored out of my mind, a shadow crossed my table. I looked up to find Justine and Kelli standing above me. Kelli wore a short red dress with a crimson hood over her head, and Justine was dressed as a sexy scarecrow.

"Hey!" I greeted enthusiastically. I hopped up to give them both a hug. "How are you guys?"

"We're great," Justine answered. "How have you been?"

What could I say to that? "I've been fine," I told her vaguely.

"Your costume is so cute," Kelli complimented.

I glanced down at my dress. "Thanks. Yours are both cute, too. So, any plans for the night?"

Justine elbowed Kelli playfully. "Kelli's volunteering for the kissing booth this year. I'm starting at the apple bobbing booth, and then I'm helping with the ring toss. Then we have the rest of the night free."

"I've been here all day helping set up, but I didn't volunteer to run any booths." At the time they were taking volunteers, I'd thought my friends would be here to spend the night with me.

Justine glanced around. "Where's everyone else? Emma? Derek? Is your boyfriend coming?"

I shook my head and opted for the easiest answer. "They were all busy tonight."

"Well, if you need some company, you can help me run my stations," Justine offered.

I smiled. "Thank you."

"Hey," Kelli said, "maybe we can meet up after we're done volunteering and we can go through the haunted trail together."

We all agreed that was a good idea, but eventually, Kelli went her own way while I trailed behind Justine and told her about Emma and Derek's breakup.

"That sucks," she said. "They made a cute couple."

Throughout the next few hours, I hung by Justine. She seemed to know everyone around, even the people I didn't know from neighboring towns. In the last 10 minutes of Justine's scheduled time at the ring toss booth, I spotted red hair in the crowd.

"I'll be right back," I told Justine before heading toward Sage. She wore an orange and white dress with matching pointed ears. "You made it! And as a fox. You look cute!" I pulled her into a hug.

She drew away from me with a smile on her face. "Thanks! So, are you working?"

I glanced back at Justine at the ring toss booth. She was smiling and handing out rings to small children. I turned back toward Sage. "No. I was just hanging out with a friend. She's almost done."

"Oh. Where's everyone else?"

Again, I went with the easy answer. "They were all busy."

She tilted her head in question. "I thought Robin was coming."

"Something came up. Anyway, we're headed down the haunted trail in a few minutes if you want to come."

"I'd love to!" Sage bounced on her toes in excitement.

We made our way back to Justine's booth and waited a few minutes for the next volunteer to come and take her spot.

"I asked a few friends to come along with us," Justine told me once she was done with her shift. "I hope you don't mind."

"Not at all," I answered as we walked toward Kelli's booth.

"It's great seeing so many people from high school again. It seems a lot came back for the weekend." Justine waved at another person she knew.

"Well, you know, our town's Halloween festival is kind of a big deal," I joked.

We met up with Kelli and then found a couple of Justine's friends.

"I'm scared," Sage faked, grabbing my elbow on our way to the entrance of the haunted trail. We followed behind Justine and her friends, with Sage and me in the back of the group.

"Oh, relax. It's just volunteers in costumes," I laughed.

"Hey, sometimes you can't tell the difference between zombies and kids in makeup. I've seen enough of those shows, and the effects are creepy."

"Don't worry. I won't let any zombies get you. I can't make any promises about the vampires, though."

Sage giggled. "I'd take care of the vampires, but I left my stakes at home."

We made it through the haunted trail unscathed, though we all jumped a few times. When we emerged from the trees, our group split up. Sage and I headed toward the aisles of booths to explore the games. On our way, I spotted curly dark hair I recognized all too well.

"Emma!" I practically shouted in surprise before we even met up with her. She was dressed in Gryffindor robes and noticed me making my way to her. "What are you doing here?" I asked as soon as I was close enough. "You're supposed to be sick!"

She shrugged. "I feel fine, honestly. I changed my mind about coming. I couldn't sit around at home knowing all this fun stuff was going on without me." She gestured around to the games around us. "I think it's silly for me to shut down just because Derek broke up with me. I can't let him control me like this. Besides, my mom and sister were coming anyway, and I figured, why not?"

Honestly, I was proud of her for realizing that moving on was the best option, but why couldn't she have figured this out tomorrow? At least if Robin stayed away, things should still turn out fine, I hoped.

Except that before I had a chance to respond to Emma, my hopes were instantly shattered. Sage tapped me on the shoulder and pointed. I followed her gaze and noticed a pirate with a peg leg walking toward us.

My face grew hot in worry. "Robin! You—you weren't supposed to come." My eyes shifted between Robin and Emma. Neither of them were supposed to be here. This couldn't be happening.

"I couldn't stay away." He stopped so close to me that I could feel the heat radiating off his body.

I worried that perhaps he could hear my heart hammering against my rib cage. The muscles in my face twitched as I tried to force the worry out of my expression, but he showed no indication that he noticed my unease.

Robin glanced between Sage and Emma. "Do you two ladies mind if I have a word alone with Crystal?"

Sage and Emma both nodded and walked off together to a nearby booth.

I looked up into Robin's eyes, my own beginning to glisten with tears. "Robin, you shouldn't be here."

His hands came up to rest on my biceps. "I couldn't stand not talking to you. Whatever it is, we can work this out. I needed to see you in person. Plus, I couldn't let my authentic peg leg go to waste."

I glanced down at his leg and almost laughed. He was right when he said I'd like his costume. When I looked back up into his eyes, though, my chest constricted, and my throat closed up. They shouldn't all be here at the same time.

"Robin," I said quietly, "I told you I didn't want you to come."

"I know, but I'm a stubborn guy. I want to talk about it, whatever it is."

"Robin, I—" I paused. It was going to happen one way or another. The three people I loved most were here in one spot, and as much as I wanted to stop it, I knew now that I couldn't control the future. It was best to simply enjoy the present.

I swallowed the lump in my throat before speaking. "I'm glad you're here right now. Let's just have fun, okay?"

He pulled me into a hug and kissed the top of my head, which really ended up being a kiss on my pointed witch hat. "That sounds like a good idea. I love you, Crystal."

I had to force the tears back. "I love you, too, Robin."

He took my hand, which helped steady it, and led me over to Sage and Emma.

"So." Emma looked between us with bright eyes. "Where should we start?"

Robin looked around before gesturing to the carnival game in front of us. "This looks like as good of place as any."

We spent the next half hour making our way down the aisle. I tried to let go and have fun, but my senses—all but my sixth one—were on full alert. I jumped when a balloon popped and tensed when a nearby child screamed in excitement.

Robin gave my hand a gentle squeeze. "You okay?"

I gazed up at him and gave a fake shrug. "Yeah. I'm fine."

I'm not fine, I wanted to say. *But if it comes down to it, I hope you will be.*

Emma hopped in excitement when her ring landed on the end of a bottle. Sage high-fived her in congratulations.

Emma turned toward me. "Let's head down the next aisle. I want to visit your mom's tent."

"No," I said too quickly. Everyone seemed to notice, and I quickly forced myself to relax. "I mean, it's a popular booth, so maybe we should wait until a little later in the night. Then there won't be a line." Hopefully my friends would forget about it or be too tired to visit her. I couldn't let the three people I loved most be together.

"Okay, well, we can at least go see how long the line is," Emma suggested.

"How about we go through the haunted forest," I countered. "There will be a longer line for it when it gets really dark out, so we shouldn't have to wait now."

"We already went down the haunted trail," Sage pointed out.

"Come on." Robin pulled at my hand. "Let's just go down the next aisle."

Emma rushed off in front of us, and I had no choice but to follow as Robin dragged me behind him.

"I guess you were right," Emma said, looking toward my mom's tent. "There is a long line."

I followed her gaze and noticed curly brown hair at the front of the line. I had the sudden urge to call out to him and get him to join our group before a sinking feeling in my chest reminded me that Emma and Derek didn't want to be by each other right now. If he wasn't hanging with us, who was he hanging out with? Hadn't he said he wasn't going to come?

I watched as my mother pulled aside the flap on her tent and a young girl stepped out. She rushed over to a man I guessed to be her dad and jumped in excitement. She was probably telling him about the fortune she'd received. Derek stepped into the tent behind my mom.

"I kind of want to try the apple bobbing booth," Sage admitted.

I pulled my gaze from my mother's tent and back to my friends. "You can go ahead. I don't really want to right now."

"Yeah," Emma agreed with me, "I'll mess up my makeup."

"I'll try apple bobbing with you," Robin offered, releasing my hand.

A moment later, a voice called my name from behind me. I turned to find Hope dressed as a unicorn rushing toward me with a smile on her face. She plowed into me and squeezed me into a tight hug.

I hugged her back. "Hey, Hope! Are you having fun?"

"Yes!" she answered enthusiastically. "Look what I won!" She held up a small stuffed animal shaped like a cat.

"That's awesome!" I answered just as Hope's mom, Melinda, caught up with her.

"Hi, Crystal," Melinda said, taking Hope's hand. "How was volleyball season?"

"It was good. I'm kind of sad it's over."

"Yeah, but at least you have another season. You'll be ready to start babysitting again on Monday, right?"

I couldn't look her in the eyes, so I stared down at the cat in Hope's hands instead. "I hope so," was all I could say.

"Well, have fun at the rest of the festival," Melinda told me with a wave while Hope dragged her off toward a new game.

I nodded back. "You, too."

I turned back toward my friends, who were giggling their heads off at the apple bobbing booth. Robin came up for air, still hopeless in the apple department. I couldn't help but laugh along when he plunged his head back under the water and fought with an apple that bounced away from him every time he came close. Sage pulled her head out of the water, and her hands shot up in victory. An apple was trapped between her teeth, and Robin was still engaged in a losing battle. Mine and Emma's laughter only grew louder, but a split second later when I heard my mother's voice, my laughter died. I turned toward the sound, facing the stage. A woman dressed as a gypsy stood at the microphone and was trying to get everyone's attention. It was the first time the microphone had been turned on all night since the band wasn't scheduled to start playing for another half hour.

Emma noticed me staring. "Crystal, what's your mom doing?"

"Can I please have everyone's attention?" she repeated into the microphone.

"I don't know," I answered Emma. "Maybe Sheryl and Tammy asked her to make an announcement." I inched my way down the aisle until I stood at the back of the grassy area in front of the stage.

Conversations seemed to die out around us, and the area grew quiet. When my mother was satisfied that she had enough of the audience's attention, she spoke again.

"I'm sorry to interrupt your night, but I have an announcement to make, and it can't wait." She glanced toward the side of the stage and then back at the audience. "It's not so much an announcement as a confession, and it's time that I spoke up."

A confession? What could she be talking about?

"Crystal," Emma repeated from beside me, "what's your mom doing?"

The hairs on my arms stood up, and I couldn't answer. More people had gathered around the stage to listen.

My mother continued. "I think it's time that Peyton Springs knew the truth." She hesitated and glanced off stage. For a moment, an eerie silence hung in the air before she spoke again. "My tarot card booth you all like, the one you all say is so accurate… well, it's for real."

My heart nearly stopped in my chest. She told me she'd never tell the community. Why was she doing this now?

She didn't stop. "The truth is, I'm not who you all think I am. Because of what I can do, I've hurt people, and it's time you all know the story of Sam Marshall."

CHAPTER 21

I didn't give myself another second to ask questions. Something was seriously wrong. I didn't know what it was yet, but I knew I had to stop my mother from telling the whole town our secret. Even she said it was best if the town didn't know. I pushed through the crowd as she began her story. When I rushed up the stairs on the side of the stage, I immediately noticed a figure standing with his back toward me. His arms were crossed over his chest, and he was staring at my mom on stage.

I drew in a deep breath. "Derek, do you have any idea what's going on? Why is my mom doing this?"

He turned to me slowly, a wide smile plastered on his face.

My pulse quickened. "Derek, what's going on?"

If possible, I could swear his grin grew wider. He spoke as if amused. "You're so stupid."

I took a step back, stunned. "Derek, what's *wrong* with you? You've never been as mean as you have lately. You haven't been acting like yourself…"

He noticed the realization cross my face, and he nodded in satisfaction.

I distanced myself another step until I gripped the railing to the stairs. My eyes widened in horror, and I completely froze in place. How could I not have realized it before? Derek had been so different lately. I had assumed something major was bothering him, but nothing made enough sense to cause such a drastic change. I should have paid closer attention, done my research, and realized such a thing was possible.

I spoke slowly. "You're not Derek, are you? You haven't been for a long time."

"Bingo." He laughed.

"Oh, my god!" I cried. Worry about my mother's confession faded as I faced the new problem standing right in front of me. "Who are you? What have you done to Derek?"

"Oh, relax," he said like we were having the most casual conversation in the world. "He's still in here." He tapped his head with his index finger. "I just needed to borrow him for a while."

"A while? How long has it been?" I quickly shifted through my memory, trying to remember when Derek had changed. It was around the time I had stayed home from school, when we held that séance. A gasp escaped my lips, and my hand flew to my mouth in shock. I knew now why I hadn't seen the shadow ghost since we held the séance. The ghost was never my father to begin with.

"You possessed him when we contacted you," I accused. That's what the explosion of energy was about. Anger boiled in my blood, momentarily masking my fear.

He began pacing, but at least he was keeping a generous amount of distance between us. It was strange to watch Derek move in front of me, knowing it wasn't him who was speaking. "Hmm... maybe you're not as stupid as I thought."

Suddenly, a lot more about the past few weeks made sense. "Derek never broke up with Emma, did he? It was *you*."

"Ah, so maybe you are a bright girl."

"My headaches? That was you, too?" My heart hammered against my rib cage, and I thought I might nearly fall over. Luckily, I was still gripping onto the railing to steady myself.

"I was wondering when you'd catch on to that one. I mean, come on," he spread his arms wide mockingly, "you only got headaches when I was around."

And my headache was only returning again. I wanted to put as much distance as I could between myself and the man standing in front of me, but if Derek really was still in there somewhere, I couldn't just abandon him.

"How did you know so much about Derek?" I asked in an attempt to make sense of it all. I forced my breath to slow. I couldn't let him see how much he was terrifying me.

He shrugged. "I didn't. I just played along. It was so simple. I claimed I lost his locker combination, and the school gave me his class schedule. When I didn't know how to get to the kid's house, I asked your friend to walk me home a couple of times. I mostly didn't talk to the kid's family.

And you were easy to convince. It's like you didn't even know enough about your friend to tell the difference."

"I did!" I defended. I knew *something* was up, but never in a million years would I have guessed it was a *possession*. I didn't even know for sure that was possible, not until now. I briefly thought back to the time Olivia Owen spoke through me. She'd done the same thing to Kelli. But I'd never thought of it as possession. She hadn't actually inhabited my body; she'd just spoken through me. Was this the same type of thing?

He stopped pacing and stood still in front of me, tapping his foot. "There's so much you still don't know, Crystal."

I swallowed, forcing my voice to remain strong. "Who are you?"

His brows shot up. "You haven't figured that one out yet?" He glanced behind himself at my mother, who was still giving her confession at the microphone.

I knew I had to get to her, but I couldn't with him in my way. I wasn't even sure which was more important at the moment: my mom or Derek?

He scoffed. "Figures she never mentioned me." His hard gaze met mine, sending my heart pounding again. He plastered a smile of amusement back on his face. "You see, Crystal, I'm the guy your mother killed."

I drew in a sharp, hot breath. "You have the wrong person. My mother never killed anyone." My grip tightened around the railing.

He threw back his head and laughed. It was the kind of laugh that sent a shiver down my spine. He began pacing again. "The wrong person? I don't think so. Not this time."

I forced myself to speak evenly even though my breathing wavered. "This time?"

"When I first saw you on the SMU campus, I thought *you* were your mother. You have the same blond hair, same blue eyes, and same nose. You see, at first, I didn't realize how much time had passed. I saw this girl around campus that I could have sworn was Theresa, and all of a sudden, it's like I woke up. The strange thing was, I still knew what had happened to me. Then you showed up, and I followed you. It wasn't until I actually saw your mother that I realized you weren't her. And then the rest made sense. They called you Crystal Frost, so I knew that meant Andrea had married David. I didn't know who the new guy was, though. Teddy? That's his name, right? So, tell me. What happened to David, then?"

The surprise on my face as he spoke was evident in my wide eyes. Could he really mean Theresa Hanson, Justine's mom? And if he knew my parents, that meant...

"You're Sam Marshall," I stated confidently. It wasn't a question.

He missed a step in his pace and then planted his feet firmly on the ground. "So, you *have* heard of me. Interesting..."

It all made sense now. Justine had said she felt like someone was watching her, and she was right. It was Sam all along. He thought Justine was her mother, and somehow that awakened his spirit. Then he'd been following her around campus.

"That's why you went into the shop asking my mom about college. You wanted to make sure she was the right person. Derek never was worried about his future."

He nodded with a haunting grin that made my skin crawl. "Right again."

"You were so interested in her, always asking to come over to my house or go to the shop. And Diane's visions? She said it was like she was seeing her own memories through someone else's eyes. She was talking about the day you died. She was seeing it from *your* perspective." Everything that happened over the last few weeks finally came together in my mind. I didn't need my sixth sense to confirm it.

"Well, I don't know anything about what things those *witches* see," Sam responded.

I had the sudden urge to punch him in the face at the term, but I still saw Derek standing in front of me and couldn't bring myself to hurt him. Derek wasn't exactly a huge guy, but I wasn't big either. I'd have a hard time fighting him.

"I see you've joined them," he said, gesturing to my costume.

I gritted my teeth but only reacted by raising my voice. "So, what is this?" I gestured to my mom on stage, who still hadn't noticed me. She was nearing the end of Sam's story. I caught a glimpse of Sophie and Diane near the stairs on the other end of the stage. They were watching my mom as warily as I was, no doubt wondering whether they should stop her or not.

Sam laughed again, and though he was in Derek's body, it didn't sound anything like my friend. "It's my revenge, of course. You were actually the one to give me the idea."

I released the clench on my jaw to speak. "How do you figure that?"

"At first, I thought I'd just kill her. An eye for an eye. I even tried a couple of times."

My breath quickened, and another piece of the puzzle came together. That's why my mom had been so clumsy lately. "The box cutter that could have slit her wrist, the crystal ball that could have cracked her skull, her tripping on the rug... That was all *you!*"

His laughter never seemed to end. "Of course it was!"

"You were there each time," I thought aloud. "First as a ghost, then in Derek's body."

"Right again. I even tried killing you when I thought you were your mother."

I instantly thought back to the bus ride back from SMU and the tree that would have fallen on our bus had I not screamed. Did that mean he had something to do with my first accident? *No,* I thought almost immediately. That happened before I visited SMU. All this stuff with Sam happened only after we spotted each other in the cafeteria that day.

"I was beginning to lose my patience," he continued. "After all, it took some extra energy to make the objects move seemingly on their own. I had to wait a bit for my energy to return and try again. I could have framed the kid," he gestured to Derek's body with a shrug, "but he didn't have anything to do with it. I just needed a body for the time being so I could actually communicate with people. It's not like you were any help with that."

I almost bit back with an explanation about why I hadn't been able to help him earlier, but he continued without missing a beat.

"Then you mentioned a better revenge is public humiliation. And you were *so* right. Now she has to *live* with what she's done!"

"Sam," I pleaded. "I can help you. She didn't kill you. It wasn't her fault. Can't we talk this out?"

He threw his head back to laugh again. It made me sick to see the satisfaction he was getting out of this.

"You can't help me," he snarled. "You can't *change* this. Besides, the secret is already out. Your mom is almost done with her confession."

"Why is she doing this?"

He shrugged. "Because I told her that if she didn't confess to killing me, I'd kill you instead."

I wanted to run, to get as far away from him as I could so he wouldn't hurt me, but my feet remained grounded. I surprised myself when I managed to spit my next words out instead of cowering away like instinct told me to do. "Why are you telling me all this?"

"I've been dying to tell *someone,*" he answered hauntingly. "And it's fun watching you try to figure it all out."

Sam glanced to my mom on stage. She was reaching her closing remarks, and we both fell silent to listen.

"I cannot take back what I did," she said, "and I can't change who I am, a wi—" She paused like the word was too hard to spit out. "A witch," she finished.

I glared at Sam, though he didn't notice. He'd made her say that; I didn't need my sixth sense to know she wouldn't use that word on her own.

The entire bandstand area went quiet for several long seconds until someone in the crowd clapped their hands and shouted. "Great story, Andrea."

Sam and I shifted to stare out at what we could see of the crowd. They weren't taking her seriously.

Sam balled Derek's hands into fists. "This was supposed to work!" He spoke as if I wasn't there.

My mother's voice filled the stage area again. "I am completely serious. This thing I can do, it's why Divination is part of our town."

An unfamiliar voice called from the crowd. "Props for being true to yourself!"

In that moment, it was clear. Half of our town didn't even believe her, and the other half accepted her for who she was.

I relaxed slightly and spoke to Sam confidently. "It appears you won't get your revenge."

He scoffed and turned to me. "You know what the cool thing about possession is?" He didn't wait for an answer. "Even though I'm in someone else's body, I still have some power."

I remembered what my mom had said about how ghosts were more powerful the longer they'd been dead. That must have been how he could possess Derek.

"It's not as much as when I'm outside the body," he continued. "You see, it takes a lot of energy to keep control of this body. After I try something… powerful, I have to rest, but since I haven't tried anything in a couple of days, I have just enough energy…" He paused as if mocking me, and then his eyes shifted to the stage lights hanging above my mother.

My gaze followed his, and in a split second, my world seemed to crash down around me. My heart slammed against my chest, and I could hardly breathe. One of the stage lights swung from its safety cable.

I didn't even think about what I was doing when I pushed past Sam and sprinted across the stage. I shoved my mother from where she stood in front of the microphone the moment the safety cable snapped.

CHAPTER 22

ealizing I'd narrowly escaped Sam's attack, I whirled toward him a second later and raced across the stage, tackling Derek's body to the ground. I pulled my fist back and momentarily caught the fear that crossed his expression. It didn't slow me down. Though it was Derek's face, I could see Sam in his eyes. My fist came down, slamming into his solid cheekbone. I pulled back again, this time aiming for his nose. Before I could land another punch, a set of hands gripped my shoulders to pull me off of Sam.

"Stop!" I screamed to whoever was behind me. I struggled away, trying once again to somehow make Sam feel pain, to get back at him for trying to hurt my mom. "He tried to kill her!" I screamed.

"Crystal, calm down," a male voice said into my ear. He gripped onto my shoulders so tightly that there was no use trying to fight my way out of his grasp. I was still too full of fury to place the voice behind me.

"Please!" I cried, finally giving up the struggle. I slowly turned to face the man who had pulled me off of Sam, and when I met his eyes, my knees went weak. I couldn't move or speak, only stare into the eyes of my father. How was this possible? He looked the same as I remembered him from my childhood and from pictures I'd saved of him. A bright glow from one of the stage lights behind him outlined his silhouette.

"Crystal," he said again.

"I—I don't understand." I looked up at him, my eyes watering and my body completely still. "How are you here?" I forced my gaze down to his hands, which were still on me, and moved my own hands to touch his. He was so solid, so real. I spoke slowly when I looked up into his eyes again. "I don't get it. How did you come back? How is this possible?"

He swallowed hard. "I'm not back. Crystal, it's you…"

He turned, and I stared past him to where he was looking. This time, I fell to my knees. My father let go of me, and my hands came to my mouth. In front of me lay my body, sprawled out next to the stage light that had crashed on top of me. My mother, Sophie, and Diane knelt next to my unmoving form.

After the initial wave of shock hit me, I was able to look back up at my father. That bright glow behind him remained.

"I'm dead?" I asked in a small voice.

He nodded somberly.

It's easier to accept death when you know there's an afterlife, but this was just unreal. I hadn't felt any pain, and I certainly felt *alive*.

"Don't move," my father said sternly.

My gaze jerked in the direction he was looking, and I noticed he was talking to Sam, who was slowly creeping toward the stairs. He stopped as soon as my father's voice boomed in his direction. Sam cowered but didn't move.

I glanced between Sam and my father. "How did I—?"

I didn't have to finish my sentence. My father understood what I meant. How was I, as a ghost, able to interact with Derek's body as if I were still solid myself?

"Sam still has one foot on this plane, so you can interact with him. Since he's still in your friend's body, those interactions will affect both the spirit inside and the body he's controlling."

"And you?" I asked. "I don't understand. I thought you'd crossed over."

My father smiled like the answer was so simple. "I did. Remember the folklore about the veil between the living and the dead being open on Halloween? Well, it's true. Plus, I haven't gone very far."

He glanced behind him, and for the first time, I noticed five other figures on stage with him. The stage lights glowed behind them, giving off the same effect they had when I first turned to my father moments before. The lights were so bright that I could hardly make out the figures' faces. My father shifted, and the light followed. That's when it clicked. It wasn't the stage lights at all. It was the light to the other side. Each spirit on stage had their own, as if each was a doorway they'd stepped through to visit me tonight. I looked back at the other five figures, and one by one, I noticed they all looked familiar. Tears welled in my eyes.

"We've all been watching over you," my father admitted.

I rose from the ground and stepped toward them, completely in shock. My eyes locked first on the tall teenage girl with blond hair and brown eyes. "Olivia?"

She nodded, and I fell into her in an embrace. Olivia was the first ghost I saw a year ago when my abilities manifested.

"Whoa, Crystal," she laughed.

I pulled away, staring into her eyes. I couldn't help but crack a nervous smile that almost made the tears go away. I sniffled. "How has life been on the other side?"

She smiled back. "It's wonderful." She'd always looked like an angel, but with the bright glow behind her, I now believed that she was. "I've kept my promises," she told me. "I've been watching over Kelli this whole time."

I blinked away the last of the remaining tears. "She's changed, and it's all been for the better, thanks to you." My eyes drifted to the faces of the next two figures. A young girl with green eyes and dark hair held onto an older man's hand. "Penny. Scott."

"We saw you," Penny told me. "We've been watching Hope and my mom this past year, and we saw you visiting Hope."

"I did. I was her babysitter. How's your mom, by the way?"

"She's doing much better," Scott answered. "Lauren is getting the help she needed."

"That's great to hear."

The other girl with them inched forward, and I recognized her, too. I'd only seen her once, but she helped me save Sage's life.

"Melissa." I greeted her like I was reconnecting with an old friend, even though we'd only ever spoken a few words to each other.

"Hi, Crystal. I never got a chance to thank you. You know, for saving my sister's life."

"Don't worry about it. I see you crossed over."

A smile stretched across her face. "I did a long time ago. I was already crossed over when I met you. It took a lot of energy to get to you, but it helped to have my sister nearby. She always gave me strength."

That explained why she'd been so transparent when most of the ghosts I saw appeared solid and why I only saw her the one time. She didn't have enough energy to come to me in full form.

Finally, I focused on the fifth figure standing next to Melissa. The girl looked a little older than me, right about at the prime of her life.

"I'm sorry, but I don't remember you," I admitted sheepishly. "Did I ever help you in some way?"

An amused expression crossed her face. "It has been a while, hasn't it? I've certainly changed." She glanced down at herself. "Don't you remember me, Crystal? We used to be best friends."

I didn't understand and immediately shifted through my memory, wondering if there was a girl I'd forgotten. It didn't make any sense since Emma had always been my best friend ever since Kindergarten. I was about to ask her name when it suddenly clicked. She was the best friend I had *before* Emma, my first ghost, my imaginary friend.

"Eva!"

She nodded.

"But you were so young. Shouldn't you look like you did?"

She giggled in amusement. "We don't always stay the way we die. The young grow older, and the old grow younger on the other side. For a while, we keep the identities we had when we died, but eventually, you realize that age doesn't really matter on the other side."

"That's... actually kind of amazing." I glanced back toward my father. "Is it time for me to go? What are you all doing here? Are you here to guide me into the light?"

He shook his head. "We're here to watch over you, Crystal. First, we have a few things to take care of, starting with Sam."

Sam hadn't moved from his position on the floor where my father had told him to stop. I wasn't sure if he was scared of my father himself or of the many spirits around him. Like my father had said, Sam was still partially on the spiritual plane, and all the other spirits around him could now interact with him. He was no longer the most powerful one around.

"Sam," my father said, kneeling down to his level. "It's time for you to let go."

The evil laugh Sam was so good at returned. "I'm not going anywhere until Andrea pays for what she did to me."

"Come on, Sam," my father tried to reason. "We were good friends. You have to trust me that Andrea would never purposely hurt *anyone*."

"We were friends a long time ago," Sam spat, still not moving from his position on the ground.

I stood behind my father, wondering if there was some way I could help, but he seemed to have the situation under control.

My father shook his head in response to Sam. "It doesn't seem that long ago to you, though, does it? You only recently awakened. That's why you're still so angry. To you, your death just happened, but it's been years, Sam. Your family has found peace. *Theresa* has found peace. Come with me into the light. You'll find peace there."

"There's nothing for me there! Everything I loved is *here*, and Andrea took that away from me."

"You're remembering it wrong," my father insisted. "Andrea was trying to save your life. Why can't you see that?"

As my father and Sam talked, my gaze drifted toward my body on stage. Emma and Robin now knelt next to me. Teddy leaned over my body and administered some sort of makeshift first aid. I couldn't really see it since there were so many people crowded around the scene. My mother had dropped to her knees just feet away, and Sophie and Diane were attempting to console her. Beyond that, a crowd of onlookers observed from the grass at the front of the stage. I recognized each and every one of them.

First, I saw Hope and her mom, who both had tears in their eyes. Emma's mom and her little sister, Kate, stood next to them. Kate raised herself on her toes, trying to get a good look. Beside them was Derek's family, including his mom, dad, and twin sisters. Sage was also nearby, her eyes filling with tears. Finally, I spotted Kelli and Justine.

They were all here, everyone I loved, everyone I'd ever helped.

A police officer was trying to push people back, telling them to give me some space. *It's no use*, I thought. *I'm already gone.* It had only been minutes since it all happened, but the ambulance that was nearly here wasn't going to be any help, not now.

Movement caught my eye, and I noticed one more person I recognized in the crowd, Justine's mother, Theresa. She pulled Justine into a comforting hug.

"Sam," I blurted, interrupting my father. "Look!" I pointed to Theresa, and his gaze followed. "Look at Theresa. She has a daughter now. She has a family."

Justine looked up into Theresa's eyes before resting her head on her mother's shoulder.

"Look at their family. Theresa has moved on, and she's found happiness." I turned to face him fully and then knelt beside him like my father was doing. "My mother didn't hurt you. She was trying to save you. You were hurt because you didn't have faith in her. If you can't have faith in my mother, think about Theresa. One day, she's going to make it to the other side. She's going to expect you to be waiting there for her, but what is she going to find if you're still seeking revenge? What will she think of you if you manage to kill one of her friends? You're better than this, Sam."

He didn't say a thing. He simply stared out into the crowd, his eyes locked on Theresa. I noticed the way they softened and brightened when he spotted her, like she was all that mattered to him. And that's when I realized the truth.

"It's not about my mother and her prediction, is it?" I asked quietly. "It never was. You weren't mad that she warned you about your death. You were angry that you never got to live the life you dreamed of with

Theresa, and you needed someone to blame, someone to take your anger out on. Sam, you can be with Theresa again, but you have to find peace and go into the light."

Sam finally tore his gaze from Theresa and looked me in the eyes. "I had so much planned for us. We were supposed to grow old together." His voice was so small that he almost didn't seem like the Sam I'd just been talking to.

"It won't seem like any time at all before she joins you on the other side," my father promised. He turned to me and rested a hand on my shoulder. "It seems like Crystal was only a child a week ago, and now she's a beautiful young woman." He looked back at Sam. "Your life with Theresa isn't the only one you get to live. Someday, she'll be with you again in another life."

Sam blinked a few times and then stared across the stage. I glanced back to see what he was looking at, but I didn't spot anything.

"That's your light," my father said.

Sam's voice grew soft. "That's—that's my dad. I didn't know…"

My father looked back toward the light I couldn't see. "He's been waiting a long time for you."

Sam swallowed hard. "You're sure Theresa will join me one day? I mean, she lived a whole lifetime without me. Will she even remember me?"

My father nodded. "You have nothing to be afraid of."

"I don't want to go," Sam pleaded. "I just found her again. She's right in front of me, yet so far out of reach."

"And you will find her once more," my father promised in a calm voice. "Be there for her at the light like your father is for you now."

Sam's eyes shifted between the light I couldn't see and Theresa, but they eventually stayed on the light. He visibly reacted as if his dad was speaking to him.

"It's time," my father said.

Sam took a deep breath. "Okay. I'll do it for Theresa. I'll be there waiting for her."

I couldn't believe what I was seeing next. It was like my eyes were playing tricks on me. One second I was seeing Derek's face, and then next, an unfamiliar image washed over it until I was only seeing Sam. His outline was so familiar, but his face was new to me. Derek's body dropped to the ground, and Sam's spirit stood.

He turned back briefly before fading away. "Hey. Tell your mother I'm sorry." And then he took two more steps before he was gone.

I quickly looked back at Derek. "Is he okay?" I asked my father, frantically searching for signs of life.

"He will be," my father promised, "but right now, we don't have much time."

"Is it time for me to cross over? Why didn't I see Sam's light and you did? Is it because I haven't crossed over yet? But I can see your light. Where's my light?" The questions tumbled out of me.

My father answered quickly like he was pressed for time. "You're correct. You couldn't see Sam's light because you haven't crossed over. You can see mine because it's a different type of doorway, if you will. You don't have one because you're not ready to go yet."

"What do you mean I'm not ready to go yet? I don't have any unfinished business. I already said goodbye to everyone. I did what you told me to do. I saved..." My voice trailed off. Why he had told me to save three people when I only needed to save my mom? Did his warning somehow change the future? How were Robin and Emma involved?

Oh. Now I knew exactly what he had meant. It never was about Robin and Emma.

"It doesn't matter right now." He stood and grabbed my hand to pull me up, leading me over to the center of the stage.

By now, there was an ambulance crew surrounding my body.

"Clear," one of the EMTs shouted before shocking my body with an AED.

I looked back toward my father. "It's no use. I'm already dead."

"That AED might not save you, but we can." He glanced toward the five other spirits on stage. "There's so much love surrounding you tonight, Crystal. It may just be enough to revive you."

My brow furrowed. "What do you mean?"

He only answered with a smile.

The six spirits on stage stepped closer to my body. They didn't even regard the EMTs next to me. My father, Olivia, Penny, Scott, Melissa, and Eva all gathered around to place their hands on my heart. I couldn't help it when I began sobbing happy tears in response. My father gestured for me to join them. I knelt down beside my own body, closed my eyes, and took a deep breath for courage. Then I placed my hand on top of all of theirs.

"Clear," the EMT shouted again.

I opened my eyes and stared down at my unmoving form. My eyes widened in shock at what I saw. A pale white glow emanated from each spirit's hand, all but mine. I watched in amazement as light originated somewhere near their hearts and traveled down their arms to end at their hands. Another pulse of light journeyed from their hearts to mine. Each time the light reached their hands, the brightness grew until it was almost blinding. I witnessed that light fill my body, bringing color back to my cheeks.

"I'm going to miss you all," I managed to say through the tears before the EMT shouted one last time and shocked my heart back to life.

CHAPTER 23

J awoke to a white room, where the sun spilled into every corner. Sorrow flowed through me, igniting my senses as if they weren't my own. I forced my body to awaken further until I realized there were hands holding mine. In the next second, I sprang up in the bed I was lying in, fully alert. The sorrow I was feeling *wasn't* my own. It was my mother's and Robin's, the two people who were hanging onto me.

I was back.

I wasn't just alive. The light my father and the other spirits filled me with had blessed me in ways I didn't think possible. My abilities had returned at full force.

But it wasn't just that. My full range of senses seemed heightened. It was like the last few weeks with my faded abilities had caused my other senses to deteriorate with them, and now that my gift was back, so was everything else. I could smell the daisies in the corner of the hospital room, and the blond of my mother's hair appeared brighter than it had yesterday—at least, I thought it was only yesterday.

"How long have I been out?" I asked before either of them could say anything.

A look a relief crossed Robin's face. "Over 15 hours."

My mother gave my right hand a squeeze. "Crystal, I'm so glad you're okay."

A grin formed across my face. After everything that happened, that statement couldn't be any truer. I really *was* okay, better than I'd ever felt, to be honest.

"Don't worry about me, Mom. I'm glad *you're* okay."

"Derek told us everything," Robin said quickly. "He told us about Sam, about the possession."

I breathed a sigh of relief. "Derek's okay?"

My mother nodded. "They took him to the hospital, too, but he's okay now. He told them he passed out because he was queasy from seeing what happened to you."

The thing was, I could actually see Derek doing that had he not been possessed.

"He told us what he remembered while you were asleep," my mother informed me.

I blinked a few times, absorbing this information. "So, he remembers being possessed?"

My mother looked toward the door. "Why don't you ask him?"

I followed her gaze, and my body relaxed as Emma and Derek walked into the room hand in hand. "Derek! Are you okay?"

His brows shot up. "Me? What about you?"

"I'm fine. What do you remember?"

Derek and Emma stopped at the foot of the bed. "I came in and out. Some if it I remember, some of it I don't. It was like I was there the whole time, but I couldn't control my own body. I wanted to give you guys some sort of sign, but I couldn't break through."

"I should have known it wasn't him," Emma admitted. "The real Derek would've never broken up with me."

Derek's expression softened as he stared into Emma's eyes. "No, I wouldn't."

Emma couldn't hold it in any longer. She flung her arms around Derek's neck and held onto him so tightly that his face began turning red.

He pulled away with a laugh. "Don't worry about me. I'm okay. None of us have ever gone through something like this. I didn't even know it was *possible* to be possessed. If it had happened to any of you, I wouldn't have guessed what was really going on, either. I'm just glad Sam's gone and I have control of my body again."

"I'm glad, too," I told him. "I feel so terrible for not seeing the signs. It's just, the possibility never crossed my mind. I thought something else was bothering you."

"Believe me, if something was wrong, I'd talk to you about it," he assured me.

The door to the hospital room clicked open again, and Teddy slipped inside. He looked from me to my mother, then back at me. "You're awake."

I nodded. "I'm fine, really."

He leaned out of the room for a moment, and a second later, Sophie and Diane entered behind him. Teddy shoved his hands into the pockets of his jeans and came to stand at my bedside. Now my whole family was here.

I turned to Robin. "I'm so sorry about everything that's happened between us recently. I just…" I honestly didn't know what to say.

"You knew," Robin accused lightly, stopping me.

I tilted my head at him, wondering what he meant.

"You knew something bad was going to happen," he clarified. "That's why you didn't want me to come to the festival."

"I figured the same thing," Emma admitted. "You were trying to convince me not to come, either."

I could hardly believe how well they knew me, but it also brought me comfort. There was no point in lying to them any longer. "I'm sorry. I knew that if you all knew something was going to happen, you'd want to try to save me, and I had to save you." My gaze drifted toward my mother as I spoke.

"But why me and Robin?" Emma asked. "If it was about your mom, why keep us two away?"

I swallowed hard, not taking my eyes off my mom. Her expression was soft, but tears were beginning to well in her eyes.

"I didn't know what exactly was supposed to happen," I told them, still looking at her. "I was just covering my bases, trying to keep you all safe. I was told I had to save three of the people I love most." That was the way my father worded it. Three *of* the people I loved most. Not *the* three people I loved most like I had been assuming all along. "In reality, Emma and Robin were never in any real danger. It was my mom and my siblings."

My mother's expression quickly shifted to one of surprise. "Siblings?"

I nodded. "I know you didn't want to know, but I can't hold it in any longer. Mom, we were both right. You're having twins, a boy and a girl."

Emma squealed. "Congratulations!"

Teddy froze, and a stunned expression fell across his face. Even as Sophie and Diane patted him on the back in congratulations, he didn't move. Only after my mother made her way around the bed and pulled him into a hug was he able to speak. "We—we're going to have twins? We're going to have twins!" He hugged my mother again.

As everyone else was congratulating them, Robin took a moment to lean over me to whisper in my ear. "Crystal Frost, what you did for your mother was incredibly brave. You never cease to amaze me."

I shrugged my shoulders up slowly. I didn't know what else to say. He was so close to me now that his lips hovered just inches above my own, taking my breath away.

His eyes shifted over my face, and then he whispered the words that let me know everything was finally okay with us again. "I am in love with you." And then his lips connected with mine. Far too soon, he pulled away to sit back down in his chair.

My mother came back around her side of the bed and wrapped her arms around me. Her voice cracked when she spoke. "I'm so proud of you, Crystal. I couldn't have done it without you."

I pulled away, a perplexed expression written on my face. "You couldn't have done what without me?"

She blinked away tears. "Admitted my secret to everyone. It was something you said just before the festival. You said your witch costume was about telling the world it didn't matter what they thought about you, that you loved yourself for who you were. It just hit me that I'd been hiding behind the idea of make-believe for too long. I wondered what I'd been doing all these years trying to hide it when you've only had your abilities for a year and already embraced them fully. I found my courage through you, Crystal."

It wasn't until she said it that it dawned on me how comfortable and confident I actually was with my abilities. And with my mom's secret out in the open, I didn't have to hide it for her sake anymore, either.

The room fell silent for a beat until Sophie spoke. "We're so glad you're okay, Crystal."

I sat up straighter in my hospital bed. "I'm better than okay."

With all eyes on me, I noticed how incredibly lucky I was to have so many people who cared about me. They had all helped guide me through every challenge I'd been through over the last year. I thought back to the day I'd visited Sage, about how I realized she'd found her calling through music and I thought I'd found mine by having to die for the people I loved. But there were people out there who believed I was destined for better things, and I was determined to fulfill that destiny. From here on out, I was no longer just Crystal Frost. I was Crystal Frost, Psychic.

ABOUT THE AUTHOR

Alicia Rades is a USA Today bestselling author of young adult paranormal fiction with a love for supernatural stories set in the modern world. When she's not plotting out fiction novels, you can find her plowing her way through her never-ending reading list. Alicia holds a bachelor's degree in communications with an emphasis on professional writing.

Lightning Source UK Ltd.
Milton Keynes UK
UKHW010313080223
416649UK00010B/550/J